DEFIANCE OF THE FALL 5

JF BRINK

aethonbooks.com

DEFIANCE OF THE FALL 5
©2022 JF BRINK/THEFIRSTDEFIER

Aethon Books
www.aethonbooks.com

Print and eBook formatting by Steve Beaulieu.

Published by Aethon Books LLC.

Aethon Books is not responsible for websites (or their content) that are not owned by the publisher.

ALSO IN SERIES

DEFIANCE OF THE FALL

Want to discuss our books with other readers and even the authors like J.F. Brink (TheFirstDefier), Shirtaloon, Zogarth, Cale Plamann, Noret Flood (Puddles4263) and so many more?

Join our Discord server today and be a part of the Aethon community.

1

VANGUARD OF UNDEATH

A sea of parasites that came pouring out of their burrows, providing a clear hint what kind of tribulation Zac and Ogras had to overcome on the 32nd level of the Tower of Eternity. The quest had told them to redirect the "Ancestral Avoli," the humongous beast whose back they now stood on. Their plan was to simply pummel the beast until it changed course, but they would have to fight their way through a sea of Avoli Parasites to reach its head.

Innumerable screeching beasts barreling was a scene taken straight out of a horror movie, but Zac calmly stepped forward as he activated his set of passive skills that empowered his undead class. A billowing cloud of Miasma spread across the area and covered the ground, which elicited an annoyed grunt from Ogras, who retreated in disgust.

Zac could only grin apologetically, knowing that the skills in his current form affected his allies as well, or at least his living allies. His Draugr class, Undying Bulwark, was meant to be used by leaders of undead armies, spreading the corruption of undeath across the battle-field. The living were just members of the Undead Empire who had yet to be turned.

The thousands of parasites didn't seem to care about the Miasma, though, and they rushed toward the two with wild abandon. The situation was a perfect opportunity to Zac, and he activated [Vanguard of Undeath] for the first time. A storm of Miasma exploded out from his body, which in turn attracted the attention of all the beasts.

Even most of those who had been running toward Ogras changed their course, as they seemed intent on taking him out first as if their lives depended on it. They flooded toward him like a tide, but Zac didn't worry in the least. He was more interested in the transformations that took place in his body.

His vantage rapidly changed as he felt himself grow, and the bones in his body creaked and groaned until he was standing well over three meters tall. That was just one of the changes, though, and Zac couldn't help but marvel at the others. His frame had received a huge upgrade in not only height but also bulk, and he stood his ground like a massive tank.

He wanted to check out his muscles for a second, but it was impossible due to the other addition the skill had brought forth. His whole body was covered in thick medieval armor that ran in black and turquoise, created by extremely dense layers of Miasma.

Even his equipment had been transformed by the skill. His shield [Everlasting] had grown to match his increased size, and the circle of fractals in the middle had changed color from white to turquoise to match the details in his armor. Was this the effect of the Neprosium being able to incorporate almost any attunement?

Even [Verun's Bite] had enjoyed an upgrade, though it seemed that his axe couldn't be infused in the same manner as his shield. A massive miasmic axe had instead formed over it, a grisly bardiche that was tailor-made for his brutal frame. The haft was almost two meters long and ended in a sharp spike.

The axe-head was one-sided and slightly larger than what felt normal for such a long weapon, with its massive half-moon edge having a diameter of at least a meter. If it had been an actual weapon, it would no doubt feel completely unbalanced, but it felt perfect in Zac's hand as he took a step forward that made the ground shudder.

An annoyed growl echoed in Zac's mind, and he realized it was Verun, who didn't seem all too happy to be covered in death-attuned energies. A thought struck Zac, and he simply put [Verun's Bite] away in his Spatial Ring, and the Miasma axe thankfully stayed on without a physical base. It did, however, seem a bit faded until he brought out his axe again.

He could soon confirm that Verun wasn't actually harmed by the death-attuned energies, but it was more akin to being close to a nauseating odor. Zac could only impose on the Spirit Tool for now until he found a better solution. Perhaps he would eventually have to invest in a death-attuned axe for his undead side.

Power coursed through his whole body, and a glance at his Status Screen gave him a start. All his attributes apart from Luck had gained a solid 10% increase, pushing his power to another level. It wasn't as great as the buff from [Hatchetman's Rage], but judging by the modest consumption of Miasma, he would be able to maintain his current form for the better part of an hour without a problem.

Increased attributes, increased size, impervious armor, and a massive weapon. Zac felt like an invincible tank after having activated [Vanguard of Undeath], and he immediately started slaughtering the parasites. Each swing of his axe caused a ghastly wail to echo across the battlefield, and corpses of Avoli Parasites were launched dozens of meters from the force of his momentum.

But Zac only had time to swing his axe a couple of times before his danger sense pricked in his mind.

The next moment, a handful of shadowlances flew up toward him, and his mind froze at the unexpected ambush. The required movements were long ingrained into his body, though, and his arm automatically moved to intercept the strikes with [Everlasting] before he even had time to question what was going on.

"Ahh! What are you doing!" Ogras screamed with frustration shortly after as a spectral projection from [Deathwish] stabbed at him in retaliation for the shadowlances.

"What am *I* doing?" Zac grunted in annoyance as he turned toward the demon, but froze for a second when he heard himself.

He sounded like a real devil, where his voice had sunk to a register that shouldn't be reachable for humans. There was also the chill of death to it, giving it an extremely terrifying cadence.

"Is this your new skill?" the demon said with complaint as he shot out another handful of shadowblades, half of which were aimed at Zac.

"I don't know what the hell you're talking about. I used a skill to transform. Can you stop attacking me?" Zac growled in annoyance as he crushed the spears with a swing of his Miasmic axe.

"Do you think I want to? Your skill messes with my senses; it's like you've given me tunnel vision. I am trying to hit the damn beasts, but I somehow end up targeting you anyway," the demon said with frustration written all over his face.

Only then did the true effect of the skill dawn on Zac. [Vanguard of Undeath] had a taunting function? This was something that had been a huge problem with his class before, at least until he got [Profane Seal].

To strike Zac in his Draugr form was to slowly kill yourself due to the combination of [Deathwish] and Zac's massive Endurance. But why would anyone hit him if they figured that out? They could always flee or target Zac's allies instead, forcing him to stomp around by himself.

But it looked like [Vanguard of Undeath] at least partly shored up that deficiency.

Ogras reluctantly started helping out by testing the limits, and they found that it did not just work on ranged skills. For example, when Ogras used his movement skill, he accidentally ended up closer to Zac rather than further away a couple of times, which would have allowed Zac to launch a strike if he wanted.

There were limits to the efficacy of the skill however, and Ogras got better and better at controlling his actions as time passed. After struggling for a bit over a minute, he managed to essentially rewire his brain, as he described it, where he intentionally aimed off-keel to circumvent the effect of [Vanguard of Undeath].

But a whole minute in a battle between elites was the same as an eternity, and it would give Zac multiple opportunities to destroy his enemies. Zac also quickly learned that he could control the effect a bit, and reducing the area he taunted lessened the mental strain on him.

Conversely, the area he could cover if he strained was pretty massive, and he realized he could easily cover the whole cage he created with [Profane Seal]. So if he managed to trap his target, he would essentially be able to force a fight.

The skill worked even better with the brainless parasites as long as he kept his taunt active. They heedlessly threw themselves at him with even greater fervor than the battleroaches back in the Underworld.

They unleashed barrage after barrage of attacks on either his armor or shield, but the strikes barely left a scratch in his current shape.

Spectral parasites kept appearing one after another as strikes against his new armor would activate [Deathwish] just like strikes at his body. Large pockets of carnage were simultaneously carved out by his Miasmic axe, each swing taking out over five of the beasts without him even infusing the axe with a Dao.

He quickly realized he had some control over the spectral axe, though it wasn't as convenient as [Chop]. Still, he was able to elongate the handle by another meter, and the edge could grow to be almost as tall as a full-grown person.

Along with his increased size, Zac had suddenly tripled his range and strike zone, which finally allowed him to mow down his enemies by the handful rather than one by one as he did with [Unholy Strike]. He realized that skills like [Deforestation] or [Winds of Decay] were still far superior to clear out a large number of enemies, but it was still a pretty convenient boost.

Zac almost felt drunk with power from using his ultimate form, and he was decimating the parasite population like an angel of death. The only thing missing was a pair of wings like the ones Ogras had, but he guessed that wasn't really on theme for an Undying Bulwark.

Better yet, this was only the first of his two new skills. Zac was about to try out the second one as well, but he suddenly stopped himself as he turned to Ogras.

"You might want to back away from the battle," Zac said. "I think my other skill might target you as well."

"And you're not just trying to mess with me?" Ogras muttered, but he still flashed away to spectate the battle from a hill far in the distance.

The Miasma in the area started to churn and swell as Zac fused more and more of his stored Miasma into [Undying Legion], but he was shocked to realize that the skill still kept craving more even after having imbued the fractal with a third of his Miasma. It actually gobbled up half of his stores before the skill was satiated.

This was a shocking cost, more than twice compared to [Profane Seal]. It was to the point that Zac started to regret trying it out on these trash parasites rather than saving it for a real battle. But it wasn't like he could refund the Miasma, so he could only keep going.

One shape after another started to rise from the hazy shroud created from [Fields of Despair]. They were humanoid skeletons that shone with sinister energy, and Zac felt their power was comparable to pretty strong Peak F-grade warriors, judging by their auras. Figures kept rising until over a hundred of them stood in formation, creating a small army.

The skeletons were all whole and without cracks, but the gear they wore was mismatched and obviously worse for wear. The swords and armor were chipped and filled with rust, but they still contained deathly energy that felt strong enough to kill the Peak F-grade parasites in a swing or two.

Zac nodded in relief when he saw the skill, as the skill quest had been a bit troubling.

It had required him to gather the resentment of 500,000 kills, which made him worry about what would happen when he activated [Undying Legion]. The fact that it would be some sort of summoning skill was pretty obvious going by the name, but he had been afraid that he would summon everyone he had killed over the past months.

He didn't feel shame or regret for all those kills, but he also didn't feel proud about the kind of person he had become. Being put face-to-face again with the victims of his carnage would have been a bit much to handle, so the nondescript skeletons were no doubt a relief.

The parasites didn't worry about where the skeletons had cropped up from, and they gleefully pounced on their new targets. The skeleton warriors themselves went to work without needing any prompts from Zac. One parasite after another got ripped to shreds, and a continuous surge of Miasma filled Zac's body as he simply watched.

The skill might have had a massive initial expenditure, but Zac was happy to see that there was no cost at all to maintaining the skill after the skeletons had formed. They kept hacking and slashing without Zac losing an iota of Miasma. It was actually the opposite, as his reserves kept getting filled thanks to [Fields of Despair].

A thought struck Zac as he watched, and he tried infusing the Fragment of the Coffin into one of the skeletons. The summoned warrior turned a shade darker as a result, and its sword started to emanate a pretty terrifying aura.

Any beast the Dao-infused skeleton cut started to immediately rot and fester, and the effect was even greater than when he used the Seed of Rot with his axe. Any parasite that was struck with the sword was turned into a pile of goop within a minute. The scene made Zac realize he had forgotten one of the weapons in his arsenal, as he always used the Fragment of the Axe when fighting with his weapon lately.

It was a good reminder that he also had such a tool in his toolbox.

2

UNDYING LEGION

Zac kept experimenting with **[Undying Legion]**, and he found that he could infuse the Fragment of the Axe into skeletons as well, but only into the few who were wielding an axe. It appeared they couldn't use weapons that he provided either, which made it impossible to hand out a bunch of disposable axes to improve their power.

But the Dao of the Coffin was a more fitting infusion anyway, so Zac felt it was fine. It didn't only improve their offensive power by a huge degree, it also made them noticeably sturdier. A couple of the skeletons were ripped apart as they were mobbed by the frenzied parasites, but those infused with the Dao of the Coffin were like stalwart defenders who never went down.

One disappointing factor was that he only managed to infuse twelve of the hundred or so skeletons the skill conjured. He wasn't sure whether this was a limit of the skill or due to him lacking control over his Daos, as Zac felt a noticeable strain to split his mental energy and imbue many targets at the same time.

Being able to infuse all of them would, of course, be preferable, but at least it was a start. It created a few skeleton commanders who could lead their brethren into battle. Zac himself joined the fight as well, taking advantage of his massive frame and weapon to carve a path of death in the hordes.

Zac also tested the offensive capabilities of the Fragment of the Coffin in conjunction with **[Vanguard of Undeath]**, and the fit was just amazing. It did not only make his conjured armor far sturdier, but it also imbued his axe with the same corrosive capabilities as it did with the skeletons.

He felt extremely lucky to have mastered the Seed of Rot from the fight inside the Inheritance. What if he had simply fused Sanctuary with Hardness to form the Fragment of the Shield instead? He would have turned into a mobile fortress, impervious but unable to dish out nearly as much damage.

Now he was a tank who spread death and decay wherever he walked. Black clouds started to billow around him as well, seeping out through the slits in his helmet as though a fire burned inside the Miasmic armor. Thankfully, it turned out his summons were completely unaffected by the corrosive mists of [Winds of Decay], even though they were neck-deep in it.

One disappointing change to Zac was that he was suddenly unable to infuse the black mists with his Fragment of the Coffin. Ever since the skill had reached Middle proficiency, he had been able to infuse it with the Seed of Rot, which kicked its corrosion to another level.

But now that the nature of the Dao had changed, he'd lost the ability to infuse the gas. Was it because there was no component of hardness to the skill?

Zac felt some disappointment with the development, but he suddenly had a spark of inspiration. If he went by the image of his latest Dao Fragment, the corrosive aspect was locked inside the hardness. Zac changed his tactic and infused his lungs with the Fragment of the Coffin instead as he breathed out another lungful of corrosive mists.

The latest gust was clearly different compared to the others. The normal mist was essentially a grayish-black, but the new mist also had a greenish hue to it, making it feel more nefarious. His guess had been correct; he simply needed to adapt his thinking a bit to make the skill work.

He made his lungs the coffin, and the skill the aspect of rot that he exhaled.

This discovery did, unfortunately, bring a whole new problem he had never encountered in his Hatchetman class. He had too many skills active at the same time. The continuous consumption of

Miasma wasn't negligible, but the real problem was related to the Dao.

It was simply impossible for Zac to infuse all his skills with the Daos at the same time. The moment he started infusing [Winds of Decay], the infusion to [Vanguard of Undeath] ended. It was also completely impossible for him to split his consciousness enough to add his Daos to the spectral projections for [Deathwish] while using it for other skills.

He was able to juggle the Fragment of the Coffin back and forth between his skills with some success, but he found himself being constantly delayed and losing focus on the battle itself. It felt like he was trying to solve a sudoku in the middle of battle, making him constantly distracted. It looked like he would have to work even harder with his exercises to improve his mental control.

Still, only being able to infuse one or two skills at a time was acceptable for now, and with everything in place, Zac allowed himself to freely rampage across the back of the Avoli. Ogras kept his distance, staying far away from the toxic battlefield Zac had created. It only took him ten minutes before a deathly silence had spread out across the back of the titan, with not a single living parasite remaining in the area.

Only then did Zac release his skills, surprised to notice that he had less than a quarter of his Miasma remaining. It wasn't due to taking damage, though. He didn't even have a flesh wound from the battle thanks to the armor, but it was rather due to the massive expenditure. If it weren't for [Fields of Despair] returning some Miasma to him, he might have turned back to his human form unknowingly.

Zac was extremely satisfied with the two new skills to his class, even if their costs were pretty big. He finally started to understand how Undying Bulwark was meant to be used. The first skills had been focused on keeping himself alive in the vanguard of a battle, withstanding both physical and mental attacks.

Then came [Profane Seal], which allowed him to trap his target in an arena that would allow no escape until one side was downed. The Seal itself wasn't that strong on the offense however, as the chains only worked on weak cannon fodder. For example, almost all of the incursion leaders had been able to either destroy or push away the chains before they could do any damage.

If it weren't for Zac's unnaturally high attributes and Daos, he would have been forced to slowly grind down his targets with [Death-wish]. He had also been able to shore up his weaknesses somewhat with [Unholy Strike] and [Winds of Decay]. But it was undeniable that both his single-target and large-scale damage was limited compared to his other class.

But that all changed with the final two skills. They added the final missing ingredient to the mix and changed him from a passive defender to a real juggernaut that could change the course of a large-scale battle.

"Had your fill?" Ogras' voice drifted over from the side, and Zac looked over to see the demon walking over, pointedly avoiding going near the parasites melted by the Fragment of the Coffin.

"This undead class of yours is just a cheat," the demon muttered as he shook his head in disgust. "I've never heard of anything like it. How is one supposed to take you down without being a far higher level?"

"Isn't that a good thing?" Zac answered with a smile.

Zac didn't need to showcase his two new aces in front of Ogras, especially now that they would have to go their separate ways after the fourth floor. But it served as a good reminder for the wily demon to not have any ideas, even if he had become a lot stronger lately with his Shadow Fragment.

Since Zac had finished trying out his new skills, there was no reason to linger on the level. They rushed to the front of the Avoli and entered its body through one of the burrows the parasites had formed.

It looked like the parasites had a somewhat symbiotic relationship with the host, as they doggedly defended the inner parts of the titan. But the two simply blasted their way through until they found the brain of the beast.

Surprisingly, it was just a bit over twenty meters across, which felt pretty small for a beast as large as a mountain range. The demon had some fun prodding the poor beast, causing one massive earthquake after another as the Avoli started to buck in pain. Zac eventually had to drag him through the teleporter that appeared after one particularly massive earthquake.

Unfortunately, there wasn't anything of value that they could find inside the Avoli, but that was simply how things were. You wouldn't always find treasure even when completing the quest; you just improved your odds of finding something of value.

The following levels went by quickly as well, as the fourth floor still wasn't dangerous enough to hamper their progress. They also learned that not every single level would immediately throw them into the thick of it. At least not in an obvious way.

The sixth level had, for example, put them in the middle of a deadly array, and if Zac hadn't been warned by his danger sense, they would have had a significant amount of life force drained without even noticing.

But just as the danger increased, so did the rewards, at least when they followed through on the quests. One precious item after another went into Zac's Cosmos Sacks or Ogras' barrels until they finally reached the eighth level.

The quest this time was nothing special, as it was yet another beast tide quest, with the small addition that an upstart force had taken the opportunity to launch a coup in the middle of the chaos. So not only had they to guard against the beasts, but they also needed to protect the mayor from assassination attempts.

Completing the level early was also a bit troublesome, as they couldn't figure out if it was the beast alpha or the matriarch of the upstart clan that was the guardian. There was a real risk that killing the wrong enemy would have some unintended consequences, so they found themselves at an impasse until reinforcements arrived.

However, that was actually a lucky break for Zac. For the first time since encountering the Beast Crystals in the underworld, Verun suddenly stirred. The Tool Spirit had finally sensed something that it wanted to eat. Zac had started to worry that the Spirit Tool had reached its limits for improvement, but that was thankfully not the case.

"Can you take care of things on this end for a day or two?" Zac asked the demon, who was standing on the wall walk next to him, overlooking the sea of beasts.

"What's that?" Ogras asked with confusion.

"My Tool Spirit is sensing something it wants to eat," Zac explained, not bothering to hide it from the demon. "I want to go take it."

"That's fine. Just go." Ogras shrugged. "We are stuck here for another two days anyway, unless you're willing to risk it by guessing which one is the floor guardian."

Zac nodded in thanks before flashing away in the direction Verun indicated. He waded straight through the sea of rabid beasts outside the town, turning everything around him into a bloody mess. He only avoided the area where the horde leader, a massive demon tortoise, stood, so as not to accidentally get dragged into a battle with it.

Thirty minutes passed, and he entered a mountain range that was ordinarily a popular spot to harvest herbs and hunt beasts. But now it was almost completely desolate, with all its occupants having been drafted into the beast army.

A howl echoed across the mountains as Verun's true form suddenly leaped out of Zac's axe, and it started sprinting in a certain direction. Zac followed with interest, and he was led into a valley with an oddly sparse Cosmic Energy.

Zac got a sense of déjà vu as he gazed at the withered trees and weeds that filled the valley, and his suspicions were soon confirmed when they reached the heart of the basin. A spiritual plant as large as a tree stood alone, and a thick bloody scent wafted out from it.

It looked a bit like a cactus or a succulent flower, with an extremely wide base and no stalk to talk about. Each leaf was almost as tall as Zac himself, and they were as thick as his thighs. There weren't any flowers or fruits as far as Zac could see, but perhaps there was something like that hidden inside the layers of leaves.

Another gleeful roar emerged from Verun's throat as it pounced on the plant, clearly wanting to bite into its leaves. But a massive shape suddenly burst out of the ground, and it immediately got into a tussle with the Tool Spirit.

Zac's face scrunched up in disgust when he saw that it was a twenty-meter-long centipede, but he still jumped into the fray with his axe at the ready. The area rapidly transformed into a sacred grove as he activated [Hatchetman's Spirit], and Zac appeared right next to one of the beast's segments.

A five-meter fractal blade imbued with the Fragment of the Axe slammed into the beast, aiming to bisect it in one swift attack, but Zac's brows rose when he saw that the strike was actually rebuffed. The centipede was still thrown a dozen meters away due to the force of the swing, but it was very much still in one piece after the attack.

Zac wasn't disappointed, though, but he rather gazed at the super-sized insect like he was looking at a pile of Nexus Coins. Just how strong was that shell?

3

TUMBLES

Chitin that could withstand an offensive Dao Fragment, along with Zac's terrifying force, was definitely a material that could be refined into some very sturdy armor. Hell, he could cover a whole ship in exoskeleton, judging by how big the centipede was.

The problem was how to kill it without completely crushing the animal with something like [Nature's Punishment] and ruining the materials. Zac activated [Inquisitive Eye] in hopes it would provide some useful information, but it only managed to find out that the centipede was level 91.

It was actually the highest-level beast Zac had fought since entering the Tower. There had been stronger beings in the worlds they passed through, such as the devil titans on the 28th level, but he had never been expected to fight those.

Zac guessed that the centipede and the massive succulent it was guarding could be considered a side quest, providing an increased challenge in return for a valuable item. Zac also realized there was no time to waste, as it turned out that the centipede was not only able to touch the Tool Spirit, but it was getting the better of it.

Verun repeatedly tried to bite through the tough carapace, but it simply didn't possess the strength to do so. The centipede easily shrugged off the attacks as it tried to strangle the Tool Spirit. Zac wasn't worried about Verun though since it had already been proven on multiple occasions that the spectral beast essentially was immortal in its current form.

At least that was Zac's guess, as the Tool Spirit had been ripped to shreds on multiple occasions, yet it was fine after sleeping it off inside the axe. It also was in line with what he had learned about Spirit Tools. The Tool Spirit was almost impossible to kill and would persist as long as the Spirit Tool wasn't broken.

That didn't mean Zac was willing to stand by while his companion was getting harassed, so he cracked his neck and reentered the fray. He freely moved between the sections of the centipede, effortlessly dodging the hundreds of sharp legs thanks to the near-omniscience provided to him by [Hatchetman's Spirit]. There was no chance of getting trapped or accidentally stabbed by one of the legs while the trees were his eyes.

Soon enough, he reached the front section and jumped up toward its head with a grunt. The centipede sensed the threat and tried to head-butt him away, but Zac shot out a fractal blade that hit the beast's head with enough force to push it to the side. Zac kept flying toward its neck unencumbered and managed to grab on to the edge of one of its protective plates.

The centipede started to wildly thrash and twist to throw Zac off, but Zac would be able to hold on even if they were thrown into a hurricane with his inhumanly strong grip. He simply allowed himself to be flung back and forth while he held on with his left hand and methodically started to swing toward the gap between two chitinous plates.

This was pretty much the same tactic he had tried against the Battleroach King without any success. But things were different this time around. The centipede didn't seem to possess any real skills for one, especially not a fractal shield to block Zac's strikes. Secondly, his corrosive power had improved by quite a bit since the fight against the battleroaches.

It just took two swings before the plating had turned from a lustrous brown to a withered gray, and another swing to completely break through the thinner protective membrane between the protective plates. The centipede noticed that something was wrong, and it rose over ten meters into the air before it swung its whole body into the ground with all the force it could muster.

The whole valley shook from the terrifying body slam, and Zac felt his mouth fill with blood even if he had expended both a defensive charge from the divine tree while also imbuing himself with the Fragment of the Coffin.

Zac's vision blurred as the centipede was up in the air again the next moment, revving up for another attempt at crushing its unwelcome passenger. But the corrosion worked extremely quickly since it had turned into a Fragment, and Zac only needed one more swing to slash through its protections.

[Verun's Bite] keened as Zac cut down into the same spot one last time, and the protective membrane crumbled like rotten wood as the axe bit into its neck. This time, he hadn't imbued the fractal edge with the Fragment of the Coffin, but rather with the Fragment of the Axe, and Zac effortlessly gored the centipede with [Chop] until the fractal blade hit the shell on the other side of its neck.

The beast flailed and spasmed in its death throes, and Zac realized he might have made a mistake when he saw himself falling toward the massive flower. It would probably turn to mush from the fall even if it was a precious Spiritual Herb.

But the whole centipede was suddenly flung away as Verun slammed into its massive body as though the Tool Spirit's life depended on it. The final push was also the final straw that broke the camel's back, as Zac felt a surge of Cosmic Energy entering his body. He jumped off at the last moment, avoiding getting inadvertently body-slammed by a carcass.

A shroud entered his axe just as Zac landed, no doubt meaning that Verun had maxed out the time it could spend outside. A burst of impressions quickly followed, and Zac realized what the Spirit Tool wanted him to do.

Zac ignored the dead centipede for now as he climbed up on the massive flower. While he had been flailing about, he had spotted what it looked like from above, and there was a large flower in the middle. The fat leaves gave way to far more delicate petals halfway in, and Zac couldn't reach the core of the flower, afraid he'd ruin it.

"You sure about this?" Zac asked as he looked down at the axe in his hand, and received an affirmative response.

Zac shrugged and threw the Spirit Tool toward the core of the flower, where it landed on a bed of pollen, causing a small white cloud to rise into the air. Just a whiff of the stuff made Zac's blood almost boil, and he felt as though he was ready to go slaughter the whole beast tide himself.

But he regained his senses in just a moment and quickly climbed down the flower again. The feeling of inhaling the pollen had been pretty similar to when he activated [Hatchetman's Rage], and Zac wondered what the effect would be like if the massive succulent was refined into a pill.

He also wondered why Verun was so interested in the flower, but he soon found a possible answer. One of the fatty leaves at the outer edge had been damaged during the fight, and a viscous liquid slowly poured out from it, staining the ground red. It really looked like the flower was bleeding.

A surge of energy from the center of the flower meant that Verun had started whatever it wanted to do, so Zac walked over to the centipede. Thankfully, only the plates around its head had been damaged, while the rest of it was intact, so Zac took out [Hunger], and he tried to carve up the massive beast.

However, Zac found it surprisingly difficult to dismantle the massive beast even if it was dead, and only after three hours had he managed to stash away the dozens of shells along with the centipede's legs. Its flesh smelled quite rancid, though, so Zac decided to leave it in the valley for the vultures.

Verun hadn't been lazing around while Zac was working on the centipede, and the massive succulent had shrunk to a noticeable degree over the past hours. Its bulbous leaves looked a bit withered, and its lustrous color had faded somewhat.

It still took the Spirit Tool a full eight hours before it had completely drained the flower, and it was completely bereft of life force when Zac walked over to fetch his axe. The Spirit Tool looked pretty much the same after having absorbed the energies within the plant, except that there now were two fractals that were lit up on the handle.

Zac wanted to see what the extra fractal meant, but he realized that Verun was unresponsive inside the axe. It either needed to rest from the upgrade, or perhaps it was still in the process of digesting the energies it had consumed.

Everything was dealt with in the mountains, so Zac immediately started running back toward the town. He had only been gone for nine hours or so, but a lot could happen in that time. And his fears were realized when he saw a thick black plume of smoke rising from the town they were supposed to protect.

He held nothing back as he pushed through the beast tide like a hurricane, but Zac breathed out in relief when he saw the demon standing on the wall walk with a lazy expression. His appearance didn't match his demeanor, though, as his face was slightly scorched, and a new scar had appeared on his throat.

"What happened to you?" Ogras said with a laugh as Zac approached, and Zac realized he wasn't much better off himself when he looked down at his bedraggled appearance.

He didn't have any obvious wounds as Ogras did, but he realized his face and hands were caked in centipede blood and mud. He had long gotten so used to being covered in gore and filth that it no longer registered, but he realized now he really needed a bath.

"A bit of a tumble." Zac shrugged as he jumped up on the wall. "What about you?"

"The same." The demon smiled.

"Have you figured out who the guardian is?" Zac asked.

"Well, it can't be the matriarch of the Oylan line, because she's already dead," Ogras said.

"Must have been some tumble," Zac snorted as he glanced at the town behind them.

There was widespread destruction in the neighborhood next to the mayor's mansion, and some of the buildings were still smoldering. Zac didn't think that the demon would go out of his way to antagonize that woman while he was away since she was possibly the guardian. She had probably launched an all-out assault at the mayor's mansion, and Ogras had been forced to step up.

"So, what do you want to do now?" Zac asked.

"We can just kill that big bugger over there by now, make some turtle soup," Ogras said, nodding at the enormous leader of the beast tide.

Zac agreed and set out, to deal with things. As expected, the battle was over quickly and without any suspense. The turtle possessed a pretty strong ice-attributed attack, but it still was much weaker compared to the centipede he had just killed. Besides, being a ten-meter turtle might be worse than being a small one.

When it realized that Zac was far too powerful, it tried to retract its neck while it fled. But its sturdy shell turned into a cage as Zac could freely enter through the neck opening. Perhaps if its bloodline was more impressive, it would have some sort of skill to shore up that weakness, but now it had nothing to rely on.

The alpha beast tried to snap Zac in half in one desperate bite with its powerful jaws, but Zac ended its life with one fluid swing. The beast horde quickly scattered when their leader was slaughtered, and Ogras joined him not much later as the teleportation array appeared next to the corpse of the alpha beast.

An hour passed as Zac quickly recuperated his lost Cosmic Energy, and he eventually turned to Ogras, who was loitering to the side. "Are you sure about this?"

"I'm sure. You go ahead." Ogras nodded. "I'll stay behind here for a while to prepare myself."

"You're not setting out immediately?" Zac probed.

"Well, things worked out pretty well for me while you were gone. The mayor treats me like I am his ancestor after I saved his life, and he just so happens to have a pretty fetching granddaughter who doesn't seem immune to the hero's allure…" the demon said with a grin.

"Well, remember we're on the fourth floor. Don't relax and get yourself killed," Zac said with a shake of his head.

"Speaking of, could you leave that array behind?" the demon asked.

"The [Voidfire Array]? I guess," Zac said as he took out the massive crystal and the six spikes from his Spatial Ring.

It was a pretty good item, but Zac felt it was better utilized by Ogras in his efforts to conquer the fifth floor. He felt confident enough without it, and he doubted that an array that he'd snatched on the 28th level would be of much use on the sixth floor or higher.

"Perfect," the demon said as he put away the array. "So, what is the plan when we exit?" Ogras added with a serious face. "Who knows what the situation will be like?"

"Do you have any ideas?" Zac asked.

"We still want a patron to get rid of that Redeemer for us, right?" the demon said.

"Right." Zac nodded.

"Then we, or rather, you, might just have to spill some blood when we leave. Kill the chickens to scare the monkeys. If you feel the situation is chaotic but manageable, immediately destroy anyone who steps up for the quest," Ogras said.

"And if it's too much for us to handle?"

"Then we can only run." The demon shrugged. "Try to stay alive until we can crush our tokens. Scream for that Peak girl to save us; perhaps that might make a couple of the pursuers back away."

"I guess we'll just have to play it by the ear," Zac said with some helplessness.

"You'd better climb pretty damn high so you'll scare all the rich assholes on the outside. I don't want to risk my life against these floor guardians only to get skewered the moment I leave. It's bad enough you'll steal my spotlight with whatever crazy apparition you'll summon."

"I'll see what I can do. See you on the outside," Zac laughed as he stepped onto the teleporter.

4

ERUDITE MASTER

It was both liberating and jarring to start a trial alone. It wasn't that Zac was worried he'd fail, but he realized how much he had relied on Galau's and Ogras' experience and knowledge as they ascended one level after another. It was mostly them who figured out a plan, while he had eventually been reduced to a simple enforcer.

While there was nothing wrong with that, Zac still felt he was missing the point of the Tower, and he vowed to do his best in completing the quests rather than steamrolling through the following floors. And it was almost as though the System wanted to help him with his goal, as it had provided him with a final challenge that wasn't related to defeating the floor guardian.

But Zac still felt some dismay, as he knew that the final trial of the fourth floor might actually turn out to be impossible.

[Learn the skill of the Erudite Master]

Zac wryly looked at the quest he got, before his eyes trailed the winding path leading up the massive mountain in front of him. This was one of the simpler quests on the surface level. The Erudite Master was both the quest target and the floor guardian, meaning that Zac could either learn his skill or simply beat him up.

Unfortunately, he had proven himself to be hopelessly bad at learning skills without the assistance of Skill Crystals. Ilvere easily learned the skill that had eluded him for months, and he did not doubt that people like his sister or Thea Marshall would only need hours to master it.

But it was a welcome challenge as well, and Zac started to ascend the mountain with determination to make the best of it. He still wasn't completely sure what the rules of his odd body were. Yrial had said he had zero affinities with all Daos, yet he hadn't encountered any bottlenecks, even when forming his fragments.

He had already learned from Galau that just forming a Dao Fragment while still at F-grade was a sign of shocking talent that would make you a candidate for focused nurturing in a clan, yet he had breezed through that challenge without any issues. Twice.

In fact, he could be said to be pretty talented in the field of Dao, though many of his insights admittedly came from Dao Treasures. But not even the one-in-a-million genius Thea Marshall or his AI-assisted sister could match up to his insights, proving that things weren't as simple as they seemed.

But the zero affinities might be related to using the Daos rather than learning them, if his difficulties with learning [Cyclic Strike] was any indication. If that was the case, it would likely become a problem in the future. Everything was based on the Dao in the end, including the very core of all skills. What if he suddenly was unable to improve his skills? Would he be running around with F-grade skills even after he had formed his Cosmic Core?

A sudden pang of danger shocked his mind awake, and he flashed to the side with the help of his movement skill only to see an arrow whizz past him where his head was just a second ago. He quickly looked around and spotted what looked like a mix of a frog and a dwarf holding a crossbow.

The frogdwarf, and Zac only guessed the gender based on the thin black mustache that ran along its extremely wide mouth, looked quite surprised to see his sneak attack failing. But Zac didn't even have a chance to capture the odd cultivator, as he suddenly turned into a stone.

It looked like one of the escape skills he had seen before, and Zac looked around in an attempt to find the frog's new location. But it was in vain, as the mountainous forest was completely still.

The tranquility of the forest did not last for long though, and Zac was assaulted by one warrior after another who all seemed to be heading for the summit. It looked like it was a free-for-all between cultivators who wanted to meet the Erudite Master, and it felt like they all competed to complete the quest.

Zac had already asked about the possibility of meeting other climbers during a trial. But as far as Ogras, or the even more knowledgeable Galau, knew, there was no such thing as floors where climbers were pitted against each other.

It was not like Zac had encountered any frogdwarves outside the Tower either, so meeting dozens of them would be a bit odd if they were real. Since the frogmen were natives, Zac chose to only cripple them a little bit rather than killing them.

Since they went out of their way to attack him, he was pretty sure they were fair game, but he still didn't want to mess up his climb due to some old monster popping out of nowhere. Besides, he was already at the end of the fourth floor. It was worth remembering what Galau had said.

Nothing was black and white, and all actions have consequences. What if the old master was one of the frogmen as well, and he got enraged by seeing his people being slaughtered by Zac? Of course, it could also swing the other way, where the frogdwarves were the enemies of the master, and the lenient treatment by Zac was seen as a sign of a weak Dao Heart.

One could go crazy going back and forth over what might create the best outcome, but this was just like real life; there was no way to control all the small details. Zac could just follow his conscience as he kept climbing.

It only took him a few hours to reach the summit of the mountain, which would give Mount Everest a run for its money. He had initially planned on taking on the floor guardian in his undead form, but after having seen the quest, he decided to stay human.

The likelihood of the old master being undead was pretty slim considering the surroundings, and the pathways of his Draugr class were a lot pickier than his human side. If he wanted a shot at learning the skill, he would have to do it as a human.

The peak of the mountain was mostly flat, and it had the area of a couple of baseball fields. There was a small pond with a few fishes lazily swimming about, and a solitary tree that looked extremely ancient was providing some shade next to it.

Apart from that, there wasn't much to see, and there wasn't even a house to stay in. Confusion entered Zac's heart as he looked around for any Erudite Master. Had he ascended the wrong mountain?

"Let me have a look at you, lad," a decrepit voice echoed from the distance as an old warrior who had been hidden by the tree stood up.

Zac sighed in relief as he took a good look at the "Erudite Master." It was not one of the frogmen, but rather an ancient-looking demon. He wasn't the same kind as either Ogras or Abyssal Demons, though. This one was a pale blue, with golden horns speckled with red.

His build was pretty much the same as a human's apart from the taloned feet and indistinct scale pattern covering his skin. He would probably have been almost two meters in his prime, but time had made him lose at least two decimeters in height.

The Erudite Master was obviously nearing the end of his life span, judging by how old he looked. Zac still wasn't an expert, but he guessed the old master had a couple of months to a year at best.

The old demon inspected Zac just as how Zac was inspecting him.

"If you want to learn my skill, put that axe away. I am a pugilist, and you will never learn it while wielding a weapon. If you just want to test your strength, you're welcome to do so as well," the demon said with equanimity.

Zac frowned when asked to disarm, but he eventually put his axe away. He didn't feel any animosity from the old demon, and he was curious about what kind of skills he had. Most of all, Zac felt this was a good chance to train against a skilled enemy. Launching [Hatchet-man's Rage] and [Nature's Punishment] to level the whole mountaintop in one all-out attack would spoil the opportunity.

"Good," the demon said before his muddy eyes suddenly turned extremely sharp as his aura rose by a shocking degree.

It was still well within what Zac could handle, but he felt the pressure was even greater compared to some of the invasion generals he had fought recently. That was saying something, considering the old man in front of him was still in F-grade.

The fact that the old demon hadn't evolved didn't dampen Zac's mood. On the contrary, it made his blood pump from excitement. Calrin had once told him that the ones to look out for were those looking very young or those looking very old.

The extremely young were the geniuses who kept pushing forward, breaking through bottlenecks without any trouble. The very old ones were those who had been stuck at their current level for centuries, and this generally led to one of two outcomes.

Either they gave up on the martial path and focused on some side interests, becoming merchants or simply enjoying retirement. Others kept at it to the very end, polishing their skills and power to the limit in hopes of finally finding the spark to break through their bottleneck.

The old man in front of him was obviously the latter type.

Zac didn't know why a man with such a dense aura as the one in front of him was stuck on F-grade, but right now, it didn't matter, as the demon emitted a sharp battle intent. The master suddenly pushed forward straight across the pond, and his movements sounded like the roars of beasts.

The demon was suddenly right in front of him, and his right hand formed a fist that shuddered with power. Zac turned to absorb the punch with his left arm, which would allow him to counter with a right hook of his own.

But shifting his body like that had actually opened him up for the old demon to knee him right in the gut, and Zac was thrown away so far that he almost fell off the mountaintop. He wasn't hurt, though, as the old demon had only used the strength of his body in the opening salvo and not empowered his strikes with either skills or Dao.

Zac flashed back with the help of [Loamwalker] in an instant, and a rapid exchange of punches and kicks commenced. Unfortunately, the exchange generally consisted of Zac punching air while being barraged by attacks from all directions.

The old demon's strikes were extremely unpredictable, and no matter how Zac tried to counter the strikes, it seemed to somehow backfire. Initially, he had tried to limit the strength he used to match the old demon, but he was already using at least 20% more Dexterity while still getting his ass kicked.

"There is a battle raging," the demon said as he once again punched Zac square in his face. "One in your mind."

Zac's brows rose in shock, wondering if the old man had somehow sensed the Splinter.

"There is the instinct of the beast brewing deep inside you, wanting to break out. But you are fighting it, attempting to maintain the heart of the warrior, defeating technique with technique," the old man explained.

"Find a balance and prepare yourself!" the demon roared as his aura suddenly started to rise once more.

The massive roar caused a storm around them, and Zac was almost forced to close his eyes. The old man was obviously up to something, and his danger sense told him it wasn't something minor. His first instinct was to fight fire with fire, beating the demon down before he could unleash his strike.

However, Zac also believed it was best to be cautious. He was on the fourth floor, after all, and it was also a boosted floor due to multiple people joining. The challenge was almost on par with what he would face when meeting the guardian of the fifth floor.

A golden halo surrounded the demon, and the air around him crackled as he pushed his hand forward like a spear. The demon was clearly using a skill this time, though Zac still couldn't sense any Dao.

The power in the attack was palpable, and Zac's hand rose to counter the strike aimed at his gut. But mid-motion, Zac noticed that the man's hand changed direction, likely targeting his more vulnerable throat.

He quickly adjusted by putting both his arms in front of his throat while preparing to counter after blocking the stab. A burning sensation in his side was like a wake-up call, and he looked down at his bleeding side with confusion.

Had the demon changed the trajectory of his attack again? But why didn't he notice? Or was the small change in muscle or stance just a feint from the start, meant to confuse him? Luckily, the demon had stopped his strike after just piercing his flesh, so he wasn't really wounded.

"Having the heart of the beast and the courage to brave any danger is commendable. Having a cool and calculating heart will allow you to turn a losing battle into victory. But your heart cannot encompass everything," the demon said as he backed away, his hand dripping with blood.

"Who are you in the end?"

5
TRUE STRIKE

Zac was about to make up some story about why he was here, but he stopped himself, as he realized the old demon was asking a rhetorical question.

"Your heart and mind are in conflict, and you do not trust one over the other," the demon said. "This is something a seasoned warrior can exploit."

Zac understood all too well what the demon was talking about, he was a bit embarrassed. This was exactly what he had chided Emily for doing back during their sparring sessions. He had been talking big about decisiveness, yet he'd found himself crippled by indecision during the battle with this old demon.

"So what should I do?" Zac said, ignoring the wound in his side. It was nothing too serious that wouldn't heal up with a normal healing pill.

"A burning heart will stop a mind from being frozen with indecision. A calculative mind will help you distinguish between decisiveness and foolishness. But in my opinion, one must be the leader and the other follower. You may be able to ascend to a greater state of understanding in the future, but it is much too early. Perhaps when you can walk the sky like the celestials in legend."

"A leader and a follower?" Zac muttered.

"Are you a warrior of instinct or a warrior of expertise?" the old man asked.

Zac first wanted to say expertise, but he stopped himself, as he knew that wasn't the truth. He wasn't some adept weapon master who followed some great set of techniques, and he hadn't trained with a weapon since he was young like most cultivators in the Multiverse.

He was more like a beast, fighting based on instinct and his superior constitution.

"It seems you understand." The old man smiled. "Again."

Zac was already moving the moment the demon disappeared, and he swung toward his right without thought or hesitation. A deep thud echoed across the summit as the demon appeared, his arm glowing with a golden sheen as he blocked Zac's punch.

"Good!" The demon laughed. "What's the use of calculating and thinking when you're an idiot?"

Zac's face scrunched up, but he had no time to refute the words as the old man launched another barrage of punches, kicks, and attempts to grapple him to the ground. He no longer tried to think or anticipate what the old man did; he only moved the way his instincts indicated him to move.

He was still somewhat of a punching bag, but it wasn't one-sided any longer. The old man had been a martial artist for hundreds of years, and trying to match him in skill had only made him weaker than he actually was. Now that he relied on instincts, he at least managed to get in a few good punches as well.

The old man suddenly jumped backward, looking a bit worse for wear from the high-paced battle.

"Good!" he said while breathing a bit heavily. "You are passable. A rough gem that can be polished through thousands of battles. See if you can understand the essence of my skill, [True Strike]. If you can learn it, you will even be able to use it with that axe of yours. Watch how I attack your left side."

Zac breathed in relief that he had passed the test to at least get a chance of learning the skill. The ancient demon had already helped him out by pointing out his weakness, so he would feel a bit bad about defeating him just to pass the floor.

So Zac got ready to defend while trying to understand the truth behind [True Strike]. He kept his eyes wide open as the old demon's left hand essentially turned into a golden spear as he slowly walked toward him. It was the same skill as the one the demon had used before when he confused Zac's senses.

The demon's eyes were trained on a spot just beneath Zac's rib cage on his left side, but Zac could oddly enough feel another spot on his body heat up. Zac tensed up as confusion filled his mind once again. His instincts told him that the demon would strike his right side, but he was obviously aiming for the left side.

At the last minute, he decided to follow his instincts to protect his right side, but he was shocked to see that the demon had attacked the spot he had looked at since the start.

"What the hell?" Zac muttered with confusion.

"Good instincts!" The demon laughed. "[True Strike] is a mental attack powered by battle intent. It confuses the instincts of the opponent, allowing you to forcibly create an opening. It is the fruition of 580 years of delving into the psyche of battle, and my grandest accomplishment. See if you can understand it now!"

A powerful golden aura congealed around the demon as he once again targeted the same left spot as before. Zac's instincts were still telling him that the demon was targeting another spot, this time his right leg. Zac quickly tried to take control of the conflicting emotions, but his brows suddenly furrowed.

His left hand moved up to block his throat with shocking speed while his whole body got infused with Fragment of the Coffin. [Verun's Bite] appeared in his right hand at the same time, and it swung down in a fierce overhead arc.

The old demon's face scrunched up in anger when his sneak attack aimed at Zac's throat failed, and he quickly jumped back as the razor-sharp claws he had suddenly grown retracted into his hand. The façade of a righteous old warrior was gone, and his ice-cold eyes were those of a ruthless killer.

After having spent so much time with Ogras, would Zac simply put down his guard due to a smiling face? The fact that the old demon had been willing to teach him from the beginning was suspicious in and of itself. There was no guarantee that the floor guardian would be a willing teacher just because the quest told him to learn a skill.

Besides, even if he couldn't trust his instincts due to the demon's skill, he could still trust the danger sense from having over 250 effective Luck. Such a cheat-like amount of Luck was pretty much the perfect counter to almost any illusionary skill like the one the demon had just tried to use, and it had screamed in no uncertain terms that a deadly attack was aimed at his throat.

"So you knew," the ancient demon snorted. "That's a shame."

The old man's aura condensed the next moment, changing from vast but somewhat weak into something sharper and more sinister. That wasn't all; his bent back started to straighten out while his features smoothed out as well. From looking like a decrepit old man with one foot in the grave, he had transformed into a man who might be past his prime, but was still full of vigor.

Zac had to say he was pretty impressed by the demon's plan. He had understood that Zac was a tough enemy from the start, and the whole charade with the demon teaching him his skill was simply an act to not only disarm his enemy but create an opening to kill him in one swift strike. Ogras would no doubt find a kindred spirit in the old demon if he encountered the same trial during his climb.

However, the subterfuge didn't mean that what he had said was false. There was truth to the teachings he shared, and Zac felt he had gained some insight into the proper mentality of a warrior. One of his weaknesses truly was that he lacked guidance from experienced warriors, which made his understanding of battle techniques somewhat shallow.

Alyn and Ogras were both knowledgeable about various topics, but at the end of the day, they were just juniors like himself. Yrial definitely had a great understanding of tactics and how to polish one's technique, but the time Zac could spend with his master was extremely limited.

"You've helped me clear up a few things," Zac said as he ate one of his regular healing pills. "Hand over the Skill Crystal for [True Strike], and I'll be on my way."

The reason for Zac believing there to be a crystal was simple. The man never had any intention of actually teaching anyone his skill, so there must be another way to complete the quest. The most obvious solution was that he possessed a Skill Crystal.

"If I kill you like the others, what good is the crystal to you? If you manage to kill me, why should I share my knowledge?" The demon laughed. "I'll take my insights with me to the grave, or bring them with me to the peak of cultivation."

"Fine." Zac sighed as Cosmic Energy flooded the fractal on his forearm. "No matter what, you did impart some of your insights, so I will fight you with all I have."

The wooden hand broke out of the air the next moment, and it rose to the sky above the demon, radiating an intractable power. It quickly formed the array as usual, and it covered the whole summit as it glowed with the emerald luster of nature.

"A hand?" The demon laughed as he saw [Nature's Punishment] hovering above him. "That is just perfect."

A red and golden brilliance rose to the sky as a clawed hand congealed above the demon. It was almost twice the size of Zac's wooden hand, and it emitted an extremely acrid stench of blood. How many had that hand killed to gain such a sinister sanguine aura?

The large claw launched a swipe toward the emerald array, and four rivers of blood rose to destroy Zac's strike. But the array only wobbled a bit from the demon's all-out strike, and a mountain tip started to emerge soon enough. A massive pressure started to spread across the summit, and the demon once again turned hunched over from having to withstand the tremendous force.

A ruthless gleam emerged in his eyes as he gave up on destroying the descending mountain, instead opting to strike at Zac with the sanguine hand. But Zac was no longer playing along, and his full aura with its dense killing intent was released like a shockwave.

A massive fractal edge also appeared on his axe, emitting the undeniable power of a Dao Fragment. One swing was all it took to completely destroy the hand in the sky, leaving the Erudite Master completely exposed to the mountain above.

The demon obviously realized that he was outmatched, and he tried to find a method to flee. But [Nature's Punishment] was almost as effective a cage as [Profane Seal] by this point, and the pressure had completely locked down the demon's movement.

"Wait, I'll teach you!" the demon said, some fear finally evident on his face.

"Too late." Zac sighed as one peak slammed into the other, causing a shockwave that even pushed away the clouds in the area.

The whole mountain shuddered as Zac witnessed the massive destruction from a distance. He had retreated to the very edge of the summit, but he had still been forced to dig his legs into the ground to not be thrown down to the foot of the mountain.

A surge of Cosmic Energy proved that his enemy was dead, and Zac quickly instructed the hand to lift the mountain again and place it to the side. The hand dissipated after letting the peak rest against a slope with a low incline. Zac thought the scene would create an interesting mystery for any mortal geologist who passed by in the future. If this world was even real, that is.

The whole summit had been completely transformed by the all-out attack. The corpse of the Erudite Master was still somewhat whole in the bottom of the crater, but he was as dead as can be. The pond was also utterly destroyed, and the water had seeped into cracks in the mountain.

The floor guardian had been dealt with, and Zac spotted the teleportation array not far in the distance. He did not, however, immediately head into it, and instead jumped down into the large hole. The skill was real if the System had made it a quest to learn it, and he wasn't ready to give it up just yet.

An offensive mental skill that was based on battle intent rather than Wisdom or Intelligence sounded like a great addition to his current repertoire, so he rushed over to the corpse to try his luck. But no matter how many times he went over the demon's body, he couldn't find a Spatial Tool.

Zac swore in annoyance, but he wasn't overly surprised. The demon had seemed pretty confident that Zac wouldn't learn the skill if he died, so it would be odd if he could loot it so easily from his body. However, Zac did make an interesting discovery as he looked around in the pit.

There was light coming from within one of the cracks leading into the heart of the mountain.

6

ROAD TO 1,000

From one of the cracks in the ground, Zac could see a flickering light. But when he peered into it, he couldn't see what the source was. It did, however, reignite Zac's hope, and he started to cut his way into the mountain with the help of his axe.

The light steadily grew brighter as he made his way down, and he suddenly found himself in a passageway that was clearly not naturally formed. There was a tunnel hiding fifty meters down from the summit, and as Zac followed it even further down into the heart of the mountain, he found that it led to an opulent cultivation cave.

Thick rugs from unknown animals covered the ground, and all kinds of ornaments and treasures were strewn around the floor. There were even small mountains of Nexus Crystals almost touching the ceiling, no doubt vast wealth for anyone in the F-grade.

The exorbitant interiors were diametrically opposite from the image of an Erudite Master, and Zac thanked the Heavens for sending the paranoid demon to his side. If Ogras' distrust hadn't rubbed off on him, he would have been completely immersed in the training session, taking the behavior of the old demon as the desire of a dying warrior to leave behind something for the world.

Even if he had survived the encounter, he would have simply entered the teleporter as it appeared.

But not everyone cared about leaving an inheritance. In fact, most wandering cultivators had no intention of doing so unless they settled down. Even in established factions, it wasn't uncommon for an old master to barely leave anything behind. All the wealth they had gathered over the years would already have been used to prolong their own life spans and to desperately try to break through.

Zac didn't know why the old goat didn't keep all of his wealth inside a Cosmos Sack, but it made things easier for him as he swept through the cultivation cave, leaving nothing behind. But he wasn't content even after that, and he kept cutting through the mountain walls for over an hour until he found a small hidden pocket with a Cosmos Sack inside.

This was what he had been looking for, as there was a rough Skill Crystal lying inside. It did look a bit worn, though, meaning it had already been used. It started to seem a bit likely that the skill wasn't even something that the demon had invented, but rather something he had found through a fortuitous encounter.

The Cosmos Sack was also filled with various high-grade treasures, at least for a wandering F-grade cultivator. There were only a dozen or so crystals, but all of them were E-grade and life-attuned, perhaps used to help prolong life. There were also a couple of pills and a few manuals, but Zac didn't go through them one by one, but rather threw them all in his Cosmos Sack.

He wouldn't mess with pills or natural treasures he found while climbing unless he could be sure what they were. If the items stayed on after the climb, he could have Galau or Calrin identify them.

He did immediately teach himself the skill, however, and a new fractal appeared right above his navel. It was a disappointing placement, as he knew that it was a pretty common position for class skills. It was close to where the Cultivator's Core would be placed, or rather close to where his Specialty Core was currently nestled.

It was no problem right now, but it was extremely likely that his class would provide a skill for that location sooner or later, meaning that he would get limited usage of **[True Strike]**. But that was a problem for the future.

Who knew, it was possible he wouldn't get a skill for that slot until he became D-grade. And this was an issue that all warriors eventually encountered. Zac was pretty lucky that he hadn't encountered any clashes between his skills so far, even though he had used up more than half of his Skill Sockets.

But sooner or later, he would have to start discarding skills to make room for stronger ones or skills that better suited his cultivation path.

Zac quickly returned to the summit after having found what he had been looking for, and to his surprise, he saw a dozen of the little beings he encountered earlier. They all silently stood in the distance, a couple of them swaddled in bandages, no doubt a result of Zac manhandling them during the climb.

Thankfully, there was no animosity in their eyes when Zac appeared, and they bowed in respect when they saw him arrive. Zac nodded in response, realizing that the demon might have been a scourge to the area. The "Erudite Master" still had taught Zac a few valuable lessons, though. It might just have been a ruse designed to let his guard down, but he could still be considered one of his teachers.

So Zac also gave the unmoving body of the old demon a small bow before he stepped through the teleporter.

[Fourth Floor Complete. Upgrading Title.]

[Choose Reward: High-Grade Strength Fruit, High-Grade Dexterity Fruit, High-Grade Intelligence Fruit]

Zac's eyes lit up when he saw the rewards, but he held off on choosing and instead opted to first check out his title.

[Tower of Eternity – 4th Floor: Reach the 37th level of the Tower of Eternity. Reward: All Stats +10. Strength +5%, Endurance +5%, Vitality +5%]

Zac nodded in satisfaction. The bonuses followed the same pattern as the first three floors of the Tower, where he first got a bonus that improved his three "main" attributes. This pattern would continue for the following two floors as well.

As for the final three floors, Zac had no idea. He assumed that he would gain Efficiency in the same manner as the earlier floors, but he couldn't be certain. Not even Galau could confidently answer what was the case, as too few people in their sector reached those floors. However, Galau did mention a rumor that the top climbers were more interested in the floor rewards than the titles.

The quality of the items that the System rewarded had steadily risen, and now it presented something that Zac hadn't even encountered in the Base Town. Attribute Fruits, and High-grade ones at that. Even the best fruits he'd gotten his hands on in the hunt were only mid-grade.

Unfortunately, there were no Luck Fruits or All Attribute Fruits, but Zac figured that those kinds of fruits still might appear on a higher floor. His eyes went back and forth between his options as he tried to decide what to get. He could immediately discard the Intelligence Fruit since it was the most useless attribute for him, but he wasn't sure which to pick among the other two.

Dexterity would help him maintain the balance, which would get especially skewed as he kept improving his Dao of the Axe. But he still chose Strength in the end, for a simple reason. He still hadn't given up his desire to reach 1,000 Strength before he evolved. He hoped that would not only provide him with better class options, but also counteract the effect of his massive Endurance pool.

He didn't want to get stuck with two tank classes because he had enough Endurance for five men.

The darkness had started to scatter as he'd made his choice, and he found himself facing a hulking warrior clad in spiked armor. He held a sword in each hand and radiated dense killing intent as he took a step toward Zac. Zac put away his Attribute Fruit while jumping away a few meters to get a better understanding of what was going on, and the quest prompt appeared just as he landed.

[End the tradition of slave deathmatches to settle disputes.]

A quest to enact social reform? How was he supposed to do that without wasting a lot of time? Was the System expecting him to make a grand speech or something? Zac shuddered at the thought as he looked around the packed masses.

His eyes instead found a likely target for a guardian, discarding any thought of completing the level the proper way. It was an extremely obese man who sat in a seat of honor, overlooking the fight while he was fed some sort of fruits by what was obviously slaves.

"Hey, I want to kill that fat guy. Will you help me?" Zac said to the gladiator. "Do you know anything about the arrays in this place?"

But the other gladiator didn't so much as react to his words, and he once again tried to kill him. Zac could only sigh as he flashed forward and punched the gladiator with enough force to throw him like a ragdoll. The man soared like a projectile straight toward the corpulent man, who looked on with interest.

A blue shimmering wall lit up just as the gladiator was about to leave the arena, and Zac noticed a small surge of energy to his left. It was a pillar just a few meters away from him, and there were a couple more just like them.

Zac didn't delay a second, and he shot out toward the fat despot while he shot out huge fractal blades imbued with the Fragment of the Axe in rapid succession. Each of them slammed into one of the pillars almost at the same time, and the barrier protecting the array flags wasn't strong enough to withstand strikes at multiple of its weak spots at once.

A snap echoed out across the arena as the shields failed, and a resounding crash followed when the pillars were turned into rubble. Seeing that over half the array flags were broken, Zac jumped toward the luxurious seats like a beast that had broken the chains holding it down.

The fat leader's cheeks jiggled in fear, and he screamed while frantically taking out a token hanging around his chest. It lit up with a hum, and Zac found himself slamming into the ground like a comet. It was a gravity array that had been erected, and it was the strongest one Zac had encountered since he'd walked through the Zethaya Pill House entrance.

To be more precise, it was exactly the same as what he had encountered, which made Zac ponder while he got back to his feet. Was this intentional? Had the Zethaya set it up so that only those with enough power to reach the fifth floor would be able to enter their store? It wouldn't be too hard for them to set something like that up.

There was one difference compared to the previous time he was inside an array like this. Zac wasn't trying to impress anyone by toughing it out with only his body. He released his Dao Field for the axe, causing one shallow cut after another to appear on the ground around him.

The Dao Field helped him counteract the suppressive force to a pretty large degree, and Zac didn't have any trouble moving about any longer. One swing was all it took to destroy a hastily erected backup shield that the fat man's bodyguards set up, and with two quick steps, he found himself in front of his target.

"Wait, I can pay you!" The man trembled.

"Is this arena yours?" Zac simply asked.

"Yes, yes!" The man fervently nodded. "I'll gift it to you. It's yours. The slaves as well!"

Zac only answered with a swing of [Verun's Bite]. However, a ruthless gleam appeared in the man's eyes, and he launched a massive burst of flames that drowned Zac before it continued to cover half the arena.

A snort could be heard from inside the inferno, and a bestial roar followed as the flames were forcibly ripped apart by a swing of Zac's axe. The merchant could only helplessly look on as his torso separated from his legs before he succumbed to death.

Zac bent over the corpse to look for anything of value, but the man didn't even carry a Cosmos Sack.

At least the encounter gave him a decent hint of the strength required for the fifth floor, and he was pleasantly surprised to realize that the strength of the arena master was roughly the same power as the bandit Lord on the floor where he'd left Galau.

It meant that the fifth floor would barely be any harder than the fourth, except that the quests would likely turn more complicated or require more advanced knowledge. Not having to deal with the 40% bonus of his enemies was pretty nice, and Zac felt that reaching the sixth floor was a given.

As for the seventh and higher, he would have to wait and see.

It was also good news for Ogras. Unless the demon encountered some sort of situation that directly countered his skill set, then conquering the fifth floor was a distinct possibility. Getting two top-tier rewards and a boost in attributes would come in handy for the upcoming fights.

The silence was deafening in the arena as Zac stood over the bisected corpse of the arena master; no one dared to either flee or speak up for fear that they would be targeted by the crazed gladiator. Zac didn't care about their reaction as he surveyed his surroundings, but his eyes lit up when he saw that the teleporter had already appeared in the middle of the arena, and he flashed over.

He had been afraid that killing the arena master wouldn't be enough, and that the real guardian was the Lord of the town or something like that. Luckily, the System had thrown him a bone, handing out an easy one on the first level.

Zac stepped onto the teleporter without bothering to explain himself to the still reeling spectators of the arena. He had started to become a bit numb to the various people he encountered, and he couldn't really be bothered to treat them differently than if they were puppets.

His mind was only focused on climbing higher.

7

COSMIC GAZE

The next level placed him in an odd world where it felt like the colors were inverted, and he walked in a forest with white trunks and black leaves under a purple sky. The System wasn't as generous on the second world, and it took him over a day to figure out who the guardian was and to trap the wily beast.

Things were pretty much the same from there on out as Zac bashed his way from one level to another. His resolve to finish the quests fell apart after just three days when he found himself utterly unable to finish a single one of the first three levels of the fifth floor.

In the end, he only managed to complete two quests on the whole floor, one assassination and one quest to locate a treasure. The assassination was done as sloppily as was humanly possible. Zac simply stormed the mansion of the target and killed him before he had the chance to run away, destroying half a city block while completing the mission. He would have been fired on the spot from any decent assassin organization after such a shameful display.

As for the treasure quest, he simply was lucky. He accidentally overheard a few clues from an old drunk outside a tavern, and he almost stumbled onto the right spot just a few hours later. Perhaps his Luck was finally reaching the point where treasures almost jumped straight into his hands of their own volition?

But even with his Luck and his decision to kill the guardians most of the time, it still took him thirteen days to complete the eight levels of the fifth floor. That was pretty much what it took to climb the first three floors altogether, although they hadn't rushed through those levels.

He did, however, spend some time mastering [Bulwark Mastery], and as expected, he had been shown several visions related to cultivators focusing on their shields. There had been some differences between the various cultivators, but the similarities were far greater between the visions related to shields compared to those he got from [Axe Mastery].

Essentially, all of them were related to defending, though it happened in different ways. Some were like Zac's class, warriors who stood at the forefront of armies, soaking up the damage and the hate so that their companions would be safe.

Others were mages or Array Masters who were able to erect massive defenses with their shields acting as the core. Only a few were also offensively geared, but Zac instinctively felt that using a shield for attacking was suboptimal and nothing that he was interested in delving deeper into.

None of the visions really resonated with him, and it made him wonder just what he should do when evolving. He had spent most of the fifth floor in his Draugr form, and he had to say that he was loath to fight without activating [Vanguard of Undeath] now.

Just getting a Miasmic axe made Zac feel a much greater connection to the class, and he knew he needed to reduce the reliance on shields for his skills going forward. If that would happen immediately when evolving, then great. If not, he'd simply have to take it step by step and gradually move toward a more axe-focused fighting style in his Draugr form as well.

The delay caused by working on his skills only added one extra day, but some worry about the higher floors started to sprout in the back of Zac's mind. He began to wonder if his problem would be running out of time rather than lack of power. How frustrating would it be if the time ran out just as he was about to defeat a floor guardian?

Or what if he got stuck altogether, wasting weeks on some level he was unable to figure out?

At least the floor guardian wasn't anything to write home about. It was a massive golem that would be able to keep the Fire Golem Leader in a pocket, as it towered an impressive thirty meters into the air. It was like fighting a moving skyscraper, a massive construct of stone and crystal.

The golem had once been a guardian construct of a long-gone force, and for some reason, it had awakened from its sealed chambers to wreak havoc on the area. Judging by the situation, it might have gone the same way as Brazla, its artificial mind slowly getting twisted over the lonely eons.

Zac adopted a straightforward approach to dealing with the construct, which used a mix of shockwaves and earth-based attacks. It also used its gargantuan limbs for straightforward attacks, which were powerful enough to crush mountains. With the help of [Chop] and the Fragment of the Axe, he managed to dismantle the giant piece by piece over an hour, all while dodging its attacks with the help of [Loamwalker].

It was a bit hard to compare the strength between the golem and the Erudite Master, but he estimated that the golem was only around 20% stronger than the demon. He would likely have been able to finish it off with either [Nature's Punishment] or [Deforestation], but Zac wanted to gain some experience in fighting against larger targets.

He knew that the reason for the small difference in strength was because the party penalty was gone, and he reminded himself not to get complacent as he ripped out a huge inscribed crystal that had been in the golem's chest.

Zac knew nothing about constructs, but he felt that the thing in his hands should be the equivalent to an Array Core, and it might be possible to repurpose it somehow if he could keep it. He left the rest of the giant where it lay. It was essentially scrap metal without the core, especially after Zac had launched hundreds of attacks on it.

[Fifth Floor Complete. Upgrading Title.]

[Choose Reward: Offensive Skill, Defensive Skill, Support Skill. NOTE: All skills will have 80% compatibility or higher.]

Zac took a quick gander at his title, and he could confirm that nothing unexpected had happened with it.

[Tower of Eternity – 5th Floor: Reach the 46th level of the Tower of Eternity. Reward: All Stats +10. Strength +5%, Endurance +5%, Vitality +5%, All Stats +5%.]

It simply gave an additional +5% to all attributes, which had officially turned it into the title providing the most amount of attributes by now. It had pushed his Strength one step further, placing it at 927 with the help of the Peak-grade Strength Fruit he'd consumed the moment he had the chance.

The title also pushed his Luck to 204, but it seemed that there was no upgraded version of his Ambidextrous title. Perhaps something related to Luck would appear at 250 points, but he didn't hold his breath for it. Zac had long realized that it was getting harder and harder to get his hands on new titles. Stocking up on two more Limited Titles wouldn't be too hard, but he needed to find a Mystic Realm or trial that fit.

That was a later headache, though, and Zac instead focused on the three rewards, a bit hesitant as to what to choose. The System guaranteed a good fit with his pathways, but the trouble was choosing what would help him the most.

There was also the issue of which class the System would provide the skill for, but he guessed that his human form was more likely. It was still his "true" Race and also the form he had been in when defeating the floor guardian. But he still kept his mind open in case he was proven wrong.

Offensive skills were the first thing Zac discarded. His offensive capabilities weren't lacking in either of his classes, especially with his two Dao Fragments to help. That left defensive and support skills on the table.

He felt he was somewhat lacking a defensive skill in his current form, as his **[Mental Fortress]** skill was of middling quality at best. It also had no connection to his Daos, making a Dao infusion impossible. Physical defenses weren't an issue, though, with **[Nature's Barrier]** and [Hatchetman's Spirit] providing extra layers of protection on top of his huge pool of Endurance.

And he didn't even need to mention the defensive capabilities of his other class.

Eventually, Zac chose to go with a Support Skill. There was no guarantee that he would get a skill to replace [Mental Fortress] even if he picked the defensive skill, while support skills could help him in all kinds of ways.

A blinding pain erupted in his head, and the world turned white as it felt like someone was pouring acid in his eyes. Even Zac wasn't immune to the soul-rending pain, and he found himself on the floor, writhing in agony for god knows how long until the pain finally subsided.

Sweat rolled down his head as he blearily looked around, and he realized that he had already been thrown into a new world, one of endless darkness and glaciers. The cold would have turned a mortal into a popsicle in a second, but Zac barely noticed it as he looked inward after having made sure there were no enemies nearby.

He wasn't surprised to learn that the skill he had just gained was ocular, as the pain he had just felt in his eyes was all too familiar. It was the agony he'd felt when he had been forced to redraw his crude pathways into the proper ones provided by his class.

It was like inscribing something on his soul, where he first had to erase his old skill, only to inscribe a new one. He had hoped that the pain would be less pronounced, like when he'd drawn the pathways for the class in his Draugr form, but there was no such luck. It made him a bit worried about his evolution, but Zac knew that was a later problem as he focused on his new skill.

[Cosmic Gaze – See through the veil of the universe. Upgradeable.]

The flavor text was a bit similar to his old skill, [Inquisitive Eye], though it felt a lot more impressive to see through the veil of the universe than to see through their secrets. The skill was also connected to his pathways, and it was a great fit, which was a step up from the disconnected fractals that had simply hovered in his eyes before.

Zac looked around for a target to try the skill out on, but the area was truly desolate. That by itself was a problem, though, so Zac started to move away from where he appeared. Safety was an illusion this far up the Tower, and he couldn't stay around in what was probably a trap. However, he still wanted to see what his new skill did, and he eventually tried to activate it on a pristine-white tree nearby.

The world suddenly changed, and the dour landscape turned into a vibrant tapestry that shimmered in silver, blue, and white. Zac almost fell down from the rapid change in his surroundings, and it felt just like when he had been drowning in Origin Dao from the Dao Funnel.

The half-dead tree was suddenly a network of blue energy that surged from its roots beneath the snow up into its trunk. It was depending on the energy of the earth rather than photosynthesis to live.

But Zac barely had time to marvel at the beautiful scene before a formless blob of energy rose from the ground and globbed onto him, and Zac was shocked to notice there were already a couple of blobs sticking to his legs and his back when he looked down. Small motes of lights were slowly leaving his body and entering the little blobs, meaning they were stealing something from him without him noticing.

The first thing that came to mind was leeches. Were these little things slowly sucking him dry of Cosmic Energy? He quickly tried to brush the things away, but his hands passed right through. However, he thankfully found that they weren't immune to his Dao Fragment, and they were quickly disintegrated after a few Dao-infused swings of his hand.

[Help the expedition team find the ice-attuned crystal mine.]

The quest appeared just as he destroyed the pack of energy balls, and Zac suddenly found himself holding a disk that was pretty similar to the beacon array that Galau had used before. He quickly put the array away as he set out to complete the quest.

It took Zac over six hours in the freezing winds to find the place he was looking for, a nondescript snow-covered hill that only reached fifty meters into the air. It certainly wasn't the kind of mountain where you'd expect to find a Nexus Crystal mine, as the energies were barely elevated above the norm in the area.

But thanks to [Cosmic Gaze], he could see that a cold blue light was slowly seeping out of the hill in a few spots, and after he cleared the area, he saw that the lights emerged from a couple of cracks. The lights only grew brighter as Zac cut his way down a couple of meters, and he could quickly confirm he had found his target, as the stone started to become studded with white-blue crystals.

He didn't immediately activate the beacon, though, but he instead extracted a few dozen ice-attuned Nexus Crystals. He only looted right around the entrance before he activated the beacon, as he felt that cleaning house would be a mistake.

The disc suddenly enlarged, and a group of humanoids stepped through, led by an ice-blue troll that was just skin and bone. He held a staff in his hand, and the whole area turned a few degrees colder when he appeared.

The troll only threw Zac a glance before he looked down into the mine and nodded with satisfaction. He did release a snort when he saw the holes in the walls, but he didn't comment on Zac snatching a little bit for himself.

"Pay him," the shaman said with a raspy voice, and another troll stepped forward and handed Zac a box.

Zac accepted the box and put it away before stepping onto the teleportation array that had been created from the Array Disk. This was what he had expected. Looting the mine would have given him a couple of ice-attuned Nexus Crystals, which were pretty much useless for him. But properly completing a quest usually brought rewards, and Zac gambled that the reward would be better than the crystals.

His new skill proved extremely helpful over the following levels, as various secrets that would have passed him right by were displayed as clear as day from his magical vision.

The skill wasn't some sort of universal key, though, and Zac quickly realized that the lights he saw through [Cosmic Gaze] were attuned energies, and most energies simply weren't attuned. But attunement was related to the Dao, which helped give him an early warning when someone infused a skill with their Daos.

More importantly, he realized that no one noticed when he used the skill on them, which was an issue that had essentially made his old ocular skill useless. Now he would be able to glean clues from his enemies without them noticing, and Zac knew it might be just what he needed when he saw the quest for the final level of the sixth floor.

[Defeat the Enlightened Three in a Dao Discourse]

8

THELIM

Zac found himself standing on a gravel road in the middle of a tranquil forest the moment he appeared in the final level of the sixth floor, and the quest to defeat the Enlightened Three in a Dao Discourse had appeared immediately upon arrival.

If Zac had been tasked with something like this a few weeks ago, he would have thought the quest meant he was supposed to expound on the Dao, proving his deeper understanding compared to these three enlightened cultivators. It would be like a theological debate between a couple of monks.

But Galau had mentioned Dao Discourses in passing, which saved Zac the embarrassment. As it turned out, a Dao Discourse wasn't something as civil as a debate in the traditional sense. There were no podiums and no moderator keeping score of good arguments. It was actually more like a battle.

However, the difference between a Dao Discourse and a normal fight was that the battle only utilized the Dao and your Mental Energy. To make this possible, there was an array simply called a **[Dao Discourse Array]**. The fight wouldn't take place between the combatants personally, since things like attributes and skills would influence the results.

The way Galau described how it worked made it sound like a Dao Discourse was like a mix of chess and a mock battle. You infused your Daos into the array, and it would conjure various phenomena or avatars that you would use to fight. For example, his Fragment of the Axe would probably be able to conjure axe warriors, or perhaps spiritual axes that flew around in the air. But it obviously wouldn't be able to summon an ice golem.

It was a battle where you benefited from creativity and tactics, but the Dao was still the focus. The stronger your Daos were, the stronger your avatars would be. Similarly, the greater control you had over them, the better you would be able to fight. You claimed victory by destroying the enemy's avatars or forcing them to concede.

Zac hadn't understood why anyone would just give up, but it turned out that one's soul was connected to the array. Every time an avatar was destroyed, your soul took a hit. This meant that the risk of death was pretty low, but you ran the risk of seriously harming your soul if you didn't know when to give up.

These types of mock battles were a popular means of both working on your control of the Dao and settling disputes in larger sects, but it was a pretty hard item to get. Why some random force in the middle of the forest had an array like this was beyond Zac's understanding, but he supposed it was simply put there by the System to create a new type of challenge.

When it came to the strength of his Daos, Zac felt pretty confident. Two Dao Fragments should by all means be pretty strong even compared to the floor guardian of the sixth floor. The problem was his control, or rather lack thereof. His amateurish finesse was already all too apparent from his inability to learn [Cyclic Strike], but that wasn't the real problem.

He was still utterly incapable of infusing multiple Daos into a single skill or attack, which was the hallmark of a skilled cultivator. His sister had been able to do it since long ago, and Ilvere was getting close as far as Zac could tell. He couldn't be sure, but he also believed Thea had mastered that technique, going by their time traveling in the hunt.

That was the greatest risk to him failing the quest, as he saw it. Infusing two Daos into a skill might not double its might, but it would still increase it by a noticeable degree. The same applied to a Dao Discourse, where using multiple Daos would result in both more versatile and powerful avatars.

He knew that he wouldn't be able to beat some enlightened culti-vators through finesse, and there was no chance of him suddenly becoming a masterful Dao controller in an instant. He would have to rely on brute force and hope that his Daos and mental strength along with some creative tactics were enough to force his enemies to give in.

At least he had [Cosmic Gaze] now to help him understand what his enemies would be doing. Daos weren't as obvious as skills, as its natural form was invisible and formless. But with his ocular skill, he might be able to figure out what Daos the opponents were using and their plans, allowing him to gain the upper hand.

There were limits to that strategy, though, as [Cosmic Gaze] wasn't some patch that solved everything that Zac currently lacked.

The new skill only elevated Zac from a bumbling idiot to a some-what capable adventurer thanks to showing him a larger picture of the truth, but it was just a small aid in the end. The levels of the sixth floor had still taken longer and longer to complete than the fifth, even with the help of [Cosmic Gaze].

Climbing the eight levels of the sixth floor had cost him a full sixteen days. Things got more complicated at every level, and the ocular skill only helped resolve certain issues. Still, Zac judged that he'd saved almost five days thanks to [Cosmic Gaze], but it was distinctly possible that the seventh floor would take over twenty days as things looked right now.

One saving grace was that the System had actually been kind enough to swap out his ocular skill in both his classes. He had thought that [Inquisitive Eye] would remain in his Draugr form, but he had been happy to be proven wrong the first time he'd swapped during the climb. His pitch-black eyes in his undead form were pretty amazing now, both being able to discern life force and the Daos.

Losing his old skill completely didn't bother Zac in the slightest, as it didn't serve much of a purpose any longer. Losing the ability to inspect beasts was a bit of an annoyance, but there were no doubt items that could serve a similar purpose in the Multiverse. Perhaps whatever the fractal version of AR goggles was?

He had tried learning [True Strike] in his undead form as well, but his picky pathways hadn't accepted the crystal. The improved sight alone were a great asset when fighting the series of guardians though. The guardians of the sixth floor were all well into the E-grade already, and after the third level, they were all at least as strong as the Battleroach King if you excluded the Technocrat's modifications.

Of course, they didn't all excel at defense the same way the massive roach did. One of them was a lightning-attuned thief, and Zac couldn't even catch his robes in his human form. Hundreds of fractal blades were shot out in his attempts to take down the Ratman, but the blades only managed to destroy the ancient ruins they fought inside.

Zac was eventually forced to swap classes mid-battle, relying on the defensive charges of his robes and one of Rasuliel's defensive treasures to not get skewered while transitioning. The moment he unleashed the combination of [Profane Seal] and [Vanguard of Undeath], the fight was essentially over, as his Undying Bulwark class was truly the nemesis of all Dexterity-based classes.

He was thankfully still able to defeat the guardians just fine without being forced to resort to [Hatchetman's Rage] or using any of his ultimate skills, which was a relief. He still used his stronger skills now and then, but it was mostly to expedite his climb. If he had been forced to go all out against the normal guardians, then what would he do against the true floor guardian?

The increasing strength of the guardians also came with a constantly increasing risk of real injuries. He hadn't been wounded so far apart from a few minor flesh wounds, but that would probably change starting on the next floor. One mistake and he would be out of commission for a couple of days, and those types of delays could prove extremely costly.

He still had a large number of arrays and other treasures in his Cosmos Sack, collecting dust. He hadn't encountered a situation that called for a [Void Ball] so far, not to mention the even stronger arrays that he had found in Rasuliel's Spatial Tool. Perhaps they would prove to be the key to speed up the fights and reduce the time he had to spend healing up.

At the end of the day, there wasn't much he could do about the lack of time, he could only keep his head down and complete the quest he was given. He could always just run in axe swinging, but he truly wanted to succeed in the Dao Discourse if possible. The last floor guardian had been related to learning a skill, and he had found a Skill Crystal.

This quest was directly related to the Dao, and the implication was clear. If he could encounter an opportunity to improve his Daos, he had to grab it. It was pretty much the only venue for him to power up without evolving, and improving any of his Daos by one step would increase his power by a noticeable degree.

"Excuse me," a deep voice suddenly rumbled behind him, and Zac turned around only to find himself face-to-face with a walking tree, its face seemingly carved right into the trunk.

It rose almost four meters into the air, where almost half of it was a tree crown that kind of looked like a set of hair for the face that was placed on its trunk.

"Ah?" Zac was only able to answer, his mind a bit on the fritz since he couldn't believe he had neither sensed nor heard a living tree sneaking right up behind him.

"You are blocking the path, young man," the tree kindly reminded him.

"Oh, I'm sorry," Zac said as he stepped to the side of the road as if by instinct.

"Are you perchance participating in the Dao Discourse as well?" the ent asked as it curiously looked at him, the movement causing its thick trunk to creak in protest.

Zac hesitated for a moment before he nodded in confirmation.

"As I thought." The ent nodded. "How about we go together? I am trying my hand as well, though I do not hold much hope for my chances. My name is Thelim, by the way."

Zac readily agreed, as he felt that this large being didn't contain any malicious intentions, and his danger sense was completely quiet as well. The tree could rather be a source of information about the scenario of the level, an opportunity to glean whether there was some Dao-related opportunity hiding somewhere.

And if the ent decided to sneak an attack, then Zac would simply turn him into firewood.

"I am just passing through the area, and I just heard about the Enlightened Three by chance. They say there is a great opportunity waiting for anyone who could defeat them. Do you know anything more?" Zac probed.

"So you're a traveler?" the ent mumbled with a thoughtful nod. "That's why I couldn't place you. Well, it makes sense that you came here."

Zac slowly nodded, not sure what the ent was talking about.

"The opportunity you heard about is the chance to enter the Pool of Tranquility. It's a pond of spiritual dew that has formed a natural formation over countless millennia," Thelim said, the leaves on his head shaking with excitement.

"What does it do?" Zac said as his heart started to beat a bit faster.

The name reminded Zac of something Ogras had mentioned offhandedly. His family apparently possessed a magical pond themselves, which was created with the help of a huge amount of treasures and a powerful array. It was a man-made trial ground that could award a Limited Title.

The elites of the clan could dive into it, and the further down they managed to go, the better the title the System awarded. Certainly, something a small clan like Ogras' could afford wasn't anything too impressive and it cost a large chunk of money to activate, but it was still free attributes for anyone allowed to undergo the trial.

The demon had wanted Zac to buy something similar from the Town Shop, but there was nothing of the sort available. But what if this pond was the same? He still had two empty slots for Limited Titles, so no matter how good or bad it was, it would still be a pure upgrade.

And even if it didn't give a Limited Title, then it was still probably related to the Dao. Was drinking the dew the equivalent of eating a Dao Treasure? The effect of Dao Treasures was pretty muted inside the Tower, but this was a free opportunity. He might even be able to take away some of the water to drink it outside.

But the next words from the ent dashed Zac's hopes.

"Every day, a few drops are added to the pool at sunrise, each droplet infused with the spirituality of daybreak and empowered by the spirit of the forest. If my kind enters, our bloodlines will be purified, but there are some benefits for normal people as well," Thelim explained.

"What kinds of benefits?" Zac probed.

"It purifies and strengthens souls."

Zac once again got excited when he heard the effect of the pool. It wasn't exactly what he had hoped for, but it still sounded like something he could benefit immensely from. His soul getting corroded by the Splinter was a constant worry, especially since the past few days.

Because the Splinter of Oblivion had finally woken up from its slumber again.

9

THE ENLIGHTENED THREE

The Splinter was once again active, but thankfully, it hadn't shown any change in its behavior. It just extended its tendrils to touch the Miasmic fractals for a bit before it calmed down and started to emit that mysterious energy into his mind just like before.

The fact that the Splinter was once again active meant that he might boil over again, and Zac didn't want another mess like the Zethaya situation on his hands. That time, only his enemies got killed, but what if he turned berserk in the middle of Port Atwood next time? He'd end up like Anzonil's disciple, forced to live far away from people.

If he could strengthen and purify his soul, he would hopefully be able to increase his resistance to the mood swings brought on by the Splinter. Not only that, but the power of the Dao also came from the soul, and having a greater soul no doubt came with all kinds of benefits to his connection with his Dao Fragments.

"Have these Enlightened Three been bathing in the pool themselves?" Zac suddenly probed, realizing a problem with the situation.

"Of course." The ent laughed, causing the leaves in his crown to flutter. "Some say that their family wanted to keep the Pool of Tranquility for themselves, but they had to provide this opportunity to the younger generations due to pressure from the surrounding forces. Why else would they be so kind as to share their precious dew?"

Zac snorted and agreed with the sentiment. There was no such thing as a free lunch; no one was so "enlightened" that they would readily hand out their resources to outsiders. It also made Zac curious just what kind of reception the reluctant hosts had prepared for them.

The two kept walking for over an hour, and the ent was happy to share his experience from living in the area. The forest they traversed was apparently beyond massive, and even an E-grade warrior would require months of travel to exit it. Thelim had never left it at all, but had rather stayed in the area controlled by his clan most of his life.

Zac already knew that Earth could be considered a very small planet even after having grown by a huge degree during to the merging of planets. It was pretty much as small as a D-grade planet could be, where the larger ones could have a surface area that was hundreds of times larger.

As for C-grade worlds, the whole area of Earth would barely be considered a clan's fiefdom, a small corner of a single kingdom. Those kinds of worlds were exceedingly rare, though, and according to Galau, there were just three such planets in the whole Allbright Empire. Seventy percent of all C-grade forces in the Allbright Empire lived on the almost incomprehensibly large Allbright World, with the rest divided on the two slightly inferior planets.

Thelim's life in the forest was pretty tranquil, with the various forest Races having pretty close ties. This wasn't because there was some sort of harmonious camaraderie brought on by their connection to nature, but rather a need to band together to defend from outside threats. The forest contained all kinds of Spiritual Herbs, and outside forces often wanted to seize parts of the forest for themselves.

That kind of conflict was pretty far from where Zac had ended up, as they were deep in the heart of the forest. Any dangerous beasts had long been culled in the area, and the only sounds were those of birds chirping and the rustling of the leaves. It was as though the peaceful atmosphere seeped into Zac's bones, and he suddenly stopped and took a deep breath.

"What's wrong?" Thelim asked with piqued interest when he saw that Zac stood still as though he were in a trance.

"I just had a small improvement from walking in this forest," Zac said with a smile after a few seconds.

"You truly are a kindred spirit. The breath of nature is dense on you; you should consider staying here for a while. It is an amazing place to come closer to our origin." The ent nodded and resumed walking.

It had mentioned that they were brethren because it had sensed the Seed of Trees in Zac. Ents were one of those Races that were extremely specialized, the opposite of humans, who essentially were talentless jacks-of-all-trades. Thelim had noticed Zac's nature attunement the second he saw him, but the ent didn't seem to notice the other Daos in Zac's body.

Zac wryly smiled as he resumed walking next to the living tree. He wondered if the ent would feel as close to him if he knew that Zac's class was called Hatchetman and that he possessed skills such as [Chop] and [Deforestation].

It was perhaps even luckier that he hadn't arrived at the floor in his Draugr form. The stench of death might have prompted Thelim to attack him rather than initiate a conversation. Zac would easily have defeated him, but he would have missed out on the information he provided.

As for the small improvement, it wasn't a lie. Zac had suddenly sensed a stronger connection with nature around him and had stopped to properly savor the feeling. Unfortunately, it wasn't an epiphany or anything of the sort, but rather an improvement to [Forester's Constitution].

The passive skill had finally evolved to Late proficiency, increasing the boost to Vitality and Endurance by a full 2% each when the effect was doubled. Zac guessed that meant that the skill would provide a 15% boost at Peak mastery, which was nothing to scoff at.

Zac wasn't too surprised that the skill had finally evolved, as he had traveled through all kinds of forests during the past fifty-odd levels, including topographies he would never encounter on Earth. It was perfect timing as well, as just ten minutes later, they reached their destination.

The wild forest gave way to a meticulously cultivated one, where each tree or bush was a work of art. They took the shapes of people, animals, and even landscapes, though they were not sapient plants like Thelim. It also didn't look like they had been pruned, but that they rather had grown into such a shape naturally.

"We're here," Thelim said as he looked around in appreciation. "The trees are slowly formed to grow into these shapes over centuries. It is a popular form of meditation here."

Zac nodded in understanding as he looked at the living sculptures all around them. It sounded crazy to him to spend hundreds of years on shaping a tree, but with life spans running into the tens of thousands, there were probably all kinds of weird time-consuming hobbies out there. The garden was only a few hundred meters deep, so they reached their destination quickly.

A large hedge reaching at least fifty meters into the air surrounded the massive compound where the Enlightened Three and their clan lived, and its gate was guarded by odd humanoids that looked like a mix of trees and humans. Their hair was green and looked like cascading grass, but they had normal skin with a pinkish hue.

"Dryads?" Zac asked with interest as his mind grasped for similar beings from Earth's mythology.

"Just so," the ent rumbled in confirmation. "As I mentioned earlier, the 'Enlightened Three' are three grandchildren of the Perenne family's matriarch. They are dryads."

"How strong is this force?" Zac asked curiously as they approached the gate.

Going by the somewhat sparse Cosmic Energy in the area and circuitously questioning the ent, it became apparent that there shouldn't be any D-grade warriors in this world. But there might still be complications if the floor guardian was in the middle of their clan.

"I've heard that the matriarch has passed level 90," the ent whispered. "She is one of the strongest warriors in the sector."

Zac nodded, but not without some confusion. The matriarch was barely strong enough to be a challenge for him, so what about the "Enlightened Three"? Zac had assumed that they were both the quest target and the floor guardians, but it felt pretty unlikely if the matriarch was only at that level.

"What about the Enlightened Three, then?" Zac asked.

"They're all Peak F-grade," the Ent said. "But do not look down on them. Rumors are that they could have evolved over two decades ago, but they chose to keep refining their souls as they pondered on their Daos. Their insight is extremely high. In fact, don't let the levels of any dryads fool you. They are the blessed children of nature, and they have an enviable affinity with nature-aspected Daos."

"I understand," Zac commented as they passed through the gates, wondering just how talented these dryads had to be that even a naturally endowed Ent was envious.

Zac's appearance drew some interested glances among the forest beings, but no one barred his entry, especially since Thelim seemed to have some renown. Zac himself was thinking of a backup plan to the quest and only threw a cursory glance at the people around him.

His best guess right now was that the matriarch was the floor guardian, but the situation was a bit complicated. The expansive mansion wasn't mobbed, but there would be over ten allied forces and a bunch of loose cultivators in attendance. Many leaders would be here to escort their young, each of them a match to the Perenne matriarch.

Could he really attack the matriarch in such a situation?

Everyone was here for the pond and its soul-strengthening effects, and Zac might end up mobbed if he did something hastily. Helping kill an outsider was a pretty small price to pay for gaining access to the Pool of Tranquility. Perhaps he would have to waste a couple of days until the event was over in case he lost the Dao Discourse, and find an opportunity to strike then.

But that was if all else failed since he didn't have the time to wait around like that.

Zac and Thelim were led to a huge glade where a banquet was held. People walked around to mingle and network, but Zac was completely disinterested in the proceedings. What was the point in getting to know a bunch of people whom he would never encounter again? He only did the bare minimum as he tried to gather information about his targets.

It was only an hour later that the members of the Perenne Clan arrived, led by a beautiful forest dryad who appeared to be around Zac's age. She had delicate features, and her eyes were slightly larger compared to a human's, giving her a very cute appearance. But Zac already knew that she was actually an old cultivator approaching eight hundred years.

It was obviously the matriarch of the Perenne Clan. Her grasslike hair cascaded almost all the way down to the ground, but Zac had already learned that it wasn't completely ornamental. The thick stalks were her weapon as well, and she could grow them over a hundred meters in an instant according to rumors.

Behind her walked a group of cultivators of various Races, each of them radiating a respectable aura. They were formerly loose cultivators who had chosen to stay behind after previous gatherings like this one, according to Thelim, and it was this very reason that the Perenne family also allowed loose cultivators to join in on the fun.

Finally, there were the "Enlightened Three." The three were like younger copies of their grandmother, two youths and a girl. Going by appearance, Zac would have guessed they were the same age as Emily, but they were closing in on one hundred years. Reaching Peak F-grade in this world was a slow and arduous process due to the sparse energy, but it also gave them ample time to work on their Daos.

"Thank you all for coming to our humble home," the matriarch said with a cherubic voice. "We are delighted to host both honored friends and new acquaintances visiting from afar.

"Our family has been blessed with the Pool of Tranquility, and it is our joy to share the gift of nature with the fated ones," the matriarch continued. "But the dew is limited, and only a select few can enjoy its effect every decade. The mandate of the Heavens is that power is needed to seize one's fortune, and the precious opportunities cannot be wasted on the subpar."

The matriarch waved her hand the next moment, and an earthquake spread through the area. Zac frowned and got ready for a fight as the ground shook and heaved, with thick roots sprouting from the ground. Zac was about to take out his axe and get to chopping, but the ent placed a massive hand on his shoulder.

"Wait, my friend," the ent said from his side. "Just watch."

Zac hesitantly nodded and held off on taking any action, and he breathed out in relief a few seconds later as he witnessed the miraculous skill of a true arborist. The enormous roots weren't an attack, but the matriarch was actually growing a massive stadium out of the ground.

TALENT

Branches and trees entwined to form expansive bleachers that were partitioned into midsized platforms that would be able to house between five and twenty people each. Even seats and tables sprouted up from the ground on the platforms.

Finally, an inscribed disk was lifted out of the ground with the help of six gargantuan roots. The platform looked like an enormous coin, with a diameter of thirty meters or so. It would be impossible to have a proper battle on such a small surface, so it could only mean it was exclusively meant for the Dao Discourses.

The disk was almost ten meters high, and its surface looked just like the forest floor. It was a bit uneven and covered in grass, with a few bushes growing as well. Two smaller platforms rose next to the [Dao Discourse Array], one on each side of it. An altar holding a football-sized crystal was placed on each of them, no doubt the control crystals the competitors would use.

"The rules are simple," the matriarch said as she was lifted to one of the highest platforms by a root that looked like a massive snake. "If you wish to participate, simply take a number. To get the opportunity to bathe in the Pool of Tranquility, you need to defeat two of my grandchildren. However, if you lose the first battle, you are out.

"Why this rule?" The matriarch smiled when she noticed some discontent among the guests. "It's to save their reserves. A Dao Discourse isn't as draining as a real battle, but there are dozens of you here. My grandchildren would turn into hollowed-out husks if they had to expend so much Mental Energy."

Of course, there was also the not-so-hidden implication that they were favoring their own. Zac didn't feel there was anything wrong with that. It was their pond, after all, and they should be able to stack the odds in their favor a bit.

Zac and Thelim walked over and got their allotted numbers from one of the servants holding a crystal, and Zac was pretty happy with the result. He was placed at the eighth spot, whereas Thelim drew second. It was perfect for Zac, as it gave him some time to observe how the Discourse worked. It sounded pretty fantastical from Galau's explanations, and he wanted to see some examples before he jumped into the fray himself.

The best would have been to play around with the array for a bit to test out its limits and various ideas, but there was no chance of that happening. The first person to challenge the Enlightened Three was one of the few wandering cultivators just like himself, and she didn't seem all too pleased at being the sacrificial lamb that had to sound out the three youths.

The woman still walked up to the large control crystal, and it lit up with power the next moment. Zac looked on with interest as large swirls of mist rose out of the Discourse Array to quickly form the avatars the combatants would use. The wandering cultivator had chosen to form a dozen soldiers, each standing roughly one meter tall.

Their swords radiated a distinct sharpness that Zac was all too familiar with, and he knew that the girl had mastered the Seed of Sharpness, and it was at High stage, judging by its power.

The dryad rather summoned a field of flowers, and Zac couldn't place what Dao they were made from. When Zac looked at it with [Cosmic Gaze], he realized its true nature. The flowers barely emitted any color to his adjusted spectrum, but there were actually vibrant roots running through the platform itself, snaking their way toward the soldiers that were targeting the flowers above.

The wandering cultivator didn't seem to sense anything amiss, and she ordered the soldiers to approach the flowers, even sending a few of them forward to scout out the plants. One of the soldiers swept his sword in a wide arc, and a rippling wave of sharpness cut down a noticeable section of them.

There was no reaction from either the flowers or the young dryad, who held his hand against the control crystal, and the guest immediately realized something was wrong even if she couldn't sense the roots digging ever closer. She hesitated for a fraction of a second before she gritted her teeth and ordered her whole squad forward in an attempt to preempt whatever the Perenne scion had planned.

The soldiers only had time to take a few steps before spears made of wood struck out of the ground, piercing the chest of one soldier after another, ripping them apart in seconds. Each strike also seemed to hit the controller as well, and she staggered away from the crystal as blood started running down her nose. She threw an unknown pill into her mouth and quickly scurried away after bowing toward the hosts.

The battle was over in an instant, and Zac didn't even get a chance to see the dryad use any hidden cards. He heard earlier that the three of them had represented the family a decade ago as well, and at that time, all three had showcased Peak Dao Seeds. Some believed that the three had gained Dao Fragments by now while others thought they had rather worked on their supplementary Daos.

One thing that Zac could glean from the fight was that tactics were just as important as strength. The dryad hadn't even bothered using any fancy techniques such as fusing multiple Daos into one stronger projection, but he had rather won using wits.

The Dao that formed the spikes was related to nature, as it felt a bit similar to his Seed of Trees, but there were also distinct differences. Zac guessed it might be the Seed of Root. He guessed such a seed could contain some piercing capabilities like those he saw just then. More importantly, the seed that the youth had used was only at Middle stage, yet it had defeated the wandering cultivator in an instant.

"How skilled," Thelim murmured. "I only sensed the roots due to my natural affinity. I wouldn't have fared any better if I were a human in that fight."

"Good luck," Zac said to his temporary travel companion as the tree stood up with a grunt.

The one-sided battle seemed to have put a bit of a damper on Thelim's mood, but he still reluctantly stepped up to the plate. His showing was a bit better, and he summoned a massive tree that released a storm of leaves to cut his enemy.

The Enlightened Three had changed representatives to let the dryads rest in between flights, and the next one conjured stone golems that withstood the barrage of leaves until they reached the tree. A few of them combined forces to forcibly rip apart the tree, at which point Thelim surrendered by unsummoning his avatar.

"Well, it was worth a try at least," Thelim rumbled with a sigh as he returned to Zac's side. "Those three siblings are truly fearsome. We both used High-stage seeds, but the amount of spirit he could instill into the avatars was night and day. He also controlled those golems so naturally, while I struggled to just send the leaves in the right direction. Both the strength of their souls and their control over their Daos are top tier."

Zac slowly nodded, but he didn't directly comment on the fight. The friendly ent was honestly fighting way above his weight class, and if this were a real fight, the living tree would have been ripped to shreds in an instant.

He only had one seed just like the first cultivator, and it wasn't even a fragment. To challenge the three dryads who had grown up with access to the Pool of Tranquility was to ask for a beating. But the young ent had already said he was mostly joining the fun to gain some experience, so he took the defeat in stride.

Only when the fifth warrior, a local scion of another powerful faction from the looks of it, stepped up to the plate did Zac see Dao fusions come to play. Not only did the man, who seemed to be some sort of nymph, fuse two different Daos into a mighty beast that pounced on his enemies, but both seeds were Peak mastery.

The dryad wasn't to be outdone, though, and he created an image of a hunter wielding a bow covered in leaves. The hunter deftly dodged the rabid assaults of the animal until it finally managed to land a lethal strike with an arrow that shone with the green light of some nature-related Dao.

It was an interesting display, but Zac felt it was a bit lackluster compared to a real fight that brought shockwaves and explosions that could be felt from hundreds of meters away. It looked a bit like level 20 warriors and beasts were fighting to the naked eye, though it looked a lot more spectacular when viewing it with [Cosmic Gaze].

Finally, it was Zac's turn to the plate, and he was eager to try out his might. He was pretty confident by this point, as none of the fights had showcased any Dao Fragments, and he had two he could bring into play. He might not be able to fuse them, but summoning two Fragment avatars should be able to handle any trouble that came his way.

Zac jumped up on the platform, and after a nod at his competitor, he placed his hand on the control crystal and started to imbue it with his Dao. He felt a prickling sensation in his mind as he tried to conjure his avatars, like his brain had suddenly grown two sizes inside his skull.

He understood what he needed to do, since connecting with the control crystal provided him with a burst of information, but there was an almost insurmountable resistance when forcing his Fragment of the Axe into the elusive mists hiding inside the platform. It felt like he was trying to grab the haze with his bare hands.

The only solution he could come up with was to steady himself and forcibly push even more of his Mental Energy into the array, and it finally worked. Eight warriors emerged through the mist, each one of them radiating a palpable killing intent and a force that caused the ground around them to be cut.

However, there were no exclamations of excitement or envy coming from the audience, but rather confused murmurs and subdued snickers. And even if Zac didn't want to admit it, he could understand why. Things had seemed pretty smooth and simple from the stadium, but he had barely managed to create the avatars in line with his imagination. Anything more was beyond his ability.

The eight soldiers looked mighty, but they twitched and flailed about in an extremely unsightly manner. It looked like they were string puppets controlled by the world's worst puppeteer. Zac also knew it wasn't some trick by the array, but rather due to his limitations.

Just conjuring the eight warriors was even more taxing than when he'd infused the Skeletons of [Undying Legion], but Zac had never gone any further than that with the skill. The skeletons didn't require constant commands, though Zac could order them about with a few simple thoughts. But these avatars didn't listen to mental commands but were rather moved by manipulating them with his soul.

This was just like any time he tried to control his Mental Energy and have the two Daos fill the fractal for **[Cyclic Strike]**. The Daos turned into spaghetti in his hands and it all turned into a big mess.

The dryad cultivator had frozen in confusion for a second, but when she noticed that Zac's fumbling wasn't an act, she sneered and pushed the small critters looking like walking radishes she had summoned forward. They didn't look as mighty as the hunter, but Zac could see that they had been created with the help of two Peak Dao Seeds.

Zac tried to think of a solution to his embarrassing situation, and he could only come up with one course of action. If he couldn't control so many warriors, then he would just have to reduce the numbers. Seven of the axe-men dissipated into smoke just before vines shot out by the radish soldiers struck them, but one soldier stayed behind and cut the attacking vines into shreds with one swipe.

Things became a bit easier with only one avatar to control, and the power crammed into its diminutive size was far beyond anything that had been seen so far during the battles. The axe warrior roared as he stumbled forward, his axe madly flailing in the air. A wave of destruction rippled out in an instant, destroying most of the seed warriors, who couldn't muster a working response to the random strikes.

Zac breathed in relief as he tried to cajole his avatar to move forward, but he stopped when he saw that the pale-faced dryad dissolved her remaining radish warriors. He first thought that he had won, but he quickly realized she was just changing tactics as a centaur wielding a simple spear appeared to replace the small vegetable avatars.

The centaur galloped forward, and a wild exchange of strikes took place between the two solitary avatars. Truthfully, it was mostly the axe-man getting hit over and over and Zac infusing even more spiritual energy to keep it standing, while occasionally releasing a massive but random swing that either completely missed its mark or grievously wounded its target.

He also tried to incorporate the Dao of the Coffin into the mix, but the only solution he could find was to completely swap out the Dao in the avatar. It changed him from an axe-warrior into an axe-wielding skeleton climbing out of a coffin, and the stone box helped protect its sides from attacks.

It did help with the defenses a bit, but Zac eventually gave it up, since swapping back and forth in some sort of pseudo-cycle only helped him drain his Mental Energy a lot faster. He had already landed a few pretty nasty hits with the avatar powered by the Fragment of the Axe, and one more was likely all it would take to completely destroy it.

But the power of the spear-wielding centaur suddenly shot up by a noticeable degree, and its previously unattuned spear lit up with a color of attunement, this one looking a bit like steel. Not only that, one shape after another started to appear on the dryad's side of the arena, each one of them emitting a respectable amount of power.

It was a literal army of forest critters wielding various weaponry as they approached Zac's solitary avatar.

Zac was forced to look up from the crystal to see what the hell was going on. Had the matriarch suddenly jumped into the mix, or had his opponent gone easy on him before? But his eyes widened in realization when his gaze swept across the two youths standing on the platform on the opposite side.

The "Enlightened Three" were actually cheating.

11

STORM

Zac had already noticed something odd with the help of **[Cosmic Gaze]**, but he initially wasn't sure whether he was just imagining things. Thin tendrils of energy seemed to be passing between the three siblings unbeknownst to him or the other spectators, making Zac believe that they were somehow sharing their spiritual power.

The tendrils were extremely minute, looking like glistening fishing lines in the air. It made Zac doubt his eyes for a second, especially since none of the spectators were commenting on it.

Or was this the advantage of having the home field? There were tens of E-grade warriors among the spectators, but none of them spoke up. It was impossible that not a single one realized something was amiss if Zac could see it with his newly acquired Early proficiency skill. They simply didn't say anything since it happened to an outsider.

It was only good for them if Zac got thrown out, as it would leave more spots in the pool for their own progeny. So everyone kept their mouths shut in a tacit agreement. Fury started to build in Zac's mind as he railed against the injustice, but he stopped his anger from running amok. He needed to find a solution that didn't end with a bloodbath.

Calling them out wouldn't work. If the spectators cared about fair competition for outsiders, then they should have spoken up already.

If this had been a real fight, he would have launched something like **[Deforestation]** by this point, laying waste to all three of them while taking down the whole stadium and crushing the [Dao Discourse Array] into pieces. But doing so would no doubt end with him not being able to access the Pool of Tranquility.

He had tried to circumvent the quests multiple times during the climb, where he had defeated the guardian first before trying to get the treasure related to the quest. That tactic had invariably failed, as the treasures were protected by all kinds of safeguards the System had put in place. One time, a bird even swooped down from nowhere to snatch a Spiritual Herb out of his hands before he could react.

Prickling pain in his mind made him realize an odd change with the array. The moment Zac noticed the reinforcements on the other side, he had ordered his avatar to back away while he tried to figure out a plan. But while his mind churned to figure out a plan, he had unbeknownst kept infusing the control crystal with massive amounts of Mental Energy.

None of it had entered the axe-man, though, since that required Zac's full attention, but it had rather formed a large formless blob of destructive energies at the bottom of the high platform. Weirder yet, the haze that rested beneath the surface had started to mix and integrate with his spiritual energy without taking any specific form.

It was like his Dao Fragment was a magnet that kept absorbing the mists in the array. Zac completely froze witnessing the spectacle, and it felt like he had woken up from a stupor. He felt as though he had been muddled for the past months, but the Dao Discourse had finally dispersed his illusions.

He had been so focused on the Cycle of Life and Death since meeting Yrial that he had ignored his unique points, and his weaknesses. After witnessing the Lord of Cycles' might, he forcibly tried to create a cultivation system that seemed fitting on the surface, but one that still kind of missed the mark. Yrial had tried helping him by having him learn [Cyclic Strike] and improve his Dao control, but it was that very skill that had made him reach an impasse.

It was time to accept reality. Creating a cycle where he integrated two diametrically opposite concepts was like trying to breathe underwater for him. It was not in his nature, and forcing such a thing would only create mediocre results.

His thoughts went to the weird ball that Yrial had played with, and he remembered how it seamlessly flitted back and forth between frigid flames and fiery ice. Did he truly need to create something like that with his Daos of Life and Death? His sister might be suited for such a path with her amazing affinities and AI to help her fuse the four elements, but he needed to find another direction for himself.

He would still keep the core parts, with Life and Death each being one half of the whole, with the Dao of the Axe being the delivery method, or perhaps the thing that bound the two together. But braiding the two together into a revolving cycle was too complicated. Perhaps he could come back to that idea when he was as powerful as Yrial, but for now, he needed something simpler.

His eyes again turned to the mists that churned under the surface of the **[Dao Discourse Array]**. By this point, he had poured more than twice the energy into the ground compared to what he had used to create the eight axe warriors earlier.

His head was pounding already, but he kept infusing more and more inside as he moved his axe-man to the edge of the stage. He suddenly had an idea and started to push his Fragment of the Coffin into the control crystal as well. However, he didn't try to fuse the two fragments or even control them after they entered the ground.

Combining the two Daos would have been impossible, but just pouring it into the control crystal wasn't too bad. It was just like when he infused his body with the Fragment of the Coffin while he infused an attack with the Fragment of the Axe. As long as he didn't need to coordinate the two to work with each other, the strain was just a fraction of before.

The second fragment still joined the growing blob of chaos in the ground, and the mists turned more violent and unpredictable. The whole array was starting to shake, and the three dryads seemed to have realized that something odd was going on. They had probably been waiting for Zac to summon new avatars since they saw him steadily infusing the control crystal with more and more spiritual energy.

Striking down all his avatars at once would have a much stronger effect, just like when one of them had defeated the first wandering cultivator. But now it looked like they didn't dare wait any longer, and they sent a few of the avatars toward the axe-man still stumbling around on the corner of the arena. However, Zac didn't care, as his [Cosmic Gaze] was trained at the bottom of the arena.

It was like he was mesmerized by the growing mass of untamed destruction hiding at the bottom of the array. Wasn't this the way things had always been when he fought? Supreme might crushing any resistance or any technique. If those three bastards wanted to create a dozen avatars with their combined energy, then he would simply drown them in an avalanche of even more energy.

There was no fusion and no adroit braiding of the two energies into something greater. This was mindless destruction, a tsunami of unrelenting force. And it was time to unleash it. However, that was easier said than done.

His mind strained to the limit as he urged the large blob to rise, but it felt like he was trying to lift a mountain with his mind. The rumbling of the arena became more and more severe, and small cracks could be seen on both the platform and the control crystal that Zac touched.

A searing pain flashed in his mind as the axe-man was cut to ribbons by the dryads' avatars, but he didn't care, as he was completely focused on the counter he had cooking below.

Finally, the blob he had infused almost his whole soul into reached the surface, and Zac was reeling by exertion by this point. Multiple capillaries in his eyes had burst, and he felt the salty taste of blood in his mouth as it freely poured from his nose.

The sounds of exclamations that had been missing earlier finally erupted among the spectators as what looked like a thundercloud rose through the ground. It was a messy mix of light gray spots and a sinister black, with the occasional flashes of bronze. It was probably impossible to tell what it was made from unless one had a skill like [Cosmic Gaze], but one thing was clear.

It was dangerous.

There was just no way for Zac to really control the thundercloud, and he could only push it in a certain direction with everything he had, forcing it forward by sheer force of will. Zac's mind felt like it would snap in two, but he refused to stop. The control crystal started to crackle as the small crystalline cracks turned into major fault lines, but they were continuously removed by the repair fractals.

The mix of Destruction and Putrefaction brought on from his two Daos swept toward the other side like a tidal wave, swallowing the stalwart army of the Enlightened Three in an instant. Explosions and sounds of clashes could be heard from within, as the three siblings desperately tried to dispel the onslaught. But it was like trying to stop a storm with your bare hands.

One avatar after another was either melted into a rotten pool by the Fragment of the Coffin or ripped into pieces by the sharp winds brought on by the Fragment of the Axe. A few simply were annihilated in a flash when the odd bronze-colored flashes appeared. There was no contest between the two sides, and all the refinement and skill the three could muster was pointless in front of Zac's insane outburst of power.

In just a few seconds, the whole avatar army was ripped to shreds, and the effect on its controllers wasn't small. The girl staggered backward and clutched her head before she fell over unconscious. The other two siblings shuddered as well, with blood pouring out of their noses and ears as they slumped down on the ground.

The two had been implicated as well, since they had assisted their sister, and their souls had been wounded as a result. However, Zac was in no position to gloat, as he wasn't all that better off. His eyes were completely bloodshot as he looked across the platform, and he had trouble gathering his wits since it felt like his head would split apart at any second.

The method of battle that Zac had chosen was one of mutual destruction. His soul had always felt pretty sturdy, just like his odd constitution, and it was only made stronger with the help of the Splinter of Oblivion. Between his soul's strength and his more advanced Daos, Zac had bet that he would be able to take the Enlightened Three out before his soul was ripped apart.

It had worked, but he was still a bit giddy, and he quickly took out an intricate box from his Spatial Tool. Inside was a blue rose seemingly made from ice, a piece of unblemished beauty. Zac didn't care about that, though, as he crammed the flower into his mouth and swallowed, allowing a cool sensation to spread down his throat and then throughout his mind.

It was the reward he had gotten from the Ice Troll back on the first level of the sixth floor. It was a soul-restoration treasure, which quickly soothed his strained mind. He had a couple of items in the same category between his shopping in the Base Town and Rasuliel's pouch, which was what had allowed him to identify it.

The icy rose was the strongest such item in his possession, and he had a feeling that he needed all the strength he could get to handle the fallout from taking out the three dryad brats in one go. The others hadn't been inactive while Zac ate the natural treasure, and the matriarch had already hurried down from the platform she spectated from.

"Elyss!" the dryad cried as she took out a crystalline bottle and poured some unknown mixture down her grandchild's throat before directing a murderous glare at Zac. "You are pretty ruthless. This is a discourse, not a battlefield."

She punctuated her words with having her aura expand around her, causing her long hair to flutter without any wind. But the matriarch's killing intent wasn't even a tenth of Zac's blood-drenched aura, and he didn't even flinch at being targeted.

"Injury is always a risk during a Dao Discourse," Zac answered with a hoarse voice, completely unfazed. "I am more curious why the other two got hurt. Perhaps you can explain?"

"They are triplets, so of course they're bound to have a deeper connection, one reaching even the spiritual level," the matriarch said without missing a beat.

"So which one of them is heading up next?" Zac said, eventually deciding not to push the issue.

He was in pretty bad shape, but the two remaining dryads were far worse off. Crushing them wouldn't be too hard by simply repeating a smaller version of the earlier storm. The Perenne matriarch's sharp eyes were locked with Zac's for a few seconds before her strained face blossomed into a charming smile.

"No need. I know these children well; they are no match for the might of your Daos. We concede this match; one of the slots to the Pool of Tranquility will belong to you," she said without a trace of the earlier animosity.

Zac, who was ready to go all out in case things deteriorated, mutely looked at the Perenne matriarch for a few seconds before he slowly nodded and walked back toward his platform. Was it over that easily? But a sudden realization made him certain that things weren't over just yet.

The teleporter to the next level still hadn't appeared.

12

POOL OF TRANQUILITY

"My friend, that was truly a… unique Discourse." The ent coughed when Zac jumped up to the platform they shared. "I have never heard of such a, uh, masculine manner of handling the Dao. And those insights… Scary, too scary. You are a walking paradox, both a child and a nemesis of the forest."

"Thanks, I guess," Zac snorted as he sat down.

"And congratulations on receiving the opportunity to bask in the Pool of Tranquility," the ent said, patting Zac's shoulder.

Zac initially only nodded in response, but he got confused when he noted that Thelim had surreptitiously dropped a small acorn that rolled into his lap. Believing it wasn't without reason, Zac looked at it with his Attuned Sight, and he saw that it contained some nature-attuned energies.

Curious, Zac instilled a minute amount of Cosmic Energy into it, and he suddenly received a short message in his mind, just like with the communications crystal he had gotten from Ogras before. There were only two words recorded, but it was enough to give Zac pause.

Be careful.

It was obviously a warning that things weren't as simple as they seemed, and Zac wasn't surprised. For one, the teleporter hadn't appeared even after the matriarch conceded. That meant that the System still didn't consider the quest finished. Hidden danger still lurked nearby. He was more surprised that the ent had gone out of his way to warn him at the risk of straining the relationship between his family and the Perenne Clan.

Zac still gave a slight nod in thanks to the ent before turning back toward the stadium. The pool would only be opened at sunset, so he would have to wait for a few more hours while the battles continued below.

Due to Zac's performance, there were cracks all over the array, and it would take over an hour before it regained full functionality. Zac tried to figure out his next course of action while they waited, but he couldn't do a lot apart from restoring his mental reserves.

Some trap was no doubt waiting for him in the Pool of Tranquility, but he couldn't figure out exactly what it was. Openly attacking the winners was unlikely, since such an action would no doubt spread and sully their reputation. It would also become impossible for them to attract any more guardians from the wandering cultivators.

Thankfully, he hadn't shown any of his actual strength, so the dryads were still completely clueless about his massive pool of attributes. They only knew that he was someone with two Early-stage Dao Fragments but also someone who had atrocious control over them. Perhaps they even thought he had fallen into some amazing fortuitous encounter that had imbued him with the two fragments without having any skills in the subject.

Zac instead started to go over the insights into his path of cultivation gained during the Dao Discourse. He had arrived at the conclusions while pissed off about the cheating, but he still felt that they held true after having calmed down.

He would put his attempts at learning [Cyclic Strike] on hold for now, unless it somehow proved extremely easy to master after having gained a life-attuned Dao Fragment. But Zac felt the odds of that were pretty slim. It hadn't worked at all while he had possessed two Peak Dao Seeds, so using the stronger Dao Fragment should only be more complicated.

There was also a need to formalize a new direction. Focusing on force rather than technique was good and all, but he needed to find a "creation" based on force and his Dao Paths. The chaotic thundercloud created from Axe and Coffin was extremely lethal, but he had only been able to summon that thing because of the **[Dao Discourse Array]**.

He also needed to figure out a way to bring his future Dao Fragment into the mix. Right now, he had unleashed a storm of Axe and Coffin, and this wasn't the fusion of Life and Death he had envisioned. There were a lot of things to consider, and it was a bit hard to theorize what was possible and what was impractical, especially since he was still lacking one of the fragments.

There was also the issue of those flashes of light that had the color of illuminated bronze. They had only appeared for a fraction of a second before disintegrating, but the destruction they'd caused had been far greater than either of his two Fragments. But even though the force was massive, he had been completely unable to sense anything from them.

He had a connection to the thundercloud even if he barely could control it, but the same couldn't be said about those lights. They suddenly appeared and disappeared just as quickly before he had any chance to form any mental connections to them.

"Hey, what feeling did you get from the bronze-colored flashes of light from within the cloud I summoned?" Zac asked as he turned to the ent, curious what the woodland being was able to feel.

"Flashes of light?" Thelim said with confusion. "I did not see any. I only sensed a mix of two Daos, the first one sharp and forceful, perhaps the Dao of the Greatsword? The other one was cold and death-attuned."

"Oh?" Zac said with surprise. "Never mind then."

Had those bronze lights not been visible to the normal spectrum? He had been using Cosmic Gaze the whole time, and he thought that the flashes were seen by everyone. But perhaps the bronze was just the color of the attunement, while the effect was indiscernible to the naked eye.

The most pressing question was what the light represented. Zac felt those sparks might be the clue to a way for him to increase his power, as there were only two reasonable explanations behind the sparks as he saw it.

The first possibility was that the flashes were related to the Splinter of Oblivion. It was a creation based on the Dao of Oblivion, which felt a bit similar to how the sparks simply disintegrated anything they touched. However, the only energy that Zac received from the Splinter was purified to pure spiritual energy by the Miasmic fractals.

Another possibility, and the one that Zac felt was most likely, was that the sparks were the result of chance fusions between his two Dao Fragments. The two concepts had combined due to friction or something else, like a nuclear fusion reaction of the Dao.

This fusion in turn had created a short-lived spark of some greater concept. If not oblivion, then perhaps something related of a lower tier. He really wanted to experiment based on this idea, because if that was what was going on, then he'd have a terrifying ace on his hands. He could only imagine the power of [Deforestation] with the additional effect of that mysterious bronze Dao.

But he could only wait for the tournament to end to get his prize and then experiment with his insights on the next level. The hours went by excruciatingly slowly, but it gave Zac time to mostly restore his frayed mind. His soul thankfully wasn't hurt, but it would probably have been if he had fought another battle. It was still overtaxed, though, and his head was pounding.

Finally the tournament was over, and all the spots were allocated. Three went to the dryads who had been fighting all day, whereas the last two each went to one wandering cultivator and one young man who looked like an elf. He had barely won the first battle, but during the second, he had suddenly burst out with a Dao Fragment, destroying the opposition with a skillful push before the dryad had a chance to adapt.

The guests left the arena to continue the festivities while the six were led by the Perenne matriarch toward a primordial forest full of gargantuan trees. Zac only nodded in thanks to the ent before he followed in tow, wondering if he would ever get a chance to repay Thelim for his help.

The group stopped after having walked for just ten minutes, but when the matriarch waved her hand, the surroundings changed. Initially, there had only been an empty spot in the forest, as the distance between the trees was pretty big, but it was now replaced with the stump of a massive tree.

This tree must have been the king of the forest when it lived, its size forming a landmark seen hundreds of miles away. The stump was even larger than the platform the Dao Discourse had taken place on, and its size dwarfed even the trees in the redwood forest he had visited with Ogras.

The group jumped onto the stump after marveling at the specimen for a few seconds, and he was surprised to see six small ponds. The Pool of Tranquility was actually on top of the tree itself.

"So what do we do?" the elf asked, and Zac looked over at the matriarch with interest as well.

"The moment the daylight ends, there will be a change in the pools. At that moment you simply need to choose one of the pools and submerge yourself. Open your mind to absorb the energies that will be released from the dew," the matriarch explained. "I will take my leave so as not to affect your opportunity. We have also prepared six isolation arrays to make sure no sudden sounds will impact your cultivation."

Zac cracked his neck and looked back and forth. The three dryads pointedly ignored him as though he weren't there, while the second wandering cultivator kept to himself. Only the young elf tried to make some small conversation where he not so subtly tried to understand Zac's origin and whether he was affiliated with any local force.

But the young elf was soon enough subdued by the atmosphere, and he simply walked over to the nearest pool, claiming it for himself. Thirty minutes later, the sun finally went down beneath the tree crowns, shrouding the area in darkness.

It was like the stump had awoken the moment it no longer basked in sunlight, and it started to radiate an ancient energy as the six pools lit up with a soothing green luster that rose a few meters into the air. Zac's headache got a lot better from just standing near them, a clear sign that the pools truly worked wonders on the soul.

The wandering cultivator and the elf gleefully jumped into their respective pools, but the splash didn't make a sound due to the arrays. Zac glanced at the three dryads, who stared right back, before jumping into one of the free ponds himself. He saw the three dryads jumping in as well, at which point he slightly relaxed and focused on the energies in the water.

It suddenly felt like he was one with the world as he took one deep breath after another, and his pores opened wide to drink in the energies of the miraculous dew. His headache was gone in seconds, and he quickly closed his eyes and sank down so that even his head dipped beneath the surface.

He was cautious about letting down his guard while being mesmerized by the opportunity, but his danger sense was completely silent. Zac finally opted to relax his guard a bit to absorb as much of the light in the water as possible. The effect was immediate, and it felt extraordinarily good. It was like his mind was a parched desert and the motes of light were long-awaited raindrops.

The process was akin to stepping into the shower when caked in mud, feeling the dirt sloughing off from his body. His soul was giving the same effect, and he actually felt it shrinking as some discordant energies seeped out of him. But Zac felt that the effect wasn't something detrimental, as the remaining spiritual energy became stronger, more condensed.

Zac had no idea that his soul had contained so many impurities, but perhaps everyone started out that way, especially mortals. Mortals didn't have any connection with the Dao, and the soul probably played a big part in that. Zac knew that the pool didn't improve affinities, but rather cleansed some impurities and helped strengthen it.

A sudden roar in Zac's mind gave him a start and ripped him out of his reverie as his heart started beating with joy. Verun had finally awoken after having slept for two full floors. But Zac barely had time to greet the Tool Spirit before he sensed an overwhelming thirst coming from the axe even while it was still in his Spatial Ring.

It was just like when the mysterious stone had appeared during the New World Government auction, and the target was clear. It wanted the mysterious liquid in the pond.

Zac didn't have any compunctions about having Verun snatch a part of the Pool of Tranquility. The dryads had tried cheating during the match, so what if he exacted some interest in return? He didn't even have time to take out his axe, when he sensed a startling issue with his mind.

There was something else there, something foreign. It was extremely well hidden, and he hadn't noticed it at all while he enjoyed the process of his mind being purified, even if he had never completely relaxed his vigil. It was as if the shadow of a whisper had snuck into his mind along with the energy from the pond. It only took him a second to realize what was going on.

How could Zac not recognize the feeling of having his mind manipulated after having fought against the far more insidious manipulation from the Splinter of Oblivion? He suddenly remembered the dozen powerful cultivators who had stoically walked behind the Perenne matriarch. Perhaps their choice to stay behind wasn't completely voluntary.

He, unfortunately, didn't have any great solutions to getting rid of the intruder in his mind, as it had already snuck past the defenses of **[Mental Fortress]**. Only after discharging a massive amount of mental energy by unleashing his Dao Fragments did the invading energy get ripped to shreds.

Zac still felt some cold sweat running down his back though. That had been way too close. Even if the effects of the dew were amazing, he had kept a constant watch against any plot of the Perenne matriarch, but her ploy had passed by his defenses completely unnoticed. If Verun hadn't shaken him awake, he might have fallen further and further into some mental vise he couldn't get out of.

Zac furiously rose from the pool, jumping onto the stump with wild eyes. The first thing he noticed was a teleportation array that would take him to the next floor, but Zac didn't even give it a second glance as his eyes turned to three specific pools. Zac refused to leave as things stood.

He wasn't done with the Perenne family just yet.

13

RECIPROCITY

The fact that the teleporter had appeared was a relief, since that meant that he had passed the trial. The System had attached a hidden requirement to the quest where he not only needed to stand victorious in the Dao Discourse, but also survive the aftermath.

The moment he noticed and dispelled the threat of being possessed, he had conquered the sixth floor and could move on to reap his rewards. But he wasn't ready to let bygones be bygones, and a wave of smoldering anger burned in his chest. If he shrugged off the attempt on his life, he would no doubt have this nagging feeling for the rest of his life, a seed of karma that was impossible to resolve.

Part of him just wanted to go on a mindless slaughter, dragging up the whole clan by the roots while leveling half the forest to the ground. But Zac knew that was just the Splinter urging him on. It seemed like the invasion of his mind hadn't just agitated Zac, but also the Splinter itself. Maybe it didn't like the competition.

He knew he couldn't do so, though. Not only was it unconscionable, but would also open a can of worms. Who knew what would happen if he started rampaging? Perhaps there were some hidden guardians of the forest keeping watch. Besides, cheating to protect their own resources wasn't really that big a deal, and the Enlightened Three didn't deserve death for their actions.

But the mind invasion was essentially an attempt on his life, and he had no compunctions with exacting at least some sort of revenge.

His aura exploded in an instant, causing cascading waves to splash all around him as his massive Dao Field drowned out the primordial energies of the tree stump. The isolation arrays cracked in an instant, exposing the five pools.

Zac didn't waste a second and leaped toward the closest pool that housed one of the three young dryads, but the man had obviously noticed the disturbance already and prepared himself. Dozens of razor-sharp roots shot toward him from within the pool before the dryad's head even breached the surface.

But the Enlightened Three weren't the floor guardians. They were simply three Peak F-grade warriors with unusually high accomplishments in the Dao, who also possessed the ability to fuse their spiritual energies together. They had been a threat to Zac before he found his path, but that threat only existed within the confines of the duel.

This was a true battlefield.

A massive fractal edge infused with the Fragment of the Axe tore the roots into shreds even if they were infused with a Peak Dao Seed themselves. All five winners had risen out of their pools by this point, most of them staring at Zac with shock. The only exception was the wandering cultivator, who gazed around with a glassy-eyed demeanor, which only strengthened Zac's conviction.

A storm of leaves reminiscent of his own [Nature's Barrier] started to swirl around the dryad as he looked at Zac with horror, but a swing infused with the Fragment of the Coffin turned them into rotten scraps as Zac barged his way through. His free hand shot forward to grab the shocked dryad by his neck, yanking him up into the air with a tug.

"WHAT ARE YOU DOING!" a scream echoed across the area, and a dozen green blades of grass shot toward Zac with such power that the air around them exploded.

The blades contained enough momentum to pierce through steel, and they seemed to be infused by a Dao Fragment as well. Zac scrambled out of the way, thankful he had grabbed one of the youths in time. The Perenne matriarch's power had somewhat superseded his expectations, but she had obviously only aimed for spots on his body far from her grandchild.

Things weren't to the point that Zac felt any fear, however, and one tree after another appeared around the area and even on top of the stump as Zac activated [Hatchetman's Spirit]. The improved vision brought from the skill directly exposed the Perenne matriarch hiding not far away within an array. She sat together with two loose cultivators, and between them was an array with an odd plant placed on it, recently ripped from the ground, judging by the soil stuck to its roots.

The blades of grass that had attacked Zac were her hair extending from within the array, and more and more stalks flew out from her head to join the battle. The blades of grass were quick, but Zac was almost impossible to catch now that he had summoned his own forest. He even felt that the effect from the skill had been boosted due to the Pool of Tranquility, and he had completely merged with the forest at this point.

The matriarch became more and more frenzied, and the two guardians also started moving toward him. The air even shuddered above the matriarch as a massive head made from tens of thousands of blades of grass appeared. A storm of leaves shot toward him as it opened its mouth, and even Zac felt some pressure from the power it contained.

But Zac had one more ace up his sleeve, and he suddenly moved his captive in front of him, aiming to use the dryad as a shield against the leaves.

"You!" the matriarch screamed in rage as she quickly stopped the massive avatar above her. "You outsiders are all the same!"

Zac ignored the comment as he flashed forward once more, this time targeting Elyss, the dryad he had knocked unconscious during the Dao Discourse. She had jumped down from the stump just like the others, but she was clearly unaccustomed to life-and-death battles since she still stood way too close.

The moment she saw Zac rapidly approaching with [Loamwalker], she realized her mistake. She didn't even try to put up a fight as she activated an escape skill while erecting a line of defenses. Zac was in full rampage mode by this point, and the dryad's restrictive vines were destroyed in an instant as he appeared before her.

A well-aimed kick shot the girl into the side of the trunk with a loud thud, but the ancient wood didn't even lose a splinter. It was rather the dryad who was hurt and fell down on the ground with a groan. She tried to get back to her feet, but Zac was already upon her again as he swung [Verun's Bite] to rip apart the stalks of grass that had aimed to save her.

"Stay down," Zac growled as he slammed [Verun's Bite] into the stump next to her while still holding on to the other dryad in a tight grip.

A massive shudder ran through the stump as Zac's axe bit into the wood, and the primordial energies surged for a second before they calmed down again.

"The ancestor!" Elyss cried in dismay, but she still didn't dare to move a single finger.

"One more move and I'll crack his neck and cut the girl in two," Zac said with a ruthless glimmer as he grabbed the second dryad and jumped on top of the stump again.

"You've hidden your power well," the elder dryad said as she joined him on top of the ancient stump. "Are you not afraid the Heavens will turn against you for returning our hospitality with such enmity?"

"Hospitality?" Zac snorted as he ripped Verun out of the tree and stood up straight. "I didn't care that these three cheated during the discourse, but since you wanted to take control of my mind, I had to act."

"We would never do something like that!" the male dryad exclaimed with fury, indignation apparent on his face. "We're not an unorthodox force! You're just here to cause trouble! Are you working for the invaders?!"

Things such as mind control and turning cultivators were considered an unorthodox path, as they clearly went outside what the Apostate of Order had envisioned when he set up the various contracts of the System. Zac personally felt it was a pretty weird distinction to make since so many forces allowed slavery, but it had something to do with the will of the System.

Zac ignored the young dryad, though he was pretty surprised to see that he seemed genuinely repulsed by the idea. He instead turned to the young elf who was watching the proceedings perched atop a tree far in the distance.

"Could you take that guy back to the party? Perhaps his mind can still be salvaged," Zac said as he nodded at the wandering cultivator, who had fallen down from the stump due to the shockwaves of battle.

"It looks like I wasn't really fated to use the Pool of Tranquility. No matter; most of the benefit comes from the initial cleansing," the elf said with a sardonic shrug.

But he still didn't move, instead opting to turn his eyes to the Perenne matriarch, who tried to kill Zac with her glare.

"Go," she simply said without her eyes leaving Zac's.

The elf bowed and prepared to leave, but he first ran forward and grabbed the shoulder of the wandering cultivator after a brief hesitation. The next moment, he disappeared in a puff of leaves that scattered all around before dissipating.

"What do you want?" the Perenne matriarch said.

"I want this pond," Zac said. "It's a small price for trying to possess me."

"Impossible," the old dryad said without hesitation. "It's not possible even if I wanted to. It's a natural formation created by the ancestor of the forest and thousands of years of accumulation. The dew will turn useless if you bring it away."

"Then release the people you've captured," Zac said after mulling it over.

"It's also impossible. The seed has been planted; the effect is irreversible. They will be guarding the forest until they die," the old dryad said with a staid expression.

"Grandma! You didn't!" Elyss exclaimed with horror.

"Every day, new outsiders enter the forest to partake in its riches. But do they pay nature back for providing them with wealth and power? No. They return to their cities on the outside and use their newfound strength to attack us, to join the invaders in their assault. Their greed is endless, their hunger insatiable.

"So what if I control them? These people would be nothing without the forest, so the least they can do is stay behind and defend it," the matriarch said with fury in her eyes, the words turning louder and louder as she spoke.

"Grandma…" Elyss said from the ground, her eyes wide with shock.

The other dryad looked shocked as well, and it was all too apparent they hadn't been aware of their grandmother's actions. Zac sighed when he heard her words, a wave of exhaustion sweeping through his body. He couldn't condone her actions, but he could understand her motivations. How far would he go to save the people of Earth? Of Port Atwood?

But that still didn't change things, and Zac threw [Verun's Bite] into the closest pool as he took out his spare axe, a High E-grade battleaxe. Verun keened in delight as it entered the pond, and the whole stump started to shake the next moment as the energies in the area ran amok.

"What are you doing?!" the matriarch exclaimed, her killing intent rising once more.

"My weapon can benefit from the dew, so he'll drink a bit since I can't take the pond with me," Zac explained.

Verun was like a black hole as it absorbed the dew, and Zac had already witnessed its seemingly endless thirst from having drained hundreds of beasts of their blood. The stump kept shaking as the water levels of the six ponds kept decreasing until just about half remained. Only then did Verun stop, seemingly satisfied with its haul.

"Don't move," Zac reminded the matriarch as he jumped down.

"So will you release my grandchild now?" she spat when Zac emerged.

"I need to do one more thing. Stay here. You should know what I'll do if you're not here when I return. I have the eggs, but I still want the hen," Zac reminded her as he flashed away once more.

He couldn't take the dew, and he couldn't save those poor souls. But there was one more item that had sparked Zac's interest, and he quickly moved through the forest toward the arena. Zac used his movement skill the whole way back, and he appeared on top of the [Dao Discourse Array] in less than a minute.

A few quick swings were all it took to separate the platform from the massive roots that had dragged it above ground, but Zac frowned in annoyance when he wasn't able to put it inside his Cosmos Sack.

"This thing can't be carried away, young man," an aged voice said, prompting Zac to turn around.

It was a kind-looking old elf, who was accompanied by the same youth who had just left the Pool of Tranquility.

"If it could be stashed away in a Pouch of Holding, Little Glamira wouldn't have been forced to hide it below ground all this time," the old man said with a smile. "The child my grandson brought will be fine, and I guarantee his safe return in front of all these people. In return, could you leave this array intact? The Perenne family are not the only ones benefitting from it."

Zac slowly nodded, though not without some unwillingness. The [Dao Discourse Array] had been his best bet at studying the mysterious bronze Dao he had somehow conjured. But not even he could carry a thirty-meter-wide pillar around on his back, so he could only give up on it. He instead turned toward Thelim, who looked at the proceedings with confusion written all over his face.

"I don't know if you or even this world is real, but I hope I'll be able to see you again. This treasure might be of use to you," Zac said as he threw the ent a wooden box.

Thelim curiously opened it to see an egg-white leaf that radiated an intense amount of life-attuned force.

"This!" Thelim exclaimed as he hurriedly closed the box so as not to let the aura leak. "This is too precious. I cannot accept it!"

The leaf was a treasure that Zac had snatched on the fifth floor. He still had no idea what it was, but it contained almost as much energies as the Fruit of Ascension. Zac didn't dare to eat it, since the leaf didn't cause any cravings in his body like most beneficial treasures did, and he couldn't figure out any other uses for it either.

It was only collecting dust in his Spatial Ring and would probably disappear when he left the Tower anyway, so he chose to gift it to Thelim instead to reciprocate his goodwill.

"If you don't want it, then throw it away." Zac smiled.

He threw one last look at the [Dao Discourse Array] before he left with a shake of his head. Some things weren't fated. He soon arrived back at the stump and finally released the poor dryad who had been dragged back and forth like a ragdoll for the past minutes.

He had nothing to say to the four dryads, who gazed at him as though he was a walking calamity as he stepped onto the teleporter, leaving the forest behind.

14

MANUALS

[Sixth Floor Complete. Upgrading Title.]

[Choose Reward: Compatible Soul-Strengthening Manual, Compatible Body-Tempering Manual, Beast Mastery Manual]

Zac's eyes made a beeline for the rewards, but his face scrunched together when he noticed that there weren't any rewards related to the Dao. He had almost been certain there would be a Dao Treasure waiting for him, but it looked like the System had a sense of humor. Or perhaps it simply didn't award any Dao Treasures at all since there was still the projection waiting when he exited the Tower.

[Tower of Eternity – 6th Floor: Reach the 55th level of the Tower of Eternity. Reward: All Stats +10. All Stats +10%.]

The title was just what Zac expected, but he still couldn't help but feel a bit disappointed. One of his goals before evolving was to reach 1,000 points in Strength, but he knew now that he had already maxed out on the benefits he could get from the Tower Title.

The next floor, if he could even pass it, would most likely add a high-tiered component to the title, not any more raw stats. It would be better if he looked at raw combat power, and it was usually more desired to keep the raw attributes down so that one would be able to enter restricted Mystic Realms. But it was far worse for Zac now that he needed to reach a certain threshold rather than stay under it.

Zac didn't have any good ideas on how to boost his Strength with the final 73 points to reach his goal of a thousand. He had only gotten 7 points from the Peak Strength Fruit, but he should be approaching the limit of what he could gain while still in F-grade. Not that he could get his hands on any more of them anyhow.

There was some Strength waiting for him when he formed his final Dao Fragment, but it wouldn't be enough. Neither Sanctuary nor Trees gave a single point into Strength, and he would probably only get the 10 points from the boost to all attributes.

Was getting a Middle Dao Fragment the only option?

Unfortunately, that was easier said than done. He had discussed the topic with Galau a couple more times after they'd discussed [Axe Mastery] when he mastered the skill. According to him, it wasn't any easier getting a Mid-grade Fragment than pushing your Race grade to D while still having a F-grade class.

A Low-grade Dao Fragment was the standard limit for almost all cultivators. As Galau explained it, over the almost million years his clan had existed, there had been no lack of geniuses who formed Dao Fragments before they evolved. But there hadn't been a single one who managed to evolve the Dao Fragment while still in F-grade.

It could technically be done, but it required both a tremendous insight into and affinity with the Dao in question. In other words, you needed to be a cultivator to evolve the Fragment. However, Zac had reason to believe that he might be an exception to this rule.

Galau had said the same thing about Early-stage Dao Fragments as well. According to him, one even needed a high affinity if you wanted to form a Dao Fragment at all. It had something to do with an F-grade warrior lacking a natural spirituality, something that only affinity could make up for.

The first grade of cultivation was based on building a foundation. You started with a weak mortal constitution and gradually improved it to be able to support cultivation and harmonize with the Dao. In fact, the youth had assumed that Zac was a cultivator based on the fact that he had formed Dao Fragments.

However, Zac hadn't encountered any problems forming his Dao

Fragments even with his nonexistent affinity, leading him to believe that there were no such restrictions for him, as long as he got some help in forming the Fragments.

That still meant he needed to encounter an opportunity even greater than the Dao Funnel or the Tower Apparition, and Zac didn't want to rely on such a long shot for the chance at pushing his Fragment of the Axe to Medium stage.

There was the possibility of utilizing his apparition on his Fragment of the Axe instead of fusing his third Dao Fragment, but Zac wasn't too sure about that gambit. It would mess up his class choices a bit, but more importantly, there was no guarantee of succeeding in upgrading the fragment.

He was pretty close to forming the life-attuned Dao Fragment, and he was almost certain he would be able to push the final distance with the help of his apparition. But the same couldn't be said of his Fragment of the Axe. He'd barely gotten used to fighting with it, and he hadn't really figured out what direction to take it.

There was a pretty large risk he would just make some improvements rather than evolving the Axe Fragment, even with the help of an apparition. If that happened, he would essentially have wasted that huge opportunity. Perhaps the following floors would present him with a solution, so Zac didn't completely give up, and instead turned his attention to the rewards.

Galau had broadened his horizons greatly during their travels, especially after the merchant realized Zac was a pretty clueless progenitor who only got integrated a year ago. One valuable piece of information after another had flooded out of his mouth to curry favor.

The subject of manuals was one such topic. Zac had been looking for something like a meditation manual to combat the Splinter in his mind since he'd returned from the hunt. Calrin hadn't been able to get his hands on anything useful, though, and Zac had been forced to solely rely on the Miasmic fractals in his mind.

But such a thing did in fact exist, along with various other types of manuals. A Soul-Strengthening Manual was a technique to gradually improve one's soul, just like the Pool of Tranquility did. It would not only make one more resistant to soul attacks and illusions, but would also increase one's spiritual energy reserves.

The soul was the power source of the Daos, and none of the attributes directly contributed in this regard. Intelligence and Wisdom didn't help you with controlling the Daos or strengthening your soul, and neither did any other. The soul's strength was pretty much inborn, though it got stronger from leveling up.

Zac had a feeling that his soul was already a lot stronger than normal, especially after having completely steamrolled the Enlightened Three with his Dao Storm. The Splinter of Oblivion had helped by strengthening it even further, and his dip in the pond had helped remove some impurities.

This manual was a chance to work on his soul even further.

Better yet, it was even possible to use such a manual without being a cultivator, so it wasn't something that he would have to throw to the Merit Exchange. There was, however, a pretty big reason as to why it was almost unheard of for cultivators to use Soul-Strengthening Manuals.

It was slow. Excruciatingly slow.

One could spend millennia refining and empowering one's soul, turning it into a diamond completely free of impurities. But you could instead have focused on improving your Dao or progressed in levels during that same time, and both would have a greater effect on one's survivability and strength.

Body-Tempering Manuals were related to special constitutions or improving one's bloodlines. Practicing a manual along with taking certain treasures or medicinal baths would slowly transform one's body to gain a specialized constitution.

Alea was such an example, though there seemed there were some problems with the method she used. Ogras' grandfather had probably been unable to acquire a complete manual, so they had jumped into it blindly. Another possibility was that they had tried to forcibly use a manual with low compatibility.

If the main reason for the scarcity of Soul-Strengthening Manuals was the slow progress, then compatibility was the main reason for there being almost no Body-Tempering Manuals in circulation. Pretty much all manuals had extremely strict requirements on things such as Race, affinities, and even bloodlines to work.

To simply train using an unsuitable manual was to court death. If

Alea was practicing with an incompatible manual, then just turning into a monster was the least of her worries. She ran the risk of dying at any moment, and considering her class and constitution, she might end up taking half of Port Atwood with her in a storm of poison.

Beast Mastery Manuals were somewhat of a mix between a skill and a mental exercise, and likely the most popular of the three supportive manuals that Zac was offered. It allowed anyone to gain a facsimile of the abilities that a true Beast Master like Verana possessed by allowing you to slowly form a connection to a beast through prolonged meditation.

One could use it to gain a mount like the floor guardian that Ogras had fought, or a pure battle companion to fight alongside you. The connection sounded a lot like what he had with Verun, and the chance of betrayal was pretty slim unless the beast got too powerful.

There were drawbacks to this type of manual as well, though. Compatibility was an issue with both Soul-Strengthening and Body-Tempering manuals, but with Beast Mastery Manuals, the compatibility issue lay with the beast. You needed certain manuals to tame certain beasts, and some beasts were simply not possible to form a connection with unless they wanted to.

Ogras was the victim of a forced connection, from what Zac could tell, where the Umbra had forced a connection that normally wasn't possible to create. He hadn't dared to experiment on himself due to the risk of death, so he had used Ogras to satisfy his curiosity after having turned into an Inheritance Spirit.

Since the System didn't mention compatibility with the manual, Zac guessed that it would have to be either pretty general or that it was like a lottery what sort of beasts that it would work on. It might turn out useful, but it might also only work on beasts that didn't exist on Earth.

In either case, the manuals weren't something that would benefit Zac in the short run, but with enough time, all of them could help him in different ways. Finding a compatible manual was extremely rare, and most were created through an arduous process of trial and failure by clans that had the resources and manpower to experiment.

A few of the peak forces in the sector would probably not possess them, but having the means to create a specialized constitution that fit your Heritage and bloodline was no doubt rare even among the strongest forces in the area.

All three manuals were also a chance for a warrior to gain more class options before evolving, so Zac could understand why they were presented as a reward. Of course, the additional classes Zac would get from a stronger soul or acquiring a beast companion probably wasn't something that Zac wanted right now.

His bottleneck wasn't his constitution either, but rather the Dao and the concept of creation.

But even if Zac didn't need them to get a better class, they were still useful in their own way. Zac guessed that this was a way for the System to provide an uncommon perk that most elites could benefit from or use to shore up weaknesses.

Indecision plagued Zac as he looked back and forth, and he couldn't reach a conclusion. All of them had benefits and drawbacks that made Zac leery to pull the trigger. The body-refinement manual would allow him to improve on his already monstrous constitution, but there were some pretty big question marks about his body.

There was obviously something special about his body, and Zac worried that the body-refinement manual he got from the System wouldn't work well with a body of Technocrat Heritage even if it said it was compatible. It might take away what made his body special in order to create something new.

Or perhaps the constitution that would be formed from a Technocrat Heritage simply wasn't in line with the cultivation path he had embarked upon, that of Life and Death.

Getting a beast companion would be a pure plus; Verun had proven that many times. But there were extremely few decent beasts on Earth, and it wasn't even sure that the manual would work on them. He was also hesitant that there were any beasts strong enough to actually make a difference. He would have to find a pretty monstrous animal to be able to keep up with his own power and growth.

As for the Soul-Strengthening Manual, it was simply too slow. Zac wouldn't see any direct benefits until after the incursions and Dominators were gone. He also wasn't sure whether the time spent grinding using such a manual would be better used to kill beasts and open up nodes. Leveling up did strengthen one's soul as well, and reaching higher grades was probably the best counter to the Splinter of Oblivion.

Zac finally made his decision, but before he claimed the reward, he paused, first opting to check in on Earth by opening the Ladder. It had become somewhat of an emotional support to see that Kenzie and the others were all alive, so Zac's eyes quickly scanned through the lists to find the familiar names.

But he suddenly froze, as the latest change in the Ladder was just too shocking.

15

NINE REINCARNATIONS

Zac was like a statue as he gazed at a particular spot on the Ladder. How had such a change come to be?

Ladder – Level
1. Super Brother-Man | 75
2. Thea Marshall | 68
3. Thwonkin' Billy | 64
4. Enigma | 61
5. Daoist Chosui | 60
6. Silverfox | 60
7. Guru Anaad Phakiwar | 59
8. Thomas Fischer | 58
9. Francis | 58
10. Lotus | 58

Ladder – Wealth
1. Super Brother-Man
2. Smaug
3. Greed
4. Enigma
5. Thea Marshall
6. Henry Marshall
7. Djinn

8. Thwonkin' Billy
9. Francis
10. The Eternal Eye

Ladder – Dao
1. Super Brother-Man
2. Guru Anaad Phakiwar
3. Thea Marshall
4. Abbot Boundless Truth
5. The Eternal Eye
6. Pretty Pretty Mega Kenzie
7. Silverfox
8. Thwonkin' Billy
9. Daoist Chosui
10. Father Thomas

The shocking change was obviously Billy and Thea having gained a massive surge in levels since he checked last. He had taken a look just a few days ago, and Thea was level 65 at that time, while Billy was level 61. That meant they had both gained a tremendous amount of energy in an instant, since less than an hour had passed on the outside since he looked.

But the real shocker was perhaps that Billy had surged to the eighth spot on the Dao Ladder. Before this, he wasn't even ranked, and Zac wasn't sure he even possessed an Early mastery Dao Seed. Zac couldn't imagine that simple giant pondering on the intricacies of the Dao, but Billy was like an onion.

Every time they met, Zac learned one more surprising layer to Billy, from the golden blood to the sleep cultivation. It wouldn't be surprising if someone like that possessed disgustingly high affinity with some Dao, and it only took him some time to figure it out. Judging by the fact that he had also gained multiple levels, it pointed toward the fact that he had gained it mid-battle.

Zac was happy for his friends, but more so, he was worried. Had something happened on the outside that would prompt Thea and Billy to take such a risk? The only way to gain multiple levels in one go was for them to defeat a powerful E-grade invader, probably a general from the undead incursion or a leader from one of the few remaining ones neighboring the Dead Zone.

Thea was aware that he would return in a day or two, yet she had risked her life in such a fight. Zac almost regretted looking at the ladder after seeing the change, as a seed of worry had been planted in his heart. But he could only shake it off and focus on his climb. He would leave this place in fifty days, which was just a few hours on the outside.

Apart from the sudden jump by Thea and Billy, nothing much had changed since he last checked the ladder, apart from the occasional movement here and there. Francis and Lotus were two new names in the top 10, though Zac had seen them in the top 30 since the beginning.

He had no idea who Lotus was, but Francis was one of the human councilors of the Underworld Council. He had usually hovered between rank 15 and 20, but he had upped his game since he had arrived to the surface. Apart from him and Enigma, there were two more councilors on the Power Ladder, though Zac only knew Gregor personally. It was the man he had met just after taking over the Union. He currently sat at the fifty-fourth position with level 55.

The other elites of Earth hadn't been idle either, and you now needed to have reached level 53 to get a spot. That meant that there were potentially thousands of people who had attained their level 50 skills by now, something that could bring a huge boost in strength to the native armies.

It wasn't bad, but Zac still felt it wasn't enough. He understood why human wave tactics were the only reliable option against incursions unless someone like him appeared. How would a single level 50 warrior take down those leaders he had fought? Even a dozen of them would be useless.

Zac couldn't see the earthlings defeating a leader, or even a general, unless thousands of people sacrificed themselves to exhaust the invader's Cosmic Energy. Even if the Undead Empire hadn't appeared on Earth, there was probably not much hope for the earthlings. He even guessed that Thea and Billy had paid some extraordinary cost to win whatever fight they had found themselves in.

The invaders would have created permanent outposts, killing or enslaving the local population as they drained the planet of all its wealth. Earth was simply too slow in responding, with only a scant few of the incursions being closed while the invaders were heavily restricted and unable to use arrays.

The movements of the other two ladders were even more static than that of the power ladder. A few names had changed as people died or stopped progressing, but it took a lot for those ladders to move. The Dao Ladder had stayed almost completely the same since the large reshuffling that the Dao Funnel brought about, except for Billy.

Half the Dao Ladder was still filled with former spiritual leaders, such as monks and priests, with the rest being talents and elites who had risen through trials and tribulations. There wasn't a lot going on with the Wealth Ladder either. A lot of names had dropped off after Zac had conquered the Underworld Union, such as Little Treasure. Much of his wealth had been tied to the Union and was now part of Port Atwood's coffers.

But Greed, another former Union member who fled, somehow maintained his spot. It meant that he either carried a massive fortune on his person, or that he possessed intangible assets like a Mercantile License. Djinn was a new arrival, but he wasn't in any of the other two ladders. Zac guessed he had found a huge treasure that had spiraled him to the top in one go.

In any case, he could breathe out in relief since he saw that all the Valkyries, Kenzie, and Emily were safe, meaning that Port Atwood probably wasn't facing some immediate danger. It allowed him to keep climbing without too many distractions. Hopefully, Thea's actions were simply the result of impatience rather than desperation.

Zac closed the ladders before picking the Soul-Strengthening Manual. The reasoning for him was simple. The Beast Mastery Manual felt pretty useless to him, but the other two were both tempting. Eventually, it came down to choosing between power and survivability.

The Body-Tempering Manual would probably make him stronger as long as practicing it didn't mess up his body, but he was already plenty powerful for his level. The Soul-Strengthening Manual, on the other hand, could help him strengthen his soul, which was something Zac desperately needed in his fight against the Splinter.

He had already sensed the difference an empowered soul could have on him during his previous fight. The Splinter had been truly agitated due to the mind invasion, but Zac had yet been able to stay mostly calm through the fight. If it had been before, he would probably have unleashed [Deforestation] in a muddled rage before he could analyze the situation.

The Splinter was a constant worry, and he needed a long-term solution that wasn't reliant on the miasmic fractals. This might be his only chance to get his hand on a Soul-Strengthening Manual, and he had to take it even if it would slow down his cultivation or make him miss out on forming a constitution.

Besides, with his path of cultivation, he would probably spend a lot of time on the sickbed, wounded from cracking open nodes by force. Galvarion had been forced to recuperate for centuries, and Zac might share the same fate even with his constitution. Tempering his soul during the downtime would allow him to keep improving even when he was hurt.

The moment he made his choice, he was immediately sent off to the next world, and he barely had time to stash the radiant crystal that appeared in his hand before the whole field around him shook as tens of thousands of bodies rose to their feet.

One quick look around seemed to indicate that he was on a battle-field between an insectoid species and a mix of their undead counter-parts and humanoid Zombies, and judging by the groans and roars from the surroundings, the undead had won.

[Rebuff the Invasion.]

Zac wasn't surprised to see the quest, and he summoned the inde-pendent fractal blade of [Chop] to start clearing out the surroundings while he got his bearings. If he was supposed to rebuff the invasion, he needed to find either the incursion of the undead, or whatever means they had used to arrive at this planet.

After that, the most straightforward thing would be to cull the leaders of the invasion, which would hopefully force the soldiers to flee. Of course, it was a possibility that the leaders were far beyond his reach, at which point he would have to figure out how to swing the war in the insectoids' favor.

But Zac suddenly frowned as he looked around the area, and his eyes started to shimmer as he activated [Cosmic Gaze]. Were the undead really the targets?

"Something is going on!" a shout echoed out from the distance as a group of humanoids rushed toward Zac, pushing the slow-moving Zombies out of the way. "Why the hell is one of the mercenaries among the children?"

Zac curiously looked and saw that the new group was drenched in darkness to his eyes. Every part of their bodies was covered in death-attuned energies, and it was easy figuring out that they were undead, though these ones were sapient. They were a mix of different humanoid species, and it looked like some of them had swapped out certain body parts.

The fact that they were all sapient meant that they were E-grade Race as far as Zac knew, but his knowledge about the undead was pretty much limited to what Anzonil had told him. Perhaps there were situations where even lower-tiered undead could gain intelligence.

"Please, my lord!" one of the humanoids shouted from afar after having stopped outside the reach of the fractal blade that was still reaping Zombies left and right. "The children are innocent! They just haven't woken up yet. Please don't waste your strength on them."

"Hmm." Zac shrugged noncommittally as he ordered his blade to return to his side.

He had already realized that something was odd even before the group of undead approached him. He had first thought that the scenario was an invasion of the Undead Empire, but the fact that the area was teeming with Miasma made Zac realize that might not be the case.

A bunch of killed Zombies certainly would release some Miasma, but this battlefield essentially felt even more death-attuned than the core of the Dead Zone, and the effect hadn't nearly been this pronounced in the battles he had fought with the undead outside their incursion.

Besides, some insectoid species were extremely invasive as well, just like the Ayn Hivebeasts. Given enough time, they would swallow a whole world, and Zac knew there were many more species like them.

The scenario became clear after hearing the exchange between the undead. It looked like he was designated as some sort of mercenary, no doubt hired to help the undead forces to rebuff the insectoid invasion. Luckily, he had some experience in dealing with insects, and the mission seemed straightforward enough.

Unfortunately, he had just been caught red-handed slaughtering people from his own side. The only solution he could come up with was to act like an aloof master, which hopefully would allow him to not sour his relationship with the Undead Empire. It was best if he could keep his alliance with the undead to gather intelligence about his target.

"Thank you, my lord," the undead said as he scurried closer, allowing Zac to breathe out in relief.

The undead was level 60 at best, just a bit better than the extremely weak corpses around them. The low levels of the people made Zac believe this was a low-tiered world, just like the one before this.

"My lord, I am not sure how you appeared here?" the man hesitantly asked as he stopped a few meters away from Zac.

"I got a bit lost," Zac said. "Can you lead the way out of here?"

"Certainly." The undead nodded. "The children won't attack you as long as you are accompanied by one of us."

Zac was slowly led out of the sea of Zombies, and he quickly learned that it was not actually a battlefield, but rather a dumping ground where they had left a mix of acquired corpses and insectoid invaders to slowly turn into true undead. Zac's arrival had stirred them prematurely, and they would be kept there for some more time to gestate.

Zac was pretty curious about the society of the Undead Empire in general, but there was one thing he wanted to check first. He quickly took out the luminous crystal he had just gotten, and he infused his mind into it to see what he had.

[Nine Reincarnations Manual]

Temper your spirit through nine reincarnations of life and death and form an impregnable soul immune to the ravages of Samsara.

Zac's eyes lit up when he read the introduction, and any regret about missing out on a Body-Tempering Manual disappeared. It looked like he had just hit the jackpot. Didn't this sound like a manual made for him with his ability to jump between being living and dead?

LORD DRAUGR

Zac had no point of reference when it came to Soul-Strengthening Manuals, but the one he held in his hand seemed to be pretty damn strong, even if he didn't have his unique constitution. It wasn't quite as tailored to his situation as he first had thought, though, and it wasn't strictly limited to people who walked the Path of Life and Death.

The method to train in the manual was to push one's soul to the peak of life before plunging it to the depths of death, simulating a lifetime. After completing enough such revolutions, one's soul would undergo a rebirth, shedding some of its imperfections and growing in strength.

If one managed to complete all nine reincarnations, they would possess what the manual called a "Nine-Samsara Soul," and it would be so strong that he essentially wouldn't even need mental protection skills like [Mental Fortress] to stay safe. His soul would turn even more monstrous than his nigh-indestructible body.

The number of revolutions one needed to complete a reincarnation wasn't clear, but judging by the language in the crystal, it would be a massive undertaking to just complete a few reincarnations, let alone all nine. But Zac hoped that his ability to swap between life and death would be able to expedite the process, though that would probably require some experimentation.

However, there were two problems with the manual.

For one, only the method for the first four reincarnations were included in the crystal. He would have to somehow find the rest elsewhere if he wanted to continue practicing the skill, and Zac had no idea where he would even begin his search for the missing pieces of a manual like this. He couldn't just jump into a bunch of Mystic Realms, hoping to be lucky.

The fact that the manual was split up could also be seen as a positive. Zac only gaining the earliest stages of the manual meant that it was probably beneficial even in higher grades. It would have been a shame if he got one that was only useful in E-grade, after which he would have to swap to a new one.

The second problem with the manual was a bit tricky as well.

Each of the reincarnations required specific environments to practice. The first reincarnation only required him to meditate within one of two specific arrays, one death-attuned and the other life-attuned. Kenzie no doubt could help him build two chambers meeting the requirements since Zac had the schematic, but she probably wasn't able to put them on Array Disks just yet.

Perhaps this was where his unique situation could come into play. If he could swap out the increasingly stringent requirements with simply swapping back and forth, he would save an enormous amount of time and resources. It seemed unlikely that he would be able to practice the manual inside the Tower, though it wouldn't hurt to try it out.

Zac put away the crystal and looked over at the undead with some curiosity. This was the first time he had talked with a sapient undead, unless you counted his encounter with the Draugr woman in his vision.

"What Race are you?" Zac suddenly asked, breaking the silence. "Oh, and what's your name?"

"Ah?" the undead who walked alongside him started.

"Is your Race 'Zombie'? Or are you a Corpselord?" Zac asked with curiosity.

"A Zombie is a derogatory term for those who still haven't awakened," the undead answered after some hesitation. "My name is Eldar, and I am a Revenant, the most common Race of the undead."

"Could you explain a bit more? What's the difference between a Corpselord and a Revenant?" Zac asked. "It seems we have the time."

"Well…" Eldar said with clear conflict on his face.

Zac understood what was troubling the Revenant, which gave him an idea. There was something he could test that might make the group more talkative.

"Wait a minute," Zac said as he stopped in his tracks.

The group of undead stopped and looked at Zac with confusion, and their eyes widened in shock as Zac's skin turned deathly pale, and he started to release a massive amount of Miasma around him. His brown eyes quickly darkened until they were two black globes leading into the abyss.

"Wha– how?" the undead sputtered with confusion on his face.

"I am Draugr. I simply used a skill to look like a human," Zac said as he turned his abyssal eyes toward the group. "I have been traveling among the living for all my life. This is the first time I actually stepped on death-attuned soil. I hope you can answer my questions and clear up some points of confusion for me."

"I – ah, of course!" he said. "I am sorry, Lord Draugr."

Zac nodded in relief. This was one of the loopholes the trio had found during their climb, mostly thanks to Ogras' predilection of talking far and wide at any tavern he could find. Their Races were never an issue, as though the System forced all the natives to be enlightened and look past Race.

However, if you mentioned your Race, they would understand you, in contrast to mentioning the Tower of Eternity. They hadn't found any use for that small feature, though, until now. The Revenants had already been respectful earlier when he was a powerful mercenary hired to help in the war, but now it was as though they looked upon an idol.

"I am sorry for the discourtesy just now," Eldar said as he bowed deeply.

"It is fine. I understand that you'd be hesitant to discuss this matter with the living," Zac said. "Now, about the Races? I have traveled with my master my whole life, and he hasn't explained all these things for me for reasons I cannot disclose. But now that I am returning to the empire, I need this information."

It was a pretty horrible excuse, but judging by the attitudes of the group of Revenants, they wouldn't question him no matter what he said.

"Ah? Yes, certainly!" Eldar hurriedly said, though he looked pretty confused. "May I ask which empire you are referring to? Our Kingdom of Zarvadar borders no force that can be considered an empire as far as I can tell."

Zac frowned in confusion for a second until he realized the problem. This world wasn't actually part of the Undead Empire. How could it be? It was part of the Tower. The inhabitants of the worlds were never aware of anything larger than their planet, and higher-grade beings were mentioned as things of legend.

That meant that he, unfortunately, couldn't milk Eldar for information about the Undead Empire. Perhaps it wasn't completely a loss though, since there were still a lot of things that he might know. There was only one undead force in the Multiverse as far as Zac could tell, and this world should no doubt be based on the situation in the Undead Empire.

"Never mind, I cannot divulge it." Zac coughed. "Now, about the Races?"

"As you probably know, most of our population comes from corpses awakening, just like the field you saw earlier," Eldar said, eager to please. "Only the powerful can conceive children of their own, so adoption is more common. And these types of children are all Revenants.

"However, the undead are special in that some can change their Races to a certain degree, though supreme existences such as Lord Draugr does not need such things. Some shed their mortal coil through a ritual to turn into pure beings of Miasma. They gain Races, such as wraiths and specters," the Revenant explained. "A few others choose to become Corpselords.

"Corpselords are a manufactured Race. They are built by taking extraordinary body parts from multiple sources, creating a stronger than average body. Their progeny inherit a mix of their parents' bodies, which can both turn out great and pretty bad. Corpselord clans are usually subservient clans to either Liches or one of the five noble Races, since they were manufactured."

"Do Corpselords have any weaknesses?" Zac asked.

"Well, combining body parts is a hard venture, and only the most skilled Liches can do it without side effects. Most Corpselords are cursed with their body parts being in dissonance. They need to take medicine to quell the effects, and they are always looking for more compatible body parts. The risk for an earlier descent into madness is also pretty high."

"Then why would a Revenant choose to become such a being?" Zac asked with confusion.

"Ah, Lord Draugr might not know, but cultivation comes hard to us Revenants. We are not blessed with your talents, and becoming a Corpselord is somewhat of a shortcut to power some choose to take," Eldar explained, not without some helplessness on his face. "Most Revenants are forever stuck at F-grade, unable to truly enter the path of cultivation."

Zac slowly nodded, remembering Mhal, the Corpselord general. His research had been related to this subject. Infusing Draugr genes into one's body would be able to increase the affinity with Miasma and perhaps even decrease the dissonance between body parts.

"Never mind," Zac said, realizing he'd asked something he shouldn't have. "Are Liches one of the noble Races?"

"Liches aren't a Race," Eldar said with a shake of his head. "It's more of a position, as well as a branching class tree. Creators of undead, Miasma controllers. That incubation field you ended up in was maintained by a group of Liches, for example. They're needed to speed up the awakening of the children. But there are also many combat-oriented subclasses."

"So what Race are they?" Zac asked with confusion.

"Most are Revenants, but the most skilled Liches are, of course, among the five noble Races. Apart from the Eternal Clan, who exclusively follow the Sanguine Path."

"I know of the Eternal Clan," Zac slowly said. "But what about the other three Races?"

"Apart from your noble bloodline, there are the Izh'Rak Reavers. Their bodies are the strongest of all undead Races, without being burdened with any of the demerits the Corpselords have. Then there are the Eidolon, the leaders of the specters," Eldar explained. "They are the only spectral Race that is born that way, never having shed their physical form through the ritual. Most believe their control over Miasma is second only to the founders."

"Do you know what the founders look like?" Zac asked. "My master never told me."

Zac had no idea who these founders were, but he had an inkling. He kind of wanted to ask to make sure, but he saw the gazes of the group of Revenants. He had clearly asked a bit too much, and Zac was afraid that going too far would label him an imposter or something, making his quest all that much harder.

"No, the form of the exalted founders are beyond the knowledge of remote kingdoms such as ours. They are the origin of our species. I am sure they live in far greater places than here. Places where the Miasma is dense enough to turn liquid." Eldar sighed, clear longing on his face.

Zac's eyes lit up when he heard Eldar's explanation. One popular theory was that the undead Races were created by one single supreme existence, someone at the level of Emperor Limitless. He would probably have become an Apostate if he appeared in this era, but this had all happened before the System arrived, as the undead had existed even before the System.

These founders might be the descendants of this grand ancestor, and if that was the case, it wasn't surprising they would be considered the greatest undead Race.

After some more questioning, he got a pretty decent understanding of the undead Races. The Draugr could be considered the jack-of-all-trades of the five noble Races. Their bodies weren't as excellent as the Izh'Rak Reavers, and their affinity with Miasma wasn't as great as the Eidolon. But they still excelled on both those subjects, making them excellent all-rounders.

The Eternal Clan followed the Sanguine Path, as Eldar called it, and there even seemed to be some confusion whether the members were really undead or not. Some believed they were rather a closely allied Race that had decided to join the undead for some reason.

"Thank you," Zac finally said after he had satiated most of his curiosity.

There was still a lot that he wanted to know, but he felt that it would be too suspicious if he kept going. He instead turned his attention to something else.

"Where are we heading?" Zac asked as he looked at the desolate surroundings.

"We have set up a fort an hour's travel from here," Eldar explained. "You and the other mercenaries were supposed to be placed under General Niksi, but now I am not sure…"

Zac understood what he meant. Perhaps it would breach some sort of protocol for some normal undead to order around a Draugr.

"I need a place with both Miasma and normal Cosmic Energy," Zac said, switching subjects.

"Certainly," Eldar said, though his face looked like Zac had asked for a huge pile of feces to be placed in his bed. "We have already erected arrays to convert the energies for our guests. I'm sure one of the Array Masters can make some adjustments."

Zac nodded in thanks as he thought of his next move. He didn't have a lot of time on his hands, but if there was one floor he should stay some extra time on, wouldn't it be this one? Where else would he be able to find assistance in grinding the levels of his skills? Where else would he get tips on controlling Miasma?

It was time to integrate into undead society.

17

WAR

"Charge!" Zac roared as he pushed forward, each step causing the ground to shudder as his frame grew and quickly became ensconced in pitch-black armor.

Ten thousand Revenant warriors roared in response, charging the insectoid army without any care for their lives as a thick haze of Miasma covered the battlefield hundreds of meters in each direction. One after another fell as they approached the defensive line, but a fanatical gleam burned in the eyes of the survivors as they kept running.

Zac had severely underestimated the impact a purebred Draugr had in undead societies. He had figured it would be something like an elite on Earth. It would elicit some admiration and perhaps jealousy, but nothing too extravagant. But he had been sorely mistaken.

He had been given a king's welcome the moment he arrived at the base camp, and the Revenant general had even offered her position to him without hesitation. However, Zac had declined, instead opting to take command of an elite troop of 10,000 warriors with the intent to train his skills.

Anzonil, the old horndog, had also hit the mark on the pull of his Race to the opposite sex. He had essentially been visited by half of the eligible E-grade females in the kingdom by this point. He had only managed to stave them off by indicating that any spread of his bloodline would be met with swift and bloody retribution by his elders.

He knew the effect wouldn't be that pronounced in the real Undead Empire, though, as there apparently had been no one from the five noble Races visiting the Kingdom of Zarvadar for millennia. Giving birth to a progeny that was even half-Draugr would skyrocket that family into the stratosphere.

The interest had barely waned from the threat of his imaginary elders, though, and joining the battlefield had as much been an escape from the incessant courtships as it was a way to improve his skills.

He had already confirmed that the floor guardian was a "breeder," which was a specialized clone of the queen. She resided in a hive that had fallen out of the sky one day, continuously spewing out new soldiers. The original script was probably to help the war efforts to the point that a large-scale attack on the hive was possible, though Zac felt somewhat confident in assaulting the place alone after getting a grasp on the power levels involved in the struggle.

However, Zac wasn't quite ready to leave this floor yet, as he had found it extremely rewarding to use his class as it was intended.

Zac was almost upon the defensive line of the insectoid army he had targeted, and he quickly summoned the massive shield from [Immutable Bulwark]. It had slightly changed shape to look like the armor he wore when using [Vanguard of Undeath], and he used it as a wall breaker when he slammed into the row of hulking insectoid brutes that held the front line.

The specialized defenders were even larger than Zac in his transformed form, but they still flew out of the way as though they were made from Styrofoam as Zac ripped into the army. A hundred skeleton warriors rose from the Miasmic mists the moment Zac had pushed his way inside, hacking and slashing in every direction.

They caused massive confusion among the attackers, which allowed Zac's subordinates to widen the breach into a massive hole. Soon enough, the Revenant army cut their way through the middle of the army, wedging themselves in and forcing the insectoids to split in the middle. The roars of battle echoed in Zac's ears, and it felt like the battle lust of his warriors empowered him.

In fact, the accumulated killing intent of an army of the dead had been the key to upgrading [Indomitable], and it had pushed to Middle proficiency during his first skirmish. He had initially thought that the only way to improve the skill was to be hit with mental attacks, but he realized he had been completely wrong.

Hundreds of ranged attacks soared toward the vanguard, and Zac infused his fractal shield with the Seed of Sanctuary, quickly increasing its size to encompass the elite core of his army. The seed was nowhere as strong as his Fragment of the Coffin, but the coffin didn't help increase the area he could protect.

Unfortunately, he would soon lose even this capability, which was the downside of abandoning the Fragment of the Shield in favor of his Life-Death duality. Whatever Fragment the Seed of Sanctuary turned into, it would no doubt be life-attuned, which would probably make it impossible to use with his current class.

Of course, the Revenant army wasn't helpless even if Zac couldn't protect them all. They formed a second layer of defense in the sky that blocked out most of the attacks, and the soldiers ripped into the insectoid ranks with brutal fervor. Meanwhile, ten massive beacons were erected, and nine enormous cauldrons were placed between them.

It made Zac remember Mhal and his elite army. He had used cauldrons as well, though the way these warriors used them was slightly different. Massive black clouds started to billow out of the cauldrons in no time, and Zac knew it was a death-attuned poison that only affected the living. Dozens of Liches instructed the mists to roll into the swarm of insectoids, wreaking havoc on their ranks.

Zac had learned that the spellcasters of the undead armies generally followed three Heritages. First were the poison masters, such as the Liches in his squad, using toxins to cause widespread death. There were also many ice-attuned mages who fused death and frost into extremely potent attacks that froze both the bodies and souls of their foes.

Finally, there were the soul manipulators who used mental attacks, curses, and illusions. However, these specialists were extremely rare and usually required inborn affinities, sort of like the purifiers on Earth. There were certainly more classes, but these three were the most common, at least in this kingdom.

Zac had thought it had something to do with affinities, but the reason was a lot more pragmatic. The spellcasters of the undead armies leaned toward classes that would leave the corpses of their enemies intact. A fireball could turn a dozen warriors into cinders, but that would mean that the kingdom missed out on having a dozen new soldiers join their ranks.

The battle quickly turned into the undead's favor, and not just because Zac mowed through the army like a bulldozer. The two sides were almost equal in strength before his arrival, and the single addition of [Fields of Despair] had tipped the scales in the Revenants' favor.

Zac had only utilized parts of the skill until now, the part that recovered Miasma from kills and the part that weakened enemies. But with an army of the dead at his command, he could utilize the skill to its full effect, where the undead around him also benefitted from the skill.

He had initially expected that all the Miasma released from kills would go to him, but [Fields of Despair] actually provided the energy to the one who landed the killing blow. So the skill didn't just weaken the enemies, but it also increased the endurance of the undead, allowing them to keep fighting.

Using skills as they were intended was the best way to increase their proficiency. Zac had managed to push [Fields of Despair] to Late proficiency after just a few fights, and the skill reaching Late proficiency actually benefitted him.

Back when he'd upgraded the skill to Middle proficiency, the only thing that changed was that the skill's coverage more than doubled. Upgrading it to Late proficiency had doubled the area once again, and by this point, it was able to cover almost a third of a battlefield this size. One more upgrade and he would probably be able to cover a square kilometer in Miasma.

That wasn't the only benefit the skill provided after getting upgraded. He could actually feel the combatants within the mist now. The effect was nowhere near as comprehensive as the omniscience of [Hatchetman's Spirit], but it was more akin to having radar and sensing everyone in the mist like hazy blips.

He wouldn't be able to use the new feature to dodge attacks, but he would be a lot harder to sneak up on this way. Hiding within the Miasmic mists would be impossible without possessing some sort of counter.

"I'm going in," Zac said to the two powerful warriors who had fought right behind him the whole time.

They were his two assigned lieutenants, each chosen due to their ability to stay alive at the head of the battle.

"We'll hold the line," Yrvos, a Revenant created from a massive Ogre, grunted as he crushed an enemy with his barrel-sized mallet.

Zac nodded before slamming one of his feet into the ground, disappearing in a puff of Miasma. He appeared in front of a group of massive ants at the rear of the army, each of them well into the E-grade. They were war beasts that the insectoids reared, and one of the most powerful weapons in their repertoire.

Sitting on their backs were a group of commanders and Beast Masters, and it seemed as though they had been expecting Zac's appearance. Ten pillars of light appeared around them, forming an array with Zac and the ants in the middle. A heavy pressure suddenly bore down on his shoulders, whereas the insectoids seemed unaffected at all.

Zac frowned as he looked around, but he still proceeded with his plans as he stomped the ground again, erecting the cage of **[Profane Seal]**. The mists of **[Fields of Despair]** were joined by the black churning clouds of **[Winds of Decay]**. He didn't imbue the mists with the Dao of the Coffin though, but he had rather chosen to imbue **[Profane Seal]** with it.

His Dao Fragment had amazing synergy with the skill, and not using the two together would be a wasted opportunity. First, it made the five towers and their corresponding gates pretty much impervious to the outside forces who tried to break in and assist their leaders. Secondly, it empowered the chains immensely.

The spectral chains had become a bit useless against the targets Zac mainly focused on with the skill, instantly crumbling from the attacks of the powerhouses. But the chains now required tremendous effort to destroy by the insectoids, making them far more lethal. They also gained a corrosive effect when they attacked and could even deal significant damage by just lashing opponents.

Zac felt as though he were mired in quicksand due to the array, and he was utterly incapable of dodging the rabid attacks from the massive ants, who tried to gore him with their sharp legs. But he had never planned on dodging anything anyways, and he started to whittle down the massive insects with the help of **[Deathwish]**.

The E-grade warriors quickly realized their plan had failed, and they jumped down from the backs of the ants to increase the pressure. But Zac was like a whirlwind of death as his massive Miasmic bardiche ripped through the thick plating of the ants and the bodies of the insectoid leaders alike.

The massive pressure he was under from the array started to take its toll, and he was starting to run a bit low on Miasma. However, Zac didn't worry as one of the gates to **[Profane Seal]** soundlessly opened while Zac kept the insectoids busy.

The doors closed again just a second later, while one pillar after another exploded as spectral warriors appeared out of nowhere, killing the Array Masters and dismantling the array in seconds. After they had completed their main mission, they started to take out the normal soldiers in the cage that the spectral chains still hadn't dealt with.

Zac wouldn't have any issue dealing with the array himself, but he wanted to use the various squads in his employ as much as possible. It wasn't due to something as noble as giving his soldiers a chance to grow through battle. Zac knew very little about the war tactics of the undead, apart from the mindless hordes of the unawakened Revenants.

Alea had partly suffered her grievous wounds due to lacking knowledge as well, not expecting to get ambushed by ghosts like that. He didn't want that kind of surprise to happen to his armies in the clash against the undead incursion.

He had unearthed all kinds of knowledge during the three days he'd stayed on this floor. One small tidbit was that the spectral warriors couldn't pass through Dao-infused surfaces or skills with enough power. That was why he'd needed to open the door for the ghosts to enter his cage. Similarly, if warriors had their Dao Field unleashed, they wouldn't be ambushed out of nowhere, as the spectral warriors would be slowed by quite a bit.

Having one's Dao Field constantly active would put a drain on one's soul, but it would be worth it in the heat of battle to avoid unwelcome surprises such as getting skewered from a ghost popping out of the ground.

With the threat out of the way, Zac methodically killed off the leaders one by one, leaving just the largest ant alive. Zac no longer had any means to see its level, but he guessed it was around level 85 and focused on Endurance. It was a perfect target for his daily practice.

"You can go," Zac said with his deep voice.

The ghosts who had remained inside the cage until now bowed before they streamed out through a gate that Zac opened, leaving Zac alone inside. Zac cracked his neck as he looked at the target dummy in front of him.

The past three days had been full of failures, but today, he'd conjure those bronze sparks no matter what.

18

REPURPOSE

The departure of the spectral warriors left only Zac and the remaining ant inside the cage, along with a hundred decaying bodies that slowly replenished his reserves with Miasma. He was still uncomfortably low on energy though, so he bit down on a pitch-black pill that turned into a thick sludge that ran down his throat. A surge of Miasma spread through his body, almost instantly restoring a fifth of his Miasma reserves.

Zac tried not to think of the foul taste of the **[Warrior Pill]** he just ate as he swapped out **[Verun's Bite]** for one of his disposable axes. It was a pill that had a similar effect as Cosmic Water but without the downsides as long as you used them in moderation. The **[Warrior Pill]** was a lot weaker than the water, though, and you could only eat one a day before side effects started to crop up.

Next he dispelled **[Vanguard of Undeath]** and shrank back to his original size. He wanted to experiment with his Daos, and he had found that his control got even worse in his transformed body. Miasma kept churning around in his body to keep the Miasmic armor and weaponry active, which might cause some interference.

Or it was just the fact that the spiritual energy needed to travel further when his body was bigger.

The air around Zac started to shudder as he unleashed his Dao Field for his Axe Fragment to the utmost. The ant seemed to sense the threat and attempted to ambush him, but Zac kept dodging as he tried to regain the feeling he'd had during the Dao Discourse.

It was obviously harder to concentrate with a massive beast trying to skewer you, but Zac felt that it was far easier to make breakthroughs mid-battle compared to sitting alone in a courtyard, meditating. The pressure and risk of death would stimulate his potential, and something new would hopefully be born from his struggle.

The atmosphere inside the cage kept changing as Zac switched back and forth between the Dao Fields for his two fragments, one moment containing invisible blades and the next second corrosive winds. He had kept trying to recreate the Dao Storm with the help of his aura over the past days, but he was simply not making any progress.

He did at least manage to superimpose the two Dao Fields for a second by force. When he wanted to release a second Dao Field, the other automatically receded into his body, but he was able to stop it by simply blocking it out. However, that caused a pretty hefty loss in spiritual energy, as the energy simply dissipated instead of returning.

There were also no bronze flashes appearing in the brief seconds he managed to keep the two Dao Fields going simultaneously. Zac figured that the density of energies wasn't enough to force a reaction when it came to Dao Fields. He could only sigh in disappointment at yet another failed experiment and move on.

If Dao Fields could be considered the gaseous form of the Dao, then directly infusing it into a weapon or skill would be the liquid equivalent and allowed for a larger amount of spiritual energy.

The Dao Storm had contained most of his spiritual energy, and perhaps that kind of density was what was needed to summon the bronze flashes. But he couldn't just crank out half his soul in one attack, but rather recreate that amount of energy in a single point to force a fusion like before.

The problem was that Dao infusion wasn't like a water faucet. He couldn't just increase the lever and have more Dao Energy flow out of his head. Until now, things had been binary where he either chose to infuse something or not. The amount of energy it cost would depend on the skill or item getting infused, and it would regulate itself automatically. Only when he was in an extremely agitated state did he sometimes manage to push beyond his limits by a small degree.

This was the problem that he had struggled with over the past three days. Trying to control the amount of mental energy that ran down his arm into his axe was like trying to push more air into a bag with his bare hands. Zac kept trying various approaches he had thought up while resting as he ran between the ant's legs, but nothing worked.

Since he still couldn't figure out any way for him to control the amount of energy, he could only try to fuse the two Daos once again. It felt like Zac's mind would split apart as he forcibly pushed his two Dao Fragments along his arms before they streamed into the axe at the same time.

It was yesterday when he had finally found a way to force both his Daos to converge. He used each of his arms like a conductor for one Fragment, only trying to push them together when they reached his axe. He only needed to use some Miasma as the method of delivery. However, there were still many problems to solve, and the first trial was the reason that he was using a temporary axe at the moment.

Verun had roared in Zac's mind the moment the two streams had entered the axe before rebuffing the two Dao Fragments. Zac first thought it was because it wasn't able to properly utilize both fragments at the same time due to it lacking materials, but his next experiment showed that there were other issues at play.

When Zac tried the same thing with a spare axe, the two fragments had entered without a problem, but the whole axe exploded into scrap metal in an instant, maiming his hands and almost blinding him. Zac had first thought he'd managed a fusion at the first try, but he quickly realized he had overestimated himself.

The explosion came from the two untamed energies along with the Miasma causing strain on the weapon rather than a fusion of the two. It was still an impressive outburst of energy, though, and the axe scraps had either been infused with the Fragment of the Axe or Fragment of the Coffin as they shot out like projectiles in every direction.

Zac figured there was an issue of speed. He would never be able to squeeze out half his mental energy for a single strike, as he had done during the Dao Discourse. He instead wanted to rely on smaller amounts of energies colliding at higher velocities. It was like the experiments on old Earth where scientists shot electrons at each other with extremely high momentum to see what kind of energies were released by the collision.

He needed to turn himself into a particle collider.

Having a plan was one thing, but finding a solution was something else entirely. A minute later, his axe couldn't take it any longer and turned into a bomb as well. Zac had learned to see the signs by this point and threw it away in time, but he froze a second later.

What about [Cyclic Strike]? He had given up on the skill for his new path, but perhaps some parts could be repurposed. The two fractals from the skill were perfectly placed on his shoulders, and he would easily be able to push his two Dao Fragments there before they continued down his arms.

The correct usage of the skill was to infuse his Daos into the two fractals and sort of braid the energies in a way that allowed the two Daos to mesh together and combine. After that had been accomplished, he could infuse whatever he wanted with this new combined energy.

Zac had never really gotten much further than infusing both fractals with their respective Daos. He hadn't even been close to finishing the type of mesh required, but that wasn't his goal at the moment. He felt like he was so close to the answer that he could taste it, and he gave the ant a quick punch to throw it away before he prepared to test his newest theory.

Having gained some breathing room, Zac then took out two daggers and stabbed one into each shoulder without so much as a grunt. Ichor started to drip down his arms and back, but he didn't care as he hurriedly activated the two maimed fractals with a smile that would no doubt look a bit deranged to an outsider.

The Dao Fragments entered the two fractals of [Cyclic Strike], but Zac didn't care at all about balance this time as he tried to force the energies to the center of the fractals as quickly as possible. Normally, it wouldn't have been possible without properly following the winding pathways, but he had carved a new path for himself.

The two daggers acted as conductors and allowed him to skip all the intricacies of the skill fractal, leaving just the part that acted as an entrance funnel, along with the core of the skill that Zac guessed was responsible for the fusion. The weapon blade allowed him to pass by over 70% of the fractal by just pushing the energy right through the metal itself.

Adrenaline started to course through his body when he realized that it was actually working, and blobs formed from his two Dao Fragments shot toward each other in his chest.

But happiness quickly turned to panic as Zac felt a terrifying buildup taking place when the two blobs merged, and he desperately tried to push it out of his body. He wasn't sure if he'd even survive if the blob exploded like his axes, taking half his torso with it.

The energy only got halfway down his arm before the ball of energy collapsed in a soundless implosion, annihilating a good chunk of his bicep as it disappeared. The pain was excruciating, but Zac was still delighted with the result as his eyes were trained on the wound.

The implosion had contained a bronze-colored spark.

Zac was in no mood to stay on the battlefield any longer, and Zac ordered the ten chains of [Profane Seal] to kill the ant who was already on its last legs from the sparring session. The battle outside had already ended as well, with Liches going through the battlefield to find salvageable bodies.

The corpses were placed in two piles. The second pile was the fallen Revenants and the insectoids who weren't salvageable, and these bodies were slated to be incinerated. He was still curious as to why it was impossible to re-reanimate a Revenant, but he put the matter aside and instead hurried back to the outpost to go over the results.

"You're back, Lord Piker," Uro, a steward that the Zarvadar kingdom had provided for him, said with a bow as Zac barged through the door.

"Is there any news from the guild?" Zac asked as he sat down with a grimace as the wound in his arm made itself remembered.

"I will enquire," Uro said and left the courtyard, allowing Zac to go over his findings.

His arm was a mess, but his short experiment with [Cyclic Strike] as a base was a huge step forward. There was a lot of work left to do, though. First of all, he couldn't keep stabbing himself with knives to create shortcuts in the pathways. It was both time-consuming and inefficient compared to using real pathways, not to mention that it hurt like hell.

Right now, Zac had only an extremely crude proof of concept that needed huge improvements to be considered passable. He would somehow need to redraw the skill fractals of [Cyclic Strike] to better fit his purpose, but he had no idea how to go about doing such a thing.

The next step was to control the fused energies long enough for him to hurt his enemy rather than himself. Right now, it couldn't be considered a weapon as much as a creative way to kill yourself, akin to creating a bomb right next to your heart. If the spark had gone off just half a second earlier, he might have lost the whole arm instead of just some muscle tissue and ichor.

The question was whether he really needed to stay any longer on this level, as these kinds of experiments could be performed while climbing.

He still had many skill upgrades waiting for his Draugr class, but he wasn't sure how long it would take to grind them out with his army. Zac guessed he would have to hear what the guild had to say before deciding whether to stay or not, and he looked up with anticipation as his steward soundlessly entered his courtyard twenty minutes later.

"A representative from the Inscriber Guild is here," Uro said with another bow.

"Let her in," Zac said, knowing that they would no doubt send Ildera again.

"Lord Piker," the beautiful vice guild master said with a curtsy the moment she entered the courtyard. "Ah! You're wounded! Let me–"

"It's fine," Zac cut her off before she used his wound as an excuse to fondle him again.

If Zac hadn't known she was a Revenant, he would have thought she was a pale human. Ildera had one of the highest levels in the whole kingdom, and she had become remarkably close to a living being as far as Zac could tell, with the notable exception of running on Miasma rather than Cosmic Energy and food.

"How did it go?" Zac asked as he took another healing pill, one specially made for his undead constitution and provided by the woman in front of him.

The formation master looked a bit unhappy about being rebuffed, but seeing Zac using the pills she had gifted him lessened her displeasure noticeably.

"I'm afraid we failed you," Ildera said with a pout as she sat down next to him. "Feel free to punish me as you see fit."

"What went wrong?" Zac asked with disappointment, ignoring the innuendo.

That Ildera had failed to create the Array Disks for the **[Nine Reincarnations Manual]** was a bit of a blow, and he started to wonder if even his sister would be up to the task.

19

BREEDER CLONE

"We weren't successful in inscribing the life-aspected formation," the undead inscriptionist said as she took out a couple of pitch-black Array Disks. "You will likely need a life-attuned Array Master for that half. I do maintain some contact with a master who might be able to do it, but it will probably require a few months."

Zac stared at the inscriptions with bemusement for a second before he looked down at the densely inscribed Array Disks. Was there really a need to leave him on a cliff like that just now?

"This is great. No need to disturb your friend," Zac assured her after he composed himself. "How many did you manage to inscribe?"

"We made six, but I assure you we use high-quality materials," Ildera said with some confusion. "They will not break even after repeated usage, so having six of them is overkill."

The first thing Zac had done after arriving at the outpost was to commission the construction of Array Disks for his Soul-Strengthening Manual. The forces he encountered in the Tower were all at least E-grade by now, and many had skilled inscriptionists who could help save some time. He still had over forty days left in the Tower, and he wanted to use the days to the fullest.

It would also save his sister a lot of effort if he could simply get his hands on Array Disks rather than having her spend weeks on creating two cultivation caves. The reason he'd commissioned multiple copies was even simpler. He needed to improve the odds of the arrays making it out of the Tower.

"What do you know about redrawing skill fractals?" Zac suddenly asked, taking the opportunity to learn from an E-grade cultivator. "Seeing as you're an expert on inscriptions, I hope you would have some insights to share."

Ildera surprisingly didn't answer, but rather looked at Zac with a troubled expression.

"I am not qualified to discuss such matters with the young master. I am sure that your elders will show you the way when you reach the point of creating, adjusting, and fusing skills," she said. "I am afraid that me intervening at this point would deviate your path of cultivation."

It appeared that using his imaginary master and elders as a shield from any questions and courtships had its drawbacks. He tried to cajole some answers for a while, but she was like a brick wall, citing that it wasn't her place to disrupt "his master's plan."

She eventually relented a bit by gifting him a handful of sheets that were actually made from the skin of E-grade cultivators. Zac's hair stood on end when he realized what he was holding, but it was apparently a material made for practicing inscribing skill fractals and pathways. It was the closest one could get without starting to experiment with their own body.

The Array Master once again tried to turn the short visit into a romantic outing after the main matter was dealt with, but she was soon enough led out from the courtyard by Uro.

"My master contacted me earlier. He ordered me to take down the Breeder within the day as a trial. I will be leaving in a few hours," Zac said when the steward returned.

Uro, the ever stoic servant, simply inquired whether Zac needed assistance or any specific equipment for his task. Zac asked for some more [Warrior Pills] after some deliberation, along with another batch of Miasma Crystals. The steward bowed and left the courtyard once again.

Ildera not being willing to help out with redrawing the fractals was a bit of a letdown, but she still had provided a lot of help. Her words had indicated that modifying skills was possible and not some cockeyed idea he had come up with. Even more surprising, she had actually mentioned that fusing skills was possible as well.

Creating skills was nothing strange. It wasn't necessary, but somewhat expected after reaching E-grade, at least if you had a higher rarity class. Those with Uncommon classes would probably get by with just buying skills, but Zac had a hard time believing someone talented enough to get an Epic class enter D-grade without having created at least one skill tailored to their cultivation path.

Modifying skills to better suit you felt pretty straightforward as well, though it was probably a lot more complicated than it sounded. Skill fractals were delicately designed networks of thin pathways that allowed Cosmic Energy to transform into all kinds of magical effects.

The skill fractals were something like an imbuement of Dao, as far as Zac could tell. Pushing the energy through the network infused the unattuned energy with higher truths, which was how Cosmic Energy turned into anything from fireballs to Zac's fractal edges formed from [Chop]. That was also why one could ponder on the Dao through studying skill fractals.

Even small modifications of a fractal would destroy the delicate pattern the fractal created, and you really needed to know what you were doing to not completely mess everything up.

Fusing two skills was another beast altogether. Zac had no idea where to even begin with such a daunting task. He could only assume that the System assisted somehow, since skill fusions sounded way too complicated to understand for someone who hadn't spent eons studying fractals.

Zac looked up at the dour sky with some wistfulness. It almost felt as though he was back on the island again during those two solitary months. An ignoramus fumbling in the dark, trying to make sense of what was going on.

He had stepped over a mountain of corpses to get where he was right now, but he was still just someone on the threshold of cultivation. In the beginning, he was like a caveman, crudely pushing Cosmic Energy into various body parts to increase his strength. But was he all that much better now, impaling himself with daggers to create shortcuts in his skill fractals?

The steward returned soon enough, and he wordlessly handed over a Cosmos Sack. Zac didn't think much of it, but his eyes widened in shock when he scanned the contents of the pouch.

"What's all this?" Zac asked with shock.

"It's from the royal family. Killing the Breeder is just a stepping-stone on Lord Piker's path, but it is the difference between life and death for the Kingdom of Zarvadar. This is a token of our appreciation," Uro said, some life appearing on his face for the first time since he had been assigned to Zac.

The reason Zac was so shocked was that there were roughly a hundred D-grade Nexus Crystals inside the pouch, along with all kinds of pills and herbs. It might not be much compared to the vast amount of wealth he'd found inside the Spatial Ring belonging to Rasuliel, but it was still the biggest haul of any single level unless you counted special encounters such as the Pool of Tranquility.

Since Zac had made his decision, he immediately prepared to set out. The commander of the outpost apparently wanted to hold a banquet in his honor, but Zac declined, as he much preferred to depart without any pomp or ceremony. Fearing some sort of commotion, he donned a cloak before he slipped through the back door of the mansion to blend in with the soldiers.

It was still a bit weird walking among the undead in their natural habitat. It was as though he were in some sort of bizarro-world where everything was similar but not quite the same. He had seen a young couple walk hand in hand, one of them a human Revenant sporting a decent amount of decay and the other a Corpselord stitched together from at least five different Races.

Another thing that had been a bit surprising was their love for scents. Almost all of the undead living in the kingdom were too low-tiered to eat and drink, so they looked elsewhere to find the satisfaction a good meal could bring. Many enjoyed complex fragrances, and most households created their own incense or potpourri.

Zac had long known about the location of the level guardian, and he switched over to his human form when he was far enough. It was still quite a distance, and it took him six hours to reach the insectoid stronghold where the Breeder Clone was located, even when he employed [Loamwalker] to its fullest.

The location wasn't very hard to find, as it was a huge crater caused by the insect hive slamming into the undead planet. The Breeder had arrived alone and quickly started to produce an army for conquest. The insectoid queen had essentially shot out a bunch of hives specially designed for space travel, and they would autonomously conquer planets they landed on before reconnecting with the main hive.

Zac deliberated for a few seconds, but he eventually decided to head in as a Draugr. He had somewhat fallen into the routine where he relied on his human form for most tasks, while occasionally switching over to Undying Bulwark when Hatchetman proved a bad fit.

This was reflected in the slanted masteries of his skills, and Zac decided to push through the whole of the seventh floor in his Draugr form unless a level was a particularly bad match.

Sneaking inside the hive was out of the question no matter what class he chose, as the whole crater was crawling with warriors. But full-frontal conflict was Zac's forte, so he started to grow from activating **[Vanguard of Undeath]** as he ran down the slopes.

Just seconds later, enraged screeches echoed across the area as Zac mowed down one warrior after another with the help of **[Immutable Bulwark].** He didn't bother killing too many of the warriors, wanting to save his Miasma. Some unlucky warriors got bisected by the massive Miasmic axe from getting too close, but most just got lightly maimed before they were thrown out of the way.

He was, however, forced to start cutting his way forward when he reached the hive, which pretty much looked like a nondescript comet. The entrance was completely blocked with innumerable warriors and beast companions, and Zac was completely drenched in a mix of blood, ichor, and green goop when he finally reached the breeding chamber.

The Breeder Clone seemed to be something like a mix of a worm and a factory, a gargantuan mound of flesh over fifty meters long. Zac barely had time to consider a course of action as a massive burst of Fragment-empowered acid threatened to swallow him whole.

He initially planned on enduring the blast before countering, but his danger sense screamed that doing so would be a monumental mistake. He could only slam his foot into the ground to teleport next to the massive insect with the help of **[Profane Seal]** and then stomp again to erect the cage.

His pitch-black bardiche swiped at the enormous slab of flesh, but he was surprised to see that the creature had a consistency like pudding. His axe went right through, but the only effect was that he almost got doused by another spurt of acid. Even worse, just seconds later, the large wound had closed.

Zac briefly considered swapping over to his other class to deal with this weird creature, but he suddenly had an idea. The ten chains all stopped killing the soldiers that kept emerging from pods that covered the Breeder's body and instead shot far into its gelatinous flesh.

The Clone violently started to shudder and shoot acid in all directions, forcing Zac to desperately scramble back and forth as he combated the tide of newly hatched insectoids that tried to rip him into shreds. However, he almost moaned in pleasure as torrential amounts of energy kept surging into his body from the Breeder Clone.

The amount of energy that the chains managed to drain from the queen was shocking, and a massive cloud of Miasma had long formed over Zac's head, as he simply had no way to store this much energy. It took a full ten minutes for the ten chains to completely drain the queen, which awarded Zac a final burst of energy that confirmed the kill.

The whole breeding chamber was partly submerged in massive pools of corrosive acid by this point, and together with the black clouds of **[Winds of Decay]**, the hive had truly turned into a hellscape for any being, living or dead. Zac wasted no time inside the hive and quickly stepped through the teleporter.

The combination of his shocking Endurance and the layers of defensive skills that Undying Bulwark provided made Zac a nigh-impervious tank, but he still looked beyond saving when he appeared in the middle of the streets of some massive town. His pale skin was sloughing off his body in multiple spots, and Zac shuffled into an alley as he threw a healing pill into his mouth.

It appeared the days of easy victories were over.

The Breeder Queen hadn't been an insurmountable enemy, but the thing had been both hard to kill while possessing unique strengths that would make her a pain to fight for either of his classes. The realization forced him to stay in place and heal up before heading out, as he didn't dare to challenge the level in his current condition.

Zac was thankfully able to reach an almost perfect condition within a few hours thanks to the pills he was given, allowing him to resume his climb. He wanted to regain the days he'd lost on the first level, sparing barely an hour a day for sleep and meditation.

But progress was getting slower and slower, and not a single level provided a quick solution.

Worst of them all was the sixtieth level, where he was trapped in an endless loop of restrictive arrays for nine full days. When Zac finally managed to break out through a bout of unhinged fury, he didn't even attempt to complete the quest, but instead opted to turn the poor guardian into a pile of meat.

The unceasing experiments into fusing his Dao Fragments were also a cause of constant delays. In fact, the largest threat to his well-being was his own training regimen. The guardians left their fair share of wounds by this point, but none of them had managed to blast one of his lungs into smithereens like he had during a particularly ill-fated training session.

Zac was essentially leaving a trail of bodies and black ichor in his wake, but that trail was at least getting closer and closer to the peak of the seventh floor.

THE TALLEST TREES

Ogras warily looked around as he appeared in the new world. Only when he saw that he had appeared on a busy street did he allow himself to look down at the gash at his side. Luckily, the mayor's all-out attack had barely missed as Ogras jumped onto the teleporter, allowing him to avoid wasting a week recuperating.

Who knew that the old goat would become so infuriated? Becoming a grandfather should be a happy occasion, after all.

That world was done with, but he couldn't help but once again wonder if these worlds were real. Would he become a father? Well, not that he wasn't one already after his years of whoring and playing around back home. There were no doubt at least a dozen little bastards with his blood running around the streets of Ter'Ferizan.

The demon's gaze darted back and forth across the street as he popped a pill into his mouth, his shadow tendrils meanwhile spreading out in search of threats and treasures. But it just looked like a some-what flourishing metropolis, though the energy density was pretty abysmal. Luckily, he didn't have to search for long, as the quest screen appeared on its own the moment he started walking.

[Become an honorary disciple of the Transcendent Master.]

The demon sneered when he saw the name. Anyone who had the gall to call himself a Transcendent Master in a place like this was no doubt an insufferable asshole of the highest order. Just the thought of becoming a disciple to such a pretentious prick made his hair stand on end. An ornery person like that would no doubt request the full ceremony with kneeling and offering thanks to the Heavens.

It didn't take a lot of time to find out that the so-called Transcendent Master was an adviser to the crown and one of the guardian pillars of this country. The title had been awarded him by the former emperor after having fought off an invasion of the Grev Reapers, whatever that was. He currently lived alone, and he accepted five honorary disciples to carry on his legacy every year.

The next trial was unsurprisingly tomorrow.

"Leech, you'd better help me this time, or I won't feed you for a month," the demon said as he sat in the hotel room he had hired for the night.

Ogras still had no proper means to communicate with Leech, but the creature living in his shadows released a few undulations, which he felt represented a reluctant acquiescence. Ogras' mouth widened into a grin as he started to prepare, and one item after another fell into his shadows, seemingly transported into another dimension.

The next day, Ogras found himself shoulder to shoulder with a bunch of middle-aged warriors, all seemingly stuck at the precipice of evolution. Becoming an honorary disciple also meant getting access to the vast fortune of the old master, which included various herbs that would help push one's constitution forward. It was a huge opportunity in a country where even a worthless stalk of grass could be coveted if it contained some Cosmic Energy.

There were three trials to the apprenticeship: Mind, Body, Heart. The Trial of Mind was essentially just a confusion array, and his grandpa had thrown him into enough of those while growing up for him to effortlessly pass through. He did, however, slow himself down somewhat so as not to garner too much attention, as that might interfere with his plans. The standards of mental strength in the kingdom were obviously wanting, and just a third of the trial-takers passed it.

The Trial of Body was just as simple, and Ogras was starting to wonder if the old goat was simply phoning it in. The old master simply said that the trial would be over when half the contestants had been thrown out of the courtyard where the trials were being held, which resulted in an all-out brawl.

Ogras had initially been planning on going easy again to stay unnoticed, but he was a bit embarrassed to realize his worries were superfluous as he found himself perfectly mediocre without even trying. Then again, he was holding back on his shadow skills and instead tried to make do with his spear skills.

During the free-for-all, he had barely needed to act to be thrown into the six specific positions he needed to reach. But thankfully, no one seemed to have noticed that a spike was shot into the ground the moment Ogras landed, and by the time the Trial of the Body was over, the six spikes formed a circle that covered the entire courtyard.

"The Trial of the Heart will test your convictions, your morality, and your loyalty to this great nation," the stalwart old master said as he stood in front of the twenty remaining trial-takers. "A crooked tree will never grow to its full potential, always forced to live in the shadows of others. As such, I will only assist those with a righteous heart."

The old master proceeded to walk toward one warrior after another, using some unknown means to figure out whether they were righteous. Ogras' heart started to beat in anticipation as the Transcendent Master got closer and closer, readying himself for battle. Ogras' eyes widened in alarm when the old master suddenly turned toward him, hostility all too apparent in his eyes.

He had been exposed.

"You!" the old man roared as a massive surge of energy started radiating from his body, transforming him from an aged scholar into a ferocious warrior.

An explosion erupted from a nearby pavilion as a shimmering sword burst through its ceiling before it shot toward the old master, but Ogras saw no need to let the Transcendent Master arm himself. A massive crystal appeared in his arms, and he slammed it into the ground while infusing it with Cosmic Energy.

Roiling waves of illusory flames inundated the whole courtyard, and the trial-takers fell over screaming, desperately clutching their heads.

The Transcendent Master seemed a lot better off, though, perhaps due to being the floor guardian. His eyes still looked bloodshot as he gripped the flying sword and slashed toward Ogras with an enraged roar.

The demon narrowly dodged a wind blade that would no doubt have cut him in two as he charged the old man with his spear drawing a majestic arc in the air. But two sharp lances of congealed shadows suddenly gored the old master from behind, leaving two nasty wounds.

The old man was obviously a seasoned fighter who would normally have been able to intercept such an attack, but his soul was currently on fire courtesy of the **[Voidfire Array]**.

Two wounds weren't enough to take the old man down. However, it did cause him to lose focus for a short moment, which allowed Ogras to launch a massive shadowlance that ripped a hole through his torso.

The old master looked at Ogras with confusion, anger, and betrayal as he fell on his back while Ogras retrieved the six spikes with his shadow tendrils. It looked like the old man couldn't comprehend why someone would assault him after his centuries of service to the kingdom.

Ogras walked over to the old man, who barely clung on to life, and looked down at him with a bland gaze. One swift strike ended it, and Ogras quickly snatched the powerful sword before it flew away.

"What's so bad about living in the shadows?" Ogras muttered as he jumped onto the teleporter. "It's the tallest trees that have to bear the winds."

———

"How did things go?" Catheya asked, her eyes never leaving the screen in front of her.

"There are no more members of the Tsarun Clan in the Base Town. However, three managed to destroy their tokens and leave," Varo recounted stoically.

"He's already passed the sixth floor, but his speed is average at best, and it keeps getting worse," Catheya muttered. "It's hard to draw any conclusions. What do you think?"

"I took the liberty of asking around some more after completing my mission," Varo slowly said. "I would venture that he is being held back by a lack of understanding of the upper floors and assisting treasures such as Array Breakers."

"Why do you say that?" Catheya asked with interest.

If Zac Piker truly was a disciple of her ancestor, then he should be well aware of all the hidden risks and opportunities inside the Tower of Eternity, especially those on the higher floors. But his speed did honestly indicate that there were some problems.

"I found something at one of the intelligence offices at the outer rim," Varo said as he handed her an information crystal.

"Super Brother-Man? Fights with an axe... A powerful native who defeated an incursion?" Catheya mumbled as she scanned the contents. "Who are these Ez'Mahal people?"

"It's a small feudal force in the sector, no one of import. Judging by their strength, I would guess that the newly integrated planet was of the lowest grade," Varo said. "The Ez'Mahal could barely be considered a High D-grade force, and a splintered one at that."

"It doesn't make sense," Catheya muttered as her brows furrowed with confusion.

Zac Piker being an integration progenitor would explain why he was so powerful without anyone knowing about him. The combination of the Tutorial, the massive amount of Origin Dao, and the various opportunities the Ruthless Heavens provide to such planets could sometimes create extreme outliers.

But it also made the connection to her ancestor all the more baffling.

"It is a bit disappointing. Perhaps I am overestimating my nose," Catheya muttered before she turned to her steward. "How far do you think he will go?"

"He will pass the seventh floor," Varo said without hesitation.

"Why do you say that?" Catheya asked, her mouth tugging upward.

"Instinct," Varo answered after some hesitation.

"That's why we're such a good combination." Catheya smiled. "I think so too. In fact, I think he might even beat the eighth."

Varo's brows rose a bit before his expressionless appearance returned, but Catheya knew it meant that her attendant disagreed.

Catheya still had a feeling about that man, even if she didn't have anything to substantiate it with.

"Do you remember Reoluv of the Dravorak Dynasty?" Varo suddenly said.

"What about him?" Catheya mumbled with disinterest as her gaze returned to the Tower Ladder.

"His brother just arrived, and he's ready for a fight."

———

"The Zethaya send their regards," a young woman said with a bow as she handed Yeorav a crystalline vial.

"Mh." Yeorav nodded as he stashed away the pills without much interest. "What did you find out?"

"It is just as your informant indicated. A confrontation between Zac Piker and Rasuliel Tsarun resulted in the destruction of the Zethaya Pill House and the death of Rasuliel. Boje Zethaya indicated that there was likely some unknown history between the two, as Rasuliel went out of his way to antagonize Mr. Piker."

"What else?"

Yara went over the details of the altercation in the Pill House, with Yeorav occasionally asking clarifying questions.

"So either he has an extreme amount of Endurance or he possessed some sort of treasure to withstand the Tsarun brat's [Abjuration of Zerthava]. Where did he get his hands on that thing anyway? Only those in the Boundless Factions can make that cursed item," Yeorav asked.

"There have been rumors of the Tsarun doing business with unorthodox forces," Yara said after some thought. "But nothing substantiated and not to the point that it has created pushback."

"That old pretender is too greedy, too impatient," Yeorav snorted with disdain. "He wants to stand shoulder to shoulder with the likes of the Allbright Dynasty and my ancestors, but his ambition has turned him insane. How can a dynasty be created on such a murky foundation?"

"Well, these events will no doubt infuriate them. Boje also let slip that Rasuliel was the one who bought the Pathfinder Oracle's

Eye a few days ago, and it is now in Mr. Piker's possession," Yara added.

"Oh?" Yeorav said with some excitement.

He knew his family had a few body parts of Pathfinder Oracles in their treasury, but there was no chance of getting his hands on them because of their ancestor's strict rules about cultivation.

The number of resources he could draw from the treasury while still in F-grade had long been tapped out. He would only be able to trade for it with an item of equal value, and it had to be something he had found himself without assistance.

The odds of that happening without him entering the depths of dozens of Mystic Realms were almost nil, but such an opportunity had somehow presented itself in front of him now. A treasure like that was something that you couldn't get your hands on even if you had the money, and he could think of multiple ways he could utilize such a thing.

His little brother was no doubt kicking himself for not having the patience to wait just a few days before attempting his climb. But luck was sometimes as important as skill.

"Has everything been set up?" Yeorav asked.

"Everyone is in position. But multiple forces are similarly preparing for when Mr. Piker emerges," Yara said.

"What have the undead been up to?" Yeorav asked.

"They haven't made any movements since they threw out the Tsarun Clan from the Base Town," she said, some confusion clearly written on her face.

"Their motivation doesn't really matter. Perhaps they just want a top-grade body to bring back home," Yeorav said as he gently grabbed Yara's hand. "It will be an all-out brawl later. Don't get mixed into this mess."

"Is… all this really necessary?" Yara sighed as she moved closer to Yeorav.

"You know how my family operates. If Reoluv ascends, I will probably just be relegated to manage a far-off corner, but if it's second brother, I'll be assassinated along with everyone close to me," Yeorav said with a pained grimace. "My only hope is passing the seventh floor and getting accepted to one of those faraway places. I'll take you with me and leave the infighting to my siblings."

Not many people in their remote corner of the Multiverse were aware, but passing the seventh floor essentially gave them a direct shot at entering massive factions that towered far beyond anything else in the sector. The whole sector was just a small corner of their domains, breeding grounds that occasionally fostered promising seedlings.

Most thought that Lord Beradan had been lucky and encountered a great master after passing the seventh floor, but he would probably still have been able to join one of those forces due to his amazing talents and his showing in the Tower.

Yeorav knew his own limitations, and he hadn't seen passing the seventh floor as a realistic opportunity. He knew he wasn't his brother's match in either talent or diligence, especially since their ancestor had taken Reoluv as a direct disciple.

Just reaching the seventh floor was a stretch without expending some treasures. Defeating the floor guardian? A fool's dream. But that had all changed now. Yeorav didn't know what that poor man had done to piss off the Boundless Heavens to this extent, but it had actually awarded everyone who appeared in the Base Town the quest.

His previous plan was to wait a decade or so and pass the sixth floor with the help of some treasures, but now a better opportunity had presented itself. It had prompted him to cash in on every favor and borrow from everyone he could think of to stock up on enough offensive and defensive treasures to conquer a minor empire.

It should propel him through the seventh floor, and with the help of the quest, he'd skip the floor guardian altogether.

He normally wouldn't stoop to such despicable levels, as he had no bad blood against this Zac Piker. He would rather meet whatever fate came his way when Reoluv or their second brother ascended to the throne, but he knew that wasn't an option any longer. His relationship with Yara had been exposed, so whatever ending he would meet, so would she.

It was a shame, but Zac Piker needed to die so that they could live.

"But that man seems dangerous, and he's already entered the seventh floor," Yara said with worry.

"Opportunities are always found in the midst of danger," Yeorav muttered as he stroked Yara's hair. "Besides, I didn't come to the Base Town empty-handed."

STRUGGLE FOR SUPREMACY

Barely healed wounds covered Zac's whole body after hacking and slashing his way through the seventh floor, and he breathed out in relief when he saw that he wouldn't face the floor guardian of the seventh floor right off the bat. Not even the thick armor of **[Vanguard of Undeath]** had been enough to prevent him from getting hurt from the increasingly intense battles.

He had already spent a full day to restore his combat strength to its peak on the sixty-second level, but he still could use some more time to rest up. His upper chest getting obliterated had cost him a second Zethaya pill, but even then, it had taken a couple of days before he dared to swap over to his human form.

Losing a lung and maiming his heart wasn't too bad when he didn't need to breathe or pump blood, but in his human form, it might have proved lethal.

Zac looked down at his token with a sigh, seeing that only twenty-seven days remained. He essentially knew that reaching the seventy-second floor was not only a matter of strength by this point, but also luck. Twenty-seven days felt like a lot, but it was only three days per floor. Getting stuck just once would probably mean his climb was over.

The time constraints also made him hesitant whether he would be able to experiment any more with his Dao Implosions. Continuously wounding himself hadn't really delayed him too much so far since he was used to fighting while wounded.

But the enemies were becoming pretty strong by this point, and the seventy-third floor entailed another steep boost in difficulty. He couldn't keep running around with maimed body parts any longer unless he knew he wouldn't encounter the guardian for another day or so.

Besides, Zac had started to realize that his goal of using the bronze flashes offensively was far, far away.

Zac had hoped that he would be able to utilize the mysterious flashes offensively by the time he reached the floor guardian, but the past days had proven that it was simply impossible. For one, he had only managed to actually force four fusions over a hundred attempts. Worse yet, each of those fusions had been so unstable that they had exploded in his face before he managed to use them for anything.

The fact that it was somewhat working felt like an indication that he was moving in the right direction, but he started to fear that he wouldn't be able to create a working system before he evolved. The question was whether his current progress could be considered a "creation."

He felt it was unique enough, as he had never heard of anyone doing what he was attempting, and it was also suited to his special circumstances. He had also arrived at the system mostly by his own effort rather than following a Heritage or a master. Yrial was a definite influence on the path, but not to the point that it could be said that Zac was following in his footsteps.

In either case, it looked like he would have to fight without using prototype Dao Implosions on this level. But he was still confident in his chances, especially in his human form. He felt that he would be able to take out almost anything with unrelenting ferocity as long as he utilized **[Hatchetman's Rage]** and **[Hatchetman's Spirit]** along with his supreme attacks, which was why he had already swapped over to his Hatchetman class.

Looking around made his brows furrow. It looked like he was in the middle of a massive arena, one a hundred times larger than the slave ring he'd wound up in after completing the fourth floor.

Zac sat on a platform rising roughly half a meter above a floor made of large tiles, and he noticed there was an array ensconcing the platform. Zac hesitated for a second before he walked over to gingerly touch it, and he found that it felt like solid rock.

It looked like he was trapped like a beast in his cage, and a Dao-infused punch to the array indicated that breaking it was likely beyond his capabilities. He grunted in annoyance but quickly calmed himself down as he sat down in the middle of the platform to rest up and figure out what was going on.

The first thing he had noticed was that his was not the only platform in the arena. He could spot at least two hundred platforms around him, but just a few had golden arrays like his own. Indistinct shapes of other warriors could be seen inside, but he couldn't make out any exact appearances of the others.

He could, however, tell that they were likely humanoids just like himself, judging by the size and shape, rather than war beasts. Was this some sort of colosseum where he would be forced to fight other gladiators to the death? If so, why hadn't he gotten any quest prompt yet?

And who was the floor guardian in this scenario? There were no spectator stands or people visible in any direction, and the arena simply ended with a vast emptiness, like they were on top of a disk floating around in space.

Was this another riddle he was too stupid to figure out? It had been a humbling experience realizing that he couldn't complete a single one of the quests of the seventh floor, forcing him to fight against the guardians instead.

Mostly it wasn't an issue of figuring out how to complete the quest. The problem was that it would take too much time, or that he didn't possess the prerequisite skills needed. Almost all the quests either required some specific knowledge or treasures to pave the way.

Even the quest on the previous floor, requiring him to unseal a tomb to acquire a treasure within, was hopeless. The array had completely stumped him, and it was designed in such a way that brute force didn't work. But he had somewhat expected such a result.

He had been going in knowing full well he would have to rely on his strength above all. But even finding the guardians was turning into a chore, which was why he barely had enough time to complete the eighth floor now.

The fact that he was stuck inside an array at the moment didn't help with his impatience to get going.

Minutes passed, and Zac started to realize what was going on. One array after another flashed into life, and another cultivator found themselves seated on a platform in the arena. After just fifteen minutes half the platforms were filled, and Zac started to mentally prepare himself for a messy battle.

The closest platform suddenly flashed to life, and Zac looked over with interest. A hazy outline of a humanoid youth could be seen beyond the golden wall, and his head swiveled back and forth for a few seconds before he sat down.

"Shit, how unlucky. A Battle of Fates. I should have postponed my climb a day," the youth swore. "Better not be any Tower Breakers today."

Zac sat some distance away from the one who had spoken up, but he could still make out the words from the guy.

His mind spun as he tried to understand the scenario. This level felt different compared to those before. The previous levels had all placed him in some sort of scenario where he already had an identity and a clear mission. But Zac knew this was different as he looked at the indistinct shapes around him.

Were these people actually real?

But where did they come from if they were real? Were they teleported here like he had been during his Sovereignty quest? Or judging by the words of the youth next to him, were these people also warriors climbing the Tower of Eternity? If that was the case, there was no way these people came from the same area as himself.

If he passed the seventh floor, he would be the first to do so for thousands of years in his sector, but the Tower tested the young generation all across the Multiverse. Scrounging up a couple of hundred people reaching the seventh floor shouldn't be too hard, especially not if it included people coming from higher-tier sectors with B-grade forces and even higher.

But that presented a problem. He knew nothing of the capabilities of such individuals or the hidden means they possessed. What if they threw out hundreds of Peak-grade arrays to blast this whole world into pieces?

There was also that term, Tower Breaker. Did that signify people strong enough to climb the whole Tower? Such a thing was unheard of in his sector, but it wasn't necessarily the case in other parts of the Multiverse.

Zac could barely comprehend the strength required for that. Even the normal level guardians of the seventh floor all possessed various unique advantages along with at least one Dao Fragment. How would the boss two floors higher look? Would it have Peak Fragments? Something even higher?

Zac hesitated for a second before he turned back toward the youth on the platform next to him.

"Hey, what's going on?" Zac said with a high whisper.

"You don't know?" the youth answered after a few seconds of silence. "You'd better crush your token, buddy. When the walls come down, blood will fall like rain."

"Do you know about the Tower of Eternity?" Zac probed.

"Are you trying to test me?" The man laughed. "Well, whatever. We're all real. We know of the Tower of Eternity. We're just unlucky SOBs the Ruthless Heavens took an interest in."

"What do you mean?" Zac probed, praying the chatty youth wouldn't stop explaining the situation.

"This is a rare scenario. A convergence of fate, you could call it. The Ruthless Heavens noticed a lot of promising climbers in the Tower at the same time, and instead of a floor guardian, we get to fight each other. Fun, huh?"

"Why would it do something like that?" Zac asked.

"To make the survivors stronger, of course. What better way to become stronger than a life-and-death battle amongst the elites of the Multiverse?" The youth snorted. "Shit, I had a pretty good chance of passing the seventh floor as well. Now I'll have to do this stupid climb one more time."

Zac frowned when he heard the youth complain. What he said no doubt meant that it was a lot harder to pass a floor like this than to fight the normal guardian. This was obviously pretty bad news.

After having fought one tough battle after another in the earlier levels of the seventh floor, he knew he would be in for a fight that would push him hard when he met the floor guardian, but he still believed it would be manageable.

But he was far less confident about the messy situation he was in right now.

"Got any tips?" Zac sighed.

"Have fun, and don't get killed. That's what my dad said when he sent me off; has worked pretty well for me so far."

Zac wanted to glean more information from the man, but the array around him suddenly started to flash as a screen appeared in front of him. Zac blanched when he read the quest, and any hope that the young man next to him was lying was dashed in an instant.

The wording in the quest was all too familiar, and nothing good ever followed seeing that line.

[Struggle for Supremacy.]

"Supremacy…" Zac mumbled with some helplessness.

At least there was no confusion about what needed to be done this time. It was a Battle Royale. It made Zac remember when he'd sat wounded and wrung out in the tunnels of his crystal mine, and the quest for the Fruit of Ascension suddenly popped up.

The System had told the inhabitants of the island to fight for supremacy back then as well, and what followed was a bloodbath. This time, things were slightly fuzzy, though. Was this really a last-man-standing scenario?

Thankfully, it seemed like the System wasn't done, and a few more lines appeared in front of him.

[Defeating each contestant rewards 1 point, in addition to all accumulated points of the vanquished.]

[Trial ends when 10 contestants remain, or when no combat has taken place for 3 minutes. Avoiding battle for more than 5 minutes counts as forfeiture of climb.]

[Ladder will display the top ten contestants.]

Zac quickly looked around and noticed a huge screen appearing in the sky. It was currently completely blank, but it was no doubt the scoreboard the System mentioned.

At least the System wasn't so heartless that it would only let one person through. Ten spots being awarded wasn't too bad since he guessed there were roughly two hundred platforms in the vast arena. That meant 5% of the people would pass. Those odds didn't seem too bad considering they were on the last level of the seventh floor, whose guardian would no doubt have been extremely strong.

The question now was what level of power was required to be considered the top 5% in a group like this. He felt pretty confident in himself compared to almost any F-grade cultivator, but he also knew that he knew nothing of how things worked with B-grade and higher forces.

Neither did Ogras nor anyone else in the sector, it seemed, as the strongest forces were all C-grade. Perhaps the strongest people would know more, but the things beyond C-grade might as well be myths for people like him.

Zac tried to figure out a strategy to last as long as possible while keeping watch for any suspicious actions inside the other bubbles. Best-case scenario, he avoided battle altogether as the others fought it out. He would then swoop in and defeat a few warriors and snatch their accumulated points.

But he knew that was probably a pipe dream. He had no ability in stealth, and most of these people probably had anti-stealth capabilities anyway. Besides, the System clearly disallowed such a tactic with its set of rules. Huddling in a corner might be seen as a sign of weakness as well, prompting him to get attacked.

Should he go the other way and blast his aura to the fullest, drowning his surroundings in his killing intent? No, something like that would probably backfire. They might consider him a raid boss and team up to take him out before turning on each other.

A thought suddenly struck him, and he took out a couple of talismans and an Array Disk. He tried activating them one by one, but he sighed in relief when none of them worked. Next he took out an amulet, a pretty weak defensive treasure he had snatched during the climb. The amulet created a shimmering shield around him, though it was dimmer compared to the first time he'd tried it out.

It seemed that the System had enforced certain rules on the floor. Expendable treasures such as talismans, offensive items, and Array Disks had been completely disabled for the Battle Royale. However, real defensive treasures like his robes seemed to work, albeit in a reduced capacity.

Not being able to use any external items might be seen as a detriment, but for Zac, that could only be considered a huge boon. He came from a newly integrated planet of a weak sector, and the things he could bring out would probably seem like a joke to most of these people.

Most scions of B-grade clans would probably be able to beat him to death with their wallets alone, and even if the efficacy was lowered, he would be in deep shit if someone took out a bunch of Peak-grade arrays. He was pretty confident in the durability of his body, but even he wouldn't survive getting blasted by twenty [Void Balls].

This leveled the playing field somewhat at least, and he took a few deep, calming breaths as he looked around. All the platforms were full by this point, and the warriors inside essentially stood rooted to their spots as they waited for the timer to hit zero.

The array flashed faster and faster, and suddenly, it was just gone, exposing him and the other warriors. The whole area shuddered as hundreds of immense auras burst out, each one powerful enough to completely steamroll anyone on Earth.

Not even a second passed before blood was spilled, and Zac was already behind in the count before he had even jumped down from the platform. A few had taken the opportunity to launch quick strikes on their neighbors for early points, and the scoreboard had already filled up with ten names.

One warrior after another released their strongest skills and transformed, and everything from tempestuous storms of energy to awe-inspiring avatars started to take form across the arena.

However, one phenomenon reigned supreme, to the point that all battles ground to a halt. Zac was primed to meet any assault, but he couldn't stop looking at the spectacle on the other side of the arena as well.

It was as though a sun had appeared from nowhere as a colossal ball of primordial flames covered an area hundreds of meters in each direction. Space itself seemed unable to withstand the heat as count-less spatial tears were scorched open before they quickly mended again.

Zac had fought various flame-aspected warriors, but nothing he had seen had come close to the heat generated in that globe. The flames contained a boundless fury and scorching heat that threatened everyone in the arena, and Zac's danger sense screamed at him to never cross the woman who sat on top of the sun.

There was no doubt in his mind that the ball contained at least a medium Dao Fragment, but the terrifying fluctuations made Zac believe that the reality was likely far scarier. Perhaps he'd even need a Peak Fragment to reach those levels of power.

The fiery globe was a stark contrast to the young woman who hovered above the sun, as her face was an ice-cold mask as she gazed down on the arena as a goddess looking down at her subjects. Zac couldn't be sure from the distance, but she seemed to be a human, from what he could tell.

Her golden-orange hair danced from the superheated air around her, giving her a supernatural aura. Zac had to admit, she was the most beautiful woman he had ever laid his eyes upon. However, he didn't dare stare too long at her pristine features, afraid that he would draw her attention and get himself in a heap of trouble.

A gargantuan avatar suddenly appeared behind the woman, a six-winged humanoid who could either be a fallen angel or a demon. It looked like it was seated inside the ball of flames, but it was still only submerged to its navel due to its towering height.

The avatar formed an odd seal with its fingers, which conjured six enormous fractal circles above its head. The sense of danger in Zac's mind surged, and he started backing away even if he was on the other side of the arena.

Six terrifying whirlwinds of purest flames rose out from the ball of flames and entered the fractals, imbuing them with their scorching heat. The next moment, the whole arena was illuminated in a blaring light as each fractal launched a condensed pillar at an unfortunate cultivator who was too close to the sun.

Five of the unlucky targets were simply obliterated, the flames not even leaving their bones or treasures intact. Only one woman, a rugged beastkin woman wielding an odd kettle with incense, managed to survive by conjuring a massive beast avatar that succeeded in blocking the flames for a fraction of a second, which allowed her to move out of the way.

She was still grazed by the attack as it slammed into the ground, and she quickly took out a pill while she kept retreating with horror written all over her face. The beastkin only got a few steps, though, before she crumpled down on the ground as she started spewing gray clouds from her mouth. A second later, she had turned into a bonfire, as the flames had somehow burned her from inside.

The scene had completely subdued the whole arena. Just getting grazed by her attacks had been enough to get yourself killed, and she was still sitting on enough flames to drown out half the arena.

The flame goddess thankfully didn't seem inclined to push things any further for the moment and instead sat down on top of the ball of flames to spectate the battles. Zac had first thought that some people would call for teaming up against the clear frontrunner, but she was completely ignored as dozens of battles erupted as people increased their distance from the stationary sun.

Perhaps she only wanted to stake her position in the top ten, and no one was foolish enough to contend for the first position when you could fight for one of the other nine spots. Hopefully, she would only strike one unlucky person every three minutes to not get kicked out, and effortlessly pass the trial.

It was a humbling reminder that the sector he came from was just a backwater corner of the Multiverse. He was probably the strongest F-grade warrior there, but there was always a higher peak. Zac had no confidence in dealing with that girl. He wasn't even sure he'd be able to handle one of her attacks in his human form.

His undead form would perhaps be able to tank a few strikes, but defeating her in that form would be impossible. The vast power of the sun would melt his Miasmic cage in seconds, and he would be turned into cinder before he would get close enough to hit her with an axe.

Was this the actual peak of the F-grade, or were there even stronger people out there?

The flame girl was shockingly not the only warrior that made Zac leery; there were two more that he knew he would have to avoid if possible. Worse yet, half of the contenders were like him, holding back to observe the surroundings. There were no doubt a few more little monsters hiding in the mix, waiting for the right opportunity to strike.

He had briefly entertained the notion of gaining the first spot as he waited for the arrays to deactivate, but now he was rather wondering if he'd even make it into the top ten.

The System wouldn't give the leaders an easy time either, as there was actually a picture attached next to their names and points so that anyone would know who they were. One person obviously wasn't prepared for that, as his face started to distort and change in an effort to circumvent the ladder. But the picture next to his name kept changing as well.

Zac had no time to worry about others, as a sword tip pierced out of thin air, aimed straight at his heart. It contained an inexorable force, and it felt like the sword was a kilometer-long slab of metal rather than just a meter. He urgently summoned [Nature's Barrier] and imbued it with the Dao of Trees to block the incoming strike, while also getting ready to activate his Dao of the Coffin in case it was needed.

A vast expanse of trees spread out around Zac as he activated [Hatchetman's Spirit] as well, but this time, the trees found competition from massive fractal swords that materialized all around him before they stabbed into the ground. He felt he was no longer in his private grove, but rather in a contested forest full of wood and steel.

The large sword pillars would have to wait, though, as the incoming strike was stronger than expected. One of the ropes on the divine tree from [Hatchetman's Spirit] snapped, providing him with another shimmering layer of defense.

Thankfully, it seemed like his layers of defense were enough to stop the attack even if it was impossible for him to imbue the nature-attuned skills with the Fragment of the Coffin. The dozens of Dao-infused leaves didn't completely manage to impede the strike, though, proving just how much power the stab had contained.

He had just activated the defensive barrier from [Hatchetman's Spirit] as an extra precaution since he felt that [Nature's barrier] should be enough to block an opening salvo. His defensive skill was based on his Endurance, after all, and even if the attack was infused with a Dao Fragment, it still had to contend with a Peak Dao Seed and over 1,800 effective Endurance.

But the attack wasn't over, it seemed. The huge swords around him started to hum like they were struck by a tuning fork, and two swords emerged out of the closest sword pillars like the massive swords were portals to some other dimension.

It was at this time his opponent finally appeared as well, rushing out of another sword pillar, ready to strike.

It was a thin humanoid with purple skin and golden eyes. His build was pretty much the same as a very lanky human with the exception that his arms seemed to have an extra joint and a thick but short tail extended from his lower back.

"Sorry about this. You seem a nice fellow, but I decided to give this floor a try," the man said as the three additional swords plunged toward Zac, each from its own direction. "And I need every point I can get."

Zac could only smile wryly in response. It looked like information wasn't free after all.

23

BATTLE OF FATES

Zac briefly wondered if the swordsman had assumed him to be a weakling due to his cluelessness about the Battle of Fates.

A burst of Zac's shocking killing intent spread out as he moved with lightning speed, his axe already falling toward the youth as a storm of leaves pushed away the three hovering blades temporarily. The man's eyes widened in surprise, but the display didn't deter him, and a sharp aura radiated from him as he met Zac's attack with the sword in his hand.

A blinding flash of light was followed by a massive shockwave when [Verun's Bite] collided with a golden sword that the youth used to defend himself from Zac's overhead swing. A small crack could be heard from the man's arm, and it was obvious he had strained to block the strike.

Zac was still pretty shocked by the guy's power, as his swing was both empowered by the Fragment of the Axe and the titanic power in his arms. But the arm holding the sword was only forced backward a bit before it stabilized again, though the man's whole body was shaking from strain.

This was the first time someone at his level had been able to cleanly block his strike as far as Zac could remember. Of course, Zac wouldn't get flustered by something small like that, and he simply geared up for another ruthless strike. The swordsman was obviously not interested in matching brute force, and he suddenly shot back almost a hundred meters while the three flying blades prevented Zac from following by unleashing a storm of strikes at him.

Zac frowned and tried to follow using [Loamwalker], but he was for some reason unable to shrink the distance with his skill. Was it the sword pillars that messed with his mobility somehow? He could only move forward the normal way, but each step was contested by a barrage of strikes that kept ripping the leaves of [Nature's Barrier] to shreds.

The swordsman thankfully didn't try to attack Zac from afar while he tried to catch up, but he rather swung at one of the sword pillars right next to him. A hymn of vibrating metals echoed out as the man unleashed a frenzied series of swings.

Zac didn't understand what he was doing, but waiting for an opponent to finish charging up a strike was the height of idiocy, so he started launching fractal blades of his own at the swordmaster every time he saw an opening between the flying swords. He received a few cuts in return, but it wasn't anything worse than flesh wounds.

But the man expertly met the incoming fractal blades with his sword and somehow redirected the force of the projectiles to harmlessly pass by him as he kept swinging at the pillar. Zac finally noticed what was going on. The swordmaster was charging the massive sword pillars with power.

They had looked pretty much like dull steel swords before, but now they gleamed with some unknown energy. Zac had realized the issue too late, and the dozens of pillars started to shoot out a cascade of sword beams toward him.

Zac did have the advantage of 360-degree vision thanks to [Hatchetman's Spirit], but knowing where the attacks came from didn't really help when you were unable to dodge. There were just too many blades, especially with the three corporeal blades already harassing him.

Resonating sword waves kept coming at Zac from every angle, and he found himself incapable of blocking them all with the help of [Nature's Barrier], as the leaves were getting destroyed faster than he could create them. He eventually chose to just rush straight through the storm while imbuing his body with the Fragment of the Coffin, but he found himself swinging through air, as the target had somehow passed through one of the sword pillars and appeared on the other side of the sword forest.

Zac growled in frustration as he instead chose to demolish one of the pillars, and one mighty swing with [Verun's Bite] completely obliterated it and caused shards to shoot out in all directions. However, Zac felt like he was stuck in some sort of time loop when he saw the splinters fly back and recombine, once again forming an unblemished sword.

Thoughts of retreat started to intrude as Zac looked for a solution, but he stubbornly threw the impulse away. The guy he was fighting didn't have the confidence to win in this Battle of Fates. If he couldn't even beat him, how the hell would he reach the top ten? This was something like a trial for him, proving to himself that he could contend with the elites of the Multiverse.

Cosmic Energy surged into his arm as a crack appeared in the air above the battlefield, allowing the hand of [Nature's Punishment] to emerge. Zac wasted no time as the wooden hand formed a seal, conjuring the enormous array that emitted an intense pressure toward the ground.

It was only then that Zac realized a potential problem. Were there punishments to summon in this weird dimension? There was nothing apart from the arena in this dimension. However, he breathed out in relief when he saw a pitch-black peak emerge from the array, bearing down on the forest below.

Those sword pillars were simply too annoying, providing the swordsman with both a powerful attack and an escape skill while also restraining Zac's movement. He wouldn't be able to end the fight while they remained, so he saw no recourse but to go for mutual destruction and sacrifice his forest to crush the pillars.

A stabbing pain suddenly flashed in Zac's mind, and it almost felt like when he'd looked upon the massive axe in his Dao Vision all those months ago. Zac looked over at his enemy with some alarm, only to see that the swordmaster had swapped out his mighty golden blade with a run-down sword in a simple leather scabbard.

Zac had no idea what was so special about the sword, but his danger sense told him that it was far deadlier than the other blades he'd had so far. He was unable to do too much about it, as he was occupied with controlling [Nature's Punishment] while blocking the hundreds of sword waves that threatened to drown him, but Zac did manage to send a few fractal blades toward the swordsman to force him to split his attention.

However, the blades only made it halfway before they were eroded by the unceasing barrage of sword blades. The fractal edges formed by [Chop] were both larger and more ferocious, but they were unable to withstand dozens of collisions.

Zac realized he wouldn't be able to stop whatever the swordsman was cooking up, so he got ready to expend another defensive charge to endure the strike while he completed the attack of [Nature's Punishment]. However, Zac soon realized that he wasn't the target.

The lanky warrior unsheathed and swung the blade in one light-ning-quick motion toward the sky, and the rusty blade was back in its old scabbard within the blink of an eye. The only evidence of the attack was a white arc left behind along the sword's trajectory.

The light didn't disappear even after the swing ended, but it rather grew and grew until it was a hundred-meter-wide half-moon that rose into the air to meet the pitch-black mountain's descent, and Zac was shocked to see the peak get cleaved in two along with the whole emerald array.

Burning pain seared his hand, and he forcibly ended the skill before the sword arc hit the wooden hand. Luckily, it seemed that the swordsman had miscalculated things as well, and he looked shocked when the two halves of the mountain kept falling rather than disinte-grating into motes of Cosmic Energy.

A massive shockwave erupted as the two enormous boulders slammed into the ground. The mountain exploded into thousands of jagged rocks, some as large as a car, that flew in all directions with terrifying momentum. The swordsman tried to escape through the closest sword pillar, but he was immediately spat back out, perhaps because most of the swords had been utterly destroyed by the massive slabs of rock.

Zac saw his opportunity as he witnessed the swordsman scam-pering back and forth among the flying gravel. He activated [Loamwalker] and inwardly breathed out in relief upon sensing that it was no longer restrained. He pushed through the chaos the moment he realized the skill worked, ignoring the twangs of pains from being pelted by the pieces of rocks flying around.

Suddenly, he was right upon the swordsman, and **[Verun's Bite]** was ready to strike.

"Wha–" the man exclaimed as he tried to phase away using some unknown means, but Zac's free hand was even faster as he grabbed the youth's arm and infused it with the Dao of the Coffin.

Zac wasn't planning on hurting the lanky warrior with his Dao, but he made a bet that it would be able to disturb the warrior's escape just like how he was able to stop Ogras from blending into the shadows. His guess was right, as the enemy's form turned corporeal again.

The man was no weakling, since he had reached the seventh floor, and he wasn't ready to give up just because he knew he wasn't Zac's match in a direct confrontation. A barrage of sword strikes harassed Zac as the man resummoned three golden swords, and each strike came from unpredictable angles and contained tremendous force.

Zac kept blocking with **[Nature's Barrier]** and **[Verun's Bite]**, all while trying to get a good swing at the man. He still had a death grip on the other man's arm, but his attempts at pushing him down to the ground proved impossible as the cultivator somehow resisted Zac's force.

But he wouldn't relent either, and he ignored any finesse as he used a meter-long fractal edge and delivered one earth-shattering strike after another while forcibly enduring the hail of sword strikes. Since Zac had captured his target, it had turned into a battle of endurance, and if there was one thing Zac was confident in, it was his ability to take a beating.

However, he suddenly remembered that he had gained a few new cards, and his killing intent congealed into a spear that stabbed into the man's back as Zac activated **[True Strike]**. Others wouldn't be able to see the spear, as it was only a means for Zac to control where he wanted to redirect the attention.

A golden disc looking like a miniature shield flashed into existence and radiated a massive amount of power as a necklace on the man's neck dimmed. It covered the warrior's whole back in an instant, defending the man against Zac's "surprise attack."

Of course, there wasn't actually an attack coming since the skill only created a threat without any real follow-up. But that by itself was sometimes enough, as the man hurriedly looked back to see what was going on and if he needed to dodge.

The movement only took a split second, but that was all Zac needed as he activated the second fractal on [Verun's Bite] while swinging with everything he had. The distraction had caused a small weakness in the warrior's defense, and that was the difference between life and death.

The fractal edge of [Chop] suddenly disappeared, and [Verun's Bite] slipped past the golden sword as it gained a sanguine glow. It finally continued unimpeded toward the swordsman, and blood splashed in all directions.

"I'm sorry," Zac muttered as his axe bit into the shoulder of the warrior. "I need every point I can get."

Zac could have just as easily aimed his axe to bite into the man's head, instantly killing him, but he decided against it. He had no grievance with his enemy apart from them being competitors in the System's game of elimination. Besides, these people probably came from powerful forces, and who knew what kind of seeds of Karma killing these people would form.

"Shit, just my luck," he said as he reached toward the token on his waist. "Thank you for showing leniency. If you're ever in Asc–"

However, he wasn't able to finish his sentence, as he disappeared from the arena before he even had time to touch his token. His weapons disappeared with him as well, which was a shame since that rusty blade looked extremely interesting. However, Zac suddenly noticed that a Cosmos Sack was lying on the ground where the sword-master just stood.

He quickly snatched it up and stowed it away, as this wasn't the time to go over his gains. Zac's eyes rather looked around for any incoming threats, but no one seemed inclined to jump him as things stood. His eyes locked with a demon who wasn't too far away, but the man quickly retreated.

Perhaps he had seen Zac's battle and felt there were easier targets to focus on first, and Zac looked down at [Verun's Bite] and saw the glow slowly retreat into the second fractal on the handle. Judging by the density of the light, he would be able to use the fractal another three or four times before he needed to recharge it with blood.

This was the resulting upgrade from Verun devouring the massive succulent back on the fourth floor, but he had only been able to utilize it recently, as the Tool Spirit had been digesting the various energies it had absorbed. The feature wasn't as flashy as summoning Verun itself, but it did drastically increase the sharpness of the edge for an instant, allowing a sudden burst of power that was hard to adjust to.

Zac had found that it was extremely effective to combine the effect with [**True Strike**], as the lapse in concentration of the enemy allowed him to make the most of the short burst in power. If he had used the fractal from the start, the swordsman would probably have been able to use one of his defensive treasures to counter it, wasting the effect.

The brief respite after the battle allowed Zac to take a gander at the situation, and he was surprised to see how frenziedly people were fighting. Was there really a need to risk your life like this? Most of these people were scions of powerful clans, and many no doubt had a second climb remaining.

There were still over fifty fights going on, and Zac saw one person after another flash out of the arena, leaving only a Cosmos Sack behind. The scene made Zac realize that there might be some special protections in place, with the System providing last-second saves before they died.

That didn't explain why everyone fought so desperately. Was it about the Cosmos Sacks? The treasures carried around by a scion of a B- or A-grade Force were of extreme value for someone like him, but it couldn't possibly be like that for everyone. Was there some other secret to this special level?

Still, many knew their limits. For example, Zac spotted a golem defeating some sort of devil cultivator, and the golem reached down and crushed its own token the second it snatched the Cosmos Sack left behind, disappearing with the spoils.

The number of contestants had dropped to less than half in just a minute, and Zac realized that things might be over pretty soon. He needed to defeat a few more people while there still were easy targets around. But just as he was about to pick a target, he felt a sudden gust of wind right behind him, making his hair stand on end.

"Hey."

24

FRACTURED

Zac rapidly spun around to find himself face-to-face with an angelic girl who smiled in his direction. She had appeared out of nowhere, and Zac frowned as he swung his axe toward her neck without hesitation. His danger sense was quiet, but his instincts screamed of danger, and Zac infused his body with the Fragment of the Coffin while the spiritual forest reappeared around him mid-swing.

But she only looked on with a smile, her eyes trained on his.

There was finally a response of danger in his mind, but it was though it was muffled, subdued to the point that he could barely feel it. That only made Zac even more certain that the girl was a real threat, and Zac strained for his swing to move even faster.

However, he suddenly noticed something was wrong. He felt as though he was moving extremely quickly, but his axe wasn't getting any closer to his target. Terror started to well up in his heart, and he tried to flee. But it was futile, and the whole world was suddenly gone, replaced with two enormous eyes, both of them only containing a blue vertical fracture that contained endless power.

Every fiber in Zac's body screamed for him to look away, but his body didn't listen to his commands as the eyes consumed his everything. A snap could be felt inside his mind as **[Mental Fortress]** crumbled like rotten wood, and then an all-consuming pain racked his mind.

His very being was being eroded, and Zac knew he stood on the precipice of death. This wasn't a death his Specialty Core could circumvent, as this was brought on by his soul crumbling, his mental force fracturing and falling apart.

He tried to move his hands toward the token attached to his side, as it wasn't worth dying just to get a better title. But any sense of his body was long gone, and his vision swam as he fell down on the ground. His mind was turning blurry, but he felt some relief when he sensed a small vibration from the token by his side.

A shocking burst of ferocity suddenly burst forward, ripping the two enormous eyes into shreds.

Boundless destruction rampaged across his mind, startling Zac's blurred consciousness awake again. It was the [Splinter of Oblivion] that had been freed from its cage and lashed out in fury. Dark and extremely potent energies ravaged across his mind. His soul was quickly becoming tainted, but the Splinter at least seemed to temporarily hold his crumbling soul together.

Zac once again regained a semblance of control of his body, and he saw the mentalist standing just a meter away from him. She didn't move an inch, but rather stood in place as she violently convulsed. Her sapphire eyes were replaced by two ravaged sockets from where black blood poured down like waterfalls, staining her dress before pooling at her feet.

Was the Splinter of Oblivion the cause of this? Was that the reason she still hadn't been teleported out? The backlash she had received seemed to have been just as serious as his own, and it seemed like a coin flip who would succumb to their mental wounds first.

It was an opportunity for him to escape from the Tower, but Zac was dismayed to find that his arm wouldn't move toward the token. The Duplicity Core had considered him on the verge of dying, and the slower automatic process of changing form had begun as Miasma started to spread through his body. Worse yet, the Splinter's awakening seemed to have canceled the automatic transfer out of here, and he was now stuck in place.

Zac would normally still be able to move in this state even if he was severely weakened, but with the shock to his soul, he had turned completely immobile. He could only helplessly lie on the ground, praying that the Splinter would be able to keep his mind intact long enough for him to change form and do something about it.

He inwardly cursed his bad luck at being targeted by a mentalist, one of the rarest class types. Did he project the image of being a rube or something? First he had been targeted by the neighbor, then this scary girl. Did she perhaps think he was an easy target since he was an axe wielder, a class choice famously favored by meatheads?

If that was her reasoning, she was unfortunately spot-on. Zac was somewhat confident he'd survive at least one attack of that insanely powerful fire mage, but his mental defenses were completely inadequate to counter the strike of a mental user who was strong enough to reach the peak of the seventh floor.

Worse suddenly turned to worst as a massive lance of darkness pierced the chest of the mentalist, instantly killing her by the looks of it. It was some sort of masked assassin wielding a meter-long spike who had appeared out of nowhere, reaping her life in an instant.

He had probably noticed that she was barely hanging on and realized it was an opportunity to reap some easy points. Worse yet, after he had killed the mentalist, he turned his attention toward Zac, who was still lying impotently on the ground. Perhaps he thought that Zac was faking it or simply immobilized since he hadn't been teleported out yet.

It looked like his avenger would turn into his killer.

A blazing pain of getting his innards shredded joined the agony of having his soul tortured as the black pike stabbed into his chest. A burst of power ripped apart his left lung, and it took everything in his power to not even blink from the attack.

He was still completely immobile, and his only chance of survival was for the man to think he'd stabbed a corpse, as death-attuned energies already spread through his body. However, he suddenly caught a lucky break as the assassin flashed away the next second, narrowly avoiding a massive arrow that caused cracks around its trajectory.

One of the spatial cracks swiped Zac's side, and he could only bear having yet another grisly wound opening on his already lacerated body.

A few seconds passed, and Zac realized he had somehow made it. The mentalist was dead, the assassin occupied elsewhere, and the rest of the cultivators had no time to worry about a corpse lying on the ground.

Zac honestly felt he was a bit lucky, even though both his soul and body were wounded beyond their limits. His terrifying Endurance and death-attuned energy had allowed him to narrowly escape death, giving him a small opportunity to survive.

Another relief was that the Splinter was quickly being pushed back into its cage by the Miasmic fractals, but Zac felt some helplessness when he noticed that yet another one of the fractals had been destroyed. That was two fractals gone from his visit to the Base Town, and he didn't know how many of them were required for the cage to maintain its efficacy.

There was also the issue of the large amounts of unfiltered energies the Splinter had left all over his fractured soul. He had no idea what the long-term effect of such pollution would be.

However, that problem was nothing compared to the fact that his soul was once again falling apart now that it didn't have the Splinter to keep the pieces together. He did have a solution, but it was just that the price was one he really didn't want to pay. His heart was full of reluctance, but he knew he didn't have a choice. His body would slowly mend, but his soul was another matter.

He arduously managed to move his hand toward his mouth, praying that no one was watching the supposed corpses. When it was finally right in front of his mouth, a small, intricate box appeared from his Spatial Ring.

The [Prajñā Cherry] was the only thing in his possession that could mend a soul as damaged as his currently was. He felt extremely apologetic to Alea, but he wouldn't do her any good if his own soul broke apart before he even got back to Earth.

A swift motion propped open the lid, and Zac immediately shoved the cherry into his mouth, stem and all, before he put the box back into his Spatial Ring. A warmth spread through Zac's mouth, but abyssal darkness was spreading through his mind even faster, making Zac lose any sense of self.

A sharp pain suddenly flared up in his leg as a large piece of rubble from a broken platform slammed into it, probably the result of a frantic battle nearby. The pain shocked Zac awake long enough to roughly chew a few times and swallow the cherry.

Zac's mind slowly descended into the darkness once more, but suddenly, there was a burst of warmth, like his soul was caressed in a hug. He still didn't regain any feeling in his body, and the clamor of battle turned into a distant susurrus.

Was this death?

A deep bell echoed in the darkness, and the bottomless abyss was replaced with a boundless sky with splashes of clouds colored pink by a sunset. The slight rustle of leaves was the only thing interrupting the tranquility of the evening. Zac realized he was on a solitary peak surrounded by arid badlands.

The rustling came from a small tree with purple leaves, and by the looks of things, the tree was the only growth for miles in each direction. Sharp cliffs devoid of any growth surrounded him, leading down toward a canyon far below. Similar rocky pillars could be seen far in the distance, though none of them seemed to have any vegetation growing.

It was only then that Zac realized his vantage was that of the tree itself, which would explain why he was incapable of movement. Was this the origin of the cherry that he had just eaten?

"Amitabha." A gentle but decidedly masculine voice drifted out from beneath his vantage point, and Zac noticed a large figure sitting right next to the tree.

Shockingly enough, he seemed to notice Zac as well, as he looked up in his direction with a smile on his face. The old man reminded Zac of Abbot Everlasting Peace from his mannerisms, though this monk was anything but human.

Zac had no idea what Race the thing beneath him was. It was generally humanoid, though extremely rotund. It almost looked like a large ball with a smaller ball on top for a head. It didn't look like obesity, though, but rather a natural feature of his species. From his massive torso, two surprisingly long and slender arms extended downward, and his hands were placed in his lap.

If one could call it that since the monk didn't actually have any legs.

It instead had two massive wings lying across the ground like a cape, and when their feathers rustled, it sounded like divine bells while shimmering lights danced about. The being looked odd, but it was definitely a Buddhistic cultivator rather than a beast, as he was dressed in a kasaya while wearing a large bead necklace.

He had a generally humanoid face, with a set of large golden eyes that radiated wisdom, a small mouth, and a normal nose. There also seemed to be a third eye in his forehead, like that of Anzonil, though it was closed at the moment. Finally, a long mane of long gray feathers ran down his head and back, held together with a string like a ponytail.

Even if the being looked a bit odd, there was no doubt in Zac's mind he was a powerful warrior. His aura was subdued, but the power in his gaze was undeniable. Besides, looking at the mysterious lights that naturally radiated from his wings almost felt as beneficial for his Dao as witnessing a Tower Apparition.

"Little cherry tree, how can you suddenly carry such fate?" the winged being mumbled before his eyes slowly lit up with comprehension. "I see... You taught this poor monk something today. Benevolence must be reciprocated, thus completing the cycle and severing karma."

Zac tried to ask what the old monk meant, but he was unable to speak or even move. He could only watch as the monk slapped his two hands together in prayer, and the sound of his hands clapping was like divine thunder that echoed through the cosmos.

Zac's mind was filled with a shocking force in an instant, and he felt a connection to the universe he had never sensed before. All living things were part of a greater whole, all connected by karma and Heaven's Will. Was this the grand truth of the universe, or was it the cultivation path of the winged monk sitting under the cherry tree?

The feeling only lasted for a second, and when he looked around, he had returned to the solitary mountain peak, while the monk was nowhere to be seen.

Zac could sense that he, or rather the cherry tree, had transformed somehow from what the monk did. It still looked the same from the outside as far as Zac could see, but there was a tremendous power hiding within.

A massive halo that looked like a setting sun suddenly exploded out from the tree as its branches started to violently shake. Buddhist hymns sang across the badlands as the tree kept growing and transforming. It had just been a bit over five meters before, but it grew over a hundred meters in an instant.

Its appearance had also taken a drastic turn, as its purple leaves were suddenly covered in golden fractals while its trunk turned almost black with similar engravings. Its canopy stretched hundreds of meters in each direction, sheltering the area from the sweltering sun.

The changes weren't over, though, as the roots kept growing downward along the hoodoo, their exuberant vitality transforming the arid rock as they descended toward the parched ground. First, it was simply moss that covered the sheer rock, but soon enough, even small trees and flowers forced their ways through the cracks, turning the rocky pillar into a living monument.

The edges of the branches started to droop as they kept growing, and soon they had formed a dome with the pillar as a center. Outside was still the sandblasted wastelands, but the area within the canopy was quickly turning into a pocket-sized paradise.

FACELESS

The vision of the consecrated tree and its kingdom slowly faded as Zac returned to his body. Before he fell into the vision, his soul had been crumbling while his body was grievously wounded, but he realized his body was almost completely healed upon waking up. A vigorous energy was gathered at his remaining wounds, and he felt them close with enough efficacy to put most of his healing pills to shame.

A thought struck Zac, and he surreptitiously opened his Dao menu, and as expected, there was a new entry.

Fragment of the Bodhi (Early): All attributes +10, Endurance +60, Vitality +80, Intelligence +15, Wisdom +50, Effectiveness of Vitality +5%.

The vision had actually managed to help him form the third Dao Fragment, and the Fragment of the Bodhi even had tremendous healing capabilities from the looks of it. However, it was his mind rather than his body that had been in a critical state, and Zac hurriedly looked inward while still maintaining his unmoving posture. Unearthing all the capabilities of his new fragment would have to wait.

A vibrant emerald force surged through his soul, encompassing the splintered pieces of spiritual energy into a warm embrace. Most of his soul was already back together, and the remaining fractures were being mended with a speed visible to the naked eye.

However, he noted with a frown that his soul wasn't uniform any longer. Whenever he had gazed at it before, it had looked like a translucent ball in his mind, and this ball had become slightly larger and more pristine after taking a dip in the Pool of Tranquility.

However, now it almost looked like some sort of tadpoles were swimming about in his soul, small fuzzy blotches on an otherwise clear backdrop. It was no doubt the remnant energies left from the Splinter of Oblivion's rampage. Not only that, but it also seemed as though some of the alien energies had crammed themselves into the cracks of his soul, turning itself into some sort of mortar as the [Prajñā Cherry] healed him.

Zac had no idea what this infiltration would result in, and it felt like this was the very thing that the Miasmic fractals had defended against the past months. The Draugr lady's cage had managed to cleanse the energies for him before they merged with his soul.

He didn't feel anything amiss or different at the moment, but he knew he couldn't trust those instincts. The Splinter had manipulated him many times before, sometimes with him only realizing it after the fact.

Seeing the situation almost made Zac want to leave the Tower early and find someone who could create the second of his Soul-Strengthening Arrays. He was losing Miasmic fractals left and right, and it felt like things were spiraling out of control. However, he knew he couldn't give up now. He had paid a steep price to remain in contention, and he wasn't ready to exit now.

The mentalist was pretty insane, but he had now transformed into his Draugr form. Reaching Middle proficiency on [Indomitable] had allowed him to infuse the skill with the Fragment of the Coffin, and the two together should make him strong enough in case another mentalist lurked in the arena.

As for anything else, he had [Immutable Bulwark] and his shield.

Zac had initially turned his focus toward his soul, but he now tried to get a grip of the surroundings while maintaining the disguise of a corpse. The vision had clearly taken less than five minutes, as he would have been booted from the arena by now otherwise.

He was still lying on the ground with the still-warm corpse of the woman who fractured his soul, and their combined blood had created a large pool that he was currently lying inside. The scene was pretty grisly, but that was a blessing in disguise, as he had at least been left alone.

Zac tried to move a bit, but he realized he was still extremely weakened even though the transformation to his Draugr form had ended. Perhaps it was due to the fact that his soul was still being pieced back together by the emerald glow. A lot of his organs had also been turned to mush by the stab from the assassin's spike, which might have left some hidden weakness even if he had been restored by the cherry and his new Dao Fragment.

Each second felt like an eternity as Zac waited for the reconstruction of his mind to finish. He really needed to fight someone since he could be kicked out of the arena any second now due to inactivity. But Zac realized he should have been careful what he wished for, as he was suddenly shrouded by a shadow.

A figure had appeared out of nowhere, a small goblin-looking humanoid no more than a meter tall, and he bent over to rummage through the clothes of the dead woman next to Zac. There was actually someone bold enough to loot the corpses while battles raged all around them? Zac made sure to be completely unmoving, and he anxiously tried to urge his body to regain its strength.

Zac didn't so much as blink when the thief started to rummage through his clothes, or even when he found the Cosmos Sack hidden within his robes. Anxiousness burned in his chest, but he finally felt a sense of completeness as his soul was finally whole again. Zac's hand snapped forward like a spear, and with the help of the Fragment of Axe, his hand became sharp enough to stab straight into the chest of the unsuspecting thief.

The man looked one part confused and two parts horrified as his torso turned into shreds in an instant. Zac almost gaped in disbelief at the scene, but he quickly snatched back his Cosmos Sack in case it would be teleported out. But the man was deader than dead, and his upper torso slid off to the side while his legs crumpled.

Zac looked down at his hand with some shock, not able to comprehend the terrifying burst of power he had unleashed. His jab had been infused with the Fragment of the Axe, but the effect was more chaotic and destructive than it should be. Was this the result of his soul being tainted?

The situation was too chaotic to investigate at the moment though, and Zac knew he would have to look into this after he left this level. He instead quickly rummaged through the mangled corpse, but he only found the Spatial Ring that seemed to have belonged to the mentalist before. As for the thief's own possessions, he could find none.

There was not even a complimentary Cosmos Sack dropped by the System, making Zac snort with irritation as he got up to his feet. Maybe thieves got the same sort of pocket dimension skills like merchants did, effectively robbing Zac of his chance to loot another scion.

However, he quickly realized his mistake and changed his face with [Thousand Faces], bearing the painful transition. He didn't think the cultivators around him had the time to completely understand what had transpired here, but he didn't want the fact of his dual class to spread even if these people were from completely different sectors.

Luckily, he was completely drenched in blood and viscera, making it nigh impossible to match him going by clothes either. Furthermore, he would soon be covered up in another layer of Miasmic armor. The large shield that appeared on his arm would hopefully also make it even harder to connect to his human side. As for his axe, there wasn't much he could do about that.

The people around him were far too dangerous for him to use [Hunger] instead of his main weapon. He didn't even dare to swap out [Verun's Bite] for a spare axe.

A wide sweep proved that he was out of trouble for the moment, and Zac thanked the gods that there was no immediate threat. He had just killed a cultivator, which meant he had some breathing room before he needed to fight again. But the situation that he was met with was a bit odd.

There were still roughly thirty people in the arena, but only a handful of battles still raged on. The others were simply looking at the others and up at the ladder. Quite a few were actually looking right at him as well, donning calculative expressions. Their discerning eyes were a bit hair-raising, but there was nothing he could do about it.

He knew he wasn't strong enough to kill everyone who might have witnessed his transformation. Zac could only pretend nothing was wrong and hope that they'd chalk up the situation to some odd transformation skill. At least he wasn't jumped by the remaining warriors, which gave Zac a chance to look up at the ladder as well.

A lot of changes had taken place in the ladder during his unconsciousness. Only the first three positions were completely unmoved, and it looked like they were content with the results as they leisurely looked around at the others. All of them had over twenty points, making it essentially impossible not to pass the trial as long as they didn't get kicked for inactivity.

The second and third positions actually seemed to be from the same clan, as they shared the same last name, but they seemed to have no intention of teaming up, judging by how far they stood from each other. Things generally seemed pretty civil, and Zac couldn't understand why some of the spectators didn't try to take advantage of the few people who were currently embroiled in life-and-death battles.

Had the remaining elites agreed upon some code of conduct while he was out of it?

Zac wasn't on the ladder, as expected, which wasn't surprising, as he had only defeated two people, one of which only provided one point. It was unlikely that the thief he'd just defeated was anything special either, and he had probably defeated one opponent at best before deciding to loot rather than compete for the top ten positions.

The problem was deciding whom to target next. Picking one of the people on the ladder would guarantee a top ten placement if he won, but the battles would no doubt be pretty rough. Fighting Iz Tayn, who still sat on top of her miniature sun, was a nonstarter, but the other nine were obviously no weaklings either since only one of them was currently being attacked.

The other option was taking on one or a few of the remaining spectators in hopes that his combined points would at least push him to the tenth spot. That tactic might end with him expending a lot of energy without anything to show for it though. Those who still stood in the arena were no doubt the elites of elites, and taking out two of them to gather points was probably harder than just one person in the top ten.

Zac soon enough made his choice and started moving, prompting most of the spectators to look over at him with vigilance. Zac ignored the gazes as a sea of Miasma started to billow out around him, followed by the massive fractal bulwark that started to hover in front of him in case of a sneak attack.

His body groaned and creaked as he activated [Vanguard of Undeath] next. Zac didn't summon his skeletal helpers this time around, though, as he wasn't too confident in their ability to help out in a place like this. Judging by the attacks he had seen, they would be ripped to shreds in no time unless he infused them with his Dao, and he would need his fragments for his other skills.

He had a feeling that the skill would change in interesting ways as it leveled up, but for now, he couldn't justify the cost of activating the [Undying Legion]. Instead, he stomped down on the ground and disappeared, and stomped down again the instant he appeared in front of a familiar figure.

It was actually the masked man wielding a pitch-black spike, the guy who had almost killed him earlier. His pseudonym was Faceless #9, and he was currently holding the seventh position on the ladder with thirteen points.

Zac couldn't deny that part of his reasoning for choosing this man as a target was fueled by vengeance for getting his innards shredded, but there was also some logic to it. He had already seen some of the man's repertoire and weapon, whereas most of the top contenders were a mystery to him.

Furthermore, judging from what Zac had witnessed, the man seemed to be an assassin-type character, which was the best match for his current form. He had already been forced to change Race, and he wouldn't be able to swap back to his human form anytime soon. Finally, there were a couple of corpses around him, which would help fuel his Miasmic reserves through [Fields of Despair].

"Wrong choice," the masked man grunted with an emotionless voice before he disappeared, and Zac's mind screamed of danger the next moment, prompting him to urgently block the back of his head with his shield.

If Zac had been a fraction of a second slower, he would probably have died then and there, as the black spike slammed into [Everlasting] with enough force to make Zac stumble forward. The sturdy shield was almost pierced straight through as well, though the fractals helped it to quickly regain its original form.

Cold sweat ran down Zac's back, but he pushed aside his lingering fear as he quickly infused [Deathwish] with the Fragment of the Coffin before it was too late. The assassin snorted and disappeared the next moment, but even he seemed a bit shocked to find himself right in front of the massive bardiche Zac wielded.

A huge gash tore open the man's chest as the spectral projection stabbed into the back of Faceless #9, but he narrowly avoided any lethal wounds. Zac tsked in annoyance as he tried to swing his axe again, but it appeared that the assassin quickly learned from his mistake, as he managed to move further away, somehow circum-venting the taunting effect of [Vanguard of Undeath].

Zac sighed in regret when he saw that his gambit had failed. He had hoped to take down the man with a surprise strike, relying on the discombobulating effect from [Vanguard of Undeath], but the masked warrior had dodged with almost impossible nimbleness. Zac did manage to leave a pretty nasty gash, but it wasn't enough to weaken him to any significant degree.

It looked like Zac would have to do things the hard way, and billowing clouds of corrosive gas started to shroud the cage as the wails of fifteen chains started to echo out of the cage, and a turquoise fractal formed in the sky.

26

A BREAK FROM THE MONOTONY

Finally succeeding in upgrading [Profane Seal] during his climb was one of Zac's greatest gains while climbing the seventh floor. The upgrade added five more chains that extended from the top of five massive tombstones that had been added to the cage, and they would be sorely needed to catch the slippery assassin.

The additional chains weren't the only benefit from the skill evolving. Dense scripts lit up with a cold aquamarine luster on top of the huge tombstones, and they formed a large fractal in the air that covered the entirety of the cage. It was a restrictive array, somewhat akin to the gravity array of the Zethaya Pill House.

It was another layer of restrictions that hindered anyone who had been caught in Zac's cage. Along with [Fields of Despair], the spectral chains, [Winds of Decay], and the taunting effect of [Vanguard of Undeath], the area within [Profane Seal] had become a real hellscape for the living.

But the man caught in Zac's trap was no normal man, and he barely seemed troubled at all by the situation.

Another warning of danger exploded in Zac's mind, this one even more urgent than before. He desperately moved [Undying Bulwark] to block his torso while infusing it with the Fragment of the Coffin. A sharp snap could be heard as the bulwark was pierced straight through as the pitch-black spike continued toward Zac's body.

Almost all of the strike's momentum had been absorbed by the defensive skill, though, and the spike didn't even manage to pierce the next level of defense, the thick Miasmic armor that covered Zac's whole body.

Zac was ready to retaliate with his axe, but his brows rose in surprise when a spectral projection suddenly appeared on the other side of the cage. He pushed the confusion aside and infused the ghost with the Fragment of the Coffin just as it stabbed the man, creating another shallow wound that instantly started to fester.

It was shocking how far the man had instantly moved after stabbing him, but the fifteen chains of [Profane Seal] moved out to trap the assassin while Zac started to release torrential amounts of corrosive mists into the cage. He had failed in taking the man down with one strike, but Zac was still confident in whittling him down using his standard approach.

The assassin tried striking Zac's vitals a few more times, but between [Immutable Bulwark] and his shield, he was able to escape unscathed, while adding more and more wounds with the help of [Deathwish]. Faceless #9 was probably the fastest enemy he had ever fought, but his defense wasn't too impressive.

Besides, the spectral projections were immutable. The masked warrior had unleashed flurries of stabs at them the moment they appeared, but the stabs went straight through their incorporeal bodies. They could only be blocked, which made them the perfect counter for people who relied on not getting hit.

The assassin suddenly appeared far in the distance, and Zac frowned as he realized the assassin was up to something. Bleeding abscesses could be seen on various parts of his arms, whereas the wounds on his body were continuously leaking pus. A smaller spike suddenly appeared in his hand, but rather than attacking Zac, he stabbed himself in his heart.

Zac's eyes widened in shock, witnessing what looked like a suicide, but he quickly realized that things were about to get rough. The man's muscles suddenly started to writhe and wriggle as black liquid reminiscent of his ichor poured out of his wounds before they coagulated, forming thick scabs around his wounds.

The nine closest chains were suddenly thrown away with enough force to cause cracks all along the links as the man stabbed forward with enough speed to become a blur, which gave the man another short breather. Impenetrable darkness spread through the cage the next moment as the assassin unleashed some sort of domain, and any clue of the man's whereabouts was gone. The man's attuned energies had completely blended in with the surroundings, rendering [Cosmic Gaze] useless.

Even his life force was hidden by the dome of darkness, rendering the unique vision brought by his Draugr Race impotent. Just as Zac tried to figure out his next step, a sharp pain erupted in his left leg, and he realized a hole as wide as a quarter had appeared seemingly out of nowhere.

The hole went straight through not only his armor but his whole leg, and he felt his black ichor pouring out of the wound. He sensed that another spectral ghost had automatically appeared some distance away, but Zac didn't have time to imbue it before it struck the assassin. What had just happened?

Another wound suddenly opened up, this time in his right arm. Zac frowned at the fact that he couldn't sense a thing before being struck, not a single warning from his danger sense that he was about to be attacked. This time, he managed to imbue the projection from [Deathwish], but Zac was still a bit worried.

Zac had already heard that there were methods to circumvent the special senses from Luck, but this was the first time he had seen it to such a degree. Was this the hallmark of a top-tier assassin?

This was a fighting style that was completely different compared to anything else Zac had witnessed during the Battle Royale. The man had no big avatars, and there were no flashy skills that emitted massive outbursts of energy. However, that didn't mean the man was weak, and it wasn't without reason that none of the spectators had dared to target him.

Zac was sitting at over 300 effective Luck, but he couldn't even begin to sense when the attacks were coming. Not only that, but his Endurance and multiple layers of defense barely impeded the man, as two grisly wounds had appeared on his body without him impeding the strikes in the slightest.

There was an extreme penetrative force between his jabs, and just one or two attacks might be enough to kill most people. The man had no doubt been able to effortlessly assassinate one guardian after another during his climb using this method, barely sustaining any wounds.

However, a muted pang of danger suddenly erupted, and Zac hurriedly protected his head with his shield, safely blocking another strike aimed at his head. Zac nodded in understanding as he realized that his danger sense at least could sense lethal strikes. It meant that the darkness hadn't changed much.

So Zac simply ordered the chains to flail about at random as he stood rooted in place, only focusing on staying alive and infusing the [Deathwish] with the Fragment of the Coffin.

Finally, there was a break from the monotony.

Iz Tayn curiously looked at the weird cage formed from death-attuned energies, and the two fighters who were grinding each other down within. Luckily, she had been gifted the skill [Sungod's Eyes] by her uncle before entering the Tower. Otherwise, she would have missed out on the melee due to the [Red Hand Shroud].

Not that the fight was anything impressive. The assassin from the Red Hand Society had actually been forced to infuse himself with their disgusting compound to keep fighting, whereas the odd one was just unusually competent at taking a beating. He would no doubt be able to make a decent living as a sparring partner at one of her family's Trial Planets.

She had been deeply disappointed that there wasn't anyone interesting in the arena after something interesting had finally happened in this dull Tower climb. The two siblings from the Primeval Lake were pretty strong, but they were still not strong enough to force her hand even if they joined forces. It was a shame that there was no one like their grand-uncle in their current generation. Then it would have truly been a clash of fates.

She felt a bit bad about scorching a few unlucky people out of frustration, but then again, it could be seen as them lacking in fate by being spawned so close to her. After that, she let the others escape in time, apart from the despicable fellows who didn't respect the proper rules of conduct. Such people could burn for all she cared.

But something interesting had finally happened. He seemed to think that no one had noticed his transformation, but everything that her sun illuminated was within her domain. How could she not see what had happened? What kind of encounter would allow one to change between a human and a Draugr?

More importantly, was he really human? It was extremely minute, but there was something odd hidden within that she had never encountered before. Something primordial.

Mixing an ordinary human bloodline with the blood of higher beings was nothing unusual, as humans in general were extraordinarily average. Her own heritage was a prime example of that practice. But the odd thing was that her own bloodline felt some pressure from that man, which she had never encountered before. At least not against someone in her own grade who hadn't undergone their bloodline evolutions yet.

That wasn't the only odd thing, and she couldn't help herself from being engrossed as she replayed the events in her mind. It didn't make sense. She saw him almost dying from his soul shattering, then somehow being saved by an errant arrow that had forced the Red Hand Assassin to move away.

He then proceeded to eat a natural treasure that somehow changed its provenance mid-consumption, and finally recovered over two minutes. All without being targeted or hit at all as battles raged all around him. It was as though his surroundings had been shifted to a separate dimension. Was it dumb luck? Or accumulated Luck?

She didn't think that even she would be that lucky if put in such a situation, and she had over 200 Luck and multiple Fate-augmenting treasures.

So Iz felt like a child who had found an odd colorful bug in their family's garden, and her eyes followed the bulky man as he tried to take down a much more skilled opponent by sheer stubbornness.

The man from the Red Hand Society was clearly one of their stronger cadets, likely someone who had survived the hellish training on one of their induction planets. Anyone who survived long enough to enter the society from one of those hellholes was an emotionless murderer who had solidified their path with a million corpses.

He kept opening up one wound after another on the Draugr, who was leaking like a sieve by this point. He was using some nurturing Dao Fragment from the looks of it, but his control of the Fragment was atrocious. Why didn't he form proper Dao Arrays on the wounds?

The humanoid cockroach tried, again and again, to catch his opponent with his axe and the fifteen chains that flailed about in the cage, but he didn't seem to possess any means to pierce through the darkness of the shroud. The assassin effortlessly moved back and forth between the attacks, bursting forward with one stab after another.

Of course, the assassin was facing his own troubles as well. He was starting to look disfigured from the wounds of the retaliatory strikes. Absolute strikes were the worst to people like him. If it were her, she could have simply formed a shield of flames to block out any such attempts, but the assassin seemed to follow a much more extreme path, lacking such tools.

He had quickly expended the few defensive treasures in his arsenal, and since talismans and arrays didn't work here, he had to endure a thousand little pinpricks infused with a corrosive Dao Fragment. However, the fragments the Draugr used were just Early stage, a far cry from her three Middle Fragments that empowered each other. Even worse, he seemed unable to properly coordinate them into something more potent.

Should she kill the assassin to make sure that the colorful bug didn't die? She had already moved a flame tendril to stand ready beneath the Miasmic cage. A quick poke and the struggle would be over.

But that would be a bit rude, not to mention somewhat embarrassing to butt in on a fight after having killed a few people for that kind of transgression. She guessed she would have to leave it up to fate.

Finally, it seemed like the assassin had had enough, and he launched a rapid succession of furious stabs as he moved quickly enough to make it hard even for Iz to follow. But the armored warrior was like an impenetrable fortress, enduring the strikes he could endure and blocking those he could not.

The failed assault was followed by an attempt at escape, and the assassin first tried to teleport out of the Miasmic cage. But he was completely unable to leave, and another special warrior attacked him the moment he tried to slip through the cracks. A furious assault on one of the towers was only met with a storm of ghosts as well, it seemed.

The moment the assassin realized that both killing the man and escaping was impossible, he instead reached down and crushed the token on his belt. Ever the pragmatists, the assassins.

The Red Hand Assassin disappeared in a flash, taking the domain with him. The Draugr stumbled around for a few seconds, seemingly unaware that he had actually won. The fifteen spectral chains kept flailing back and forth inside the cage as he stood hunched over, ready to eat another stab.

Only after twenty seconds passed did the man have enough presence of mind to look up at the sky. He had appeared in the sixth spot, meaning that the battle was won. Only then did he slowly start to move toward the Cosmos Sack, leaving a trail of black goop in his wake.

Iz was unsure what to do. The man was very interesting, but he was some random person from another part of the universe. Was there any point in trying to look into his secrets? There were a lot of oddities on his body, but who didn't have a secret or two? But it was *interesting.*

Of course, there was one easy way to test if they had some connection of fate. She instructed Uyirrik to get to work, and Iz's bloodline familiar formed another seal as she channeled a piece of her **|World's End|** into the array.

Someone who was dead obviously couldn't carry any fate or secrets worth fretting over.

27
FATE

Zac felt like a block of Swiss cheese as he desperately rotated his new Fragment while eating healing pills like they were candy. Whatever that assassin had infused himself with had made him disgustingly durable, and Zac couldn't believe how many Dao-infused strikes it took to force him to give in.

Scabs had covered almost every part of the man's blackened body, and he'd looked more like an undead compared to Zac himself by the end. It appeared that whatever the black spike infused into the man's body had forcibly kept the assassin going while instantly patching up his accumulating wounds.

But the layered corrosive effects had finally proven too much, forcing the man to crush his token. The encounter had been too close for comfort, though, and Zac wasn't sure whether he would have been able to endure if it weren't for his new Dao Fragment that kept patching up his lacerated body. Zac shook his head as he arduously moved over to the spot where the assassin had left the arena, and bent over to pick up the Cosmos Sack he'd left behind.

A glance at the sky confirmed that he was pretty much safe from elimination at this point. He was in sixth place on the ladder with 18 points. He had a shot at reaching even higher since there was only a 3-point difference between the fourth and his spot, but he wasn't sure his body would be able to take it.

He had barely defeated the assassin even though his class was a direct counter, and he was running low on Miasma due to the massive loss of ichor. He did pop a **[Soldier Pill]** to restore some of his reserves, but running low on Miasma wasn't the only issue. Zac looked down at **[Everlasting]** with a sigh.

The shield currently had multiple holes after getting brutalized during the fight. The fractals of the shield were thankfully still intact, and the holes were slowly closing themselves by the automatic repair function. However, its structural integrity was breached, and the weakness would transfer over to **[Immutable Bulwark]** as well, meaning his defenses were compromised by at least half until the shield had restored itself.

There was also the issue of the Splinter. The side effects of having one's soul filled with the Splinter's corrosion had started to make itself known during the latter half of the fight. A smoldering fury had started to build as he got increasingly wounded, and it was a strain to stay in place.

His subconscious had been screaming at him to destroy every-thing, to bravely rush forward and crush everything with the axe in his hand. That was obviously lunacy, though, as he couldn't even see his own hand in front of him, much less his target flitting about in the darkness domain.

The impulses had luckily calmed down the moment the battle ended, and Zac felt like himself again after just ten seconds. But it proved that prolonged battles could turn a bit iffy in the short term. Any thought of retreat had been long thrown out of his mind as he fought, and he would rather have died than given up in the heat of the moment, even though he was just inside a trial.

That fact alone made Zac leery about entering another battle. Getting a higher position would probably improve his reward, if past experience was any indication, but he wasn't ready to die just to get a better placement. But it might not be up to him if he entered another battle, but rather the Splinter.

All this combined made Zac unwilling to fight until getting a better handle on his situation. In fact, he wanted to keep **[Profane Seal]** active until the trial ended as a protective measure, but he felt that he was losing control over the skill, meaning that it was reaching its limits of how long it could stay active. He could only reluctantly release the skill as he tried to appear as intimidating as possible to avoid getting attacked the moment he was exposed.

Thankfully, his Miasmic armor from [Vanguard of Undeath] automatically repaired itself, and it should be impossible to see all the wounds covering his body. Along with the swirling clouds of his [Fields of Despair] and [Winds of Decay], he should look just as menacing as when he was at full strength.

However, not even a second had passed after the cage went down before alarm bells once again went off in his mind, and he saw a massive pillar of fire bearing down at him with terrifying momentum. He barely had time to adjust [Immutable Bulwark] before the beam was upon him, and it suddenly felt like he was being burned alive.

Flames burst out in all directions as the attack slammed into the bulwark, and the fractal shield only managed to block parts of the shocking amount of energies before the excess energy went around its edges. Zac was soon enough trapped within a corridor of flames, barely holding on.

He was slowly being pushed back as [Everlasting] started to lose its shape from the heat. Each second felt like an eternity, as Zac could only focus on holding on. He had seen what had happened to the beastkin warrior by just getting grazed by a beam just like this one, and he couldn't let it hit him. His defensive fragments and sturdy constitution might be able to handle the flames, but he wouldn't bet his life on it.

Zac's whole body was shaking from the strain, and much of the Miasma he had just restored with his [Soldier Pill] had been expended as his wounds reopened. Finally, he wasn't able to hold any longer. Perhaps if he had been in peak condition, he would be able to withstand such an attack multiple times, but now there was simply no way.

The shield cracked, and Zac reached down toward his token to escape before it was too late. But no flames waited behind the crumbled bulwark, only the vast sky. Just a few errant sparks remained, but Zac barely dodged them by ungracefully frog-leaping forward. It looked like he wouldn't share the same fate as the poor beastkin woman at least, but a furious rage just as potent as the flames had erupted in his mind from the brush with death.

His vision turned a bit jagged and monochromatic as he glared at the woman sitting atop the sun. The air twisted and turned around him as he lifted his bardiche, and his arm swelled from a massive infusion of Miasma from [Unholy Strike]. Blood would be repaid with blood.

Only at the last second did he manage to wrest back control of his mind, and he was shocked at what he had almost done. He had just been about to infuse his weapon with the Fragment of the Axe before throwing it at Iz Tayn.

Not even mentioning if such a crude attack would ever reach her before Verun was turned into ash, just what was he thinking? That crazy powerful cultivator was the last person he should antagonize, especially considering she only seemed intent on attacking once, judging by her demeanor.

The power in his arm still needed a release though, and a powerful slam into the ground caused a massive rift that stretched fifty meters forward as the Miasmic mists swirled around him. Zac quickly turned back toward the scorching sun afterward as he readied another [Undying Bulwark] just in case.

The two stared at each other for a few seconds, until Iz Tayn finally broke eye contact as she turned to the other participants, who looked at the spectacle with confusion and trepidation.

"This has gone on long enough. Start fighting right now or leave if you're not in the top ten," the woman said with a bored voice before she turned and pointed at Zac. "Not him, though. We are connected by fate."

Her eyes once again turned toward him, and Zac felt like she was looking at an interesting curiosity. Had she witnessed his transformation and wanted to dissect him like he had been warned by his master? Warning bells went off in Zac's mind when he saw her look, and he slowly started to back away even further from her.

Thankfully, she didn't seem to have any interest in attacking him again and instead chose to spectate the six battles that erupted as a direct result of her words. More than half the remaining warriors had targeted someone else, whereas the rest crushed their tokens with downcast expressions.

No one did target Zac, though, and he didn't make any moves either. He had already been hesitant to fight any more due to his wounds, and gaining the attention of that pyromancer didn't allow him to split his attention. He needed to be alert enough to counter anything that she had planned, or at least flee fast enough before being burned alive.

The battles took less than two minutes, and Zac was pushed down to the eighth position in the end as two warriors, one unranked and the other the previous tenth-spot holder, managed to accumulate enough points to pass him. The moment the fighting was over, ten pillars of light emerged, and Zac realized that one of them was placed on top of the platform where he'd started out.

The others realized what was going on, and over half the winners rushed toward their respective platforms as fast as their legs could carry them, none of them interested in staying behind. There was nothing to gain by staying in the arena, but everything could be lost if Iz Tayn decided to burn everything to the ground.

Only the two cultivators from the same family slowly walked toward their respective teleporters after bowing toward Iz Tayn, receiving a small nod in return.

Everyone seemed loath to stay in the arena, but perhaps no one was as motivated to flee as Zac himself. He couldn't care less what fate the insanely powerful pyromancer thought she had with him; his only interest was getting to the teleporter. But horror gripped his heart as the bored voice echoed out behind him.

"Wait, Mr. Bug," Iz Tayn said, and Zac's eyes widened with alarm when he saw that the scorching sun transformed into a massive river that snaked toward him.

There was no way he would wait to see what this maniac had in store, especially after she actually referred to him as a bug even though his name was on full display in the ladder. He redoubled his efforts at reaching the teleporter, but he was forced to stop in his tracks when a towering wall of flames rose to block his path.

If it had been someone else's flames, he would have simply run straight through, but he didn't dare to do something so foolhardy here. He quickly launched a wide swipe with [Unholy Strike] empowered with the Fragment of the Axe, but the strike was quickly swallowed up by the wall of flames like a pebble in a lake.

Zac turned around and saw that the girl was almost upon him, and his instincts screamed at him to get out as he saw a white flame forming above her hand. He desperately tried to think of some way out, but he could only come up with one solution.

His Miasmic armor dissipated into a gust of smoke as he shrank back to his normal size, and he stabbed his shoulders with two daggers as he ran straight toward the wall of flames. A massive surge of mental energy pushed into the two fractals of [Cyclic Strike], and Zac felt a mix of fear and anticipation when the two fragments actually fused into a bronze flash.

A roar echoed out across the arena as he punched the wall of flames with all he had, and a five-meter-wide void was created as the bronze spark sprang out of his fist and erupted in a fierce implosion that simply deleted the flames barring his path. Zac was flush with elation at finally being able to use the bronze flash for something useful, but he had no time to think about that now as he jumped straight toward the teleporter that was just twenty meters away.

He glanced back in midair just in case, only to see that Iz Tayn was only ten meters away. She donned an incredulous expression as she watched Zac soar toward the teleportation array, but Zac was unclear whether it was due to his incredibly stupid technique or because her wall got breached.

However, her expression soon turned thoughtful as she pushed two fingers into the white-hot flames she had conjured. A small glob of flames covered in dense fractals was quickly extracted, and Zac cursed from surprise when she flicked it toward him with a small smile.

He quickly moved his bulwark and infused it with the Fragment of the Coffin as he braced for impact, but his defenses weren't enough. The small flame shot straight through [Immutable Bulwark] and hit him in an instant. The stench of burnt flesh spread out in an instant as a burn mark as large as a fist appeared on his chest.

Zac growled with pain as he quickly applied the Fragment of the Bodhi on the wound, but he was relieved to see that the flames seemed unable to spread as they had with the beastkin. It still hurt like hell, and he shot a furious look at the girl, who had stopped in her tracks.

"Goddamn lunatic," Zac spat through gritted teeth as he disappeared through the teleporter.

28

DREAMS

Hot, hot flames and darkness. Billy didn't like it. Billy tried to get away, but it kept following wherever he went. But suddenly, the hot darkness was gone, and Billy saw he was on the mountain again.

"You were having a nightmare," the statue said.

"Billy told you, Billy won't listen to you, statue-man!" Billy snorted with disdain as he glared at the twenty-meter statue. "Trying to trick Billy that Billy is not human!"

The statue-man loudly groaned in response. Did he finally realize that Billy was too smart to be tricked?

"Remember, I only told you that you have Titanic blood due to your ancestry? It has simply awoken in you, pushing your mundane human bloodline aside," statue-man said, using a soft voice like a woman. "You are a descendant of mine; remember how I awakened your bloodline transformation?"

"Keep trying to trick Billy with big words," Billy muttered as he started to turn over rocks and rip up bushes.

"What are you doing now?" the statue finally said after some silence.

"Billy is looking for a way out. You think you can trap Billy here? Billy is a genius, Alien-man said so himself. Billy will find the door," Billy muttered as he started digging a hole.

"Look – listen. I am not trapping you, remember? I simply created this world so that I can guide you in your dreams. Isn't it working? Aren't you stronger after waking up?" the voice said with a sigh.

"Stupid statue, everyone feels better after a good night's sleep. Mama always says so," Billy snorted as he shot another despising glare at the huge statue looking like a human.

The statue was a bit annoying, even if it looked almost as handsome as Billy himself. Statue-man had big muscles like Billy, and he held a really big hammer that looked good for thwonkin'.

But statue-man was always trying to trick Billy, so Billy had tried to break it. But the stone was very hard; even Billy couldn't thwonk it to make it go quiet. Billy did manage to drag it away once, but the next night, it was right back. But Billy would one day find a way to thwonk it for good.

The trouble was that Billy always forgot about this stupid mountain and statue-man when waking up. Statue-man said that it was to protect him from enemy forces, but Billy believed that it was just so that Thea wouldn't help Billy figure out a way to thwonk him. Thea was almost as smart as Billy, and she had a lot of books.

Billy bet that at least one book could tell him how to make a statue shut up. Mama always said that books had all kinds of smart things written down.

"Lord, help this child," statue-man groaned.

"Billy is an adult," Billy muttered in response.

"Never mind." The statue sighed. "What happened to you? You have pretty serious wounds. I can only help so much through this dreamscape."

"Are you peeping at Billy? Mama said that peeping Toms get no dessert," Billy said with a scowl.

"We are connected through our bloodline. I can tell without peeping," statue-man said.

Billy hesitated for a bit, but he eventually decided to tell statue-man what had happened. Statue-man was a bit stupid and a liar, but he had helped Billy a few times with getting better at thwonkin'.

"Bad guys are attacking Billy's friend's town while he is away. Billy came to help. Their boats had a lot of fire," Billy muttered before his face lit up with glee. "But Billy thwonked one of their boats, and now the Zombies and lizardmen are fish poop."

"Good! A real man is true to his brethren and ruthless to his enemies," statue-man roared. "But your enemies are pretty strong. Why don't you draw the array I imparted to you, and I'll–"

"Billy won't fall for your tricks!" Billy cut off statue-man. "Billy knows that statue-man wants to use the drawing to escape Billy's dreams!"

"Ai, this child's bloodline might actually be too pure for his own good. The other emperors would laugh if they heard how hard it was to get a disciple."

"What did you find out?" Adriel asked as he gazed down at the ocean waves.

"It was Thea Marshall and Thwonkin' Billy," the ghost answered with a hollow voice. "They managed to sink one of the advance vessels before being forced to retreat by the Bishop. They were both wounded in the conflict and will likely not be able to fight for a week or two."

Adriel nodded with satisfaction. Those two weren't a real threat to his plans, but they had been a constant annoyance for a few months now, like two flies who refused to go away. It was good to hear that they had finally been brought to justice, and he knew that Krisko would perform a rite of thanks to the Founders upon hearing the news.

Besides, it was good news for another reason. Neither Super Brother-Man nor the two incursion leaders who chose to join his banner had participated in any of the raids that tried to impede their progress. The human champion was truly held up somehow, perhaps even sent off-world by the Ruthless Heavens.

If they hadn't captured a couple of the living to gain access to their Ladder, Adriel would have thought that the man was wounded after enduring the tribulation. But he was clearly still at level 75, proving he hadn't taken that step just yet.

"Our soldiers?" Adriel asked.

"Less than 5% survived from the vessel," the scout reported. "There are extremely bloodthirsty beasts in the waters; some of them seem to be controlled by the powerful contracted cephalopod."

"What about the arrays on the ship?" Adriel asked, cutting to the heart of the matter.

"We managed to recover them." The ghost nodded.

"Good." Adriel sighed with relief.

Losing a few hundred Revenants born on a world with such abundant Origin Dao was regrettable. These were among the first to awaken, and they would no doubt have become strong subordinates. But the mission could still be considered a win as long as they managed to plant the arrays.

The alignment would commence in five days, and as long as they managed to trap Super Brother-Man on his island kingdom until then, he would have won.

The brains of the zealots must have been scorched by their flames, as they still believed that they could actually kill the target in the middle of his own kingdom. Adriel knew better. He was happy to let them fight it out as he placed the spatial locks down.

Of course, if that was only what was needed to be done, he wouldn't have needed to send his strongest clones to this remote corner of the world. He had a secret mission to fulfill, handed to him straight from his master's master.

Who would have thought that some great powerhouse from the Empire Heartlands was touring their remote kingdom? With the distances involved, there might not be a single guest for tens of thousands of years, and usually not people with this kind of clout.

More importantly, the great master had a treasured disciple who craved unique bodies for experimentation, preferably ones leaning toward the Three Great Arts. And didn't he have a prime body waiting for him here? Thankfully, his master had managed to hear about it and quickly contacted him.

This was his shot at greatness. Between the contribution of aligning a world with such a unique Mystic Realm and gaining the favor of that great master, he might actually have a chance at gaining a Teleportation Token to the Heartlands. He had heard that treasures that could cause two forces to fight to the death in this remote sector were sold like they were worthless sticks of incense over there.

Adriel had already promised the body to Harkon, but he would have to get out of that contract even if it meant killing his old friend.

He could only pray that they had managed to keep the poison girl alive long enough that she hadn't decomposed or been cremated.

His hollow eyes looked out across the waters, cursing the zealots for building such bulky vessels rather than the small skippers that their enemies used. They would long have reached the islands if they could move even half as fast as the ships the humans utilized.

But they were so close that Adriel could taste it by now, and he could already sense markings left behind by Mhal even without the help of the tracking arrays. They would be there in less than a day, and without the human champion there, they might be able to completely conquer the town.

It was time to make all his dreams come true.

"You were right! He passed the seventh floor. Only took him something like twenty minutes too!" Leyara said with excitement, prompting Pretty to look over. "How did you know?"

"I had a feeling," Pretty said with a smile.

"You know something, I can feel it," Leyara said with a pout. "I can't take it! Just look at the chaos below! My sister disciples will be green with envy when they hear of this spectacle. Our sector might never have seen anything like it!"

Pretty Peak sighed as she looked down at the crowd that kept growing by the minute. Three-quarters of the climb was over for Zac Piker, and he could be dropping out at any moment now that he had reached the eighth floor.

One fight after another had erupted, as the square was only so big, and forces fought for the opportunity to be closer to the array. Mr. Piker would be drowned in a deluge of attacks the moment he emerged from the teleporter, and everyone wanted to be the one to land the killing blow.

Pretty felt some helplessness as she saw the commotion. She wasn't sure what she was supposed to do in this situation. The man had a minor connection to her uncle, but she couldn't be expected to deal with a mess of this magnitude, right?

"What are you thinking about? Do you want to join? I am sure

Prince Yeorav would give some face and let you set up camp next to his array," Leyara said. "Might be a good chance to make a connection? He's pretty handsome and less muscle-headed than his cultivation-maniac brother."

"I told you I'm not joining." Pretty sighed. "Besides, Yeorav has a Dao Companion already."

"So what's wrong?" Leyara asked as she took out a bottle of wine.

"Zac Piker has a small connection to my family, and I'm not sure what to do," Pretty finally admitted, but regretted it the moment she saw her friend's exuberant expression.

"I knew it!" Leyara screamed with excitement. "Secret boyfriend? Hiding him from your crazy grandpa?"

"What?" Pretty snorted with a roll of her eyes. "It's my cousin who knows him. Uncle Greatest sent Average on a training mission, and they met Zac Piker by chance. Mr. Piker beat the crap out of Average, and my uncle was impressed by his performance."

"He's from the Allbright Empire? But why haven't we heard of him before?" Leyara asked with confusion.

"I'm not sure if he's actually from my empire or not. He was sent to an abandoned planet in the Red Zone for a quest by the System. I think my cousin was used as a prop for him," Pretty explained.

"Well, Average is only seventeen. Beating him up shouldn't be too hard; he has barely started setting up his foundation." Leyara shrugged.

"Well, my uncle said there's something miraculous about Mr. Piker," Pretty said. "But he refused to say what when Dad asked."

"Well, that's not surprising. He beat the seventh floor. There's no way he hasn't had some unique encounters," Leyara said.

"So what do you think I should do?" Pretty asked.

"You can't stop what's going on down there, even if you team up with that mysterious Draugr," Leyara said as her eyes started to radiate with a white glow. "There are multiple arrays down there at the limit of what this place allows, and the powers are chaotic enough to indicate that there are at least a dozen offensive treasures in the mix."

"So he's doomed?" Pretty sighed. "It doesn't make sense that the System would create a scenario like this. We finally see a great genius emerge in this sector, only to have him die by the hands of a thousand pieces of trash?"

"Well, perhaps things will turn into an all-out brawl where the preparations are used on competing forces rather than on Mr. Piker. Or perhaps he has concocted some sort of counter. Who knows?" Leyara said, though she looked less than enthused about Mr. Piker's chances. "But I think the System will only require him to survive for a short moment to consider it a pass."

"Well, he's had almost a hundred days to prepare, and hopefully, he'll have found something that can assist him." Pretty nodded.

"Well, it doesn't hurt to get ready just in case," Leyara said thoughtfully as she adjusted her dress to show a bit more cleavage.

"What are you thinking about now?" Pretty asked with exasperation.

"Well, if he actually survives long enough for the quest to expire, wouldn't he become this sector's number one Prince Charming?" Leyara said as she started applying some makeup to her already immaculate face. "This is a prime opportunity to snag both a dashing husband and an amazing seedling for our forces."

GAINS

[Seventh Floor Complete. Upgrading Title.]

[Choose Reward: Evolution of *[Verun's Bite]*, Duplicity Core Upgrade to E-grade, Upgrade of Port Atwood to World Capital]

[Additional Reward 8th place: Limited Title Slots +1, Peak F-grade All Attribute Fruit]

Zac's pitch-black eyes went back and forth between the three choices, the pain and exhaustion almost completely blown away. Then again, the black dimension seemed to have some sort of suppressive effect on wounds, so he probably wouldn't be as chipper when he left this place.

A quick look down at his chest proved that the crazy girl had left a burn mark that almost looked like a fractal, but the wound showed no signs of spreading at least. However, that didn't provide much comfort, as there had obviously been something off about that piece of flame she had shot at him.

His best guess was that she had formed some sort of Karmic tie to him for some reason. Iz Tayn came from some top-tier force, though, and Zac hoped that the distance to his remote sector would prove too far away to make it worth tracking him down. If it was even possible since she was just an F-grade cultivator.

However, the encounter with the crazy flame girl wasn't enough to put a damper on his feelings at the moment. He had passed the seventh floor, a feat that only happened once every few millennia in a star sector with trillions of cultivators. And there were no two ways around it, these rewards were amazing.

Better yet, they were clearly custom-made for himself, which was a first since he'd entered the Tower. The reward for clearing the sixth floor had been pretty great too, but it was still something generalized apart from the compatibility.

Was it because he had cleared a high-tiered floor, or was it because there had been a special event?

Even better, there was actually a bonus reward for reaching the eighth place, and it provided something he had never even heard of before. Getting a fourth slot for Limited Titles was an extremely powerful boon, and Zac started to understand why so many had been fighting tooth and nail even to the point that some died.

Getting another spot for Limited Titles wasn't as simple as having another title. If that was it, then Zac wouldn't have been so excited, since he already had thirty of them. Limited Titles had never been too important for Zac until now, simply because he hadn't encountered any such opportunities so far.

But Galau had properly described the roles of Limited Titles during their climb. The merchant had already confirmed that getting real titles would get harder and harder, and most people got almost 80% of their titles during the F-grade. That was why some called normal titles "Foundational Titles." They set the foundation for your entire cultivation journey.

Limited Titles were something that you could continuously improve, though, and there was almost an unlimited number of opportunities for such titles in the Multiverse. They were the lure the System used to keep pulling cultivators into deadly trials and unexplored Mystic Realms, and they just kept getting better the more dangerous the trial was.

One single Limited Title snatched from a deadly D-grade trial might be even better than the Tower Title he had worked for the past seventy days. Getting another Limited Title slot was essentially getting a 15–20% boost to your power, provided you could get a good title that provided Efficiency.

The reward might not be useful at the moment, but Zac would quickly be able to acquire a few Limited Titles after leaving Earth. As for the scions who risked their lives, it was understandable as well. This was a reward that no amount of treasures, wealth, or guidance could provide, and they no doubt had a bunch of top-quality Limited Titles to choose from through their forces.

Not only that, the System even threw in a small bonus in the form of an All Attribute Fruit, which was equivalent to a pretty good Low-tiered title. That was the most valuable of all the Attribute Fruits, even more so than Luck Fruits. Zac was extremely thankful that he hadn't given in to the fear in his heart that had told him to cut his losses after narrowly surviving his soul getting crushed.

The rewards from this floor alone far eclipsed the rewards from the first six floors combined.

It also made him wonder just what the others received. Take Iz Tayn, for example. She was already strong to the point that it felt like she had somehow snuck inside the Tower while being E-grade. Just what level would she reach after getting her individualized reward plus whatever reward was awarded for the first spot. Did she get multiple Limited Title slots?

Remembering the traumatizing encounter where he almost died made him think of something else, and he reluctantly turned his eyes away from the rewards. Zac wasn't quite ready to make a choice, so he first opened his Status screen to check something, and just as expected, he had taken a huge step forward.

Name: Zachary Atwood
Level: 75
Class: [F-Rare] Hatchetman
Race: [E] Human
Alignment: [Earth] Port Atwood – Lord

Titles: Born for Carnage, Ultimate Reaper, Luck of the Draw, Giantsbane, Disciple of David, Overpowered, Slayer of Leviathans, Adventurer, Demon Slayer I, Full of Class, Rarified Being, Trailblazer, Child of Dao, The Big 500, Planetary Aegis, One Against Many, Butcher, Progenitor Noblesse,

Duplicity Core, Apex Hunter, Heaven's Chosen, Scion of
Dao, Omnidextrous, Eastern Trigram Hunt – 1st, Tyrannic
Force, Achievement Hunter, The First Step, Promising
Specialist, Tower of Eternity – 7th Floor, Heaven's
Triumvirate

Limited Titles: Frontrunner

Dao: Fragment of the Axe – Early, Fragment of the Coffin –
Early, Fragment of the Bodhi – Early

Core: [F] Duplicity

Strength: 980 [Increase: 75%. Efficiency: 163%]
Dexterity: 498 [Increase: 60%. Efficiency: 155%]
Endurance: 1282 [Increase: 80%. Efficiency: 163%]
Vitality: 673 [Increase: 65%. Efficiency: 163%]
Intelligence: 264 [Increase: 60%. Efficiency: 155%]
Wisdom: 386 [Increase: 60%. Efficiency: 155%]
Luck: 243 [Increase: 80%. Efficiency: 155%]

Free Points: 0

Nexus Coins: [F] 6,830,543,287

Zac's stared with confusion at his attributes, unable to compute the
changes for a few seconds. It was a welcome problem, though; he had
gained too many points. He already knew he would get a small boost
from fusing his last two Dao Seeds, but that alone couldn't explain the
growth. But he soon enough realized what was going on as he kept
opening menus.

The first thing he checked was the Dao menu. He had taken a
quick look during the Battle Royale, but he hadn't had the time to
properly look at the attributes at that time.

**[Fragment of the Axe (Early): All attributes +10, Strength +110,
Dexterity + 80, Endurance +15. Effectiveness of Strength +5%.]**

[Fragment of the Coffin (Early): All attributes +10, Endurance +80, Vitality +50, Intelligence +15, Wisdom +60. Effectiveness of Endurance +5%.]

[Fragment of the Bodhi (Early): All attributes +10, Endurance +60, Vitality +80, Intelligence +15, Wisdom +50, Effectiveness of Vitality +5%.]

Gaining the Fragment of the Bodhi was all thanks to the [Prajñā Cherry], and Zac wondered if the Zethaya had even known the true value of that thing since Boje had considered it a soul-healing treasure. Then again, they did cherish it to the point that they weren't willing to part with it for money, so they probably knew that wasn't the limit of its capabilities.

There wasn't a lot of change to his attributes as far as Zac could remember, with the Fragment essentially only adding the +10 to all attributes and a little bit of Wisdom. However, he noticed how similar its distribution was to the Fragment of the Coffin. The weight of attributes was almost identical, with just the focus on Endurance and Vitality being switched.

Getting the Fragment of the Bodhi rather than something like the Grove or the Forest was a bit unexpected, but perhaps not as much as getting the Coffin. Zac had read up on Buddhism a bit since learning that it was an actual cultivation system in the Multiverse, so he knew a little bit of what the word represented.

The Bodhi was a divine tree that the Buddha gained enlightenment under, and the word was the term for true Enlightenment, the escape from the cycle of reincarnation. The only issue was that such a Dao sounded related to Buddhism, and he wasn't sure how good a fit that would be to his current cultivation path.

Ogras had joked about him embarking on the path of ascetic cultivation like a monk, but he wasn't ready to take a vow of silence just yet.

But his instincts told him that it wouldn't be an issue. The name of a Dao Fragment wasn't important; what mattered were the concepts the Fragment contained. The main focus of the vision hadn't been the Buddhist praying, but rather how the cherry tree had changed after the blessing. It had turned into a divine tree that became the guardian of the desolate badlands.

It didn't only provide the whole area with vitality, but it also empowered everything within its domain. Normal weeds and grasses had become full of life and power, quickly growing far stronger than they would be able to on their own. From what Zac could tell, the healing he had enjoyed was just part of the picture. The Fragment might have a huge impact on his Hatchetman class, as many of its skills were related to nature.

What would happen if he turned the wooden hand of [Nature's Punishment] into a divine hand?

Getting the third Fragment early was a huge relief to Zac, and it took a lot of pressure off. It was a shame that it came at the cost of the soul-mending medicine, but now that he had passed the seventh floor, he should have a stronger position for bargaining when he exited. Perhaps he could buy another one from some powerful clan who wanted to make a connection with him.

It also meant that the chance of gaining something from the Tower Apparition was a lot higher since he now could upgrade any of his three Fragments. Ideally, he wanted to upgrade the Fragment of the Axe, but it wasn't completely necessary at this point. Any of the three would allow him to gain an Arcane class, as long as the System considered his new path to be unique enough to be called a "creation."

He couldn't wait to experiment some with his new fragment during his ascent of the eighth floor. He had finally managed to use the bronze flash for something useful just now, and it had been shockingly effective. It felt like confirmation that he was on the right path, and he needed to capture the moment of inspiration and expand it to his new Fragment as well.

Of course, getting the final Dao Fragment wasn't the only surprising gain from the seventh floor. He had not only upgraded his Tower Title, but he had actually gained another one, the first one in a good while. He had assumed that he wouldn't get any more titles before evolving unless he got something from his massive pool of Luck, but it appeared he had underestimated himself.

[Tower of Eternity – 7th Floor: Reach the 64th level of the Tower

of Eternity. Reward: All Stats +10, All Stats +10%, Effect of
Attributes +5%]

[Heaven's Triumvirate: Attain three Dao Fragments while still at
F-grade. Reward: All Stats +5%. All Stats +5. Effect of Attributes
+5%]

The Tower Title had upgraded, but not quite as expected. Instead
of boosting his three main attributes, it had directly provided +5% efficiency to all attributes. That meant one would probably get the perfect
10/10/10 from completing the eighth floor. But then what would
happen on the ninth? Did it provide a separate title?

The guy earlier had mentioned "tower breakers," and from context,
it sounded like someone who would be able to defeat the whole Tower
of Eternity. Was Tower Breaker perhaps the name of not only the
achievement, but an actual title?

Zac unfortunately knew that the ninth floor was out of his reach
unless the rules drastically changed on the final floor. The progression
of strength had been pretty even during the climb, and he knew that he
would start entering true life-and-death battles on the eighth floor.

Even defeating the guardian wasn't a given, and he had already
decided to start looking for clues to amazing inheritances as a backup.

Time was a precious resource, so Zac held off on choosing a
reward a while longer and instead sat down to recuperate while he was
in this special zone. Getting chased down by Iz Tayn had only worsened his wounds from the battle with Faceless #9, and he needed to
give himself and his poor shield some time to rest up.

[Everlasting] almost looked like a melted clump of metal, but it
was truly a tenacious item, and it was slowly regaining its original
shape. Just like his body, it would probably be in serviceable condition
within a few hours.

However, the situation with his soul wasn't as easy to fix. The
verdant glow had completely disappeared by now, leaving his soul
whole. But his soul had inexorably changed after the experience. It
was now crisscrossed by black lines where the fractures once were,
reminiscent of a kintsugi bowl. There were also some splotches here
and there, marring the picture even further.

He had already felt the effect during the battle earlier, where bloodlust had coursed through his body, almost to the point that he was ready to run straight into a sun. Zac was afraid that the effect would only become worse as the corruption grew. The energies might even start damaging the Miasmic runes from the outside.

He quickly needed to find a solution.

THE HAYNER CLAN

The mental defense skills available to either of his classes were of no help against the Splinter. For example, [Indomitable] formed a formidable wall around Zac's soul, but it didn't help when the threat was already a part of him. The [Nine Reincarnations Manual] might help, but he still hadn't found anyone who could create the second Array Disk required to practice it. Having just one of the arrays was useless, and he couldn't even begin to practice the first reincarnation.

The Fragment of the Bodhi did seem to be able to stabilize the situation somewhat at least, just like his Seed of Trees had constrained the Draugr bloodline that had been implanted in him. It was a losing battle, though, and it was probably only a matter of time before something went wrong.

The only solution that Zac could think of for the moment was to keep the energies in check as best he could, and hopefully, he'd find something to use during the last day that had been allocated for the Base Town. Or perhaps he was worrying over nothing, and his soul would slowly grind down the infected parts since the main body of the Splinter was still locked away in its cage.

Thirty minutes quickly passed as Zac almost went into a trancelike state where he tried using his new fragment to the utmost while absorbing E-grade Miasma Crystals and healing pills. Some fresh hell was no doubt waiting outside his special zone, and he needed to be at his best.

He was still far from top condition, but it should be enough for him to survive the initial chaos and properly rest somewhere else. He would rather have stayed inside the black dimension for a few more hours, but the whole zone had started to shudder, indicating that it was time to leave.

The problem was what reward to choose, as all of them were extremely tempting. He knew that the evolution of the weapon wasn't something as simple as an upgrade from Middle to Peak E-grade, but it was rather more akin to a bloodline evolution of a beast. It might provide Verun with a matching attunement to his own, or swap out the materials with ones of far higher quality.

The somewhat humble origins of his axe hadn't been a problem so far, but it would sooner or later start to fall behind, or even get stuck in a bottleneck. It needed fortuitous encounters just like himself, and this was a great opportunity to improve his companion to something with greater potential. It would probably also help during the final remainder of the climb, and he would need every advantage he could get.

As for the Specialty Core upgrade, it spoke for itself. He already had the [Pathfinder Oracle Eye] in his possession, so it was not completely needed in his case. But the eye was an amazing treasure that could be used for almost anything, it seemed, and upgrading his core this way would free up the treasure for other uses.

As for upgrading Port Atwood to a World Capital, Zac wasn't as clear what it would entail. It would no doubt come with a slew of advantages to his force in general, and it would probably also give him some sort of title for being the one who founded the capital after integration. It would provide access to all kinds of new businesses and other beneficial buildings as well, since it was a common requirement in the Town Shop to have the World Capital.

Indecision gnawed at him for a minute, but he knew he couldn't stall forever. His eyes eventually went to the middle option, and he picked the Duplicity Core upgrade. His reason was simple; his core was a unique mutation, and there were no guarantees the eye would be able to upgrade it even if he ate it after evolving.

Meanwhile, the System termed it as an upgrade, and there shouldn't be any chance of the upgrade failing. Evolving Verun would have been nice as well, but Verun was ultimately a pretty common Spirit Tool, and finding other opportunities to improve it shouldn't prove impossible. Even his Pathfinder Eye could upgrade the Spirit Tool if need be.

Besides, Verun was still keeping up at his current power without a problem, especially after he had managed to light up another fractal on its handle. He would probably need to reach level 100 or so before the axe started to fall behind.

As for the World Capital, he had great confidence in accomplishing that on his own, provided that he didn't get himself killed first. Taking that option would ultimately only speed up the process, and he felt it wasn't worth it. It would perhaps have given him a better title for getting the World Capital while still in F-grade, but he wasn't lacking for titles.

The choice was made, so Zac waited to be teleported to the start of the eighth floor. But nothing happened for a few seconds until a startling change took place in the empty space. A densely inscribed circle appeared beneath his feet, and it illuminated him in a golden luster.

A volatile surge of energy entered his body the next moment, and Zac had to force himself to stay still instead of rolling around in pain. The colossal amount of power streamed straight toward his core, and he didn't dare make a move for fear that he would ruin what was happening.

Who would have known that the System would force an upgrade immediately rather than hand him some pill?

The pain thankfully only lasted for less than a minute, and Zac could only guess it wasn't a big deal for the System to upgrade a simple F-grade Specialty Core, even if it was a mutated version. Zac wanted to inspect the upgraded Specialty Core, but the surroundings changed as he was teleported to the next world.

The massive bulwark from [Immutable Bulwark] was conjured within a second of arriving as he hefted the somewhat restored [Everlasting], and [Indomitable] defended his mind from taking another hit. The cherry had worked wonders, but he guessed the soul was still a bit vulnerable after having almost crumbled to pieces.

It was lucky as well, as a massive blade slammed straight into his shield just as Zac appeared in the new world. A pained roar followed as [Deathwish] retaliated the strike. But even then he didn't get any respite as his danger sense hollered in the back of his mind, forcing him to jump to the side as the air itself where he stood was ripped open.

[Seize the Hayner Clan's defining treasure before the invaders.]

Zac sighed in disappointment even though he saw the quest was related to a defining treasure. He had been down this road before during the past floors, and he knew things weren't so simple. First of all, he was thrown onto some desolate beach without any civilization nearby, and he had no idea where this Hayner Clan was located.

But that was just the start of his problems. Right behind him was a massive pillar that stretched into the sky, and one warrior after another appeared around him. The soldiers were beset with attacks from a defending force that didn't ask any questions but rather tried to kill anyone that appeared.

The situation was all too familiar to him. It was an incursion.

However, the chaos was still a bit different from the one he was used to. It looked like he had arrived just minutes after the pillar appeared, yet an army full of Peak F-grade to powerful E-grade warriors was already fighting back with great ferocity. The attacks he had just avoided came from the defenders, who looked like a mix of humans and trolls.

They stood almost three meters tall and had pale green skin. They seemed to favor physical combat as well, and even the strike he'd barely dodged had come from an explosive arrow attack. Zac could understand the words the humans streaming out of the pillar screamed, but the defenders spoke in an unintelligible guttural gibberish.

How would he find out where the Hayner Clan was? And who was the guardian in a scenario like this? He seemed to be allied with the raiders, but also not, judging by the wording of the quest. He could liken it to being an infiltrator who had joined the incursion with hidden motives, so everyone was an enemy.

Was the incursion leader the guardian, or was it perhaps the patriarch of the Hayner Clan? As for actually finding the treasure, he had already given up on it. He knew that even if he found the clan, there would be all sorts of hurdles to jump in order to get the treasure, hurdles he didn't have the time nor the skills to deal with.

Eventually, he could only find one solution to his situation, and Zac searched the area until he spotted a human radiating a sinister aura as he commanded his troops to take down the defending armies. Zac steadied himself as he activated **[Profane Seal]**, appearing in front of the man without warning.

The man looked extremely shocked to be attacked by one of his own, but he immediately reacted as a huge bird made from hundreds of flying daggers appeared in front of him as he flashed away. However, the cage was already erected, and Zac steadily grew to his towering form as Miasma covered the area.

The flying daggers assailed him like an angry swarm of bees, and Zac was quickly forced to actively block with **[Immutable Bulwark]** as he noted that the daggers were infused with a Dao Fragment and could cut straight through his Miasmic armor. The fractal shield thankfully held, though, and Zac saw Dao-empowered specters appear around the incursion general in an instant.

However, most of the specters' strikes were diffused with some sort of small shields that appeared around the leader, with only a few of them managing to land an actual blow on him.

Zac knew he had taken the strength of the potential guardian too lightly at that moment. He hadn't mentally adjusted due to the increased difficulty because he hadn't fought a real floor guardian at the end of the seventh floor, but rather a bunch of cultivators. It made him still think of his competition as roughly the same as the sixty-second level, forgetting about the sharp increase that came with the final levels of a floor.

The man was also an incursion general, which Zac had ample experience in defeating without exerting any herculean effort. It had made him confident in deflecting the small blades with his impervious armor, but he received a rude awakening as over ten daggers bored into his body and reopened some wounds.

If that was all that happened, it would have been fine, as such small weapons weren't any threat to Zac's towering physique. But a blistering pain started to radiate from the wounds in an instant, and

Zac felt the world lurch for a second before he found his bearings. He realized what was going on in an instant; the daggers were poisoned.

Luckily, both the spread and impact was largely contained the moment he activated the Fragment of the Coffin. But it was nothing like when he'd fought the corroded monkeys back on the third floor. The Coffin didn't make him magically immune to all poisons; it only strengthened his resistance to it and allowed him to refine it.

This poison he was struck with was on a completely other level compared to what he had absorbed before, and it seemed to also be empowered by a Dao of its own. It wasn't life-threatening as far as Zac could tell, especially with his Draugr body's natural resistance against poisons as well. But it would still take some effort to refine it all.

"You are not one of ours!" the man roared from the other side of the cage, a large festering wound having appeared on his arm.

Zac didn't answer as he was focused on combating the poison spreading through his body, while simultaneously making sure that he wasn't cut by any more of those small daggers. He noted that a concerted effort to break through from the leader's soldiers was already underway, and he knew his time was limited.

He quickly pushed his taunting effect to the limit as he rushed toward his target, with ten of the fifteen chains targeting the general. The other five started to take out the people who had been caught inside the cage along with their leader, and these people quickly turned into nourishment for him. The incursion leader managed to stave off the chains, though, by allocating a large number of his flying daggers to fight them off.

A poison master was a decent counter to his build since intangible attacks like poison or illusions wouldn't trigger [Deathwish], but that didn't mean Zac was helpless. He could still retaliate if the man used daggers rather than pure poison attacks like Alea, and he also had his massive bardiche to strike back.

The ground cracked beneath his feet as Zac ran straight toward the incursion leader, but the man seemed intent on stalling as he was swallowed by a hurricane of blades before he was whisked away. Unfortunately for the man, he hadn't realized he was under the effect of

[Vanguard of Undeath], and the general suddenly appeared only five meters away from Zac.

Zac's arm was already bulging from cramming it full of Miasmic energy from **[Unholy Strike]**, and the sounds of ghastly wails filled the cage as the massive black axe crashed into the whirlwind just when the general appeared.

The axe went straight through the general's torso, but Zac felt no elation, as the swing provided no resistance, and it looked like he had struck a pile of mud as the invader's body fell apart into a rotten pile on the ground. The general had escaped his killing blow.

FATED

Danger sense erupted in Zac's mind the next moment, and he desperately swiveled **[Everlasting]** to block a strike coming from behind. A dark-green lance had appeared out of nowhere, aimed straight at Zac's core. Zac tried to dodge, but his bulky body wasn't quick enough, and he barely managed to reposition himself before the lance slid right through his armor as though it were made of paper before continuing into his side.

Radiating pain spread throughout his body, and Zac felt like he was being bitten by a million fire ants. But the lance pushing straight through his body had one upside; the incursion leader was suddenly well within his range. The man was pretty quick, but he was nowhere near as fast as the assassin he had just fought.

Zac let go of his shield as he grabbed on to the poison master before he could slink away again. His grip covered half the invader's torso, and there was no escaping now. The warrior seemed to realize the problem, and a green blade appeared in his hand as he tried to cut Zac's arm off with one swift motion.

A black shield appeared around Zac's arm as he hurriedly threw out a talisman from his Spatial Ring. It was something he had gotten from the undead level, a defensive treasure that could be used almost instantly. It wasn't strong enough to completely block the strike, but it absorbed enough momentum for the Fragment of the Coffin along with his conjured armor to block out the rest.

Wet crunching sounds emerged from the poison master's body as Zac's grip closed like a vise. The man started wailing in pain as he desperately tried to morph away, but Zac was flooding the guy with his corrosive Dao, making it impossible to change his form.

However, the man seemed completely unwilling to give in even when half his torso was crushed, and a storm of daggers rushed toward them both in an attempt at mutual destruction. Zac was forced to quickly cut the man in two to finally sense a burst of energy enter his body as the flying daggers lost their power and fell down on the ground.

The invasion leader had almost been as durable as himself, launching destructive strikes, even though half his body was crippled. Perhaps he was just like Alea, forced to focus on Vitality to counteract the effects of the poisons he used.

Zac felt as though both his body and mind were on fire from the poison, but he still released the cage of **[Profane Seal]**. The fighting between both sides had mostly subsided, and they gapingly looked on as the massive form of Zac walked forward, holding the crushed incursion leader like a ragdoll in his almost grotesquely large hand.

"This invasion is over. Return or die," Zac said to the humans, his gravelly voice sending shivers down the spines of the listeners.

Seeing most of the humans flee toward the incursion pillar, Zac turned to the massive trolls. They hesitantly looked back at Zac, probably unsure whether he was an ally or just a bloodthirsty lunatic.

"Do you understand my words now?" Zac simply asked as he forcibly tried to quell the storm raging in his mind.

"We understand, Warmaster," one of the trolls said as he stepped forward. "Why did you help us?"

"I am following a prophecy that took me to your world. I am looking for the Hayner Clan," Zac said.

Following a prophecy was an excuse that Ogras had used multiple times when searching for information upon arriving at new levels. It didn't really explain why they were there, and neither did it divulge whether you were an ally or a foe. Furthermore, a lot of people read into it whatever fit their point of view, which made them accidentally divulge some extra information.

"The Hayner Clan?" the troll mumbled with a frown. "Are they the cause of this cataclysm?"

"They have something in their possession that should not exist on this planet," Zac said, neither confirming nor denying the troll's question.

"So it is them," the troll growled. "Delving into the taboo. They pretended to be our saviors, bringing words of warning, but they were actually the harbingers of our doom."

It turned out that the Hayner Clan was an ancient clan full of sages who delved into the mysteries of the Heavens. They had warned the forces of this world that a great war was coming, that invaders would come to disrupt their way of life. It had allowed the forces to ready themselves for war, but it had also inadvertently helped Zac gain an excuse for why he was looking for them.

However, a frown quickly formed beneath Zac's helmet while listening, as it quickly became apparent that the family focused on the Dao of Karma, just like Abbot Everlasting Peace. Fighting those kinds of people was notoriously annoying since they were often able to anticipate your next move.

Did the Hayner Clan already know they were targeted by him? Perhaps they had even gone underground the moment he arrived, which would make Zac's mission even harder to complete.

He had already confirmed that the incursion leader wasn't the guardian of the level. No teleportation array had appeared when he killed the poison master, and he was pretty sure by now that he would have to actually find the Hayner Clan to advance to the next floor. After asking about the general state of the world and getting a decent map of the area, Zac left the trolls to deal with the aftermath of the incursion.

However, Zac only ran for twenty minutes before he stopped and took out another healing treasure along with some general antidote pills. With the number of pills he had eaten over the last hour, the effect was drastically reduced, but he needed to do something about the poison rampaging through his body.

It had been a struggle to just stand upright and talk with the trolls. They were very congenial after he had killed the incursion leader, even calling him Warmaster, but that friendliness might have taken a sharp turn if they found out he was in an extremely wounded state. Dealing with poison was his strong suit, but the wounds had stacked up to an almost unmanageable state by now.

He knew he was running out of time to reach the top of the eighth floor, but he still needed to take a moment to rest. At least the last level had finished extremely quickly, which saved him a few hours, even though the final levels of each floor usually were pretty quick to deal with. It wouldn't be the end of the world if he spent a couple of hours healing up from the aftermath.

Taking the opportunity of the downtime, Zac first looked inward, checking out his new and improved Specialty Core. Its size and coloring were pretty much the same, but the density of fractals covering its surface was on a whole new level. The inscriptions were so fine that he couldn't discern them all with his spiritual vision.

There was also an indefinable upgrade in the quality of the Duplicity Core. It almost felt like it had been a cheap plastic ball before, but it was now upgraded to solid metal. The quality and composition were essentially improved. However, Zac quickly started to feel some confusion as he tried to understand the changes the upgrade had brought.

The reason was simple; there were none. The line in his Status screen had been updated to say **[E] Duplicity**, but that was about it. It didn't provide any more attributes, and there was nothing else that seemed to have changed.

It was a pretty big disappointment, as it currently awarded 5% Strength and 5% Endurance, based on the two main attributes of his classes. Zac thought that those boosts might increase from the upgrade, which was another reason he'd opted to take the Specialty Core upgrade as an award. If his boost went from 5% to 10%, then his Strength would have passed 1,000 by now. But it seemed like that wasn't meant to be.

However, it wasn't a complete loss. He had only seen those things as a bonus if he got them. The main point was that he would be able to evolve his two classes without having to worry whether his Specialty Core would be able to keep up. Besides, Yrial seemed to indicate that the speed of his transformation should improve as the core evolved. He didn't dare to try it out right now, as he was both poisoned and wounded, and his Draugr form was better at enduring such a state.

Not gaining any boost to his Strength was disappointing, but he had gotten his hands on another Peak Attribute Fruit, which would allow him to almost reach his goal. As long as a Medium Fragment increased the boost to All Attributes, he would breach 1,000 Strength no matter which of the three Fragments he managed to upgrade from the Tower Apparition.

As for whether he would manage to upgrade his Dao from the apparition, he felt it almost was a given by now. He had reached the eighth floor, something that only happened once every few millennia. The strength of the apparition he would summon should be on a completely different tier compared to those he had witnessed before, and the effect was reportedly boosted significantly when you were the one who conjured it.

After having rested up for another hour, he felt strong enough that he didn't need to solely focus on recuperation. Most of the poison had already been converted to energy, with just a few Dao-empowered remnants lingering on. Those remnants would take a while longer to grind down, but they weren't a threat to him at all.

Seeing the situation stabilized, he first took out the Peak Attribute Fruit and ate it. A warmth spread through his body, and he quickly checked the Status screen for the result. A quick mental calculation let him know that he had gained 8 to All Attributes, which would have to be considered a pretty good result.

However, his Strength had only gained 7 points, pushing his total to 992. It was only one point less than the other attributes, but it proved a somewhat disappointing fact; he had hit the cap for how much Strength he could gain by eating treasures. Adding the fruits from the hunt, he had gained a total of 25 points in Strength before he hit the limit.

An attribute limit of twenty-five was as good as it got in the F-grade, as far as Zac could tell, where most people were only able to gain 15–20 points from Attribute Fruits. However, he had held out some unspoken hope that his odd constitution would also apply to this situation, where his limits were a lot higher compared to normal. But it looked like his body had to follow the same rules as everyone else.

But there was not only bad news waiting after he looked through his Status screen. His Luck had shot up to 257, and it had provided a title just like he had hoped.

[Fated: Gain 250 Luck at F-grade Reward: Effect of Luck +5%]

It wasn't anything special, truthfully, but Zac guessed it was fair enough. His Luck was so high from having gained so many titles, and if the System kept giving titles for those kinds of accomplishments, it would essentially mean he was getting rewarded for getting rewarded. Besides, even if the boost was pretty small, it was still a high-tiered title that boosted Luck. Such a thing was extremely hard to come by.

Zac closed the screen and turned his attention to the two Cosmos Sacks and the Spatial Ring he had gained during the last level. A smile of anticipation spread across his face as he scanned the contents of the first pouch, wondering what kind of treasures the elites of the Multiverse would carry around.

A blank look of confusion spread across his face, though, as he first scanned the swordsman's sack. Zac couldn't figure out what was going on. He would have expected a Cosmos Sack from someone like that to be filled to the brim with all kinds of mysterious items, but there was even less inside than his own Cosmos Sack.

The first thing he noticed was one of the golden swords. It was one of the three that the lanky humanoid had controlled with his mind and that had kept harassing him throughout the fight. But he couldn't find the other three swords he'd used even after scanning the contents multiple times. Had the System simply snatched a part of the losers' treasures at random as they left the Tower? Because that was what it looked like after going through the contents.

He did, however, spot the old sword in its tattered scabbard. It was something that had piqued Zac's interest due to its dangerous aura, and Zac curiously took it out from the Sack. Upon looking at it from such close proximity, it felt like the sword was something that had been left to rot in some storehouse for millennia before being picked up. The leather scabbard was extremely faded and dried out, and it looked like a strong wind would turn it to dust.

However, his mind started to scream of danger the moment he

gripped the hilt, and a furious presence suddenly urged him to draw the sword and paint the world red. Zac groaned and quickly threw the sword to the ground, but it took him over ten minutes to regain his composure. The presence had awakened the **[Splinter of Oblivion]** inside its cage, and it furiously railed against the Miasmic fractals.

It felt like when he had been possessed by the cursed ghosts during the hunt, as violent impulses had tried to take over his mind. Zac looked at the old sword with some lingering fear, unsure what he was dealing with.

Was it a Tool Spirit that had gone insane?

NOUVEAU RICHE

Brazla had only turned a bit schizophrenic and annoying over time, but he wasn't strictly dangerous. However, it was possible that some Tool Spirits turned sinister as they went insane. Zac knew there had to be some benefit to the sword, though, as the swordsman had used it as an ace. The half-moon attack had contained a shocking sharpness that cut both his mountain and array apart; was it perhaps only possible to conjure such an attack with this sword?

Zac was loath to carry the weird sword around, and he tried putting it back into the Cosmos Sack again. But the sword refused to enter the pouch, and Zac soon realized the sacks left behind were temporary pouches just like the one he'd gotten from the hunt. He threw the sword into his own sack instead as he turned to the next items in the pouch.

The bag contained an assortment of pills along with a small mound of crystals and a couple of manuals. However, Zac refrained from touching those, afraid that they would be protected like Mhal's manual was. They possibly contained skills and cultivation techniques whose quality was unrivaled in his sector, and such things would no doubt come with high-grade theft protection.

The bag from the masked man was a lot more ominous. It contained over a hundred heads from a dozen different Races, each of them placed in their own densely inscribed boxes. Their eyes were sewn shut, and a talisman was pushed halfway into their mouths. Why the hell was this man carrying around something like this?

It didn't seem to be part of his class, since he never used any heads to fight. Was this some sort of morbid way to create talismans? And if Zac only got part of their accumulated treasures, just how many heads had Faceless #9 been carrying around in total? Apart from that, there were a bunch of vials and assorted treasures, including five identical spikes that the assassin had stabbed himself with during their fight.

Zac hesitated for a second before he transferred two of them to his own Spatial Ring. He wasn't sure exactly what these things were, but they'd allowed the assassin to fight beyond his normal capabilities. The spikes probably had even worse side effects than his [Hatchet-man's Rage], but he might be forced to go all out upon exiting the Tower in a few days.

Just like with the swordsman's pouch, there was another pile full of an assortment of items in one corner, likely things the assassin had picked up inside the Tower. However, after seeing the heads, he was in no mood to look too closely at what had captured the interest of such a lunatic.

Finally, there was the Spatial Ring belonging to the mentalist, the Spatial Tool that Zac felt held the most promise. The two sacks had been dropped off by the System, but this was the real deal that was taken from her person. And he only needed a glance to realize he had hit the jackpot. It looked just like what he expected a wealthy scion's Cosmos Sack to look like. First of all, the space inside the ring was well over ten times the size of Rasuliel's Spatial Tool.

The dimensions were also extremely clearly defined compared to the somewhat hazy borders of his own ring. According to Galau, that was a sign of high-quality craftsmanship and proof that its space would stay stable for a long time. Cosmos Sacks only stayed functional for a decade or two before they needed to be swapped out, and Rasuliel's ring was probably an old hand-me-down from the looks of it.

But the ring he had just gotten his hands on was no doubt recently produced, and it would hold together for thousands of years before its subspace deteriorated. Seeing the amazing Spatial Ring raised another question in Zac's mind. Were these items protected from the general rules of the Tower, or did he risk losing them as well?

Seeing as they were the personal items of trial-takers, Zac leaned toward the former, but he guessed he would have to exit the Tower to make sure. His first instinct was to swap out his subpar ring, but that might cause him to lose all his possessions. Perhaps he should use as many items as possible before leaving the Tower, just in case. But he knew that using up the contents of the Spatial Ring would be nigh impossible.

There were at least ten thousand E-grade Nexus Crystals neatly stacked in one corner. However, they were somewhat different from his own, as they all seemed to be covered in some sort of engravings. Zac took out one of them, and he was surprised to see that it didn't leak a smidgeon of energy. He hesitated for a few seconds longer, but he eventually tried to absorb the energy.

It was extremely uncomfortable to absorb energy from a Nexus Crystal in his Draugr form, and it felt akin to drinking tainted water to parch your thirst. Cascading waves of nausea hit him, but he only needed to continue the absorption for a few seconds to confirm his hunch.

The energies inside the crystal were actually released at twice the rate compared to a normal one, as the inscription formed some sort of energy transfer array akin to his Mother-Daughter Array that had been put into the Merit Exchange long ago. It was a pretty luxuriant method since it was used on simple unattuned crystals, and the cost of the craftsmanship was no doubt far beyond the value of the crystals themselves.

The inscribed Nexus Crystals weren't the only types of crystals in the ring. Another, far smaller pile of crystals sat next to the mountain of Nexus Crystals, each of them looking like a block of ice. Zac had never seen such a resource previously and took one out to get a better look. The crystal was cool to the touch, and mysterious emanations spread from it, and Zac immediately felt a reaction as he held it in his hand.

The reaction didn't come from his body, though, like when he was near a great natural treasure, but it rather was a prickling sensation from his soul. Zac had a pretty good guess what it was after remembering just who had been the owner of the sack, and he could quickly confirm it was some sort of Soul Crystal.

The crystal didn't seem to be attuned, but instead something that contained mental energy. He had never heard of anything like it before, and it had never been on display in any of the shops in the Base Town. A soothing sensation entered his mind the moment he started absorbing it, and he felt his drained soul rapidly regain its vigor.

This would be a great asset in speeding up his climb. Better yet, if these things worked like Nexus Crystals, he might even be able to use them to strengthen his mind. If direct absorption didn't work, he might still be able to use them together with his Soul-Strengthening Manual.

It was also a huge relief to see that there seemed to be no response from the pieces from the Splinter of Oblivion swimming about, meaning that he could use the Soul Crystals without worry that he was harming himself. He didn't want another Cosmic Water situation on his hands, after all.

Apart from the Soul Crystals, there were a plethora of dresses, all of which sported dense sets of inscriptions. It looked like the mentalist actually had a full wardrobe of defensive treasures, and if Zac wasn't wrong, then all of them seemed to be Spirit Tools. There were also dozens of rings, earrings, necklaces, and bracelets, each a defensive treasure that looked more powerful than anything he'd seen in the Base Town.

He doubted that the rules wherever the mentalist came from differed; these items had to be low E-grade treasures at most to be taken into the Tower of Eternity. However, there was undeniably a difference in quality among items of similar grade. These things probably only used the energy of a low E-grade treasure, but what they could accomplish with that amount of energy far surpassed what Zecia craftsmen could accomplish.

Using expensive treasures as though they were normal clothes was another level of wealth that Zac hadn't encountered before. Almost everyone he knew pretty much wore the same getup every day after getting graded clothing. It was the same with himself. The white robes he got from Yrial were the strongest defensive wear he had, and they possessed self-repairing and self-cleaning features. Wearing other clothes seemed silly by this point.

There was also a large number of pills, raw materials, and natural treasures that seemed valuable enough to make him doubt his eyes. There were also a few soul-mending treasures, but Zac wasn't too sure whether they would be strong enough to replace the cherry in regard to helping Alea. Their energy fluctuations were a lot stronger than equivalent pills in his own possession, but they were far weaker compared to the cherry he had eaten.

There were also a bunch of things Zac couldn't understand, such as a large metallic head, what looked like a massive drum that had a diameter of over five meters, and all kinds of odd trinkets. Perhaps they were specialized tools that could assist in specific tasks, but Zac didn't have time to go through them one by one.

He did, however, spot something he recognized. There was a large leaf with ten luxuriant prayer mats placed on top. Zac was perhaps way off base with his speculations, but he was pretty sure he was looking at a flying treasure, one of much higher quality than the one he'd lent his sister. It seemed to have been crafted from a natural treasure, with both natural and inscribed fractals combining into an extremely exquisite pattern.

It was a shame that flying treasures were disabled in the Tower of Eternity. Perhaps the System considered having one to be too large an advantage and restricted them completely. It would have saved Zac a huge amount of time if he could have used one, as he spent days just traveling on each floor.

Finally, there was the pile of random items that seemed to be just flung into a corner of its own, no doubt the things she had found during her climb. Zac wryly smiled as he looked at the treasure trove, and he almost forgave the woman for destroying his soul.

Zac hesitated for a few seconds on how to deal with the three Spatial Tools before he poured out all their contents one by one. He had no inspection skills and no knowledge worth mentioning in appraisal, but there were some ways to tell what was good and what was not.

Every time he had encountered a beneficial natural treasure, he had been able to feel his whole body itching as it craved the energies the item contained. It was the same with **[Verun's Bite]** as well. Zac eventually found six treasures that elicited such a response in his body.

He also discovered four items that Verun seemed interested in: two slabs of metal, a piece of bone that was almost pink, and an odd rock. However, the axe was only able to absorb the rock, while it could only roar in anger at the other three items. Perhaps they were materials that could assist in upgrading the quality of the axe, but reforging a Spirit Tool probably required the assistance of a skilled Blacksmith or Inscriptionist.

Soon enough, everything in the two Cosmos Sacks was transferred to his own spare Cosmos Sacks, at which point they dissipated into motes of light. The high-quality Spatial Ring stayed behind, even though Zac had emptied it of all its contents. Zac was pretty sure that it was a permanent item, but he wouldn't risk the vast wealth inside on a hunch. He also stowed away the natural treasures that elicited such a strong reaction in his body, albeit not without some reluctance.

He would put Calrin on figuring out what to do with these items. The Sky Gnomes seemed to be thieves as much as merchants, and they probably knew what hidden dangers there were to owning loot like this. He didn't want to add a bunch of B-grade forces to the list of Earth's enemies due to ignorance.

Having dealt with the treasures, he sat down and redoubled his efforts on restoring his body, this time with the additional support of Soul Crystals.

Zac set out five hours later, which was a lot better than what he expected, going by the state his body had been in. The combination of the Fragment of the Bodhi and his newly acquired Soul Crystals helped supercharge his recovery, building on his already shockingly high Vitality. Since he was pretty much healed up, he swapped over to his human form in order to move quicker.

Unfortunately, things didn't go quite as smoothly for the rest of the level as in the beginning. It quickly became apparent that the Hayner Clan was very aware of his existence, as they had disseminated the news that a dangerous solitary invader threatened their whole world. Zac had been beset by everything from righteous citizens to large bandit gangs as he headed toward the lands the Hayner Clan controlled.

But Zac was like a moving calamity, essentially fulfilling the Hayner prophecy whether he liked it or not. All obstacles were destroyed in the quickest manner, as Zac had no time to spare. Most opposing forces were destroyed with utter prejudice, apart from a few unlucky souls whom Zac caught and dragged along to question on the move.

However, he suddenly stopped in his tracks just as he was about to enter the domain of the Hayner. An old troll wearing a voluminous robe with a star pattern stood in the middle of the road, and from the looks of it, he was waiting for Zac. The old man seemed to be blind, judging by his milky-white eyes, yet he stared straight at Zac like he was peering into his soul.

"Catching a glimpse of heaven's secrets can be both a blessing and a curse. It told me that the key to my family's survival was stopping you," the man said, and surprisingly enough, there was a kindly smile on his face. "Karma brought us together, but severing Karma is Heaven's Path."

Zac was about to respond, but suddenly, he found himself without any ground to stand on as an enormous sinkhole hundreds of meters across swallowed them both up, causing them to barrel into the abyss.

33

PAWN OF FATE

Zac's heart hammered with horror as he plunged further and further into the abyss. He tried to find something to hold on to, but he found himself pelted by one rock after another as massive boulders detached from the walls and slammed into him with the force of a speeding truck. There was no way that this wasn't the work of the old Hayner patriarch.

He did, however, notice that the old man had fallen inside as well, and he was some ways above him. But his situation didn't seem nearly as bad. The old seer was sitting on a piece of land as he sailed toward the bottom as well, but not a single boulder hit him or even came close. Zac glowered in anger at the man who had caused this mess and quickly charged up a [Chop].

However, a second after he launched the strike at the old man, a massive boulder slammed into the fractal blade, resulting in mutual destruction. Zac was about to charge up another strike, but he was thrown off course by another boulder. Was all this really a coincidence, or was this what it was like to fight against a Karmic Cultivator?

It would take more than some errant rocks to take him out, though, and Zac stopped trying to hit the man and instead focused on the depths below. They had fallen for almost fifteen seconds already, but Zac noticed the dive was about to have a very abrupt end, as the ground below was quickly rising to meet them.

Zac only had a second to think, and without any better options available, he activated a defensive charge of his robes along with another talisman as he infused himself with the Dao of the Coffin. He couldn't actually die or get seriously hurt from just falling in standard gravity, but he didn't want to risk getting knocked out, as he suspected the old man had some means to deal with the landing.

Zac landed like a comet, causing a massive crater with himself in the epicenter. Zac felt the taste of iron in his mouth, but he ignored the pain and scrambled to his feet to meet the next wave of attacks. A massive boulder had appeared seemingly out of nowhere, but Zac cut it apart just in time to see the shockwave of his own crash landing buffeting the old man's descent.

It actually allowed him to land as smoothly as if he had only jumped down from a small incline, and Zac couldn't help himself from swearing at the scene.

"You are quite adept at resisting Karmic manipulations. I am Ter'Erian Hayner, former patriarch of the Hayner Clan." The old man smiled when he noticed Zac's glare.

"Why did you do this?" Zac growled, his anger already building. "You should have realized that trapping yourself in here with me can't end well for you."

"Even a blind old man can see how powerful you are. My descendants aren't your match. So I nudged events a bit to create this place for us since I learned of your coming," he said. "Of course, nature had already laid the groundwork."

Zac looked around, and he had to say he was pretty shocked by what a Karmic Cultivator could do. The hole they found themselves in was the biggest one he had ever seen. It was hundreds of meters wide, and its edges were almost completely sheer. The sky was still visible far above, but even he would have some trouble getting back up in short order.

"Do you have the clan-defining treasure on you?" Zac asked.

"The [Star of Aryaldar] is placed on top of a flying treasure. The flying treasure has also been reinforced with an illusion array and an isolation array, and my descendants have been instructed to keep flying across this vast continent for twenty-three days before returning." The man smiled.

"Twenty-three days," Zac repeated with an even stare.

"Indeed. The star is the core of our Heritage; we cannot lose it. We sacrificed much to glean a path out of this calamity. The longer it is hidden, the better, and after twenty-three days, the treasure will be safe. You might still be able to find the treasure if fate is on your side, but are you in a position to worry about that?"

A surge of anger flashed in Zac's mind, as the pieces of Oblivion seemed energized. But Zac quickly calmed down as he tried to understand the situation. The Hayner Clan was obviously the real deal since they had indirectly inferred the rules of the Tower even if they didn't know about its existence. Twenty-three days was how much time remained of his climb.

The treasure would be safe in twenty-three days, as he would have been thrown out of the Tower by then. But Zac suddenly froze when he realized what the old man had said.

"What do you mean position to worry?" Zac frowned.

"A celestial stone will fall into this hole in a short while," the old man said, some ruthlessness finally shining through his congenial facade.

"A celestial stone?" Zac muttered with confusion until his eyes widened in alarm. "A goddamn meteor?"

"My clan worked for a thousand years to form a Karmic Link with one of the stones sailing about in the vast beyond, gently nudging it closer to us. It became our clan's guardian and judgment, and when better to use it than now?"

These people were lunatics. That was the only thing Zac could think of as he looked at the old man with an aghast expression. Dragging a meteor down on top of his own head to take out a threat to his clan was beyond overkill. Even if his mission succeeded, he would have destroyed half his country from the impact, along with getting himself killed.

Zac also knew that there was no way that the old man would let him climb out of the hole in peace. He could only take him out as quickly as possible and pray that he was the level guardian. A storm of energy exploded around him as he activated [Hatchetman's Rage], and it almost looked like a sea of flames was conjured by his wrath.

He hadn't used the skill too often, since he was worried that the mental effect of the skill would synergize with the anger that the Splinter was always fanning in the background, but now was not the time to care about such things. A towering power made him feel flush with potential, and he almost welcomed the descent of the meteor to test his mettle against it.

However, he quickly snapped out of it and instead focused his attention on the old man. Each upgrade of the skill had prolonged the effect of the boost by ten full seconds, so he still had less than a minute to finish the fight before he would enter a weakened state. However, that should be more than enough to settle the fight.

Zac shot toward the old man as he shot out five fractal blades in an instant, with a sixth starting to whirl around him like a buzzsaw. The air screamed from the power in the blades, as they contained the highest power Zac could muster. However, it almost looked like the old man was a hologram, as he flickered the moment the attacks were supposed to hit him.

The fractal blades passed right through and crashed into the sheer wall behind the old man, causing massive scars in the rock that ran for dozens of meters. Zac didn't exactly understand how the old man had dodged without moving, but he guessed he was messing with fate somehow. But Zac still rushed forward, confident that there had to be some limits to what the man could avoid.

However, the ground suddenly crumbled beneath his feet just as he was about to attack the Hayner patriarch, which completely robbed him of his momentum and made him slam into the ground. A crystalline staff appeared in the Hayner patriarch's hands just as Zac was about to get back on his feet, and Zac summoned a storm of leaves to protect himself from whatever strike was coming.

A shudder in the air lifted Zac from his feet and threw him dozens of meters away. However, his danger sense hadn't warned him of anything, and as far as he could tell, the attack hadn't harmed him in the slightest. He felt some disorientation for a second, but he regained his wits after shaking his head, and soon enough, he was back on his feet. The old man had conjured a massive avatar behind him by this point, a shimmering priest holding a large crystal toward the heavens.

Reality suddenly shifted, and Zac saw dozens of versions of himself split off from his body. A few rushed toward the old man, whereas others started channeling Cosmic Energy into his arm. There were even two massive spectral axes from **[Deforestation]** that appeared in the sky.

His mind was a confused jumble as competing ideas and impressions clamored for supremacy, and he felt his cosmic and mental energies rapidly drain into the different versions of himself. Zac suddenly roared at the top of his lungs as he stomped on the ground with enough force to cause cracks to spread over ten meters in each direction. Five explosions followed in quick succession as Zac pushed toward his target.

It felt like he was forced to push through solid matter to advance, and it was as though his mind was being dragged toward the other incarnation of himself. But it wasn't enough to stop him, and Zac was soon upon the old man again. **[Verun's Bite]** fell, its sanguine glow illuminating the surroundings.

Zac stood panting to restrain his rage as he looked down on the old man on the ground. A massive wound ran from his shoulder down to his navel, and he was almost split in two by Zac's strike. He looked down at the troll with some confusion, as he hadn't actually expected his strike to hit that easily. The idea had been to push him a bit further to expend his defensive treasures, after which he would finish him with **[Nature's Punishment]**.

But perhaps he had overestimated the old man.

"How?!" The ancient troll coughed with confusion in his eyes as he was bleeding out on the ground. "Why are you immune to the pull of fate?!"

Zac wasn't completely sure what the old man was talking about. The weird illusion he had been put under was pretty annoying, but it could barely be considered a nuisance due to draining his energy. Was it supposed to do something more?

Perhaps he had his almost inhuman pool of Luck to thank for avoiding any serious harm. Karmic warriors seemed to fight by slightly augmenting causality and fate in their favor, but Zac had a huge amount of Luck that did the same thing. The special attribute might be the best way of countering these kinds of people.

The battle was over as the man lay dying on the ground, and Zac could breathe out in relief when he saw that a teleportation array had appeared a few meters away. Killing the guardians was never a requirement unless it was stated in the quest; defeating them was all that was needed. However, most of the battles so far had ended with a fatality, as the guardians were seldom good people.

The battle hadn't been too exhaustive, and he was completely unscathed. However, he still wasn't too elated with the results. Normally, he would have stayed on the floor an hour at the least to recover from his weakened state and calm his mind, but he knew that wasn't an option this time.

A massive ball of fire had appeared in the sky by now, and Zac knew he would have to leave within a minute.

"Why did you go this far?" Zac asked as he looked down on the old man. "You should have seen that I didn't really want your life."

"Sometimes drastic measures are needed to push fate in the direction one desires, Warmaster." The old troll coughed. "Or should I say trial-taker?"

"You know?" Zac said with surprise.

"Even the Heavens aren't perfect. Fragments and pieces slip through," the old man wheezed. "However, that knowledge is what led you to our doorstep. I peered too deep, and I cannot be allowed to live. At least my family is ignorant of the truth, and the calamity will hopefully end through my death and your disappearance."

Zac looked at the old man for a few seconds, but he had no idea what to say. What could one say in a situation like this? It might be true that he was being used as a real Hatchètman by the System, taking out those in its net who had learned too much.

"I'm sorry things ended this way." Zac sighed and started to walk toward the teleportation array.

"Freedom is an illusion, trial-taker." The old seer coughed as Zac stepped onto the platform. "Are you any freer than us?"

Zac took one last look at the old troll. The seer's face had turned into a grotesque mask of anger and irreconciliation as the blank eyes stared up at the sky. Zac wasn't sure if he was looking at the meteor that was fast approaching or the heavens above.

"I am Ter'Erian Hayner, and I am more than a pawn!"

34

OUT OF REACH

The encounter with the old seer was pretty jarring, but it wouldn't stop Zac from moving. He had his goals, and he knew that one couldn't get anywhere in this world without knocking out the competition. It was not a matter of Ogras-induced cynicism, but rather a reality forced onto everyone by the System. If there was no conflict, then one would be created.

Hearing the old seer's final words indicated that the worlds he traversed might all be real, but did it really change anything? He could only shrug off any hesitation and insecurities and head toward the next guardian.

Climbing the eighth floor presented a new kind of torture as Zac desperately pushed through the levels. He had almost completely given up on sleep by now; his rest was slightly slowing down while revolving the Fragment of the Bodhi to help recuperate his exhausted body and keep the Splinter in check.

He had realized that the Splinter wasn't as intrusive when his mental state was in perfect condition, but problems quickly arose after having expended a lot of mental energy. He almost fell into a rage after every straining battle, and he quickly had to restore his mental energies to not go out of control. By this point, he needed to pretty much constantly travel with a Soul Crystal in his free hand to stay lucid.

The problem was that every time he used his Dao, he felt as

though the Splinter's corrosion was slightly more ingrained into his soul, for good or bad. It did seem that the Dao he forced into his attacks kept getting stronger, but it came at the cost of his mind getting slowly eroded. Zac could only push back against the effects as he kept climbing.

He considered stopping using his Daos altogether until he found a solution, but that would eventually just slightly delay the inevitable. Besides, not using his Daos would effectively end his climb. He couldn't defeat any enemies without them, and he was not ready to stop climbing.

His experiences in the Tower had completely remolded him, pushing him toward a peak he didn't even know existed. It had resulted in his mind being invaded, but Zac started to believe that his best bet at finding a solution was to keep climbing. The seventh-floor rewards were customized for his needs, and perhaps the eighth floor would be even more tailored to his needs.

And what did he currently need more than something to control the Splinter?

He might even find a solution before reaching the seventy-second level, as the eighth floor was a veritable treasure trove. It was almost torture to traverse one world after another and hear about shocking treasures that would drive anyone mad, knowing that each of them was just out of his reach.

The sixty-fifth floor seemed to contain an ancient array left behind by a long-extinct Race. It would be able to awaken one's "hidden potential," which, according to rumors, meant gaining a huge surge of attributes and perhaps even awakening a constitution. But it was locked behind the floor's quest, and Zac simply couldn't complete it. So he could only take out his frustrations on the guardian before moving on.

The next floor contained what Zac guessed was a top-tier E-grade Axe Spirit Tool, but it was in the hands of a Peak E-grade warlord. This one wasn't quite as alluring as the previous floor, but it would still be a huge boon to have an alternative to [Verun's Bite]. This was especially true, as it was rumored to have "a corrosive attunement," making it an extremely good weapon of choice for his Draugr form.

Zac initially thought that he was doomed to not get his hands on it, but news spread that the warlord had suddenly died just as Zac was about to finish things up on the floor. He couldn't join the fight for the warlord's hoard, though, as he was running out of time. He could only grit his teeth and move on to the next floor, leaving the treasures behind.

It almost felt like the System kept throwing out more and more alluring baits in his path in an effort to stop him from climbing any further. It was to the point that Zac wondered if it was some sort of trial that tested his determination, and Zac staunchly kept his eyes on the prize as he kept moving toward the next levels.

Missing out on all the treasures was a big disappointment, but he did make some startling progress with his experiments. Zac had almost reached a 40% success rate in forming the bronze flashes since getting to the eighth floor. He still needed to use his crude method of stabbing himself in the shoulders, but with the help of the Fragment of the Bodhi, he was able to keep experimenting even after accumulating one grisly wound after another.

Zac had initially been afraid that the experiments would worsen his mental condition even more, but he soon realized it was the opposite. His mind actually calmed down after having shot out a bronze flash. It almost felt like some sort of mental bloodletting where the darkness in his mind was expelled through the Dao Implosions.

The explanation that Zac felt was most likely was that the Splinter of Oblivion had a part in the creation of the bronze sparks somehow. Perhaps it acted as a base to what the two fragments would fuse into, like a blueprint to the higher Daos. That would explain the increased success rate of forming the bronze sparks compared to his trials during the seventh floor.

Before, the only energies from the Splinter that suffused his soul were the small amounts of purified energy that the Miasmic fractals slowly let out of the cage. But now his soul was completely infiltrated. The improvements felt like a small silver lining to the mess he found himself in, but there were still some parts that he hadn't figured out.

Things weren't working out as he had hoped with his third Dao Fragment. No matter how many times he tried, he simply couldn't form some equivalent of the bronze flash when trying to fuse the Fragment of the Bodhi with the Fragment of the Axe. The same problem arose when trying to fuse the Bodhi with the Coffin.

Only the combination of Axe and Coffin worked, leaving Zac wondering just what was missing. Did the second fusion require another method of activation to work? Or did it only work because the destructive flash leaned toward Oblivion rather than Creation?

His utter failure was another hint that he was on the right track about the Splinter, but he still wasn't completely convinced. The two Grand Daos of Creation and Oblivion were extremely high concepts, and pretty much all lower Daos should contain hints of both of them. The Bodhi wasn't pure Creation, and the Coffin wasn't pure Oblivion.

Not even the higher concepts of Life and Death that he was striving for were pure Creation and Oblivion. So it was a bit odd that he couldn't mix the Fragment of the Axe, which by itself should lean toward Oblivion, with the Fragment of the Bodhi.

There was no real way for him to verify what was really going on at the moment. For now, he could only take the opportunity to self-medicate while working out the possibilities and limitations of the bronze flashes. It seemed that desperation had played a part in managing to actually use the Dao Implosion.

His left arm was a mess after having ruptured dozens of times, but he had managed to successfully destroy a strong beast in the heat of battle once with the help of the Dao Implosion. The key seemed to be adrenaline, or rather, battle lust. When he was just experimenting while traversing the worlds, he was too calm, and that led to him being too slow in moving the bronze spark out of his body.

It was as if he was energized, then the blob of energy he created would be energized as well. Zac even tried to slap himself and roar at the top of his lungs to get his blood pumping, but it wasn't very effective. Only his true fight-or-flight responses seemed to be working, perhaps as they activated some primal part of his brain.

His theory of the origin of the flashes also gave Zac some clues into what needed to be done to somewhat formalize his "creation." The largest problem was that he had no control over the energies he created, and he could only push it forward. But perhaps there was a solution; he needed to take control of the Splinter of Oblivion.

If the flashes were truly created with help from the debris of the

Splinter, then he needed to somehow form a connection with it. It would allow him to guarantee a successful formation rather than leaving things up to fate. It would perhaps even allow him to stabilize the volatile energy long enough that he could infuse it into skills rather than just throwing it away like a hot potato.

Messing with the Splinter would come with huge risks, though, and Zac wasn't confident at even attempting to open the Miasmic cage in his mind before his soul was a lot stronger compared to now. It once again came back to a lack of time. He wished he could jump into some time chamber and practice **[Nine Reincarnations Manual]** until his soul was strong enough to withstand the Splinter's influence.

However, Zac didn't spend all his time on the bronze flashes, as they were still somewhat of a long-term goal. He had gained many other new upgrades that needed to be better understood, such as his new Dao Fragment.

One slightly surprising benefit was just how much stronger the Fragment had made his Hatchetman class.

Zac was currently assaulting a massive army on the sixty-seventh floor, and he was being pelted from all directions as he tried to reach the princess in the middle of the army. He was somewhat confident that she was the level guardian, and Zac had immediately set out toward her army the moment he learned of her insane crusade.

This level was the same as the previous ones on the eighth floor. He had quickly learned of rumors talking about a divine tree that was about to bear fruit. Elites from all over the world were getting ready to compete for the natural treasure, as the fruit seemed to possess the capabilities of opening the "third eye."

The effect of the third eye, or the soul's eye, sounded a lot like his danger sense after asking around, and he felt that combining the two might almost turn him permanently omniscient like when he used **[Hatchetman's Spirit]**. But he could only ignore the temptation while cursing the fact that he was too slow. If he had another month left in his climb, he could have cleaned up on these last levels, but now he didn't have the leeway to take any detours.

Targeting one of the amazing treasures that appeared on each level now would essentially erase any chances of completing the floor, so the treasure had to be more tempting than an upgraded title and a tailor-made reward from the System itself. And while the treasures thus far had all seemed extremely valuable, they weren't quite at that level so far.

That didn't make the situation less frustrating, though.

Luckily, he had a whole army to take out his annoyance on, and a storm of purple leaves flew around him as he waded into the army that desperately tried keeping him at bay. It was [Nature's Barrier] that had changed its appearance after getting infused with the Fragment of the Bodhi and reaching Peak mastery.

Not only had the leaves become shockingly sturdy, but the skill even provided a restorative effect in the eye of the storm now. It was just like the hidden world within the cherry tree's canopy in the vision. If Zac had had the fragment while fighting the swordmaster in the Battle of Fates, he probably wouldn't have needed to use any other defenses than this skill.

His defensive skill wasn't the only one that had benefitted from gaining the Fragment of the Bodhi. Pretty much every single nature-aspected skill in his repertoire became stronger in one way or another, just like how Coffin added all kinds of effects to his death-attuned skills.

The forest created from [Hatchetman's Spirit] now provided a defensive sphere from the outside. It wasn't too useful for Zac at his current stage, but it would help with keeping allies safe in large-scale conflicts. The skill had also reached Middle proficiency on the last level, since he was pretty much forced to activate it during every battle now.

One surprising skill that benefitted from the Dao Fragment was [Loamwalker]. Not only did it increase the distance he could travel with each step, especially inside forests, but Zac even felt a mysterious energy rising from the ground and entering his body with every step. The energy was an earthy brown when he looked at it with [Cosmic Gaze], and he guessed it was earth-attuned energies.

He didn't have a use for the attuned energies, but being able to move much faster was a godsend.

The fabric of space cracked as Zac closed in on the princess' command tent, and a wooden hand covered in leaves and flowers quickly emerged, causing verdant lights to fly around its fingers in an exuberant dance. An outsider might think that the vibrant image might mean that the massive hand was about to bestow a blessing on the lands, but the reality wasn't quite so benign.

Zac had quickly figured out the fundamental use of the Fragment of the Bodhi apart from the healing. Life mutated and grew far beyond its normal means within the canopy of the consecrated cherry tree, and Zac was able to bestow that same effect to his skills. That meant that it wasn't simply a defensive or offensive boost to his nature skills, but rather a foundational empowerment.

[Nature's Barrier] naturally became even better at defense as the leaves mutated, but the hand instead evolved in a more forceful direction, which was evident by the terrifying aura it had started to radiate. A two-hundred-meter-wide array appeared as an immense pressure, forcing the average soldiers down on their knees.

An enormous sword saint appeared in the sky above the command tent, likely the avatar conjured by the princess he was targeting. She was currently on a path of carnage to earn the respect of her father, but her path was littered by the bodies of innocent civilians who were unlucky enough to live too close to the border of a rival kingdom.

Zac had no moral issue with taking someone like this out. She didn't respect the lives of others to attain her goal, so why should he respect hers? The massive sword saint aimed her sword at the core of the array, which also meant that the wooden hand above it was targeted.

Destructive energies started gathering around the avatar, but Zac wasn't worried, as an unassuming trunk descended from the core of the array.

LITTLE BEAN

The single tree looked like any ordinary one apart from its lack of branches. But it quickly grew into a tremendous spike, like the finger of a forest god. It just took a second for it to grow to a size that almost eclipsed the mountains he had pulled through the array before, and the tip of the tree pushed straight toward the command center beneath.

A shocking burst of energy rippled out from the massive avatar's weapon, and multiple layers of the protective membrane of [Nature's Barrier] were decimated even though the princess aimed at [Nature's Punishment] rather than in his direction.

A hollow with a diameter of almost fifty meters was punched straight through the wooden spike, but hundreds of branches grew from the hole and merged to restore its original form. Zac felt a huge strain on his mind from the increased consumption, but he could only grit his teeth as he pierced the avatar with his punishment.

The avatar only managed to ineffectually rip off a few layers of the branch before it was forcibly dispelled, and the branch passed through the chaotic energies as it slammed straight into the command tent where the princess resided. The ground heaved and cracked, and Zac felt a surge of energy enter his body,

A shudder went through his body as a storm of Miasma spread to every inch. The hundreds of leaves around him disappeared into motes of lights, and the verdant forest of [Hatchetman's Spirit] was gone a second later. Only the towering tree remained as a testament of his earlier attacks.

That didn't mean the army was safe, though, as billowing clouds of corrosion and Miasma quickly spread out before the warriors had time to understand what was going on.

This was the true power of the upgraded core, and it was the only feature that mattered as far as Zac was concerned. It was disappointing that it hadn't provided any attributes when reaching E-grade, but the transformation only took a second now as long as he used Yrial's Transformation skill.

Not only that, but he had also learned that he could now transform twice before he needed to wait for an hour again. In other words, he could now almost completely freely use his two classes in one battle as long as he had a second to spare during a fight.

Zac stomped the ground and appeared next to the massive branch that was stabbed into the ground, just in time to see a part of it explode as his target emerged. She was drenched in blood, and one of her arms hung limply to her side, but she still radiated the aura of someone with fight left in her.

The cage of [Profane Seal] was erected with the branch in the middle, and five of the chains cut into the massive piece of wood. A surge of energy entered Zac's body as he started his usual whittling down of his enemy.

It was one interesting perk he had found from being able to quickly change between classes. Most of his skills disappeared when he changed classes, but there were two exceptions. The first exception was the punishments he could summon through [Nature's Punishment], like the tree he was able to call forth since gaining the Fragment of the Bodhi.

It was teeming with life force that the chains could steal and then feed to his Draugr form. This synergy was why he opted for the tree rather than the massive mountain he usually used.

It made him even more unkillable, as the piece of wood turned into an enormous battery that would keep him going far longer than he would be able to without. It was to the point that Miasma steamed out of his body due to overconsumption, which further aligned the surroundings in his favor against living enemies.

The second skill that lingered was **[Winds of Decay]**. The skill was made from his breath, so it didn't matter that he changed class, as the mists remained. This wasn't as much of a boon, though, as the skill targeted him the moment he changed to his human form. It didn't bother him thanks to his huge pool of Vitality, but it was still pretty uncomfortable to stand inside.

The Miasmic cage shook as the two clashed one time after another, but soon enough the princess couldn't stand it any longer. Her body was covered in festering wounds as the armor-clad Zac towered above her.

"Why?" she asked with fury and despair in her eyes. "Who are you?"

"Fate, I guess," Zac answered as his bardiche fell.

Zac didn't swap back to his human form just yet, as he wasn't sure what would await him at the other side of the teleporter. He rather just restored his reserves to peak condition before he stepped through to the next realm.

It felt like he was being squeezed for every piece of potential he had, and he was embroiled in constant battle as he kept going. At least it kept the Splinter mostly satiated as he ripped through the later levels of the eighth floor. Unfortunately, he never heard of any treasures or inheritances that seemed able to restrain the corruption in his mind, and this continued all the way to the seventy-first level.

The second-to-last level of the eighth floor would no doubt be a real nightmare, but his all-out push the past weeks had at least made sure he had over three days to complete it. **[Verun's Bite]** was already high in the air to counter any sneak attack, and Zac had equipped **[Everlasting]** and changed into his Draugr form just in case of a sudden assault.

But when the scenery changed, he realized there would be no ambush this time around the moment he stepped through the teleporter. The surprising stillness even seemed to subdue the Splinter in his mind, and it crept into the back of its Miasmic cage.

He was in a small cabin that was best described as futuristic. The whole wall in front of him was just one massive screen that seemed to be showing a blueprint, and another wall displayed a majestic nebula and stars that were fixed in the distance. Zac almost forgot he was in the Tower of Eternity for a second as he looked around with excitement.

Was he on a spaceship?

That was the immediate conclusion, judging by the screen in front of him, unless he was reading the blueprint completely wrong. The map showed an elongated vessel that looked pretty sleek apart from a large circular bulb in the middle, and Zac found that he was able to zoom in and out by touching the screen.

The first thing he could see was that the ship was just massive. He was currently in a section that seemed to house thousands of cabins, just like the cabin floors on a cruise liner. The cabin he was in was around twenty square meters, and while it was less than a tenth the size of the largest cabin, it was still a decent size.

Each cabin had a series of numbers or letters marked, though Zac couldn't read them. He guessed it was either the name or serial number of the person who lived inside. Some cabins were pretty large, but they had over twenty numbers attached, meaning they were probably barracks or shared domiciles.

Perhaps the cabin belonged to some sort of middle-management or a petty officer on board the space cruiser. The huge number of cabins only took up a small section of the total space on the ship, though, and he saw that there were more sections just like it. If not for the shape and the two massive thrusters at the back of the vessel, he would have thought it was a space station rather than a ship.

He tried to engrave every detail into his mind in case he needed it later, but it seemed the resident of this cabin only had limited access, as over half the ship was blacked out except the general outline. Perhaps those sections were critical parts of the ship only accessible to authorized personnel.

Zac eventually backed away and tried to figure out his next step. A quest screen conveniently appeared after he retreated, indicating what needed to be done.

[Stop the *Little Bean* from returning from its expedition.]

Zac wasn't overly surprised to read the contents of the quest after seeing the surroundings, but some hesitation crept into his heart as he looked at the wall displaying the vibrant nebula in the distance. This *was* still the Tower of Eternity, right?

Or had the System sent him out on an actual mission to mess with its enemies, the Technocrats? Since meeting the Hayner patriarch, he had started wondering if he was actually ever inside the Tower, or if he was just sent to various corners of the Multiverse like when he'd completed the Sovereignty quest.

A muffled swishing sound interrupted his thoughts as the door leading to his quarters suddenly opened, displaying a young man who was looking down with a troubled frown at a screen that hovered in front of him.

He entered the small cabin without even looking up, and he only noticed something was wrong when a gray object ripped through the air straight toward his head. His eyes widened in shock when he looked up, only to find himself face-to-face with Zac, and an orange shield started to materialize around him.

But it was much too late, and [Everlasting] slammed into his head with enough force to throw him into the wall, knocking him out cold. Zac hurried over and dragged the man further inside the cabin and sighed in relief when he saw that the cabin door closed by itself.

Things calmed down again, but Zac stood frozen for almost ten minutes, waiting for some backup to come rushing through the door. But it looked like his actions had gone by unnoticed, allowing him to breathe out in relief. Zac didn't put away his weapons, but rather just hunched down to take stock of the man whose cabin he had been thrown into.

It was a human just like himself, or at least mostly human. Some parts of his body seemed to be mechanical, which Zac guessed made the man a cyborg. His clothing made him believe he wasn't a warrior like the other cyborg he had met, but rather some sort of noncombat personnel.

He had also all but confirmed Zac's suspicions that this was a Technocrat vessel.

The shield that he had smashed through was clearly of technological origin, just like those in the Technocrat incursion, though it was a bright orange instead of the red ones back then. Apart from the shield, there were no signs of any weaponry on him. The man wore a uniform made out of cloth, and there was not a single fractal anywhere on them.

His build wasn't anything to write home about either, and when Zac activated [Cosmic Gaze], there was almost no response either from the man or the surroundings. It made Zac guess that he was on a vessel belonging to the Machine God Faction. Both Transcenders and Technomancers would possess at least some equipment connected to cultivation.

Zac quickly found the source of the shield, a small bracelet on his arm, and after having taken it off, he started to look for any piece of detachable technology on him until he finally poured some water over the unconscious man.

"Wha? How?" the man sputtered as he wildly looked around, making Zac realize that the guy even had mechanical eyes. "Who are you?! How did you manage to board the *Little Bean*? We just fell out of subspace!"

"Never mind that," Zac said as his pitch-black orbs pierced into the man's augmented vision, making him flinch. "Tell me what I need to know, and I'll let you live. If you're not willing to cooperate, I don't mind killing and reanimating you. You will help me one way or another."

"No, please!" the man cried, clearly horrified at the prospect of being turned into a Zombie.

Being a Draugr had its advantages, and there was no way for the guy to know that Zac didn't even know how to turn someone into a Revenant. None of those he had killed in his undead form seemed to have shown any inclination to turn, at least, meaning there was probably some hidden component to it.

"Have you heard of the Tower of Eternity?" Zac asked first, wanting to check on his earlier suspicions.

"The Tower of Eternity?" the man said with confusion. "Never heard of it. It's not related to our corporation, I swear!"

Zac nodded in relief, but he suddenly froze. His answer sounded similar to all the others during his climb, but there was one significant difference. He actually mentioned the Tower by name, which had never happened before. They had always responded with some sort of confusion and completely glossed over the mention.

"What is your name, and what is your mission?" Zac asked as he settled in front of the man, who had slowly inched toward a corner of his cabin.

"I am Jaol. I'm just a comms officer of the *Little Bean*, no one important!" he said.

"A comms officer?" Zac repeated. "Know this. If you send out an alert through any hidden gadgets that end with me cornered, then I'll kill you first before trying to fight my way out."

The man quickly nodded his head, but Zac noticed his eyes darted toward his arm where Zac had taken off the wristwatch.

"Where is the *Little Bean* heading?" Zac asked, and pushed the axe toward the man once again when he seemed hesitant to answer. "Answer me."

"We're heading to the closest outpost, but we've fallen out of subspace," Jaol explained. "It's because of that thing. I guess that's why you're here? It has created too many anomalies for our engines to handle. We were forced out of subspace until our engineers can fix the damage."

Zac's interest was piqued when he heard about the situation aboard the ship. It was clear that the leaders of *Little Bean* had found something that they wanted to bring back to their forces, but it was obviously something pretty amazing if it could mess with the entire vessel and its advanced technology.

It also gave him a lead in completing the quest in the normal manner. If he could take out the engineers, or somehow sabotage the repair efforts, then he would essentially be done with the mission? The best thing would be to blow up the engines altogether, but Zac guessed that they would be pretty hard to get to. But it felt entirely possible that the chief engineer would be the guardian if it wasn't the captain.

"What have you found out about the item?" Zac urged, not wanting to let on he had no idea what the guy was talking about.

"It keeps bending the laws of physics in unpredictable ways, fusing and changing matter without following any of the known rules.

It really deserves being a shard from the **[Spark of Creation]**," Jaol exclaimed, excitement seemingly making him forget he was a hostage at the moment.

"Spark of creation?" Zac repeated, his eyes widening.

Didn't this sound a bit too familiar?

ROAD OF NO RETURN

The more questions Zac asked about the item the Technocrats had found, the more certain he became. The item truly seemed to be the equivalent of the Splinter of Oblivion in his mind. The Technocrats had found it on a low-tiered world at the edge of some sector, though they hadn't realized its true origins initially.

Apparently, the Technocrat Factions often released swarms of drones that floated about in the Multiverse, and now and then they'd pick up odd energy fluctuations from valuable materials. Beauty was in the eye of the beholder, and some things that might seem useless to cultivators could be extremely valuable to the Technocrats, and vice versa.

This time, though, they knew that there was a special item rather than raw materials, and it would be discovered sooner or later. Orders were quickly sent out from above, and they tasked the ship Jaol worked on to retrieve it before the local factions realized there was a treasure under their nose.

The Shard, which was what they called it, had long since fused with a humanoid cultivator, which had created a series of shocking changes in both his physique and his surroundings. The man was F-grade like Zac himself, and he had managed to stave off the effects for almost five years before he started to succumb to the influences of the item.

The Splinter of Oblivion was like an insidious whisper that caused its user to become an avatar of destruction, a madman who couldn't stop fighting. It had been the same for everyone Zac had seen in the visions, with the exception of the Draugr woman. However, the effect of the Shard of Creation was completely different, according to the Technocrat.

An item of Creation sounded like something positive to Zac, but that truly hadn't been the case for the poor cultivator. If the Splinter turned people into powerful lunatics, then the Shard turned them into monsters. The moment the man lost control, he had started transforming and growing.

New limbs, weird tumors, hair, horns, and all types of appendages had started growing on the man, who quickly changed from a normal biped into a massive blob of flesh. Some parts of him had even changed their composition completely, turning into rocks, precious metals, and constructs that moved about.

There seemed to be no limits to his changes as long as he didn't run out of energy. He had completely drained the area he lived in by the time the Technocrats had arrived, and they believed he would keep absorbing energy until his soul couldn't take it any longer.

Of course, the man had become a raving lunatic by the point the Technocrats arrived. Being forcibly turned into a monstrosity that kept growing and changing had to be unimaginably painful. They had obliterated the being with orbital attacks, turning multiple square kilometers into a smoldering hellscape, leaving only the Shard intact.

The task force quickly loaded the items and hurriedly fled. The attack on an integrated planet with advanced weaponry had launched a wide-scale quest of retribution, and they had been forced to fight their way out of the sector while constantly dogged by Spiritual Vessels and the powerhouses steering them.

The Shard was now kept in a secured field that was designed to isolate energies, but it kept causing trouble to their vessel through bursts of creation that slipped through. It had turned a motor into a sentient golem and changed a highly condensed liquid energy into something that smelled like wine.

It had already forced the *Little Bean* out of subspace six times, and if it weren't for the multiple layers of redundancies and skilled technicians, the ship would have been turned to scrap metal stuck in the middle of nowhere. A few of the crew had wanted them to drop it off at a desolate planet and let someone else pick it up, but the captain was adamant about being the one who brought it in.

"How long until you return?" Zac asked.

"Two weeks," Jaol hurriedly said.

"I will capture more people, and if they give another answer, I'll come back for you, understand?" Zac said, his pitch-black eyes boring into the comms officer.

"One day if we get the subspace engines running," the comms officer hurriedly corrected himself as he repeatedly bowed his head in apology. "We would have already been picked up if the Shard hadn't completely destroyed our antennas as well. I have worked on opening up a line of communication for days now, but we are lacking some components."

Zac slowly nodded with a snort. This sounded more like a situation that the System would arrange. The engineers might be able to get the system up and running at any moment, at which point he would be barreling toward an enemy stronghold. He would need to delay the efforts or quickly tackle the guardian if he wanted a shot at defeating the level. But there was one thing Zac didn't really understand.

"Can't your people scan this area if you're so close?" Zac asked skeptically. "Just one day of travel."

"One day in subspace can be both close and impossibly far. We would pass through multiple dimensional layers. Our space station doesn't have that advanced scanning equipment," Jaol said.

"How strong is the most powerful warrior on your vessel? And how strong is your chief engineer?" Zac probed.

"Strongest warrior?" Jaol said. "The captain is a Class-3 Transhuman, and the chief engineer is only lacking a few critical upgrades to reach late Class-2. My readings are telling me that you are somewhere in the range of early to middle Class-2. Why not just leave instead of throwing your life away? I will not say anything."

Zac only glared at the Technocrat without saying anything, making him shrink back toward the wall again. Classes were likely the equivalent of ranks to the Machine God Faction, where Jaol had mistaken him for middle E-grade. It made Zac a bit curious about the mechanical eyes he employed, but now was not the time.

Hearing that there was a D-grade warrior on the ship was problematic. He wouldn't be able to run rampant and simply cut his way through to the engineering bay. If the captain suddenly showed up, his only recourse would be to crush his token.

However, the real issue was the Shard. Should he go for it?

It felt like the System was presenting him with an alternative to assaulting the eighth-floor guardian. He could either target the engineers and the engine to delay the ship, or he could snatch the Shard of Creation.

In a perfect world, he would be able to do both, but either action would no doubt expose his presence on the ship and result in a massive response. With someone like the captain on board, he wasn't very confident in completing either task, and doing both seemed nigh impossible.

The question was what he wanted the most. The past levels had pushed him pretty hard, and he wasn't completely confident in a fight against a floor guardian of this power level. But the rewards would no doubt be shocking as well. The gains from the seventh floor had been extremely suited for him, and the completion reward for the eighth floor should be pretty amazing as well.

On the other hand, finding a Shard of Creation was a once-in-a-lifetime opportunity. He had long thought about finding a counterweight to the Splinter in his mind in order to restrain it, and this was his chance. This desire had only increased over the past weeks since his soul had been infiltrated.

Shooting out bronze sparks every now and then to weaken the Splinter was a patchwork solution at best, but sooner or later, it wouldn't be enough. It felt like he was a pressure cooker waiting to explode, and this might be his only option on hand. The item was just the kind of thing he had envisioned, and Zac felt it wasn't a coincidence he had been placed here. It was a temptation that he could either follow or choose to ignore.

But did he even dare to absorb such a thing?

The ending of that poor sap who had fused with it previously sounded beyond horrifying, and he didn't really have any means to counteract it apart from his Soul-Strengthening Manual and the Miasmic fractals inside his head. He also didn't dare place his hopes on a second old master popping out of nowhere and giving him another set of fractals to house the Shard.

The optimal scenario was that the Shard would enter the Miasmic cage, and the two items would restrain each other. The worst-case scenario was that some unexpected chain reaction would take place, causing a massive eruption in energies that would blow both him and the *Little Bean* into smithereens.

There was also the issue of agency. The words of the Seer back on the 73rd level echoed in his mind. He had said that Zac was just as much a pawn as he in the eyes of the System, and perhaps he was right. It couldn't be seen as a coincidence that the System first presented him with the Splinter of Oblivion at the specially created Hunt on his planet, and just a few months later put him next to a Shard of Creation out of a trillion possible scenarios.

What was the goal of the System here?

It felt like he was being led by the nose down a path rather than creating his own destiny, and he wasn't sure for what purpose. It was one thing if the System simply wanted to make him stronger and found a suitable solution for him. But everything he had heard about the System indicated that it wasn't so benevolent, and also not hands-on to this degree.

Was the System treating him like a prize hog, feeding him with these two treasures? But to what end? Considering his Technocrat Heritage, he felt like it couldn't be anything good. Or was it the mysterious Draugr woman who somehow influenced his fate? He had no idea what cultivators standing at the peak were capable of.

But was there anything he could do about it, even if he was being manipulated? He needed power, and he had started down a road of no return the moment he got mixed up with the Splinter. Things were already spiraling out of control, and this might be his only opportunity to strike a balance in his body.

Hesitation gnawed in his heart for a few seconds, but he eventually decided to go for it. The Splinter was uncommonly silent in his mind, and he guessed it was because it sensed the presence of its opposite. He needed to make this effect permanent by bringing the Shard with him.

There were a lot of logical reasons not to take such a massive risk, but every fiber in his body told him to consume it. It felt like he was a puzzle, and the Shard was the final piece to finish the image. This wasn't the decision he would have made before the integration, and it probably wasn't even the decision he would have made just a few months ago. But he had realized something during his climb.

One needed to push oneself to achieve anything worthwhile.

On the surface, it might have seemed that Zac had almost pushed himself beyond what was possible, but most of his actions had been forced out of need. But here was a difference between risking your life to survive, and risking your life to push yourself to greater heights. He had mostly done the former, but he knew that he needed to take some risks to keep his momentum going.

Things might very well turn to shit, but even the random cultivator on an unintegrated planet had managed to stave off the insanity for a few years. If things truly didn't work out, he would still have time to save Earth and deal with the Dominators and even have a couple of years to find a way to rip both the items out of his body.

Besides, the very fact that he was probably being manipulated into consuming both these items felt like an indication that he wasn't going to die from it. Why would the System or some mysterious peak being go through all the trouble of manipulating his fate and the Tower of Eternity if the end result would be him simply dying? There were a lot of easier ways to kill a puny F-grade warrior.

Since he had made his decision, he could only walk forward, taking things as they came.

CLEARANCE

"Where is the Shard stored?" Zac asked after having made his decision.

"It is in a restricted holding bay, with multiple layers of defenses around it," Jaol said, his eyes widening upon the realization that Zac wasn't deterred by the presence of the captain. "The captain will come the moment he hears his cargo is being targeted. He is part-owner of the whole vessel, and it has taken a lot of damage from this mission. If the mission fails, he will face disastrous consequences, but if he succeeds, he will gain centuries' worth of resources."

"How would I gain access?" Zac pushed, ignoring the warnings.

"You can't," Jaol said without hesitation. "I have no idea how to get inside!"

"Think harder," Zac growled as a black mist started to steam out of his mouth, adding an acrid smell to the cabin.

"I-I... You would need to have special authorization. But it is impossible for you! You have no neural implants, and even if you get inside, there are extremely strong autonomous Class-2 Guardians inside," Jaol exclaimed.

"Don't you have access cards or something?" Zac said with a frown.

"Cards? Like a medieval key?" Jaol said with incomprehension. "Why would we have such a blatant security risk as keys that can be stolen?"

"I guess that means you'll have to take me there." Zac smiled.

"Are you crazy?! You will be spotted in ten seconds after leaving this place. There's no one on this ship who has eye augmentations that even slightly look like yours," the comms officer staunchly refused. "We'll both be dead within a minute."

Zac snorted as he activated his Transformation skill, and the never-ending black in his eyes quickly gave way to white sclera and irises. His deathly pale complexion gained life, and he was once again a normal human, at least outwardly indistinguishable from a Technocrat human.

"Wha–" Jaol sputtered as he looked up and down at Zac incredulously. "How is such a perfect transition possible? Not even the chimeral Transcenders are able to do something like this before reaching Class 3."

"What's with these classes you're talking about?" Zac muttered. "Isn't it just grades?"

"We refuse to use the classifications of the Cursed Heavens," Jaol said haughtily before remembering he was a hostage at the moment. "Uh, no offense."

"So you're just being obstinate? Each class represents a grade?" Zac confirmed.

"Well, yes." Jaol coughed.

"So can we go? And remember, our fates are bound together. I die, you die," Zac reminded his hostage.

"You can't." Jaol sighed after a short silence. "That's what I've been telling you. You have no implants, so the ship will consider you an intruder. Only people with clearance will be able to walk around this ship. I don't even understand how you can stand in my cabin without detection."

Zac glared at Jaol before he looked around. The implicit meaning was that the Technocrat had expected a rescue, but none seemed to be forthcoming. Zac's brows furrowed with contemplation as he tried to figure out what was going on. Was it the System that protected him? The problem was that he had no idea if that protection extended out of the cabin he found himself in.

"So how do I get clearance?" Zac asked.

"Get clearance? Impossible. You aren't even connected to the

Multiverse Network through implants or your sigil; getting clearance is impossible. If it had been so easy, we would have been infiltrated and extinguished long ago."

Zac felt a bit helpless as he looked around the room before he spotted a few small holes in the wall not far away. Did spaceships have air ducts? They should have, considering how many people were aboard. Perhaps if he cut through the floor, he'd find whole service levels he could traverse instead. But before he could ask about it, he suddenly had a thought, and his head snapped back toward Jaol.

"Sigils?" Zac said, an idea suddenly popping up in his head. "Like this?"

He took out the necklace that Leandra had left with his father before disappearing. He still hadn't found any use for the thing, but it was obviously more than a simple piece of metal. It had vibrated and moved about in his Cosmos Sack when he met the Technocrat researcher back on Earth, and it might have other functions that would be useful now.

He wasn't really worried about attracting his mother's enemies either, as he had been transported god-knows-where by the System. If anything, it might rather throw Firmament's Edge off the scent by thinking Leandra had popped up on this vessel.

The small token suddenly shuddered, making Zac worried he had activated some hidden alarm, but it quickly calmed down again. However, the Technocrat hostage wasn't as calm as he looked up and down at Zac with confusion and fear.

"This is impossible!! How did you get such clearance?!" Jaol almost screamed.

"What are you talking about?" Zac said, starting to get a bit exasperated by the rapid change of his captive's emotions. "And keep your voice down."

"A – I…" Jaol sputtered with clear hesitation on his face.

"Remember, if I get pushed into a corner, I'll take you out before anything else," Zac muttered and pushed Jaol with his axe when it looked like the comms officer was planning on cooking up another lie.

"I swear I don't understand! I don't recognize that insignia, but it has somehow given you Level 4 access on our ship! Even I only have Level 2 access. It uses some archaic access code I have never heard of before, designating you as a council inspector! What council?!" Jaol blabbered.

Zac looked down at the necklace in his hand with mixed emotions. It looked like his mother had come through for him after all. He had already known that she was probably some sort of big shot among Technocrats before something happened to make her turn traitor, and this seemed to further confirm it.

But where was she? Why had she left Earth and her family alone, even to the point that her husband had died from the integration? Long-repressed emotions threatened to run rampant as he held the sigil, but he quickly gathered his wits and focused on the task at hand.

"Is Level 4 access enough to get to the Shard?" Zac asked.

"No," Jaol said. "It gives access to all parts of the ship except critical areas that need the captain's direct authorization. In other words, special authorization."

"Who has special access?"

"Just two people as far as I am aware. The captain and Dr. Fried," Jaol said.

Messing with the captain was obviously out of the question, which only left him with one option.

"Who is Dr. Fried?" Zac probed.

"Uh, no idea," Jaol said.

"Jaol…" Zac growled threateningly.

The comms officer hesitated for a few seconds before he eventually reached toward his eyes and literally pulled them out of their sockets. Zac couldn't stop himself from gaping in shock as the man handed his eyes to him. Zac unconsciously accepted them with confusion before he looked back at Jaol with utter befuddlement.

The comms officer didn't say anything, but Zac noted that he had pointed his head down, and it almost looked like the empty sockets were staring straight at Zac's waist. Zac tried to follow the lack of vision, and he suddenly had a hunch of what was going on. He immediately stowed the two eyes into his Cosmos Sack.

"I put your eyes in my Spatial Tool," Zac said as he looked at the Technocrat with interest.

"I know, I just lost connection." Jaol nodded.

"What's going on?" Zac asked.

"I don't want any hard evidence of divulging information about Dr. Fried. He comes from a powerful corporation." Jaol sighed. "Dr. Fried was sent by Deramex Dynamics, our employer's employer. He's an expert at force fields, and he is in charge of keeping the Shard of Creation restrained."

"Sounds like he's doing a pretty shit job," Zac muttered as he tried to look anywhere except at the two empty sockets that stared right at him.

Was this what it felt like talking with him when he was in his Draugr form?

"Yes, well." Jaol shrugged. "I don't understand how that works, but he has set up multiple layers of restrictions around the Shard in the middle of the *Bean*. I've heard from a few guards that the problems we've seen are just the tip of the iceberg of what goes on within the containment field. Dr. Fried has said that the Shard does not like being without a host, and it resents being trapped."

"Likes? Resents?" Zac asked with shock. "It's alive?"

"It's beyond me. Perhaps alive in the sense that a virus is alive?" Jaol ventured.

Zac felt like it was an apt description after having observed the Splinter in its prison over the past few months. It wasn't an inert object, but it also didn't feel sentient.

"What strength is the doctor?" Zac asked.

"I think he's late Class-2?" Jaol said hesitantly.

"Is he strong in combat?" Zac asked with a frown.

"I am pretty sure he's a pure researcher," Jaol said. "Their combat strength is on the lower end, but they no doubt have some means to protect themselves."

Zac grunted in affirmation. This was exactly what he hoped for. The plan he had come up with was pretty simple. He'd use the necklace to get to Dr. Fried, kidnap the researcher, and use him as a key card to the Shard. Seeing as the doctor seemed to have a pretty high status, he might even be able to use him as a hostage to blow up the engines and pass the stage afterward.

"Do you know where to find him?" Zac asked.

"I can point you to his lab on the map," Jaol quickly said. "It's not too far; you'll be able to get there easily."

"Point on the map?" Zac smiled. "We're going together."

Jaol froze for a few seconds before he deflated with a sigh.

"Alright... Is there anything else I need to know about the doctor?" Zac asked.

Zac asked a few questions to gauge his strength, but Jaol didn't seem to know too much. The researcher spent almost all his time split between his lab and by the Shard. He was also pretty haughty and barely socialized with the crew. He even seemed to have taken a superior stance toward the captain even if he was just a Class-2 noncombat class.

But that was fine with Zac. It meant that he would get his opportunity as long as he managed to get to the laboratory to set up an ambush.

"Okay, let's go," Zac finally said after he had asked everything he could think of.

"Well, you're still looking a bit..." Jaol hesitantly said.

Zac looked down at himself and immediately realized the problem. He looked like someone doing cosplay with his ancient robes and weaponry. It wouldn't take an AI to figure out something was wrong if he walked down the corridors wearing cultivator's robes. His first idea was to take clothes from Jaol, but waving around an axe for months while focusing on Endurance and Strength had made his build pretty bulky.

Jaol was a head shorter and probably weighed a hundred pounds less, so getting into his fitted uniform was impossible. It also seemed that the clothes they wore didn't have an automatic fit like his robes. Sending Jaol out for a disguise was out of the question as well. The Technocrat would probably rat him out the second he was out of earshot, so Zac had to go with the second-best option.

"Call someone here. Someone with a similar build as mine," Zac said.

"A-alright. I need my eyes back, then," Jaol said, and soon enough, he pushed the two orbs back into their respective sockets.

"So weird," Zac muttered.

Jaol didn't dare to comment, but he rather summoned a screen that appeared in front of him, looking a bit like the status screens that the System used. Zac saw a bunch of faces flash by on the screen until

Jaol's eyes lit up. The screen disappeared the next moment, and Jaol slightly turned away.

"It's Jaol. Something is wrong with these calculations; could you assist me? I'll owe you one," Jaol started muttering into thin air. "Well, it's a bit inconvenient; could you come to my compartment? Yes, I am sorry, I'll provide 10% of this month's salary as compensation."

"Well?" Zac asked.

"A colleague will come over in a minute. He is off for the day, so no one will feel it out of place if he's not around," Jaol said, a small smile creeping up on his face for the first time since getting captured. "His build is pretty similar to yours as well."

"Why do you look so happy about this?" Zac asked with a raised brow.

"He's kind of a work rival, and we're up for the same promotion," Jaol said, looking a bit embarrassed. "If I have to live through this calamity, I might as well drag him with me."

"Fair enough," Zac snorted as he walked next to the door. "But no funny business."

UNDERCOVER

Jaol hurriedly nodded in response to Zac's warning as the ship schematic on the wall changed to a large array of complex schematics and diagrams. They didn't have to wait long until the sliding door opened, and a burly man stepped through, his eyes trained on Jaol, who stood by the screen, seemingly in deep thought.

"You'd better not be lying about pay–" the man said, but didn't get any further before he was on the ground, twitching.

"Undress him and take away anything that he can use to warn people," Zac said.

"That's impossible. He has implants like everyone else. The moment you try to tamper with them, a warning will go out," Jaol said with a shake of his head.

Zac thought for a few seconds before he took out a vial and threw a pill over to Jaol.

"Feed him this," Zac simply said.

"If he dies, you will be exposed," the comms technician hesitantly said as he looked down on the pill with trepidation.

"It'll just make sure he won't wake up for a day or two," Zac explained.

A minute later, Zac inspected himself in a monitor, and it felt like he was on some science fiction show, as his clothing completely matched that of Jaol's. The clothes of the poor man who was now slumbering in Jaol's sleeping pod were a bit long and snug, but it was a passable fit that shouldn't arouse any attention from a casual glance.

"Let's go," Zac said as he cracked his neck. "Take me to Dr. Fried's laboratory."

"I–" Jaol said before he sighed and shook his head. "Fine, let's go. Try not to speak. If anyone asks, we're heading toward the research department because the scanning equipment has been broken by the Shard. This is actually true, but it's a low priority compared to the engines. It would have been better if I had a gift. Some might see this as me taking the chance to suck up to the doctor."

Zac nodded, feeling it wasn't a bad idea.

"What kind of gift?" Zac probed.

"Rare materials and stuff like that. Something I could pretend to have picked up on the planet we just visited and wanted to use as a bribe," Jaol thoughtfully said.

"I have a few things," Zac said before he froze as he looked down at his Spatial Ring.

He hurriedly reached for his pouch, but he breathed out in relief when he saw that all the items were still there even though he wasn't inside the Tower. But what did that mean? Were all his items safe? Or would the confiscation still happen the moment the trial ended? Perhaps it was even possible to cheat the System this way by sending out everything he had gained. But he obviously couldn't trust Jaol to come through and send his amassed wealth back to Earth.

Even if Zac somehow managed to make Jaol obey, did the Technocrat even have the ability to follow through? They could be anywhere in the Multiverse right now, and there was probably no way for some random Technocrat to find his sector, let alone Earth. Zac eventually threw out a handful of random materials he hadn't figured out the use of.

"This…!" Jaol said with wide eyes as he looked at the items that emitted strong fluctuations.

"So?"

"Ah? Yes, yes," Jaol hurriedly said as he reached out and took one of the items, a piece of purple wood.

It was something that Zac had picked up on the sixth floor. He had noticed that a tree survived even though Zac fought right next to it.

The bark was extremely durable and was even able to resist being cut with the Fragment of the Axe twice. Strangely enough, the whole tree withered when Zac cut it down to bring with him, leaving only the plank-sized piece of lumber intact.

"A piece of wood is actually valuable among Technocrats?" Zac asked curiously as he saw Jaol's excitement.

"Well, no. It is rather the unique energy signature of the material that is valuable. We can extract it and infuse it in an alloy to make a stronger material," Jaol said without taking his eyes off the piece of wood. "My preliminary reading says that it should be able to increase the durability of many alloys by some degree."

Zac shrugged, and the two finally left the compartment, and they found themselves in a luxuriant hallway. It didn't feel cramped at all like how it often was with cruise liners back on Earth, but the hallway was almost ten meters wide with occasional seats and greenery. There was even a small artificial river running along the middle, creating a soothing atmosphere. Zac wasn't there to sightsee, though, and they hurried toward the center of the ship.

Soon enough, they reached a door that seemed to be a checkpoint between sectors, and Zac noticed how stiff Jaol looked as he waited for it to open. But the door slid open without any issue, making them both release a breath in relief as they kept going. It looked like the insignia left by Leandra really worked like some sort of universal key.

It only took a few minutes of walking for the surroundings to quickly change. Zac remembered the map he had studied, and they now were in the sector where the cabins housed over ten people each. The hallways had become a lot more cramped, and there were even missing platings and exposed wires seen at spots.

Zac was surprised at the stark contrast between different parts of the ship. Jaol's compartment and the section around it were hypermodern, with not a speck of dust in the fancy hallways.

"This looks more run-down than what I would have expected," Zac muttered with a low voice as they passed through the barracks and a large mess hall. "It's like this part will fall off at any moment."

"Well..." Jaol coughed. "We're a freelance freight-class vessel bought from an auction selling off the inventory of a defunct company. The ship itself is well over four thousand years old and long due for an overhaul. The section where I and the higher-ups live was refurbished five years ago, but this section…"

"Four thousand years?" Zac exclaimed with surprise.

A thousand years wasn't much in the world of cultivation, but he knew how quickly technology failed back on Earth. A machine holding together for a couple of decades was almost a miracle, and this spaceship had stayed in one piece over thousands of years and countless missions?

"Are there no teleporters on the ship?" Zac asked after they had walked a while.

They had passed through a seemingly endless number of passageways and were currently passing through what seemed to be a large mess hall. They had passed some people by now, but Zac was relieved to see that they only shot Jaol, or rather, the piece of lumber in his arms, a curious glance before continuing with their business.

"There are a few for emergencies," Jaol said after a few seconds. "But we can't use them. They require a lot of energy to power to use. In other words, it is a waste of money."

"Jaol!" A voice reached them from the other side of the shabby mess hall, and Zac looked over to see a stout woman wave and walk over toward them.

"Deal with this," Zac simply said with a low voice before he looked away.

"Ah, Kerven." Jaol weakly smiled as he turned around to face the woman, who curiously looked at them. "I thought you were on duty today?"

"Can't do anything until the changes stop. The thing is acting up again," the woman muttered as she curiously looked back and forth between Zac and the piece of wood in Jaol's arms. "What are you up to? Isn't this your day off?"

"I, ah… I was planning on seeing if I could pick Dr. Fried's brain about our problems. This is just a small token of my appreciation."

"Uh-huh," she said with a raised brow before she shrugged. "Well, I won't keep you."

Zac's eyes followed her as he walked away, and some killing intent started to leak as he frowned. The Splinter in his mind had woken up a few minutes ago, demanding blood to be spilled. Jaol's eyes widened in horror as he sensed the dangerous aura that Zac was leaking, and he tried to drag Zac toward the exit.

The door closed behind them, and Zac took a ragged breath before he shot the technician a look.

"Let's go," he said and started walking again.

"We're almost there," Jaol answered with a sigh.

It took them almost half an hour to reach the center of the ship, the massive ball that contained both the containment field for the Shard of Creation and Dr. Fried's temporary lab. Luckily enough, they didn't meet a single guard until they reached the laboratory itself, and Zac felt the ship was a bit overly reliant on the AI and the security doors.

He couldn't be sure, but it seemed like it shouldn't be too hard for an assassin-type cultivator like Faceless #9 to cause severe damage to a ship with as lax security as this.

However, the door leading into the lab was guarded by two men wearing some sort of tactical gear and holding some sort of energy batons. They didn't feel like real warriors to Zac, but rather security guards who were there to make sure that no one peeked at the researcher's lab without authorization.

"I am Jaol Kresson, junior deputy of the Communications Department. We're here to see Dr. Fried if possible to ask a few questions about how to deal with the recent disturbances from the cargo. I brought a small token of my appreciation that I think will pique the doctor's interest," Jaol said with a slimy smile as he stepped forward.

"The doctor is out," the guard slowly said after having looked at the piece of spiritual wood for a few seconds. "Let me–"

He didn't get further, though, as Zac moved forward like a ghost and punched the guard straight in his face as [Everlasting] appeared from his Spatial Ring and slammed into the other guard simultaneously. One of the soldiers went down, whereas the other one required another jab before he lay unmoving on the ground.

"Hurry," Zac said as he grabbed the two unconscious men and carried them into the laboratory.

Jaol quickly bent over and wiped a spot of blood before he followed with a face as white as a mask. Zac guessed he hadn't seen a lot of action up close, and the situation was getting a bit tense. He had no idea if his actions just now had caused some hidden alarm to go off, but he had acted on instinct when he saw the guard activating his communication device. Jaol looked at Zac like he was a lunatic, and Zac started to worry that the comms officer might do something stupid from desperation.

"Stay calm," Zac whispered. "We'll stow these two in some corner, and after I've captured Dr. Fried, you're free to go."

"Yes, yes." Jaol fervently nodded. "How did you know the door to the lab would open?"

"I–" Zac said with raised brows. "Huh. I just figured it would open like all the other ones?"

Jaol's mouth opened as though he wanted to say something, but he slowly closed it again and instead helped move the two guards so that they were hidden beneath a desk in the inner part of the laboratory.

Zac fed them a double dose of his knock-out pills even if the guards were just early E-grade at best. He didn't want them waking up any time soon even if he started to cause a ruckus when the doctor returned. However, because he had acted so fast, he had no idea where the doctor was or when he would return. He didn't dare walk around and look for Dr. Fried, though, as Zac wasn't meant to be here. He could be stopped at any moment, at which point the jig would be up.

He could only hope that the doctor would return to the lab soon enough. But the minutes passed as the two sat in an increasingly oppressive silence, and Zac was starting to get worried. His eyes were slowly growing bloodshot, and his mind was awash with murderous thoughts.

The Splinter was making itself known, and the effect was even worse than usual. Was it angry because of the close proximity to the Shard? Zac could only bear with it for the moment as he took out a Soul Crystal to try to soothe his soul.

"Your ship isn't quite what I was expecting," Zac finally grunted, grasping for some topic of conversation to distract himself. "It seems you're using a lot of old technology together with newer ones."

"Old technology? All technology is old," Jaol said, seemingly more than happy to break the silence.

"What do you mean? Don't you come up with new things and improve?" Zac said with a frown. "Isn't that the whole point of your factions?"

"Where did you hear that?" Jaol asked with confusion.

"I–" Zac said, but stopped himself when he realized he had no idea.

He had just assumed that the Technocrat Factions were somewhat like Earth before the integration, constantly figuring out new things. But then again, the Technocrat Faction was billions of years old. Had they reached a point where they couldn't progress any further?

THE MACHINE GOD FACTION

"We're in the forty-third age right now," Jaol said, seemingly understanding Zac's thoughts. "Each age represents the pinnacle of technology taking a step forward, which usually resulted in a trickle-down effect that empowered the whole Technocrat Faction. But almost all of these ages took place in the early stages of the System Era, before it was as powerful as today. The current age has lasted for over seventy million years."

"So you keep doing the same thing over and over again, with no improvement?" Zac asked.

"Isn't Heaven's Path the same?" Jaol muttered. "Cultivating and fighting, doing the same over and over again."

"I guess," Zac acceded. "So how do you improve? How do you become more powerful?"

"Work and save Bits; buy upgrades for myself," Jaol slowly said. "I've been working on this freight for four years, and I was planning on performing my fourth overhaul with my savings along with the reward for completing this mission. But now…"

"So money can simply solve all your problems? You get rich enough and you'll instantly shoot to Class-3?" Zac probed with interest.

Jaol hesitated again, seemingly unsure whether he should answer.

"I don't believe that this is some secret information of your faction. I can probably buy an information packet anywhere explaining this in detail," Zac said.

"Well, I guess you're right. I doubt I can get in any more trouble than I already am." Jaol sighed.

I wouldn't be so sure about that, Zac thought.

Zac wasn't about to say that he not only wanted to steal the Shard but also destroy the ship's engines if possible. In fact, he had been consciously vague about what he wanted to do just in case there was some built-in warning system in everyone's head that woke up if he mentioned stuff like "blowing up the engine" or "stealing the cargo."

There was no telling what safeguards the ship had against its employees. Jaol was pretty forthcoming, but Zac had already noticed that the Technocrat had tried to hide vital information to trip Zac up multiple times. There was no way he'd warn him that there were certain things he couldn't say without sending an alert to the captain.

"So? What's stopping you from shooting up to Class-3?" Zac asked.

"Well, first of all, I don't have the money for such an upgrade. But secondly, my soul isn't strong enough." Jaol explained. "I would need to drastically strengthen it to be able to support that level of power. I honestly doubt I'll ever get there unless *Little Bean* suddenly strikes it rich with a lucky encounter."

Zac was about to say that it was a bit unscientific for a Technocrat to believe in souls, but he stopped himself after realizing that really wasn't the case. He only needed to look inward to see irrefutable proof that the soul existed. Ignoring that in favor of some sort of atheistic technology-centered worldview was akin to burying one's head in the sand by this point.

"You're a soul cultivator?" Zac instead asked with interest, some alarm bells going off in his head after his recent encounters.

"Not as the people following Heaven's Path would see it," Jaol said after some hesitation. "Did you board our ship without even basic knowledge of our capabilities?"

Zac only glared in response, making Jaol shrink back again.

"Well, I think you people call us the Machine God Faction, and I guess that is accurate. Our 'cultivation' is essentially slowly upgrading our body parts one by one. For example, my eyes have been improved, along with most of my organs. I no longer require food, but I rather run on energy cells."

"You're turning yourself into robots?" Zac asked with shock.

"Is it any different with you? Your body is a biomechanical machine controlled by electrical impulses from your brain and nervous system. We are simply upgrading the machine we were born with to become stronger and more durable. The captain is completely augmented by this point, for example," Jaol said, some jealousy evident in his eyes.

"So he's immortal?" Zac asked with surprise. "If you can call a robot that."

"Robots and Transhumans are different things," Jaol said with a shake of his head. "Transhumans have souls; robots do not. The captain is not immortal since his soul will continue to age until his lifespan runs out. True consciousness is the foundation of life, and it is not something that can be created out of thin air. At least not until the Machine God awakens. At that point, we'll all be able to digitize our souls and reach immortality."

"So that's what you're fighting for?" Zac asked curiously.

The vision was reminiscent of how some people on Earth wanted to download their minds into computers and live forever. Some had even believed that the technology for something like that would be invented within their lifetime, if the integration hadn't taken place, that is. It looked like the reality wasn't quite so simple, as the Machine God Faction had been working toward that goal for billions of years.

"Well, the big shots are, I guess?" Jaol said. "Most of us are just trying to live our lives."

"So what's the point of upgrading your soul if you're a machine? You said your soul is too weak to become Class-3," Zac said.

"As we upgrade our bodies, our components become increasingly complex while the materials become more and more exotic. But more importantly, the components are infused with the deeper truths of the universe, what you call the Dao. The soul is the core of a being, and it is connected to every component. The stronger a module is, the larger the demands are on your soul. If your mind is not strong enough, you won't be able to control it. Worst case, the components will put such a strain on your mind that your soul breaks," Jaol explained.

Zac felt that it was an interesting alternative to traditional cultivation. They somehow directly infused their bodies with the Dao rather than learning it, and used their souls as some sort of spiritual battery. It seemed like a mortal would be better off as a Technocrat than cultivating the normal path, by the sound of it. The only cultivation that mattered was that of the soul, and anyone could do that, even himself with his zero aptitudes.

"So you still need to cultivate using Soul-Strengthening Manuals to progress?" Zac snorted. "Isn't that bit ironic?"

"Soul strengthening was there long before the System, so it's not really a part of Heaven's Path. Besides, our methods are more refined," Jaol said.

"More refined how?" Zac asked urgently, almost moving over to search the Technocrat again for soul-strengthening secrets.

Fixing his soul was a top priority, and he wasn't above abusing whatever means the Technocrats had. He didn't have the ingrained distrust, or even hatred, of the Dao of Technology like many of the old forces of the Multiverse. He'd use any tool that he could get to protect himself and the people around him. If the Technocrat had some bioengineered elixir to give his soul a power-up, he'd drink it in a heartbeat.

"We train through the Neural Network. Our company gives access to a decent algorithm, and as a comms officer, I can use the facilities twenty hours a week," Jaol said with some pride.

It turned out that all the Technocrats were connected to a virtual universe through their implants. But it wasn't actually virtual, as one's soul entered the network as an avatar. It was perhaps more apt to call it a synthetic spiritual world, where distances were irrelevant, as it existed in another plane of reality.

It honestly sounded like something that should have been created by a great mentalist faction, but it was constructed by the Technocrats. It was the piece of technology that defined the sixth era, and it was still considered one of the five greatest inventions among the Technocrat Factions. It only went to show how important the soul was for them. It was the whole base of their identity, whereas their body was just a transient and exchangeable coil.

Inside this world were training facilities where one could slowly strengthen their souls with the help of some sort of advanced algorithms. There were both public facilities where one could train in return for an hourly fee, but the results in such places were pretty average. Most corporations had their own soul-strengthening algorithms, and getting access to those kinds of facilities were one of the means to attract talents to their force.

Even more conveniently, it turned out that Technocrats could access the network while sleeping, so they could work on their souls at night without disturbing their daily routines. Stronger people could even allocate a part of their minds to constantly train inside the network while going about their day.

Zac couldn't help but feel a bit jealous at the convenience of the Neural Network. It was accessible from almost anywhere within their domains, and it was even possible to reach it from much of integrated space. How convenient would it be if he could gain access to such a place?

"Can anyone enter?" Zac asked.

"Of course," Jaol said, but Zac felt like his robotic eyes were a bit teasing. "You just need to implant a neural device or be given access by one of the other two factions. That will mark you as a member of the Boundless Path, though, and you wouldn't be able to live peacefully among cultivators."

Zac wryly smiled and discarded the thought. He had enough problems on his hands, and there was no need to make the whole Multiverse his enemy just to get access to those training facilities, especially when his own Soul-Strengthening Manual was probably equivalent to some of the best training algorithms.

"Wait, what are these Boundless and Heaven's Paths you keep mentioning?" Zac suddenly asked. "Is it the same as orthodox and unorthodox forces?"

He remembered seeing the Boundless Path being mentioned during the quest to take out the Technocrat incursion, but he had never heard much about it since then. People in his sector only divided factions in orthodox and unorthodox, as far as he could tell.

"It's related, but also different. I feel that you cultivators don't really understand our factions because they bunch us together with a bunch of lunatics," Jaol said.

"How so?"

"We're not some heretics trying to tear the world apart. We just want to live free from the control of an insane AI run amok. What good has the so-called System brought to the world? Endless strife and suffering, and for what? Nurturing soldiers for a war that is long over?" Jaol said with conviction in his eyes. "Yet we're being hunted from all directions because we threaten the interest of the powerful factions who rely on the System to stay in control."

"Do you really think that the universe would be so much better off if you managed to destroy the System?" Zac snorted, though what the Technocrat said did somewhat resonate with him.

"At least we would be free," Jaol muttered.

"You still haven't explained the difference," Zac reminded him.

"The System is a guidance system, but it's also a limitation. A prison. The Boundless Faction are those who don't want to bow down to a false Heaven," Jaol said. "The factions who follow the Path of Technology are part of the Boundless Faction, but so are many cultivators. Some of the cultivators are sinners who try to take shortcuts through nefarious means, but there are also righteous factions."

"Why would normal cultivators choose to cultivate outside the System?" Zac said skeptically. "It seems to create a lot of problems for oneself for no gain."

"Because the Path of Technology wasn't the only path that got cut off when Emperor Limitless began his mad experiment. Some paths are missing; others are broken," Jaol said.

"How do you know all this?" Zac asked. "No offense, but you kind of seem like a nobody."

The comms officer glared at Zac before he quickly remembered where he was and deflated again.

"Everyone knows. The origin of our factions and our goals is something that everyone learns in school," Jaol said. "Besides, my teacher told us that the stronger you cultivators are, the more likely you are to belong to the Boundless Faction. The pinnacle warriors and emperors can see the truth of the false Heavens, and join the Boundless Path to continue their journey."

Zac obviously wouldn't believe something Jaol had been told by some war-time propaganda teacher, but perhaps there was some truth to it. Why would people decide to go against the System? Were there some problems that arose at the higher grades that forced people away from the conventional path?

But then again, did it matter? He had never heard of anything like that in his sector, so even if it was true, then it was some problem that was far, far away from him. He had barely taken the first step of cultivation, and he wasn't much better than some random hillbilly.

"Where do you get the components, then? Just buy them at a market, or do you make them yourself?" Zac asked.

"You need to contract a manufacturer or work for a company that has manufacturing lines. It's another thing that separates good corporations from upstarts," Jaol said. "Almost all my components are acquired at a discount through my employer."

"So companies are essentially like sects?" Zac asked. "They both provide body upgrades and Soul-Strengthening Manuals?"

"I guess you could say that." Jaol slowly nodded. "Corporations have a database of components that provide high synergy with each other. So the best is to move up the ranks within the company to get access to matching parts of the same series. There's a high risk of compatibility issues arising if you mix and match at random."

40

DR. FRIED

It sounded to Zac like corporations had something very similar to the Heritages of the traditional factions. But instead of cultivation manuals and instructions on what classes and titles to get, the Technocrat corporations instead had manufacturing blueprints and lists of components that worked well together.

"Is everyone in your company equally strong if you have the same components, then? Sounds like a weakness for a force," Zac said skeptically.

"Well, some parts are custom made to fit with our soul frequency, and compatibility with standard components differs between people," Jaol explained. "So there will always be some differences. Most importantly, even if our components are the same, our talent and souls are not."

"Does it matter where you buy the components from, as long as the compatibility is high? Isn't it the same no matter where you go if all technology is old?"

"I'm sure two swords crafted by two different Blacksmiths are not the same. One might have better materials or benefit from a secret crafting technique. It's the same with us. There are billions of Class-1 materials out there, meaning there is an almost endless number of combinations of body parts to choose from.

"A good component might perform a few percent better than a similar one from a competitor, and certain components might have a synergy that improves performance even further. These incremental advantages really stack up when you consider the number of components a single Transhuman carries. Elite Class-1 Transhumans from peak forces can easily annihilate a Mid Class-2 Transhuman with shoddy components," Jaol said.

Zac nodded in understanding, and he felt it a bit humorous how similar things between Technocrats and cultivators were, even though they were of completely opposing philosophies. The situation was exactly the same as the one he found himself in. He had gained one incremental advantage after another with the help of his titles and second class, and these small advantages had stacked up into something immense by now.

There was no comparing himself with an average cultivator like the weaker demon warriors. He would be able to take them out by the hundreds, if not thousands, by now. The System played favorites, and the average cultivator was nothing but fertilizer for the elite few.

"So you can't change jobs if you want to keep upgrading?" Zac asked. "Because of component synergy."

"There are often some rules where we can still contract our old employer for a set amount of years after changing jobs, but most choose to do a large overhaul of components to re-form their core if they change forces. This will incur a huge cost, but it will allow them to incrementally improve by swapping out components one by one again with the help of their new employer," Jaol said. "Real elites are even given welcome packages of full component sets upon getting headhunted."

The two kept talking as they waited for the doctor to return to his office, and Zac quickly got a pretty decent understanding of the Technocrats, or at least the Machine God Faction that Jaol belonged to. And just as he had expected, they weren't better or worse than any other people he had encountered before.

They simply represented a different worldview compared to the factions working within the System's rules. But it was also clear that they weren't any better than the ruthless factions that could slaughter each other for a little bit of wealth.

The struggle for resources was extremely intense, and there were huge societal differences between the classes. The lower classes worked themselves to the bone to be able to upgrade to higher classes and provide a better future for their progeny, or just to prolong their lives with the technologies that emulated the effects of Race upgrades.

Meanwhile, the massive corporations and families kept almost all of the wealth and technology to themselves, almost making themselves into gods among men. Zac himself wasn't very convinced by Jaol's worldview. Personally, he felt the System was like the weather. You couldn't control it, and it sometimes screwed you over, but it was part of life. It certainly had a hand in a lot of the struggle across the Multiverse, but things might become even more chaotic if it disappeared.

Zac wasn't just interrogating Jaol to make conversation and distract himself from the whispers of the Splinter, but it was also to understand the technology he had back home. He had gotten his hands on whole production lines and massive fabricators, so he had hoped he'd be able to produce massive weapons that would be able to blow the Great Redeemer to kingdom come if he showed up.

But it appeared that there were multiple issues with his plan. Not only would such powerful weapons be powered by his soul, but he would also need the blueprints for that kind of weaponry. There was also the issue of his fabrication machines. The ones he owned were no doubt Class-1 fabricators and would therefore be unable to manufacture higher-class items.

Finally, there was the issue of retaliation. Small infractions didn't seem to bother the System, but if you went too big relying on technology, you'd land in a heap of trouble, just like the *Little Bean* did by launching orbital strikes.

He also wanted to know as much as possible of how cultivation worked among Technocrats to better be able to help and protect his sister. With Jeeves in her head, she could be considered a Technocrat, and it looked like he would have to somehow come up with a Soul-Strengthening Manual for her. Normal components put a strain on a Technocrat's soul, and he could only imagine that miraculous technology like Jeeves would be even more demanding.

He even tried making Jaol download the soul-strengthening algorithm he used, but it seemed as though there were heavy restrictions to stop any such theft. Zac also wasn't comfortable letting Kenzie onto the Neural Network because of the risk of being exposed. At least he hoped she hadn't found her way onto the network yet. The System was blocking Earth from the Multiverse, and he could only pray that it also included the network.

Unfortunately, it looked like the doctor was quite tied up somewhere, and over an hour passed without anyone entering the lab. The long bout of inactivity along with the raving Splinter started to take its toll, and Zac eventually had no choice but to stab his two shoulders and resume his experiments.

A fountain of blood erupted in all directions as a bronze flash burst out through his arm and decimated some machinery nearby, leaving Jaol gobsmacked at the other side of the room.

"What's taking so long?" Zac panted as his murky eyes, filled with killing intent, were trained on the comms officer.

"I – ah…" Jaol stammered after he saw the outwardly unhinged actions of Zac. "I don't know. If it's alright with you, I can access our network to see if anything has happened."

Zac thought for a moment before he walked over next to the comms officer as he dragged out the bleeding daggers from his shoulders.

"Do it. No funny business," Zac reminded him.

Jaol hurriedly nodded as a screen appeared in front of him. A series of screens and rows of text appeared in rapid succession, and Zac had no way to understand what was going on. Was this what it felt like for his grandfather when Zac had set up his computer back before he passed?

"Something odd has happened," Jaol eventually said. "There are over ten incident reports due to mutations, causing problems all over the ship. There are usually some things that need fixing since we acquired the cargo, but not to this degree."

"The Shard has become more active?" Zac asked with a frown.

"It seems like it," Jaol said before he shot a hesitant look at Zac. "It seems to have started shortly after you boarded the ship."

"So you don't think the doctor will be coming back here? He's busy putting out fires?" Zac asked.

"I don't think so. He has never helped with repairs before. I think Dr. Fried is more interested in taking readings of the Shard than helping the *Little Bean*, but that also means he probably will come back here to go over the results sooner or later," Jaol ventured.

Luckily, they didn't have to wait too much longer, as the door suddenly opened, and Zac sat poised to strike. However, instead of a person, a small ball flew inside, and alarm bells went off in Zac's mind.

He pushed forward to rush out of the laboratory, but his eyes widened in alarm as **[Loamwalker]** refused to activate. Only then did he realize that he was in outer space, whereas the skill needed to be connected to the earth to work. The ball detonated in a massive shockwave the next moment, and Zac found himself thrown into a wall as he was almost blinded by a piercing light.

His ears were ringing, and he was completely blinded, but his eyes weren't the only way for him to see what was going on. Dozens of fractal trees rose from the metallic ground inside the lab and the area outside the next moment, and Zac was once again inside a forest.

The augmented vision from **[Hatchetman's Spirit]** showed that a dozen robots were waiting outside, seemingly controlled by two Technocrats standing behind them with an array of screens in front of them. There was also a somber-looking Transhuman wearing a white robe spectating from behind, and Zac easily recognized Dr. Fried from a picture Jaol had shown him.

His conventional vision was just a blur from the grenade, but he still navigated himself outside as a storm of leaves spread out around him.

"It's an intruder!" one of the two guards exclaimed with shock.

Had they just thought they were dealing with some corporate espionage or some curious crewmember who wanted to take a gander at the doctor's research? Zac felt he had caught a lucky break as he shot out a rapid series of fractal blades. The blades managed to destroy half the machines, but the remaining ones unleashed an unrelenting barrage of attacks. Both the Technocrats were unscathed as well, as dense shields had blocked the two strikes he had launched at them.

Zac dodged most of the attacks even if he was blind, but he found out that the projectiles automatically detonated into a kinetic storm that contained some mysterious energy that almost completely ignored the leaves of [**Nature's Barrier**] and caused painful wounds across his body.

But to a warrior who had an effective Endurance of over two thousand, the lacerations could barely be considered a wound at all, and Verun lit up with a sanguine glow as Zac appeared right between the two controllers. A wide arc of death ended with the two Technocrats falling into puddles of blood and what looked like mercury, but Zac had already moved on to his real target.

Zac grabbed the throat of the old researcher before he had a chance to react at all. He looked pretty much like a normal human in his thirties, except for his skin being silver. Was this the mark of higher-tier components? The mechanical parts of Jaol were easily discernable, but Zac could barely tell that the throat he was gripping wasn't actually skin.

"I am working for Deramex Dynamics," Dr. Fried said with a calm voice as he looked into the eyes of Zac. "You should know the price we've paid for retrieving this item. I do not know which force you belong to, but we will respond in kind if this mission goes awry. My private emergency vessel is untraceable and anchored at the end of that corridor; it requires no authorization to use. Leave now, and this will be the end of it."

"The Undead Empire would welcome your company's attempts at revenge. I am sure some Lich would find your weird bodies an excellent source for experiments." Zac smiled, ignoring the offer.

Blaming the Undead Empire for his actions had become almost instinct by now. Someday Karma might come knocking, but for now, they made an excellent boogieman to blame all evil on. It was less convincing when he was in his human form, but the undead probably had a bunch of living lackeys that got things done for them in the life-attuned territories.

The doctor only snorted in response, and Zac's eyes widened when the man's head disintegrated into nothing as a massive blast was released from the torso of the researcher. There was no warning at all, and Zac was flung into a wall with a searing pain in his chest. However, he managed to activate one of the defensive charges of the robes hidden beneath his sci-fi getup at the last moment, which absorbed over half of the damage.

The surprise attack wasn't the real issue, though; it was the fact that the doctor seemingly had blown his own head up. How would he use the man's special authorization to get to the Shard if he was dead?

"Behind you!" Jaol suddenly shouted, and Zac looked back only to see a floating head fleeing in the distance.

A cannon ball ripped through the air and knocked the head into a wall less than a second after the shout, and Zac flashed over and picked up the seemingly unconscious Dr. Fried. There was no stream of energy entering his body at least, which indicated that the Technocrat was alive. In fact, he hadn't even got any energy for "killing" the two controllers, and Zac was starting to suspect that he needed to destroy the souls of the warriors of the Machine God Faction, or at least destroy some sort of core component.

Zac looked down at the head in satisfaction as he jogged back toward Jaol. He had barely needed to use any energy to capture his target, which would allow him to go all out against the defenses surrounding the Shard.

The Machine God Faction didn't have key cards, but this was the second-best thing. Now that he knew that the head could teleport, he was also infusing it with the Fragment of the Coffin to keep it in place, which hopefully would work with Technocrat tech as well.

As for whether the doctor was actually unconscious or acting, he didn't care. Unless the man had planted a bomb inside his head, he was likely not a threat any longer. It was fine by him if he wanted to play dead as long as he managed to get past the massive security doors and their accompanying shields that were currently blocking his path.

Jaol had moved out from the lab sometime during the battle, and he was currently looking at the destruction around him with dismay. Zac felt a bit bad about the fate waiting for the guy, but he suddenly had a thought.

"Do you use Nexus Coins?" Zac asked.

"No, but we can trade them for Bits for a small fee," Jaol mumbled with a hollow voice.

Zac nodded and transferred 100 million Nexus Coins to the comms officer. Jaol's eyes widened in shock, probably because 100 million Nexus Coins was more than he'd make in a decade, perhaps a lifetime, at his current post.

"You no longer need to stay undercover on this ship." Zac smiled as he said this with a voice that carried far and wide, which quickly changed Jaol's face from excitement into horror. "Thank you for your assistance. I wouldn't have come this far without you. There is a ship down that corridor, according to the doctor. I suggest you take it before reinforcements arrive."

With that, Zac flashed away with Dr. Fried's head in his grip.

Jaol looked at the receding back of his captor with mute incomprehension for a few seconds before his eyes turned to the two unmoving controllers on the ground. Indecision gnawed at him, but only for so long.

He rushed inside the lab, and he quickly put everything valuable and untraceable into his Subspace Container. He would need every resource he could get if he had to flee to a lawless zone where Deramex Dynamics wouldn't be able to find him.

41

DESOLATION

Zac's large donation was compensation for pushing Jaol's fate off course, but it wasn't completely born from benevolence. Such a huge sum would draw massive suspicion toward the comms officer, and his end would no doubt be pretty horrible if he stayed on the ship.

But the same probably held even if Zac hadn't done it. The guy seemed pretty shell-shocked, and Zac was afraid he didn't understand the severity of the situation. This way, he'd forced the guy into action to save his skin. It was both an apology and a threat. Jaol could take that money and escape, taking the knowledge of Zac with him.

Of course, the easiest solution would have been to kill Jaol, but it wouldn't sit right with him. Zac's actions of reciprocity with Thelim, the ent back on the sixth floor, had opened his eyes to an important truth. Giving back or severing Karma wasn't only vital for Karmic Cultivators, but everyone.

If he had cut down Jaol after having received help with the heist and all that valuable information, it would have festered like an untreated wound in the back of his head. So he could only rely on this little ploy to deal with him instead. The money was a huge sum to most people in the F-grade, but it was almost nothing to Zac, especially after looting the mentalist. Just one of her dresses was probably worth five times that amount, and there were over a dozen of them.

He was already rushing toward the containment center, but Zac was observing the young Technocrat through **[Hatchetman's Spirit]**.

He saw Jaol run inside and snatch some things from the laboratory before fleeing toward the escape vessel as fast as his legs could carry him.

Zac nodded in satisfaction as he ran to the metallic gates guarding the room housing the Shard, and he breathed out in relief when they soundlessly slid open without prompting. He was thankful he hadn't gone full muscle-brain as he had initially considered, as he saw the doors were over two meters thick with three layers of hidden energy shields within.

There was no way he would have been able to cut through such an arrangement in short order.

The interior chamber was massive, with a ceiling height of well over a hundred meters. It was inside the core of the ship, the monstrous spherical construction that had given the ship its name. The cubic chamber that housed the Shard just took up a part of it, though, even with its impressive size. It was a good reminder that the ship was like a flying city, and he wondered if completely crippling it had ever been on the table for an F-grade warrior like himself.

Roughly fifteen Technocrats were standing inside the room, and they looked up with shock at the intrusion. None of them seemed like a threat, so Zac rather focused on the giant ball with a diameter of one hundred meters in the middle. It was the outer shielding that protected the ship from the Shard, and dozens of tubes as large as a man ran along the floor from the right, likely powering the thing up.

Zac could barely discern another, far smaller, shield inside the ball. But further within, there was just a radiant light, like they had captured a miniature sun. He couldn't actually see the Shard of Creation, but he was sure it was within the core. This was somewhat proven by the fact that the Splinter in his mind was fully raging by this point, pushing the Miasmic cage to its limits.

He was considering how he could use the doctor's head to pass by the defenses when an alarm suddenly started blaring out from hidden speakers, and dozens of robotic sentries rose from the ground. The seemingly empty containment chamber had turned into a battlefield in an instant. The Technocrats didn't seem to be combatants, though, as they fled for their lives through a smaller exit in the back.

Zac didn't stop their escape, as they were essentially civilians, and he had given up subterfuge by now.

Bad turned to worse as a pang of danger in his mind prompted him to quickly discard the head, just in time before it exploded in a concentrated gush of purple plasma that effortlessly melted the reinforced ground where it landed. Zac couldn't believe the professor would up and kill himself.

But Zac's brows rose when a cylindric box inside the inner layer released some steam and opened up, at which point Dr. Fried stepped outside, completely unscathed. Soul transfer or a backup body? The Technocrats were full of weird means.

"Thank you for carrying me the last stretch," the doctor snorted as a series of clanking sounds echoed out from within his body. "Good thing I kept a few spares in case something happened with the treasure."

Zac wanted to retort something clever, but he couldn't come up with anything before he was bombarded with attacks from the robotic guards that had repositioned themselves to protect the power supply of the shield.

It seemed the sentries had only held back due to the presence of Dr. Fried's head, but now they weren't restricted any longer. Zac furiously charged the closest machine as he released [Nature's Barrier] along with [Hatchetman's Spirit] to turn the surroundings into his domain.

He knew his time was limited, as the captain could appear at any moment.

He needed to break through the shield in front of him, but the machines kept blasting him with concussive projectiles that threw him off-balance. It wasn't enough to hurt him, as the leaves still absorbed most of the damage, but it did slow him down considerably.

Three furious swings with [Verun's Bite] crushed the thick shield protecting the robot, and another one cleaved it in two. He tried launching a few fractal blades at the shield next, but they were actually shot down in midair by the remaining sentries. Zac grunted in annoyance and glanced at the machines, but he didn't have time to figure out his next step before his danger sense went off again.

He quickly flashed away with [Loamwalker], and it was just in time as a substantial explosion erupted where he had just stood, making him realize the machines were triggered to blow up the moment they were out of commission.

"It's useless." The voice of Dr. Fried drifted over, and Zac's eyes widened when he looked over.

A massive machine had appeared seemingly out of nowhere, looking like a mix of a walking crystal ball and a mecha. It had eight sturdy spider legs that held a platform in the air. On top of it, a ten-meter crystal ball rested, and it resembled the containment shields a bit. Finally, there was a platform on top that the doctor himself stood on.

Over a hundred thin arms reached down from the upper dais, and appendages ending with small satellites pointed at the crystal ball from every direction. It looked to Zac like they were used to restrain the ball in the middle, and he could understand why. A chaotic swirl of febrile energies rushed around inside the crystal, and Zac started to wonder if the crazy researcher had turned the Shard of Creation into a weapon.

Zac launched a series of fractal blades at the outer shield as he spread the storm of leaves to block any attempts at shooting them down. However, the fractal blades ineffectually hit the shield, only creating small ripples even though they were infused with the Fragment of the Axe.

"I told you." Dr. Fried laughed. "As long as the sentries are standing, you won't be able to destroy this shield, and the captain will be here long before then."

Zac growled in annoyance when he saw the researcher sitting on top of the weird machine with a smug grin plastered across his face, and he launched another series of fractal blades at the shield. But it was completely useless like the last time.

He quickly realized that his current strategy wouldn't work. The bots were too durable, and they focused on slowing him down rather than taking him out. He quickly forced a storm of Cosmic Energy toward the fractal on the right side of his chest, and soon after, the first axe of [Deforestation] appeared above him.

The bots were just too annoying, and he would rather fell them in one big swing. His arm swelled as he swung [Verun's Bite] in a wide arc toward the group of sentries that protected the massive array of tubing. The machines had proven a tough target for [Chop], but against the [Axe of Felling], they were little more than pieces of lumber, and they fell apart and exploded in an instant.

"You fool!" Dr. Fried cackled when he saw Zac launch his massive strike. "Did you really think that the shield was reliant on exposed power lines? Who would design such a shoddy defense?! You cultivators are really not much better than animals."

Zac only snorted in response, but he was honestly a bit surprised that it didn't seem to have any effect at all. He had still managed to destroy most of the robots, and he was sure that the massive tubes at least provided some power to the shields. Perhaps it was only running on some auxiliary power right now, and the doctor was only putting up a brave face.

Besides, it wasn't like Zac was all out of options.

Veins popped out all over his arm as he forced even more energy into the skill fractal, and the flaming axe appeared next, causing the very air around it to twist and combust. Zac didn't waste a second as he launched it straight at the shield, empowering the strike even further with the Fragment of the Axe.

The cutting flames of [Infernal Axe] slammed into the containment field with the force of a tidal wave, and flames were pushed in all directions, incinerating everything around them. Dozens of expensive-looking machines were reduced to scorched pieces of scrap, and even large sections of the floor were turned into molten pools.

But the shield endured. Some cracks had appeared across its surface, but they were quickly mended. Zac tsked in annoyance when he saw that the containment held. He hadn't expected that the outer shield could withstand the second strike, even after losing its main power supply.

"You're decent enough for a cultivator, but how can you match up to my lovingly crafted isolation sphere? It can even restrain the Shard, so what can a fiddling little h– ah?" the doctor ranted, but was interrupted as a pulse suddenly spread from within the core containment.

Zac couldn't believe his eyes when he saw the molten plasma around him turn to mud, and trees and mushrooms appeared out of nowhere inside the huge room, causing the shield to flicker a few times before it died out. Zac and the researcher mutely stared at each other for a second, both obviously shocked by the turn of events.

Was the Shard helping him?

It seemed as though the Shard had destroyed the backups while Zac took out the outer power source. The question was whether this was a random act of creation, or whether the Shard was sentient and had some plan of its own. But Zac couldn't focus on that right now, as the air twisted and turned as Dr. Fried seemed ready to launch his final attack with the weird machine.

But Zac had one more card up his sleeve, and he endured the pain as he pushed almost a third of his Cosmic Energy into the fractal of [Deforestation], initiating the third and final swing. His bones creaked and groaned as he pushed his arm forward, but he wasn't the same person as when he'd attempted the swing in his battle with Salvation.

A terrifying axe appeared in the air, and even Zac felt some palpitations in his heart after sensing the aura. It was an ashy-gray single-bladed axe with a long edge that almost formed an inverted S. The poll and shoulder of the axe seemed to form a robed being whose four arms ran along the cheek of the axe-head.

The shaft was straight and unadorned, ending at a spiked knob, showing none of the craftsmanship of the intricate axe-head. But the most striking aspect of the axe wasn't its incongruous design, but rather the desolate aura that spread out around it.

A tremendous resistance pushed against him as Zac almost finished the swing, but he roared and struggled to complete the motion with everything he had. He felt a sharp pain in his forearm as accumulated wounds from past levels reopened, but he didn't care. Zac could have activated [Hatchetman's Fury] to effortlessly finish the swing, but he didn't dare to be under the influence of that skill at the moment.

The scientist had noticeably quieted down, as he no doubt understood the power of the attack Zac had brought forth, but he didn't flinch as he frantically tapped at a console in front of him. It looked like the rampant surges of power inside the crystal were being magnified, but they were still being contained.

"Die!" the researcher screeched as dozens of the machine's appendages rapidly reshuffled to no longer envelop the ball, but rather expose the side facing Zac.

The sphere started to destabilize, and a second later, the crystal cracked as a terrifying surge of destruction rippled toward him. Zac's mind screamed of danger, but he was unwilling to back down, as canceling his strike now would not only cause a backlash but also put it on a long cooldown. It was also unclear whether [Nature's Punishment] would even work in a place like this, as there was no nature to draw from.

His destructive capabilities were, in other words, quite limited, and his other class wouldn't be any help in breaching the core containment field either. He could only meet fire with fire and bet the house on his ultimate strike. Zac roared in defiance as he finalized the swing even though his arm was strained beyond its limits.

A gray wave silently swept forward as the sinister [Axe of Desolation] matched the swing, and the whole ship shuddered as the two monstrous attacks collided.

CREATION

The whole room violently shook as the wave of ash collided with the vibrant beam. There were no explosions, though, and the collision of the attacks was very different from anything Zac had witnessed before, and it led Zac to believe that Dr. Fried really had managed to harness at least a small part of the Shard of Creation.

The energies that had been contained inside the crystal ball contained the ability of inception, and weird items kept popping up one after another, each stealing a bit of the momentum from his attack. A massive blue icicle appeared from nowhere and shot toward Zac, but it crumbled into drifting ash from the wave of desolation before it even had time to pick up any momentum.

There were rocks, waterfalls, and scorching flames that appeared to hinder the wave of desolation and strike at Zac, like all the elements of the world had combined to take him down. However, the third swing of **[Deforestation]** was the pinnacle of Zac's power, and it wasn't enough to just throw some rubble in front of it.

The gray cloud was noticeably diminished as it pushed through the construct's attack, but it still had almost half of its energy remaining when it finally exhausted the beam and swallowed the odd machine along with the doctor on top of it. There was still no explosion, and the mecha only shuddered before falling apart. It was as though the thing was a burnt-out log that turned into a pile of ash when prodded.

The doctor's face was frozen in a visage of fear and incomprehension as it crumbled as well. Zac knew the man was finally dead, body and soul as well, as he felt the surge of energy entering his body. A quick look around unfortunately indicated that the doctor wasn't the level guardian, as no teleportation array had appeared upon his death.

The largest threat was dealt with, but Zac didn't rest, as only half his objective was completed. He flashed forward, running past the pile of dust that was once the doctor and his battle platform. He wanted to stay in the wake of his own attack, though he kept a healthy distance, as he didn't want to turn into another dust pile.

The wave had lost even more energy from killing Dr. Fried, but it was a large-scale attack capable of taking out tens of thousands of people, so it continued forward in the limited space of the inner containment field. It finally reached the core that housed the Shard itself, another spherical shield with a diameter of no more than ten meters.

A tremendous shockwave suddenly threw Zac back across half the room, but his eyes lit up when he saw what was going on.

The last burst of power inside the [Axe of Desolation] had managed to crack open the final shield, and radiant tendrils reached out from the breach. They looked like condensed sunlight but almost moved around like the tentacles of an octopus as they gingerly felt around outside the containment shield.

It looked just like when the Splinter in his mind was searching for cracks or weaknesses inside the Miasmic cage, and Zac knew his opportunity had presented itself. He flashed forward with [Loamwalker] as far as he could until he left the spiritual forest of [Hatchetman's Spirit], at which point he started to run normally. He needed to snatch the item before the shield healed.

"HALT!" a tremendous roar suddenly echoed from behind, and the power in the voice alone was enough for Zac to stumble as bloody gashes appeared all over his body.

Zac knew this was the end-run, and he scrambled to his feet and kept going, ignoring the mounting sense of doom from his danger sense.

However, it quickly became too much, and he glanced back and spotted an infuriated metallic humanoid approaching. The cyborg's speed was way faster than his own, and it was upon Zac in an instant.

Terrifying energies surged around him, and Zac desperately activated a Bodhi-infused [Nature's Barrier] to protect himself.

However, a flashing light almost blinded Zac, and he felt a stabbing pain in his mind as all the leaves were shredded to pieces in an instant. They didn't even impede the Technocrat for a second as he reached for Zac's throat.

Zac swung his axe with all he had at the incoming hand, but [Verun's Bite] didn't even leave a mark, as it was blocked by a thin energy layer covering the hand. Conversely, the hand released some sort of counter, and Zac felt the Spirit Tool yowl in pain from the clash. Zac already understood who this was, and he wasn't surprised that his attack didn't work.

This was the captain, a true D-grade Hegemon. Even if he was the lowest rung among D-grade warriors, there was no contesting him while still in F-grade.

But the clash had fulfilled its purpose, and Zac was shot backward like a comet from the counterforce, straight into the core containment area. Zac prepared himself to swap classes if needed to block another strike, but he realized the man had stopped some distance away with a sinister smile. A small pang of pain suddenly flared up in the back of Zac's head as he hit something within the light, and Zac immediately felt an odd force invade his body.

He realized that he had accidentally hit the Shard, and he quickly tried to reach for his Tower Token to teleport out as planned. However, he only had time to see the Technocrat captain shouting a bunch of orders before the world turned white.

A crackling sound full of ebullience echoed out into the void, each snap exuding the primordial Dao. For untold ages, the [Spark of Creation] left its mark on the universe, its conceptions growing ever larger and more intricate. But suddenly, its revelry was encroached upon.

His breath was the Dao, and his hand was the earth, and when he moved, the Heavens shied away. He gripped the Spark and clenched with enough force to tear the fabric of reality to shreds. The shockwave shattered the Dimensional Core that the Spark had turned into its nourishment, the explosion destroying innumerable planets.

Unwillingness. Desperation. Desire. The spark shattered, its remnants fleeing to all corners of the myriad planes. Creation was never over.

A great sage sat upon his platform with a kindly smile, and with a wave of his arm, he brought forth his miracles. Magical scenes covered the night sky, scenes of unfettered creativity and depth. The crowd was busy gaining inspiration from the apparitions above, and no one heard the despondent wails from the captives below as their very souls were being used as fertilizer for the sage's false gifts.

The warrior's arm quickly grew and formed a massive scythe as he swung it in a wide arc that decimated the closest attackers. His eyes were already hollow and his face a sallow mask, but there was no going back now. He released a bestial roar as he rushed into the thick of the Verith Tribe's Truthslayers, and a shockwave of metal and flesh exploded out from him like a detonation of a Taboo Treasure.

Wings containing boundless force stretched out for hundreds of meters in each direction, like two canopies shrouding the earth. Each flap of the gargantuan bird's wings brought forth storms that ravaged the plains below as it traversed its prison. It hated its inability to soar higher, and it released a cry of desolation. A shudder pushed the clouds away as the wings grew yet longer. Blood seeped out from its body and fell like rain, but it didn't care as it soared ever higher toward the stars above.

The young monk desperately prayed for tranquility as he climbed the lonely peak. He couldn't stay at the monastery any longer; he couldn't risk the lives of his brothers. But the whispers never ended even after reciting the mantras. It would be so easy to give in to desire, to grasp the power that resided within. One thought to turn dreams into reality, one wish to challenge fate itself.

Zac had once again found himself captive within a storm of visions showing an unceasing number of fates. Most were pretty horrible, and any lingering notion that the Shard was the "good" to the Splinter's "bad" was finally gone. Those who had found themselves in possession of a Shard mostly seemed to be just as wretched, just with a different flavor. Coming in contact with concepts that were too far beyond comprehension was to play with fire; you were bound to get burned sooner or later.

The flashing visions suddenly stopped, and he found himself looking at a solitary figure from above. However, this time, there wasn't a Draugr lady calmly sitting within a lake of Miasma in silent contemplation. Instead, there was a cultivator perched on a terrifyingly tall peak under a shimmering night sky.

He wasn't Draugr, or any other undead Race for that matter, but rather, a humanoid alien with ashen-gray skin. The alien almost looked human with extremely fine features, making it hard to discern its gender. It did, however, have four eyes, one normal set and another one placed almost to the side of his head. The cultivator probably had 360-degree vision thanks to this feature.

The warrior radiated a dense and powerful aura full of verve, and even if Zac couldn't put his finger on it, he somehow felt like the cultivator was the exact opposite of the Draugr lady. The whole peak was drowned in a vibrant shimmer as northern lights in all colors imaginable danced around him. It was a beautiful spectacle, but the cultivator didn't seem to care, as his or her eyes were closed in meditation.

"Hm?" the cultivator mumbled, and judging by the cadence of the voice, he was no doubt a man.

The alien looked up from the ground, and his two sets of eyes seemed to focus on the spot where Zac's spirit hovered. Zac's emotions surged in anticipation as he tried to speak, but he was simply a blob of consciousness without any opportunity to communicate. But it really looked like the System had prepared another fortuitous encounter after all.

"Be'Zi mentioned meeting a child following her path just this way, and now you arrive at my doorstep just moments later?" the man said with a spurious smile. "I wonder what the Villainous Heavens has planned this time?"

The elation Zac felt was slowly doused as he listened to the seated cultivator. Even though the expressions on this man's face were more amicable than the cold visage of the Draugr, he still felt less welcoming.

"Creation and Oblivion. Broken peaks and an ocean of despair.

The cycle continues," the cultivator muttered before he smiled again. "Will you break it? Or will you drown as well?"

Zac didn't understand what the hell the odd cultivator was speaking about, but he was more worried about whether he would provide assistance or not. He felt fine at the moment, but he knew that a storm was probably brewing inside his body back at the ship. A storm that would have no problem crushing him, body and soul, if not dealt with properly.

"The Villainous Heavens brought you to me, but why should I bow to the bindings of fate?" the alien continued, his four eyes gaining a ruthless gleam.

Zac's danger sense was quiet, but his instincts still screamed of danger as the lights surrounding the peak started to flash with increased intensity. Zac suddenly sensed his soul being crushed by immense pressure, like he was being thrown into a black hole. But a sudden shudder from beneath the mountain froze the northern lights, and the pressure disappeared in an instant.

"Mh?" the man said as he looked down at the ground again. "Very well. Let the threads of fate run their course. I hope you will survive long enough to provide my wife and me with some entertainment. The eons are growing tedious, after all."

The man pointed a finger at Zac, and his surroundings rapidly closed in and disappeared. Zac realized that the man had sent him away, and he was a bit disappointed over the fact that the four-eyed master still refused to help out, even though he obviously had a connection with the Draugr lady.

Had the path the System laid out for him gone awry due to the cultivator's reluctance to assist, and if so, what did that mean for him and his odds of survival? Frantic thoughts swirled in Zac's mind as his vision turned black, but the voice of the cultivator drifted into his ears just before his vision disappeared completely.

"Creation is a miracle, but it is also a drug. It will satisfy your desires until you are nothing but a ball of cravings, a husk of a man. But through temperance and austerity, Creation will bow to your will."

43

PERCEPTION OF REALITY

"Two days remaining," Ogras muttered as he looked out the window of the small farmstead. "I guess it's about time."

"What's that, darling?" the lithe woman purred in Ogras' ear.

"I need to go out for a bit," the demon said with a smile as he pinched the bare bottom of his little savior.

"You shouldn't walk around too much with those wounds of yours," she said with some admonishment in her eyes. "You were on death's bed just three weeks ago."

"Didn't I prove just how healthy I was yesterday?" Ogras said with a cheeky grin and received a roll of the eyes in return.

He had been pretty confident in defeating the fifth-floor guardian after his experience with the Transcendent Master, but the fight had pushed him way harder than expected. The enraged beast had been a perfect counter to him as well, too stupid to be tricked.

Things didn't really turn for the better in the following three levels as he looked for an inheritance to end his run with. His wounds kept accumulating until he almost died at the hands of the assassin who guarded the gates to the 49th level. If it weren't for the defensive treasures he had commandeered from Galau, he might have actually met his end then and there.

Thankfully, he'd managed to escape from the assassin's pursuit, and he'd quickly disappeared into one of the neighboring kingdoms.

However, the wounds were too severe, and he had fallen unconscious outside this Uynala's farmstead.

"Are you sure you don't want to enter the path of cultivation?" Ogras asked as he looked at the girl lying in the bed.

"Only problems will come from that. Life is beautiful because it is short. Why would I want to prolong it just to fill it with bloodshed?" Uynala said with disapproval. "Look at that wound on your chest. Is it really worth it?"

Ogras only smiled in response as he finished dressing and walked out of the small house. He didn't have a specific place in mind, but rather simply chose to walk a while to loosen up. One day on the inside meant roughly fifteen minutes on the outside. He might find himself in deep shit real soon and needed to be ready.

The massive gash in his chest was still a bit troublesome, but he would be able to fight at full power without issue. Hopefully, it wouldn't come to that. Zac should have reached a floor high enough to scare off any attempt on their lives, and if not, he would serve as an excellent lightning rod for their attacks until they tired themselves out.

The demon found himself on top of a small hill soon enough, and Ogras took a deep breath as he looked around at the quiet vale where he had stayed the past days. The world of cultivators and immortals was almost completely cut off from this little community. The strongest person he had encountered was an old hunter who was level 29.

People worked their fields and lived off the land, without strife or any real suffering. Their lives were short but fulfilling. Uynala would probably marry someone from the community, and their three weeks together would turn into a hazy memory of an adolescent escapade.

"Is it worth it…?" Ogras mumbled as he looked up at the sky. "Definitely."

He donned a mask and robe and crushed his token the next moment, not sparing the house and his savior another look. A brief bout of darkness shrouded his surroundings until the world exploded into colors.

The beautiful lake was hidden deep within the mountains, untouched for thousands of years. Not a ripple could be seen on its surface, making it seem like a perfect mirror that reflected the heavens above. If one looked from a certain angle, it would be impossible to discern which sky was real and which one was fake.

A scream suddenly broke the tranquility of the secluded mountain as a harried cultivator desperately fled for his life. A group of warriors was hot on his heels, and the man's back was covered in wounds. He looked back and forth, but there was nowhere to hide. He knew he would have to make a final stand if he wanted to break free.

An hour later, the same man slowly breached the crest of the mountain housing the tranquil pond, and his eyes lit up when he saw the inviting waters. He had barely survived the ordeal, and he was grievously wounded and without provisions. But at least he could drink his fill.

The man dipped his hands in the pond, causing a ripple to spread across the tranquil surface. If the man hadn't been completely focused on quenching his thirst, he would have noticed a shocking change in his surroundings. Just as the pond rippled from his actions, so did the sky above.

Heavens and lake mirrored each other, and it was impossible to tell which was which.

But his mind was occupied with thoughts of escape, and he lamented the fact that he couldn't simply sprout wings and fly away, leaving his problems behind. He was so engrossed in his escapism, he didn't even notice how the air behind him shuddered as two crystalline wings appeared on his back. He only kept drinking the icy-cold water, feeling it was the most delectable thing ever.

He finally managed to quench his thirst, and the moment his hand left the pond, the ripples disappeared, once again turning into a mirror. The man looked down at his reflection again, feeling that he wasn't as harried any longer.

There was something odd about him, though, but he couldn't put his finger on it. Did he get the feeling because of the wound across his chest? No matter. The important thing was that he would be able to keep moving for a bit longer.

He jumped off from the ground, his wings vigorously pushing

through the air to lift him into the sky. The warrior soon soared among the clouds and set off toward the sunset. Each beat of his wings filled his tired soul with a sense of freedom as trees and hilltops flashed by beneath. But his sense of euphoria slowly dimmed and was replaced with a creeping unease.

Something was wrong.

He had sensed it before, and the feeling only became more and more palpable as time passed. It was like he was dream walking, where the world wasn't true and correct as he had always known it.

The wings!

Since when did he have wings?! What were these crystalline monstrosities attached to his back? Was this some curse the guards of his family had placed on him before being struck down? But he had never heard of anything like it.

Incongruous emotions clashed in his mind, memories of a life in the heavens, and memories of a life on the ground. But the memories of soaring among the clouds soon shattered, turning into crystalline shards that floated away.

He was elated at grasping the truth, but his eyes widened in horror when the wings on his back disintegrated, turning into shards just like the false memories. Without any means of flight, he plummeted toward the forest below, and a large thud echoed out across the desolate mountain as he slammed into the ground.

The wounds of the warrior had worsened, but he was at least alive. The false memories were gone, and his pursuers were half a world away. A sense of freedom once again filled his soul, and it allowed him to rally the energy to keep going.

Dreams of his boundless future started to form as he walked across the unknown forest, but he suddenly felt the creeping unease return. He started running to escape the mounting dread, but it only worsened as time passed. What was happening to him? Who was messing with his mind, his perception of reality?

And what else about him was false? Something was no doubt the origin of the undeniable unease. He looked down at his hands and froze in place. Were these hands really his? Or were they figments of his imagination just like his wings?

The answer soon presented itself as the hands fractured and turned into crystal shards that started drifting toward the sky. But as more and more of his body fragmented and split off from his body, the heavier his apprehension became.

These memories that were left in his mind, were they real or more figments of his imagination? They turned more and more disjointed, and soon enough, they were filled with nothing but short bursts of faces and places that he couldn't name or place.

Am I even real?

A swirl of crystalline fragments floated into the sky, and a ripple spread out as they breached the surface. The small crystals kept falling until they fell onto the bed of the tranquil pond, joining the millions of other ones just like them.

Ogras found himself standing on top of the teleportation array, and he took a deep breath beneath the mask before he sat down and went over his final gain of the Tower of Eternity.

"Reality is perception," Ogras muttered with a frown.

A surge of energy inundated his body as his understanding coalesced, and he felt a new path opening up before him. He had gained the Seed of Mirage from the inheritance trial, and he had quickly incorporated it into his fighting techniques as a means of distraction.

But was the way he looked at the concept too shallow? What if false could be true, and true be false? How could someone defend against something that was neither real nor fake, while simultaneously being both? His eyes stayed closed for another five minutes until Ogras finally took another deep breath and opened his Dao screen.

Seed of Mirage (High): Dexterity +15, Intelligence +35, Wisdom +10

It looked like he had gained 5 Dexterity and Wisdom along with 20 points into Intelligence. It wasn't a huge amount, but it did push his somewhat lacking Intelligence a bit further. He had never planned on focusing on the attribute even though it was beneficial to some of his skills, but he would gladly take it when it came for free.

Only after having secured his gains did he bother to check on his surroundings, and his expression immediately soured when he saw what was going on.

"Shit..." Ogras muttered as his eyes met the hundreds of glares from the mob waiting outside the protective shielding.

Had something happened to Zac's climb that emboldened these fools? Or did they have a false sense of security by their numbers? They would find that numbers were meaningless in a battle of elites, and if they got swept up by the chaos, it was their problem.

At least they couldn't target him until he stepped off the platform, but he knew that was only a temporary protection. The human cockroach would have to find a more permanent solution for their trio.

The array suddenly shuddered, and a pale Galau appeared the next moment. No apparition appeared upon his exit, but he still sat down with closed eyes as he took out a pill from his Cosmos Sack.

"You're late." Ogras grinned beneath the mask, quickly pulling himself together. "Just missed my apparition, and it was a pretty good one. By the way, do you have a tool to check what level that guy has reached? Hello?"

"Ah?" Galau suddenly said. "Mr. Azh'Rodum? It has been a while. I am glad you are fine. What did you say just now? You want to see the Tower Ladder?"

"What happened to you?" Ogras asked with a raised brow. "Trouble at the desert town?"

"Ah – well," Galau said with a weak smile as his hand reached for his Spatial Pouch again. "Negotiations fell through at the last moment. I got a bit greedy, I am afraid, wanting to make a big transaction right before I left."

His face turned even whiter the next moment, and he looked ready to puke. Ogras looked on with incomprehension before his eyes widened in understanding. He quickly reached for his own Cosmos Sack, and a second later, his expression was an exact copy of the merchant's. So many barrels of fine liquor gone.

"It's that bad?" Ogras asked, trying to find some solace in the sorrows of others.

Almost a third of his barrels remained, though, and most importantly, he still had the treasure he got for defeating the fifth floor. That thing alone was worth more than everything he had stashed away combined. Together with what that asshole had provided in the inheritance, he stood a chance to open up two of his hidden nodes in one go, provided that he survived, of course.

"It's worse than I expected," Galau confessed with an almost crying expression, but he still took out an opaque crystal. "At least I could keep some of m– WHAT IN THE HEAVENS?!"

"What?" Ogras asked with a frown.

"He's reached the 71st level," Galau sputtered, incredulity evident on his face. "Almost at the gates to the ninth floor."

"Monster," Ogras snorted with a shake of his head, even though he wasn't as calm as he let on. "We'll see if it's enough to deter the group of starving Gwyllgi waiting outside the gates."

44

INDIGESTION

Zac took a deep breath as he found himself back in his body, and he was almost surprised to see that he was still in one piece after the four-eyed cultivator had refused to provide him with a cage for the Shard. He did sense a new power coursing through his body, but it didn't feel too bad. His whole body was pins and needles, but there was nothing like the all-consuming rage and insanity that the Splinter sometimes brought forth.

Even the Splinter seemed to have been subdued by the alien presence in Zac's body, and the railing against the Miasmic cage had completely stopped. This alone made Zac pretty hopeful for the future, as this was exactly the sort of effect he had hoped to gain by taking this huge risk. Satisfied that he wouldn't up and explode the next minute, he quickly took in his surroundings.

The radiant lights that had previously lit up the core chamber were gone, and he found himself sitting on the metallic floor. He reached for the token fastened to his belt, but he stopped himself when he realized that there was no threat.

The initial plan was to snatch the token and escape if he encountered the captain, but he realized that might not be needed now since the core containment shield had been erected again with him inside it. Three massive machines that had appeared while he took his spiritual journey powered the sphere from the outside, each of them shuddering with power.

Just outside the energy cage, the metallic Transhuman stood guard, staring at Zac like a praying mantis. Beside him were a few Technocrat scientists who were busying themselves with dozens of panels in front of them. It had been impossible to make out the orders the captain shouted earlier, but Zac quickly put two and two together as he looked at what was going on.

Jaol had mentioned a drastic increase of issues on the ship, and Dr. Fried believed that the anomalies appeared because the Shard wanted a host. Perhaps the Technocrats hoped that him absorbing the Shard would result in fewer problems, which was something they desperately needed until they were out of harm's way.

"I don't know what your plan was, but I'll be keeping an eye on you until we return to our domain. Deramex Dynamics will no doubt pay even more for the Shard being delivered in a compatible host," the silver Transhuman said, confirming Zac's guess.

Zac ignored the man as he touched the shield, only to feel a painful zap that traveled along his arm. He wasn't worried in the slightest about being imprisoned; it was actually the opposite. This was the perfect outcome for him since they couldn't possibly know he would disappear the moment he cracked his token.

Since his safety was guaranteed for now, he wasn't too anxious to return, and he would rather wait things out for a few days to see whether any unanticipated changes arose within his body. He also didn't want to exit too early, as he had made an agreement with Ogras and Galau. Perhaps he would even be able to figure out a way to complete the mission on this level and then test his mettle against the floor guardian.

However, his eyes widened in shock when he looked down at the token. It showed that less than two days remained in his climb. How was that possible? He'd had over a week remaining when he arrived on the ship, allowing him to allocate over three days to finish this level before moving on to the floor guardian. There was even the chance of fighting for a treasure if one appeared on the 73rd level, in case he defeated the eighth-floor guardian quickly.

He had pushed himself to the limit over the past weeks, but the System had somehow invalidated his efforts and stolen time from his climb. But a sudden realization made him want to curse out loud. He wasn't inside the Tower any longer. He hadn't even considered it until now, but it appeared as though he had been forced to complete this level under normal temporal conditions. He had spent an hour and a half on this level, which pretty much was the equivalent of six days of climbing time.

It also meant that his climb would end in less than thirty minutes unless he managed to get to the next level.

Even worse, were there perhaps other changes to the rules he had taken for granted? Would he even get sent out if he crushed his token at this point? Panic started to build in his body, and he was no longer as calm and collected as before. He desperately started to look around for an opportunity to escape, wishing for some solution to present itself.

A deep thud made his whole body shudder for an instant before a shockwave of creation spread out, causing the environment to turn into a chaotic mess of random shapes and colors. The shockwave was contained within the shield though, and it seemed as though the power was slowly drained by the three large machines.

"It's pointless." The captain's voice could be heard from outside, but Zac couldn't bother with it, as he had more pressing issues to deal with.

The Shard had awakened.

A shudder traveled across Zac's whole body as it felt like he was being ripped apart, and the next moment, hundreds of bleeding cracks appeared across his body before quickly closing again. What had changed? The thing had been quietly moving about his body like a curious animal, but suddenly, it was frenetically releasing power to the point that Zac had trouble withstanding it.

Desire. Was this what the cultivator in the vision had warned him about? Zac had suddenly wished for a way to return to the Tower, and the Shard of Creation started rampaging a moment later. Worse yet, the Splinter had woken up from the massive fluctuations in his body, and Zac felt his mind tremble as it pitted itself against one of the Miasmic fractals.

It almost seemed as though the two Remnants were creating some sort of loop where they kept agitating each other further and further. The visions he saw were pretty grim, but it was nothing like this. The

Shard was going haywire in his body, pouring out an ever-increasing amount of unfamiliar energies.

It was just like when he was drowning inside the pond of Cosmic Water, except that this time, the energies came from one of the highest Daos in existence. There was no telling what would happen next, and he briefly considered whether he should crush his token in hopes that he would get sent out after all.

However, Zac eventually decided against it. His situation wouldn't be any better in the Base Town than here, and there was a complicated situation waiting outside. He would need his mental faculties to deal with whatever the forces in the Base Town had planned, and he would rather try to deal with this mess on board a Technocrat vessel than among the elites of his sector.

If he left the Tower of Eternity like this, there was a decent chance that the tragedy of the Zethaya Pill House would repeat itself, this time perhaps causing trouble of irrevocable levels.

Zac knew he needed to get rid of this excess energy before he exploded, and he desperately tried to force the energy out into his arm just like when he'd experimented with the bronze flashes. If something was going to explode, it was better if it was an appendage. Ogras had lost an arm, but it hadn't really slowed the demon down at all.

However, the energies from the Shard of Creation weren't that easy to manipulate. Besides, his whole body, including his arms, was already crammed full of power. Zac briefly lamented that he couldn't expand his arm to contain the energies like with [Unholy Strike], and his eyes widened in horror the next moment as his arm turned into a macabre slab of sinew and muscle that kept growing until it slammed into the entrapment a few meters away.

The shield wobbled for a bit, but it didn't break, but Zac didn't care about that as he frenziedly wished for his arm to get back to normal over and over in his mind, in hopes that the Shard would comply. And Zac was almost ready to cry when he saw his arm twist and turn until it returned back to normal.

In fact, it was actually better than normal. There had been a few wounds and a crack in one of his bones earlier from launching the third swing of [Deforestation], but the arm was completely unblemished now, even missing a few recent scars that had yet to fade away.

It was both a relief and cause for worry, as he wasn't sure whether this was really his old arm, or rather something that the Shard of Creation had reforged from nothing.

Worse yet, he felt that while the rapid transformations had expended some of the energies of creation building up inside him, it had also expended something from him. He wasn't sure what, but it was something other than Cosmic Energy or Mental Energy. However, Zac barely had time to feel a sense of relief before all hell broke loose.

He sensed another buildup of energies in his chest, but it refused to budge in the slightest this time. Instead, it shot toward the Miasmic cage with furious momentum. The Splinter wasn't about to be outdone, and the whole cage shuddered as it started to release unprecedented levels of power.

Zac desperately tried everything he could think of to stop the inevitable, but the two forces crashed into one of the seven remaining fractals at the same time. The pain in his mind threatened to turn him insane, but his mind felt like a small ship lost on a raging ocean. The Miasmic cage barely held, but Zac sensed that the fractal had started leaking from the crash.

The two Remnants had failed in destroying each other, but their war was turning Zac's body into a ravaged battlefield as even higher amounts of energies rampaged around, and he was barely cognizant of the fact that he was on the ground, screaming his lungs out as the air around him crackled before it broke apart.

"What is he doing?!" the captain screamed from outside, but Zac barely heard it over the roar of the powers clashing in his body.

The whole core containment was already painted red as his body kept crumbling before being forcibly restored by the Shard. The pain was excruciating, but that was only a minor inconvenience compared to the cost. Zac had finally recognized the pain deep in his soul that came each time he expended the Shard's powers. It was feeding on his life force.

His mind was a hazy mess, but he still understood that he needed to expel the excess energies even if it came at a cost of his longevity. He arduously got back on his knees and started punching the ground, each punch containing enough Strength to cause the whole room to shake.

The alloy was made to withstand terrifying power, but each punch expelled some of both the two Peak Daos of Creation and Oblivion. Oblivion turned metal to nothingness as Creation turned his hand into massive sledgehammers. The entrapment had only been meant to keep the waves of Creation inside, but that was only half the force inside Zac at the moment.

It just took a few seconds of rabid punching for a deep hole to form, and he suddenly found himself falling face-first over twenty meters onto a subfloor that seemed to be some sort of service level.

The pain startled his muddled head awake for a second, and he quickly stopped swinging to instead look around. All kinds of pipes ran along the walls and into the floor and ceiling above, and there were no signs of any Technocrats anywhere.

"Lower the shield!" a voice roared from above, and Zac desperately looked around for an escape route.

He started running toward what he believed was the rear end of the ship, and the aura around him kept increasing as Creation and Oblivion started to seep out of his body. Wherever he passed, destruction followed, either in the form of utter annihilation or rampant mutation.

The waves that radiated from him had been contained while he still was within the shield, but now he was like a walking radiation sphere that ruined everything around him no matter if he wanted to or not. But that was fine with Zac, as it both lessened the stress inside his body while it worked toward completing the mission.

Hopefully, he'd break enough to make a teleportation array appear, which would send him back to the Tower and its elongated spacetime. As long as he left soon, he would still have a day left to deal with this mess.

A sense of danger suddenly cut through the pain and confusion, but he felt himself getting punched before he had a chance to even erect any defenses. A biting cold spread through his body as a massive hole was blasted open in his chest, the force throwing him through multiple walls. It was the captain who had caught up, and it looked like he was no longer interested in keeping him alive. Half Zac's torso was gone, and it was barely held together by a few thin strings of flesh.

Zac felt death creeping forth, and not like when he changed his Race to Draugr. This was a true death. He was full of reluctance, as there were too many people counting on him back home. And the Vibrant energies surged in his body, and Zac was startled awake by excruciating pain as his torso grew back in an instant.

Cold sweat ran down Zac's forehead as he shakily got up on his feet and glanced down at his perfectly intact chest. Was this why the Technocrats had launched an orbital strike on the previous host? He briefly wondered what Ogras would say after seeing such a disgusting regeneration speed, but he knew it came at a cost. He had lost even more of his longevity, and it was not a small amount as far as Zac could tell.

Worse yet, the captain was already charging up another strike.

PINK

Zac barely had time to release another set of leaves and activate a defensive charge of his robes before the captain was once again in front of him, his fist crackling with power. However, just as the captain appeared in front of Zac, the two slivers decided to once again try to destroy the Miasmic cage, and a massive wave of wild energies blasted out from Zac's body.

Everything within fifty meters was destroyed in an instant. Some parts had been annihilated or at least destroyed with complete prejudice, whereas some of the surroundings had been twisted and transformed beyond recognition. A dozen large crystals had also appeared out of nowhere, making the area look like a quartz mine.

The captain wasn't unscathed either, and his chest lit up as a wave of dozens of shields spread out around him. However, these shields obviously hadn't been augmented by Dr. Fried, as they proved utterly incapable of hindering the aura of Creation and Oblivion that radiated out from Zac.

The shields cracked like brittle glass, and the captain was suddenly inundated in the energies of the two Remnants. His body twisted and mutated as other parts just withered away, but he shot back with enough speed to break the sound barrier. The wave subsided, and Zac once again found himself in control of his body, and he looked up with bleary eyes only to see the captain's body quickly re-forming itself to peak condition.

It looked like killing a D-grade warrior wouldn't be so easy.

The captain had learned his lesson, though, and he no longer seemed interested in getting up close to Zac. Perhaps he had wanted to minimize the damage to his ship that way, but the detonation seemed to have been too dangerous for comfort. Instead, he raised his arm toward Zac, and a dozen miniature drones were released from his arm and created a circle in the air.

Streams of power emerged from his arm and connected with the drones, and a simile of an array was formed. A ball that seemed to be a mix of electricity and plasma was quickly formed within the circle, and Zac's danger sense once again startled him awake from his muddled state.

Zac was still dealing with the aftermath of the shockwave himself, and fleeing from the captain was out of the question. He just hesitated for a fraction of a second before he sent the command to his Specialty Core, and he almost fell over again as a surge of Miasma joined the chaos within his body.

But the transformation finished in time, allowing Zac to barely erect [Immutable Bulwark] before a terrifying beam of energy slammed into him.

The captain was going all out to take him down, and his latest attack was causing even more damage to the ship than Zac's own efforts. Everything around him melted as he was pushed back over a hundred meters, but his defensive skill had protected him from getting incinerated at least. However, Zac saw that the shield was about to break after just a second of defending, and he scrambled out of the way at the last moment.

He had hoped that the beam would shoot past him and blast a hole in the hull, but it winked out the moment Zac dodged it. His danger sense screamed again, and he resummoned the large fractal bulwark to block his upper body as the captain, or rather, his detached arm, appeared in front of him.

[Immutable Bulwark] cracked in an instant under the pressure of the D-grade warrior's punch, and Zac was thrown through two walls before he slammed into what could either be a massive pipe or some sort of tunnel.

Scorching pain suddenly radiated from his leg, and Zac miserably got out of the indent that he had caused. An almost blinding light drowned the area the next moment as the dented metal was incinerated from the contents within. A beautiful yet terrifying stream of light coursed through the conduit, and Zac's eyes widened at the display.

The light didn't give off any heat or aura of power like a Cosmic Energy, but it still almost amputated his leg by just grazing it. His usually impervious body had proved wholly incapable of stopping it, and the pain was excruciating. The good news was that the captain had stopped over a hundred meters away, and he didn't seem to be readying himself to activate another beam.

Was it just fear of another shockwave, or was it fear of damaging the power conduit behind him? It was probably one of the main lines of power that ran this whole ship, as far as Zac could guess. What else would require this much power in a reclaimed old freight vessel?

His first instinct was to blow up the pipeline, but the problem was that he had sort of already done that by slamming into it like an infuriated barghest. The thick metal tubing was dented and twisted, but the stream of light seemed wholly undeterred. The parts of metal that blocked its original path had simply been incinerated, allowing the energy river to continue on its intended trajectory.

It made him believe that the piping itself might actually be there to protect others from getting themselves killed, or prevent things from getting into the energy feed. The stream itself was controlled through some other means, which made it much harder to blow up.

He had a sudden bout of inspiration as he quickly stabbed his shoulders with two knives as he stared into the eyes of the Technocrat. The Fragments of the Bodhi and the Axe poured into the two fractals on his shoulders, and his whole body felt some reprieve as a lot of the backup energies inside his body poured into the fractals as well.

An extremely large blob had formed in his chest in an instant, and it started expanding at a shocking pace. Zac frantically pushed it out of his chest and into his arm as usual, but the ball of creation was as large as a beach ball by the time it reached his elbow. Zac gritted his teeth and pushed half of his left arm straight into the stream of energy with one instant motion.

The pain of getting his arm singed off up to the elbow was almost enough to make him black out, but a spastic mess of flesh grew out and replaced the lost forearm in an instant as Zac repeatedly wished for a hand just like before when his arm was destroyed.

"What have you done!" the captain screamed with fury before he launched toward Zac with murder in his eyes.

A billowing wave of killing intent caused his whole body to shudder, and he urgently reached for the token again. However, his eyes widened when he realized that his newly created hand was completely without strength and coordination. It flopped around like a wet noodle, and he couldn't even grip properly.

However, the whole thing became moot before the captain had a chance to arrive. A scorching pain enveloped him as a huge explosion of pink and blue flung straight through a meter-thick wall. Multiple bones creaked in pain, but he had thankfully been able to infuse his body with the Fragment of the Coffin along with expending a defensive talisman.

One explosion after another rocked the whole vessel, but he unsteadily got back to his feet in case the captain showed up again. But the only thing he saw was blue and pink flames spreading in every direction, and immense structural damage. Zac's eyes lit up at the scene, and he quickly looked around for a teleportation array.

Fleeing from the captain had already caused an excessive amount of damage to the ship, and he refused to believe that the chain of explosions that he could feel in his bones wasn't enough to get the job done. Just as expected, just twenty meters away, a teleportation array had appeared, and Zac lunged at it, as he knew he was running out of time.

However, just as he was about to step onto the platform, the whole ship heaved as a massive crack opened up beneath his feet. Zac desperately tried to reach the array, but his surroundings turned to a blur as he was flung away from the spaceship decompressing.

A distance of hundreds of meters was opened up between Zac and the Technocrat ship in an instant, and the momentum kept pushing him further and further away. He panicked for a second, but he soon enough realized that the Miasma in his body was keeping him safe, though the expenditure was pretty taxing.

Another shockwave from the distance caused Zac to spin out of control as he was pushed even further, and he started to flail his arm to regain control. And surprisingly enough, it worked. He realized he could actually shoot out a burst of Miasma to somewhat mimic the effect of a propulsion engine. It allowed him to right himself soon enough, and he finally got a good look at the surroundings.

Pieces of metal were spinning about all around him, and in the distance, a series of explosions harried the gargantuan vessel he had just fallen out of. The dome of the bean in the middle of the ship had completely buckled, and the shockwave he had just felt was no doubt one of the enormous thrusters in the rear exploding.

A beautiful wave of the radiant destruction was currently spreading outward like a supernova explosion, but he seemed to be far from the blast zone. Guilt rather than happiness filled Zac's mind as he witnessed the scene. He hadn't really considered the implications of his actions when he'd infused the unknown pink spark into the river of energy.

He had subconsciously compared it to pouring sugar in a car tank to stall the engine, but this was much worse. Tens of thousands of people lived and worked on that ship, and he had turned it into scrap metal. Thankfully, the vessel had some fail-safes installed, as blue shields spread across the breaches that leaked atmosphere, meaning that most of the Technocrats were probably safe.

Zac breathed in relief as he thought of his next move. Usually, the teleportation array followed you if you kept moving, pretty much urging you to move on to the next level. Would it be the same in outer space?

There was nothing to lose from trying, and he quickly looked for any clues. Thankfully, the familiar array was just a few dozen meters away from him, attached to a piece of wreckage from the *Little Bean*.

A sudden collision inside his body forced him to puke a mouthful of blood that instantly turned into an ice sculpture, which rudely informed him that the two slivers in his body wouldn't even take a break after being thrown into space. He ignored the pain as he propelled himself toward the array with the help of a burst of Miasma expelled from his hands.

The array lit up the moment he floated into it, and a brief bout of darkness provided some reprieve to the chaotic war that had resumed in his body. But the struggle for supremacy between the two artifacts immediately started up again the moment he appeared in the next world.

Zac tried to get a grasp on the situation at the 72nd level, but another clash made him double over and puke another stream of blood that this time turned into sanguine butterflies. The little bugs flittered about for a couple of seconds before they exploded, causing wide-spread destruction to the area around him.

He tried to rouse a response to the reignited war, but he knew he was in pretty bad shape. He had plenty of Miasma and ichor to spare, but his constitution and soul were drained after being inundated in Creation over and over again. The adrenaline coursing through his body during the escape had kept him going, but the brief sojourn into outer space had cooled him down.

A quest prompt appeared in front of Zac's eyes, but his fuzzy mind couldn't make out what the screen said as his body suddenly expanded ten meters before shrinking back again, the agony enough to make Zac scream out loud. Another burst of energies threatened to burn his path-ways clear, and he desperately pounded down on the ground with enough force to cause a massive explosion that caused gravel and dirt to fly in all directions.

Zac zealously clung on to the parting words of the cultivator in the vision, using it as a foundation to steer back on course. The cultivator had told him to restrain himself and not wish for anything, and by now, he understood all too well what he meant by restraining desires. The moment he had an errant thought, it was immediately fulfilled, but the results were seldom what he hoped for.

It was like the Shard of Creation was an evil genie that sort of fulfilled his wishes, but in a way that seemed to backfire while also draining him of longevity. Should he try releasing a couple of flashes to tire out the Shard? The Splinter was also causing trouble, but it was still contained in its cage even if the fractal was leaking pretty badly by this point.

But releasing flashes was like putting Band-Aids on a sinking ship, and he needed a permanent solution. Should he try to expedite their attempts at breaking open the cage? It would happen sooner or later anyway, as they kept slamming into the Miasmic fractal, and perhaps it would allow him to trap both Remnants inside.

But something suddenly cut through both the pain and confusion as Zac's danger sense suddenly screamed that his life was in danger. It was not from something within, but rather from someone or something attacking him again.

The Splinter brought forth an all-consuming fury that threatened to burn Zac alive as hundreds of eyes spontaneously grew on his body to see what had accosted him. But the vision scared Zac straight, and the eyes shrank back into his body.

It was an actual dragon from mythology, a primordial beast over a hundred meters long.

46

DRAGON

Had dragons actually existed on Earth once upon a time? That was the only way Zac could explain it, going by how stunningly similar it was to the depictions he had seen since he was a child. It looked like a traditional black dragon, though its scales were tinted slightly red at the edges. Two great horns adorned its head, and sharp spikes ran along its spine down to the edge of the thirty-meter-long tail.

Only then did Zac realize that he had been dropped off right in front of an enormous cave mouth, which probably led into the dragon's den. What caused the surge of danger was a blade of power that was rushing toward him, seemingly caused by a swipe of the dragon's claws. Had he awakened the dragon and pissed it off by causing a ruckus at its doorstep?

Zac had to push down a primordial fear as he prepared himself for battle. There was no way that this big thing wasn't the floor guardian. One good thing about the situation was that the dragon emitted an immense pressure that seemed to have subdued the Remnants to some degree.

The swipe slammed into the bulwark the next moment, and Zac nodded in relief when he felt that the attack's power was immense but a lot more manageable than the Technocrat captain's. He completed the transformation of **[Vanguard of Undeath]** before he stomped down on the ground as he activated all his passive skills. An explosion of Miasma erupted as Zac appeared right beneath the dragon's chest, and the cage of **[Profane Seal]** rose from the ground the next instant.

Even the hundred skeletons of **[Undying Legion]** appeared and surrounded the enormous beast, and they staidly moved toward it without any fear of death. It was a pretty huge Miasma expenditure, but Zac figured that he would throw everything in his repertoire at the big bastard before swapping back to his human form, as he still had one change remaining.

But Zac still felt a bit stumped as he looked up at the beast. How the hell would he take this thing down? He had grown to a hulking behemoth himself, but he wasn't even close to reaching the dragon's chest with his axe. The thick legs looked extremely fortified as well by thick scales, and it was not like they were very good targets anyway since the thing could fly.

However, the dragon gave Zac no time to form a proper battle plan as it stomped at him with one of its frontal claws. Zac quickly scrambled out of the way as he took out the five strongest offensive talismans he had been given by the undead kingdom. He threw them all toward the scales on its chest, and a huge explosion of ice and poison rocked the whole area the next moment.

Zac's pitch-black eyes widened in surprise when the vision cleared to display completely unblemished scales. The dragon was still infuriated by the attack, and its long neck curved as it tried to catch Zac in its massive maw. Ten spectral chains slammed into its head with enough momentum to veer it off course before they tried to find a way beneath the scales to burrow into its body.

The scene gave Zac an idea, and a spectral chain suddenly flashed over to him and looped a few rounds around his body before it hoisted him up in the air. His arm swelled to almost ridiculous proportions as he forced as much Miasma as possible into it with **[Unholy Strike]** while the chain lifted him toward the dragon's softer underbelly.

The creation energies worked in his favor this time, and it felt like there was no limit to how much Miasma he could infuse into his biceps. It just kept growing to accommodate. He still didn't dare to overdo it, though, in case he harmed his main arm. His left hand was still barely serviceable since it was re-formed, though he felt that he was gradually regaining control over it. But he couldn't afford that sort of thing happening to the arm he used to wield [Verun's Bite].

Zac growled as he swung the massive black bardiche with everything he had, and the power was actually so great that the whole beast was pushed back a few meters. A small stream of blood leaked out from the wound, and Zac's eyes lit up as he saw his chance. The first swing had been infused with the Fragment of the Axe to cut through the thick scales, but his second swing was instead infused with the corrosion of the Fragment of the Coffin.

Zac wasn't done there, and he breathed out a cloud of corruption into the open wound as he frenziedly swung over and over to cause as much rot and fester as he could. But he only managed to swing four times before the beast roared and moved with shocking speed. It almost looked like it teleported as the bleeding chest was replaced by a scaled tail barreling toward him.

The shield of [Immutable Bulwark] quickly moved to block, but he was still slammed into the ground like a comet while the spectral chain was fractured into pieces. The other fourteen tried to worm their way into the open wound in retaliation, which stopped any follow-up from the beast.

It didn't help Zac much, though, as the dragon's attack had been infused with some sort of Dao Fragment related to brute strength. The armor of his transformation had broken apart all along his back when he slammed into the ground with enough force to cause a small earthquake. It felt like half the bones in his body had broken from the impact, but he suddenly felt a lot better as a cold and soothing stream of energy surged across his body.

Zac's first guess was that the Shard of Creation had yet again healed him at the cost of even more of his life span, but the feeling was completely different this time. There was not that aching hollow feeling that had accosted him the last times, and he crawled up from the ground with confusion just in time to see twelve of the closest skeletons crack and crumble into dust. What was this?

Only then did the real use of [Undying Legion] dawn on him. They were not only soldiers but also decoys that took damage for him. He had not used the skill a lot since trying it out against the Avoli Parasites, and when he did use the skill, it was only on weaker enemies. The skill cost a lot, and he didn't want to waste any Miasma in tough battles, which meant he had only seen the surface use of the skill.

Since he hadn't really been hurt until now, he hadn't witnessed the secondary use of the skill: damage transference. He wasn't given a hundred lives, though, judging by the fact that over ten skeletons had been destroyed from one single strike. But it was still enough to let him keep fighting a lot longer. He also wasn't sure how strong the effect was.

For example, he doubted the skeletons could deal with a massive wound like the one where he'd gotten his whole torso blown to bits.

However, Zac's problems had just started, as he found that the dragon was looking down at him with malice in its eyes. It almost seemed enraged at the fact that its mighty tail hadn't even managed to hurt him. Its wings started to furiously beat, causing torrential winds that made the Miasma and corrosive mists billow into the air.

The turquoise fractal in the sky was obviously strained, as large cracks appeared on it before they mended themselves, but it stopped the dragon from going airborne. The beast did, however, manage to rise onto its back legs, and Zac felt a foreboding sensation as a very familiar light lit up deep in the open maw.

An unceasing stream of scorching flames slammed into Zac the next moment, and he could only turtle up on the ground beneath his fractal bulwark. The flames carried a terrifying heat, and it felt like he was being boiled alive inside his little bubble. Less than a second passed before he felt that all the skeletons outside had been turned to ash, and he even sensed that the whole Miasmic cage struggled to withstand the sea of flames that covered the whole area by now.

The shield of [Profane Seal] finally broke a few seconds later, and Zac received a strong backlash that made him groan in pain. Even the thick bulwark started to show signs of tearing as small cracks let droplets of flames through.

He felt a scorching pain in his leg as one of them dripped right through a crack in the armor, but the burn was healed by the Shard of Creation at the cost of even more life force. Zac knew he needed to finish the battle quickly. He couldn't let the Shard keep draining him to heal his wounds, or he'd return to Port Atwood as a senior citizen.

The flames finally abated, and Zac looked around only to see scorched earth in all directions. All the skeletal soldiers were gone, as was the cage trapping the beast. Even the vast swathes of Miasma and corrosive mists from [Winds of Decay] had been singed clean, leaving only superheated air.

Zac saw his opportunity, as the dragon seemed pretty drained from having expelled a small ocean of flames, and Zac quickly swapped back to his human form. Lush growth rose from the ashen fields as the domain of [Hatchetman's Spirit] emerged, and Zac launched a series of fractal blades at the open maw of the dragon.

However, the Fragment-infused blades only caused minor scars on its face before they broke apart, and Zac knew he would have to use something stronger than that. Cosmic Energy surged in his body as he activated [Nature's Punishment], and the wooden fist emerged from the crack in space before it flew toward the exhausted dragon.

But another pulse from the Shard made Zac's hand twist and deform. Shockingly enough, the same thing happened to the wooden hand, and it suddenly looked like a misshapen stump. The scene thankfully only lasted for a second before both of them turned back to normal after Zac shouted in his mind.

He had accidentally put too much focus on his hand from activating the skill, which the Shard had interpreted as desire.

A grand peak emerged from the enormous fractal in the sky the next second, and it shot straight down toward the head of the dragon. Zac wanted to end it once and for all with one massive strike, but he was dismayed to find that he had underestimated the sturdiness of a dragon's skull. Blood poured down from its head like rain, but it resisted the downward push with a furious roar.

It looked like it refused to give up in a battle of pure strength, and its whole body trembled as it tried to throw away the mountain pressing down on it. However, its head had been noticeably pushed down toward the ground, and its throat was only five meters in the air while its whole body was fixed in position.

Zac knew he wouldn't get a better opportunity than this.

This was his final shot, but he knew that any attack with [Verun's Bite] wouldn't cut it against the thick plating protecting the dragon's throat. There were only two things in his repertoire that had a shot at killing this thing in one go. The first option was the third swing of **[Deforestation]**, but it was impossible to launch the skill again after such a short duration.

Besides, he didn't have time to wind up three consecutive strikes before the dragon managed to divert the mountain. He was already feeling that he was losing control of **[Nature's Punishment]**.

The second option was more fraught with danger, but he had already come to a point of no return. He felt that both the Remnants were already building up for another strike at the fractal cage, and he knew that the rune was already teetering on the brink of collapse. His best shot at surviving whatever came next was to exhaust both the slivers first.

Two knives appeared in his hands, and he stabbed them into his shoulders before he tried to launch what should be his ultimate move. He hadn't tried this before, but he saw no real alternative. A normal bronze flash was extremely strong, but the implosion area wasn't large enough to wound a beast of this size.

The pale pink flash he had managed to summon on the Technocrat ship might work, but he still had no idea what it actually did. It might even heal the dragon rather than hurt it for all he knew.

Besides, either of those attacks would only exhaust one of the Remnants, and he wanted to tire both of them out before the Miasmic cage broke open. He needed to see if he could create a new flash by fusing Bodhi and Coffin in hopes it would create a mix of the two. That would involve both the slivers, and it should release the strongest force he could muster.

If that couldn't kill a dragon, then nothing would.

He was extremely drained already, but he still pushed more mental energy into the two fractals on his shoulders than he had ever done before. His vision was turning blurred, but he forcibly held on to his consciousness as he jumped toward the dragon's throat. The two Fragments entered the modified **[Cyclic Strike]** without issue, and streams of energies started to converge in the middle of his chest to merge as usual.

But the moment the two energies tried to merge in his chest, the Remnants turned insane.

47

CHAOS

The Shard of Creation stormed toward the Miasmic fractal while pouring out unprecedented amounts of energies like it was suicidal, and the Splinter responded in kind. The rune cracked in an instant, causing a chaotic storm of energies that left a new set of cracks in his soul. However, a fractured soul wasn't actually his most pressing issue, as something terrifying was brewing in his chest.

The two streams of energy resisted being merged. Meanwhile, the dual skill fractals were like funnels that didn't stop infusing the two energies, causing more and more opposing energies to gather in his chest. Zac wasn't even providing any mental energy to the skill any longer, but the energy was rather ripped from the two Remnants. He couldn't understand what was going on; nothing like this had happened before when forming a flash.

However, the two Remnants seemed completely uncaring about the shocking amounts of energy they were losing. Dozens of tentacles shot out of the cage the instant the gap was created, all of them targeting the Shard hovering outside. It met the assault with radiant tendrils of its own. Dozens of clashes took place in an instant, but the battle was quickly slowing down as the two Remnants started to look faded and listless.

It was too much.

Zac couldn't even begin to prepare a strike in this condition, and he was horrified to find himself locked in the air as massive surges of power radiated around him. In fact, it seemed as though the whole area had been forced to a halt, as neither the dragon nor the descending mountain moved in the slightest. However, the wind still blew, and Zac briefly noted a bird flying in the sky above, proving that time hadn't actually stopped.

Both Zac and his foe were just locked in place as a bomb was growing inside his chest.

Finally, the situation reached a tipping point just as the two Remnants seemed to be on their last legs. They no longer fought, but their tentacles rather gripped each other for support as they teetered on the brink of collapse. Meanwhile, the pressure in his chest had built to such a degree that the two sides no longer were able to resist the merge, and the two streams finally fused into a new energy.

However, that was anything but good news, as Zac was still frozen, and this new creation contained such terrifying force that Zac was almost scared out of his mind. Just its existence was breaking apart Zac's body, but he was utterly incapable of moving it even an inch.

Zac screamed with desperation in his mind, fervently wishing for the Spark of Creation to push the thing out of his body. His desire was thankfully granted, and a spear of white metal was forged by some of the leftover energies spread through his body. It emerged from his chest and shot toward the throat of the dragon with the terrifying creation residing within.

The universe suddenly stopped as time and space unraveled, and a hazy pattern emerged as the fused energy exploded.

Zac was still stuck in the air, and his eyes were glued to the thing he had brought forth into the universe. It emitted an unlimited sense of vastness that threatened to turn him insane. It felt like it was trying to force the whole universe into his mind, but his soul was already bursting at the seams from just being subjected to an insignificant corner of the whole.

He needed to look away, but he wasn't even able to blink. Zac was forced to witness the profundity of the universe and the end of his existence.

The dome of heaven suddenly cracked as boundless lightning spread across the horizon. They were the only things that moved in this world of gray, and the lightning seemed to accumulate right above his position. Zac tried to look up to see what was going on, but his eyes were still fixed as they had been before the world stopped. He could sense a terrifying pressure from above though, like he was being gazed upon by an indifferent god.

Power, supremacy, but also happiness?

There was no way for him to comprehend the series of events, but he was relieved to see that the odd pattern in front of him was starting to fade. His mind was right on the brink of a meltdown, and he fervently prayed he would be able to withstand the insane pressures until the gray rune was gone.

A pure pillar of lightning suddenly slammed into the pattern from above, but it was forcibly dispersed by a deep shudder emerging from within the rune. Another blast followed immediately after, and this process repeated eight times with increasing intensity until a golden beam of lightning descended.

Its might was even a match for the mysterious rune, and it wasn't as easily dispersed as the earlier bolts.

Zac felt multiple shudders deep in his soul, but the final lightning bolt was like an unmovable fixture. Only after ten seconds did it dissipate, but it left behind a pillar of golden fractals so densely inscribed that Zac couldn't even begin to comprehend what they were meant to do. The pattern inside seemed intent to escape, and a world-ending amount of energy ravaged inside the cage.

The world shook, and the universe seemed to be cracking as Zac's vision faded to black.

A shudder ran through his body as he was startled awake, and he scrambled to his feet as he looked for threats in all directions. It felt like his eyes were full of sand and his head turned to mush, but he was alive. The dragon lay unmoving next to him with a massive hole in its throat where the mysterious rune had appeared. The summoned mountain was lying beside it, making an odd addition to the environment.

There wasn't any sign of either the gray pattern or the terrifying lightning. The massive dragon was completely unscathed apart from the hole in its throat, even though it should have been reduced to ash by the lightning strikes that had struck the pattern right beneath it. It almost felt like what he'd witnessed while the world had stopped was a dream.

But he knew that what he had seen was all too real, and he had an inkling of what was going on. The gray pattern he had summoned was something the System desired, and it had slowly created a situation for Zac to provide it on a silver platter. He had sensed the greed of the Heavens, and the jubilation when the pattern was trapped.

He had been played.

Zac had a pretty good idea of what the thing he summoned was as well. It was Chaos, or more likely a small fragment of it. It was the origin of the Dao, and just looking at it had almost driven Zac insane. If the System hadn't swooped in to steal the thing, he would have probably died then and there.

He didn't even have the energy to be mad about being used as an incubation chamber for the System. What could he do? Scream at the sky like a raving lunatic? A sigh emerged from Zac's lips as he looked down at the token by his side. It looked like he had been unconscious for over twelve hours, giving him some time to finish things up on this level and recuperate, but nothing more than that.

His climb would end at the entrance of the 73rd level.

He took a deep breath as he looked up at the sky, and he felt a sense of peace, for the first time in months it felt like. But the tranquility made him freeze in realization as he finally noticed that the two Remnants had been completely quiet since he woke up half a minute ago. He quickly turned his sight inward, and he almost reeled in shock at the drastic changes that had taken place.

The most important changes were obviously the ones that had happened to his Miasmic cage. Only six Miasmic runes remained as expected, but they had gotten company. Six golden fractals teeming with power had been added to the mix, forming an alternating circle in his mind. The construction seemed extremely robust, as though the two sets of runes formed something greater than the sum of their parts.

More importantly, the cage already housed the two Remnants. Was this the System's method of reciprocity, some sort of reward for Zac providing it with the Chaos Pattern?

The two Remnants were still entwined by their tendrils just like at the end of the fight, and they still seemed completely listless. They didn't move or struggle at all, and they felt faded, almost dying. They had been forcibly drained in order to form that special blob, and it seemed that it had almost taken all the power they had in the end.

Zac took a shuddering breath as he sat unmoving for a few seconds. He had made it after all. The two Remnants had glommed on to each other and formed a mutual restriction, while his cage had upgraded to an unprecedented level. Of course, he knew that he couldn't completely count on the issue being solved.

The Remnants couldn't even be destroyed by a warrior who was able to crush a black hole with his bare hands, so he doubted that getting slightly overtaxed would take them out. Besides, he wasn't confident in putting all his trust in the System's restrictive fractals. What if the System suddenly decided it wanted another Chaos Pattern and started prodding around in his head?

He still needed to quickly upgrade the strength of his soul to make sure he could handle any future problems. Besides, he still hadn't given up on his path after his recent troubles. On the contrary, he felt more confident about his choice than ever, which meant that strengthening his soul was still a top priority.

Fusing the Coffin and the Bodhi again was obviously out of the question, at least for the foreseeable future. But the bronze flash and its Bodhi-based equivalent were still very much on the table. He just needed to create a proper foundation first. He was currently like a kid with matches, playing with things he didn't understand.

He was shocked at the recklessness he had displayed during the latter parts of the climb as he looked back on the past weeks. He had not only risked his life untold times by creating the bronze flashes, but he had headed straight toward the Shard without any regard for his life.

Was it the Splinter that had egged him on toward his own path of destruction? Or was it the System that was somehow messing with his sense of reason in order to achieve its goals?

The current breather he had been given would hopefully give him the time he needed to work on his soul and figure out a way to control the high-grade energies to such a degree that he could reliably use them.

There was no need for him to go to the lengths that he had to forcibly try to tame the flashes while still being a beginner cultivator. The glimpse of the Chaos Pattern had proved that he was in way over his head, and he needed to learn to walk before he could run.

However, it wasn't all good news; his soul had once again gone through a change after his encounter. A set of white scars had been added to the black tendrils, making his whole soul look checkered. However, both the black and white scars seemed ephemeral and dim, like they were about to fade away. It looked like they had been completely drained just like the real slivers.

At least his soul seemed to have been healed by the Creation's infiltration, but Zac still swallowed one of the soul-healing treasures he had gotten from the mentalist just in case there were hidden wounds he couldn't spot.

It did clear his mind a bit, though it obviously wasn't able to expel the two high-tiered energies that had infiltrated his soul. There were no Creation-based globules of energy in his soul, but there was still a decent amount of leftover energies spread across his body. It was just a pittance compared to what he had spent in the final clash, but it would be able to help him out in a pinch.

As long as he didn't accidentally let his mind stray and waste it, of course.

His soul getting marked by the events didn't feel too surprising, as it had been the unwilling conduit as the two Remnants were drained. However, another change was pretty startling. The two fractals on his shoulders had changed. The torrential amounts of energies that had coursed through the crude shortcut he had made had actually remolded the skill fractals, making the pathing permanent.

But that was not all, as fine markings lined the paths, creating patterns way beyond his comprehension. They were not fractals, and neither were they formed in the inscription language that was commonly used in the Multiverse. They felt more primal, like they were natural markings created by the Dao itself.

The fractal on his left shoulder had clearly been marked by the Shard of Creation, whereas the right one gave off the desolate aura of the Splinter of Oblivion. This could be both good news and bad news, but Zac wasn't ready to experiment whether it would cause any trouble when forming the bronze sparks.

Not that he was very sure that he'd actually be able to form one, judging by how pale and faded the scars on his soul were.

Apart from that, his body was in decent condition, except for the horrifying cost of life force. He would have to ask an expert to make sure, but he believed that he had lost decades from the intense usage of the Shard. If he had kept going like that for a few days, he would have died of old age, or at least reached an advanced enough age to make further cultivation impossible.

There was no way that using the Shard for recuperation was worth it, as it cost way more of his life compared to slowly recuperating with healing pills.

At least the Shard's forced healing regimen had helped him prepare for what waited outside the Tower. The long bout of unconsciousness had also restored most of his missing Cosmic Energy, and he would be able to reach peak condition before the deadline was up. Only two hours remained in his climb, and his two companions had probably already emerged.

If he knew Ogras, he would probably want to maximize his benefits by witnessing both his own and Zac's apparitions. He didn't immediately enter the teleportation array, though, but rather turned to the unmoving body of the dragon.

His climb might have ended prematurely, but there were still treasures to be claimed.

48

AN OLD FRIEND

"Worst dragon ever," Zac muttered with disgust as he emerged from the dragon's den.

He had expected to be met by a veritable sea of treasures upon entering the cave, but the only thing that had waited for him was an enormous mat and a small mountain of raw fire-attuned crystals. Certainly, the mat seemed to have been woven from extraordinary materials to create a soft and luxuriant feeling, but it was a far cry from the dragon's hoard he had been expecting.

At least there was the actual carcass of the dragon itself. Such a beast was no doubt a living treasure, and he needed to harvest it before moving on. He had already given up on any hope of finding treasure on the ninth floor, so he needed to make the most of this beast.

However, Zac didn't simply put the whole thing into a Cosmos Sack, but he rather chose to methodically harvest its body piece by piece. It would be a huge shame if the whole dragon turned to dust the moment he left the Tower, and this way he would at least be able to guarantee that some parts would make it.

Zac tried to pry off as many scales as possible, along with its two massive horns. He also dug out what he believed to be a Beast Core from its head, though he was a bit surprised since those things usually only appeared after reaching D-grade. The dragon was extremely powerful, but Zac suspected it was still in early E-grade, if even that.

He had heard a bit about dragons from Galau. They were terrifying beasts and among the most naturally endowed creatures in the Multi-verse. They could grow impossibly large as well, making Zac believe he was only dealing with a youngling or a mixed-blood dragon.

Still, leaving anything behind would be a waste, so he even poured out almost all his containers to fill them with dragon blood. Enough blood to fill an Olympic-size swimming pool entered his dozen or so canteens and the magical barrels of liquor he had bought.

He did feed a lot of it to [Verun's Bite] as well, but not enough to accidentally cause another upgrade. It took hours, sometimes days, for [Verun's Bite] to absorb treasures, and Zac was about to potentially face an army waiting outside the gates of the Tower. The Spirit Tool was extremely interested in the Beast Core also, but it would have to wait.

It was a waste, but he could only pray that the Dragon Core would turn out to be real, as he might need Verun's special skills for the upcoming battle. He had somewhat counted on the bronze flash to act as an ace, but there was no way that the Remnants were in a position to provide help anytime soon.

He had tried summoning a bronze flash over twenty times while carving up the beast, but nothing happened. The two Fragments entered his reworked fractals just fine, but when they met in his chest, they just turned into an impure mix of the two fragments that soon dissipated, just like the failed attempts from before. Something had clearly changed, as he'd had almost a 50% success rate before.

The transformation of the fractals on his shoulders might be causing problems, but he was pretty sure that wasn't it.

An hour had passed since he had woken up by now, and he started to see some patterns of how things might go from here on out. It quickly became clear that the Remnants were really capable of some sort of self-restoration. Small motes of energies appeared from within their bodies, even though no Cosmic or Mental Energy had entered the cage.

However, it had been a slow grind for a pitiful amount of energy.

Things only went even worse for the Remnants from there, as the new cage created some sort of suction just moments after the motes of energy formed. The energy was instantly ripped out of the Shard and

Splinter, leaving only a fraction behind. The rest was purified and funneled out into Zac's body.

The purified energy from the Splinter made its way to his soul, as usual, subtly strengthening it. However, the energy from the Shard rather went into his body, where it seeped into his cells, which greedily gobbled it up in an instant. Zac didn't feel any difference in his body, but he guessed that it would slowly improve his constitution.

The amount that he got was far lower compared to before, and he was not even receiving a tenth of the purified energies he'd gotten from the Splinter before he entered the Tower. That was fine with Zac, though, as the gifts from the Remnants always came with deadly downsides.

Focusing on just himself for the time being felt a lot more pertinent. It seemed like he had touched upon some of the massive secrets of the Multiverse, and he was slowly forming a few theories based on what Jaol had told him about the System and what the four-eyed alien had said. But all those things were too grand, too complicated, and not something he wanted to get involved with.

He could mess with the broken peaks of the Boundless Path when he had reached A-grade and was bored with life. Until then, the Chaos Patterns and the skies full of lightning could stay as far away as possible, as far as he was concerned. He wasn't even in a mood to start experimenting with the flashes again before he had got his Soul-Strengthening Manual up and running.

Actually, it seemed that his mind was agreeing with his reluctance to get involved, as his memory of the Chaos Pattern he had just witnessed was growing foggier by the minute. He couldn't remember any details any longer, and he wouldn't be surprised if it would completely disappear from his memory in a day or two.

It was a pain to dismember the extremely sturdy dragon, and Zac was quickly running out of time. So he finally ran into the carcass and chopped its insides into massive slabs of meat and threw them into his Cosmos Sack. Finally, he threw the mangled remains into the sack as well and called it a day.

There was one more thing Zac wanted to do before he left the floor, though, and he took out an inscribed box containing an unknown fruit. It was one of the natural treasures he had found during the climb.

He still had no idea what it did, but he figured that his body knew what it was doing, as it urged him to eat it.

He was somewhat certain that the items he had pilfered during the Battle of Fates would stay, but the same couldn't be said about these things. He wanted to follow Galau's advice and eat them rather than have them return into the System's hands the moment he left.

It was only thirty minutes later that he snapped out of his state of vivid hallucinations and bouts of extreme gastrointestinal distress. His whole body was covered in a film of extremely foul-smelling oil, and he felt weak like he had been afflicted with food poisoning.

The natural treasure hadn't actually been toxic, but it rather looked like the treasure was the kind that helped expel impurities like pill toxicity. The problem was the way of expulsion. Some things needed to be processed into pills before being eaten, and that scary fruit was probably one of them. He had less than thirty minutes remaining, but he still spent ten of those vigorously scrubbing off the foul gunk. The smell was making him nauseated, which was saying something, considering he could be covered in blood without noticing it nowadays.

Zac reluctantly discarded any idea of eating more of the treasures as he stepped into the teleporter with a tired sigh.

[Eighth Floor Complete. Upgrading Title.]

[Choose Reward: [Two Extremities Physique Array], [Divine Investiture Array], [Yin-Yang Arhat Soul Array]]

Zac found himself in the familiar black dimension, and he almost felt some wistfulness that this was the last time he would come to this place. Of course, the wistfulness wasn't brought on by nostalgia, but rather that this was the last of the rewards. He first opened his title screen to sate his curiosity.

[Tower of Eternity – 8th Floor: Reach the 73rd level of the Tower of Eternity. Reward: All Stats +10, All Stats +10%, Effect of Attributes +10%]

The upgraded title was just as he had expected after seeing the change on the seventh floor, and he was suddenly extremely curious about what would change upon finishing the whole Tower. Was there a secret title waiting at the top after all? However, his attention was soon diverted from the Tower Title when he noticed that there was a new addition to his ever-growing list of achievements. And it was an odd one.

[Terminus – Gaze upon the Terminus.]

There was only a short description and no reward, the first empty title Zac had encountered thus far. Zac guessed the Terminus either referred to the lightning sea or the pattern that he could no longer remember, but he didn't understand why the System would add a title if it wouldn't dole out any attributes.

Perhaps someone in the Base Town would know, but he felt that keeping this experience to himself was for the best. Stuff like the Dao of Chaos involved the System itself and the peak individuals of the Multiverse, and just talking about it might bring a calamity upon his head.

He could only close the title screen with mixed emotions and instead turn his attention to the three arrays up for grabs. However, the rewards honestly had him a bit stumped. He understood the words as he read them one by one, but he had some trouble understanding what they meant.

Zac was surprised that the rewards didn't feel as tailored to his situation compared to the previous floor. Truthfully, they even seemed worse compared to the ones he had been awarded after succeeding in the Battle of Fates, as each of them had represented a clear and almost immediate boost to himself or his force.

Was there an element of luck where you could either get a good set of reward choices or a subpar one? Or were the arrays perhaps even better than the seventh-floor awards, but Zac was too ignorant to tell? He looked back and forth between the three options, and he felt some helplessness at the fact that he didn't know what any of the three arrays did.

The first array, the [Two Extremities Physique Array], might be some sort of training array to form a unique constitution. It might even be an extremely suited constitution based on the name. Two Extremities could refer to life and death, or perhaps even Creation and Oblivion. Remolding his body to be able to withstand the two Remnants seemed pretty amazing. That might just be wishful thinking, though.

That would mean that the award was an upgraded version of the Body-Tempering Manual, an array that would directly awaken a life and death constitution. However, there was another possibility, based on the wording of the first and third rewards. One was called a Physique Array, and the other a Soul Array.

That kind of wording was a bit reminiscent of War Arrays, and it made him remember something: the Fire Golem down in the Underworld. Parts of its body had been engraved with crude fractals, and he had learned this was a common way for constructs to improve their power.

Was the same thing possible for humans? Was it perhaps an array that would be engraved to his body, somehow boosting it beyond its normal capabilities? He guessed something like that would work like a synthetic constitution or something, where it provided similar boosts.

Whichever way the array worked, the end result was most likely the same. It would probably directly increase his combat power by improving his body, almost like having a private War Array. It would give a direct and convenient boost to his Strength, and it was definitely a viable choice.

As for the [Divine Investiture Array], he had no idea. Judging by the name, it might be something that could improve a person or an item. Divine Investiture, maybe it meant that it could bestow Heaven's Blessing. Perhaps it was something like the array that he had passed when he climbed the eighth floor, but a greater version? Or was it related to fate?

Getting the System's blessing didn't sound too bad right about now, and it sort of felt like the System owed him one after the last two levels.

Then there was the final reward, one related to the soul. He would have preferred one that mentioned caging rambunctious slivers, but this one rather seemed geared toward taking advantage of the odd scars covering his soul. It seemed to be based on the concept of duality just like the Constitution Array, but he had no idea what a "Soul Array" could do. Did it improve one's control over the Daos, perhaps?

It did, however, include the word Arhat, which was a Buddhist term. He didn't know if that would cause any issues with his cultivation or his recently acquired manual, but he guessed that anything he got from the eighth floor would be compatible with him. An Arhat was a perfected being who had reached enlightenment, so perhaps the Soul Array would be able to push his soul to a perfect state?

Zac looked back and forth between the options, but he truthfully didn't need to look too long before he decided on the third option, the **[Yin-Yang Arhat Soul Array]**. It wasn't that he felt it was perfect for his situation, as he honestly had no idea what it did, but he'd obviously take anything that helped his soul at the current juncture.

The other two options were probably great as well, but they were luxuries compared to a necessity. His arm reached toward the hovering prompt in front of him, but he suddenly froze in shock as the silence of the special dimension was broken.

[First choice will grant you power. Second choice brings rectification of regret. Third choice will lead you down an alternative Path.]

Zac didn't know how to react when he heard the emotionless voice in his head. A year had passed, and he had almost forgotten those early days of the integration, but it all rushed back to him at that moment.

The System was once again directly speaking with him.

49

BEWARE THE TERMINUS

Zac froze like a deer in the headlights as he looked in all directions. Back when the integration first took place, he had been completely clueless, unaware of just how powerful a thing the System was. But now he was all too aware just how mighty it was, and the attention put him under immense psychological pressure.

However, he knew this was a rare opportunity, and he needed some clarifications.

"Was it you who pushed me down this path, who put these two Remnants in front of me?"

**[Yes. User qualified for unique empowerment scenario.
Congratulations.]**

Zac felt some fury flare up at hearing the same annoying emotion-less congratulations as he did when the two last spoke, but he quickly restrained himself this time and instead focused on what was important.

"Are we done, then?" Zac asked, his heart pounding. "You won't mess with me any longer? I gave you that pattern, and you provided me with protections against the fractals."

**[Reciprocity has been achieved, and balance is maintained.
Beware the Terminus.]**

"What does that even mean?" Zac asked with some bitterness in his voice, but he was only met with silence.

"What regrets are you talking about? And what alternate path? Please elaborate," Zac tried instead, as he didn't understand what the hell the System had been talking about earlier.

Unfortunately, it looked like the System wasn't any more talkative this time around, and it had left after delivering a few cryptic lines. Zac once again looked upon the screen with the three rewards, his earlier resolve completely crushed. Could he trust the System? Or was it messing with him once again?

His thoughts about the first reward didn't change, as the comment was in line with his own thoughts. But the other two threw him for a loop. What did an alternate path mean? Did it refer to his soul cultivation, or was it something much bigger? Would it tamper with his nascent Creation based on Life and Death? Would it actually force him to embark on Buddhist Cultivation, forgoing his current classes?

And what the hell did rectification of regret mean?

He had done things he wasn't too proud of since the integration, but he would say there was only one real regret: not reaching his father before he was murdered. It couldn't possibly be an array that could resurrect the dead, could it? Or was it rather related to his inability to cultivate? The more he thought about it, the more likely it felt.

Wasn't that exactly what Divine Investiture meant? The ability to cultivate was based on one's affinity with the Daos, something that he was completely lacking. What if this array could rectify that deficiency in his body, allowing him to embark on the path of a true cultivator?

There were a lot of secrets related to his body, secrets that might make him want to stay a mortal. But he also knew that things would get extremely rough the further he walked down the path of cultivation. Things weren't too bad right now in F-grade, but the situation would get much worse for each grade, as far as he knew. This might be his shot at getting the final, and greatest, boost to his power, becoming a proper cultivator.

Zac finally went with his gut and reached for the second option.

Zac chose the **[Divine Investiture Array]** based on his guess that the System wasn't actively messing with him. Why would it even bother? It was in control of the rewards, after all. He wasn't interested in changing his path, which would potentially make the **[Yin-Yang Arhat Soul Array]** useless. And between rectifying regret and strength, he chose the former.

He had plenty of Strength from a bunch of other sources, and a Constitution Array wasn't required for him to deal with the issues on Earth. He hadn't even seen anyone in his sector utilizing this kind of thing, and it didn't come up when Galau talked about constitutions. It was probably some sort of high-tiered boost not available in his sector, but people did just fine without them.

Rectifying regret was more in line with his purpose of cultivation. He didn't really care about power for power's sake, and not all his troubles could get solved by becoming stronger. Perhaps the **[Divine Investiture Array]** would make him a cultivator, or perhaps its function was something else entirely, but it didn't matter.

He didn't want to experience some tragedy in the future and realize it could have been prevented if he hadn't been too greedy for more power.

Zac didn't immediately pick the reward, though, but he first started putting one ring after another on his fingers before moving on to bracers, earrings, and necklaces. It was the jewelry he'd looted from the mentalist, each of them a pretty strong treasure that contained one charge either of offensive or defensive nature.

He had seen a couple of similar items by now, and he could tell that all of them were E-grade items made with craftsmanship you couldn't find in the Zecia sector. It was like he was decked in treasures that each could release an attack or shield at the very limit of what you could bring into the Tower of Eternity.

The most important point was that while they were heavily suppressed inside the Tower of Eternity, they'd work just fine in the Base Town. The items were clearly made for a woman, but he wasn't in a position to be picky at the moment. The whole square could be full of people wanting to rip him to shreds for all he knew, and every small advantage would make a huge difference.

He actually wanted to don a few dresses as well to improve his defenses even further, but he was afraid that he'd ruin any chances of finding a patron if he came out looking like a maniac.

He looked down at his body a second later, satisfied with the result. Ogras had once told him that wealth was one of the greatest weapons, and he was inclined to agree as he looked at the glistening treasures covering his hands and arms. It was like he suddenly had ten lives, though each item spent was probably the equivalent of losing hundreds of millions of Nexus Coins, perhaps even billions.

Zac also had enough Creation Energy in his body for one major restoration, but he didn't want to use it unless absolutely necessary. He finally prepared one of the spikes of Faceless #9 in the sleeve of his robes, but he was even leerier about that spike compared to the Creation Energy. It might be lethal for outsiders to use, and he would only stab himself with that thing if he really didn't see any alternatives.

Normally, he would have entered the new floor as a Draugr to defend against surprise attacks, but he, unfortunately, couldn't do that, as he was exiting the Tower. Zac wasn't ready to expose his second identity, which meant he would have to defend against any potential assault with treasures and his nature-based defensive skills.

Zac took a few deep breaths before he picked the **[Divine Investiture Array]**, and the next moment, he was teleported to the 73rd level. He crushed his token the moment he arrived, but his danger sense already screamed in alarm.

He activated one of the defensive charges of a ring as he created a massive fractal edge that he swung in a grand 360-degree arc. A dozen massive rats were turned into mincemeat, and his whole body was drenched in blood and viscera in an instant. It wasn't exactly how he wanted to look upon exiting the Tower, but perhaps it would give off an intimidating impression.

A glance at his surroundings showed that he had been thrown into the middle of an endless rat tide that relentlessly tried to swarm him from every direction with furious abandon, and he was forced to fight them off, as their teeth seemed to be able to bite straight through the shield he had summoned. Even the leaves of **[Nature's Barrier]** were getting ripped apart and swallowed by the crazed beasts.

Thankfully, he only needed to fight for ten seconds before he was teleported out of the Tower of Eternity, where the Dao Apparition awaited.

The stone slate floated through the vast cosmos, just as it had since there was only darkness. Ancient lines marred its surface, every single groove and turn containing seemingly boundless profundity.

It spoke of the grand tenets of the universe, but very few had the ability to glean any of its secrets. So it continued its solitary journey toward eternity. It silently passed the grand warriors who traversed the stars, and not even ancient existences born from stardust itself could sense its presence.

But all journeys must end.

A remote and solitary planet shone like a green gem; the stele imperceptibly adjusted its trajectory to head toward it. It breached the atmosphere not long after, and it finally settled down in a secluded valley.

The stele settled down gently on the ground, as though it weren't encumbered by gravity in the slightest. However, a simple touch of the slate made the whole world tremble, causing earthquakes and extreme weather to ravage the whole planet for months before subsiding.

The primordial stone plaque sat in its valley undisturbed, but the planet slowly changed from the fundamental truths it espoused. War ravaged the continents, and enough blood was spilled that crops refused to grow in the soil. Countries rose and fell like the turn of the seasons, grand warriors becoming kings before turning to dust.

One day a one-armed man found himself in the valley. His army had been utterly defeated in battle, and he needed a safe harbor to hide from his enemies. He hadn't lost through lacking skill or tactics, but through inferior numbers. It filled him with irreconciliation that a fool had defeated him, but there was nothing to do about the situation. Reality wasn't fair.

There was something alluring about the valley, though, and the general soon forgot his anger as he scoured its nooks and crannies until he found the ancient stele. He was unable to take his eyes away from the patterns covering the surface, and it felt like they were the most beautiful things in the universe.

He sat down in front of it as though he was possessed, his eyes never leaving the stone for a second. The seasons passed as the man pondered upon the stele, silent and unmoving. Months turned to years, and years turned into millennia. Forces emerged and fell soon after, great triumphs and defeats replaced each other one by one on the continent.

However, no one ever visited the secluded valley. No one even spoke about the mountains that shielded it from the surrounding countries. It was as though it was separated from the world, a dimension of its own. It was just a man and a stone, and eons of silence.

A storm suddenly erupted in the valley, and the millennia of tranquility ended. The cultivator shuddered, as though he was brought out from a dream.

"War," he muttered as he got on his feet and looked to the stars.

War was the motor of progress, and blood was needed to turn the wheels of fate. He bowed to his master before walking over to take away the monument, as he felt there was still much to learn. But no matter how he strained and pulled, it wouldn't move the slightest. Cracks spread for tens of thousands of meters around him, but the monument refused to be moved.

The man sighed in disappointment, but there was no real anger in his eyes. There was just tranquility, and the burning fires of conflict. Increasingly powerful waves started to emanate from his body until he suddenly disappeared in a massive explosion. The next moment, he stood in space, looking down at the planet below.

His homeworld had once been without end in his mind, a battlefield whose scale beggared comprehension. But now the scene was too small, just a small ripple in the universe not worth mentioning. He needed a grander arena to progress further. The warlord waved his hand, and a moon was ripped from its trajectory and crushed into an unadorned lance of stone and steel.

Its materials were nothing special, but space still broke from the slightest movement of its tip.

He looked down at the planet, or rather the now-ruined valley where he had spent most of his life. If it wasn't meant for him any longer, then it might as well continue its journey toward the next fated one. Being stuck on this small corner was an insult to the grandeur it represented.

He swung the lance with one swift motion, and space trembled as a wave of unfettered destruction carved off a section of the planet, sending the continent spinning toward the endless black. The universe needed war, and war needed more than one general.

A stone slate floated through the vast cosmos, and it would continue doing so until there was only darkness. Ancient lines marred its surface, almost every single groove and turn containing seemingly boundless profundity.

WAR

"He made it to the 72nd level after all!" Balios said to his uncle. "He might even make it the whole way."

"He's almost out of time. There was less than a day remaining when he finally managed to pass the 71st level. Even if he defeats the guardian now, he will be exhausted and most likely wounded," Ubrok answered, but there were clear signs of hesitation on his face.

"Still," Balios whispered. "Perhaps we should stay out of this? Even Lord Beradan only made it to the 65th level. No matter if he passes or not, he's still someone we shouldn't get involved with. We're just sticking our necks out while the real Lords will reap the eventual rewards. The promised payment for assistance is not worth our lives."

"You are right. Let's back away," Ubrok finally relented. "We cannot get involved with the second coming of the Eveningtide Asura; our force will not be able to withstand the fallout no matter which side stands victorious. Let's back away and enjoy the apparition in peace. I might even be able to improve my Dao Seed after all these years."

Balios hurriedly nodded in agreement, and their group of eight started making their way back across the square. They weren't alone in choosing retreat over the quest reward and the private bounties provided by a few scions. The heated competition for the front-row seats of the square had quickly died down as Zac Piker had knocked down one level after another, eclipsing all the sector's geniuses for the past hundreds of thousands of years.

Things had calmed down as Mr. Piker, or rather Lord Piker, found himself stuck on the 71st level for almost a week, but the moment he'd reached the final level of the eighth floor, people started to worry. Some had already backed away, and there were not many willing to take the place of the deserters.

A million years had passed, but the lessons that the Eveningtide Asura engraved into the souls of the people of the Zecia Sector were still vividly remembered. Opening yourself and your family up to that level of vengeance was not worth the potential prize or remuneration. However, the group only managed to retreat a hundred meters before a commotion broke out across the square.

"Seventy-three!" a cultivator screamed with shock, causing some panic to finally appear even in the eyes of the staunchest of warriors.

A few still remained, clearly intent on betting it all, but most people started running for their lives. However, the fleeing cultivators stopped just a few seconds later because the Tower started releasing an immense pressure as waves of power radiated across the whole town, far beyond what anyone had ever seen before.

Greed fought with fear, but the allure was too great. Witnessing a ninth-floor apparition from a front-row seat was too enticing to give up, and the whole square sat down on the ground as if they were of one mind. Balios froze in hesitation, unsure whether he should flee further or join the others. The hesitation only lasted for a fraction of a second as he hurriedly took out his prepared mat as he gazed up at the sky.

The pressure emitted from the Tower kept accumulating, and fewer and fewer managed to hold their backs straight. A few even started bleeding from their ears from the immense aura of the Tower of Eternity. It was as though the Heavens themselves had descended upon the Base Town, standing in judgment.

But the pressure was suddenly gone, and Balios' eyes widened in shock as the Tower flickered before it suddenly disappeared as well. Taking its place was a stone plaque whose size was a match to the Tower of Eternity. Balios' eyes were drawn toward the mysterious scars covering its surface, and his mind turned blank the next moment.

It was only sometime later he woke up from his trance, but he was shocked to realize he couldn't remember a thing, not even how much time had passed. But something had changed inside his body, and it felt like his blood had been replaced by fire. The drums of war echoed in his mind, and his arms bulged as he subconsciously dragged out [Skylark], his azure blue Azrathir Spirit Tool.

The sword hummed in response, seemingly influenced by the odd state of its master.

The teleportation array lit up, and the whole square collectively held their breath as the man they had been waiting for the past day reappeared. However, this was not a hero's exit, but rather that of a beggar. The man's aura seemed strong and stable, but he was completely covered in still-wet blood. He was also decked out in odd jewelry that made him look like a robber who had absconded with a maiden's jewelry box.

His rough state wasn't surprising, as he had passed to the 73rd level at the last possible moment. He was probably putting up a brave front, and he quickly sat down and closed his eyes, enjoying the protection of the array. Zac Piker had overtaxed himself, forgetting that there was another trial waiting for him outside.

Balios' eyes were slowly turning bloodshot, and a wordless agreement passed between him and his uncle. The group no longer had any interest in retreating, but instead slowly made their way back toward their position.

"The quest! It changed!" another man suddenly shouted.

The flames of war were already drowning out most of Balios' thoughts, but curiosity overcame bloodthirst, and he slowly looked away from the blood-drenched man to instead check out the changes of the quest.

Fatebreaker (Unique, Limited): Kill Zac Piker within the time limit. Reward: Ten free levels in the Tower of Eternity.
[00:01:00]

Balios' eyes threatened to pop out of their sockets as he read the reward. What was going on? If the previous reward had been unprecedented, then the current one was beyond comprehension. Had Lord

Piker spent his whole climb cursing the Heavens, and this was his retribution?

The whole square was like a kettle that threatened to boil over at any second, and Balios' eyes were locked on the humanoid treasure trove. A few minutes passed, and Balios almost lashed out at his neighbors in a bloodthirsty rage, his muscles shuddering as he tried to keep his impulses in check.

But finally, the man stood up and turned toward the square.

"I–" Lord Piker said, but he stopped when the protective array suddenly winked out like it just ran out of power.

Everyone gaped in incomprehension for a second, but chaos took hold of the square the next moment.

Zac appeared on the teleportation array, and he breathed out in relief when he saw that the defensive array was still up and running. He needed to quickly consolidate his gains, so he sat down on the ground after nodding at Ogras and Galau, who were mutely staring at him with eyes as wide as saucers.

He was relieved to see that all the defensive treasures he had equipped before exiting were still there, as was the valuable Spatial Ring that had belonged to the mentalist. He was pretty certain at this point that all the loot he had snatched from other climbers was still in his possession, though the same probably didn't hold true for the other valuables he'd picked up during the climb.

The other two didn't say a word as Zac closed his eyes, and he could understand their stunned expressions.

Not even he had really expected to pass the seventh floor, let alone the eighth. But all that could wait until later, as he needed to focus on the vision he had just witnessed. It felt as though he had sat right next to that man for tens of thousands of years, appreciating the stone stele and its mysteries. Just looking at it had filled him with a desire for conquest, a bit like when he used [Hatchetman's Rage].

The runes spoke of the survival of the fittest, about the need for conflict. Through battle, the weaker sides would get cleansed, or "weakness leaving the hive" as the Zhix would call it. The strong would get stronger, and the universe would benefit as a whole. It was evolution, continuous betterment by discarding what didn't perform.

Zac wasn't sure what concept the rune represented, but he felt that it was either a Dao of Conflict or a Dao of War. The man in the vision had leaned toward the latter, but he had also been colored by his past experiences as a general. The man had only grasped a snippet of the truths the stele contained, but that part alone had turned him into a terrifying powerhouse that made him break through multiple grades without any other assistance.

The main takeaway for Zac was the connection between war and creation; war always had a purpose. It might be held to protect your beliefs or to punish evil. War might erupt over resources, or to take out a hated enemy. It might just simply be the pursuit of strength. Purpose and conviction were what separated a warrior and a beast or a madman.

This meant that the concept engraved upon the stele wasn't based on Oblivion, as it was not mindless destruction. It was creation through destruction, where you built your future through conflict. It felt like one of the most fundamental fusions of the two peak concepts after looking at the ancient runes, but the Dao Fragment it resonated with most was his Fragment of the Axe. Perhaps all weapon-related Daos were children of the Dao of War.

A swing empowered by your conviction would move faster and hit harder than an empty attack. As long as he fought for what he believed in, he would be able to push himself much further than if he fought with hesitation or reluctance in his heart. He had combined many aspects of heaviness and sharpness into the Fragment of the Axe, such as sharpness through speed and heaviness from momentum.

But he now added the reason for swinging his axe into his Dao.

Energy surged around him as he felt his insight coalesce, and his body was flush with power in an instant. He opened his eyes and activated his Dao screen to see the result, and he was extremely satisfied with what he saw.

Fragment of the Axe (Middle): All attributes +20, Strength +225, Dexterity +120, Endurance +15, Wisdom +50. Effectiveness of Strength +10%.

It was a massive boost, though Zac looked at the additional all attributes with mixed emotions. He had hoped to maintain his massive lead in Luck against general cultivators, but it looked like deep insights into the Dao would be able to bridge some of the gap. Of course, he would still maintain a commanding lead thanks to his large number of titles that improved upon his base Luck.

Perhaps he shouldn't be too surprised about the increased Luck stemming from a deeper understanding of the Dao. Gaining Dao Seeds and Dao Fragments was just forming a stronger connection with the heavens, which in turn should improve one's fate.

The evolution of his Fragment of the Axe wasn't the only thing that he had gained from the vision. The stone stele had almost been all-encompassing, and he felt like he had created a foundation for improving both his other Fragments as well. Both the Fragment of the Coffin and the Fragment of the Bodhi were at the lowest possible level until now, but Zac now had something to build upon when he came back.

Taking the first step forward toward an upgrade had always been the hardest for him, but upgrading the two Fragments was only a matter of time now. It wasn't to the point that he felt one week of meditation would do the trick, but he still believed that he would be able to take the next step within a few months even if he didn't enter any life-and-death battles.

Unfortunately, he couldn't revel in his latest gains at the moment, as there were some pressing issues to deal with.

"Are you okay?" Ogras asked with a hoarse voice as Zac stood up, and Zac noted a slightly manic look in the eyes behind the mask he wore to cover his features.

"Not my blood." Zac shrugged. "I'm in perfect condition. I killed the guardian over twelve hours ago. What's going on?"

"People started to leave, but then the apparition appeared, and the quest changed. We're in deep shit," Ogras growled.

"It changed?" Zac exclaimed with shock. "I'll deal with this. Stay behind me if I can't convince them to back away. I'll activate a defensive treasure I found."

He turned toward the square, and he immediately understood what Ogras meant. The field in front of the Tower was only half-filled with cultivators from all sorts of Races, but people were rushing toward the center square from every direction.

"I–" Zac said with a carrying voice, but he was cut short as the shield in front of him suddenly disappeared.

His mind blanked out as he found himself exposed to a whole army waiting to kill him. He had hoped to work out a diplomatic resolution, but he realized that was a fool's dream as a collective roar spread across the square. His eyes widened in alarm, and his danger sense was already going off the charts.

The Spectral Forest of [Hatchetman's Spirit] appeared in an instant, and [Nature's Barrier] followed right after. He infused the Fragment of the Bodhi into the leaves without hesitation and spread it to cover his two companions as well. The two of them backed away as far as they possibly could, each of them erecting a few layers of defenses of their own.

He didn't understand what was going on. It felt like he and the System had struck an accord earlier, and it had even gone so far as to help him out by directly speaking to him. But then it followed it up with dialing up the bounty on his head to the point that it made these people froth at the mouth.

Was the System unhappy with his choice?

MAN VERSUS WORLD

Over a hundred attacks teeming with power soared toward him, and the whole sky was shrouded by the multifarious display. Zac's fractal leaves condensed to cover a smaller area to create more layers of defense, but the defenses were quickly ripped to shreds by the onslaught.

Zac was far stronger than anyone here, but the attackers weren't weaklings by any means. This was a low-grade sector, but everyone present was still the strongest of a generation, all intent on taking him out. There was only so much [Nature's Barrier] could block before the leaves were exhausted, and he knew that he couldn't just sit around like a target dummy.

[Verun's Bite] keened with delight as Zac's arm was almost turning into a blur. One fractal blade after another radiating terrifying energy ripped into the storm of attacks, crushing most of them without even needing to clash. The extreme power that radiated from the Middle-stage Dao Fragment was enough to utterly dominate the weaker strikes, and they were ripped into swirls of Cosmic Energy.

However, if each of his fractal blades was like a powerful elephant, then the weaker attacks were like a sea of rabid hyenas that slowly managed to whittle them down. There were just too many attackers, and he felt his waves of fractal edges slowly getting pushed back as more and more cultivators joined the fight.

It was a bit disappointing not to be able to utterly crush his enemies with sheer might, but it was still a massive show of force that he could almost create a stalemate when exchanging blows with hundreds of the top geniuses of the sector. He also knew that it was a testament to just how powerful a Mid-grade Dao Fragment was.

His weapon was just average if you discounted the uncommonly high spirituality of the Tool Spirit, and [Chop] was as basic a skill as they came. However, each blade still managed to crush a dozen beautiful and intricate skills that sailed toward him before they ran out of steam. Of course, if he didn't do something soon, he might get himself or his two companions hurt.

However, Zac was prepared for exactly this kind of worst-case scenario, and Cosmic Energy streamed toward his neck.

Mysterious fluctuations spread out from his position the next second as a massive eye emerged out of the void. It was one of the treasures he had taken from the mentalist's Spatial Ring, a necklace with an eye that actually seemed alive. The conjured eye didn't move, but it rather just stared at the sea of cultivators and the incoming attacks. A mystic ray of blue light spread out, and the attacks cracked in an instant, leaving not a single one intact.

Dozens of warriors fell back with blood pouring from their eyes, their souls definitely hurt by the clash. It caused a lull in the battle, and Zac figured this was his last chance to stop the madness before it got out of hand.

"Stop now, and I won't cause any trouble for you or your clans," Zac roared at the top of his lungs. "But I will kill everyone who stays behind, no matter Heritage or affiliation! This is your only warning!"

His voice was filled with power, and the air shuddered around him as his blood-drenched aura was unleashed to its fullest. He hoped to wake these people up from their greed-fueled battle fervor. However, the effect of his words and his aura was far worse than he anticipated, and not a single one seemed willing to back down.

It was like they had eaten stimulants or some sort of berserking pill.

A few had been killed or incapacitated by the massive eye, but new warriors filled the ranks, and Zac could see that the streets were filling up with people who wanted to join the chaos. Just defending wouldn't cut it, and he needed to go with Ogras' idea. Kill a few chickens to scare the monkeys, as the demon called it.

Another defensive treasure cracked on his hand, causing a shimmering fractal made from churning waters to appear in the air. Torrential typhoons shot toward the cultivators and swallowed up even more attacks, but a few still slipped through and slammed into his newly formed leaves. The storms weren't as effective as the mysterious eye in pushing back the attackers, but it gave Zac enough time to charge up [Deforestation].

Zac was going all out from the start. If the first swing wouldn't convince them to back off, then there was a tsunami of flames waiting. If people still hadn't managed to curb their greed, he would release the [Axe of Desolation] and end the battle altogether. The massive woodcutter's axe materialized above him, and Zac immediately initiated the [Axe of Felling].

You could say that he had started this battle with this very attack just before he was forced to flee into the Tower, and he would end it the same way.

"Stop its activation!" a shout echoed out across the square, and Zac was suddenly covered in uncomfortable energy that made the Cosmic Energy in his body feel slow and listless.

He quickly activated the first defensive charge of [Hatchetman's Spirit], but his eyes widened when the attack passed right through the emerald shield and drilled into his chest.

"It's a curse, a rare type of mental attack!" Galau screamed from behind. "You can break it by force or treasures; look inward!"

Zac's eyes lit up, and he looked inside, allowing him to spot crude runes covering the skill fractal for [Deforestation]. He rotated a storm of Cosmic Energy to slam into it, and three forceful pushes cracked it wide open. It caused light internal bleeding as well, but it wasn't a big deal for someone like Zac.

However, that was just the first of dozens attempts to tie down the massive axe in the sky. It was covered in ten layers of restrictive arrays as well, and no matter how hard Zac struggled, he wasn't able to move his arm forward. It was a type of counter to his attacks he had never seen before, and he couldn't figure out any quick fix to launch the skill.

His axe was already tied up in the swing, making it impossible to send out any fractal attacks to destroy the restrictions. [Nature's Punishment] was liable to destroy the axe as well, not that Zac was able to unleash both the attacks at the same time. Ogras seemed to have understood the issue, as a beam of darkness slammed into the restrictions from behind, but only the outermost of the many layers of restrictions were broken.

"Don't worry," Zac said as he looked back. "I'll deal with this."

He felt thankful that the demon was willing to stick his neck out in a messy situation like this, but Ogras was honestly more of a liability than an asset at this moment unless he had completely transformed during the time since they'd parted ways in the Tower. He could only activate yet another of the onetime treasures, and he felt a large chunk of Cosmic Energy leave his body as a thousand golden swords shot toward the restrictions around the [Axe of Felling].

The restrictions were ripped to pieces before the swords continued toward the mob and caused widespread carnage as the summoned weapons slipped straight past hastily erected shields and into their bodies. However, the [Axe of Felling] was already dissipating, and Zac had lost his connection to the fractal axe. Nothing happened as Zac swung [Verun's Bite] over and over until the massive woodcutter's axe dissipated.

Zac growled with annoyance and tried to resummon the axe, but he was shocked to find that the skill wouldn't activate. It seemed that [Deforestation] had been put on its cooldown since the first swing had technically been initiated. Zac didn't even know that an outcome like this was possible, and he scrambled for new ideas to deal with the mob and their next salvo of attacks.

Zac activated another one of the treasures, an offensively geared ring that released an invisible force that made the whole square twist and bend. Dozens fell to their knees screaming, their eyes and ears bleeding as they clutched their heads. It looked like the mentalist had been in possession of multiple mental attack treasures in addition to her terrifying skills.

The attack gave Zac a short breather, and he turned toward his two companions, who were still hiding in the back.

"How do I defend against more curses?" Zac asked.

Galau only hesitated for a short moment before he took out a small doll and threw it over to Zac.

"Pour some energy into this. It will take your place. But curses are very hard to plant when the target is anticipating it," the merchant hurriedly said as his eyes darted back and forth in search of any lurking threat. "You can also guard your fractals with your Daos if they try it again."

Zac nodded in thanks before he turned back toward the enemies. Losing **[Deforestation]** to such a trick was a huge blow, but he wasn't out of options just yet. Cosmic Energy surged into his hand instead, and the sky above him cracked.

He also activated **[Hatchetman's Rage]** for good measure, as he was confident that the Splinter was in no condition to cause any trouble at the moment. The leaves surrounding him suddenly lost the beautiful fractals covering their surface as the wooden hand emerged from its separate dimension. Zac needed to make this one count, so he chose to infuse the attack with the Fragment of the Bodhi rather than his defensive canopy.

However, the wooden hand barely had time to move more than ten meters before it was almost blasted to pieces by three beams of light that converged right at its position. Zac endured the pain in his own hand and looked around, realizing that three attackers were holding identical mirrors covered in fractals. It was no doubt an array, and if there was one, there were bound to be more arrays waiting to be activated.

A shockwave spread out from his original position as he flashed forward, two massive avatars appearing in an instant as a bracer on each of his arms cracked. One formed a vast cloud of darkness that covered the sky. Everything that entered it disappeared, including the beams of light. The other was a kneeling warrior without features, and he enclosed Ogras and Galau in a protective embrace.

The second treasure was activated to prevent the attackers from taking his two companions hostage in case he needed to enter a melee with the mob, whereas the first one would let him complete his skill. The vast clouds allowed the hand to move forward shrouded in darkness, and it quietly managed to erect its emerald array above the chaotic army.

However, its activation was by no means uncontested, as over twenty avatars and powerful attacks rose to meet it.

The combined power of the dozen elite warriors was barely able to hold back the descent of the punishment, and Zac found it difficult to make any headway. Zac was considering whether he should try to cause some chaos by jumping into the fray or perhaps weaken their coordination with another treasure.

Finally, he also decided to make a move himself. It would put Ogras and Galau at some risk, but he felt he needed his hands to get a bit bloodied if he wanted to end this thing. Perhaps the mob thought he kept using treasures because he wasn't actually that strong, which emboldened them to keep going. It would put him in harm's way of his own punishment, but he was durable enough to withstand some friendly fire.

He was just about to flash forward with **[Loamwalker]** when a group of cultivators suddenly appeared out of nowhere at the front of the army. Most of them radiated a powerful aura that could almost match the weaker warriors in the Battle of Fates, and Zac knew that the true elites of the sector had made their move.

Zac wasn't worried in the slightest, rather, the opposite. He believed if he managed to take out these people, then any cohesion in the army would crumble, and he would only need to defend against some weaklings for another minute to make it out alive. Zac directly charged at the quintet, but he didn't have time to move before each of them produced a different treasure in their hands.

"Four Gates!" one of the men shouted, and one massive doorway appeared in each direction around Zac.

The doors cracked open, and four densely inscribed hands emerged, each one forming a different seal. Zac noticed there was a group of warriors behind the man who had created a War Array to support the summoning, but he didn't have a chance to even attack before he was beset by a series of hallucinations.

Not only that, it felt like the world was twisted and inverted. He saw that his hand moved when he tried to walk, and the world was suddenly upside down. It was like all his wires had been crossed, and just making the smallest movement needed great focus. Eating one of the mental pills and cracking another defensive treasure did alleviate the symptoms somewhat, but it was still a struggle to understand what was going on around him.

Zac knew he would have been able to improve the situation by infusing **[Mental Fortress]** with the Fragment of the Bodhi rather than Fragment of the Coffin, but the still-struggling **[Nature's Punishment]** would be destroyed if it lost its Dao empowerment. He really needed to take out these five new arrivals; he arduously split his attention from the wooden hand to shoot out a series of fractal blades toward the group.

"Six Directions!" a second cultivator shouted with a shaky voice as Zac launched his attacks, and six elongated fractals formed a circle in the sky.

Zac growled in annoyance when he saw that he had been trapped by a shield that blocked his strikes with only the smallest of cracks forming, and he realized that it might be even sturdier than the cage he created with **[Profane Seal]**.

But these people would soon understand he wasn't someone they could trap so easily.

RESTRAINED

Zac realized that breaking through the thick shield would be difficult from the outside, but the wooden hand was already presiding above the army outside the shield. He needed to create an opportunity to let the punishment descend, which would hopefully ruin the array as well. He had a few options, but he ultimately chose to utilize one of the rings on his finger, which was part of his rapidly diminishing stock of offensive treasures from the mentalist.

He hoped that the mental attack would be able to breach the Six Direction's shield, as it seemed physical in nature. It was unlikely they had prepared mental defenses after his display upon entering the Tower, after all. The ring on his finger cracked, and Zac breathed out in relief when he saw the almost imperceptible wave slip through minute cracks between the six fractals and descend on the army.

Another burst of Cosmic Energy entered Zac's body as several cultivators instantly got their souls crushed, and many of the skills blocking [Nature's Punishment] failed as warriors were forced to withstand a massive trauma to their souls. It seemed as though the group of five in the front were protected by some unknown means, and they didn't even flinch as the wave passed them by.

The offensive treasure had fulfilled its purpose as the avatars that blocked [Nature's Punishment] lost their vigor in an instant, and a massive branch finally managed to emerge from the emerald fractal in the sky. Chaotic storms of Cosmic Energy caused massive waves in the sky as warriors threw out defensive treasures and all sorts of talismans as a last-ditch effort, but everything was pushed aside or crushed as the massive branch descended.

Only at the last moment was the wooden punishment stopped by a prismatic shield that reminded Zac of a soap bubble. Zac kept infusing the skill with more and more power, and he felt like he was just missing a little bit to break the last line of defenses. One cultivator after another fell beneath the shield as they were overtaxed by the pressure, but the replacements were seemingly endless.

Zac suddenly had an idea, and he took out an impressive-looking talisman from his Spatial Ring and threw it toward the army with a roar. The eyes of quite a few warriors widened in alarm, and they quickly refocused their efforts to defend their minds from yet another concussive wave. The army had already been beset by two Peak-grade soul-harming arrays, and many were probably hanging on by a thread.

However, no mental attack emerged as the talisman cracked in front of the prismatic shield. Instead, a weak shield sprang up and covered a patch of dirt.

The prismatic shield burst apart the next moment, and the wooden finger headed right toward the army with world-ending force. The branch slammed into the large square cobblestones of the square like the finger of an angry god, and the whole area shook and heaved as Zac was inundated in a massive amount of Cosmic Energy. At least fifty people had died from the initial attack, and even more sported grisly wounds from the shockwave.

However, the attack wasn't over just yet.

Hundreds of sharp branches grew out of the tree and stabbed everything in its surroundings, causing another wave of carnage. It was just like when the spectral chains of [Profane Seal] targeted the living inside its cage, and desolate cries echoed across the core area of Base Town as one cultivator after another was impaled.

Only then did the emerald array in the air dissipate while Zac lost his mental connection to the tree. It remained in the square, though, its branches filled with the unmoving bodies of dozens of fallen warriors. It had turned into a twisted monument drenched in the blood of the elites of the sector, and hopefully, it would serve as a reminder to choose life over wealth for anyone who had any ideas about Zac.

Unfortunately, it seemed as though the group maintaining the two powerful arrays around him had come prepared, and another shield protected them from the fallout from **[Nature's Punishment]** as they prepared their next moves. It was becoming increasingly apparent that this group of five was the largest threat unless there were even stronger people lying in wait in one of the palaces that lined the square.

"Heaven's Punishment!" "Hell Suppression!" two more cultivators shouted in unison as Zac scrambled for a way to break the stalemate, leaving only the young man in the middle of the group of five unoccupied.

A vast array in an unblemished white appeared in the sky, and it felt like his body was slowly being ground to dust just by being covered in its light. Zac wanted to get out of the way, but a pitch-black array suddenly covered the ground he stood on, and he helplessly fell down onto the cobblestones from an immense pressure.

Zac's whole body was immobilized by an almost unbearable weight, and the whole square around him cracked even though it was made from some mysterious material that hadn't even scarred until he brought out **[Nature's Punishment]**. The four arrays were no doubt at the absolute peak of what could be brought to the Base Town, and they had even formed a system to create an even stronger effect.

Just moving his arms was a struggle, and Zac started to worry for the first time as he saw the leader of the group prepare what would no doubt be the finale. He considered activating another defensive treasure preemptively, but he quickly decided against it. He was running low on Cosmic Energy by this point, and each activation took a good chunk of his reserves. He'd only activate another talisman if he saw a lethal attack coming.

He was also out of offensive treasures, leaving him unable to deal with any of the four arrays restricting him. He was almost out of options, and he knew he would have to pay a price to deal with this situation. However, he was unwilling to keep his head bowed down to some warriors relying on superior numbers.

He remembered the feelings of irreconciliation of the general in his vision, the frustration of being bested not by skills or hard work, but by being overwhelmed by sheer numbers. He would have done well to remember that general's painful lesson, but he had walked into this fight with a feeling of superiority, that numbers were irrelevant to his superior might.

But he had been met with ingenious tactics and boundless ferocity, proving that not even someone who had stood shoulder to shoulder with the elites of the Multiverse was safe. Death could come at any time, from the most unlikely of perpetrators.

Veins wiggled beneath his skin across his body as he forced himself back on his knees. The pressure was terrifying, but he was slowly adapting to it with the help of his insights into the Dao of Heaviness. Thin layers of skin were peeling off from his face and arms before rising toward the array above like he was spontaneously falling apart, but he ignored the pain as his wild eyes were trained at the group of warriors.

The whole shield shuddered as Zac flashed forward and cut into it with [Verun's Bite], the weapon radiating sanguine light that painted the group red. The woman controlling the array paled from the backlash, forced to take a step back. It did hold against his assault, but Zac was just getting started.

Power and rage coursed through his veins as he slammed one time after another, each strike containing enough force to split mountains. His whole body creaked and groaned from the pressure, and wounds were opening up from just moving about, but he kept swinging his axe with relentless ferocity.

The woman controlling the Six Directions array was empowered by a retinue running a War Array, but the supportive cultivators fell down with bleeding orifices as they were being overtaxed. Cracks started spreading across the shimmering wall, and just a bit would be enough to break through and reach these people.

As long as he got into melee range, things would be over, as no one here was his match in such close proximity.

Zac's eyes were filled with blood from the immense pressure from the combination of the suppressive array and [Hatchetman's Rage], but the leader of the five looked into his eyes with equanimity as he took out a large box and pointed it toward Zac. Zac's danger sense screamed for him to move, but he first sent a mental command into his axe.

A swirl of mysterious energies slipped through the cracks Zac had caused in the shield, and the primordial beast appeared in all its glory a second later. Zac wasn't the only one who had undergone a drastic change during the climb; Verun had received its own share of opportunities.

The beast was actually a bit smaller compared to before, but it was more condensed, more corporeal. It was still five meters long and reached almost three meters into the air, making it a massive beast compared to anything that had lived on Earth at least. Its huge maw with its gnarly fangs looked the same as before, but the number of eyes had actually increased on its head.

It now had two sets of eyes, all four of them seemingly moving independently of each other as they looked for targets. Swirls of blood also slowly rotated around its paws, and Zac sensed a hint of the dragon's primordial aura from the Tool Spirit. It released an earth-shattering roar after having finally being allowed to make an appearance, and it ferociously pounced on the cultivators in the square.

Zac had initially wanted to force his way out of the shield, but he knew enough to listen to his danger sense. So he jumped back to avoid whatever the leader had planned. He didn't know what was inside that box, but it felt extremely dangerous, even to him.

Being forced to back off at this critical juncture was a disappointment, but the shield was seriously weakened, and its controller seemed to be running out of steam. Verun was also causing mass panic among the cultivators outside, and together with the mass casualties from [Nature's Punishment], he pretty much only had the five elites and their retinues to worry about. And he still had something that could easily turn the tide.

Zac was still a bit hesitant, though, as he took out the rusty sword from his Spatial Ring.

However, he had witnessed the power of the sinister weapon himself during the Battle of Fates. That swordsman had been able to utterly destroy [Nature's Punishment] with the help of this cursed weapon, and if Zac hadn't deactivated his skill in time, he might even have lost his hand. It was his best option to end things in one go, especially now that the rabble had been mostly routed with the help of the massive tree's descent.

Besides, he didn't want to waste any more of the mentalist's jewelry. He would have wasted too many treasures before even returning to Earth if he continued like this, and those things might be crucial in the upcoming fights against the Dominators and the Undead Empire. Zac gripped the dried-out leather of the hilt, and his wounds opened all over his arm as he forcibly started dragging it out of its scabbard.

Blood fell on the ground like rain, and Zac roared into the sky as a storm of voices entered his mind. Odd veins started traveling up his arm from his sword as well, like the weapon was trying to fuse with his body. Even the exhausted Remnants shuddered from the intrusion into his mind, but they weren't in any condition to affect the course of events.

Zac suppressed the voices with everything he had as he strained to finish the attack quicker.

It almost felt like he was trying to complete the third swing of [Deforestation] by unsheathing the blade, and a huge chunk of his remaining Cosmic Energy was swallowed by the sword in an instant. But Zac didn't care, as he felt that a horrible power was brewing within the sword, and his arm bulged as he finally managed to drag out the reluctant weapon before the veins could spread above his elbow.

A piercing wail echoed across the square, and Zac's vision doubled from the mental shock, but he still swung the weapon in a wide arc toward the cultivators running the arrays. He wasn't sure whether there was a trick to using the weapon, so he tried to mimic the form of the swordsman as best he could remember.

The familiar white half-moon thankfully appeared, but it was covered in the same red pulsating veins as those snaking up along his arm. The strike had felt like a pure sword strike when the lanky swordsman used the weapon back on the seventh floor, but now it really felt like something an unorthodox cultivator would use. It hadn't weakened the power of the strike, but rather, the opposite.

Zac moved his mental energy and started infusing the blade with the Fragment of the Axe for good measure. Zac got a rabid pushback from the weapon, but Zac growled and crammed it in, no matter what the crazy voices were screaming. The blade shuddered, and a few cracks appeared, but it quickly mended and continued to expand as it picked up more and more speed as it rushed toward the shield, now empowered with Zac's most destructive Dao.

It was like the edge was tapping an unceasing fount of power, and was soon so large that the whole army would be hit if it managed to break out from its cage. Most of the surviving warriors had already started running for their lives after realizing their attacks passed straight through Verun's body, and seeing the corrupted half-moon broke the will of the few remaining cultivators hoping to fish in muddy waters.

Only the five cultivators stood their ground, and they seemed to have some confidence in the layers of restrictions they had superimposed on the square.

"Breath of Cosmos!" the leader shouted, and he finally opened the box that he had held in his arms until now.

A cloud of stardust emerged from the chest, and it drifted straight through the shield and toward the incoming attack. The whole blade was soon covered in a glistening cloud, and it looked like a beautiful nebula. The aura of madness that the half-moon emitted was completely swallowed by the dust, and Zac sensed that the cloud was slowly grinding it down.

However, Zac's attack pushed forward with undeniable intractability, and it was like the mysterious cloud that had caused such a strong reaction in Zac's mind only managed to nip at its heels. The leader looked extremely surprised at the turn of events before some worry started to show on his face.

"Release your greatest attacks!" the leader shouted as Cosmic Energy started to surge around his body.

"This is not what we agreed upon!" another of the five retorted. "You guaranteed that the [Five Dimensional Seal] would restrain him! Does this look restrained to you?!"

53

CLASHING FATES

The man who had spoken up wasn't the only one who looked at the leader with fear-induced anger, but another two of them seemed to be ready to leave then and there.

"I'll increase the compensation. Besides, he is still restrained even if he's not incapacitated. We just need to break this attack and we'll have won," the man said.

The man looked unreconciled, but he still complied, and he took out a green finger from his Spatial Tool and swallowed it. The next moment, he swelled over five times in size while an enormous cauldron appeared behind him, and he launched a punch that shuddered with power toward Zac. The attack caused a cascading series of putrid explosions to rock the area, and a few unlucky cultivators who had been maimed from the fight earlier were consumed as well, turning into brittle skeletons in an instant.

The four elites followed suit, and all of them either transformed from an ultimate skill or caused an avatar to appear behind their backs. One of them seemed to be a lightning cultivator, and another summoned a beast that looked even more dangerous than Verun. The Tool Spirit roared in defiance, but it still stayed away from the five due to Zac's command and kept routing the stragglers.

Zac was a bit out of it from the increasingly intrusive screams emerging from the tattered sword, but he could still hear their discussion. He was initially confused just who these five people were, as they were of mixed Races and dressed completely differently. It didn't seem like they belonged to the same force, and this notion was only reinforced when they released their ultimate skills.

From the conversation, it looked like a group of elites had decided to band together in order to incapacitate him. Zac guessed they had kept their aces in hopes that they would be able to snatch the final prize the moment he was lying within the arrays, unable to even lift a finger.

The two sides clashed, and it felt like the world had frozen before cataclysmic waves of attuned energies spread in all directions, drowning the whole square in color. There was a very clear divide in the sky, with Zac's side being white with red streaks, and the other half being a mix of colors representing the five elites.

It looked like there was a stalemate taking place, but Zac knew things weren't that simple. His attack was one single wave of unadulterated power, whereas the other side was a mostly disjointed mix. It was only a matter of time before his attack would break through, at which point things would go south very quickly for his enemies.

The leader of the group seemed to have realized what was going to happen as well, and he immediately took action. However, he neither tried another counter nor tried to run away, but instead, he slapped a talisman onto the back of the woman next to him, the cultivator responsible for the "Six Directions Array."

She disappeared in a puff, leaving the others flabbergasted.

Their side had already been on the losing end of the confrontation, and they had suddenly lost a fifth of their power along with the powerful shield protecting them. The four remaining attacks crumbled in an instant, and the half-moon seized the opportunity and pushed forward with a final leap of madness.

One of the masters tried to run, but it seemed as though he was bogged down in a quagmire. He released a soundless scream as the half-moon bisected him, but Zac's brows furrowed when he saw that the blade actually seemed to swallow the man. The red veins crept out from the edge and latched on to the cultivator, and his body was drained in an instant.

Most of the retinues that infused the five through War Arrays met the same fate, and only the leader of the quintet managed to hold on by expending a series of defensive treasures. Zac finally couldn't take the strain from holding the sword any longer, forcing him to put away the cursed thing, which caused the half-moon to disappear after releasing a wail of discontent.

Zac flashed forward the next moment, and he activated the first fractal of [Verun's Bite] again, intending to end things then and there. The mob of cultivators was mostly dealt with, but as long as the man who had organized the assault was alive, he wouldn't feel safe. He was in front of the leader in an instant, and his axe shone with a sanguine glow as it fell toward his head.

However, before Zac's attack had a chance to connect, a necklace lit the man up, and Zac felt an all-consuming pain as the defensive charge of [Hatchetman's Spirit] crumbled in an instant. His chest had been turned into a bloody mess yet again, and it was almost as bad as yesterday when he'd gotten punched by the Technocrat captain.

Thankfully, Zac still possessed the final energies that the Shard of Creation had released during its rampage, and he quickly urged it to re-form his torso before he passed out. It almost looked like time went in reverse as his body re-formed in an instant, but the fact that his robes were broken and tattered was proof that he had been at death's door just a second ago.

The richly dressed youth gaped in shock and dismay as Zac's axe bit into his body. The richly decked man tried to push the axe-head out of his body, but Zac utterly overpowered him as he released a storm of rampant energies that turned the man's insides into a mess.

He somehow managed to stay alive, and their eyes met as the man clung to life.

"I'm sorry. You needed to die for my dream to come true. My ending is well deserved." The cultivator weakly smiled before his volume rose to be heard across the square. "I risked everything for power, but I failed. My ending has no relation with my clan."

Zac didn't say anything, and the man died just a few seconds later. A lot of murmurs erupted from the cultivators who had spectated the battle from a safe distance, and a lot of people seemed to be recording the events into information crystals.

Being recorded was pretty much expected, so he didn't care, but he rather readied his still bloody axe for any follow-up attacks. As expected, his mind suddenly felt a pang of danger, and he quickly turned around as **[Everlasting]** appeared on his arm.

However, the assassin who had wanted to take advantage of the moment Zac let his guard down found himself impaled on a black spear as Ogras appeared out of his shadows. A burst of shadows ripped the man to pieces, and the demon walked up next to Zac as his face dripped with blood.

"It's over!" the demon shouted. "The quest is over, and Lord Piker has withstood the Trial of the Ruthless Heavens. We understand the allure of the reward and the effect of the apparition, so we'll let all enmities stay behind and dissipate in Base Town as we leave. But any further attempts on our lives here or out in the open world will be met with a vengeance of extreme proportions. If not today, then later."

A snort escaped from Zac's nose even if he understood the severity of the situation. It was just like Ogras, appearing at the last moment, looking like a heroic defender of justice with his spear pointed at the skies. Zac knew full well that the demon was nowhere near as confident as he wanted to appear, but it was for the best that Ogras dealt with the fallout.

Zac naturally understood what Ogras was doing. He was trying to minimize potential threats that could crop up in the future. They already had the Zethaya, Tsarun Clan, and the Great Redeemer to worry about, and causing a grudge with dozens of more families would do neither him nor Earth any good.

He could only hope that the forces of the sector would take the death of their scions in stride. A few people dying should barely be noticeable for these huge forces, as thousands died every day in their struggle to become stronger. Such was the life of a cultivator.

If that wasn't enough, the various forces would hopefully restrain themselves out of fear of what he might become in the future. He had reached the ninth floor, something that only had happened once in recent memory, which should be a huge indicator of great potential for the people in this sector.

Thankfully, it looked like no one wanted to fight any longer. Perhaps it was because the quest had ended, or perhaps it was because he was still essentially unscathed while the bodies of his enemies littered the whole square. The corpse tree rising almost fifty meters into the air was also a poignant warning to anyone arriving late.

It was a relief, as he was currently pretty exhausted. Along with the backlash from activating [Hatchetman's Rage], he wouldn't even be able to muster half his power right now. But there was one thing that cut through the fatigue: greed. Just as there were bodies strewn everywhere across the field, so were there Spirit Tools and Cosmos Sacks.

His eyes turned to the man lying in front of him, the presumptive leader of the other side. He walked over toward the corpse and bent down to take the Spatial Ring on his finger. However, he stopped when he saw a man from the sidelines take a few steps toward him.

"Ah, Lord Piker, I mean no disrespect. But you might not want to take that man's possessions," a man hesitantly spoke up from the distance. "That is Yeorav Dravorak, of the Dravorak Dynasty. You might want to let them take his body and belongings back."

Zac looked down at the body in front of him without a change in expression, but some waves still rose in his heart. Was this the brother of Reoluv, the man whose Tower Apparition had given him the Fragment of the Coffin, and the greatest genius in the sector for thousands of years? And more importantly, the Dravorak Dynasty was a peak force in the sector. How would they respond to one of their princes dying?

Was this why the man had spoken up right before his death?

But at the same time, wasn't it too late by now for a show of respect? If the Dravorak wanted revenge, would him giving back the man's body make any difference? If this had been inside the Tower or in the wild, then Zac would definitely have looted the body before destroying it, but this had taken place in front of hundreds of people.

He wasn't sure what the custom was regarding this, and he glanced at the demon for assistance.

"The young prince was an honorable man, facing his fate with equanimity," Ogras said. "His companions can claim him and his belongings. However, that only goes for the young prince. The rest bet their lives for power and wealth, and their possessions are Lord Piker's rightful claim for standing victorious. Everyone is free to claim the bodies of the deceased, to give them their final rites."

Zac glanced at the expressions of those standing in the distance, and from the looks of it, the demon's way of dealing with things wasn't anything uncommon. However, his eyes widened when he saw the woman whom he had just fought return. Her eyes were bloodshot as she looked down at Yeorav Dravorak before her eyes moved to meet Zac's.

Zac felt the demon next to him tense up, gearing up for a battle, but Zac stopped him with a shake of his head.

"I am sorry. I–" she said before she looked down again with a shake of her head. "I am sorry."

She bent down and gingerly picked up the body of Yeorav before she slowly walked away from the square with the man in her arms. Zac's eyes followed the woman's lonely back as she carried the body to the edge of the square before she squatted down. It didn't look like she was planning on avenging him or anything, but rather that she seemed at a loss of what to do next.

Zac only shook his head with some heaviness.

It sounded like that man had desperately needed to get the reward for taking him out, to the point that he had been willing to die for it. That didn't really make him evil, but rather someone out of options. Zac knew the feeling all too well, having been forced to make decisions that went against his conscience to protect those around him.

Ogras would probably have killed the lover as well if they hadn't been inside the Base Town, where his actions might have triggered another quest, but Zac had no such intentions. It might be akin to releasing a wolf back into the forest, but what trouble could she possibly cause compared to Yeorav's family?

Zac didn't even have the energy to start speculating about the aftermath of killing a scion of the Dravorak Dynasty, and instead focused on the task at hand.

"I am Zac Piker, and I am not connected to any force," Zac said with a hoarse but carrying voice.

He had long considered what he should say if he ever got to this point, and he was glad to see the eyes light up among many of the scions.

"There is a man calling himself the Great Redeemer heading for my planet, intent on sacrificing everyone on it for an evil ritual. I believe he is currently a Peak D-grade warrior, and he has some knowledge of the Dao of Karma, but that's all I know," Zac continued.

This was the plan. He'd simply lay the cards on the table. He had no bargaining skills, and his time was limited, so he wanted to create a sense of urgency. There should be a lot of C-grade forces interested in making a connection with him, and everyone would want to be the first to tie him to their chariot.

The scions looked a bit confused about the sudden change in topic, but a few eyes lit up in comprehension as they realized what was going on.

"I come from a weak recently integrated planet, and no one will be able to stop him. Taking care of a D-grade Hegemon would be a small task for many of your ancestors, but it would be a favor I would forever remember. I am wi–" Zac said, but he was interrupted by a man who had just walked out of one of the palaces.

"Wait! I know that man!" the youth said with surprise. "He's the excommunicated son of the Heliophos Clan! They have been looking for him for tens of thousands of years!"

Zac's eyes lit up when he heard the news. Things would only become easier if the man was actually a fugitive. Perhaps he could even count on this Heliophos Clan to deal with the problem for him.

But the drastic change in expression among the people quickly doused Zac's excitement.

54
FRIENDS AND FOES

People who had already spoken up of their support suddenly looked troubled, and a few others were even walking away without hesitation. Just what was going on? He quickly looked over at Ogras, but he shook his head in confusion as well.

Zac could only guess they were another peak force, and he looked over at Galau for confirmation.

"Ah… This…" Galau stammered, clearly unwilling to broach the subject in front of such a large audience. "I think you should speak with the Heliophos Clan before doing anything else."

Zac slowly nodded as he looked at the troubled faces of the people around him.

"Is there anyone here who belongs to the Heliophos Clan?" Zac asked.

"The Heliophos Clan isn't a combat-oriented family, so they don't climb the Tower of Eternity," the youth from earlier said after the silence had stretched on for a while. "They are a solitary clan focusing on divination and fate augmentation."

Zac inwardly groaned in annoyance when he put two and two together. These people didn't want to risk causing a rift with a clan full of Karmic Cultivators. They might find that their clan was on the brink of ruination a few hundred years later without knowing what had happened. No one wanted to be the one to take out the Great Redeemer if it meant making such a troublesome enemy.

He was about to ask the merchant to clarify just how powerful the Heliophos Clan was, but he suddenly noticed that the crowd was giving way for someone to reach the front. Was there actually someone who could speak for this odd clan here?

"Now that was something else," a slightly amused voice said, and young cultivators hurriedly scurried out of the way to give room to a young woman.

Zac looked over and almost took a step back in shock, as the woman looked almost identical to someone he had seen before. The newcomer was almost a picture-perfect copy of the mysterious Draugr lady who had given him the Miasmic fractals in his mind, and whose presumed husband he had just met in another vision.

Behind her, two Revenants walked in pace, one of which radiated an aura that was at least comparable to the man he had just taken out. If such an elite was just an attendant, then the Draugr might be frightfully powerful, even if Zac couldn't gauge anything from her appearance alone. Add to that the vast resources of the Undead Empire, and this small group might be an even bigger threat compared to those he had just fought.

However, they didn't emit any killing intent, but rather, the opposite. It was like the Draugr was looking at him like he was some long-lost brother or something. Was this a huge coincidence? Or was this the System messing with his fate somehow? He warily stared at her, trying to figure out what her aim was.

"You don't need to worry about me. I'm not even from this star sector. I wouldn't care even if you killed everyone in this place." She smiled. "In fact, I'm a friend, and I come bearing gifts."

Almost forty bloody heads appeared in front of her the next second.

"I... encouraged a few forces to stay away from this matter, as I wanted to meet with you," she said as she looked down at the heads like they were a pile of garbage. "I also dealt with the Tsarun Clan for you so that we would be able to talk uninterrupted."

"What do you want?" Zac asked suspiciously before he looked down at the heads with a grimace.

It wouldn't be an exaggeration to say that things had deteriorated into an irreconcilable feud with the Tsarun Clan after this.

It made no sense that this Draugr wanted to make friends with him. The Undead Empire wasn't strictly xenophobic, but they seldom mingled with the living. Or did she simply need a strong F-grade ally for some task? Or more likely, was she able to sense his connection to Be'Zi somehow?

"I think it's a discussion best held in private," the Draugr said, not offering any clues.

"A – my friend," a familiar voice said as Boje Zethaya scurried forward. "I feel terribly apologetic about the mess caused by my inattentiveness the other day. Why don't you use my family's abode to conduct any meetings you might have?"

"Well, shall we?" the Draugr said as she sauntered toward the Pill House with the powerful-looking Revenant silently walking behind her.

Zac only hesitated for a second before he decided to check things out. This girl wasn't even from this sector, which meant she had a pretty strong backing. Traveling between sectors was something that only the extremely powerful or the exorbitantly wealthy could do.

It was a possibility that she came from some big-shot family of the Undead Empire, and she might even be able to solve the problem on Earth with a few words. One newly integrated planet couldn't be very important in the wider scope of things. It was absolutely worth exploring further.

He first turned to Ogras and Galau, who had walked over as well, but still stood some distance apart from the gathered mob.

"Will you two be fine?" Zac asked.

"I-I need to talk with my cousins," Galau said with a slightly hollow voice.

"Tell me if you need help with anything." Zac nodded.

"I'll come with you after dealing with the battlefield. You talk with the Draugr; I'll stay outside and see if I can find out some more about that clan. I don't believe there isn't a single force that's brave enough to stick their neck out and help deal with that old goat coming for us," the demon said.

Zac nodded as he looked around at the square full of corpses. His eyes moved to a corpse lying just a few meters away, a stocky humanoid holding a beautiful blue sword that hummed with spirituality. Ogras looked over as well, and a shadow tendril brought over the sword.

"Water attuned," the demon muttered. "Might be suited for old man Trang."

Zac nodded before his eyes turned toward the merchant who was scurrying toward one of the roads leading toward the outer sector of Base Town. However, he didn't get far before one scion after another approached him. Finally, two stunning beauties dispersed the crowds before they led Galau to a palace facing the square.

"They seem to know him. The Peak girl?" Ogras muttered as he shot a glance at the merchant just as they walked into the grand building.

"Perhaps." Zac nodded. "We haven't done anything evil in his presence, though, and the Peak family might prove our best shot at dealing with this mess. Let them sound Galau out while I talk with the Draugr."

Zac left the demon to deal with the cleanup, and he only personally took the Spatial Tools of the three elites who had assisted Yeorav before he walked toward the Pill House. He couldn't stop his curiosity, however, and he took a look at his Status screen as he walked.

Name: Zachary Atwood
Level: 75
Class: [F-Rare] Hatchetman
Race: [E] Human
Alignment: [Earth] Port Atwood – Lord

Titles: […] Promising Specialist, Tower of Eternity – 8th Floor, Heaven's Triumvirate, Fated, Peak Power
Limited Titles: Frontrunner, Tower of Eternity Sector All-Star – 14th
Dao: Fragment of the Axe – Middle, Fragment of the Coffin – Early, Fragment of the Bodhi – Early
Core: [E] Duplicity

Strength: 1253 [Increase: 81%. Efficiency: 199%]
Dexterity: 590 [Increase: 60%. Efficiency: 170%]

Endurance: 1453 [Increase: 99%. Efficiency: 189%]
Vitality: 784 [Increase: 84%. Efficiency: 189%]
Intelligence: 293 [Increase: 60%. Efficiency: 170%]
Wisdom: 494 [Increase: 60%. Efficiency: 170%]
Luck: 285 [Increase: 86%. Efficiency: 179%]

Free Points: 0
Nexus Coins: [F] 6,862,770,130

Zac wryly smiled as he looked at his Status screen. He had been worried about being able to reach 1,000 Strength at all, but he had suddenly shot way past his goal. However, he quickly realized that all of it didn't come from his upgraded Dao Fragment, but there were actually two new titles as well.

[Peak Power: Reach 5,000 Attribute Points while still in F-grade Reward: Effect of Attributes +5%]

As expected, there was another title for reaching a monstrous number like 5,000 attribute points while still at F-grade. However, he wasn't as sure about just how rare it was any longer after witnessing the Battle of Fates and his Mid-grade Dao Fragment.

One Dao Fragment awarded 550 attribute points, which together with the effect of titles closed in on a thousand points. If someone had a couple of them, or perhaps even a Late-stage Dao Seed, then reaching 5,000 attribute points wouldn't be all too difficult. However, that wasn't all he gained, as he had actually gained another title, though this one was limited.

[Tower of Eternity Sector All-Star – 14th [Limited]: Attain the 14th best all-time result in the Zecia Sector. Reward: Strength, Endurance, Vitality, Luck +6%. Effect of Strength, Endurance, Vitality +6%]

He was honestly a bit surprised about being only the fourteenth position. It was still an extremely good result, but he had only heard of the Eveningtide Asura. But then again, the sector was probably extremely old, and outliers were bound to appear now and then over millions of years.

However, he noticed that his recently gained title related to the Terminus was missing in his Status screen, though he could still find it if he opened the actual title screen. It was a bit odd, but he honestly felt it was for the best. What if some old monster had the ability to spy on his Status screen? Having seen the Terminus might only cause a bunch of problems for him.

Interestingly enough, it also looked like the System had finally decided his status screen had become too wordy, and it had shifted to only showing the five latest titles on his Status screen. Normally, he would have looked through his screens a bit longer to see if anything else had changed, but he had things to do, and time was limited.

He soon walked through the passageway into the Pill House, and there was no array impeding him this time. Zac almost felt as though he had dreamed that the place had been turned into a pile of rubble just one day ago, as the place looked almost like a carbon copy of its predecessor.

Boje was already waiting in the lobby, and Zac was personally led by the man to the second floor.

"Let us know if there's anything else you need," he said as he stopped outside a room.

"Do you have any more of those cherries?" Zac asked before walking inside.

"A – no? I thought you…" Boje stammered a bit, looking a bit confused.

"I had to use it on myself in the Tower, so I need another soul-healing treasure for the intended recipient," Zac explained.

"Oh, I see," Boje said with a troubled face. "I am afraid I don't have anything on me. If you give me a week, I'll be able to send for something from my family, and I'll be happy to directly gift it to you."

"I'm leaving today," Zac said with a shake of his head. "See if you can find out if anyone has something that would work."

"We'd be happy to," Boje said before he handed Zac two tokens after some thought. "This Teleportation Token leads to one of our main stores, and the insignia gives you the status of an esteemed guest. You will be able to order a medicine tailored for your friend there, and our resident Alchemist will concoct it for you. Such a pill would not have any secondary effects like the cherry might have produced, but its healing efficacy will be at least of the same level, probably higher considering it won't be limited by the Base Town's restrictions."

Zac's eyes lit up, and he gladly accepted the two tokens. He wouldn't personally go there until he could be certain about his safety, but he might be able to send someone else there if he couldn't find any solution for Alea in the short run.

"Thank you. You can speak with Ogras if there is anything else." Zac nodded.

He couldn't help but feel some sort of vindication as he stepped inside the room. Last time he had come here as a nobody, a supplicant begging for resources. Now he was a big shot who got things done with a wave of his hand, and he'd be lying if he said that it didn't feel pretty nice.

"I didn't have a chance to introduce myself earlier." The Draugr smiled as Zac closed the door behind him. "I am Catheya Sharva'Zi. I am from what you would call the Empire Heartlands."

"Why have you come to this remote corner of the universe, then?" Zac asked with some confusion. "Shouldn't be anything of interest here."

"My master is looking for a certain opportunity to break through," Catheya said. "He received some clues that made us pass by this frontier region. But he suddenly had a bout of inspiration and had to enter seclusion for a few years. I got bored and chose to visit the Tower."

Zac only wryly smiled as he sat down. Having a sturdy backing like a powerful master to depend on seemed to allow for a pretty leisurely lifestyle.

"Did you know? It has been over a million years since someone breached the eighth floor in this sector," the Draugr said as she glanced at the Revenant standing by the side.

He nodded and produced an exquisite teapot out of nowhere and expertly poured Zac a cup before he lit a stick of mild incense.

"The Eveningtide Asura." Zac nodded, ignoring the drink for now.

"Yes," Catheya said. "You two are more similar than you might think. He was a progenitor as well."

Zac frowned as she looked at the Draugr. Had she found out about Earth and was planning to use it against him?

"I mean nothing by my words." Catheya smiled as she handed over a crystal. "Take a look for yourself."

Zac gave Catheya another glance as he quickly scanned the contents.

"Ez'Mahal," Zac snorted, some fury erupting in his chest again.

Those scumbags weren't content with treating the earthlings like cattle, but they even dared to place a bounty on his head? He wondered what their reaction would be after hearing about his deeds inside the Tower of Eternity.

"It seems you have looked into me while I climbed. Why? I have no connection to your Undead Empire," Zac said as he stashed away the information crystal.

"I wouldn't be so sure about that," Catheya said with a smile. "I was somewhat convinced when I saw you when you entered the Tower, but now I am certain. You and I are connected, I know it. You even smell like one of us."

Zac didn't say anything, but he was pretty surprised about her last comment. Did he actually smell like a Draugr?

QUID PRO QUO

Iz Tayn slowly walked through the vast gardens in her home, not sparing the divine flowers a second glance until she reached a burning mountain.

"Hello, Uncle. Is Grandpa awake?" she asked, and the ground started to shake the next moment.

Enormous pieces of rocks rearranged themselves, and the mountain turned into a golem hundreds of meters tall. Its whole body was covered in extremely dense scriptures to the point that not a single inch of its body wasn't covered with fractals. Iz always liked looking at the mysterious patterns while meditating, but she had other things to do today.

"Master has been expecting your return; he is awake," the enormous golem rumbled as it stretched out a finger that was over a dozen meters wide.

Iz disappeared in a puff of flames the next moment, and the fiery flowers and red sky were replaced with the boundless cosmos. In front of her, a scorching sun hovered in the void, with an impossibly large man sitting on top of it. The man looked to be an amalgam of man and flames, and the heat he emanated far eclipsed the sun beneath him.

It was Mohzius Tayn, her grandfather.

Iz was just a speck of dust compared to the terrifying size of her ancestor. However, the scale of the cosmos somehow changed, and the gargantuan man was suddenly the same size as Iz herself, and the sun even smaller than her own **[World's End]**.

"How did it go?" the middle-aged man asked with a warm smile.

"Fifty-one days," Iz said as the bored expression she usually wore outside became increasingly animated. "You lied! It wasn't exciting at all. The last guy was pretty tough, but it was just one long slog."

"Ha!" Mohzius laughed, and the star beneath him flickered as it shared the man's mood. "Old Man River's descendant in your cohort took over eighty days to break the ceiling. I can't wait to see his face when he hears about this."

"My age group? Theleferos is almost twenty thousand years old," Iz snorted, but she was still secretly happy about her grandpa's expression.

Seeing his smile was more valuable than the titles and new treasures she'd received, since she knew her grandpa had been pretty down since her grandma had to leave.

"Still the young generation." Mohzius smiled. "By the way, haven't you only been gone for a few days? Why didn't you stay and play with your friends? I am sure we have a nice house by the Tower."

"What friends? Just a bunch of people who only think about benefits and getting stronger all day," Iz muttered before her eyes lit with excitement. "I met someone interesting inside the Tower, though! But I need your help, Grandpa."

"Hm? Met someone? A boy?" the old man said, a frown quickly appearing on his face.

"Yes, but I just found him interesting," Iz hurriedly explained.

"Bringing someone out from that spatial fold is quite troublesome," the man muttered. "Your uncle can't do it without getting hurt, and I can't leave this place for the next few centuries."

"No, he's not someone from that place," Iz said with a shake of her head as she described her encounter on the seventh floor.

"Dual classes and dual Races? And you say he's a human rather than a wanderer?" her grandpa said, looking a bit interested. "Sounds like a mutated constitution or a twinned soul. Perhaps even the fusion of two individuals with interwoven fates."

"But he somehow managed to remove the marking just after I returned. Can you help me?" Iz entreated.

"That is much easier." The man nodded, and a small mote of flame split off from the sun and entered Iz's forehead.

A small rune emerged a few seconds later, and the man grabbed it in his hand.

"He seems to have completely blown up his torso to rid himself of the mark," Mohzius said with a smile. "A gutsy fellow. But he didn't notice the branding on his spirit body. I strengthened it a bit; he won't be able to remove it easily now. But why do you want to see him?"

"No particular reason." Iz shrugged. "I was bored, and he was interesting, so I thought I would go visit and take a look. Besides, he called me a lunatic; he owes me an explanation."

"Remember not to go around causing trouble in the lower realms," the man sternly said. "Most people are just trying to live their lives."

"I know, Grandpa," Iz muttered.

"Fine," the old man eventually relented. "You can go when you have undergone your next bloodline evolution and formed your first Dao Branch."

"But that can take years!" Iz exclaimed.

"Just the blink of an eye." Mohzius smiled. "Better work hard."

"Fine. I'll go and break through now. Goodbye, Grandpa," Iz Tayn said before she looked up at the stars. "Goodbye, Grandma."

The next moment, she disappeared from the remote star system, leaving the giant sitting on his sun. However, a massive claw ripped through the fabric of space, and a scar even larger than the celestial body appeared the next moment.

An eye of impossible proportions gazed down through the tear, and just its gaze put tremendous pressure on the whole star system. However, the giant wasn't worried in the least, but rather looked up with a smile matching the one that was usually reserved for his sole granddaughter.

"It seems you're well on the way to getting better. Just a few dozen millennia and you might be able to descend," he said with barely restrained elation.

"I didn't hear everything just now. Has little Iz met a boy? And you actually wanted to send her into his arms?" a booming voice echoed across the cosmos.

"Iz is more talented than both of us, but she lacks the drive and curiosity to walk toward the Terminus. I am hoping that she will find something worth fighting for, like how I fought for you all those years ago," Mohzius said, his smile widening.

A snort could be heard from within the void, and the whole star system shook in response.

"If my granddaughter runs away with some man before I can even meet her without afflicting her with my fell Karma, I'll fight it out with you, old man," the voice said as white flames danced in the eye. "How dare he call my beautiful granddaughter a lunatic. He'd better not come to this sector of space."

"Yes, dear." The old man smiled as he closed his eyes, some wistfulness flashing in their depths. "You should go back now. I can only hold back the Heavens for so long."

———

"How do you know my ancestor? Is she your master?" Catheya asked point-blank, her pitch-black orbs boring into Zac's eyes.

Zac was about to respond, but he suddenly felt a small pang of pain in his chest. He was already feeling pretty wretched after the fight, and he started to wonder if the cursed sword had left some lingering threats.

However, he felt fine except for the exhaustion, and a quick inspection couldn't pinpoint any issues, so he returned his attention back to the Draugr sitting in front of him.

"It's not what you think," Zac finally said after the pause.

"Then what?" she said, leaning forward in eagerness.

"There is an incursion of the Undead Empire on my home planet," Zac slowly said, ignoring the question. "Can you deal with it?"

Catheya froze for a second before she wryly sighed.

"No. I am willing to pay a lot for information pertaining to my ancestor, but I cannot help you in that regard," she said with a shake of her head.

"Why not?" Zac said with a frown. "One small planet shouldn't matter to you guys."

"It doesn't really, but there are a few iron-clad commandments in the empire. The first one is cohesion. Undead kingdoms cannot go to war against each other. Skirmishes for unclaimed resources are okay, but full-scale wars are banned. The second commandment is the Commandment of Conquest," she said.

"Conquest?" Zac repeated.

"All the kingdoms of the empire have a quota to expand, and no one is allowed to hinder a crusade. I could take over the incursion if I could somehow make my way to your planet, but I would still be bound by law to conquer the planet," she said.

"Why?" Zac said with incredulity.

"Do you know the history of our people?" Catheya asked.

"I just know the Undead Empire is older than the System." Zac shrugged.

"Well, the undead Races are older, but the Undead Empire is not," she said. "Do you know about the Darkness?"

"What? The Darkness?" Zac said, the rapid change of topics throwing him off-balance.

"When the System was born, the universe was drained of its energy to feed its usurpation of the heavens. The path of cultivation was cut off," she said.

Zac nodded in understanding. Alyn had told him about this while she was explaining the origin of the System.

"For most Races, it was a great inconvenience, but for the undead Races, it was a calamity. Our existence is dependent on death-attuned energies, and when the universe was being drained, so was our life-line," Catheya said.

Zac's eyes widened in understanding. This was something he hadn't considered. If all Cosmic Energy was suddenly gone, then Zac would live as he did before the integration. But his Draugr side would be screwed.

Even just sitting around would slowly expend Miasma, though nowhere near the amounts that were expended during battle. But he would no doubt die within the year if he didn't have any Miasma Crystals to top himself off.

But Zac remembered that the Darkness, as Catheya called it, had lasted over a million years. How did the undead Races survive for so long? He could only imagine that more powerful warriors required a lot of Miasma just to survive.

"The founders and the undead princes searched the whole universe for pockets of energies that could sustain us, but over 95% of our population succumbed before we found the Heartlands. Since then, there's been a standing order to realign the universe, because if the whole Multiverse is death-attuned, we'll never be without a lifeline again. So we will never stop expanding."

"That's… crazy." Zac sighed.

"Well," Catheya said with a smile, "only the fanatics take the mission seriously nowadays. But conflict is still the cornerstone of progress, and the Ruthless Heavens is very much in favor of the way we're doing things, as it causes conflict everywhere. That by itself provides us with some special benefits. Besides, we cannot disobey the commandments since they are coded into our bloodlines by the Primo."

"The Primo?" Zac asked.

"I cannot discuss the Primo," Catheya said with a shake of her head.

Zac sighed with a nod. He could only guess that the Primo was either the founder of the Undead Empire or the current emperor. It didn't really matter, though. What mattered was the fact that there was no way for the Draugr in front of him to settle the incursion.

However, the undead incursion was just the first of the many threats that Earth was facing, and he was pretty confident in dealing with it on his own after all his recent gains.

"What about the thing I mentioned out in the square? You said you're not from this sector, so you wouldn't care about offending these guys, right?" Zac probed.

"I'm not sure how I would be able to help with this matter. He sounds like someone on his last legs. I doubt he would care for a second that your planet was under the protection of some old master, unless said master was actually standing guard over the planet," Catheya slowly said. "I also don't carry anything that can kill someone that strong with any guarantee, since items of that grade can't be taken to this place."

"Can't your clan do something?" Zac asked with some help-lessness.

"My master probably wouldn't mind killing that guy if I asked him. He has no love for the unorthodox cultivators. But we have no means to find him. He could be anywhere in this sector, and his being versed in the Dao of Karma makes him twice as slippery. Do you have a token to summon my master if needed?"

"A–" Zac stammered, realizing that there were glaring issues in his plan of getting a patron.

"I am willing to join a force as long as they can provide protection of Earth," Zac said.

"Well, that might work, though not with me. Undead kingdoms and forces cannot form alliances with the living, with you being targets of conquest and all. We could strike an unofficial partnership, though." The Draugr smiled. "But there are a lot of problems with this plan."

"Problems how?" Zac asked.

"Is my ancestor alive?" Catheya smiled, but the effect was extremely creepy if you combined it with her pitch-black Draugr eyes.

Zac sighed and mulled it over for a second.

"She was alive three months ago to the best of my knowledge. Or well, alive by undead standards, I guess?" Zac said. "What problems?"

"She's really alive?!" Catheya exclaimed, even standing up in excitement.

Zac was pretty sure by this point that the Draugr lady in his vision was an ancestor to the one in front of him, one that seemed to have gone missing. Had she perhaps left her clan behind due to issues stemming from the Splinter of Oblivion? She was clearly extremely powerful, and if she went mad, it wouldn't be just a small Pill House going up in smoke.

She might blow up a whole planet.

It was a great bargaining tool for Zac, though. She clearly was anxious to learn about her ancestor, and she seemed to come from an extremely powerful faction of one of the oldest forces in the Multiverse. She was probably the most knowledgeable person he had met, perhaps with the exception of some of the scions he had met during the fight on the seventh floor.

It was time to get his money's worth.

"The problems?" Zac reminded her.

"Well, you can technically join a faction, either as an ally or a subordinate. But that doesn't mean that you can get the help you need," Catheya said after having composed herself. "First of all, travel will not be possible, as your world probably hasn't met the requirements to connect with the Multiverse. You can't even teleport to local factions; how are you going to teleport to other factions of the sector?"

"So there's no hope?" Zac said with some bleakness.

"Well, most people here have tokens to give out. You could technically form an agreement now, and then use the token to fetch a powerhouse to assist you. The one going would need to be a planetary leader though, since others wouldn't be able to bring anyone back while the planet is closed off," Catheya said.

"How do you know this?" Zac asked. "Seems like a pretty specific rule."

"I've led an incursion myself," Catheya explained as if it was a matter of course. "That's how I met Varo over there. I guess you could say he was that planet's version of you. Anyway, the rules are pretty much the same for an invader, so I read up on how things worked. It's a bit more convenient for the invader, though, as the world immediately gets integrated after the conquest is done with, becoming part of their force. But you will still be cut off for a hundred years even if you win."

Zac's eyes turned toward the silent Revenant, and he couldn't help but shudder. Would this have been the fate of him and Kenzie if he hadn't managed to accumulate enough power? The Revenant seemed to feel the gaze, and he opened his eyes and looked over at Zac.

"That was him; I am me. We're nothing but strangers fated to never meet," Varo said before he once again closed his eyes.

ARCANE

"Oh?" Io said, looking up from his position in the middle of the Data Array.

The thousands of screens around him faded away as he stood up and walked out, taking in a fresh breath of air for the first time in almost a year. He didn't like to be away from his array for too long, so he made a beeline toward the restricted area in the middle of the sect.

Io was just a Peak D-grade warrior, but he was still let into the Hidden Realm without any hassle after flashing a token. A guard even arranged for transportation to where he needed to go, and he stood in front of the Lake of Solace after just a couple of hours.

Being friends with a Grand Deacon had its benefits.

"Oh? I thought I would have to drag you outside for you to leave your little cave," a laughing voice echoed out across the lake.

"I experience far more in the Data Array than I could ever do with my own two eyes," Io said with a smile as he drifted over to the small island in the middle. "How are things on your end?"

Io and A'Feris came from the same world, so Io had helped him gain his footing in the sect, which had formed a friendship that had lasted for eons. A'Feris had passed him by in terms of cultivation long ago and was now one of the true elites of the force.

"Same as usual," A'Feris said with a smile as he poured a cup of tea for his old friend. "Something is lacking. I need some impetus to take the next step, but it eludes me."

"You still look quite calm," Io commented.

"Well, my road has taken me further than I ever expected. Even if it stopped here, it wouldn't be the worst of fates." A'Feris laughed.

"How about taking a disciple?" Io smiled. "Some have found the experience rewarding and have even managed to break through their barriers that way."

"Why would I want to get bogged down with one of those snotty brats who keep relying on their elders to solve all their little problems?" A'Feris snorted with derision before he looked at Io with suspicion. "Wait, why are you saying this right now? What have you found out through your array? Or do you have some descendants you've hidden from me?"

"I just received a report of an outlier in the Zecia Sector," Io said as he took a sip of the tea.

"Zecia? I haven't heard of it," A'Feris said. "What sort of outlier?"

"It is one of the frontier sectors that could tentatively be said to be within our domain, though ownership of those sectors is quite contested, as you know," Io explained. "Someone just reached the ninth floor of the Tower of Eternity, though just the entrance."

"Tower of Eternity?" A'Feris muttered. "Haven't heard of that place in a long time. So who was it?"

"His name is Zac Piker, but that's all I know," Io said. "It is likely a pseudonym, though."

"That's it?" A'Feris laughed. "Is this the limits of the so-called Living Library?"

"I am guessing he is a wandering cultivator or a planet progenitor. The established forces in that kind of place don't have the means to nurture that level of elite, so those who appear are the results of a series of lucky encounters. Of the fourteen people who have passed the eighth floor in the Zecia Sector, eleven of them have been unattached," Io said.

"A gem in the rough," A'Feris muttered. "What path is he following?"

"I just found out about his existence; no real information has leaked out yet," Io said. "One of our agents will know more in a few hours. I thought I'd let you know before others learn of it. I will only be able to block the information from leaking for a day or two."

"Discipleship…" A'Feris muttered as his fingers ran along the grisly weapon that never left his side. "We will see. It's not just a matter of convenience, but also of fate. He might be someone worth nurturing, but he needs to walk a similar path as mine. Otherwise, both our times would be wasted."

———

It was a pretty odd situation.

The man had essentially been killed by Catheya and turned into a Revenant, but he still seemed happy enough to follow her. But Zac knew that "realignment" wasn't anything evil in the eyes of the undead after his stay at the undead kingdom during his climb. It was the same as waking up someone who had been sleepwalking.

"What if I sign a contract with the scions here?" Zac asked as he turned back to Catheya, getting back to the topic at hand. "Something along the line that they cannot attack me and promise to provide assistance in return for me joining their force."

"The people here are just juniors; they can't speak for their elders," Catheya said with a shake of her head. "Besides, there are ways for the elders to forcibly break the contracts, as the difference between them and you is so vast. Then they can simply make up some reason for why they apprehend you before they steal all your treasures and dig out your secrets. They might even hand you over to that Heliophos Clan to curry favor."

"So what should I do?" Zac asked. "I can't be the first guy who has needed to hire someone much stronger than me."

"Of course not. But you have stood out too much. You definitely have a bunch of secrets on you, to the point that even I am extremely curious. Maintaining reputation in the face of such a huge potential gain is nothing." Catheya smiled.

Zac slowly nodded, and he remembered Yrial's situation. He had almost lost his life multiple times to so-called righteous factions who wanted his treasures without paying for them. There was no right and wrong in the Multiverse; there was only power and benefits. Crushing a token to arrive at a foreign force full of D- and C-grade Hegemons would be like serving himself up on a platter if there were no safe-guards in place.

The fact that the Great Redeemer was from a powerful clan of Karmic Cultivators only made the situation messier.

The only force he felt he could somewhat trust was the Peak family, but he wasn't completely ready to put his life in their hands. But it was a last-ditch solution if everything else failed. He could head over to their place if he got a token from Pretty. Even if he ended up captured, he would probably have a better ending than whatever the Great Redeemer had planned.

"Do you have any solution? Just preventing him from finding my planet is enough for now," Zac said as he explained the situation with the Dominators and the beacon he had destroyed with the help of the old Abbot.

"Cutting off any Karmic ties before he reaches your plane is your best bet, as it doesn't matter how close or far he is from your planet then. He will not be able to find you through the spatial folds of the sector without any guidance, at least not while the Ruthless Heavens is shrouding your world. And I do have something for that, actually," Catheya slowly said as she turned to the Revenant behind her. "Go fetch the eighth and twenty-third treasures."

"The local chapter will require remuneration," Varo slowly said.

"That's fine," she said with a disinterested wave.

The man nodded and blended into the shadows with a bow.

"What are the treasures?" Zac asked with interest.

He probably had a lot of good things in his bag, but he had no idea what most of them were. Besides, even if they were valuable, there was no guarantee that they'd be able to help him with his current predicaments.

"The eighth treasure is called [Lantern of Fate]. Anyone it illumi-nates will have their Karmic ties exposed, and you will even be able to destroy the ties with enough effort. The wearer will also be immune from forming Karmic ties when it's activated," Catheya said.

Zac's eyes lit up, as it sounded like a treasure that produced the Karmic ties that the Abbot had allowed him to see for a short while.

This was exactly what he needed to make sure there were no lingering ties between Earth and the Great Redeemer after he had dealt with the Dominators. It could solve any potential issue stemming from his repeated contact with the Redeemer, and make sure that nothing was wrong with those who had almost been possessed during the activation of the Dao Funnel.

"And the twenty-third?" Zac asked with mounting excitement.

"A top-quality E-grade treasure of erasure. Use it on the corpses of the underlings of the Redeemer, and any hidden Karmic Links should be severed. We use those kinds of treasures before we create new subjects with... troublesome histories. No one wants an insanely strong ancestor to come for you to reclaim the body of a descendant," Catheya said with a wry smile. "Normally, an E-grade treasure wouldn't be powerful enough to break a true Karmic connection with a Hegemon, but with the System's shroud, it should be more than enough. Those links must be as weak as can be, considering he still hasn't found your planet."

"Both these two items are yours in return for the information I'm looking for. You will have to sign a contract saying that the treasures cannot be used against the forces of the Undead Empire though," she added.

"Deal." Zac nodded without hesitation.

It was a bit disappointing that she wasn't able to directly help with either the Great Redeemer or the undead incursion. However, he wasn't really worried about the invaders any longer. He had gained far more than expected during his visit to the Tower of Eternity, and he had great confidence in dealing with the Lich King.

He had hoped to get some help with the incursion to be able to delay his evolution. He had made a lot of improvements in the Tower, but he had been too rushed to make gains. If he could have a couple of months to figure out what was going on with his Dao fusions and what to do about the two items in his head, he would probably be able to get even better classes.

"So...?" Catheya asked with a raised brow.

"Let me see the treasures first," Zac said with a smile, taking a cue from the paranoid demon.

"Fine," she snorted.

"By the way, do you know the requirements from the System for it to consider one's path a 'creation'?" Zac asked instead as they waited for the Revenant to return.

"Big appetite, already grasping for an Arcane class?" Catheya smiled.

"Something like that," Zac said, not denying it.

He had passed the eighth floor of the Tower of Eternity. It shouldn't come as a shock that someone like him wanted to get the best possible rarity for their class.

"You should think long and hard before taking that step," Catheya said.

"Why wouldn't I want to get an Arcane class?" Zac asked with some skepticism.

Was this another lecture like that of Alyn? To pursue greatness through mediocrity.

"Have you changed your view of cultivation since your world got integrated?" Catheya asked.

"Of course." Zac nodded.

"Will you change it again?"

"Probably," Zac responded after a short deliberation.

"Well, there you go." Catheya smiled.

"What?" Zac said, not following the logic.

"The Arcane class gives you a bit more attributes and a few other benefits, but you shouldn't think of it as something as simple as the next step after Epic rarity. Getting an Arcane class is confirming your path of cultivation, and doing so is irrevocable," she said.

"Irrevocable? What does that mean?" Zac asked with confusion.

"It means that you cannot change directions any longer. The path you choose will be the path you will have for the rest of your life. If your creation is substandard, then your path of cultivation will be cut short," Catheya explained. "Arcane classes are probably extremely rare in this sector, but they are more common where I am from. However, most people hold off on choosing them until later in their life."

"What's the difference between choosing now and later?" Zac asked, though he had an inkling.

"We're just children," Catheya said. "Our understanding of the Dao and the universe is shallow at best. Choosing an Arcane class this early is like choosing your future profession as a child. You don't know what you are doing. So people wait until their understanding becomes deeper and the creation becomes more refined.

"You lose some attributes, but trying to maximize attributes is a fool's venture in any case," the Draugr continued. "What is important is your path and your Dao. They will take you past the bottlenecks; a few extra points in Strength will not."

The room turned silent as Zac looked down at his hands with a frown. He would have to confirm that she was telling the truth about Arcane classes, but what should he do if it was the truth? He felt that his creation was extremely high tier since it followed the path of Life and Death, which might even be turned into that of Creation and Oblivion with the help of the Splinter of Oblivion and the Shard of Creation.

But was that enough? There were still huge obstacles to overcome. He still couldn't use the energies as he pleased, and he was essentially fumbling in the dark about most aspects. Besides, he wasn't even sure if his ideas would even work any longer after the changes just before he left the Tower. The pathways to [Cyclic Strike] had been rebranded, and he hadn't been able to confirm whether they even worked like before.

What would happen if he chose an Arcane class based on such rickety foundations? His whole future might be ruined since he grasped for too much, just like Alyn had warned him of.

The silence stretched on for another four minutes until the Revenant returned with two boxes.

"This is the lantern." Catheya smiled. "Be careful not to use it constantly. It consumes life force to run."

"Life force? How much?" Zac said with a frown.

"One minute's use will result in a year lost when used." The Revenant spoke up after the Draugr shot him a glance. "Ten years if you have reached the early D-grade. It is not strong enough to protect the fate of those stronger than that."

Zac nodded in thanks. It was a bit creepy to pay with your life to use an item, especially after already having lost so much of it to the Shard. But just using it for short durations wouldn't be too bad, especially as he was about to evolve and get a new chunk of life span any day now.

"So, about the information?" the Draugr said.

"I don't know if the one I'm thinking of is related to you, but you look just like a younger version of the one I saw," Zac said as he stowed away the two treasures. "I think her name is Be'Zi."

"So you really have met her?!" the Draugr almost screamed as she leaned across the table. "Is she in this sector?"

"I don't know," Zac said. "We met in a vision since we walk similar paths. She bestowed me with something to protect me. Perhaps that's what you can sense from me."

"Why would she help you, though?" Catheya said with confusion.

"She believed it was fate we met." Zac shrugged. "According to her husband, she seemed to place pretty great emphasis on such things."

"Her WHAT?!" Catheya shouted as she slammed the table. "WHO?!"

TWILIGHT HARBOR

Catheya looked extremely shocked at the prospect of her ancestor having married, or perhaps having remarried, as she'd already had descendants before.

"I didn't get his name." Zac coughed before he described his appearance.

"Our ancestor has run off with an Aetherlord? What?" Catheya mumbled as she sat down with a thump. "Well, better that than some human, I guess. No offense."

Zac only snorted in response, not taking the thing to heart. It was not like he was lining up to date someone who wasn't even alive.

"Why hasn't she returned, though?" Catheya asked. "Where is she now? How was her mental state?"

"I have no idea where she is," Zac said. "I saw her sitting in a dark cave with a sea of liquefied Miasma slowly rotating around her. It felt like a drop of that pond would be able to instantly kill me. She seemed normal; a bit cold, I guess?"

"So why hasn't she been back for so long?" she muttered with some despondency.

"She didn't say. I saw them for less than a minute," Zac said, but he spoke up again after some hesitation. "But the path we walk has side effects. You saw what happened to this place the other day. She might be afraid of hurting her family if she lost control."

"Madness…" Catheya muttered. "I feel like you are still keeping some secrets from me though."

"Some things aren't of any value to you, but they pertain to my cultivation path. I know that the two of them cultivate opposite Daos, and I think they are forming some system between them. That might be why your ancestor can stay alive," Zac added after some thought, feeling he hadn't provided much information in return for the treasures.

"The husband also spoke of broken peaks and seemed to carry resentment toward the System."

"Broken peaks…" Catheya muttered. "The Boundless Path? This might be important. I need to speak with my master."

"Stuff like that is beyond me. I'm just a newly integrated progenitor; I don't have any experience with stuff like old ancestors." Zac shrugged. "Can I ask something else?"

"What?" Catheya said, though her interest in keeping up the conversation seemed to have waned somewhat now that she had the information she wanted.

"What ways are there to gain more Limited Title slots?"

Catheya was someone from a higher sector than the one he lived in, which meant that her knowledge might be unrivaled compared to all the other scions in the Base Town. She also didn't care about offending any local force like the Heliophos Clan, so he needed to milk her for as much knowledge as he could before he returned to Earth.

"Limited Titles… Just what did you encounter in the Tower of Eternity?" Catheya said, her crestfallen demeanor replaced by one filled with curiosity. "Did you encounter a trial?"

"A what?"

"A special event inside the Tower. You encountered one, didn't you?" Catheya asked.

Zac hesitated for a few seconds before he slowly nodded.

"The fate you carry must be pretty immense," Catheya muttered. "Then again, that was already all too apparent from the events outside."

"Fate?"

"The amount of attention the Heavens put on you. It is both a blessing and a curse." Catheya smiled.

Zac weakly smiled in return, knowing the sentiment all too well.

"So, Limited Titles?" Zac said.

"It's extremely rare. My master is deemed to have great genius partly because he has four Limited Slots. There are people with more, but I don't know how they have gotten the other one. There are only a few generally known means to gain such a boost, and the Tower and its equivalent trials are the only ones I have heard of before D-grade," Catheya said.

"Why is there a limit at all?" Zac muttered. "Why doesn't the System not just have normal titles? Isn't its goal to make people powerful?"

"Tell me what trial you encountered." Catheya smiled.

"It was called a Battle of Fates; it replaced the 63rd level," Zac said after deciding if the trade of information was worth it.

"That's a rough one, but its mortality is pretty low." Catheya nodded. "It's a decent one to get as long as you're adept at combat."

"So, titles?" Zac said.

"Did you know that cultivators today are stronger than they were pre-System?" Catheya said.

"Isn't that the point of the System?" Zac responded, not understanding where Catheya was going. "Making warriors stronger."

"Yes, but I am talking stage by stage," Catheya explained. "The average cultivators of today are slightly worse than the average ancient cultivators, but the elites are almost twice as powerful, going by the records. Can you guess why?"

"The titles?" Zac ventured, having a vague sense of what the Draugr was getting at.

"Exactly. Skills, cultivation manuals, bloodlines, and Daos. All this existed before the System, though the mediocre of today would never manage to cultivate in those times. Even the weakest cultivators back then had decent talent. However, titles didn't exist back then," the Draugr said. "It's still not completely understood exactly what the Ruthless Heavens does when giving out titles, but the consensus is that it can be seen as an extremely exact, but minute, bloodline evolution. A title improves our base constitution by a small degree.

"However, nothing comes without a price. It definitely costs the System energy to improve the fundamental aspects of a warrior, and the Heavens is running at maximum capacity as far as we can tell, constantly integrating new realms. It can't expend unlimited resources on every person, especially as its core directive is to manufacture warriors as efficiently as possible," Catheya said.

"The general belief is that it's pretty cheap for the System to award titles to warriors who are still in the earliest stages of cultivation. Giving 5% to Intelligence to a F-grade cultivator is barely anything. But providing 5% Intelligence for an A-grade prince? That would require terrifying amounts of energy," the Draugr continued.

"But even if you get the title early, you'll still get the same boost when reaching A-grade later," Zac countered.

"The Heavens won't provide that energy. You will need to collect that yourself through killing or cultivating." The Draugr smiled.

"So if you have a bunch of titles, your cultivation will be slower?" Zac asked with surprise.

"Yes. The amount of energy a warrior requires to level up differs from person to person. A higher potential will require more energy," Catheya explained as a matter of course. "It's not noticeable in the F-grade, as the System subsidizes everyone, but elites generally gain levels slower. That's why most factions force their general warriors to use lower rarity classes. They'll shoot up to their bottlenecks far quicker, and a few might even break through with the extra time on their hands."

"So the System provides the titles as rewards, but you have to provide the energy required to maintain them yourself," Zac concluded.

"Exactly." Catheya nodded.

"And the Limited Titles?" Zac asked.

"The Ruthless Heavens still needed an extra incentive for people to enter dangerous places. Often people return empty-handed from such ventures, but if they at least could get a title out of it, more are likely to risk their lives. This dramatically increases the death rate among cultivators, but those who survive are stronger and more experienced." Catheya smiled. "Besides, if you have a limited number of titles, you will gradually upgrade them, and it will create a smaller strain on the Ruthless Heavens.

"Of course, that's just the general theory. Another is that titles are actually unrealized potential. There is only so much potential that the System can dig out from a person, so it can't provide unlimited titles and needs to set a limit," Catheya added.

The two kept talking for almost an hour, where the two kept going tit-for-tat for information. She obviously didn't know as much about the Dao or cultivation as Yrial, but she had the viewpoint of someone who was born in a top-tier faction. That came with all kinds of snippets of information that accumulated into a huge advantage.

Catheya was more interested in his experiences and kept asking about whether he had encountered any cursed Mystic Realms or performed rituals on battlefields. Zac realized she was trying to understand why he "smelled" like a Draugr, but he kept that secret to himself as he extracted one piece of information after another.

For example, he learned that it was possible to control one's Dao to the point that you could actually form arrays with the mental energy before infusing it into skills. It would increase the boost even further and sometimes even change the way a skill worked. He had never heard of anything of the sort before, which meant that it probably wasn't a widely known technique here. Of course, that wasn't something that was fated with Zac in any case.

However, the real shock was learning just what a [Divine Investiture Array] was, and he almost exploded in anger when doing so.

It was actually an array to create or alter Spirit Tools. It could either take raw materials or an already existing Spirit Tool, and it would create something new with it. It was extremely sought after, as you could create a Spirit Tool with extreme growth potential that was uniquely suited to one's own battle style and Daos.

It was a very convenient item, and Catheya even went so far as to offer 800 billion Nexus Coins for it, probably everything she had brought into the Tower of Eternity, but it didn't detract from the fact that the System had screwed him over yet again. How was an array like this supposed to "rectify regret"? Had it straight-out lied to him, or did it refer to the fact that [Verun's Bite] was starting to lag behind, which could be considered regretful?

"You don't understand how great such an array is. It can potentially create an item that will follow you for the rest of your life. An item you buy from a Blacksmith will always be influenced by the creator's Dao and path and limited by his lack of skill, creating frictions that become more obvious the further you progress," the Draugr explained with exasperation.

"The [Divine Investiture Array], on the other hand, can create an unblemished item that is a direct bridge between you and the Heavens," Catheya continued as she looked at Zac like he was an idiot. "Having a perfectly suited weapon is even more important than having a perfect cultivation manual; it's a top-tier reward of the Tower. I would have tried tricking it out of your hands if you didn't have a Karmic connection to my ancestor."

Zac slowly nodded in understanding, though there was still a sense of frustration about the situation. It sounded like something he could use, however, and he contemplated upgrading Verun after returning to Earth. He had gathered quite a few materials during his climb, and he would be able to get some more in the Base Town.

He had the Pathfinder Eye and pieces of a true dragon, along with metals, bones, and other odd materials that had attracted the Tool Spirit's desire. It should allow him to elevate [Verun's Bite] to a terrifying level, which might be considered rectifying regret in some roundabout way.

Another valuable piece of intel appeared a few minutes later, when the Draugr asked where he had got his hands on a Sword Slave.

"A what?" Zac asked after hearing the unfamiliar term. "Do you mean one of the avatars I conjured? They were defensive treasures."

"No, I mean the old sword you used at the end," the Draugr snorted. "I am guessing you looted those defensive treasures from some poor girl during the Trial, judging by their design."

"Oh, that one. I picked it up during the Battle of Fates as well," Zac explained, not commenting on the fact that he was still wearing a bunch of jewelry.

He probably looked a bit weird, but he would be in a weakened state for a while longer, and there was no way he'd take off his defensive treasures in front of the Draugr.

"You should be careful about that item and have whatever the human equivalent to a Cleansing Lich is take a look at you," Catheya said.

"Just what is it?" Zac asked with some worry, making a mental note to have Sui check up on his condition. "It feels a bit like a Spirit Tool, but it's still different."

"I guess you could call it a cursed object. A piece of a cultivator's soul has fused with that weapon, either through accident or through a ritual. The skill you used is most likely one the warrior knew before dying," Catheya explained. "Judging by its appearance, its state is unstable, and it even tried to fuse with your arm."

"The man I took it from didn't seem to get any backlash from using it," Zac said, hoping the Draugr would have a solution.

The power of the attack he had unleashed was somewhere between the second and third swings of **[Deforestation]**, and if he could use the weapon freely, it would be a great ace to take out if needed. But his arm did feel a bit uncomfortable now that Catheya mentioned it. He had just thought it was the general state of weakness from **[Hatchet-man's Rage]**, but perhaps there was something more.

"Then he must have had some means to counteract the side effects of the weapon," Catheya guessed.

"So what's the point of having one of these cursed swords instead of a normal Spirit Tool?" Zac asked.

"There really isn't one. Spirit Tools are generally more convenient, as the Tool Spirits are more compatible to reside in a weapon. It's either a sinister cultivator who makes them with mass sacrifices to suit their warped paths or as a punishment. Imagine, capturing the soul of your enemy and forcing it into an old rotten sword? It's pretty impactful." Catheya smiled. "Of course, I'd personally make them into my followers instead."

Zac shook his head with disgust before his thoughts went back to the youth back on the platform. Had he actually done something so cruel as to trap the souls of his enemies as punishment? It didn't fit with the righteous swordsman image he projected. But Zac was soon dragged out of his thoughts as someone knocked at the door.

Varo slowly walked over and opened it up to show Galau standing outside.

"I'm sorry to interrupt," Galau said as he repeatedly bowed toward

Zac and Catheya. "Ms. Peak and her friend have waited to speak with you for some time now… I wonder if you might be available today?"

"Interesting fellow," Catheya muttered as she stood up. "We're done here in any case. Here, take this. I believe it might become useful to you someday. You need to upgrade your Nexus Hub quite a bit before using it. You can contact me through the Eldritch Archivals there."

It was another Teleportation Token, though it looked more refined compared to those he had seen until now.

"Does this lead to the Undead Empire?" Zac asked as he looked at the Draugr in askance.

"No," she snorted. "If you showed up at a teleportation array in the Heartlands, you would get snatched up and realigned in seconds. This token leads to Twilight Harbor, an interesting place in a frontier sector neighboring this one. That sector is even younger than Zecia, and things are very chaotic and exciting. You could call Twilight Harbor a 'Gray Zone,' one of the few places where the living and dead intermingle."

"Didn't you say that wasn't allowed by the empire?" Zac asked with a raised brow.

"It's not. But I never said that all undead are part of the empire, did I?" the Draugr said with a smile as she left the room.

CHALLENGED

Zac looked over at Galau, who shook his head in confusion.

"I thought they were all part of the same empire as well, even if it was a pretty weak connection for local kingdoms," the merchant said. "Perhaps that's only true for the Zecia Sector?"

"Where is Pretty Peak now?" Zac asked, dropping the subject.

Zac was a bit surprised that the token didn't lead to Catheya's home planet, as he would have expected her to want to stay in touch. But she probably believed that he would never go to the Empire Heartlands, and felt it a waste of a token.

She couldn't know that it was a place that Zac was actually interested in visiting sooner or later, in order to find opportunities for his Draugr class. That would have to wait until he got a surefire way to hide his unique condition, though. Greatest was only a D-grade warrior, after all, and Zac doubted that the bracer he'd made would be able to fool anyone in such a place.

Twilight Harbor sounded like an interesting place as well, though, and it might serve as a safer substitute to the Empire Heartlands. Leaving one's planet while still at the F-grade was nigh suicidal, though, as any random Peak E-grade warrior might be able to kill him. He needed to reach at least a level of strength where he could escape from a D-grade warrior if needed.

"Lady Peak and Lady Lioress are currently resting in a neighboring room," Galau said.

"Lioress? Who's that?" Zac asked.

"I'm not sure. Her first name is Leyara. My guess is that she is a disciple of some of the hidden peak experts of the sector, judging by the way others treat her," Galau said with a low voice. "They might both be able to get in contact with the Heliophos Clan for you, which isn't easy, from what I've heard."

"Let them wait a few seconds more," Zac said as he indicated Galau to come inside instead. "Did you hear any mentions of the Great Redeemer outside? Are the claims credible? I'm thinking that cultivator who spoke up might have been messing with me as revenge or something."

"Have you seen the man you mentioned?" Galau asked, receiving a nod in response.

"Is this him?" Galau asked, and a face along with some text appeared on a screen the next moment.

"That's him," Zac confirmed with a sigh.

It was obviously the man he had seen twice, though his age was somewhat younger compared to the real-time avatar he had conjured when breaking the beacon. It looked like he wasn't lucky this time around, and the Redeemer really was part of the Karmic Cultivator clan.

"Well, his real name is Voridis A'Heliophos. He is not technically part of the Heliophos Clan, hence the prefix. He is presumably an illegitimate son of one of the grand elders of the family. It's said that the elder came back to the clan with a five-year-old child after having traveled for a few centuries, and he said the boy was his son," Galau started explaining as he took out a crystal.

"It's hard to get details since it seems like a touchy subject with the clan, but apparently, the boy seemed to have some unique gifts, and he was heavily nurtured even if he wasn't part of the real bloodline. But something happened, and Voridis couldn't form his Cultivator's Core, so he fell out of favor within the clan, much to his and his father's dismay.

"He got desperate, both due to his own remaining life span growing shorter by the day, and to prove himself to his clan again. He left the clan and came back as a D-grade Hegemon two hundred years later. However, the elders noticed something was wrong with his

Karma even though it was buried deep. It was eventually exposed that Voridis had used a taboo ritual that was powered by the deaths of millions of people," Galau said.

"So why is he still out causing trouble if he was exposed?" Zac asked with a frown.

"His father pled for leniency, and the patriarch relented and only exiled him after crippling his cultivation and putting a Karmic curse on him. They planned to let him live out his life as a mortal on a desolate planet to understand the plight of those he had killed.

"A thousand years later, another sacrifice was exposed, and it soon became apparent that it was Voridis who had regained his ability to cultivate and had just re-formed his Cultivator's Core. That was tens of thousands of years ago, and he still hasn't been caught by his family. There are at least four taboo genocides linked to him. The System has handed out multiple quests for his death as well, but he is still alive," Galau narrated, clearly reading off some information packet.

"Taboo?" Zac asked. "Like unorthodox?"

"Exactly. What he's doing is going against the will of the Heavens. That man wasn't talented enough to form a core by himself, but he didn't want to risk his life in Mystic Realms in hopes of finding opportunities that could allow him to break through. Instead, he chose to sacrifice mortals to change his fate. That is one of the most taboo actions to the Heavens," Galau explained.

Zac slowly nodded as he went over the information that Galau had provided. The origin of the Great Redeemer didn't change anything. The good news was that the Heliophos Clan seemed intent on dealing with their embarrassment, but the bad news was that the father seemed ready to cover for him even after all his transgressions.

It also meant that killing Voridis might cause all kinds of issues for Earth, as someone like a Grand Elder of a C-grade Karmic Clan probably could mess with a single D-grade planet without much effort. Perhaps focusing on making Earth harder to find rather than dealing with the man himself was really the better course of action.

There should be no cause of conflict between Earth and the Heliophos Clan if Earth simply hid away until the Great Redeemer had died or moved on.

Zac also noted that the merchant's wealth of knowledge seemed a lot broader right now compared to his comments after the fight.

"You've been busy since we exited," Zac commented.

"Ah, well." Galau coughed. "Gathering the information was mostly done by the two misses; I am just the messenger. Incidentally, why don't we head over and say hello?"

Zac shot an even glance at the merchant, waiting for an explanation.

"Well, you know what happened with the Tsarun Clan, and then the fight as we exited. I was afraid that it might implicate my family after all, but thankfully, I managed to form a connection with the Peak family. That way I won't return to my family like a criminal," the merchant confessed. "I'm sorry."

"Isn't knowing me enough of a boon now that the bounty is lifted?" Zac asked with confusion.

He wasn't trying to be arrogant, but he was the first person to conquer the eighth floor in an extremely long time in the sector, which no doubt hinted at him being a future powerhouse. Shouldn't such an accomplishment be worth something?

"Honestly, it's still not decided whether knowing you is a boon or a curse," Galau said with a wry smile. "It's unclear what the attitude of the Heliophos Clan and the Dravorak Dynasty will be. That will affect whether you will be seen as a murderous fugitive or a pride of the sector until you are strong enough to speak for yourself."

"I guess I overestimated myself." Zac snorted. "Before we head over, can you look into a few things for me?"

"Look into?" Galau said, his interest clearly piqued. "Treasures?"

"Exactly." Zac nodded.

He had spent over an hour with Catheya, but he hadn't been completely focused on their conversation. His hand had imperceptibly moved toward the Cosmos Sacks now and then, and he glanced at their contents.

There were a lot of things missing, but there was even more remaining. For example, almost the whole dragon was left intact, apart from some scales and the messy remains he'd thrown inside at the end. Both the massive horns and the Dragon Core were still there, which was a huge relief, as they were probably worth the most of the beast.

"Do you know what this is?" Zac asked. "Be careful. It comes from an elite assassin."

Galau gingerly took the spike and turned it over as his eyes flickered with light.

"There is a liquid inside," the merchant slowly said. "That is the real treasure. The young master from Zethaya might be more knowledgeable about it."

"I'm not comfortable with exposing what I found just yet." Zac smiled. "Please keep these things to yourself as well."

"Of course." Galau hurriedly nodded.

Zac took out one item after another from his Spatial Tools, and the eyes of Galau grew even wider.

"I've never heard of items with such craftsmanship appearing in the Tower of Eternity," the merchant mumbled. "Is it a special perk of the higher floors?"

Zac wouldn't expose the fact that he had taken them off the body of an elite from another part of the universe. He was afraid that would hurt resale value in case he decided to swap them for cold hard cash instead.

It turned out that over twenty of the odd trinkets in the mentalist's Spatial Ring were Array Breakers that could take out specific types of formations. It wasn't anything related to evolving or fighting, but rather items that were probably used to expedite the climb for the young mentalist. Galau couldn't pinpoint exactly what sort of arrays they worked against, though, as that would require some experimentation.

He was a bit surprised that there were no treasures geared toward evolving among the things he had picked up from the three elites. They should all have been right at the precipice before evolving, so why weren't they preparing? Or was there perhaps no point for people like them to carry around such items, as they could simply visit their clan's storage rooms?

Galau also had no idea what the odd heads that Zac had found in Faceless #9's Cosmos Sack were. He could confirm that they were some sort of unorthodox arrays that had trapped the souls of the previous owners, but he said that experimentation was the only way to know for sure what the arrays did.

It was either that or hand them over to an Array Master who could slowly decipher the inscriptions on the talisman, but Zac didn't know anyone like that at the moment.

Zac could only nod with some defeat and hope that the Sky Gnomes back on Earth knew more, even though the Thayer Consortium wasn't nearly as powerful as Galau's clan. They were, however, once a C-grade merchant clan, and a lot of knowledge should remain even if they had fallen to their current pitiful state over the past centuries.

The two soon enough left the room. The Zethaya scion was actually waiting outside, and Zac already knew the results of the Alchemist's inquiries, judging by his expression.

"I am afraid that there are no treasures to heal old wounds in the Base Town. Plenty of people have brought pills that can heal a recently wounded soul, such as our Zethaya's [Serene Soul Pill]. But you would normally only bring items like the [Prajñā Cherry] if you plan on selling or trading it," Boje explained with a pained expression.

"That's fine. I guessed as much." Zac sighed. "You don't happen to know a way to block out Karmic Links for a whole planet?"

"Is this about the Heliophos traitor?" Boje thoughtfully said. "It's an unusual problem. Perhaps there are arrays that can provide such an effect, but I would have to confer with a proper Array Master."

Zac nodded in thanks as the Alchemist walked off again, and his eyes turned to a woman who stood in a doorway not far away. It was one of the two ladies who had snatched up Galau earlier, and judging by the trademark purple hair, it was no doubt Pretty Peak.

"He's happy you're not holding a grudge." Pretty smiled. "Outliers like you are a nightmare for large clans. Come inside, and we can discuss your predicament."

Zac nodded and followed her inside, where the second girl waited. She stood up to greet him when he appeared, but Zac noticed that her smile looked a bit forced. Her eyes repeatedly went toward the various jewelry that decked his hands, while occasionally darting over to Galau to the side.

Had the merchant said something weird?

However, she soon snapped out of it and introduced herself as Leyara Lioress, calling herself the personal disciple of "the Void

Priestess." That didn't mean anything to Zac, but judging by Galau's reaction, it seemed as though she was a big shot in the sector, or at least in the Allbright Empire. Zac marked down the information for later before he introduced himself.

"I'm Zac. Nice to meet you," Zac simply said.

"I am Pretty Peak, but you can call me Divine Fist," Pretty added from the side, drawing a blank stare from Zac.

"Don't mind her." Leyara giggled from the side as she walked closer to Zac, causing a puff of perfume to waft over. "Pretty was finally allowed to change her name a year ago after forming a Midgrade Fragment while still in F-grade. But she can't decide on a new name."

"Yes, I've met your cousin." Zac coughed, surprised at how much stronger she seemed to be compared to her cousin. "How is Average?"

"He's current–" Pretty began, but Zac's attention was suddenly diverted by a System prompt that appeared in front of him.

[Lordship of Port Atwood Challenged]

"Lordship challenged?!" Zac swore out loud as he saw the prompt as he glared at the two girls; his dense killing intent started leaking a bit. "Who?"

"It's not us. Such a prompt means your capital is being attacked," Pretty said, her equanimity slightly cracking in front of Zac's aura.

Zac shot up from his seat upon hearing the news and started to walk out the door without another word.

"Wait," Pretty said from behind, and Zac looked back to see both the girls throw a Cosmos Sack over.

"We'll contact the Heliophos Clan for you," Pretty said. "We should have heard back within a month. You can read in the crystal how to contact me without exposing yourself."

"A small greeting gift from me," Leyara added as well.

"Thank you both." Zac nodded and left in a hurry to find Ogras.

"What did you give him?" Pretty asked her friend after Zac had left the room, noticing that her friend had acted a bit unnatural since Zac Piker had arrived.

"You heard the merchant's descriptions," Leyara said with a slight blush. "And you saw what he wore. Many geniuses have unique interests and tastes, and you have to adapt to circumstances."

"You didn't…" Pretty exclaimed, her eyes widening in disbelief.

TRAPPED

Zac rushed out of the meeting room and found the demon sitting in the lobby downstairs, surrounded by a handful of scions. Ogras looked up and instantly realized something was wrong with Zac's expression. A moment later, the demon had flashed over and a barrier of shadows shielded their conversation.

"The town is being attacked," Zac simply said with a low voice. "I got a prompt by the System."

"What?!" the demon said with surprise. "Who would be able to attack the island?"

"I'll go deal with it right now," Zac said. "It doesn't look like we'll be able to get any force to help us out against that guy anyway."

"No," Ogras said with a shake of his head. "I asked around. It seems a few C-grade forces in the sector have gone from rulers of their areas to beggars after having crossed that clan. One weird calamity after another befell their factions until nothing was left. They are definitely not some benign monks, and no one wants to be the next one to fall."

"You can stay behind a bit longer while I deal with this," Zac said after thinking it over. "I got something that will be able to see Karma threads at least. See if you can find anything else that can help us hide our planet better, like arrays or obscuring treasures."

"I'll make some inquiries. Many still want to make a connection to us even if they will stay out of the way of the Heliophos Clan," the demon said. "I'm sure I can squeeze all kinds of good things out of the people here. There might be something useful in the sacks I looted as well. I haven't had a chance to go through them yet."

"Might as well make the most of the situation." Zac sighed. "I've already asked Boje Zethaya, but see if you can find any soul-healing treasures. My soul cracked, and I was forced to use the treasure during the climb, and I don't have anything to heal Alea now. And get some materials for upgrading weapons as well."

The demon looked shocked before he wryly looked at the people around.

"I'll ask, but if the Zethaya descendant can't find anything, I doubt I will fare any better," Ogras said. "But the girl is strong, and we still have time. We need to focus on that old bastard coming for us. I'll see what solutions there are."

"Good. I got a token from Boje anyway, so we can always send someone over for a healing pill," Zac agreed as he took out the Tower Token. "When will you come back?"

"I'll sort things out quickly before returning as well," Ogras said after some thought. "Give me an hour or so."

Zac only nodded and cracked his token, and ten seconds later, he was back on Earth.

It almost felt surreal to be back in his secluded courtyard after moving through dozens of worlds that might have either been real or imaginary. The experiences over the past hundred days had been life-changing. Some parts had far exceeded his expectations, but for other things, he had come up short.

The increase to his power compared to when he left Earth just ten days ago was almost incalculable, yet he had still failed in either getting a real solution in the fight against the Great Redeemer or a cure for Alea. It wasn't all hopeless, though, as Ogras might be able to come back with something that would help them shroud Earth from any Karmic trails.

But there was no time to rest. He was still not completely recuperated from the showdown outside the Tower of Eternity, but he had thankfully relied heavily on his accumulated treasures to tide that tribulation. It left him with a decent amount of Cosmic Energy to spare, though the side effects of **[Hatchetman's Rage]** were still there to a certain degree.

There were no obvious sounds of battle that he could hear, so he rushed toward his Nexus Node. His first instinct was that someone might be trying to tamper with his private node while he was away, like a spy trying to snatch his lordship from under his nose. But the house with the node was empty, and it didn't look like anyone had messed with it either.

Zac quickly walked out of the building and was about to head toward the town, when a shocking explosion erupted to the south. Trees were almost flattened to the ground, and Zac felt the shockwave deep into his bones even though the explosion came from hundreds of meters away. There was only one thing in that direction, the shipyard.

"The Creators?" Zac muttered with confusion before he flashed away.

A massive plume of flames rose to the sky the moment he passed the final layer of trees, and Zac was forced to cover his face from the intense light. The explosion earlier must have taken place somewhere out on the water, but Zac could feel the heat all the way from where he stood.

Zac was about to rush toward the Creator offices, but he noticed that a familiar figure had appeared in front of him without him noticing. It was Rahm, the Creator liaison.

"Lord Atwood, it has been a while. I hope you are well?" the stoic Creator said, seemingly unperturbed by the fact that the whole area had been turned into a blazing inferno.

"I'm fine," Zac said. "More importantly, what is going on? Are there attackers on the island? Or is this an experiment?"

"It is not an experiment, unfortunately," Rahm said. "It would appear that you are being invaded. Multiple large ships have breached your shores, and there have been sounds of conflict for a while now. The explosion just now was one of the ships trying to breach our arrays."

"Do you need assistance?" Zac asked.

"No," a booming voice echoed as the familiar spider-golem emerged from the offices. "It's so rare I get to see some action, and I hold no love for either the fanatics or the unliving. There is no way these children will be able to breach our fortifications, so you can rest easy. Nothing will be able to anchor on this side of your living quarters."

It was Karunthel, the Creator foreman, who had shown up. He looked pretty much the same as before, with the noticeable addition of a cannon radiating a terrifying amount of energy that had been mounted onto his torso. The spider golem was turning more and more into a killer robot every day.

"What?" Zac blurted with confusion. "Are they *both* attacking us? They are supposed to be mortal enemies."

"I guess you youngsters gave them a scare. Should've finished them off sooner, though; now they're crawling all over the island." Karunthel shrugged as he inspected Zac.

"Brat, your aura is getting nice and condensed. But if you would accept a piece of advice, don't get hung up on perfection. Cultivation might not be a sprint, but it is not a marathon either. You need to maintain momentum and keep pushing forward. The second you stop, it will be much harder to start running again," he said.

"Thank you," Zac said, though he couldn't really focus on the advice after hearing the whole island was under attack. "I will soon evolve. So you are fine here?"

"They have already realized we're a Mercantile Structure and will soon move on." Karunthel laughed. "And I am not allowed to blast those rats who are staying outside the shields. Not within the job description. But I've expanded the shield to the maximum area that I am allowed, which will keep part of your coastline safe at least."

"Thank you. I'll visit you once this is dealt with." Zac nodded before making a beeline toward Port Atwood.

Zac rapidly moved through his private forest like a specter, each step with [Loamwalker] moving him fifty meters forward. Urgency and some confusion made his mind muddled as he tried to figure out just what was going on. Had the two bitter enemies really put their differences aside just for him? He had never heard of anything like it.

And more importantly, how the hell had they found these secluded islands so easily? It had taken months of exploration to find the mainland, so finding his small island would be like looking for a needle in a haystack.

He could only pray he wasn't too late yet again. With both him and Ogras gone, and Alea in a coma, there was pretty much no one who would be able to rebuff an assault. He could only thank the System that it was kind enough to provide a warning that his people were under attack.

Another massive shockwave erupted in the distance, containing enough power to almost throw him off his feet. A plume of golden flames rose into the sky, and Zac remembered Ogras' descriptions of the zealots' powers all too well. Fury started to smolder in his mind, fiery anger at the people who dared launch such a massive strike at a town full of civilians and noncombat personnel.

The world shrank around him as he pushed **[Loamwalker]** to its limits. The towering flames came from the northeast, some ways inland from the coast. It was the part of Port Atwood that contained the Academy and the structures related to his army. It seemed the attackers knew what parts they needed to take out first.

Was there really a spy on the island?

Port Atwood had thankfully overhauled its defenses since the last waves of attacks, and his people should at least be able to hold out for a while even against the Undead Empire. Back then, he barely had the resources to run a simple town protection array, but Port Atwood had been a Global City for quite some time now.

He had given his subordinates almost free rein with the town's funds in order to develop Port Atwood, and he saw waves of flames slamming into a sturdy crystalline barrier as he approached the battlefield. Four massive fractals shone in the sky, and one of them suddenly lit up.

A tremendous surge of chaotic energies cut straight through the seas of flames with such force that space was ripped open, and a thundering explosion could be heard as the attack hit something on the other side of the ten-meter-tall wall.

It was clear that the town had added some great new defenses, but both the Undead Empire and the Church of the Everlasting Dao were terrifying forces with extremely deep Heritages. A golden ball slammed into the crystalline shield protecting the wall the next moment, causing massive cracks all over as streams of fire shot toward the people standing guard on the wall walk.

Zac's eyes widened with anger as he saw the gouts of flames pour down toward his army, who were desperately trying to maintain the barrier. The ground cracked beneath his feet as he leaped forward, and a storm of leaves spread out to create a vast canopy to block out the rain of fire.

"Lord Atwood!" a Valkyrie suddenly screamed, and hundreds of hopeful eyes were turned in his direction.

Zac only nodded in response as he flew toward the golden ball in the sky with furious momentum, and his body was hardened by the Fragment of the Coffin as his fist slammed into the molten core. A shockwave spread out in all directions from his punch, and a few warriors were even thrown off from the wall as the golden ball was twisted and deformed before it was flung away.

Another shudder spread through the earth as the ball landed some distance outside the wall. Zac himself landed on the wall walk, and he tried to understand what was going on outside. However, the only thing that met his gaze was a sea of flames that spread in every direction outside the city wall.

The lunatics had set half the island on fire, it seemed.

"What's going on?" Zac asked as a familiar demon rushed to his side.

It was Harvath, one of the demon captains who had accompanied him in the Underworld and the earlier incursions.

"We discovered six massive ships heading this way about a day ago, carrying both the undead and zealots of the Church of Everlasting Dao," Harvath explained between pants. "We tried to stop their advance with repeated raids using our smaller vessels, but we only managed to sink two of them before our ships were too burned to continue attacking."

"The Undead Empire has really teamed up with the Church?" Zac asked incredulously, still having trouble believing it was true.

"It appears that way," Harvath said. "Three of the remaining ships sailed for our island, with the final one veering off for some reason. We fear that other settlements might have been hit."

"You don't know?" Zac asked with a frown.

"They are somehow blocking our teleporters. It is like this island has become isolated from the rest of the world. We have lost connection to all other locations on our teleportation list. We could still tele-port within the island until recently, but we lost that ability a few minutes ago. We have sent out scouting vessels but haven't gotten word back," he said.

"How's that possible?" Zac muttered with a frown.

"General Ilvere believes the ship might have dropped some manner of spatial disruption arrays into the ocean as they sailed toward us," Harvath said. "But we don't know."

Zac frowned when he heard about the block. It seemed to be the same technology as that which almost got Alea and his whole army killed. He hadn't expected being troubled by such technology right as he returned, and he didn't have any real way to solve it. The simplest method would be to destroy the jammers, but he didn't even know what they looked like.

Were the invaders trying to imprison him on this remote island?

6 0

SOWING DISCORD

"How do things look with the undead incursion?" Zac asked after making sure that another molten ball wasn't coming their way. "Have you found out how long until it activates?"

"The array has already been activated," the demon said after a brief hesitation. "Half the sky of the main continent is reportedly covered with a green array."

"WHAT?!" Zac almost roared, his eyes widening with shock. "Since when?"

"Four days ago." The demon sighed. "But it is not converting the world as of yet; it is currently drawing energy from the planet. Your sister and the human champions have worked hard to slow it down for your return, but I am not sure how much time there is left. Lady Atwood will likely know more."

"Okay, where is my sister right now?" Zac asked, his mind reeling after getting bombarded by a series of unwelcome news the past hour.

His miscalculation of the time he had remaining had caused massive repercussions for Earth, and he felt a wave of shame upon thinking back to his meeting with Thea just before leaving for the Tower. He could only pray that he had returned in time to set things right.

"She is fighting at Azh'Rodum," Harvath said. "She is holding the invaders back with your swarm of flying machines."

"My machines?" Zac repeated with confusion before he remembered the drones.

She had actually gained control of the drone swarms, which Zac guessed wasn't surprising considering Jeeves. Some fear flickered in his heart, but he knew he couldn't blame her for taking them out. If now was not the time to use them, then when? But another point of confusion suddenly entered his mind.

"Wait, Azh'Rodum? What are they doing so far inland?" Zac asked with a frown.

"We don't know. They first tried bombarding us from a distance where we couldn't retaliate, but our shields were too strong for those attacks. So two ships stayed outside this town while they prepared for a siege, while the largest ship sailed north," the demon captain explained. "We believe they might be targeting the Vein through the mine."

"Who went with her?" Zac asked.

"Most of the Valkyries, along with Ilvere and a squad of E-grade demons. Azh'Rodum is not as strongly defended, and it is the gateway to the Nexus Vein, so most of our elites went there. Our task here is simply to hold out until you and the young lord returned, or until the threat inland was averted. The young master... is he here?" Harvath asked as he looked around.

"Ogras is still in the Tower of Eternity; he is fine. I got a prompt that Port Atwood was under attack, so I returned early. Ogras will return a bit later after he has dealt with some matters over there," Zac explained as his mind went over the details.

Some things didn't make sense. His force had been in combat for over a day. Why hadn't the System warned him? He also suddenly remembered the spike in levels for Thea and Billy roughly twelve hours ago in real time.

"Are Billy and Thea on the island?" Zac asked.

"Yes, it was only thanks to them we managed to sink one of the ships before we were pushed back." Harvath nodded, some respect shining in his eyes. "They are currently on bed rest. Janos had to hypnotize the big one to prevent him from running out and bashing the invaders with that nasty club of his. They will be fine in a week or two."

Zac sighed in relief when hearing those two were fine. It looked like they actually had risked their lives to protect his people. But it made him all the more confused why the alert had only warned him just now.

"Did something change a few minutes ago?" Zac suddenly asked.

"A few minutes ago?" the demon repeated. "Nothing special has happened except our communications being blocked. They did also start shooting those massive balls at our shield recently. We can't see them any longer because of the flames, but the zealots set up large siege tools some distance from here."

Zac slowly nodded in understanding. It seemed that the System only gave out a warning at the last moment, which was a valuable piece of information. He couldn't rely on the System as a warning call to protect his home. This time, he was lucky enough to be able to get back to town almost instantly, but that wouldn't always be the case.

He really needed to erect a more permanent protection that would withstand any threat on Earth.

"I can't see anything in front of me; what are they doing on the other side of the flames?" Zac finally asked.

"Our vision has been blocked for a while now as well. It's almost exclusively the cultists who have set up camp outside. We received a report that the situation is almost the opposite at Azh'Rodum before we lost contact. There's almost only undead warriors up there."

"I'll deal with the attackers here before heading to Azh'Rodum," Zac said. "Try to find out if they've erected some sort of array anywhere. We need to break the arrays blocking our communications."

With that, he simply jumped out from the wall and landed in a sea of flames that rose over a dozen meters into the air. He had just jumped twenty meters or so, but his vision was completely blocked in both directions, and he was forced to activate the Fragment of the Coffin to not get burnt. A thought suddenly struck him, and his Specialty Core activated.

The undead and the cultists might be working together on the surface, but things weren't very harmonious from the sound of it. Perhaps he could cause some confusion within their ranks with his alternate form while also letting his Hatchetman class rest for a bit.

Both the main skills of Hatchetman were on cooldown, after all, along with **[Hatchetman's Rage]**.

Granted, he was still pretty confident at defeating this army even with Hatchetman in a weakened state. His power had almost doubled in the ten short days since he'd left Earth, while the invaders still should have some small restrictions to their power. Not only that, but he had also gone through all sorts of life-and-death encounters, sharpening his skills to the utmost.

His body grew as the pitch-black armor covered his body, and Zac caused the flames surrounding him to die out with one massive swing of his bardiche. It put him face-to-face with the zealot army, and he was delighted to see their anger and confusion as a sea of Miasma spread out around him as he started running toward their front lines.

"You! What ploy is this!" a massive roar echoed out from the army, and a huge lizardman decked in thick armor shining in gold and red pushed past the inquisitors at the front.

Zac didn't answer, but he instead took out one of the enormous Unholy Beacons from his Cosmos Sack and slammed it into the ground like he was planting a flag. It immediately started spewing out Miasma, though most of it was burned away by the surrounding flames. But this was more about sending a message than getting more death-attuned energy, and the effect was immediate.

"Heretic! Your sins will be judged today!" the infuriated Bishop roared, and Zac couldn't help but snicker beneath his helmet as the undead liaisons were mobbed by infuriated cultists.

There was no time to waste, though, as his sister was fighting for her life as far as he knew. The only reason he didn't rush to Azh'Rodum right away was that he believed her to be somewhat safe with the help of the drone swarm he had left on Port Atwood. She also had access to the Town Shop, meaning she could keep buying one defensive layer after another as needed.

He still didn't want to waste time with the crazy zealots, though, and he stomped down onto the ground to teleport into the middle of the army. However, he was surprised to find himself rebuffed, and he stumbled a bit as he appeared right outside a golden shield that had appeared in front of the army.

"We have fought your kind for millions of years. Did you truly think we didn't come prepared?!" The Bishop roared with mad laughter.

Zac knew he was putting himself at a disadvantage by fighting as an undead against the cultists, as they had whole armies dedicated to fighting the Undead Empire. However, he saw it as an opportunity to fight in an adverse situation, and he still felt he had the strength to prevail. There was no way he wouldn't be able to deal with these guys head-on unless the leaders of the two incursions had shown up on his doorstep.

But that would be fine with Zac as well, as killing those two would essentially end the incursions and threat to Earth.

His arm swelled as he forced it full of Miasma for [Unholy Strike], and the whole area shook as the shield was beset by a series of furious swings empowered by his improved Middle-stage Dao Fragment. Almost a dozen of the robed priests standing behind the shield hunkered over after the first swing, with a few even starting to bleed from their ears.

A storm of golden flames beset him as Zac tried to force his way through the shield, but he kept them at bay with [Immutable Bulwark]. However, he noticed with some surprise that the flames were like sticky napalm, and they stayed on the fractal bulwark and slowly whittled it down. It was like the flames and the Miasma canceled each other out, and Zac felt a far higher than normal consumption just to maintain the fractal shield.

His reserves of death-attuned energies were thankfully immense due to his almost inhuman attribute pool, and he kept providing the bulwark with more and more energy until he managed to create a crack in the wall. He forced himself through in an instant; he was upon the cultists like a fox in a henhouse.

Two burly clergymen tried to take him down by swinging scepters that contained the same fiery energy as the ranged attacks. Zac blocked one of them with his axe, and the other one got slammed with [Everlasting] with enough force to be thrown dozens of meters away. Zac heard a crunching sound after the man was hit with the shield-bash, and he felt a surge of energy not long after he fell onto the ground.

"Regroup!" the leader from before shouted, but Zac didn't want to give them any time to retreat to a safe distance.

He stomped his foot onto the ground once more, and the cage of [Profane Seal] rose from the ground and captured almost the whole army along with the siege tools that had been shooting out the molten cores at the City Shield. However, he was unable to spread his corrosive breath along with Miasma from [Fields of Despair] to cover the cage, as waves of flames kept dispersing the mists.

Zac finally gave up on his usual tactics and instead started fighting by hand as he commanded the fifteen spectral chains to target the weaker warriors. Ghosts kept appearing in the cage as well as hundreds of the cultists tried to destroy the gates and the towers of [Profane Seal], only to hurt themselves.

A hundred skeletal warriors also emerged from the ground, and they formed ten squads that moved across the cage to take out stragglers and interrupt the zealots' attempts to form a proper defense against the chains. Unfortunately, it seemed as though the cultists were quite adept at fighting skeletons, and Zac felt himself losing subordinates at a rapid pace.

However, it wasn't like the life and death of the skeletons mattered, as long as they fulfilled their purpose. The whole cage was an utter mess soon enough with battles taking place everywhere. Errant flames and Miasmic gusts made visibility almost impossible, and Zac was only able to make sense of the situation with the help of [Cosmic Gaze].

A tremendous wave of golden flames threatened to swallow Zac whole as the siege weapons launched a barrage meant for shield-breaking right at him, scoring over fifteen zealots by mistake. He swiftly cut the projectiles apart with a Dao-infused swing, and he started taking out the operators the next moment.

One siege tool after another entered his Spatial Ring as the controllers were cut into two, and the situation was turning gradually in his favor, as each chain soon held multiple desiccated corpses while they whizzed around. The head priest had been suspiciously silent until now, though, but Zac finally spotted him through the flames.

Two wings sprouted out from his back, and he rose over a dozen meters into the air even after the suppressive effect of the turquoise fractal sealing the cage. A glowing orb of flames over fifteen meters across emerged behind his back, making him look like an apostle of the sun. However, it still looked a bit hollow in Zac's eyes, as he had witnessed the true flames conjured by Iz Tayn.

"Weight of the Heavens!" the priest roared, and a massive array appeared in the sky above the cage the next moment.

Zac's eyes widened at the sight, but it still wasn't enough to make him despair or even worry. He had faced a lot stronger arrays just a few hours ago, and Zac still had almost half his treasures remaining if need be. Besides, the restrictive array from [Profane Seal] didn't only put pressure on the people inside, it also acted as a protection from outside interference.

But Zac realized that the cultists were going all out as he spotted nine priests who had kept out of harm's way until now, each of them holding a metal sun toward the sky that seemed to burn the controllers alive. He directed a chain toward each of the priests, but they were immediately rebuffed by a fiery wall of flames whose heat was enough to turn the spectral fetters into motes of Miasma when they got too close.

A few seconds later, the nine priests were gone, replaced with nine hovering suns positioned in a circle at the edge of the cage.

The nine glowing suns were clearly related to the array that had lit up in the sky above, but the main controller was no doubt the Bishop, who was still hovering up in the air. Zac growled in frustration over the lack of ranged options in his Undying Bulwark class, and he opted to try out his recently invented tactic again.

A spectral chain made a few loops around his chest before it hoisted him up, but he only managed to rise five meters before the Bishop launched a stream of fire that destroyed the midsection of the chain. Zac helplessly fell down again, wondering if he actually had to waste one of his single-use treasures on a simple general.

"A lowly cretin wants to rise toward the sky?" the Bishop roared. "The Boundless Heavens won't abide it!"

METEORS

The Bishop's golden array lit up the next moment, and a fiery meteor several times larger than the one that had slammed into the City Shield began its descent, its fall accompanied by a rain of fire so hot that the air itself was incinerated.

Zac realized these maniacs weren't called zealots by chance, and over a hundred of their own would die if that thing slammed into the ground in the confined space of [Profane Seal].

"We wanted to use this strike on the native Lord, but taking out an elite from the five cursed Races is a worthy trade." The Bishop laughed from the sky.

The meteor rammed into the Miasmic fractal acting as a dome for the Miasmic cage the next second, and Zac knew in an instant that it would only hold for so long before cracking. Zac started running toward the edge of the cage along with the surviving cultists, but he was forced to carve a path of blood, as the lunatics seemed ready to sacrifice their lives just to keep him within the blast zone.

However, the normal cultists had no means to even impede Zac's escape, and he reached the edge of his cage just as the turquoise fractal broke apart, transmitting a blowback to Zac that made him stumble for a second.

The meteor regained its momentum in an instant, but it actually managed to change its trajectory, and it went straight for Zac. He growled in annoyance as he activated [Immutable Bulwark] and infused it with the Fragment of the Coffin. The fractal wall grew to its maximum size, reaching almost twenty meters across, but it could still barely cover a third of the meteor as the two collided.

Zac felt like he was being subjected to the gravity of a sun as he was locked in a battle of man versus nature. His whole body trembled from the strain as the pressure was transmitted from the skill into his body. A few zealots tried to take the opportunity to strike while Zac was occupied, but they found themselves turned into desiccated husks from a few spectral chains that hovered around Zac like sentinels.

The meteor thankfully lost its momentum fast enough, and Zac pushed the fiery ball toward the largest clump of soldiers with a grunt, and it landed among them with a massive outburst of flames that rushed in every direction. The soldiers had desperately tried to erect some golden shields to stop the meteor as well, but they were nowhere near as powerful as Zac and his fractal bulwark.

The shields had broken in an instant, and the cultists were either turned to paste or burned alive.

Screams could be heard from every direction, and not even Zac was completely unscathed even if he had managed to change the trajectory of the array. He had lost a large chunk of Miasma to maintain the massive shield as it was pressed against the flaming meteor, and he was still beset by the waves of flames that instantly covered the entire cage after the impact.

He also felt that the whole cage was being pushed toward its breaking point. The dome in the sky breaking had already damaged [Profane Seal], and cracks now covered both the towers and gates of the skill. The only thing maintaining the skill right now was probably the infusion of energy from the fifteen spectral chains.

However, Zac didn't enjoy that kind of energy boost, as [Fields of Despair] was completely countered by the all-consuming flames. The Miasmic haze hadn't been present at all during the battle, and he hadn't gotten even a smidgeon of Miasma from the large number of killed zealots. It was the first time he had met a perfect counter to so many of his skills in his Undying Bulwark form, and he felt it wasn't by chance that the Church of Everlasting Dao and the Undying Empire were such bitter enemies.

Zac quickly readjusted his shield so that it shrank just to the point that it covered his body. It was just in time as well, as waves of fire and molten stones shot toward him. The heat was blistering, but it was somewhat manageable by circulating the Fragment of the Bodhi through his body. His first instinct was to dispel the cage and regroup, perhaps even change back to his human form to gain some ranged capabilities to take out the Bishop and the stragglers.

However, Zac eventually decided against that course of action. Instead of fleeing from the scorching heat of the meteor, he ran toward it. The ground shuddered beneath his feet as he ran as quickly as his bulky transformation allowed, and he ignored the burning heat that was transmitted straight through his armor as he started scrambling up the burning meteor.

The Bishop was still floating in the air, the flames seemingly having no effect on him, and he started to rise even higher when he noticed Zac's approach.

There should no doubt be a limit of how long an E-grade warrior could stay in the sky, but Zac wasn't willing to let the Bishop run amok until he ran out of steam. He wanted to end things quickly since his sister was waiting for him, but he was out of offensive treasures that could kill the flying man in one go.

Hoisting himself into the air with the spectral chains had already failed spectacularly as well, so he could only move as quickly as he could until he reached the top of the meteor to use it as a springboard before it was too late. The Bishop launched a storm of flames in his direction, but he simply punched through them as he jumped toward the lizardman in the sky.

The meteor cracked beneath Zac's feet as he put everything into the hulking leap, and his arm was already swelling in size in preparation for the final strike. The Bishop snorted and flexed his wings, but ten spectral chains whipped at him from behind to push him down. It was the final hurrah of the spectral chains before **[Profane Seal]** was destroyed by the flames.

Eight of the chains were incinerated as they tried to destroy the radiant sun that shielded the Bishop, but the sacrifice released a dense storm of Miasmic gases that allowed the final two chains to pass straight through the globe of fire unscathed. The Bishop was forced to stop ascending to avoid the attack, which kept him in Zac's trajectory.

The wings of the cultist suddenly covered his own body in an embrace and Zac realized the man was using some sort of movement skill. However, that was just what Zac hoped for, and he swung his axe the moment he saw a burst of flames appear in front of him. The massive bardiche fell, cutting straight through a golden fractal and luxuriant armor.

The large meteor lost most of its heat in an instant, and three thuds echoed out across the battlefield as Zac and the two bisected pieces of the Bishop landed on the scorched ground. A large surge of energy entered his body, but he also felt a backlash as the Miasmic cage finally broke apart.

Zac would have thought that seeing their leader getting cut in two would douse the fighting spirit of the surviving zealots, but he had severely underestimated just how crazy these people were. Most of them started emitting extremely condensed fires from their mouths and eyes, and they heedlessly ran toward him as their bodies started swelling.

Some fell onto the ground before they even got close to Zac, their bodies turning into bloated balloons before exploding into cascading flames. It reminded Zac of the man who had exploded when he saved Kenzie from the New World Government at the border town. The whole area shuddered as dozens of eruptions went off one after another as the soldiers tried to bring Zac with them down to hell.

The pitch-black armor from [Vanguard of Undeath] was already in a haggard state after climbing atop the meteor, and the blasts were quickly ripping apart the remaining layers. Zac blocked out the attacks he could with [Immutable Bulwark], whereas the few remaining skeletons absorbed some of the attacks for him.

Thankfully, the battlefield turned quiet soon enough, with just him and a few dying cultists remaining.

His hair was singed clean off, and burns covered a large part of his body, but one of the two invading armies were dealt with at least. The cultists hadn't even managed to harm him apart from some surface burns, but they had been a surprisingly hard nut to crack. It looked like most, if not all, of the incursion restrictions were gone by this point.

Normally, he would have wanted to sit down and go over the battle at this juncture, as it felt like he had gained a lot from the fight. But there was no time, and Zac turned back to his human form before he walked back through the burning wreckage toward Port Atwood's wall.

He jumped up with a grunt, appearing next to the demon captain and a few Valkyries who had waited for his return.

"I've dealt with the leader and the army, but be careful," Zac said as he cracked his neck. "There might be more hiding."

Harvath slowly nodded as he looked out across the destruction outside the wall, mute disbelief apparent in his eyes.

"Have you found anything about the array jamming?" Zac asked as he took out one of his healing pills to deal with the burns.

"I'm sorry, we didn't dare to leave the wall while you fought in case we would become a liability. We'll start cleaning up the battle-field and looking for the array right away," Harvath said as he started awake.

"That's fine." Zac nodded as he took out his new flying treasure, the large inscribed leaf. "I'm heading inland. Be careful, most of the cultists chose to blow themselves up, but perhaps there are reinforce-ments on the ship."

"We'll be careful." Harvath nodded. "Don't worry, and let us deal with the aftermath."

Zac jumped on the treasure the next moment, and it soundlessly rose to the sky before it shot away with enough speed to rip the clouds in two.

It felt a bit bad to leave Port Atwood while there were still enemies remaining. He had dealt with the army, but who knew what other things the cultists had planned. It was all too apparent just how far they were willing to go to take out their enemies, and he wouldn't be surprised if they had more nasty surprises in store for his island.

However, there was only one of him, and he needed to prioritize where to strike for maximum effect.

The speed of Zac's new flying treasure was just shocking, and he wasn't sure whether he would have been able to hang on if it weren't for the protective array that blocked out any wind. He didn't have any means to make an exact measurement, but he felt that the leaf would be able to keep up with a modern fighter jet.

At least it felt like he moved a lot faster compared to when he had flown in a commercial airplane before the integration.

It wasn't all thanks to the high-quality craftsmanship of the vessel, though. He had actually noticed that he could infuse the leaf with the Fragment of the Bodhi, which boosted the treasure's speed by around 30%. He believed he could push the thing even further if he had some nature-attuned crystals to feed into the sockets rather than normal E-grade Nexus Crystals.

It would normally have taken Zac hours to reach Azh'Rodum by foot, even if he used **[Loamwalker]** to speed up, but he was closing in on the center of the island after just fifteen minutes of travel. He was anxious to reach the demon stronghold, as he didn't want to repeat the tragedy of arriving just a few seconds too late again.

Finally, he saw the battlefield ahead, or rather the massive clouds of Miasma that covered a huge section of the northern parts of the island. The undead forces had no doubt set up a large array of Unholy Beacons to form such a vast cloud, but he frowned in confusion when he saw that there wasn't much of a battle raging.

There was a hovering line of sentries protecting the whole flank of Azh'Rodum, and there were over a hundred craters on the ground outside, along with a few scorched bodies. It looked like there had been a few minor skirmishes that had been ended with laser beams by his sister, but the complete lack of damage to the town fortifications indicated that the undead army wasn't even straining itself to take over the town.

However, the defenders were desperately launching attacks at an aquamarine shield from the walls of Azh'Rodum, with dozens of projectiles hitting the barrier every second. It almost felt like the roles of invader and defender had been swapped. Zac guessed that something was brewing within the cloud of Miasma that needed to be dealt with, and quickly, judging by the fervor of the attacks.

He didn't even touch down inside the town to get a grasp on the situation, but he rather chose to fly straight toward the Miasmic shield. Just when he was a hundred meters from the shield, he pushed off while simultaneously stowing away the treasure. Tremendous amounts of Cosmic Energy swirled around him as he shot toward the shield while **[Verun's Bite]** drenched the area in a bloody hue.

This time, he would be the meteor.

62

FIGHTING FATE

The air screamed around Zac as he shot toward the turquoise shield with the speed of an airplane, and even he got a bit worried he was playing a bit fast and loose with his life. However, he threw any hesitation into the back of his mind as he conjured a fractal blade that was as large as himself. He was perfectly capable of making it even larger, but he needed to contain the impact to a smaller area.

The blade first changed color to a gleaming silver as he imbued it with the Fragment of the Axe, but the sanguine glow quickly spread from [Verun's Bite] as well to cover the whole fractal edge. This was the most power he could release without utilizing [Hatchetman's Rage] or the slumbering Remnants, and he could only pray that it was enough to punch a hole in the massive array.

The world froze as Zac's attack cut into the shield with all the power he could muster, but an enormous shockwave that dispersed the clouds of Miasma soon followed. Hairline cracks spread for hundreds of meters in each direction, and Zac managed to squeeze through the hole in the barrier before it healed.

However, the point of impact was over a hundred meters in the air, and he had no means to control his descent. The collision had also caused him to completely lose balance, and any hopes of a hero's entrance were dashed as he slammed into the ground face-first. Another shockwave, this one a lot smaller, spread out from the point of impact, instantly killing the closest Zombies. He scrambled back to his feet while wiping away some of the blood running from his nose, and he took stock of the situation.

The insides of the array were shrouded by dense swirls of Miasmic haze, and his skin crawled from the contact with the condensed death-attuned energies. The extremely limited sight made it impossible to see any clear threat to Port Atwood, and instantly getting mobbed by enraged elite Zombies didn't make things easier to discern.

Fractal blades shot out in each direction as swathes of destruction were carved into the undead hordes. However, these were the best of the Zombies, and the fractal blades were whittled down before they reached too far. Each strike still killed over fifty Zombies, but the blades broke apart from a storm of counterstrikes after that.

Zac activated **[Cosmic Gaze]** in hopes of making anything out, but everything became a haze of varying degrees of gray. However, he did spot spots with more condensed energies, and he shot toward the closest target.

A few seconds later, he found himself in front of an Unholy Beacon, and Zac wasn't surprised by the sight at all. What did make him frown in consternation, however, was the array surrounding it. There hadn't been anything like that around the beacons he had seen until now, and he guessed it was some sort of secondary array that was powered by the beacon.

The beacon was guarded by a hulking Corpse Golem that swung at Zac the moment he appeared. However, Zac's physique was beyond monstrous by now, with an effective strength reaching 2,500. Zac countered the punch with his own, his fist not even a tenth the size of the massive undead construct.

A thundering explosion echoed out as the arm of the golem blew apart from the force, and it was cut in two the next second as Zac slashed it with a lazy swing as he stepped toward the beacon. He couldn't make out its purpose, so Zac simply cut a few lines to ruin the inscriptions before he ripped the beacon out of the ground and stashed it in his Spatial Ring.

Zac was a moving calamity as he moved from beacon to beacon at his utmost speed, and he had stolen ten beacons in less than three minutes. Some of them had launched massive outbursts of death-attuned energies at him, but Zac had managed to dodge the waves of death with the help of **[Loamwalker]**.

One of them had actually detonated just as he was about to stow it away, but the vibrant energies of the Fragment of the Bodhi were able to neutralize the attack. He still hadn't spotted any leaders, so he could only keep going in hopes that they would be forced to show their hand sooner or later.

A large shudder echoed out when he ripped another beacon out of the ground, and he saw that the shield finally flickered before it dissipated.

It had been pretty smashed by his tremendous momentum when he'd launched himself at it, but it had soon healed itself after he pushed his way through. But now it looked like Zac had caused too much destruction within the shield, to the point that it could no longer maintain its functionality. The highly condensed Miasma within the barrier started to spread out as well, but Zac knew that it would sooner or later be cleansed by the pure energies of the world.

However, his confusion only grew while looking around as visibility steadily grew better. He couldn't see any high-grade siege tools or anything else that would separate the thousands of Zombies from normal elites. But he finally spotted a group of hooded beings in the back of the army, guarded by five hulking E-grade Corpse Golems.

Zac immediately rushed toward them, carving a line of true death through the Zombie horde. The hooded warriors didn't react to his approach, but the golems readied themselves for battle and started rushing toward him. However, these golems were only marginally stronger than those who had guarded the Unholy Beacons, and Zac needed less than a minute to turn them into small hills of rock-hard flesh.

The hooded warriors had started fleeing, but he effortlessly captured one of them while blocking the escape of the others. It tried to struggle out of his grasp, but Zac was surprised to find that it was pitifully weak.

"What are you planning?" Zac growled with anger as he ripped the hood from the Lich's head.

However, what met Zac's gaze wasn't the Lich King or one of his generals, but just some random Revenant that couldn't have been higher than Level 60. Zac crushed its neck in frustration before he captured the others, getting the same results.

Just what was going on?

It quickly became apparent that this was all a big diversion, and that the undead weren't actually interested in conquering Azh'Rodum. But what was the point of sacrificing their own without any gain? Was it to trick the Church of the Everlasting Dao? Or was the real mission taking place somewhere else?

Zac's first thought was the mines, just like how Harvath had guessed. Were they trying to mess with his Nexus Vein somehow? If the real leaders had entered the confusing mess of subterranean tunnels beneath the island, it would be extremely annoying to root them out, as his own force still hadn't completely mapped the nigh endless number of narrow passageways that ran beneath the surface.

However, he suddenly saw someone running toward him, decimating all the Zombies that tried to impede her path with a barrage of attacks based on the four elements. Zac flashed over to Kenzie, who immediately threw herself in his arms. He really wanted to catch up and hear what had happened since he left, but he saw how frazzled she had looked as she ran toward him.

Something was wrong.

"Are you okay?" Zac asked. "What's going on?"

"I am fine, but someone is tampering with the arrays in the valley since some time ago!" Kenzie said with worry as she released him. "I stationed a few sentries on the mountain just in case, but I can't get a hold of them now with the jammers. I'm afraid they're up to something over there. I've been trying to head to the mountain, but the undead swarm anyone who leaves the town. We've tried breaking out, but their shields were too strong."

"I'll deal with it," Zac said as the leaf appeared again beneath his feet. "There are no elites here, it seems. I think this whole army is a diversion. I'll be back in a bit."

The next second, he was hundreds of meters away, speeding toward the secluded valley.

Panic coursed through Zac's body as he infused the flying treasure with the Fragment of the Bodhi. He had handed over control of the network of arrays he had erected around the island to his sister upon leaving, so he hadn't noticed anything wrong at all since arriving. His thoughts were a mess as he tried to figure out the purpose of whoever had breached the arrays.

Were they looking for Alea, or did they have some other agenda?

Was it because of the mutated Tree of Ascension? That thing would no doubt be of huge value for anyone dabbling with poison, perhaps even after having reached E-grade. However, there should be no way that the Undead Empire knew about it, as access to the valley had been completely restricted after Zac took control of the island.

Besides, things wouldn't end well even if the invaders weren't there specifically for Alea. Would they simply let her rest in peace after seeing her next to the Tree of Ascension? Of course not.

Zac and his sister had placed strong protective arrays around the whole valley to keep people away, but the invaders were either extremely strong or adept at breaking arrays. The inner shield protecting Alea's Stasis Array wasn't much stronger than the outer one, and Zac was doubtful that it would prove a challenge to whoever had encroached upon the valley.

Less than five minutes had passed since he'd left the outskirts of Azh'Rodum, but he felt like it had been hours when he finally breached the crest leading into the valley. He immediately noticed that there was something wrong with the outer array covering the whole valley like a dome. It was still intact, but it felt completely drained of energy like it was just there for show.

The leaf shot straight through it, and he was at the core of the valley in seconds. However, his fears were soon realized as he spotted four hooded individuals sitting in a circle around Alea's stasis array, right next to the [Tree of Ascension]. An intricate array covered the ground around the stasis array, and Zac sensed extremely pure fluctuations of death-attuned energies from the crystals powering it.

Zac jumped down from the flying treasure and rushed forward like an enraged beast, his axe already shining with a sanguine glow. The air popped around him as his aura billowed out without restraints, and even the slumbering Splinter stirred in his mind from Zac's towering fury.

"So you are he–" the closest man said with a hoarse voice, but he couldn't even finish his sentence before he was obliterated by a world-ending punch, turning into scraps of flesh that rained down upon the area.

The three others quickly rose from their seated positions around the array and unleashed what looked like a swarm of jumbo mosquitoes at him, but Zac ignored them as he unleashed a Dao Field based on his strongest Dao Fragment. Many of the bugs died from the sharpness of the domain, but even more managed to resist as they assaulted every piece of exposed skin on his body.

The spectral forest of [Hatchetman's Spirit] rose from the ground, and an emerald shield protected Zac from the gnats as he cut through the swarm. The hooded warriors released another barrage of what seemed to be poisonous insects and airborne toxins, but everything was destroyed by Zac's furious assault.

The second robed warrior was quickly cut into a dozen pieces from a furious barrage of swings, and the third was literally ripped apart the moment Zac caught him with his free hand. Only one final warrior remained in just a couple of seconds, and Zac had him caught in an iron grip as he took ragged breaths due to barely restrained rage.

He had gotten even angrier as he had seen the Stasis Array at close distance, as it had obviously been tampered with. The golden glass was replaced by a murky black sheen, and he couldn't even see Alea's body inside due to an extremely dense violet cloud within the glass. He couldn't even tell whether she was alive or dead while standing just a few meters away.

"Tell me, what have you done?!" he roared as he ripped off the hood of the man, exposing a man who looked like a corpse that had been left out in a desert for weeks.

"Fractured soul, not living, not dead," the man wheezed with a laugh. "I was anointing her to become an elite of our empire, but now it's all for naught. You might as well put the girl out of her misery."

"Tell me how to fix this!" Zac screamed into the man's face, his anger towering to an unprecedented degree.

"Death is the destination for all. You can't fight fate." The desiccated husk of a man laughed, and Zac's danger sense soon erupted, forcing him to throw the man away.

The hooded Lich exploded into an enormous cloud of gasses that were no doubt extremely toxic, but a few wide swings with **[Verun's Bite]** pushed the cloud north and toward the edge of the island.

Zac only took a cursory glance at the surroundings before running over toward the glass array that had kept Alea's soul from crumbling any further. However, he stumbled after just a few steps, and his mind started to become cloudy. He quickly ate one of his best antidotes as he circulated the Fragment of the Coffin in an effort to refine the invisible toxins that must have made their way into his body.

Helplessness threatened to immobilize him as he looked down at the array. He somewhat regretted not bringing his sister in his hurry to get here in time, but he instinctively knew there was nothing she could do in front of something like this. He ripped out the four crystals powering the array, and they were no-doubt D-grade Miasma Crystals from the fluctuations.

Extremely condensed streams of death-attuned energies tried to infect his body without him even trying to absorb anything, but his Specialty Core just trembled a bit as it absorbed the infiltration. Zac put the crystals into his pouch as he swung his axe a few times to ruin the intricate layout of inscriptions covering the ground, and the array instantly lost any remaining strength.

The array was stopped, but his heart still hammered as he gripped the glass coffin cover to push it away. But before he even had a chance to move the lid, an invisible shockwave erupted from within, and his surroundings changed the next instant.

63

FRAGMENTS

"GET OUT!" Yasera screeched, her eyes muddled and unfocused from the Hera Leaves. "You keep taking up time and money; what are you good for?"

Tears pooled in Alea's eyes, but she knew her mom was not herself at the moment.

"I'll be useful, I promise," Alea said as she shuffled out of their corner of the communal space, her eyes downcast to avoid the mean stares of the others.

She quickly found herself on the streets, the two burly guards at the door only sparing her a glance as she vacantly stopped after a few meters. What should she do? Mama was not well, and they had no money.

Alea already scrounged food outside most days, but the shop-keepers had started to become wise to her tricks. There was only one solution left. She needed to start working as well.

The madam had said that she should wait a while longer, but Mom needed money now. So Alea tried to still her beating heart as she looked back and forth along the street to find a willing customer.

She finally spotted a young man who seemed to have recently passed the Age of Adulthood. He wore mostly ragged clothes just like most people in the slums, but there was something about him. There was an energy around him that made him feel the same way as the scary man who always followed the madam around.

The energy of a cultivator. Besides, he looked very handsome even if he had a lazy expression, and the dirt on his body seemed to be recently applied compared to the ingrained filth some walked around with. He would no doubt have some coin to spare, and compared with most of the men who entered the Tea House, this one seemed a lot better.

She slowly walked up toward him before he had the chance to walk away, and quickly gathered her courage as she looked up at the man, who was over two heads taller than her.

"Yo-young master, ho-how about having a cup of tea with me?" Alea stuttered as she desperately tried to mimic the ladies of the White Lotus Tea House.

The young man with the lackadaisical expression looked down at her with surprise, and she tried to give off the innocent charm that Madam Sai said would be her best weapon for the next few years. However, Alea became uneasy when she realized that he didn't have that gleam in his eyes that was so easy to discern. The expression that meant that the man was no longer thinking with his brain.

Was he too young to be interested in these kinds of things? Alea still wasn't sure how everything worked, but she was confident she had seen even younger men entering the private compartment in the Tea House.

"Why did you call me young master? Do you recognize me?" he said curiously as he walked closer.

"Ah, no?" Alea said, some fear taking hold of her heart.

Had she made a mistake and said something she shouldn't? Madam Sai always said that words were the most dangerous things, and one wrong word could cause a lifetime of suffering.

"Then how did you know that I am rich? I am not wearing anything expensive, and both my face and my clothes are dirty," he said as he took another step closer.

"That," Alea said, looking back and forth, trying to figure out a way to get out of the situation.

She pleadingly looked at the two guards behind her, but they pointedly ignored her. Had they already realized that the young man was too dangerous to mess with?

"I'll give you an E-grade Nexus Crystal if you tell me," the young man said.

Alea's eyes widened in shock when she heard what he said. An E-grade Nexus Crystal was a huge fortune. One aunty in the Tea House had been tipped one once, and she had been able to eat her fill for over a year on that, even after having given the Tea House their share.

Could she make that much money by just answering a few questions? Her instincts said no. Things that seemed too good to be true always came with hidden dangers. More than one girl in the Tea House had disappeared after being offered a handsome reward to visit a patron in their homes.

Some believed they had found a better life, but Madam Sai said they were usually sold into slavery, or even turned into some sort of materials for evil cultivators.

"My patience is only so long," the young man said as he took out a shimmering crystal from nowhere and waved it in front of her.

Alea's heart started to beat rapidly, and she was unable to take her eyes off the mesmerizing crystal in his hand. She had never seen anything so beautiful, and it radiated amazing amounts of energy.

"Your clothes look worn, but they are new. The wear doesn't seem natural. It is like you have rubbed the clothes against a stone to make it look worse than it is. It's the same with the face, it's dirty, but your skin is healthy and clear," she said, the words tumbling out of her mouth as quickly as she could form them.

"I guess I overestimated my disguise." The youth wryly smiled as he threw her the crystal.

Alea's eyes lit up as she clutched the crystal, quickly placing it inside a hidden pocket within her dress. The youth looked at her with amusement for a second before he seemingly had thought of something.

"Here, hold this for a second," he said, handing her another crystal, though this one was a smoothly polished sphere that didn't emit the same beautiful colors.

Alea didn't dare to say no to the young master, so she gingerly gripped the ball, and she noticed that the young man's eyes lit up when it started to gleam with a mysterious purple shimmer.

"Are you sure about this?" Ogras asked with a serious expression.

"What's there to think about?" Namys growled from the side as she glared at Alea. "The Lord has spent so much time and effort on this. Why are you hesitating?"

"Namys." Ogras sighed before he turned back to Alea.

Alea looked down at the large vat with trepidation, knowing that she might never be able to leave once she entered the bubbling pool.

The young Lord didn't know this, but she had found out that there had been three before her. Three young women who had died while attempting this. Her knowledge about constitutions was shallow, but she had learned from the old master who had instructed the nine of them that the risk of dying was extremely high unless there was a great fit between you and the manual.

And that risk only increased when you were dealing with deadly poison.

But this was the path she had chosen. If she died, she would at least have died at the peak of beauty. Her thoughts went to her recent return to the White Lotus Tea House, the first visit in six years. Her mother, the beautiful goddess wrapped in the finest garments, was gone, replaced by a wretched hag.

Her face had been pocked by scabs, and her skin sallow from overindulging on alcohol and Hera Leaves. The lithe and graceful curves were gone, replaced by sagging skin and festering sores.

Yasera hadn't cared where she had been. She hadn't even bothered looking for her after she left with Lord Azh'Rezak. Her mother had only demanded money or liquor after having seen the quality of the dress and jewelry she wore. Alea had turned away without another word, ignoring her mother's cries as her childhood crumbled around her.

"I'm ready," she said as she let her dress fall to the ground, show-casing her pristine body.

"Good," Ogras said, trying his best to appear unperturbed by the scene as he handed her a shimmering Beast Crystal. "The main component of the medicinal bath comes from a swamp creature named [Er'Harkath Marshwalker]. They are known for their ability to store all kinds of poisons in their body without harming themselves. Try your best to fuse with this thing as quickly as possible."

Alea nodded, and after one deep breath, swallowed the crystal whole as she stepped into the pool. This would be either the first step on the path of cultivation or the last day of her life.

―――――

"Is that him?" Ilvere whispered with incredulity as he gazed at the human in the distance. "I can't believe that guy toppled the Azh'Rezak Clan singlehandedly. While wearing lady's garments."

"Progenitor. Odd advantages," Janos muttered.

"Why is he even alive?" Namys growled. "He's a threat to our Lord, especially now that he's doubly weakened. Alea, shouldn't you do something?"

Alea's mouth curved upward as she looked at the man, trying to imagine the scene that Lord Ogras had described. One human dressed in Vesarith's dress and drenched in blood, running around causing havoc. It somehow felt like the world had just turned a bit more interesting.

"Lord Azh'Rezak hasn't told us to do anything, so why should I?" Alea smiled as she stood up and adjusted her dress.

"What are you doing?" Namys wheezed as she saw Alea skip toward the human.

―――――

"Are you heading to the mines again?" Alea said with a smile as she walked next to Zac.

"Yeah," he said, looking a bit perturbed.

"Why don't I join you?" Alea said, snaking her arm around his.

"I have a lot to do." Zac sighed, helplessness evident in his eyes.

It was a refreshing difference compared to those meathead warriors at the compound she had trained with, a bunch of men with overblown egos and rampant aggression. This guy was the strongest warrior on the island, but he didn't even know what to do with himself when she teased him. It was both intriguing and a bit frustrating.

"I know, learn about the Ruthless Heavens?" she said, pushing her breasts toward his arm, the response leaving nothing wanting. "I know. I know all that basic stuff as well. I can teach you just as well as Alyn can. And wouldn't it be nicer with just the two of us?"

Her heart hammered in her chest as she hurried away from the gazebo, and she immediately jumped onto the teleporter taking her to Azh'Rodum.

Just what had she done?

This had been the perfect opportunity, but she had ruined it all by poisoning him because of that stupid impulse. She regretted stepping into that bath for the first time since gaining this odd constitution. For the first time, the gains didn't seem to match up to the costs. Of course, a larger part of her knew that absorbing the essence of the swamp monster was the only reason she had been able to save Lord Atwood at all during the final beast wave.

Without it, she would just have been another bystander.

She walked up to the secluded rooftop garden in her mansion and lay down on the recliner, her eyes absentmindedly looking up at the stars. The blue sky that once had felt so cold and glaring felt soothing for the first time since arriving to this odd world.

He was drifting away. The sturdy back kept growing, now towering like a mountain in front of her. It was this cursed situation that pushed him toward the Heavens themselves. It should be a joy seeing the man she loved growing stronger, but she couldn't help but feel pangs of loneliness as the two drifted further and further apart. She simply couldn't keep up. No one on Earth could.

Zac was leaving again soon, this time for the Underworld, and a changed man would no doubt return. She had somewhat managed to improve their situation after her mistakes, and there was no longer that thinly veiled disappointment in his eyes when he looked at her.

But that didn't change the reality they found themselves in. He was

Lord Atwood, the de facto leader of a world, and perhaps even a future elite who would make his name known in the whole sector.

She was just Alea, a prostitute's daughter who hadn't even earned the right to take a last name. She had thought that becoming a cultivator would change her fate, but she was still that same dirty child from the slums, looking up at the gods soaring through the skies toward their faraway palaces.

How long would it be until they looked at each other like strangers?

———

Zac was inundated in one vision after another, snippets of Alea's life flashing past him. He had a vague understanding of what was going on, and the knowledge was terrifying. Alea's soul was rapidly falling apart, and fragments of her soul released the visions for him.

He didn't know how this was possible, as it had never happened with all the people he had killed until now. But one thing was certain; Alea was not long for this world if this kept on. Suddenly, another shudder emerged from the coffin, but this time, Alea's voice rather than another vision entered his mind.

"I'm not ready. I want to follow you."

DESPERATE TIMES

Zac's mind was already thrown into disarray after witnessing one snippet after another of Alea's life pass by his eyes, the storm in his heart only grew stronger after hearing her plea. His thoughts churned as he desperately tried to figure out a way to salvage the situation. Once he was back in his own body again, he immediately lifted the casket, only to be met by a horrifying sight.

Alea's body had been turned completely black, and dense waves of corruption and death radiated from her body. Gases leaked out of her pores as well, and Zac was forced to quickly close the lid again, as the noxious fumes almost made him keel over after a single breath.

That scene alone made him furious enough to almost spontaneously combust, but he restrained his anger as he searched for a solution. However, there were simply no treasures in his possession that would allow him to save her life.

Her soul was falling apart, and her body was no longer fit for a living being as far as he could tell. But her last words echoed through his mind, and he refused to give up as long as there was a chance that he could save her.

His first idea was to turn her into a Revenant somehow, as that would at least allow her to keep "living" in a sense. However, not only would that erase Alea and create a new personality, but it might turn her into a subordinate of the Lich King. It was those robed Liches who had initiated the process, which might have left some sort of mark.

Also, he had no idea how to actually turn someone into a Revenant.

"Follow me…" Zac muttered as he stared down at the crystalline casket, and in his desperation, he suddenly thought of something.

He didn't have any idea whether what he did was insane or not, but when the idea was born, it refused to leave. So Zac took out an object and placed it on top of the lid.

It was the [Divine Investiture Array].

This was the only solution available to him. Her soul was already a problem that was out of his league after having lost the [Prajñā Cherry], and with the Lich messing up her body, she was way beyond his means of salvation. He wasn't even sure whether a D-grade healer would be able to bring her back from the brink of death, let alone his paltry E-grade pills.

But what if she became a Tool Spirit, a being that was essentially immortal? He had recently learned about two pieces of key informa-tion. First, living beings could be turned into Spirit Tools, or rather "Sword Slaves," through sacrificial rituals. Second, the [Divine Investiture Array] could pretty much turn anything into a Spirit Tool.

If he turned Alea into a Tool Spirit, she would be able to live on, just like Brazla. It was obviously a messed-up solution, but one that would fulfill her wish and keep her "alive." The universe was full of magical things that he couldn't even imagine, and perhaps he would be able to turn her back into a living being again in the future.

He decisively infused a stream of Cosmic Energy into the [Divine Investiture Array] before he could change his mind. A massive pillar of gold shot down from the heavens and slammed into the valley with enough force to completely obliterate all clouds for tens of kilometers in each direction.

A groundswell of energy rose from the depths of the mountain to meet the golden pillar, and Zac found himself submerged in a surge of power so dense that it was almost a liquid. He did not doubt that he would be able to gain multiple levels in minutes from staying in a magical place like this upon reaching E-grade, but that wasn't why he had summoned these energies.

He suddenly felt a spiritual nudge from beneath the lid, and Zac refocused on the coffin Alea lay inside. His eyes lit up in excitement upon sensing it. Zac couldn't be sure, but he felt it was an agreement to his plan. Perhaps she could understand what was going to happen after being in the middle of it.

However, nothing happened with the casket, and the energies simply seemed to swirl around it as Zac felt the spiritual signal from within weaken. Zac's mind spun for solutions, trying to figure out what the problem was. Was the array not enough?

Zac emptied his Spatial Ring of anything that might help with her situation, and a stream of golden energy emerged from the [Divine Investiture Array] and snatched a third of his Soul Crystals before starting to go over the other things he had taken out. Zac didn't mind in the least, as he suddenly felt Alea's presence once more from within the coffin, making it seem as though the Soul Crystals had condensed her soul again.

The next thing to be selected by the golden tendrils was the fossilized bug that radiated an unceasing aura of corrosion. Zac had picked it up on the third floor of the Tower, but he believed that it was a lucky find, as neither Ogras nor Galau had been able to even get close due to the aura it emitted. He thought it might fit with Alea and her constitution, so he took it out as well.

However, it wasn't enough, and he felt Alea's spirit slowly weaken again.

Panic welled up once more, and he gritted his teeth and took out an intricately inscribed jade box and opened its lid. The tendrils of light pounced on the contents with a palpable desire, and Zac wasn't surprised, considering what the box contained; the [Pathfinder Oracle Eye]. The auctioneer had said that it was perfect to improve a Spirit Tool's spirituality, and it might just be what was needed.

The cost was pretty shocking, but he had already gone so far as to expend his [Divine Investiture Array]. It was too late to hold back.

Zac's eyes suddenly widened in alarm as another tendril reached out behind Zac and picked up [Everlasting], which he had poured out of his Spatial Ring along with the rest of his treasures. Zac was about to take the shield back, but he stopped himself after some hesitation and let the golden light use the E-grade defensive treasure as another ingredient.

It wasn't even a Spirit Tool, and he could always get another shield elsewhere.

The tendril also reached behind him and ripped off a few of the largest branches of the [Tree of Ascension] while a storm of gases was dragged out from the underground where the Amanita Mushroom resided. Only then did the array seem satiated, and the tendrils receded back into the crystal as a Golden Cocoon formed around the Stasis Array.

"Thank you…" a silent whisper suddenly echoed out in his mind, but its volume grew lower and lower toward the end, as though Alea were moving away from him.

"Are you okay?" Zac asked, but a sinking feeling spread through his chest, as there was no answer. "Alea?"

The silence stretched on, and Zac started to panic, as he couldn't get an answer from Alea no matter what he did. He wanted to go closer, but he was instantly rebuffed by the powerful force from the [Divine Investiture Array].

Zac could only anxiously wait for the light to dissipate. Time passed as more and more energy was infused into the cocoon, but Zac didn't move a muscle. He knew there were no doubt a dozen things that needed to be done on the island, but he refused to leave until he had seen this thing through. Only two hours later did the lights finally dissipate as the cocoon cracked, revealing the item within.

The large crystal Alea was recuperating inside was gone, as was his shield and all the materials he had poured into the array. In their place was only one thing, a massive black coffin.

The coffin was just over two meters long and seemed to be crafted from a mix of the wood from the [Tree of Ascension] and some black crystal or smooth stone. The two materials formed intricate patterns all across the surface, though they didn't seem to be fractals as far as he could tell. They were more akin to the markings of the stone stele he had seen in the vision, though they obviously didn't contain that kind of power.

The coffin's shape was traditional with the top being slightly wider before narrowing again toward the bottom. It looked nothing like the translucent glass studded with Divine Crystals of before, but rather a rugged and completely opaque box that carried a heavy and almost solemn aura.

There were two sets of fractals covering the lid as well. First was a circle placed at the wider section toward the top, and the other set was two lines of inscriptions that ran parallel along the length of the lid. The fractals almost reminded Zac of a funeral wreath with two ribbons hanging down.

Finally, there were thick pitch-black chains that were wound around the whole coffin a few times, and Zac was surprised when he realized they actually emerged from holes in the side of the coffin. A quick estimate told Zac there were over five meters of links wound around the ominous item, and there were perhaps even more chains waiting inside the coffin itself.

All in all, it felt like an extremely somber item, and Zac was pretty shocked at how it had turned out. He wasn't sure what he had expected the [Divine Investiture Array] to do, but at least it wasn't something as drastic as this. It had completely repurposed the items he had thrown inside in just two hours, a feat that would no doubt be utterly impossible even for great artisans like the original Brazla.

But the amazing craftsmanship wasn't really what Zac was interested in right now. He hurried over to the coffin and tried to open the lid, but no matter how hard he strained, he was utterly incapable of moving it even an inch.

He growled in frustration as veins bulged across his arms, but he could eventually only give up. He tried peering into the six holes the chains emerged from on the sides, but there was nothing but darkness inside the coffin. Zac tried shining a light inside with an illumination crystal, but it was as though the light was swallowed the moment it entered.

Zac sat back with a blank look, his determination slowly being swapped out by confusion and depression. Just what had he done? Making Spirit Tools from living cultivators wasn't just considered an unorthodox method, but a downright evil one. He felt like a mad scientist playing god, and he had no idea what would come of this.

"What have you done?" a furious voice said from the side, and Zac looked over to see Ogras walk over with bloodshot eyes, his eyes darting between the coffin and Zac.

"She said she wasn't ready to leave, that she wanted to follow me," Zac mumbled with a hollow voice. "Her soul was falling apart because of those damn Liches. She wasn't ready to let go, and this was the only solution I could think of."

The demon stared at Zac for a few seconds while Zac simply looked at the coffin with a lost expression.

"So what is this?" Ogras finally said as he looked at the coffin. "Exactly what did you do? I can't sense her presence any longer."

"I got something called a **[Divine Investiture Array]** from the eighth floor. It could turn anything into a Spirit Tool. I also added the **[Pathfinder Oracle Eye]**, and it seems the process swallowed my shield along with a bunch of the treasures I have gathered so far," Zac explained.

"This... This is not right," Ogras said with disgust on his face. "It goes against the natural order. How will her soul find rest or enter the cycle of the Heavens this way? You have cursed her."

Zac could say nothing in response, bleakness washing over him as he felt some disgust with himself. The silence stretched on with one man brooding and the other man stewing.

"You threw a shield worth over a billion into this, and it was one of the cheaper materials?" Ogras finally said with a grimace. "The things you expended here would be able to pay for the foundation of a great faction."

"I figured that if I could turn her into a Spirit Tool like Brazla, she would be able to stay alive. We could find a way to turn her back into flesh and bone in the future." Zac sighed as he looked up from the coffin. "Do you know if it's possible?"

"No idea," Ogras said. "Anyway, we can't stay here."

"What's going on?" Zac asked.

"We're being invaded, remember?" Ogras snorted. "There are still enemies to deal with even after your rampage; we need to clear them out so we don't leave any hidden threats. Besides, we are running out of time to deal with the unliving. Your sister may have bought us some time, but we're still cutting it close."

Zac nodded before he walked over to the coffin. He silently looked at the beautifully crafted surface and the chains that kept the thing sealed before he slowly reached down to put it in his Spatial Ring.

But the coffin suddenly shuddered and started shrinking as the chains moved about. In just a second, the coffin had shrunk to just half a decimeter's length, and one of its chains had formed a loop through the top holes of the coffin.

Zac realized what was going on, and he didn't hesitate to put the chain over his head to wear it as a necklace. The moment the coffin touched his chest, a weak tendril emerged from the treasure, but there was no voice accompanying it this time. It still gave some comfort to Zac, and he desperately clung to the idea that Alea was still inside there, but that she was simply too drained to communicate at the moment.

THE NEXT STEP

Confusion and guilt plagued Zac's conscience about what he had just done to Alea. But the deed was done, and he couldn't stay in this secluded valley and second-guess himself forever.

The two jumped onto Zac's flying treasure, setting off toward Azh'Rodum. As they flew, he got an update of the situation from the demon. Ogras had returned thirty minutes ago, at which point order was mostly restored to the island. The Valkyries had discovered the jamming array that blocked out any communication and teleportation on the island and deactivated it somehow.

They were still locked out from the rest of the world, but Kenzie and the other experts were working on multiple solutions while multiple squads had set sail to look for hints of similar arrays. Even the Creators were furiously producing new vessels to replace the destroyed ones, and they had already delivered three carracks in record speed.

They reached Azh'Rodum soon enough, and Zac was relieved to see that the Miasmic clouds were mostly dispelled by this point. He saw hundreds of warriors walking through the forests in groups, likely looking for stragglers who had wandered off from the rest of the Zombies. An inquiry told him that his sister and the demon generals had already returned to Port Atwood, and they'd taken the teleporter back as well.

The scene in Port Atwood was pretty similar to the one in Azh'Rodum. The raging flames had been doused by now, but much of the southern edge of the island had been completely ruined by the wildfires. Thankfully, they sat right on top of a Nexus Vein, and the dense energies would restore the greenery in a year or two.

The two walked over to the battlefield, where the bodies of the fallen cultists were still being examined for lingering threats. The few who survived Zac's onslaught had either tried to go out in a blaze of glory or were summarily executed by one of the demon armies. Zac didn't care about that, as there was no middle ground with these two forces.

He saw his sister standing at the edge of the battlefield as a dozen drones roved back and forth across the area. It was the same ones who had stood sentry around the Technocrat incursion, and Zac guessed she was looking for any survivors who tried to play dead. The demon generals were nowhere to be seen, though, perhaps occupied elsewhere.

Of course, her search was a bit redundant considering that demon warriors and a few nauseated humans were cutting the head off every corpse just in case. It was both to kill the stragglers and to prevent any corpses from rising again.

Their approach was quickly noticed, and Kenzie ran over with worry written on her face.

"What happened? Is Alea okay?" she asked the moment they appeared.

"It's complicated." Zac sighed. "We'll talk about it later. How are things here? How are the losses?"

"Around two hundred people died from the invasion, almost all of them during the battles at sea before they reached our island," Kenzie said. "We mostly stayed within the arrays after they arrived, though, so very few people were hurt."

Zac closed his eyes as he took a deep breath. Another two hundred people dead, and that was probably just a drop in the bucket compared to the losses on the main continent. But he couldn't do anything about it, and he slowly opened his eyes and indicated for his sister to continue.

"The threat was essentially over after you arrived. We're mostly cleaning up and rebuilding by this point. We've also figured out a means of communication, old-school radio signals. A few engineers and the Ishiate tinkerers have managed to strengthen the signals of old machines to the point we can communicate pretty great distances, but it's only in Morse code."

"That's good." Zac nodded. "Do the ships you've sent out have these things?"

"They do, and we've actually found the missing cultist ship already thanks to Mr. Trang's companion. It is sailing away from us, toward Mystic Island, I think." Kenzie sighed. "We have sent over half of our remaining ships to harass it, but it will take a few days to catch up. Ilvere is leading those ships."

"I'll deal with it," Zac said with a frown, preparing to take out his Flying Treasure again.

"Just let it be," Ogras said from the side. "Our time is limited, and we can deal with the stragglers another day. It should take them a few days to reach that island, perhaps over a week if they're constantly under harassment. We already have elites stationed there, and they can just jump into the Mystic Realm and close the spatial tunnel, allowing us to reclaim the island at a later date."

Letting the invaders have free rein in his archipelago went against every fiber in his body, but he knew that he didn't have much of a choice, as there were bigger fish to fry.

"How long do we have until the Realignment Array activates?" Zac asked

"We broke a couple of key pillars before we had to stop," Kenzie answered. "I can't be sure, but we think it will take around six or seven days to complete unless something changed in the last day. But the sooner it's stopped, the better. It's draining our planet; who knows what long-term effect that might have."

"What about the arrays blocking our teleportation array?" Zac asked. "I heard you were working on some sort of solution?"

"We haven't located any more arrays apart from the one on this island," Kenzie said with some helplessness. "So we are still locked out from the main continent. Worst case, you can try flying over to Cogstown and use their teleporter; it's possible it hasn't been impacted by the spatial disruption."

"That will cost us a few days, though," Ogras interjected. "And we don't know the situation on the mainland."

"Calrin and I have looked into these types of arrays since what happened to Alea and the army," Kenzie said. "I figured they might block out all the teleporters around the Dead Zone after they activated the Realignment Array. They found a simpler solution by just blocking this island. But I do have something that might work."

"You do?" Zac asked with surprise.

"Blocking arrays is a standard tactic during conflicts in the Multiverse," Ogras added from the side. "It's almost impossible to catch your targets if they just keep teleporting away. Just look at the insectoids and their war. They have tried to catch the followers of the old Redeemer for months, but they just keep teleporting away from any compromised hive."

"So there are solutions?" Zac asked.

"It boils down to whether your or your opponent's methods are better, and that's why I'm not sure," Kenzie explained. "We managed to get our hands on a [Spatial Reinforcement Array], and it should technically be able to stabilize the subspace or whatever long enough for you to teleport to the main continent."

"That's great!" Zac exclaimed, a weight lifted from his shoulders.

"Well, it's just that we're dealing with two ancient factions; their jamming arrays are probably pretty strong. I'm not sure what would happen if our array breaks apart before your jump is completed. You might be thrown out in the middle of the ocean, or you might be torn to pieces by spatial rifts."

"Oh," Zac muttered. "So it's either waste a day or two getting to Cogstown in hopes that their teleporter still works, or risk getting ripped apart?"

"Pretty much," Kenzie said with a weak smile.

"Just teleport." Ogras shrugged from the side. "With your luck, you'll be just thrown out right in front of the Lich King even if the array breaks."

Zac only snorted in response before he turned back to his sister.

"Can I do anything to help with the spatial array thing?" Zac asked. "I've gathered all kinds of items during my climb."

"I don't think so," Kenzie said. "Some treasures might be able to make the array stronger, but I don't know how to do that."

"That's fine. Where are Thea and Billy?" Zac asked. "I heard they helped out while I was gone. Oh, and where are the Tal-Eladar? I haven't seen a single one since returning."

"Billy and Thea are recuperating in a mansion next to the hospital," Kenzie said before her face scrunched up. "As for the Tal-Eladar…"

"They didn't come," the demon snorted. "I told you that you can't rely on those wily beast tamers."

"Is that true?" Zac asked with a frown as he looked over at his sister, and her face told him everything he needed to know.

"We sent a distress call, but they delayed and delayed until our teleportation array was blocked out," Kenzie said with some anger.

Zac knew that the Tal-Eladar had just stayed behind as business partners, but he was still pretty angry that they simply chose to cower to the side when their ally was being attacked like this. This was the second time Verana had refused to get involved with the conflicts on Earth, and it had become abundantly clear that they couldn't be relied upon for anything important.

"Well, I'm sure they'll regret their choice sooner or later," Zac finally said after a short silence, which elicited a knowing snort from Ogras.

"So what happened in the Tower of Eternity?" Kenzie asked with some worry. "Ogras said that you caused a mess, but things turned out mostly fine?"

Zac glared at the demon, who just grinned back at him.

"Well, I got a pretty good result and made some allies, but I might have also made some enemies as well. I had to suddenly leave due to getting a prompt about Port Atwood being invaded, so I don't know about the fallout," Zac said as he took out the [Heaven's Secrets Array]. "More importantly, can you install this thing on my Nexus Node later when you have the time? It can help with my evolution."

"Oh?" Kenzie said with interest as she looked down at the array. "It shouldn't take too long. I'll go deal with it right now. I'm done here anyway."

Zac nodded before he left his sister to visit his two friends, with two Valkyries accompanying him to catch him up to speed as they walked. They reached the mansion soon enough, where the guards wordlessly let him in with a bow. He indicated for the Valkyries to stay outside as he entered, and he quickly spotted where the two were recuperating with the help of [Cosmic Gaze].

A few quick steps brought him to a large bedroom on the second floor, and he entered after softly knocking on the door.

"You're back," Thea said with a weak voice from her bed facing a window looking out at a beautiful garden. "Your intelligence was incorrect. They made their move early."

"I heard." Zac sighed as he sat down next to her bedside.

He was inwardly relieved, though, that Thea seemed fine, with all her limbs intact. He did spot a wound on her stomach that was lit up with Miasmic energies, though. But it didn't look as bad as the one he got himself from Mhal, and it should heal up as long as she slowly ground down the lingering Dao with her own.

"I'm sorry," Zac said. "And thank you for helping my people while I was away. Who knows how many would have died if you weren't there."

"So? Have you dealt with everything?" Thea said as she turned to look at Zac, her piercing blue eyes staring evenly into his.

Zac was silent for a few seconds, thinking it over. There was honestly more he could do to improve his current power while still in F-grade, a lot of untapped potential, as Catheya would call it. But more importantly than that, there was a burning desire that was eating him alive.

There had been a desire smoldering in his chest since the events in the valley, the desire to unleash an unprecedented level of vengeance upon the so-called Lich King for what he or his subjects had done to his island and Alea. Zac's face was without expression, but a fire burned in his eyes as he looked down at Thea.

"I am evolving right now and heading toward the core of the Dead Zone the moment it's completed," Zac said, and he felt a momentum building in his body the moment he made his choice. "The undead incursion will be gone within a few days."

LOVE'S BOND

Zac didn't immediately leave the mansion, but rather gave some of his best healing pills to Thea. He was about to leave her room to visit Billy as well, and Thea surprisingly jumped down from her bed to join him. The giant was even worse off than Thea, from what she said.

He had taken the brunt of the attacks after changing into a massive form to sink the ship, and this time, Zac hadn't been there to block out the attacks with **[Nature's Barrier]** like during the hunt. Billy had been badly burned by the flames of the cultists, it seemed.

It was easy to figure out what room the giant resided in, as the whole room shook from the massive snores from within, but they stopped when Zac walked into the room.

"You're back!" Billy rumbled as he woke up. "Help Billy a bit! A stupid horny guy keeps tricking Billy, making him forget how to leave this place! All horny people seem tricky, could use a good thwonkin'."

"Don't let your fans hear that," Thea snorted from the side as she walked inside as well, prompting Zac to look over with confusion.

"He has over thirty suitors among the demons on this island," Thea said with some bemusement. "It's a bit surreal."

"Of course it is super real. Billy is the most dashing prince. Mama always said so." Billy nodded with a complacent expression. "But Billy doesn't like horny girls."

"Uh, you should just call them demons." Zac coughed, the anger in his gut somewhat dispersed by the giant's antics.

He couldn't stay for too long, and he had to leave after making sure Thea and Billy had everything they needed.

"I'm sorry about how things turned out. I underestimated the Undead Empire and put too much trust in the words of Void's Disciple. I was sure I had a few more weeks," Zac apologized again just as he was about to exit.

"It's our fault as well." Thea sighed as she sat down next to Billy. "We didn't adapt quickly enough to this new reality, forcing the whole burden onto your shoulders. We played politics and fought for benefits when we should have been fighting for our lives and our futures."

Zac sighed as well, not knowing how to respond, and he left the mansion in silence.

"You really are evolving?" a voice said from the side, and Zac looked over to see Ogras standing there.

"I am." Zac nodded before he wryly smiled. "Did you know that Billy is pretty popular among the female demons?"

"Well, it makes sense. He's even bulkier than the Abyssal Demons, and rumors are circulating on the island that he has some powerful bloodline that increased his strength even further." The demon shrugged. "Between his constitution and his potential, he's one of the best bachelors on this world, perhaps even better than you since you're a mortal."

Zac only shook his head in bemusement before he got back to the matter at hand.

"I need to take down the undead incursion quickly. Do you think I can do it without evolving?" Zac asked as the two walked toward his private section.

"It's hard to say," the demon said after a while. "Normally, I would have said yes, but we're running out of time. The Lich King seems adept at arrays, judging by what we have seen so far, and he has no doubt turned the core zone into a fortress over the past year. He doesn't even need to maintain the shield for that long, just a few days will do, and he will have won."

"You really think his arrays are that strong?" Zac asked skeptically. "I even managed to break the arrays in the Base Town."

"That's different; those were mobile arrays powered by F-grade warriors," Ogras said with a shake of his head. "The undead array will have hundreds, perhaps thousands, of Unholy Beacons powering it. He might even sacrifice tens of millions of Zombies to give the defenses a boost until the realignment is complete."

"Still," Zac muttered, but he knew the demon had a point.

"Sieges can take years, decades even, to slowly grind down the defensive arrays, and that's with proper equipment we don't have. You need to be a lot stronger to crack them in an instant," the demon said. "The normal method would have been for us to bring millions of fodder to blast attacks on the shield to weaken it before we made our move. But there's no time for that either."

Zac slowly nodded. He had somewhat hoped for the demon to convince him otherwise, but it truly looked like he needed to get a few power-ups to increase his certainty of success. He wasn't willing to bet Earth's future that he was able to break through the defensive perimeters and destroy the Realignment Array within one week without evolving.

"Where's my sister?" Zac asked. "Has she installed the array?"

"She's still trying to figure out the thing," Ogras said. "But you need to slow down."

"What? You know we're running out of time," Zac said.

"Just a few hours have passed since you exited the Tower. You have fought half the sector's geniuses and then fended off an invasion. You even turned Alea into a heaven-cursed necklace. You're not stable at the moment; you can't evolve in your current state," the demon said. "Honestly, if you were the scion of some clan, you would probably have been forced into silent meditation for at least a year to regain a sense of tranquility and balance."

"So you just want me to sit around?" Zac said with disbelief. "The planet is dying as we speak."

"We are all dying," the demon snorted. "Don't ruin everything now by rushing into things. Sit down and heal up and calm your mind at least. A few hours spent now will save you a lot of time in the long run."

Zac was somewhat unwilling, but he knew that the demon was right. He wasn't in his right mind at the moment, and he needed to cool off. But he still felt like a child who got sent to take his nap as he walked back to his courtyard and sat down.

His thoughts were a whir as he tried to calm down, and his mind kept jumping between the various things that needed his attention, each more urgent than the last. But slowly circulating the Fragment of the Bodhi helped him relax his tense muscles, and his thoughts slowly followed. Visiting the Tower of Eternity was supposed to give him a breather to decompress, but things had gone increasingly out of hand with the Splinter and then the time crunch to complete the climb.

He felt more wound up than ever, especially after what he'd gone through with Alea. It was a mindwarping experience to be blasted by someone else's memories and emotions like that, and Zac could still barely discern what was he and what was Alea.

His eyes slowly opened, and he looked down at the black five-centimeter casket hanging on its chain around his neck. He still didn't know whether he had done the right thing or not. What if he had completely damned Alea by turning her into something like the Sword Slave he had snatched from the swordmaster? The voices that had invaded his mind while using the thing had sounded beyond wretched.

The one solace in his mind was that the System had said that the **[Divine Investiture Array]** was a rectification of regret.

If Alea had died in front of his eyes like that, then he would have regretted it forever. To be just too late to save her not just once, but twice would have been too much to take. The System was essentially omniscient, and perhaps it had already known that things would end up like this. It did make him a bit pissed off that the System didn't provide a better solution to save her, but he guessed the System was more interested in making him stronger than it was in saving the poison mistress.

However, his actions had no doubt caused some complications to his plans. A lot of his materials had gone into the **[Divine Investiture Array]** in his frenzied attempts to save the demoness. It also meant that he no longer had any way to upgrade his axe, except letting it slowly eat various treasures. Of course, most items meant for Verun had gone to Alea, but he at least had the Dragon Core still.

The real question was what sort of item he had created. He had initially just been focused on saving Alea's soul, but the array was meant to create a perfect Spirit Tool. This became doubly important, as **[Everlasting]** had been thrown into the mix, leaving him without anything to activate half of his skills.

It might even affect his coming class choices for all he knew, so he needed to understand what he was dealing with.

He tried sending his mind into the coffin to see if he could glean anything, but it was impossible. Zac suddenly had an idea and released a drop of blood onto the necklace, which was immediately swallowed.

A stream of information entered his mind the next moment, and Zac felt the same sort of connection as he did to his robes and **[Verun's Bite]**. He felt a sense of sourness when he realized that either Alea or the System had named the chain-covered coffin **[Love's Bond]**.

There was still no active response from the demoness even after having bound the treasure with his blood. The coffin was still in a "passive" state like his robes, where he could use it, but he couldn't sense any Spirit Tool's sapience. This was the norm for an E-grade Spirit Tool, though, with the tool-awakening Spirituality usually happening at higher grades, if ever.

However, the stream of information had broadened his insight of what a Spirit Tool could do, and a mental command made two chains rush out from the holes on the side of the coffin and latch on to his left arm as the coffin rapidly grew in size.

It took just a fraction of a second before the coffin had become almost as tall as Zac himself while keeping the width of a normal coffin. But it was a lot thinner compared to what should be expected, with a depth of just fifteen centimeters. It had actually turned into a shield.

However, that was just one of its functions, and another mental command prompted the chains to snake around his torso as the coffin moved toward his back. It grew a lot shorter as well, making it almost resemble a coffin for a child or perhaps a gnome.

Four more chains reached out from their respective holes, each of them dancing in the air as though Zac were a snake charmer. He was already used to this kind of fighting from the chains in **[Profane Seal]**, and commanding them was almost as natural as moving his own limbs. The chains shot out in an instant, and four trees in his courtyard had holes punched through with such force that they barely shuddered from the impact.

The chains didn't have the life-sucking ability of the spectral chains, but there seemed to be some inherently corrosive effect attached to them, perhaps an addition provided from the mysterious fossilized bug he had thrown into the mix. It wasn't immediately noticeable, but the holes in the trees started to wither after a few seconds as well like they were being assaulted by some sort of invasive rot.

Furthermore, the chains were actual corporeal links made by top-tier materials like Neprosium, compared to the far more fragile fractal chains that his skill conjured. There was no way that a casual swing of an E-grade warrior would be able to break them apart as they could do with the spectral copies.

That meant that the chains were essentially a combination or fusion of hardness and rot, which made them a perfect fit for using together with the Fragment of the Coffin.

However, Zac didn't take the time to experiment with all the possibilities of the chains at the moment, so he retracted them back into the coffin. He was extremely relieved that there was a second form of Alea's new form since he was somewhat leery about using the coffin in its shield state. What if he encountered some powerhouse who managed to break it? What effect would it have on his chances of restoring her to her demon form?

The chains themselves looked like his Neprosium shield but slightly darker, so they wouldn't break so easily. Besides, Neprosium had excellent healing capabilities even if that happened. The chains would probably just re-form if the links broke as long as he retrieved the material.

It still felt weird to consider using Alea as a Spirit Tool, but he also knew that was what she'd wished for. At least he prayed that was what the spiritual connection had implied. She wanted to accompany him in his journey, and leaving her in a corner of his Spatial Ring felt even worse than using the treasure.

He would need some time to think of the pitch-black coffin as [Love's Bond] rather than Alea, but he would make the best of the situation. Besides, that might be his best shot at actually getting the poison mistress back.

Zac had asked about Spirit Tool upgrades while talking to Catheya since they had broached the subject when discussing the **[Divine Investiture Array]**. Much of what she said hadn't been anything new, but one thing had stuck out. Using the same weapon a lot and for a long time gradually formed a bond that was helpful in all kinds of ways.

It would allow a warrior to squeeze out more potential during a battle, and it would even help with upgrading the Spirit Tool. That was why most elites wanted a powerful weapon that could follow them during their whole Cultivation Path rather than repeatedly swapping out their weapon for a stronger one. Nurturing this bond was the same as nurturing the Spirit Tool, so using the coffin in battle might actually be the best method to heal her soul, odd as it might sound.

A chain snaked around his throat as the coffin shrank again, and it soon enough had returned to its passive state. Zac finally tried imbuing the Spirit Tool with his three fragments, but he found that the coffin, unsurprisingly, resisted the Fragment of the Axe. Imbuing it with the Fragment of the Bodhi worked, but he couldn't sense any direct effect when doing so.

But when he tried imbuing the skill with the final Fragment, he was shocked. The surprise didn't come from the fact that the defensive fragment entered the Spirit Tool effortlessly. After all, if the Dao of the Coffin didn't fit this Spirit Tool, then nothing would. The surprise came from something else.

The Fragment of the Coffin had evolved.

AGAINST THE NATURAL ORDER

Zac quickly opened up his Dao screen, and as expected, there was a change.

Fragment of the Coffin (Middle): All attributes +20, Endurance +190, Vitality +120, Intelligence +35, Wisdom +65. Effectiveness of Endurance +10%

Zac still didn't know when the upgrade took place, but he guessed that it mainly came from creating a coffin-type Spirit Tool. He had sat as though he was in a trance, witnessing the whole process, and something about the experience had helped him break through.

Of course, more things had contributed to the upgrade. He had taken the first step toward upgrading the Fragment from witnessing the Dao Apparition of the War Stele, and he had fought both in the life-and-death battle against half the Base Town, followed by the battle against the cultists.

These battles had set the foundations for the evolution, and the magical activation of the **[Divine Investiture Array]** was probably the final spark that upgraded the Fragment. However, these things were just the latest additions. Alea had been the spark of inspiration for the formation of the Fragment of the Coffin since the very beginning.

The vision of her lying in the stasis array had felt like a perfect mirror of the blood-drenched lotus he'd witnessed during his Dao Vision. The two visions had merged into the Fragment of the Coffin, and the recent events were a continuation of that reality. Zac couldn't exactly pinpoint what concept was added to the Dao Fragment, but he slowly started to form an idea.

He had long since started to walk the path of life and death, but only the Seed of Trees had properly incorporated this concept so far. The Seed of Rot was clearly death-attuned, but that seed was mostly propped up by fortuitous encounters. The concept he had incorporated into the Fragment of the Coffin was one he already had brushed upon before: life through death.

There were some differences, though. The insight related to trees was more akin to how a seed would grow from the ashes of a burned-down forest, gaining life through death. However, the insight he gained now was based on embracing death for a shot at life.

He knew that he essentially had killed Alea when he turned her into a Spirit Tool. Even if her consciousness awoke again, she wouldn't be living. But Alea dying was the only way for her to live. The insight contained the willingness to go against the natural order, whereas the earlier insight was based on making the most of the natural order.

They were the same, but also the opposite.

Zac felt it was an extremely important step in the creation he was building for himself, a realignment of his Dao so that it would better fit as one half of the whole. Getting a second Middle-grade Fragment would no doubt improve his choices upon evolving as well, but for now, he focused on the gained attributes.

The improved attributes weren't too surprising, apart from the boost to Endurance being slightly smaller than expected. That was the best-case scenario, though. He had reached a terrifying 1,692 Endurance in his human form after the latest upgrade, and while he still was some ways from the attribute cap of 2,500, he still needed to be careful. A few more titles and another Dao upgrade and he might hit the ceiling.

He had only lost three points in Strength from reaching the limit of the F-grade, but a loss at this stage could be huge in case there were complications for him to upgrade his Race to D-grade.

There wasn't cause to worry just yet, though, and Zac refocused on **[Love's Bond]**. He already knew that there were also actually two skills in the Spirit Tool already to match the two fractals on the handle of **[Verun's Bite]**, but he wouldn't use them now, as they had pretty big cooldowns.

A long cooldown was fine with Zac, since that meant that the skills were a lot stronger than normal. It was just like how his ultimate skills, except **[Vanguard of Undeath]**, couldn't be used over and over.

All in all, he felt that his new Spirit Tool was even better than expected. The more he thought about it, the more he felt it would be extremely easy to incorporate **[Love's Bond]** into his fighting style without it affecting the fighting style he had come up with for himself.

It almost symbolized his whole creation in a sense. It was an extremely good fit with most of his skills in his Undying Bulwark class, while also adding something new to the table. It perfectly mirrored his Fragment of the Coffin as well, and he would perhaps be able to move them both toward the Dao of Death over time.

But the Spirit Tool also represented life and rebirth through Alea's soul and the purpose of its creation. If things progressed as he hoped, he would be able to turn Death into Life and give Alea back her life again.

He could even think of some interesting possibilities with the sparks he could create with the help of the Remnants. Getting them under control was a long-term plan, but perhaps he would be able to use the chains as a delivery method in the future.

In the final attack against the dragon, he had used Creation Energy to form a spear to house the spark, but perhaps he could simply put the sparks into the coffin and shoot them out with a chain. He could only imagine the destructive potential of a Neprosium chain infused with the purest destruction.

He wouldn't need to force it or change himself to adapt to the shield, and the System had upheld its end of the bargain and created a Spirit Tool suited just for him. The process had even given him a second Mid-tier Fragment, which might allow him to get a fitting Arcane class. After having upgraded a second fragment, he couldn't help but start fantasize about what options he might see when touching the Nexus Node this time.

With his previous usage of **[Hatchetman's Rage]** leaving him in a weakened state, Zac spent another hour resting up before heading to the Nexus Node. He had gotten mostly better during his talk with Catheya, but he wanted to be completely rid of any lingering threats to his evolution before taking that step.

He already had the ticking time bombs in his head to worry about.

Truthfully, the undead incursion wasn't the only reason why he wanted to evolve as quickly as possible; there were two more reasons. The first was the two Remnants in his mind. He knew there was a tribulation waiting for him when evolving. It was the final test before reaching E-grade, and he would normally be completely confident in passing.

However, the two Remnants in his mind had already proven extremely adept at causing chaos at the most inopportune times, and Zac was afraid that they would flare up during the tribulation. It was better to smoothly evolve into E-grade now while the Remnants were still drained and in an inactive state.

The second was that he was getting dangerously close to the limit of how many attributes he could have. With the Fragment of the Coffin having evolved just now, his wiggle room was becoming limited. There was also probably a title waiting for reaching E-grade first on the planet, and then there was potentially something for surviving the integration, closing the most incursions, and becoming the world leader, and so on.

There were potentially a lot of titles waiting for the moment he managed to close the final incursions, and he wanted to have the ability to enjoy the bonuses. His plan was to immediately eat the **[Fruit of Rebirth]** and the two Race-boosting pills he'd gotten in the Base Town while flying toward the core of the Dead Zone.

It might not be enough to completely pass into D-grade Race, but it would at least set up the foundations and both increase his longevity and unlock some of the attribute cap of having a D-grade Race.

Zac finally felt he had both figured out what he needed to do and calmed his mind, and the next thing was simply for him to evolve so that he could set out toward the undead incursion. He walked over to the Nexus House and found that Kenzie was still installing the **[Heaven's Secrets Array]** he'd bought during an auction in Base Town.

"How are things?" Zac asked when he arrived, nodding at Ogras, who stood to the side as well.

"I'll have this array installed in half an hour," Kenzie answered as she blew a wisp of hair away from her face. "Are you okay?"

"I'm fine. I'll be able to get a breather when the undead are dealt with." Zac sighed.

"Have you decided what to do to get to the mainland?" Ogras asked.

"If we haven't managed to stop the disruption by the point I'm ready to leave, then I'll risk it and use Kenzie's stabilization array. The area that was jammed by the undead the last time was enormous, and I'm afraid that going to Cogstown will just be a waste of time," Zac said.

"Fair enough." Ogras shrugged.

"I'll get Calrin's uncle to help me set it up," Kenzie said. "He's pretty skilled with arrays, but he can only help with things that we buy through Thayer Consortium. Something to do with the limitations of the Mercantile License."

"That little blue bastard should be thankful that we don't throw him into a spatial tear to search for a safe passage for us," Ogras muttered from the side.

Zac snorted and was inclined to agree. The Sky Gnome's small act of giving him a protective ring had caused a ripple effect of almost incomprehensible proportions. It had led to the Zethaya Pill house blowing up, and him gaining infamy through slaughtering over a hundred scions of the Zecia Sector.

Who knew what trouble waited for him when venturing into the vaster stage of the sector?

However, the demon's words also made him think of something else, and he turned to Ogras.

"Can you have the Sky Gnome and his appraisers come over?" Zac asked. "We need to make a preliminary tally of the gains. I want to see if there's anything useful we can bring to the Dead Zone."

"Sure," Ogras said with some excitement as he flickered away.

Zac turned to his sister and handed her his Cosmos Sack. His most important Treasures had already been moved over to his new Spatial Ring after it was confirmed that it didn't disappear. Most of the stuff he didn't have any direct use for had been thrown into the Cosmos Sack to be either appraised or added to the Merit Store.

"I'll go talk with Brazla for a bit," Zac said.

"Is this about Alea?" Kenzie asked as her eyes darted to the necklace around Zac's neck. "Ogras told me what happened."

"I was too late again." Zac sighed. "This was the only thing I could think of."

Kenzie silently looked at her brother, but her eyes spoke volumes.

"I… I just couldn't sit and watch her die." Zac coughed, dodging the meaning of the stare.

He truthfully wasn't sure how he felt about the demoness even now. He had thought about her a lot during the climb, and seeing those snippets of Alea's memories had rekindled the memories of those months they had spent almost attached at the hip after he'd closed the Demon incursion. They had gone through ups and downs together, and he knew her even more intimately than Ogras in a sense.

If this had been before the integration, he would no doubt have believed it was love. But the past year had numbed him, made him almost unable to think about anything except getting stronger. First, it was to find his family; then it was to save Earth. He had never stopped to consider things such as love, especially not after Hannah's betrayal.

But all of that was moot now that she was a coffin.

"So you think you can bring her back in the future?" Kenzie asked instead after seeing her brother's brooding silence.

"That's what I hope. I'll go talk with Brazla; he might know more," Zac said with a pained face. "Provided he's in a talkative mood today."

"Say hello from me; it's been a while since I've had time to visit him. This thing will be up and running when you're back," Kenzie said as she turned back to keep working on the [Heaven's Secrets Array].

Zac smiled as he flashed away with [Loamwalker], and he found himself in front of the Towers of Myriad Dao in a few seconds. His Dao Repository had always looked gaudy, but now that he had witnessed the awe-inspiring Tower of Eternity and its mysterious apparitions, it looked even worse.

The lights were blinding but hollow, completely lacking the

mysteries of the universe. Zac kept his opinions to himself though as he walked inside the repository with a staid expression.

"So you survived after all." The ever-annoying voice drifted over as Brazla descended from a golden light appearing out of nowhere.

The Tool Spirit was decked in golden armor with multiple golden and gem-studded swords attached to his back. Zac wasn't sure, but he guessed that he was copying the creator of the Blademaster Inheritance this time, perhaps inspired by the war outside.

"I thought more capable owners had descended on the island for a moment, but I guess the Great Brazla has to make do with you for a while longer," Brazla added as he threw Zac a scathing glance as he conjured his throne.

"I'll try to live up to your expectations." Zac sighed. "My sister sends her regards."

"I–" Brazla said, but he suddenly froze as he stared at the necklace around Zac's neck. "What's that?"

INVITATIONS

"This craftsmanship," Brazla muttered with glowing eyes as he teleported closer. "It almost matches that of the Great Brazla himself. But why does it have a False Spirit within?"

"That's what I came to talk to you about. One of my people was dying, and her soul was crumbling. The only thing I could think of was to use a **[Divine Investiture Array]** to lock her soul in a Spirit Tool in hopes of saving her life."

"Using the holy array for such a purpose," Brazla muttered. "Sacrilege. My creator would have turned you into blood mist if he heard about you wasting such a chance on something so frivolous."

"I was out of options and got desperate," Zac admitted. "I came to ask you, do you know if I can bring her back?"

"Bring her back?" Brazla asked as he looked at Zac like he was an idiot. "Why would you want to do that? As long as the girl's spirit heals, she can become a True Spirit. You will have to break some rules to upgrade her, but you already seem all too willing to dabble in the taboo."

"What do you mean?" Zac asked.

"This thing will not be able to improve the normal way. You need to find... creative solutions to upgrade it. Solutions that the Heavens won't be too happy about," the Tool Spirit said, clearly taking pleasure in Zac's misfortune.

"Why would I need to upgrade the Spirit Tool, though?" Zac asked. "I just want to return her to life."

"Upgrading a weapon will upgrade the spirituality residing within. Just look at the dumb mutt inside your axe. You will need to upgrade this thing if you want to heal the girl," Brazla said.

Zac frowned when he heard the news. This was clearly bad. He had never had any desire to go against the System by becoming an unorthodox cultivator, but it was exactly what he needed to do to upgrade [Love's Bond], from the sound of it. Even weirder, it almost felt like the System was pushing him in that direction, as it was the System that had given him the array.

Just what was it planning?

Was this another type of trial it wanted to have him survive? If he stepped on the unorthodox path, he would be turned into a pariah like the Technocrats, and people might get quests to kill him just by coming close to him. Or was the System planning something else entirely? Something related to the Terminus?

But first of all, Zac needed to know if there even was a point to going down that road.

"If I make her a new body, can I put her soul into it and give her back her life?" Zac asked.

"No idea." Brazla shrugged with disinterest. "Seems pretty stupid."

"Haven't you ever hoped to become living? To become able to cultivate just like your creator?" Zac probed, hoping to elicit some response.

"Why would the Great Brazla ever want to become a fleshbag cursed by mortality? I am perfection, unsullied by time, and I will walk these halls long after both you and your planet have turned to dust. I might not be able to cultivate, but I am eternal," the Tool Spirit harangued, and shining lights started appearing all around him like he was a god's avatar or something.

"But do you know if it's possible? Someone as knowledgeable as you must surely have figured some things out," Zac entreated.

"My creator once mentioned that Spirit Tools can reach a sublime state where they are virtually indistinguishable from cultivators, but he had never seen it himself. Of course, the Great Brazla wouldn't degrade himself to the point of being mistaken for a lowly human. But all things are possible," the Tool Spirit admitted. "Turning a False Spirit back into someone living is probably possible."

"So it's possible after all." Zac sighed in relief.

"It might be possible, but what you want to do is going against the natural order," Brazla snorted. "It's akin to bringing back those from the dead. It might be achievable for the great characters of the Multiverse, but what does that have to do with a piece of trash like you?"

"I'll work hard and get there sooner or later," Zac said. "As long as it's possible, it'll be fine."

A derisive snort was all the Tool Spirit deigned to respond with before he dissipated again.

Zac felt as though a huge weight was lifted from his shoulders as he walked back toward the Nexus House. Brazla was obviously a bit fuzzy on the details, but it really seemed that returning Alea into a demon was within the realm of possibilities. That was all Zac could ask for right now. He knew the process would likely be a long and arduous one, but at least he knew he hadn't completely messed things up.

The knowledge gave him a sense of purpose beyond saving Earth as well, but for now, he needed to refocus on the task at hand. He needed to get his items appraised and deal with the realignment.

The thought of his items suddenly reminded him of the two Cosmos Sacks he had stowed away just before leaving Base Town. They were from Leyara and Pretty, and curiosity made him take a look before returning to his sister.

The Cosmos Sack he got from Pretty Peak just contained three crystals and a Teleportation Token, but he was surprised to see that one of them was a Skill Crystal. He didn't immediately touch it, but rather turned his attention toward the middle crystal, which seemed to be a communication crystal. He infused some Cosmic Energy into it, and the next moment the voice of Pretty Peak appeared in his mind.

I engraved this thing because some things should not be spoken aloud. You should not rely on the Heliophos Clan dealing with the threat to your planet. There are some unsavory rumors about that clan among the top forces of the Zecia Sector.

Divination comes with a cost, one that few are willing to pay unless absolutely necessary. One cannot divulge Heaven's Secrets wantonly. But being able to glimpse the future is also an extremely addicting power, from what I have heard.

Zac suddenly remembered Lord 84th, who'd stopped Abbot Everlasting Peace from saying too much. The reincarnated Buddhist had said essentially the same thing. Did divination perhaps mess with the plans the System had set in motion across the Multiverse and was therefore punished? Or was it simply that such a heaven-defying ability couldn't be powered by something so basic as Cosmic Energy?

Zac shook his head as he kept listening.

Many believe that the Heliophos Clan is searching for means to avoid the side effects of Divination and Karmic Manipulation. They are already suspected to have been gravitating toward unorthodox means for tens of thousands of years.

It's possible that Voridis is performing his mad experiments with the clan's tacit blessing, and that they even have covertly protected him from capture by manipulating events behind the curtain. I don't understand how Voridis has survived pursuit for so long otherwise.

I bet they can't wait to find out what scheme that lunatic has concocted in case they can use it for themselves.

Zac sighed when he heard the explanation. Yet another method to deal with the threat of the Redeemer seemed to have been ruined then and there. It looked like hiding was his only option, but as long as he cut any Karmic Links in time, they were likely safe.

After meeting Catheya, he finally had a better grasp of just how a star sector was constituted. She had likened a star sector to a book, where each page was a dimensional layer. A star sector was, in other words, not a coherent galaxy teeming with life, but rather parts of multiple planes stacked so close to each other that dimensional travel was possible.

Not even singular forces were constrained to a single dimension. The Allbright Empire was comprised of planets and continents across thousands, perhaps tens of thousands, of realities. Some planets in the empire might actually exist in the same dimension, but so far away from each other that it was infinitely faster to use interdimensional travel rather than normal travel to go between the two planets.

It was akin to wormhole technology that Zac had seen in science fiction movies, where space was somehow bent and twisted, and traveling out of the main dimension was like taking a shortcut compared to moving in a straight line.

The whole thing was extremely confusing, but the biggest takeaway was the difficulty of finding one's way without a marker. The Redeemer was probably traveling toward Earth or another seeded planet at this very moment, but he needed to move through multiple dimensions to get here. As long as any Karmic Link was cut off before Voridis was within a few dimensional layers of Earth, then finding this place was almost impossible.

Especially while the System's shroud was still in effect.

This was also why Flying Treasures that could travel between worlds were expensive to the point that even D-grade warriors were often confined to their own world, or at least their solar system. The vessels didn't only need to have the capability to fly through the vacuum of space, but they also needed the capabilities to push through dimensional layers.

It was a bit uncomfortable to think about, but Zac's only recourse was to hide Earth so that Voridis fed on some other poor planets instead of Earth. He could only pray that the people of Berum would manage to take out all the remaining members of the Medhin Royals on their side, as no one deserved getting culled by a lunatic like the Redeemer.

That would be the best-case scenario, where all the seed planets managed to hide from Voridis. He already looked as though he wasn't long for the world, and a hundred years was a long time. Perhaps the issue would be dealt with by the time that Earth was properly integrated into the Zecia Sector.

I will contact the Heliophos Clan for you, the message continued. But you truly shouldn't expect much. You can still get in touch with me by visiting Jaera at the Blossom Rose Sword School that's close to Trasteria, the city where the Teleportation Token leads. She is an elder there, and a disciple of my father.

Trasteria is located on the main continent of the Allbright Empire, a vast place full of opportunities. You can simply use the token to move to a place with more opportunities if you want. But you should know that your situation is precarious. Standing out too much without backing can cause an endless amount of trouble to arrive at your doorstep.

The universe is full of lunatics ready to risk everything to progress one step further on the road of cultivation, and some might believe you might be the key for them to take that step.

I hope you will be able to survive the following centuries; the Zecia Sector needs a beacon.

The second information crystal was a comprehensive introduction packet of the Allbright Empire, its forces, and even some Mystic Realms that provided good Limited Titles. There were also a couple of identities that Zac could freely assume with the help of the attached skill, which was of the shapeshifting variety. It was like he was about to enter the witness protection program or something.

The skill was called **[Shared Identity]**, and it worked a bit differently compared to **[Thousand Faces]**. The skill he got from Pretty seemed to be able to create a greater transformation, where even one's aura could be changed by a certain degree, but it came with only three "preloaded" identities.

He could essentially take one of these three shared identities, but he wouldn't be able to change his face as he wished like he could with **[Thousand Faces]**. Zac held off on learning the skill for now, but it wasn't impossible he'd use it in the future. It would be pretty convenient to step into the shoes of someone with a proper background, but he didn't know if there were hidden strings attached to taking the name of one of these three men.

Zac turned his attention to the second Cosmos Sack next, but his expression froze when he noticed its contents. There were only two things inside, a short note and a frilly piece of fabric.

A small greeting gift to remember me by. I am not allowed to hand out Teleportation Tokens to the Void Gate, but I would be happy to entertain you if you have the opportunity to stop by. We can talk about fashion and our futures under the light of the Void Star.
–Leyara

Zac blankly looked at the note, his mind unable to compute what was going on. The strained smile of Leyara suddenly flashed by in his mind before he remembered the apologetic face of Galau. Just what had the merchant divulged during their meeting? Would he be known as some sort of deviant in the whole sector because of that one level in the Tower?

A sigh escaped from his mouth as he stowed away the Cosmos Sack, unsure what to do with the "treasure." He could only reluctantly put it into his Spatial Ring, as it would be weird throwing it out in the middle of his forest. However, things didn't get much better when he returned to the Nexus House, where Kenzie stood next to a rack of exquisite dresses, while three Sky Gnomes eagerly went through the mound of treasures.

"Why are there so many dresses in your sack?" Kenzie asked with a weird smile when she noticed his return.

"I was about to ask." The demon laughed from the side. "I thought I absconded with the most 'treasures' back then, but I see that I still have much to learn."

"Are you planning on wooing someone? Is it Thea?" Kenzie asked before she shot him a hesitant look. "Or don't tell me…?"

"Don't be silly." Zac sighed. "The seventh floor had me fighting actual scions from other parts of the Multiverse. I looted my new ring and those dresses from a girl who targeted me."

"Do you think any trouble from that will lead back to Earth?" Ogras asked with a frown.

"I doubt it?" Zac said hesitantly. "It kind of looked like my human side was killed by the girl I looted, and she was killed by someone else in turn. I fought the rest of the battle in my Draugr form. I don't think the System would allow problems to follow you back home, right? Perhaps it's possible to do something to 'cleanse' the items if needed?"

However, he honestly wasn't as sure as he let on.

CHOICES

He had already noticed it back during his meeting with Catheya, but there was something wrong with his chest. Iz Tayn had left a burn on his body that he hadn't been able to get rid of with healing pills. However, getting his torso blown apart and re-formed by Creation Energy had dealt with that problem.

Or so he thought.

He still couldn't see any mark on his body, but he had felt a slight pain in his chest multiple times now, but the feeling was gone before he had a chance to react, making him almost doubt it was ever there. He couldn't see anything amiss, but the fire mage had seemed to come from a real powerful force.

She might have all kinds of means of tracking he had no idea about.

"The Thayer Consortium happens to be skilled in those kinds of endeavors; we'll happily help in this regard... for a small remuneration," Calrin said as he gave a prim bow. "Young Lord, it is good to see you again."

Zac didn't immediately greet the wily merchant, but he rather gazed at the Sky Gnome for a few seconds as his thumb rubbed the defensive treasure that he'd received from Calrin before he left for the Tower.

"Did you know that the ring you gave me would cause trouble

with the Tsarun Clan?" Zac asked while he tried to gauge the slippery merchant's face for any lies.

"No way!" Calrin said, looking genuinely shocked. "It is just a defensive treasure that has been kept in my family. I just wanted to make sure that you, my great benefactor, wouldn't meet any untoward end during your first sojourn into the cultivator world!"

"Well, your small gift led to the destruction of the Zethaya Pill House and the death of almost a hundred elites of the sector. Including a Dravorak princeling," the demon snorted from the side. "Oh, and a main branch Tsarun scion along with all their members at the Base Town. Thayer Consortium might become famous across the whole sector over the following years as the rumors spread."

"It – ah? Dravorak as in the Dravorak Dynasty?" the Sky Gnome said, his face aghast. "Did they see the signet as well? I mean, it wasn't my intention to cause any trouble. I don't understand what's going on."

"Just what happened during your climb?!" Kenzie exclaimed with shock from the side after glaring at the Sky Gnome, who quickly busied himself with the pile of treasures by the side.

"It's complicated." Zac sighed. "I got spotted by one of Calrin's old enemies, but the problem was that I didn't handle it well. Things got a bit out of control from there, and a bunch of people tried to kill me. But it was mostly sorted out."

"Sorted out?" Ogras snorted from the side, but he didn't add any more oil to the fire after a glare from Zac.

"Well, we also learned a few things about the origins of the Redeemer. For now, make sure that no one in Port Atwood mentions where they come from if they decide to head to the Tower of Eternity. My identity might be a bit delicate," Zac said after some thought as he turned to Kenzie.

"If I may, young master," Calrin said from the side, "what level did you reach?"

"Seventy-third level. The entrance of the ninth floor," Zac said, not bothering to hide the truth.

"Ninth floor!" Calrin screamed while the appraisers looked up from the pile of treasures for the first time, shock clearly written all over their faces.

"Monster! True monster!" the Sky Gnome muttered before his face lit up again. "But that's for the best. With you as a guardian, the Thayer Consortium will reach unprecedented heights. I, Calrin Thayer, will not only have led my family out of a calamity, but toward the heavens themselves!"

"What are you getting so bigheaded for, you little bastard?" Ogras snorted from the side. "You'd better think of new ways to provide benefits to your shareholders instead. A big tree might give you shade, but it also requires a lot of nutrients."

Zac slightly smiled at the antics, but he didn't correct the demon. He still couldn't tell if the Sky Gnome had exposed his connection to the Thayer Consortium on purpose or not, but it had caused heaps of trouble regardless. The little merchant would have to work extra hard to make up for the chaos he had caused.

But he knew that he would have to rely on the Sky Gnome to a certain degree after meeting Catheya. He'd had no idea that elites required more energy to level up compared to weaker cultivators, which honestly made him worry about his own situation a bit.

Not only were his attributes almost ten times higher compared to a normal cultivator, but he also had high efficiency on the attributes. Add to that he had a second class to level and the even more troubling issue of him being a mortal. All that combined made for an extremely torturous leveling experience that would require terrifying amounts of bloodshed and treasures to reach the peak of E-grade.

As for the grades above that, he didn't even dare think about it.

"How long until you've gone through everything?" Zac asked instead as he turned to Calrin.

"We'll have a preliminary answer for you in two hours," Calrin hurriedly said. "You can focus on your cultivation with ease."

Zac nodded before he turned to Ogras.

"So do you have any advice? The information crystals I have only mentioned the three tribulations," Zac asked. "Heart, Body, and Soul. It said that using treasures to pass is impossible and that you have to rely on your own prowess. Then it just went on to say that one should have an elder nearby in case of a mishap."

The information crystal was something he had bought in Base Town during the first week he stayed there. He had bought a bunch of general information crystals that contained all sorts of things that were good to know. Most of it was things that any teenager belonging to a cultivation force would know, which was why they cost almost nothing.

However, that also meant that they didn't delve too deep into any topics, only giving an overview.

Buying the crystals had been the first step toward self-reliance for the humans of Port Atwood. It wasn't that he didn't trust Ogras' or Alyn's teachings, but their worldview and knowledge were influenced by growing up in Clan Azh'Rezak.

What worked there wasn't necessarily optimal for Port Atwood, so it didn't hurt to get another source of knowledge. It wasn't anywhere near as comprehensive as Thea's library, but it was a start.

"It differs," Ogras said as he looked at the Nexus Node while Kenzie was putting the finishing touches to the support array. "It tests you in one of three ways, depending on where the Ruthless Heavens feels you are lacking. The tribulation will strike at your weakness, and either you pass or you fail."

"What happens if you fail?" Zac asked.

"Anything from mild wounds to death, depending on how badly you performed and whether someone could disperse the tribulation for you." The demon shrugged. "But truthfully, I've only met one who failed his trial so badly he was forced to give up on cultivation. Obbu-rak, a guard in my home. He undertook the trial drunk out of his mind; it ended with him going insane."

"Insane? Just what did he encounter?" Zac asked with a frown.

"The Body Tribulation is essentially the Ruthless Heavens beating you up, and you just have to bear it. It is to test that you have created a foundation sturdy enough to keep building upon. I doubt you'd get that one, considering your monstrous constitution," the demon said with an envious glance. "It is the most common trial for Dexterity- and Intelligence-based classes."

"And then?" Zac urged.

"Next there is the Spirit Tribulation," the demon continued. "Your soul is attacked in a way that neither skills nor items can protect you from. You need to use your soul and Dao to defend yourself. The soul is the connection to the Heavens, and it needs to be strong enough to withstand the weight of the Dao," Ogras said.

Zac grimaced as he heard the description. His soul was already in a pretty fragile state after having been forcibly torn apart and mended twice in the past month. It was a patchwork upon a patchwork, where the slightest thing might set off a chain reaction beyond his control. However, his soul had become pretty sturdy from the series of harrowing experiences, so he still felt some confidence in case he got that one, at least while the Remnants stayed inactive.

"Finally, there is the Heart Tribulation. You will be thrown into illusions and temptations, and you will need to break free. The Heavens test your conviction and mental fortitude. A sturdy body and soul is needed to walk the path of cultivation, but a resolute heart might be even more important," the demon continued. "This is the trial that turned Obburak into a simpleton, by the way."

Zac slowly nodded as he listened to the options. The third one didn't feel too difficult either. His mental state should be a lot sturdier compared to most peak F-grade warriors after his countless life-and-death battles. Many cultivators who had reached this point had never even left their own clan's estates, and this kind of trial might be pretty difficult for that kind of greenhouse warrior.

Still, it was a relief that the risk of death or crippling was pretty low. He could still fail, but he would at least be able to heal up and fight the Undead Empire in his current condition.

"Is it the same for all the rarities, or are there more things to be wary of when talking Epic classes or higher?" Zac asked.

"Perhaps Epic and higher have different trials apart from the normal three; I wouldn't know," the demon slowly said. "But they will no doubt be more dangerous. Each increase in rarity means a sharp increase in difficulty that accompanies the tribulation."

Zac looked at the crystal with mixed emotions. He wasn't sure if he was ready. He wanted to consolidate his gains and stabilize his foundations before attempting this. But time waited for no man, and he couldn't hold off any longer.

Hearing about the losses out on the ocean and seeing the scorched landscape outside his home had been a stark reminder that every day he spent accumulating his strength was another day of disastrous losses across the world.

Perhaps he would be able to enter the heart of the Dead Zone and take out the Lich King without evolving. But perhaps he wouldn't. With the situation looking like it did, there would be no second chances or do-overs. If his assault failed or even got slightly delayed, the whole world would fall.

He could not have that on his conscience.

"It's done," Kenzie said as she looked up with a tired grin.

"Thank you. Try to rest up." Zac smiled, a pang of guilt blossoming in his heart again.

He had heard from Ogras just how hard she had fought to keep things together while he was gone, and her unstable aura clearly indicated that her soul was overtaxed. He had already learned from Jaol that using high tech was draining on the soul, and Jeeves was no doubt as high tech as they came.

"Here, take these with you as well," Zac said as he took out a stack of Soul Crystals. "They'll help restore your mental energy."

"Where did you get those?" Ogras said with wide eyes, his hand already reaching out to snatch one from Kenzie.

"Here, take this," Zac snorted and took out a few more after he slapped away the demon's hand. "I got these Soul Crystals from the mentalist cultivator on the seventh floor as well."

"It's called a Soul Crystal?" Ogras asked curiously as he tried absorbing it.

"No idea, that's just what I called it." Zac shrugged. "They didn't have these things on your home planet?"

"I don't think I've ever heard of crystals like this in our sector at all," Ogras muttered with a frown. "Perhaps our sector simply doesn't produce them. Trade between sectors is pretty difficult, from what I've heard, and only the top people do it. Nobodies like us will have to make do with local products."

"So I won't be able to restock on these things?" Zac muttered with disappointment.

He had thought that might be a real possibility after not having seen a single Soul Crystal during his time in the Base Town, but he had held on to some small hope that was because he'd only been there for less than two weeks. But judging by the demon's reaction, he wasn't so lucky.

He suddenly regretted using Soul Crystals like candy during his climb, but he also knew that they had played a large part in him managing to break through the eighth floor. But he would have to be more careful about any expenditure going forward, which was fine now that the two primordial Remnants were restraining each other.

With the array installed, Zac couldn't wait any longer, and he walked over to the large crystal with brisk steps, anticipation making his heart pound. The moment Zac touched the Nexus Node to initiate the upgrade, a screen appeared in front of him, but it was vastly different compared to the sparse rows of information he had seen the last time. He almost completely forgot his surroundings as he eagerly read the boxes.

Free Attributes Gained Per Level: 10

Base Attributes Gained Per Node 76–100:
Common, Uncommon: Base Attributes: +6
Rare, Epic: Base Attributes: +7
Arcane: Base Attributes: +8

Base Attributes Gained Per Node 101–125:
Common, Uncommon: Base Attributes: +14.
Rare, Epic: Base Attributes: +16.
Arcane: Base Attributes: +18.

Base Attributes Gained Per Node 126–150:
Common, Uncommon: Base Attributes: +22.
Rare, Epic: Base Attributes: +25.
Arcane: Base Attributes: +28.

[Option 1.]
Name: Gatekeeper of Sukhavati [E-Epic]. Divergence from Hatchetman.
Attribute per Level (x1/x2/x3): Vitality +10, Endurance +8, Wisdom +5.

First Skill Gained: Chains of Samsara.
Paradise is waiting, but only the worthy may step past your gates.

Name: Undying Warlord [E-Epic]. Divergence from Undying Bulwark.
Attribute per Level (x1/x2/x3): Strength +12, Endurance +10.
First Skill Gained: Profane Annihilation.
Unstoppable. Undeniable. Unmatched.

[Option 2.]
Name: Vessel of Destruction [E-Arcane]. Upgrade of Hatchetman.
Attribute per Level (x1/x2/x3): Strength +38, Agility +5 Endurance -10.
First Skill Gained: Avatar of Wrath.
Only through destruction can creation take place. Become the harbinger of a new era.

Name: Nature's Lament [E-Epic]. Divergence from Undying Bulwark.
Attribute per Level (x1/x2/x3): Endurance +10, Wisdom +11.
First Skill Gained: Touch of Anguish.
Paradise is a lie, a putrid tomb of unimaginable horrors.

[Option 3.]
Name: Edge of Arcadia [E-Epic]. Upgrade of Hatchetman.
Attribute per Level (x1/x2/x3): Strength +14, Vitality +8.
First Skill Gained: Rapturous Divide.
Even paradise needs a butcher, an unrelenting storm of violence.

Name: Fetters of Desolation [E-Epic]. Divergence from Undying Bulwark.
Attribute per Level (x1/x2/x3): Strength +11, Endurance +8, Wisdom +5.
First Skill Gained: Blighted Cut.
Bind them to your calamity. Sever their path. Emerge alone.

[Option 4.]

Name: Gaia's Apostle [E-Epic]. Upgrade of Hatchetman.
Attribute per Level (x1/x2/x3): Strength +5, Vitality +12,
Wisdom + 5.
First Skill Gained: Gaia's Eruption.
The champion of verdure, unmatched and unkillable. Upgrade of Hatchetman.

Name: Wall of Bones [E-Epic]. Upgrade of Undying Bulwark.
Attribute per Level (x1/x2/x3): Endurance +18, Vitality +5.
First Skill Gained: Profane Phalanx.
The living can only run in fear as the tide of bones moves forward.

[Option 5.]
Name: Warmaster of Hecate [E-Epic]. Divergence of Hatchetman.
Attribute per Level (x1/x2/x3): Strength +15, Vitality +7.
First Skill Gained: Nature's Fall.
Empowered by the Sacred Yew, the Warmaster becomes Death incarnate.

Name: Risen Asura [E-Epic]. Divergence of Undying Bulwark.
Attribute per Level (x1/x2/x3): Strength +12, Endurance +11.
First Skill Gained: Winds of War.
Not even death can chain down your furor.

DECISION

Zac looked at the options with mixed emotions. He had succeeded in the sense that there actually was an Arcane class available, a class called Vessel of Destruction. However, it didn't have another Arcane to accompany it. It was instead matched with an Epic class called Nature's Lament.

He had been hesitant about what he should do after hearing Catheya's description, and this only muddied the waters further. With Arcane classes locking in your future path, there was a real risk that picking just one Arcane class while leaving the other at Epic might have some unanticipated ramifications.

If there had been a set of two Arcane classes, he might just have ignored Catheya's warning and followed Yrial's advice to shoot for the stars, but now he wasn't so sure.

His instincts told him that he needed to create a functioning system between his two classes where both sides moved toward a common goal. He had felt there were some compatibility issues with his second class for some time now, and there was a real risk that his Draugr side might turn into a bottleneck if he wasn't careful.

Zac slowly read the description of Vessel of Destruction. It felt most likely that it was based around the Splinter. It seemed to utilize the rage and madness that the Splinter radiated, and the class would perhaps even help him in harnessing the bronze sparks. It also provided a skill called Avatar of Wrath, which sounded like some sort of boosting skill in the vein of [Hatchetman's Rage], or perhaps something more akin to [Vanguard of Undeath].

However, nothing indicated that it also incorporated the Shard or the balance between the two forces, and neither was there any such indication on the accompanying class. It wasn't surprising, though, as there simply hadn't been enough time for him to get acquainted with the pink flashes and the Shard of Creation.

He'd only had access to it during the frantic escape from the Technocrat vessel and the subsequent battle against the dragon. That was nothing compared to the months of carrying the Splinter and the weeks of constant experimentation with the bronze flashes.

The Dao requirements had been fulfilled after reaching Middle mastery with the Dao of the Coffin, and there was no doubt in his mind that he had gone far beyond what was required to generate enough merit for a second Arcane option. He had conquered the eighth floor of the Tower of Eternity. He had taken down a literal dragon before forcing the elites of the whole sector to give in.

He had taken out a whole Technocrat vessel, and he had closed almost all the incursions of a newly integrated world. He had even witnessed the "Terminus," the origin and the end of the Dao itself. If he didn't have enough achievements by now, then who did?

That meant there was a problem with his "creation."

There was a fuzzy image of his future cultivation in his mind, one based on a few defining features of his power. It was a path of duality, exemplified through his two classes, his opposing Daos, and the two Remnants in his mind. But there was still nothing that really tied these three pairs together. He also had no actual idea what the bronze and pink flashes he created were, or even how he was supposed to properly use them.

He knew that there was no way for him to gain a quick fix to upgrade Nature's Lament to an Arcane option, so he could only drop the issue for now. Cultivation was measured in centuries, even millennia, and he had ample time to figure out the missing pieces of his cultivation path.

There were all sorts of logical reasons why he shouldn't take the

Vessel of Destruction, but the word "Arcane" was like a target that kept drawing back Zac's eyes. The class was clearly powerful, and it would both provide more attributes from the base attributes while almost ten extra attribute points per level.

It was an extremely lopsided class, but his unique situation with bonus attributes would cancel out the huge downside of negative Endurance. He was frozen in indecision for a few seconds, but eventually, his fears of the potential risks overcame the lure of the potential rewards.

He was giving up on an Arcane class for E-grade.

Zac slowly read through each of the four other options instead, not too surprised with the rarity of them. He had already expected to be presented mostly Epic classes, perhaps with a few Rare ones peppered in. The only question was how many options he would be provided.

There was no denying that his visit to the Tower of Eternity had been worth it in terms of options to choose from. Not only did his options max out at five, but every single class apart from Vessel of Destruction was Epic. Most of them were new as well, with only Undying Warlord remaining as an option from his previous inquiry.

The [Heaven's Secrets Array] was also showing its worth, and the information he was given was just on a completely different level compared to last time. It didn't just provide him with information about what attributes the classes provided, but even revealed the names of the skills he would gain.

Zac already knew about the base attributes after having spoken with Ylvas and Catheya, but it was still eye-opening to see the numbers in person. It was not without reason that Ogras had said that Low-tiered titles were useless for anything except leveraging them into Medium- and High-tiered counterparts.

Even a Common-class warrior would gain the equivalent of a top-tier flat attribute title every level while still early E-grade, excluding Luck of course. Furthermore, that boost would increase further at reaching Middle E-grade, and then once more upon reaching High E-grade. If things followed the same pattern as F-grade, then there might also be a bonus waiting at the peak of E-grade.

And that wasn't all. The actual class gave another round of attributes on top of the base, and a quick glance proved that an Epic class seemed to give another 20 to 25 attribute points, in addition to the 10 free attribute points. That meant that a Low E-grade warrior with an Epic class would gain almost 80 attribute points per level, which was in line with what Ylvas had said – that the attribute gains were almost ten times those of F-grade.

The real question on Zac's mind was how this base worked for him. Judging by the description, it seemed like a done deal that he would get the class-specific attributes from both classes, along with two sets of free attributes, as he did level his classes separately. But would he also get two base packs per level?

It would make a huge difference, as more than half of the attributes came from the base attributes awarded upon breaking open a node. If he didn't get the base attributes twice, he'd "only" get 50% more attributes compared to a normal cultivator, drastically reducing his advantage.

Another piece of information that the array added was whether the evolution was an upgrade or a divergence. Zac guessed that meant that the new class would either build upon the earlier class or move it away from its predecessor in some other direction.

For example, Edge of Arcadia and Gaia's Apostle were both clearly related to the Hatchetman class, but judging by their attributes and skills, they went in different directions. Edge of Arcadia seemed to focus more on axe-work, whereas Gaia's Apostle leaned toward nature skills like **[Nature's Punishment]** and **[Hatchetman's Spirit]**.

A divergence would instead stake out a new path, perhaps only partially relying on the earlier class. It wasn't surprising that he saw mostly divergent options for his Draugr class after splitting up its Dao Seeds with hardness going into the Coffin and Sanctuary going into the Bodhi. It might result in some of his old skills becoming obsolete, but Zac already knew that going in.

Zac knew he needed to make a decision, and he first excluded the fourth option. The Draugr class seemed to be purely defensive, which was the very thing he wanted to move away from. Gaia's Apostle didn't really resonate with him either, even though **[Nature's Punish-ment]** had been one of his main skills for dealing with tough opponents.

The other three options both had strong points and demerits, but

Zac eventually discarded the first option as well, leaving him with options three and five. Undying Warlord seemed like a good fit for him, as it probably was just like his current class with a higher focus on offense. However, the problem was with the class "Gatekeeper of Sukhavati."

The class didn't provide a single point in Strength, which indicated a significant step away from his current fighting style. Even worse, it seemed to be lopsided in the sense that it was based on both the Bodhi and the Coffin. He didn't want those two Fragments going into the same class, as he wanted for each class to represent one of the concepts of life and death, or Creation and Oblivion.

The third and fifth options both seemed to fulfill all his goals for his new class. The Draugr classes seemed to be geared much more offensively compared to Undying Bulwark. Risen Asura gave the feeling of pure violence and oppression, like he would become an unstoppable killing machine that refused to die until all his enemies had fallen before him.

The Fetters of Desolation was a bit less clear, but he still felt it was a very good match. The name of the class didn't really sound like something he'd want to use, but there were some good indications that it was still suited for him. The first indicator was the skill Blighted Cut. It sounded like a weapon-based attack, and perhaps something that took advantage of the corrosive elements of the Dao of the Coffin.

The flavor text also made him think of a restriction-based warrior who entrapped and weakened his enemies before he delivered the killing blow. That seemed like a good option to him, as that was the main way that he used his Undying Bulwark class. He trapped his enemies in the Miasmic cage, then whittled them down with [Winds of Decay], [Deathwish], and the spectral chains.

If the enemy tried a desperate strike, he took them out with [Vanguard of Undeath] and [Unholy Strike].

Of course, these were still just hypotheses, but there was undeniably something about that class that pulled at him. He wasn't sure whether it was the advertised Karmic Guidance that was supposed to be included in the [Heaven's Secret Array], or if it was because of his recently acquired Spirit Tool.

As for the two classes for his human side, both of them had strong points.

Arcadia contained the meaning of becoming one with nature, which was exactly the direction he wanted to take the class based on his life-aspected vision for his path. But it still had Strength as its main attribute, which clearly indicated a warrior archetype together with the flavor text and skill option.

However, Warmaster of Hecate had provided an interesting twist to his envisioned path. Hecate was a goddess of witchcraft, death, and poison. It was a fusion of Death and Life, while still being a warrior-type class with a connection to nature. This fit well together with the "Risen" part of the other class, which seemed based on his recent insight of Life from Death.

So one of the options blended life and death, incorporating a nascent duality of his two main concepts into both the classes. The other option was more neatly separated with his human side representing life and nature, and his Draugr side representing death and desolation.

The question was whether he wanted to fuse these two concepts right now and build upon it, or if he was better off progressing in the two paths separately until he understood more about what the paths entailed.

Eventually, his eyes turned to the third option, the combination of Edge of Arcadia and Fetters of Desolation.

He decided to go with this option for two reasons. First was the fact that Warmaster of Hecate was a divergence of Hatchetman, a class he felt perfectly suited for him. He would rather upgrade his human side and get a divergent class for his Draugr side.

The second reason was that he felt it was too early to start mucking about and fusing the two concepts of life and death into one single class. He wasn't even sure if that was the form his "creation" would take in the future, and he didn't want to walk down that path before he had come to a conclusion there.

However, he didn't immediately start the evolution, but rather turned toward his sister and Ogras, who curiously looked at him.

"It's working." Zac nodded.

"Well, no shit," the demon muttered. "You've been standing still with a disgusting grin on your face for five minutes. Are you ready to evolve?"

"I'm going now." Zac nodded.

"None of us can help you if you mess up, so you might as well do it in your courtyard, where you won't be disturbed," the demon said. "You will have a minute or so before the tribulation descends."

Zac nodded in agreement, as it sounded like the best option.

"This might take a while, but make sure I'm okay if I haven't emerged in a day," Zac said as he took out the dozen Array Breakers from his Spatial Ring. "And focus on identifying treasures that will help in the battle against the Undead Empire. I'm pretty sure that these are all Array Breakers; see which ones might be of use against anything the Lich King uses."

"We'll certainly extract their secrets by the time you're done." Calrin hurriedly nodded, obviously eager to rack up some contribution.

"Good." Zac nodded before he turned back to the Nexus Node and picked the third option before having a chance to change his mind again.

[Tribulation will descend in 1 Minute]

"Good luck," Kenzie said from the side, but some excitement was evident in her eyes. "You're making history here."

"I'll be back soon." Zac smiled before he flashed away, quickly returning to his courtyard.

The moment he entered, he activated his layered arrays before he sat down on his prayer mat. He doubted it would be of any help, but it did help him calm his mind a bit better as he waited for the minute to pass.

Finally, it arrived, and he felt himself being surrounded by a mysterious energy. He couldn't figure out what it was made of, but it felt a bit reminiscent of the sky of lightning he had witnessed when the Chaos Pattern had appeared. Of course, it was an extremely watered-down version.

He was just about to close his eyes and brace for the tribulation when two prompts appeared in front of him.

[Heart Tribulation Descends. Struggle for Survival.]
[Spirit Tribulation Descends. Struggle for Survival.]

"Shit," Zac muttered before his world was consumed by pain and fire.

HEART

Zac growled from the pain as it felt like his soul had been doused in kerosene and lit on fire. The torment made it almost impossible for him to form a coherent thought, let alone erect some sort of defense.

Not that there was any. He knew that skills and items were useless in a case like this, and he could only bear it. The pain was agonizing, but it wouldn't actually hurt his soul unless he gave in. He repeated the word "endure" over and over in his mind, turning it into a mantra of perseverance.

The pain was well beyond what he had expected for a tribulation, though; it was almost up there with other terrifying ordeals such as his dip in the Cosmic Water pond. Did everyone have to endure suffering of this magnitude, or was he given special attention because he chose an Epic class?

However, he didn't have time to form any hypothesis before his surroundings blurred, and he suddenly found himself in his bed. Zac looked around in confusion, his past experiences turning muddled and indistinct as a slender arm reached around him. He smiled and turned over, coming face-to-face with his new girlfriend.

"What is it?" Hannah asked as she scratched his beard with a wink. "Can't sleep?"

"Something like that." Zac smiled as he dragged her closer to him.

"Hmm," Hanna hummed as she leaned in for a kiss as her hand reached downward.

Zac's body was quick to respond, but he froze just as he was about to reciprocate her actions. How did he get here? Why did things seem so off?

"What's wrong?" Hannah panted in his ear, her hand stopping just as it was about to reach inside his underwear.

Lust fought with unease, but Zac finally shook his head and climbed out of his bed, his head darting back and forth with a wildness in his eyes.

Something wasn't right.

A heavy sense of wrongness encompassed him even though everything in his studio apartment looked like it should. But a shocking pain in his mind almost made him keel over, and he held his head in his hands as the world turned blurry.

"Zac? What's going on? Should I call an ambulance?" Hannah asked with fright as she ran over, but Zac's eyes widened when a knife suddenly appeared in her hand and sank deep into his chest.

"You're not real," Zac growled, finally remembering what was going on. "This is not real."

"Yes, isn't that what you like to tell yourself after you discarded me like trash?" Hannah sneered as the world collapsed.

Anxiety burned in Zac's chest as he urged the flying disk to move faster, but it felt like he was flying through solid matter as he saw his beleaguered army in the distance. Alea stood in the front, desperately fighting to create an opportunity for the army to survive. But it was for naught as she was cut down where she stood by a group of spectral assassins.

Zac finally managed to push through the solidified air as he landed next to her, and he quickly put a healing pill in her mouth. But it barely had an effect as the wounds kept bleeding, staining the ground in a crimson hue.

"Why didn't you save me?" Alea cried as she looked up at Zac with desolation in her eyes. "I loved you. I bled for you. But you only saw me as a tool to further your goals."

"I–" Zac stammered, but he had no chance to form a response before one sobbing voice after another spoke up around him.

"Why did you give up on us?" a Valkyrie cried. "You were supposed to lead us out of misery, not into it."

"Why?" a dozen dying soldiers cried in anguish, their wails growing in agony and sorrow by the second.

"Why?!"

"WHY?!"

The chorus grew louder and louder, and Zac felt like his mind was splitting apart. A wave of pain came from nowhere at that very moment, making him fall over in agony. He arduously got to his feet again, and he tried to explain himself to the angry mob of corpses. He didn't mean for anyone to die. He was trying to do the right thing, but he was just one man, unable to save everyone.

But the words didn't come. It felt like when he was in a dream where he wanted to throw a punch, but he was wholly impotent to actually urge his hand to move. He wasn't even sure whether his explanation could be considered a legitimate excuse, but it was moot, as he couldn't even vocalize a single word. Zac only helplessly fell backward, the screams growing ever louder in his mind.

Alea crawled closer as he mutely sat on the ground, leaving a trail of blood and intestines behind her. It was with great exertion she managed to drag herself up along his torso, completely drenching Zac in blood while doing so. She whimpered in pain as she enclosed him in a final embrace, her head resting on his shoulder.

"Was this all a game to you?" the sorrowful voice of the poison mistress whispered in his ear. "You played around in the Underworld, looking for opportunities to level up. You left us to fight one of the strongest forces in the Multiverse. You sent us to our deaths. You're the leader; you should join us."

"Join us!" the chorus echoed as a storm of poison seeped out of every pore of Alea's body.

Zac felt muddled from the blazing pain in his head, but his danger sense screamed for him to wake up.

No!

Zac ardently recoiled in his mind, and the world around him cracked like a broken mirror.

Shame and self-blame threatened to drown Zac as he stood in front of Thea's sickbed. Her piercing blue eyes had lost their luster as she hollowly stared at him, and her ragged breaths told him she already hovered at death's door.

"I thought we had formed an understanding during our time in the Hunt. But the moment we left, you forgot about me, discarded me for the next shiny thing. Was that all I was to you? A means to an end during the hunt?" she asked with a voice so weak that it was barely audible.

"Billy was true in his sincerity toward you. But were you sincere toward him? Or were you just patronizing him while abusing his naiveté and strength? You didn't even bother going in person to help with his incursion; you rather sent a subordinate to steal the main achievement from him," Thea continued, despondency creeping into her voice.

"That's not—"

"Yet we came here, leaving our own people to fend for themselves. Just so that you wouldn't have yet another excuse to avoid doing the right thing. We bled for you. Why won't you do the same?" she said just as her eyes grew blank, her final breath leaving her lungs.

Panic made Zac's heart beat like a drum, but he suddenly calmed down as he looked at the unmoving body of Thea Marshall.

"You're alive, and I will save you all," Zac growled as the world crumbled.

He had dreaded this moment, but Zac was finally here. His fingers fidgeted with nervousness as he walked across the field toward the man sitting on a rock. His steps were unsteady from the mounting pain in his head, but this thing couldn't be held off any longer.

The man looked up on hearing Zac's approach, his disfigured face scrunching up in anger upon seeing who it was. David slowly stood up with the assistance of a cane, and he spat at the ground the moment Zac arrived.

"I was captured, tortured, left for dead. All because I used to know you," David said before Zac had a chance to greet him, his face contorting in anger and pain. "I wake up screaming every night, drenched in sweat, because of what that lunatic put me through. But you didn't even come to visit me. You threw me out of your mind as you stowed me away on this desolate island, where I wouldn't be able to remind you of what you've become."

"Hannah," Zac said, but he was interrupted by David, whose fury was quickly mounting.

"Hannah was traumatized, manipulated, and abused. First by the Lord of Eyes, then by the infiltrators, and finally by your little demon lover. You couldn't even wait for a second to cast her away the moment she finally regained a sense of stability. All because she didn't fit with your 'new self,' the great lone-wolf warrior who consorted with demons," David spat.

"But perhaps it's for the best, no?" the mutilated man said as he swung his cane at Zac. "Better to be a castaway than turned into a cursed piece of jewelry."

Zac tried to catch the cane, but another wave of pain made him space out, and he found himself on the ground as David desperately tried to pummel him.

"It's all your fault!" he screamed, but he was forced to stop as he spat out a mouthful of blood from the exertion.

"I'm sorry," Zac said through gritted teeth as he woke up from his stupor, once again realizing he was inside an illusion. "The way I treated you isn't right. I will visit the real you when this is all over."

The world dissipated in a haze, and he was surprised to find himself in a very familiar place, this time completely aware he was still undergoing the Heart Tribulation. It was his childhood room where he had lived until he moved out at twenty-one. However, it looked vastly different from how it did before the integration. It was rather decorated exactly the same as when he was a child.

That wasn't all, as he could actually see himself lying asleep in his bed. Why was the System showing him this? It was no doubt another trick of the Heart Tribulation, but why was it so different compared to the other ones that preyed on his emotions? Why had he come here like some sort of Ghost of Christmas Future?

A wave of agony suddenly burst through the illusion, and Zac found himself soundlessly screaming into the room. The waves of pain were getting worse, and Zac was getting worried that the other tribulation was running amok with him stuck in these visions.

Becoming aware that this was all an illusion obviously wasn't the key to getting out, so he started to look around for any clues on how to break the illusion. But there was no clearly identifiable clue to help him escape, and he could only turn to the sleeping form in the bed.

It was a surreal feeling to see himself as a ten-year-old. Things he had completely forgotten were reproduced with perfect crispness as well. There were his posters and the orange lava lamp that always was turned on when he went to bed but inexplicably turned off when he awoke. Of course, it was his parents who turned it off as they checked on him, but today, it was still turned on in the middle of the night.

However, that small detail wasn't the only thing that was a bit off.

There was a note of discordance in the memory, the sounds of agitated voices seeping through the door. The two voices gradually grew louder, but Zac still couldn't make out any distinct words. The fact that it felt like his head was splitting apart didn't make things easier either. He tried to move closer to the source of the commotion, but he found himself stuck next to the bed, or perhaps rather stuck to his younger self.

However, the argument taking place outside his room was soon enough to wake up the ten-year-old version of himself, and Zac was filled with trepidation as he saw himself getting out of bed. He looked just as confused as Zac felt, but he still silently moved over toward his door. Zac thankfully moved in accord, and they got closer to the source of the sounds.

"… to the doctor," Zac heard as they inched closer, and he could finally confirm that it was his father's voice, though the voice sounded frantic in a way that he had never heard before.

Young Zac seemed to come to the same realization as he slowly turned the doorknob and created a small crack in his door without making a sound. It was just enough for some light from the corridor to bleed inside, along with the voices. The voices of his parents.

"Doctor? What would some mortal doctor be able to help me with?" Leandra snorted, her voice dripping with disdain. "Besides, I am telling you I am not sick."

"Darling, calm down. You just had a baby; don't get agitated." Robert seemed to try to placate her.

"I'm not agitated. I'm just telling you what needs to happen," his mom answered with a cold tone that Zac had never heard before. "I guess I can consider myself lucky that the pain of childbirth startled me awake."

Zac frowned as he listened in on the conversation from his vantage as a silent specter behind his own body. Was this actually a memory of his, or yet another lie shown by the System? Because he couldn't remember this ever happening in his real life, though his childhood had always been a bit hazy.

But judging from the discussion and how old he looked, this might just be the night when his mother disappeared, never to be heard from again.

THE FINAL ERA

"Did you really plan on leaving and just leaving a note? What about Zac? What about our daughter?" Robert wheezed, his franticness turning to anger mid-sentence.

"Don't mention that little monster. And I am doing this for our daughter. She is destined for greatness," Leandra retorted. "Against all odds, she is an actual match. She will finish what her ancestors started hundreds of millions of years ago."

Another wave of pain intruded on his mind, but Zac growled as he forcibly pushed it away with far greater fervor than he had done before. He refused to be disturbed by the other tribulation at this point. He wasn't sure if this was all real or not, but he needed to hear what his parents were saying.

What the hell did she mean by calling him a monster? And what was with the ambiguous wording of his dad? His mind was running a mile a minute, but he had no chance to digest the words of his mother before she spoke up again.

"You know what? Why am I even–" his mother continued before a muffled scream followed by a thud came from the room on the other side of the corridor, his parents' room.

And the room where his sister slept.

"I'm sorry, Robert." Leandra sighed, her voice barely audible through the door. "In another lifetime, perhaps."

Terror was clearly written on the face of his younger self, but Zac still saw himself slowly open the door and sneak outside. There was a shining light coming from the next-door room, and he steeled himself before he glanced inside.

Only to lock eyes with Leandra, who stood next to the crib, an unconscious Robert by her feet.

"You heard us?" she said as she looked at the younger Zac with an unperturbed face.

His younger self didn't say a word, but he only looked down at the unmoving form of his father before his eyes turned back to his newly born sister, who still radiated a red light from her forehead.

"Some things have been set in motion that cannot be stopped. You were the first, and she is the second. Perhaps this is for the best. I was never happy with the original plan in any case," she said with a calm voice as she looked down at him. "And the Heavens proved me right."

Zac observed his mother as a specter behind his younger self, and it felt like a wave of memories were awakened by the familiar face. However, there was a difference between the gentle woman that hazily appeared in the back of his mind and the woman in front of him. The gentleness was utterly gone, replaced by far uglier emotions hiding within her eyes as she looked down at his younger self.

Disgust and rage.

He, or rather, his ten-year-old self, was clearly in shock by the turn of events, but he still spoke up.

"Is Kenzie sick?" he said hesitantly as he fearfully took a step toward the crib.

"You want to protect her?" Leandra laughed. "Well, perhaps you can be good for something. I can't stay here. My awakening has already alerted the Cursed Heavens and some other old bastards. Someone will need to stand guard as we rebuild from the ground up."

It looked like his younger self received a shock the next second, and he fell over right next to Kenzie's cradle. The present Zac was still there, though, and he looked down at himself before his eyes once again turned back to Leandra.

It at least looked like she wasn't aware of his existence, in contrast to Be'Zi and her husband, who could sense his presence in his visions. She gave the two unmoving forms on the floor a long look before she once again focused on Kenzie, but Zac couldn't understand what she was doing.

She stood unmoving with her hand on his sister's infant head for a good ten minutes, but there were no changes and no energy fluctuations as far as Zac could tell.

"It can still be salvaged," she breathed in relief as she took a step back.

The next moment, she bent down and put her index finger against his forehead, and a shudder ran through his ten-year-old body. Finally, she walked over to a cabinet in the room, and a familiar item appeared in her hand: the pendant. She placed it next to a paper before she took one last look at the room where she had lived the past ten years.

"Keep her safe. I'll be back to claim her after I've dealt with this mess," she mumbled down at Robert, or perhaps himself. "She is carrying the fate of the Final Era."

A rift opened up in space the next moment, and she walked right through it without a second glance.

Confusion muddled his thoughts as he tried to make sense of the vision. Was this really what had happened twenty years ago when his mother disappeared? Had she wiped his memory of the actual events, planting the story of her mysterious disappearance?

And what was with her reaction to him? Zac didn't remember her fondly due to her abandonment as a child, but he had to admit that she had been nothing but a good mother before she disappeared. But the eyes of Leandra had been those of a fanatic on a mission, almost reminding Zac of Salvation.

There was one possibility that came to mind and refused to leave: Robert wasn't his biological father.

It might even be possible that Leandra wasn't his mother, but his instincts told him they were mother and son. They had a lot of similar features, especially their eyes, which looked identical. But perhaps her hatred was a projection of any animosity she carried for his biological father?

That was the only reason he could think of that would explain the hatred from his own flesh and blood.

Leandra's grand proclamations of carrying out the will of the ancestors and the "Fate of the Final Era" also felt extremely ominous, and not something he wanted Kenzie to get embroiled in. But was it really up to him, or was their mother really coming back to take Kenzie away?

A mother reuniting with her children might seem like something good, but there was something deeply wrong with the way Leandra had looked at Kenzie as well, though there wasn't the unmasked hatred she held for Zac. Was Leandra just using her as nourishment for Jeeves, where the mysterious AI was using Kenzie and her soul as an incubation chamber until the point that Leandra came to steal it?

That would explain why the AI had taken so long to awaken. It only happened months after the integration was over, according to his sister. Had it fed on her soul until that point, slowing her progression and weakening her potential?

Then again, all this was just conjecture, his frayed mind running amok from not knowing whether this was real or fake. Was this just the System messing with his head, preying on his fears, causing a bout of paranoia that would trap him in this illusion forever? Or was it trying to create a rift between himself and his mother, making sure that he never joined Leandra's camp?

Did the System have other plans for him?

Zac's mind was a mess, and he felt a weird sense of disconnect with reality like he had been living a lie his whole life. The whole room around him started to twist and contort like it tried to superimpose on his own sense of reality.

His emotions started to spiral out of control, but Zac quickly stabilized his thoughts. He knew that these feelings were mostly fake. This was the Heart Tribulation. The System had shown him an illusion that had caused a crack in his mental fortitude, and it had tried to push him toward insanity from there.

But his mind wasn't so easily shaken, not after all the things he had gone through in the past year. He had looked at the Terminus and survived; how could this compare? Perhaps the things he had seen were real; perhaps they weren't. There wasn't much that he could do about it in either case if he didn't get stronger.

The fact that their mother might have ulterior motives about Kenzie had been something that Zac had considered a real possibility since the moment he'd figured out their origin. Witnessing this scene did nothing to change that. He would still keep his guard up for anything that might come his way.

It was the same with his own Heritage. Perhaps Robert wasn't his biological father, but so what? He had been as real a father as any could have been. The fact that there might be some other guy out there didn't matter in the slightest to Zac; he could just be considered a sperm donor at best if it even were true. There was no point in looking into the matter any further.

It was far more important to keep improving and getting stronger.

Only then would he be able to achieve his goals; only then would he be able to feel a sense of safety and freedom. He needed to become stronger to protect his sister and everyone else who had come to mean something to him over the past year. To protect Earth itself against those who wished it harm.

The room drenched in the red glow cracked, and he found himself back in his body, the real one. He didn't know exactly what had changed, but he somehow felt stable, like he could face anything with a calm heart. Was this a hidden benefit of succeeding against the Heart Tribulation?

He breathed out in relief, but he quickly remembered that he wasn't out of the woods just yet. He'd just overcome the Heart Tribulation, but there was still the Soul Tribulation to deal with. Just before he was dragged into the illusion, he had felt like his soul was lit on fire, and it had made itself remembered multiple times during the hallucinations as well.

Another wave of terrifying agony assaulted him the moment he remembered his predicament, setting his whole world on fire. He screamed in pain, but he quickly activated the Fragment of the Axe and spread it across his whole soul. The soul was the connection to the Dao, and his fragments would be able to dampen the effect of the tribulation, from what he knew.

And thankfully, the searing pain quieted down by a noticeable degree the moment his soul was covered in a dense layer of his Dao. It was just like when he'd used the Seed of Trees to ward off the corruption in the wound that Mhal left in his side. However, the mysterious energy that had descended upon him was still there in full force, meaning he wasn't safe just because his tactic had worked out.

Zac quickly looked inwards and breathed out in relief when he saw that his soul was fine apart from some small wounds that could be fixed with a normal Soul-Healing Pill. It was a lot better than he had feared after having felt those bouts of agony during the Heart Tribulation, and nothing compared to the time after the Shard had ripped it apart and ensconced itself in the tears.

But one part was a bit worrying. The scars were still there, and not only did they seem more integrated with his soul, but they had now regained some of their luster. Had they somehow managed to feed on whatever energy the System used to put his soul under pressure?

The pain quickly got worse, though, making Zac unable to gather any further clues from the scars. The Dao energy of the Axe was somehow losing its efficacy, but Zac had an idea and swapped to the Fragment of the Coffin. The pain became manageable once more, and Zac soon set into a cyclic pattern where he moved from one Dao Fragment to another to handle the Soul Tribulation.

Zac lost track of time as he just focused on enduring, but it gradually grew harder as the effect grew steadily worse, even if he kept swapping between Daos. However, a sudden shudder from within his soul suddenly blasted his defenses straight open, giving the tribulation energy free access to his soul.

However, Zac felt no pain at all as two whirlpools appeared, one black and one white, and they dragged the Tribulation Energy into the abyss with extreme fervor. Zac was shocked to see that the energy didn't go into the scars though, but the other side of the whirlpools were clearly inside the cage that housed the two Remnants.

Both of them seemed enlivened, and they started fighting with each other once more. However, they quickly calmed down and focused on absorbing the unwilling Tribulation Energies. Zac tried to figure out a way to break the connection, but he couldn't destroy the two whirlpools no matter what he did.

However, it thankfully looked like he had the System on his side this time. It seemed that it considered him having passed the second tribulation as well, as the Soul Tribulation was actually becoming food, and the energies around Zac dissipated the next second. Better yet, the fractals of the cage woke up once more and stole most of the energy from the Remnants.

They looked clearly upset about the situation as they slammed their tendrils against the walls, but the cage didn't even shudder as it continued its siphoning. A few minutes later, a surge of extremely pure energies seeped into his soul and body, and he felt extremely invigorated. The wounds on his soul closed by themselves, and he felt a huge surge of power coursing through his body.

He had made it; he was finally an E-grade mortal.

A FRAYED WEB OF UNCERTAINTY

What had changed?

Who had made such a mess of his Karma, turning it into a frayed web of uncertainty? Finding the source of the Karmic turbulence had proven futile, though, with connections having formed from every single direction. There was a larger overlying cause, but any attempt of his to scry the source was met with failure.

Voridis hesitated for a while longer until he finally made a decision. There was a populated world just one jump away, and Voridis realigned his vessel after casting an obscuring haze to confuse any potential pursuers. He needed to know what was going on. Had the orthodox faction among the elders finally made their move?

That was the only explanation Voridis could think of as he descended upon the planet. The humanoids of the town he chose fell to the ground as their futures were drained clean, but these morsels wouldn't even pay for the delay to his plan. Only the mayor was left alive, turned into a marker to enable his return.

Anger bubbled in Voridis' chest as he located the Nexus Hub and teleported away after donning his disguise. He was finally reaching fruition of his goal, thousands of years of planning on the cusp of producing results. His wretched circumstances over the past eons would all change as long as he succeeded, but something was threatening to ruin it all.

A brief bout of darkness swallowed him before he appeared in a simple tower.

"Identification," the golem rumbled with a threatening tone, but it backed away when Voridis flashed his token as a member of the Hephasar.

Voridis' identity was stolen, of course; the token was taken from the body of one of their chieftains. But they wouldn't know for a few centuries, as the corpse of the man was currently soaring through the outskirts of the sector, attached to a meteor.

The chieftain's family still believed him to be traveling the Zecia Sector in search of opportunities to form his inner sanctum, when it was just his body kept "alive" by special means. Voridis snickered at the thought as he flew straight toward the floating palace in the distance, the local chapter of the Hidden Whispers.

Just emitting a hint of his aura, modified to be unrecognizable of course, was enough for him to immediately receive VIP treatment. He was led into an opulent room where an elderly man waited. Voridis inwardly snorted in annoyance when he realized the old man was not only Peak D-grade as well, but also wearing multiple layers of protection.

So much for free information.

"What do you wish to know?" the man said with a smile as they sat down.

"Voridis A'Heliophos," Voridis said with a growl.

"Oh, you too? Well, it is no wonder." The old man smiled, his eyes never leaving Voridis in search of any clues.

"Hmph," Voridis grunted noncommittally, though he was extremely anxious to know what the man meant.

It really looked like there was something wrong, to the point that it was already spread to the better information houses within a day.

He wanted to trap the old bastard's soul and drain it of its secrets, but he knew he couldn't cause any waves in this place. There was a C-grade Monarch presiding over this town, after all. Voridis normally wouldn't have come to a place like this at all, but he was afraid some backwater information house wouldn't have the information he needed.

"What does sir need to know? I am afraid we have no clues about his current whereabouts. But we have gathered his known movements over the past few millennia," the old man said. "We are also buying any pertinent information."

"I heard there are opportunities related to his capture from certain channels, but I just emerged from cultivation," Voridis said. "I need to know what rewards there are."

"I understand. Sir can buy the relevant information for 10 D-grade Nexus Coins. The price is steep due to how fresh it is; these things will not become public knowledge for some time." The old man smiled.

"Hmph, old thief," Voridis snorted, but he still transferred the money without hesitation.

A few minutes later, he was returning toward the Nexus Hub with haste, not wanting to spend one second longer in this place than necessary. He paid the exorbitant fee and teleported away, once again returning to the remote town at the edge of the Zecia Sector.

Voridis culled the mayor as well before he flew off in his vessel, not leaving a soul behind who could bear witness to his appearance. He quickly performed his obscuration rite before he jumped back to the original plane, only then feeling safe from pursuit once more. He didn't immediately set the course toward the closest beacon, though, but he started reading the contents of the missive he'd just bought.

He needed to know who would have to pay the ultimate price for messing with his plans.

However, Voridis' anger was exchanged for exhilaration the more he read, even if he paid more than 10,000 times what a report on some F-grade brat was worth, no matter how impressive. Ninth floor? Known across the sector? Exalted masters of the upper realms asking about him? How was it possible that he had lucked into such a huge windfall?!

A soul embraced by the fate of a world, a world steeped in the Energy of Inception. Two Fulcrums, and one world would be born from the death of another. But what if the Fulcrum of Fate was powerful enough that it could impact the whole sector? His plan no longer seemed like a long shot, but almost a foregone conclusion.

It felt like his worn body was injected with stimulants as his mind ran thousands of simulations to make sure that his original design for his Fulcrum Array would still work. He might need to make some alterations to capitalize on the external Karmic Links, but it was definitely possible.

As for any repercussions, he didn't care. That brat would disappear long before the Shroud of the Ruthless Heavens dissipated, turning him into an interesting but forgettable side note of the Zecia Sector's history. No one would mourn or avenge the death of an unattached F-grade brat.

The question now was how to locate which of the seed worlds held the key to his ascension.

"What is your impression of the situation?" Theos asked.

"It's tricky. Voridis is extremely crafty, but Zac Piker is no doubt in possession of multiple Teleportation Tokens. If Voridis makes a mistake, a lingering threat might be created, one that would lead to the demise of our clan." Reolus sighed as his milky-white eyes gazed toward the stars. "I can't see it..."

"I know." Theos Heliophos sighed. "Voridis will never back away from such a convergence of Karma, even if I send out Geros in person. I should have followed the whispers of fate and killed that boy. I became too greedy."

"We all did," Reolus muttered from the side. "So what do you want to do?"

"Spread the news. I will perform a Fate Augmentation to the person who brings Voridis to us, dead or alive," Theos said after a while. "Make a show of looking for him as well, but no need to draw upon the Eyes of Heaven. We'll show our stance, and let the chips fall where they may. We are not yet facing a choice between calamity and fortune."

"Voridis will either find him or he won't." Reolus nodded. "It has nothing to do with us. But what about those people from the higher planes?"

"They won't cause any storms in this remote place over a single child, at least not until someone claims him. There's no lack of talents in the higher planes, and even if they miss out on this seedling, another one will come along in a millennium or two from another sector," Theos said.

"They failed," the sturdy man growled as the golden flames in the brazier died out, ending the telepathic communication.

"Perhaps this was the Boundless Heavens punishing us for consorting with the cursed Races." Vicar Uld sighed as his hand created the sigil for a blessing. "Bishop Kyhv-Elerad and our brothers have joined the embrace of the Heavens; it is a small consolation at least."

Uld had honestly been skeptical about the excursion from the beginning, which was why he'd sent Kyhv-Elerad and kept his trusted subordinate Trovad next to him. Both of them were zealots and fools, but Kyhv-Elerad had already cozied up to Arkensau. And he couldn't have that.

He really missed Bishop Orsiccas, the only other leader of the mission team who knew the true purpose of these invasions. Sending his confidant over to secure the body of the Monarch-Select had been a massive miscalculation, one that had left him alone dealing with these maniacs for months.

"Did we manage to retrieve any of the bodies?" Uld still had to ask. "I would like to send them back to be interred among the other martyrs."

"None made it back after stepping foot on the island." Trovad sighed. "Only the vessel aiming for the spatial tunnel survived."

"Shame," Uld muttered, feeling the pinch of missing an opportunity to make some money.

"Some good news has emerged from the Incubator Realm, though," Trovad added. "We have managed to seize and purify one of the towns on the second layer. Our scribes are already working at gaining control of the systems. Inquisitor Arkensau has entered the depths."

Uld nodded with equanimity, but a pang of annoyance flared up in his chest upon hearing that name. This was supposed to be his opportunity, his chance to garner massive amounts of credit with the Zecia

Chapter. But who would have expected the Grand Cardinal to send his own disciple to this remote planet to take charge of the invasion?

He had thought that this would be his chance to get transferred out of the Zecia Sector to one of the real Cathedrals of the Everlasting Dao. To be anointed in the holy flames and born anew as a true elite of unlimited potential. But that bastard was stealing it under his nose, and he was unable to do anything about it.

"Have we located the inception point of the Dimensional Seed yet?" Uld asked. "We're only a few months away from its completion."

He still couldn't believe that a treasure like a Dimensional Seed could be found in a remote sector like the Zecia. He had never even heard of such a thing before the Grand Cardinal himself explained what it was and the importance of acquiring it. There shouldn't be enough energy in this area of space. Just which of the heretic factions was it that had created this Mystic Realm?

That seed held the promise of endless possibilities. It could be the core to create a Hidden Realm of almost unimaginable size. Imagine, controlling a Hidden Realm that would slowly grow to the size of an empire. But in contrast to a normal empire that was beset by threats in all directions, you would be a true hegemon as long as you controlled who could enter through the spatial tunnel.

A Hidden Realm of that quality was unheard of in a small place like Zecia.

But that wasn't the reason the Grand Cardinal wanted it. There was one more usage for the seed, from what Urd understood. It could be used as a foundation upon creating the Inner Sanctum of a C-grade Monarch. It would help create a world so powerful that it might even have enough potential to take that mythical next step.

The vaunted B-grade.

The Grand Cardinal couldn't use it for himself since he had already formed his inner world, but Uld was willing to bet that he planned on trading it for some opportunity to break through his current bottleneck, or to be transferred to the Embrace of the Boundless Heavens. Even Uld himself was tempted to take the treasure and run, but he knew that was impossible with the Martyr Array engraved into his soul.

There was no escape, only obedience.

"We haven't found it yet; the spatial anomalies are too numerous, rendering our arrays useless. We have been forced to search manually, but those natives know the depths far better than us, leading to setbacks," Trovad said.

"Well, Inquisitor Arkensau is the best suited for handling the natives," Uld said.

"What about the last vessel and the Monarch-Select?"

"Have them investigate whether they can destroy the entrance," Uld said. "We will not be able to hold that place, it seems, but we might at least be able to stop the Monarch-Select from entering."

"What about Super Brother-Man?" Trovad asked with a smoldering anger. "With all due respect, are we leaving him after what he's done?"

"The Monarch-Select has no choice but to assault the cursed Races if he wants to protect this planet," Uld said with a small smile. "We will find our opportunity there; we will be able to end both the natives and the unliving in one fell swoop if the Heavens provide. Inform Inquisitor Arkensau about the return of the Monarch-Select. He will no doubt be interested in joining the Holy War."

Trovad's eyes lit up with fervor upon hearing the term Holy War, and he quickly left the chapel after saluting. Uld looked at the receding back of the Bishop with some disdain before he started to plan his next move.

If he played his cards right, he might be able to realize all his goals. If all three of those powerful bastards died, he would be half done. Only those monstrous insectoids and the slippery bastards inside the Mystic Realm would stand between him and the Dimensional Seed.

Those were odds he was willing to take.

THE SECOND STEP

Zac took a deep breath as he looked around, a sense of calmness filling him.

He had done it, he'd passed the first true bottleneck of cultivation, the watershed that separated those who had a shot at immortality and those who were destined to stay at the bottom of the pyramid. He had been a bit worried about complications arising due to his weird body without any affinities, but it looked like he had been worrying about nothing.

Then again, he certainly understood why most warriors waited to consolidate their gains before evolving, some taking years to ready themselves for the tribulation. He hadn't been prepared for just how perilous it would be. However, things had gone above expectations, all things considered. Getting dual tribulations was pretty rough, but he almost felt he was lucky it had happened.

The Heart Tribulation was much harder than the Spirit Tribulation in his case. Enduring pain was his forte by now, but he had been drawn into those visions that preyed on his insecurities way too easily. If it weren't for the constant waves of pain, he might have forgotten himself for real, which would have made it so much harder to extricate himself.

He might even have failed that tribulation altogether.

It was dealt with now though, and he wouldn't have to worry about the next tribulation for quite some time. The Remnants had fallen asleep again, it seemed, but they didn't look quite as wretched as before. However, it was a good sign that they'd immediately started fighting each other rather than the cage the moment they got energized, and perhaps he wouldn't have to keep living in dread of their awakening.

But he made a mental note to mention the arrays for the Soul-Strengthening Manual to his sister. Perhaps she could work on it while he dealt with the undead threat.

He cracked his neck and looked down at his watch, extremely surprised to see that almost fourteen hours had passed since he sat down. It felt like the tribulations hadn't taken more than half an hour. Something had messed with his sense of time, it seemed, most likely the five visions.

But it still was better than his allotment of one day, and it gave him some room to figure out his situation. He opened his Status screen to see what was going on.

Name: Zachary Atwood
Level: 75
Class: [E-Epic] Edge of Arcadia
Race: [E] Human
Alignment: [Earth] Port Atwood – Lord

Titles: […] Tower of Eternity – 8th Floor, Heaven's Triumvirate, Fated, Peak Power, Monarch-Select
Limited Titles: Frontrunner, Tower of Eternity Sector All-Star – 14th
Dao: Fragment of the Axe – Middle, Fragment of the Coffin – Middle, Fragment of the Bodhi – Early
Core: [E] Duplicity

Strength: 1704 [Increase: 91%. Efficiency: 199%]
Dexterity: 708 [Increase: 65%. Efficiency: 170%]
Endurance: 1871 [Increase: 99%. Efficiency: 199%]
Vitality: 1136 [Increase: 89%. Efficiency: 189%]
Intelligence: 434 [Increase: 65%. Efficiency: 170%]
Wisdom: 721 [Increase: 70%. Efficiency: 170%]

Luck: 321 [Increase: 91%. Efficiency: 179%]

Free Points: 0
Nexus Coins: [F] 6,862,691,291

There weren't a lot of things that had changed to the Status screen from his evolution, apart from his attributes having increased by quite a bit. However, Zac was a bit surprised he was still level 75. He had assumed that he would move to level 76 upon evolving, but it looked like he was wrong in that regard. It seemed that evolving was just shedding the limiters on your body, but you would still have to do the work yourself.

He opened his Class screen next, and he saw one of the major sources for his massive boost in Strength.

Class: [E-Epic] Edge of Arcadia.
Strength +100, +10%. Vitality +50, +5%.
Level: Strength +14/28/42, Vitality +8/16/24, +10 Free.
Skills: Rapturous Divide (LOCKED)

The class itself gave him an impressive 100 flat Strength, which turned into almost 200 thanks to his titles. He guessed that his Draugr form provided a similar boost, but he held off on swapping over for the moment, as there were more things he wanted to check out first. Another reason for his increased attributes rather was his new title.

He was also a bit curious about his first E-grade title, and he focused on the line that said "Monarch-Select." Titles would get harder and harder to get now that he had evolved, so anything he got was likely based on a real tough accomplishment.

[Monarch Select: First to Reach E-grade in World Reward: Base attributes +50, Luck +5, All Stats +5%]

The term "base attributes" was the same as the one he had seen on the prompt where he'd chose which class to upgrade. It looked like any Low-tiered title he got now wouldn't give +All Stats any longer, as the boost to Luck would be too overpowered. That was a relief for

Zac, though, as it meant it would be easier for him to maintain his advantage.

The flat attribute bonus was enormous, though; 50 points in each attribute was a noticeable boost even for him, especially with his extreme multipliers. A single title gave him 305 raw attribute points, which was almost as much as he got from gaining 50 levels while in F-grade. Add to that yet another multiplier, and he had gained big from not letting anyone else snag this unique title.

He had thought that the attributes gained from his Dao Fragments would be the only thing that mattered for a while, but he now knew that wasn't the case. Both his levels and Limited Titles would provide massive boosts that would be equally impressive.

It really made sense now that he could take care of dozens of Early E-grade warriors without breaking a sweat, but started struggling against Middle E-grade warriors. Peak E-grade was still impossible for him to deal with, even the weakest ones.

Just breaking open all nodes alone would rack up to something like 1,300 points in each attribute by the time one would have reached level 150. Furthermore, someone who had reached Peak E-grade couldn't be complete trash, as such people would have been weeded out long before then. They would have a bunch of titles and Daos to supplement those attributes even further.

There was still a long way for him to go.

The name of the title made him think of something else as well, and he opened the Quest screen next. As expected, there were new quests that had appeared in the previously empty menu.

Second Step of Sovereignty (Unique, Limited): Enter the Trial within one Year.
Reward: Unique E-grade Structure (Quality based on performance), Qualification to stake claim on World. (0/1)

Zac's eyes lit up with glee as he saw the new quest. He had been pretty sure that he would get something like this upon evolving, and he had been proven right. The quest where he had killed the Star Ox had only been called the first step, which heavily indicated it to be a chain quest.

That quest had given him the ticket to the Tower of Eternity, which had turned out hugely beneficial to him, so he had high hopes for the follow-up quest as well.

And the rewards really didn't disappoint.

Every unique structure that Zac had seen had come with enormous benefits to a nascent force. Brazla was pretty annoying, but the value of the inheritances and the Skill Repositories was enormous. The Creator Shipyard was perhaps even greater, with the ability to upgrade its grade perhaps even all the way to B-grade. Even Thea's Library was a valuable asset.

Qualification to stake claim was likely related to upgrading one's town to a World Capital, and himself from a Lord to whatever the equivalent was of someone ruling over a whole planet. However, the upgraded title wasn't directly given as a reward, making Zac believe there was some hidden catch to the qualification.

Perhaps it would activate some sort of quest that pitted him against the world, and he wasn't sure if he was ready to do that while the Dominators were still around. But as long as he dealt with them one way or another, he felt confident that no one on Earth would have anything to say about him becoming the de facto leader of the planet.

The contents of the quest itself were equally as vague as the last one, though. It looked like he would be teleported to another world once more. However, after having completed over 70 levels in the Tower of Eternity, it didn't feel like a challenge to do one more.

The only issue was that of what level the System expected him to be before undertaking the trial. For the last quest, he had been given a month before he needed to activate the quest, but this time, there was a full year. It was great for Zac, who had his hands full at the moment, but it also made him wonder what level of strength was expected to complete the quest.

However, the Sovereignty quest would have to wait until he'd dealt with the more pressing issues, and he rather turned his attention to another quest that had appeared.

**Rapturous Divide (Class): Split Life and Death. Reward:
Rapturous Divide Skill (0/1).**

The second quest was far more inscrutable than any other skill quest he had gotten before now. Split Life and Death? What did that even mean? It made him long for the easier tasks back in F-grade, which essentially told him to go chop a tree or kill some monsters. It really felt like he had finally left the beginner village of a game, and the difficulty suddenly spiked.

Life and death were related to his path, though. Was the System testing him? Or perhaps even pushing him to experiment until he managed to push his creation to the next level. He already knew that there would be less hand-holding in the E-grade, and that was probably even more so for Epic-ranked classes.

They were on the precipice of forming their own cultivation paths, and it made sense that the System tried to encourage you in that regard.

It also probably meant that his other class, Fetters of Desolation, had a similarly inscrutable quest to gain the [Blighted Cut] skill. The name might sound simpler compared to [Rapturous Divide], but he doubted that meant it was a weaker skill or an easier quest. [Chop] was a pretty simple skill, but it had become a staple of his fighting style, something that could be used in almost any situation.

Apart from the quests and the updated class, there was not much new in the Status screen. However, there were still differences to explore, and Zac turned his vision inwards. His outward appearance was the same, but that couldn't be said for his interior. Almost completely new pathways had been branded onto his body after he passed the tribulations.

The pathways were far more intricate compared to before, and there was a sense of spirituality radiating from them that had been completely missing before. His skills were thankfully all still there, and from the looks of it, the fit of his skills was at least as good as before. However, that might not be the case on his undead side, as he had chosen a divergent class.

Zac eagerly started to experiment with his new pathways; it felt as though he could cram massive amounts of Cosmic Energy into the pathways without damaging them. That would no doubt allow him to generate far more power in his attacks, provided that the skill fractals could accommodate all that extra energy.

However, even though the flow of Cosmic Energy far eclipsed anything he'd felt before, he still noticed dozens of spots in his pathways that worsened the circulation. They reminded Zac of stagnant ponds in the middle of a river of Cosmic Energy, disrupting the flow and tainting the outlet.

They could be found all over his body, but they seemed to mainly be in "critical" spots, with almost two-thirds being found in his head and torso. But there were also places like this in every major joint and next to the locations that housed or could house skill fractals. Were these hazy ponds the nodes he needed to break?

It was as though these stagnant pools in his pathways both contained some sort of leaks while simultaneously blocking the flow. With this happening all over his body, he felt he could only use his body to a fraction of its real potential, and it was no wonder that fixing these trouble spots by breaking open nodes would boost one's attributes.

His mental image of nodes had been completely different compared to how these things looked. He had pictured something like a pressurized tank he needed to push more and more energy into until it finally popped. But it seemed like it was more like a clog in a pipe that needed to get flushed.

But even with all these obstructions in his upgraded pathways, there was no denying that the speed with which he could circulate Cosmic Energy had increased by at least five times. That was pretty huge as well, as it would drastically cut down on recuperation time since it meant he would be able to absorb Nexus Crystals a lot faster.

He still was barely better than Thea, who was still in F-grade, but he was doomed to fall short in this regard when compared to elite cultivators. But with his Vitality and Endurance, he would be able to keep fighting almost continuously, which would be needed if he wanted to move through the levels quickly.

CLASHING VERSIONS

Since he was done with checking what he needed to in his human form, he finally swapped over to his Draugr side. The process activated as usual, but Zac frowned when he felt that it took almost three seconds to transform, which was a lot worse compared to before he evolved. Was it because the pathways had become more complicated, and swapping them out took more time and energy?

However, there was still a solution. The transformation skill Yrial provided was geared toward the F-grade, and it could hopefully be upgraded to once again shrink the time it took to change forms. The skill was unfortunately something that the C-grade ghost had put together without much thought, and it had neither proficiencies nor an upgrade path.

Zac would either have to figure out a way to recreate the skill or wait until he could enter the Inheritance Trial again. He could only put the issue aside before opening his Class menu once again, as there were some things he wanted to confirm there as well.

Class: [E-Epic] Fetters of Desolation.
Strength +50, +5%. Endurance +50, +5%. Wisdom +50, +5%
Level: Strength +11/22/33, Endurance +8/16/24, Wisdom +5/10/15, +10 Free.
Skills: Blighted Cut (LOCKED)

Zac was a bit surprised that he had gained equal parts in the three attributes from the class, even though he would gain more than twice the amount of Strength compared to Wisdom at each level. But that was great news for Zac, as he was already pretty lopsided toward Strength with his class choices, while his low Mental Defense was his biggest weakness.

A quick mental calculation confirmed what Zac had expected. The per-level gains from his old classes remained, but the flat class bonuses had been swapped out. For example, Undying Bulwark had provided 10% Endurance and 5% Vitality before, but 5% of the Endurance and all of the Vitality was swapped out for Strength and Wisdom.

There was still a net gain, as the flat attributes increased drastically, but it was still a bit of a shame. One of his strong suits was his almost inhuman Endurance, but that advantage would slightly weaken in favor of the massive amounts of Strength he would rack up during the E-grade. Perhaps it might even be worth putting some of his free points into Endurance to maintain the lead over normal cultivators.

He opened his Quest menu next, and interestingly enough, the Sovereignty quest wasn't there in his Draugr form. Was the quest chain perhaps connected to the Race he was when the integration started? He still hadn't gained his Draugr form when completing the first quest, after all.

There was a skill quest, though, and Zac breathed out in relief when he read the task.

Blighted Cut (Class): Kill an evolved being of equal or higher level with a single nonlethal cut. Reward: Blighted Cut Skill (0/1).

The quest for Blighted Cut was thankfully a lot more straightforward compared to the one for **[Rapturous Divide]**. However, it was still not a free win by any means, as it seemed to put very high demands on the corrosive effects of his Dao. That was at least Zac's takeaway, going by the name of the skill. He needed to make a nonlethal attack lethal with the help of his caustic power.

The Fragment of the Coffin contained a decent corrosive effect, but it always required him to stack up numerous wounds to create an effect strong enough to cause real harm. For example, Faceless #9 had been completely covered in rotting wounds by the time he finally gave up, but it wasn't enough to actually take him out.

It meant that he would have to make some inroads into the death aspect of his cultivation path as well to complete this quest. Perhaps the System felt that he had utilized too many Dao Treasures to prop up the Seed of Rot, leaving the foundation lacking.

Zac shook his head as he turned his sight inward, and unfortunately, it looked like the bad news would just keep coming. His pathways had been re-formed just like in his human form, but there were some other changes. The once-perfect fit of the class skills was ruined for multiple skills, mainly those that dealt with pure defense.

However, he noted that the fit for [Profane Seal], [Deathwish], and [Immutable] was just fine while the fit of [Winds of Decay] had actually improved. This was just what Zac had expected though, where he moved away from a defensive class toward a more offensively geared one.

But more importantly, the nodes looked completely identical in his Draugr form as in his human side. The effect the nodes had on the flow of energy through the pathways wasn't exactly the same, as the two sets of pathways differed from each other. But the nodes themselves were in the exact same position.

It was clear to him that the nodes weren't actually a part of the pathways themselves, but rather something tied to his body. However, they didn't feel corporeal at the same time, but rather, intangible. Zac suddenly had an idea as a knife appeared in his hand, and he stabbed his leg, aiming right for a node.

Black ichor started dripping down his leg, but the bleeding quickly stopped thanks to Zac's massive pool of Vitality. However, Zac was more interested in the fact that the node he'd just struck showed no reaction at all from being stabbed. It ruined one idea he had where he would forcibly rip the nodes open and rely on his inhuman durability to recuperate. It simply didn't work.

The situation clearly hinted at a situation where he would only need to break open each node once. This was great news for his leveling speed, but it was horrible news for his attribute gain. Of course, he would have to confirm his hypothesis by actually cracking open a node and gaining a level, but it looked pretty clear-cut from where he sat.

There was one more thing he wanted to consume before he ended his seclusion, but he first wanted to tell his sister he was fine.

However, the scenes from the tribulation repeated in his mind upon thinking of Kenzie, and he was unsure what to think. Was their mother really on the way back to take his sister somewhere? And judging by the malice and madness in her eyes, she might just kill Zac along with the whole planet if she was in a bad mood.

Her ability to simply conjure a spatial portal out of nothing proved she was a big shot, though he had already suspected as much. Not only was she involved with a peak force like Firmament's Edge, but her necklace seemed to be some sort of ghost key that gave blanket access to Technocrat facilities.

The necklace by itself was a cause for concern, and he took it out of his Spatial Ring and looked it over. Reaching the E-grade, unfortunately, hadn't increased his skills of discernment, and he still couldn't find any clues of how it worked. However, the moment he touched the token with his mind in an attempt to look inside, a drastic change occurred.

The token hummed to life and floated up into the air by itself. [Verun's Bite] was already in Zac's hand as he jumped up in alarm, though confusion plagued his mind. He had tried scanning the medallion the same way dozens of times, but there hadn't been any response until now. What had changed? Was there something different about his mental energy after evolving? Or was it the Remnants?

However, Zac had no time to get to the bottom of things as a familiar figure appeared in front of him. His mother.

"Zac, my son," Leandra said with a smile marred with longing.

"Mom?" Zac said, his mind thrown into chaos once more. "Is that you?"

He had just seen a crazed incarnation of his mother during the Heart Tribulation, but now a completely different Leandra stood in front of him. Her demeanor was in stark contrast to the one the System depicted. There was happiness, but also sadness as she looked upon Zac.

"It looks like the integration took place after all." Leandra sighed, not answering his question. "I am glad you are fine, and evolved at that. Where is your sister? Is she okay?"

"Kenzie's fine. Is this really you or an AI?" Zac asked, some doubts worming into his heart when he heard his mother immediately asking about Kenzie.

"It seems you have learned a few truths." Leandra nodded. "You are not speaking with the real me, but a synthetic AI based on me. I left it in the necklace, and it activated now that someone of my blood has reached the E-grade."

"Why wait until now?" Zac asked with a frown.

"My identity is a bit complicated. I am an enemy of the System," Leandra freely admitted. "I couldn't allow any clues of my existence to appear on the planet right after it got integrated. The Cursed Heavens would have spotted me, which would have put your lives in danger. It should have taken you a while to reach E-grade, and the System has long turned its gaze elsewhere."

"What's going on?" Zac asked, trying to calm his chaotic mind to not miss any details. "Why did you leave back then? Kenzie was just a newborn."

"My family, your family, has been working on a miraculous device with the help of some of the greatest minds of the Multiverse for longer than you can imagine. But things turned awry, and most of our clan died. Some people we thought were friends betrayed us in our moment of weakness out of greed, causing even greater losses," Leandra said, pain and anger flashing in her eyes.

"I was badly hurt, but I managed to barely escape. I set course for your homeworld, as it was a desolate rock far from either integrated or controlled space, where our family once hid a small laboratory. The base was abandoned after the experiments were concluded, to not draw the attention of the System, but I discovered it in our family's archives. I scrubbed any knowledge of it to make it a safe harbor in case I needed it," Leandra said with a wry smile. "Who knew that the desolate world would have turned populated in just a few dozen millennia?

"My wounds were too harsh, and a safety protocol kicked in where I lost my memories and any aura that could lead my captors to me. Robert found me as I wandered around in your world in a daze, and we had you two years later." Leandra smiled. "But when I had Kenzie ten years later, there were complications, and the pain woke up the real me from its recuperative slumber.

"My aura was noticed by both the Heavens and my enemies, and I was forced to flee Earth shortly after Kenzie was born. I couldn't risk leading my enemies to you, especially not while I wasn't strong enough to protect you. I don't know where the real me is, but I am sure I am still working hard on finding a solution so that I can return to your side," Leandra said.

"Is Kenzie here as well? The time I can stay here is limited. I want to see her before I go," Leandra said.

"She is out in the wilderness, training," Zac lied. "She will be back in a week or so. Can you wait until then?"

Zac felt he could see a spark of turbulent emotions flash in her eyes, though it was quickly masked with a forlorn disappointment.

"Well, there will be time for us to meet in the future." Leandra sighed. "Be careful, you two. Don't mention your connection to me; it will cause you trouble. And stay away from the Mystic Realm that seems like a science fiction movie. Some unknown force found it and set up their own experiments after we abandoned the place. It may be extremely dangerous, depending on what they did there. I didn't have a chance to scout it out myself."

"Are you really coming to get us?" Zac asked, his heart beating in fear-mixed anticipation.

"Earth is a low-tiered world with no strong points. The Multiverse is a magical place that you cannot even imagine. Staying there will only harm your future," Leandra said with a shake of her head. "You need land, resources, and opportunities to reach your full potential. Earth is lacking on all three fronts. Staying there is a waste of your future.

"Remember to protect your sister. I left a protective AI with her that will be able to help her out, but it is just an assistant in the end. It's not infallible," his mother added. "I must go now, or your location will be discovered. Stay safe, Zac."

With that, she was gone, and the medallion once again turned into an inert ornament as far as Zac could tell. He stood frozen for a few seconds, unsure of what to believe. Seeing another version of Leandra just after seeing the vision hadn't really made him clearer on whether his mother was a friend or a foe, or which version was the real one.

But there were a few snippets of information that probably were true, as they were mentioned in both encounters. First of all, it really didn't look like she had left willingly. In both versions, she seemed forced to leave Earth because her presence was made known.

Secondly, she was coming back. One version felt like a farmer who wanted to harvest her crops, and the other was a loving mother who wanted to provide a better future for her children. His heart wanted to believe that the second version was the true one, but something held him back. There was a voice whispering in his mind that all the projection said was just a cover story to make sure he didn't mess up her plans.

Then again, he had become pretty paranoid over the past year, and his opinions were already somewhat swayed after having been shown the original vision. Perhaps that was exactly what the System was aiming for by creating a Heart Tribulation like that, just as he had initially suspected.

But the real question was, did he dare to risk it? Could he really allow his mother to return?

76

HEARTBEAT

Zac wasn't sure. Was he willing to bet his and Kenzie's lives on his mother being a friend who wanted the best for them, or should he start looking for ways to actively hide from her just like he was planning to do with the Great Redeemer? Perhaps the two plans could be fused, making sure neither party could find their way to Earth.

The more Zac thought about it, the better the idea seemed. He would try to stop Leandra from finding them, at least until they could protect themselves from whatever she had planned. One piece of good news in that regard was that she had been wounded just thirty years ago or so. It might seem like a lifetime to him, but it was just the length of a single round of meditation for high-grade powerhouses.

Getting wounded enough to lose your memories at that level must mean that her enemies, possibly the rulers of Firmament's Edge, were extremely powerful, and healing from such a battle could take centuries. It was just like the Great Redeemer and his nasty scar that radiated terrifying energies. He would probably carry that wound for centuries before he could completely heal.

Leandra might be unable to come back for the time being due to being forced to focus on recuperating. She had been awoken ahead of time, and perhaps there were repercussions for that. The longer he had to prepare, the better he could hide himself and his sister. He would begin with the lantern, but he had a feeling that a Technocrat's tracking wouldn't be based on something like Karmic Threads.

Perhaps there were anti-Technocrat arrays that would stop her from finding Jeeves. The orthodox forces had been fighting the Technocrats for millions of years; there should be all kinds of solutions in circulation.

Zac stood up with a grunt and walked out of his courtyard to let his sister know he was fine, but he was surprised to find a drone hovering just a few meters outside. He knew it must have been Kenzie who put it there, and she came running a few seconds later as expected.

"You did it," Kenzie said with a wide grin, and Zac nodded with a smile, inwardly thankful he had erected his obscuring arrays around his courtyard before he evolved.

Zac knew that he would have to tell her about his visions sooner or later, but now was not the time. However, he couldn't help but feel a sense of foreboding as he saw the undeniable similarities between Kenzie's and Leandra's features.

His mother's appearance had always been a bit blurry in his mind, but it was refreshed upon seeing her twice in short order. And Kenzie really took after Leandra, no matter if you spoke of the slightly curled hair or their hazel eyes. Her appearance was a stark reminder that Leandra might come to collect at any moment, and it reignited his desire to become stronger.

And the first step toward that end was to open his first hidden node.

"I'm fine," Zac said as he looked around. "I passed the tribulation without any issue. I just wanted to tell you that before I headed inside again."

"What's going on?" Kenzie asked. "Do you need to undergo the tribulation twice because of your two Races?"

"No, I actually got two tribulations, but they descended at the same time, so it's dealt with. I have gathered a few things I can finally use now that I'm E-grade," Zac explained. "I can use a few of them while heading toward the Dead Zone, but some need to be taken while in seclusion. I'll be away for a few more hours."

"Is it dangerous?" Kenzie asked with some worry. "You just passed the tribulations. Don't you need to stabilize your foundation or something?"

"It should be fine," Zac said, though he honestly had no idea.

Yrial didn't explain exactly what would happen when he used the **[Eye of Har'Theriam]**, apart from that it would break open a hidden node. If you were lucky and knew to listen well, it could also expose more of the hidden nodes spread through your body, but only the one node was essentially guaranteed.

However, the Lord of Cycles never divulged if there were any dangers to absorbing the treasure. Taking normal pills to gain a level wasn't dangerous, from what he had gathered. It mimicked the method used when cultivating, but it sped up the process drastically. It would hurt a bit, but you wouldn't cripple yourself from opening a node this way.

It was nothing like forcing them open by cramming the nodes full of Cosmic Energy.

But opening a Hidden Node was his best shot at getting a direct power spike before setting out to the Dead Zone. He would be able to force a few nodes open as well while traveling, but he had no idea what to do about the skill quests for the time being. He didn't have any Dao Treasures either, at least not that he was aware of.

So the Hidden Node had the highest priority.

"Alright, I'll keep helping old man Gemidir with the Array," Kenzie said. "Be careful."

"Don't let that old thief scam you." Zac smiled before he returned to the courtyard.

Zac erected the restrictive arrays once more, and he sat down as he took out the box he bought during the trial, the container that held the **[Eye of Har'Theriam]**. It was the most valuable item available in the inheritance, except for Yrial's lock of hair, that is.

He gingerly took it out, and the whole courtyard was suddenly drowned in cascading waves of energy. The fluctuations were extremely exotic as well. They neither felt like Attuned Energies or Dao Energy, but rather something he had never encountered before. Of course, it could simply be a higher-tiered attunement that he was too stupid to recognize.

The so-called **[Eye of Har'Theriam]** didn't really look like the eye of a beast, which wasn't a surprise, since it actually wasn't one. The Pathfinder Eye he recently expended to create **[Love's Bond]** was actually part of a slain beast, but this thing was something else entirely. It was rather a natural treasure, a convergence of specific energies that had been given physical form.

It was an object created by chance from some unknown event in a dead universe, something that had proven extremely hard or even impossible to reproduce. It meant that the supply was extremely limited, and not something that normally would appear in the hands of someone like him. The name came from the fact that the crystalline clump had a discoloration in the middle that somewhat looked like an eye.

Zac didn't eat the treasure, but he rather took off his robe to leave his chest bare before he pushed the item against his navel. Next, he simply started infusing the thing with Cosmic Energy. The small rock was like a bottomless abyss, swallowing everything Zac threw at it. But it was finally satiated after Zac had spent more than half of his reserves, and the treasure started to sink into his body.

He had expected to feel a scorching pain like he had put a piece of coal against his flesh, but nothing of the sort happened. It rather felt like he suddenly had eaten a massive feast, making him a bit bloated. The treasure was quickly getting ready to do its thing, and Zac focused his mind again as he observed the changes.

The slightest fluctuation could be a clue to another hidden node going by how Yrial had explained it, and he didn't want to miss a single thing.

The amount of energy Zac could sense from the **[Eye of Har'Theriam]** was just shocking, like he had swallowed dozens of high-grade pills in one go. His own Cosmic Energy was just a fraction of the whole, something to mark the treasure with his own aura. However, the energy ball didn't spread out across his pathways and, but it rather set up camp close to his Duplicity Core.

One tendril after another reached out in various directions of his body, like they were some sort of scouts that looked for their target. After having looked around for a bit, they returned, looking slightly expended. This repeated over and over, and Zac tried to engrave every movement and every pause in his mind.

However, he started to worry as time passed. He and Yrial had briefly wondered whether he actually had any Hidden Nodes due to his unique constitution, and things weren't looking too good right now.

The ball of energy had almost halved in size over the hours as it sent out one tendril after another in search of a node, but it hadn't found anything of note just yet.

Zac refused to give up unless the ball of energy completely ran out of steam, so the search continued until there was finally a change. Zac felt a surge of victory as one of the tendrils froze after having dug into his heart. One tendril after another joined it until there suddenly were ten of them reaching inside, clearly having found what they were looking for.

The next moment, the main energy ball pounced like a predator going for its prey.

Only then did Zac see what the treasure was doing. A major section of his pathways ran through his heart, and six normal nodes were surrounding it. However, there was now a small distortion added to the mix right in the middle. Zac was 100% sure that it hadn't been there before, since he had gone over his whole body after his evolution.

Or rather, it hadn't been visible to his internal vision.

However, the Eye had managed to find it, and the small disturbance was quickly enlarged as the ten tendrils of the [Eye of Har'Theriam] poured massive amounts of the mysterious energies into the hidden node. Another stagnant pond quickly appeared, though this one looked completely different to the other ones he had seen so far.

It looked like an actual black hole, and any energy that entered it was swallowed without a hint of where it was going.

A shudder spread across his body as it suddenly felt like he had two hearts, each one beating to its own tune. The new addition was deeper and slower, like the beat of a war drum. Each beat became heavier and heavier as the hidden node was getting unlocked by the remaining energies of the [Eye of Har'Theriam], and Zac finally couldn't hold on as he spat a mouthful of blood.

He was shocked to see that the blood actually looked like brown sludge, but he didn't get a chance to even consider any course of action before he felt a crack in his heart, and a surge of energy stormed into his mind.

Zac had once again been thrown into a vision, finding himself on an utterly lifeless piece of stone soaring through the vast cosmos. There were no stars around him, leaving the area almost completely shrouded in darkness. The weak light from a distant nebula was all that illuminated the surface of the celestial body, and was the single feature that barely stood out against the bleak surroundings.

It was a man, or Zac at least guessed it was a man going by the muscular build, stoically sitting on top of a prayer mat. His features were shrouded in darkness, and most of his body was covered by a simple robe, giving no indication of who it might be. He was completely unmoving as well, utterly blending in with the surroundings to the point Zac would have thought he was a statue or a corpse if it weren't for one detail.

The heartbeat.

A heavy heartbeat beat once every few seconds with such vigor that ripples pushed out from around the cultivator's unmoving form. But more interestingly, it looked like there was a pushback the next moment, like a receding wave. The counterforce dragged dense amounts of energy into his body before the man's heart beat once more to send out another ripple to gather even more.

It felt as though his heartbeat was absorbing the power of space itself, and even the stars in the distance flickered as if they were affected by the beat as well. It was like this man was an actual black hole, taking everything from the surroundings for himself. It was no wonder that the meteor he was sitting on was completely devoid of life and energies. He had no doubt already consumed it all.

Was this some sort of cultivation method based on the heart? Or was it simply the effect of his unique constitution? Was he traveling across the cosmos like a locust, draining any area he passed of its vitality?

Zac quickly realized that the meteor was moving with shocking speed as well. They were rapidly closing in on a sun and looked like they could collide at any moment. However, the man was completely oblivious to his surroundings, and Zac soon understood why. The sun was completely helpless in front of that man's heartbeat, and a massive chunk of flames was ripped from the enormous sphere in an instant.

An odd crack in space appeared above the man's head, and the stream of flames was swallowed without leaving a morsel behind. Zac was flabbergasted at the scene, as just a fraction of those streams of flames was far more condensed than the whole scorching sun that Iz Tayn had summoned during the Battle of Fates.

Finally, there was a change in the man's demeanor as they whizzed past the dimmed-out sun. Steam rose from his body as he slightly shuddered, and Zac looked on with a mix of confusion and anticipation. It appeared as though the heart cultivator might have swallowed a bit more than he could chew, and Zac was curious to see if he would show some way to deal with the fallout.

Zac had found himself in the very same predicament a couple of times, after all, and he had only survived by the skin of his teeth.

There was also one more question burning in Zac's mind. Was this man in front of him an ancestor of his, either living or dead? Dao Visions showed you people who were walking the same general path as you, such as the Axe-Man and the Immutable Defender, but this wasn't a Dao Vision. It was a vision brought forth from his own body, a hidden node in his heart.

And such a vision would probably be based on an ancestor of his.

77

VOID HEART

Hidden nodes could generally be categorized into two types, from what Zac had gathered. There were the Racial Nodes that most cultivators of the same Race had, such as the Three Gates. Pretty much all humanoids had these three hidden nodes, with one important exception. They could have been swapped out by Inherited Nodes provided by your bloodline.

Perhaps there were more types out there, but those were the two that Zac could gather intelligence on.

People with strong enough bloodlines had hidden nodes more specialized for their paths, and these types of Inherited Nodes were one reason that families with amazing bloodlines churned out so many powerful warriors. However, he was a bit confused by what he saw, as the most likely source of any bloodlines and Inherited Nodes was no doubt his mother.

However, the shuddering man in front of him definitely didn't look like a Technocrat. He was emitting a terrifying force from his body, like his average-sized frame contained endless power. It was the same sort of fierce aura like he had sensed from Greatest, one of a warrior who used his own body as a weapon.

However, Zac felt this man was on par with those supreme existences he had seen in his previous visions, rather than some D-grade warrior.

Finally, the man stopped shaking, but plumes of steam still rose from his body from the heat he emitted. A small dagger that seemed able to tear space apart by its very existence suddenly appeared in his hand, and he stabbed his leg in one swift motion.

A torrent of blood shot to the sky, and Zac was shocked to see the amount. The wound had closed itself in a fraction of a second, but hundreds of liters had poured out in that short window. Weirder yet, the blood didn't actually freeze from the glacial cold of the vacuum of space.

In fact, it did the opposite, as it suddenly combusted like it was gasoline rather than blood, lighting up the meteor for a short moment before the area was once more plunged into darkness. It looked like expelling the burning blood had drastically improved the man's situation, and he had once again returned to his statuesque demeanor.

The heartbeat the only proof that the man still lived.

Zac slowly woke up from the vision, but he somehow still heard the man's pulse deep in his soul. Each thud made Zac's blood rage like it followed the mysterious man's heart rather than his own. With every thud, their hearts synchronized a bit more until Zac's heartbeat was perfectly in tune with the hooded man's.

His blood started coursing through his body at unprecedented speeds, but he felt no discomfort at all. It was like his heartbeat was in tune with the universe, and a small ripple spread out from his body before space stabilized itself again.

A crackling sound from the sky woke Zac up from his reverie, and he was shocked to see a massive swirl up in the sky. Massive amounts of Cosmic Energy had gathered into a whirlwind of untamed power, and Zac's eyes lit up in anticipation as he waited for the energy to descend.

However, elation quickly turned to confusion before he was filled with annoyance. The energy had no intention of entering his body as it did with the mysterious cultivator in the vision, but it was rather dispersing again now that Zac no longer heard the deep heartbeat. Zac's dreams of a few free levels crashed and burned just as they were born, and he instead turned his attention to a screen that had appeared in front of him.

[Void Heart – An all-encompassing heart born from the primordial void.]

Zac looked at the screen with some confusion, trying to understand just what this new node meant. It was clear that it was an Inherited Node he had opened, rather than something like the Three Gates. But the problem was that there were a huge number of these Inherited Nodes, and people rarely divulged them.

A hidden node was like a secret weapon of a clan, and one of the most guarded secrets. This had made it impossible for Zac to gain a decent understanding of Inherited Nodes, like what limits and capabilities they usually had. But he had learned a thing or two from Galau, who had freely admitted that his clan possessed no Inherited Nodes.

Getting an unknown Inherited Node rather than one of the Three Gates could be both good and bad for him, as Inherited Nodes ranged from being extremely overpowered to utter trash. **[Void Heart]** seemed to be a node that helped with cultivation rather than giving a direct boost to his power like the common nodes like the **[Flesh Gate]**.

But the description was unfortunately of the less informative variety.

The "all-encompassing" was no doubt referring to the man's ability to seemingly absorb any energy, as he swallowed anything he passed, even a sun. There was also no doubt an element of energy gathering to the node, evidenced by the convergence of Cosmic Energy in the sky just now.

Unfortunately, improving energy absorption might mean that it increased cultivation speed, which would be pretty useless to Zac since he couldn't cultivate. What if this **[Void Heart]** kept gathering massive amounts of energies around him, but he could only look at it from a distance, unable to take it for himself?

Wouldn't that be a novel method of torture?

But the vision gave him an inkling that it might not be exactly the case. There seemed to be two components to the ability that the node provided, judging by the vision. The first was the heart, and the second was the blood. The heart seemed to swallow the energy of the area, which was related to some sort of absorption, though not necessarily one related to normal cultivation.

The man also exsanguinated himself on purpose, and there was clearly something wrong with the blood. Zac's best guess was that it was a node that would allow him to absorb various types of energies better than a normal warrior, but that kind of absorption would fill his heart with impurities or toxins.

The exsanguination would in turn allow him to simply flush the toxins out of his body. It was a system of keeping the good and expelling the bad. Something like that seemed to match with Zac's impressions of his own body as well. He had survived his body getting crammed full of all kinds of weird energies until now.

There was the Cosmic Water, then the storm of Miasma in the Dead Zone, and finally, the high-grade energies of the two Remnants in his mind. His body was clearly unnaturally resilient to all kinds of energies, and this Hidden Node might actually be the first step toward taking advantage of this, more than just surviving.

It was just a hypothesis, but one easily tested. Zac took out a Miasma Crystal from his Spatial Ring and absorbed some of its energy. At first, he felt extreme nausea having condensed death-attuned energies in his system, but something mysterious soon happened.

The death-attuned energies entered his pathways and were shot in a few quick revolutions through his body, but each time they entered his heart, the nausea lessened. A few minutes later, the feeling was gone altogether, but there instead was a chilliness in his veins. Zac took out his axe and drew a small cut on his arm, and blood that was slightly darker than normal started dripping down on the ground.

It was barely discernible, but then again, he had only absorbed death-attuned energies from the Miasma Crystal for a short duration. Perhaps his blood would turn into the black ichor altogether if he kept at it long enough.

This quick experiment clearly indicated he was on the right path with the node, but this obviously wasn't the right way to utilize the hidden node. It would be a lot more efficient to simply use a normal Nexus Crystal in this case, as there would be no need to waste time and energy on cleansing it.

But some things might work, such as Natural Treasures. A lot of herbs and other Natural Oddities contained massive amounts of energy, but they were too chaotic and toxic to ingest unless made into pills or concoctions first. And sometimes even that was impossible. Besides, this sort of refinement always led to a significant loss in energy, at least among pills made by normal Alchemists.

Perhaps it wasn't the case with top-tier Alchemists in the Multiverse, but it wasn't like Zac had access to those kinds of people.

He didn't dare try that out right now, though, as he might be badly wounded if proven wrong. But if he was right, then he might have found the key to leveling up quickly in E-grade, perhaps even beyond. He might not be able to gobble up a sun anytime soon, but he might be able to bargain hunt for energy-rich items that were normally too chaotic to turn into anything useful.

He really wanted to find the little blue merchant and requisition some items immediately, but he knew that such experiments would have to wait until after the undead horde. Instead, he left his courtyard, only to find Emily waiting some distance from the gates. She was lazily throwing rocks at a drone that deftly dodged the small projectiles.

Zac was a bit surprised to see the teenager here, as she was out at sea last time he heard, boosting the Intelligence for the scouts and water mages in charge of searching for the jamming arrays.

"You're back! But why do you look the same?" Emily added from the side as she suspiciously looked him up and down. "And what did you do just now? I thought you were about to upgrade the Nexus Vein or something."

"It didn't work out, unfortunately," Zac said with a smile. "You'll have to make do with the normal one for now. And why would I look different?"

Suddenly, a fiery axe appeared in her hand, and she threw it at Zac.

"WOW!" she screamed as she looked at Zac with wide eyes. "Monster! At least you got stronger. A lot stronger. How am I supposed to beat you up now?"

"I guess you'll have to work harder," Zac snorted.

"Aren't people supposed to become more handsome when evolving? But you're still the same monk as ever," Emily said, waving at Kenzie, who was coming over as well.

"You're thinking of Race upgrades." Zac sighed with some exasperation as he ran his hand across his once-again bald head. "I haven't upgraded that yet. I thought you were helping the others looking for the jamming arrays?"

"I returned when I heard you were back. I'm coming with you to fight the Zombies," Emily said, her face scrunching up with stubbornness when seeing Zac's frown. "You might need me. What if you're just too weak to win? Wouldn't you feel stupid if you got stuck outside an array, just lacking 10% Strength to get through?"

"Fine." Zac sighed. "But you should know that even getting to the mainland will be risky."

"I'm going as well," Kenzie suddenly added from the side.

"What? Why?" Zac said, just stopping short of staunchly refusing.

"Calrin and I figured out a few of the Array Breakers while you evolved, but you probably won't be able to use them," Kenzie explained. "They either take a few weeks of study or general knowledge of formations. So I need to go as well."

Zac really didn't want to bring his sister to the heart of the Dead Zone, but he knew that he might not have much of a choice. It was all hands on deck right now, and Kenzie might be the foremost expert on arrays among all the natives of Earth. There were more skilled people among the Sky Gnomes and the Creators, but he couldn't bring them for something like this due to the limitations of the Mercantile System.

"Alright, alright." Zac sighed before he turned to the demon who had appeared to the side as well. "Did you evolve as well?"

"No," Ogras said. "Me evolving won't change the grand scheme of things in the battle with the undead. I need a month or two to consolidate everything. So what classes did you get? Epic? Or even Arcane?"

"It's too early for me to get an Arcane," Zac said. "It's not a good idea to get that rarity before you really know what you're doing, from what I gathered."

"Well, I guess that excludes you. So what did you end up with?" the demon said, almost leaning forward in anticipation.

"What about you?" Zac snorted. "There's no way you didn't check out your options while I evolved."

"He did, like two seconds after you left." Kenzie smiled from the side. "But he won't say what options he got."

"Why aren't you working on that reinforcement array?" Ogras said with some exasperation.

Zac laughed, but he was inwardly a bit worried about the demon. Was there some trouble with his evolution? He had seemed pretty intent on evolving the moment they returned based on their discussions in the Tower, but something seemed to have changed his mind.

He knew that the demon had a Rare class right now. Was he perhaps lacking something to get an option? Or was it the opposite? Did he feel that he was on the verge of getting enough merit to be provided with an Epic class, and closing out the undead incursion might give him the final push to take that step?

Thankfully, it wasn't critical to Zac's plan that Ogras had evolved. He mainly wanted to bring the demon for his obscuring capabilities, and those seemed to be mainly based on his Dao of Shadows. Getting a boost to his main attribute, Dexterity, probably wouldn't make those skills any stronger.

The fact that Ogras wouldn't be as strong wasn't a huge deal either, as he would personally deal with the Lich King. However, as Zac looked around at the three people, he was reminded that no man was an island. Certainly, none of these people were nearly as strong as him in direct battle, but they all brought something to the table that would increase the odds of success.

He realized now how foolish his initial idea to deal with the Undead Empire alone was.

"I've done what I can about that array," Kenzie said as she pointed toward the house housing Zac's private teleportation array. "The old gnome is performing the finishing touches over there."

"I'm thinking of leveling up immediately," Zac said, changing the topic. "Is there any problem for me to start taking the pills I've prepared?"

"Not that I'm aware of," Ogras said. "That's usually how it goes. Of course, most people spend years at the peak of F-grade to solidify their progression. But you should be fine. You're a meathead who finds your path in battle anyway. I'm not sure sitting down and meditating will do you any good. Just eat it and then stabilize your foundation by bashing Zombies."

"Sounds good to me," Zac said as he took out one of the pills that would give him a level.

It wasn't the **[Four Gates Pill]** with spirituality he'd found during the Hunt, though. He wasn't sure if he wanted to eat that thing right now or save it for when he hit a roadblock. It might even be something that he could use to open up more hidden nodes in the future.

There were no guarantees, but Zac felt he had a pretty good idea about the location of one hidden node at least, thanks to ingesting the treasure earlier. He had observed every movement of the energy tendrils from the **[Eye of Har'Theriam]**, and it had sent its tendrils to one specific spot multiple times, and they had stayed there with hesitation for a bit before moving on.

This node was close to a crossroads of pathways on the top of his head. He obviously couldn't be sure, but he believed that the node the tendrils had found might be the **[Spirit Gate]**, one of the three common Hidden Nodes. It supposedly increased your control over Mental Energy by a large degree, which was something Zac desperately needed.

His control was atrocious because of his nonexistent affinity to the Daos, but opening the Spirit Gate might allow him to at least control his Daos to the same degree as most cultivators did. He probably wouldn't reach the level of people like Catheya or Iz Tayn, but it was at least something.

His goal wasn't to become the most powerful man in the universe or anything, but he still wanted to maintain his ability to punch above his weight class. Being an elite was the best deterrence, after all. People still spoke about the Eveningtide Asura in hushed tones after a million years. He wanted to create that same effect so that Earth would be left alone without him having to guard the planet day and night.

Of course, there was no guarantee that the pill he picked up during the hunt was any good for opening hidden nodes, and he didn't want to take the gamble just yet. Judging by the power it contained, it might even be able to break open nodes at high E-grade. Besides, he still knew nothing about his **[Void Heart]**.

Perhaps he would see far better results if he waited to take that pill until he could maximize the benefits with that node somehow. There was a chance that the node might have an impact on the absorption of pills, after all. But until then, there were still a bunch of normal pills he could take.

He couldn't wait any longer, and he took out one of his normal leveling pills. Zac really wanted to know how leveling would work in E-grade. The attribute gains were split between opening nodes and gaining levels, and he still didn't know if the node breaking needed to be done in both his forms.

"And eating these kinds of pills won't weaken or wound me before the battle?" Zac asked.

"It'll hurt, but not like forcing it open with excess energy," the demon said as he looked on with curiosity.

Zac nodded and popped the pill in his mouth as he sat down. The pill felt like a small sun that ran down his throat before it hit his stomach. However, the energies didn't set up camp like the [Eye of Har'Theriam], but it rather shot out like it had a life of its own.

The little packet of energy surged around his body with shocking speed until it suddenly stopped at one of the weak spots in his right arm. Zac was a bit surprised, as he had simply assumed that it would go clockwise from where his Duplicity Core was placed, but it looked like it was random.

The intensity of the pill energy kept increasing as a huge amount of warmth streamed into the node, and Zac was shocked at how much energy the unassuming bead had contained. It was just like Ogras had said, it hurt a bit, but it wasn't too bad, it almost felt like he was getting pinched. However, his brows started to furrow as time passed.

Over twenty minutes had passed, and the pill was starting to lose its steam. However, the node showed no signs of changing, and the pill finally petered out. Zac felt the same, but he opened his Status screen to be sure. But just as expected, he was still level 75.

"Wasn't this thing supposed to guarantee a level up to level 80?" Zac complained as he opened his eyes and turned to the demon. "What now?"

The demon looked perfectly jubilant as a grin spread across his face.

"I guess there's some justice in the world after all," Ogras snorted.

"If you gained levels quickly on top of everything, the rest of us might just as well have given up."

"Well?"

"I don't know? Take another one. You should have a few." The demon shrugged as he looked at Zac as though he was an interesting oddity.

He also threw a Cosmos Sack at Zac, who caught it with an inquisitive look. It wasn't like Ogras to freely give out any gifts.

"These are some of the gifts I gathered from the rich bastards in Base Town earlier. There should be a few dozen such pills inside. I handed most of it over to the gnomes to categorize," Ogras said as a grin spread across his face again. "Now let's see how many you need to eat to break open the first node."

Zac sighed, but he could only oblige. He took out a second pill that guaranteed the same effect, and he was relieved to see that the pill energy stopped at the same node as the last one and continued the work there. However, his frown quickly returned as the pill energy quickly drained while the node stayed the same.

Only at the last second did he felt something change in his body. It was like he had cracked his neck and suddenly felt looser. His body felt lighter, and the energy surged through his body with greater vigor.

Zac quickly looked inward and saw that the weak spot had completely transformed. The murky pond that sucked energy had changed into a slowly rotating whirlpool that kept moving from its own momentum. It reminded Zac of the Dao whirl he had experimented with a bit during the time he'd tried to keep the Draugr wound in check with the Seed of Trees.

A quick check on the status screen showed him that he had gained 7 points to the base attributes, but surprisingly enough, he hadn't gained the extra Strength and Vitality from gaining a level in Edge of Acadia. He frowned in annoyance and ate another pill, ignoring the demon's snicker from the side.

Ten minutes later, the whirlpool had gone from a slightly weak swirl into a surging but stable whirlpool that empowered rather than weakened his pathways. He had finally gained a level and reached level 76 in his Edge of Arcadia class. It looked like two pills weren't quite enough for both opening the node and gaining the level, but the third one did the trick.

He would probably have been better off using a Nexus Crystal after the node was opened, as breaking the node was the hard part. After that, he only needed to gather enough energy to qualify for a level increase. But he had been a bit impatient, and the condensed energies in these pills were far more efficient for this purpose, though they left some toxins behind.

Having to use three pills wasn't great news when only one was supposed to "guarantee" a level, but it also wasn't too bad, especially after having gotten his new hidden node. However, there was one more problem. He didn't gain anything for his Draugr side, it seemed, neither levels nor nodes.

Zac gave it a thought before he activated his Duplicity Core, and he changed into his Draugr form for the second time this day. A glance at his Status screen proved what he already knew: Fetters of Desolation was still at level 75. However, there was an interesting change when he checked out the node in his right arm.

It had actually turned into a whirlpool as well, but it was so weak that it was almost completely unmoving. It was far worse than it had been in his human side at any point in time, and it looked like it could die out at any moment. It was obviously lacking energy, perhaps the full amount needed for a level.

Node-breaking was something that affected both his classes simultaneously, it seemed, but he would need to fill the nodes with energy separately. That, unfortunately, confirmed that he wouldn't get a second set of base attributes and that he no longer would get twice the amount of attributes from levels compared to others.

This was a pretty big blow to his unique advantages. His massive pool of raw attributes was his greatest ace against the cultivators who could fuse their Daos and empower their strikes with their cultivation manuals. He would still get more points than others, but the difference was nowhere near as big any longer.

It was a very important reminder that he couldn't relax in the pursuit of power. You needed to keep pushing yourself and keep finding new opportunities to advance. If he couldn't steamroll people with raw stats any longer, then he would simply have to find another advantage. The first thing that came to mind was the **[Nine Reincarnations Manual]** that hopefully would be able to make his soul strong enough to handle the Remnants.

The second thing was the possibility of getting rewards for closing down the last incursions and reaping the rewards.

"How are your preparations?" Zac asked as he got back to his feet. "How soon can we leave?"

"We're ready anytime," Kenzie said as she got up from the table she had summoned while Zac focused on leveling up.

"Good. There's no time to waste," Zac said. "We're heading out in one hour. Get a defensive squad of Valkyries as well."

"I can protect myself," Kenzie disagreed.

"Yes, but Emily is a support class who needs guardians. We're going all out here, and we have no idea what we might be facing," Zac said. "I'll be able to unleash more power if I know you guys are safe."

"Fine. We'll get everything in order." Kenzie nodded. "Meet back here?"

"I'll go see if I can get some goodies from that slippery bastard we picked up in the underworld," Ogras muttered. "Knowing you, things will turn pretty chaotic over there."

With that, he disappeared in a puff of shadows, and Emily sat down on a rock and started to play with her tomahawks. Kenzie sent out a drone before she walked back to the Teleportation House, no doubt to make sure the stabilization array would be installed in time.

"Good," Zac muttered as he simply sat down under the sun to start stabilizing his mind. "In one hour, we'll assault the undead incursion."

As long as we don't get ripped apart by the spatial turbulence, Zac added in his mind.

TURBULENCE

"You sure you need me for this?" Ogras said as he looked at the modified teleportation array with some trepidation. "It might cause less strain on the array the fewer people who go; it might be better if I just stay behind after all."

"This is our only shot, and I might not be able to deal with this alone," Zac said. "Besides, what are you whining about? Even a teenager is going, and you're afraid?"

"Sending two or ten people won't really make a difference to the array," Kenzie added from the side, a hint of schadenfreude in her eyes. "As long as we enter at the same time, we have as good a chance of surviving as when going alone."

"Don't speak such unlucky words," Ogras muttered, but it looked like he had resigned himself to going with the rest.

"Is there anything we need to know?" Zac asked the old Sky Gnome to the side.

"The moment the **[Spatial Reinforcement Array]** activates, it will cause a clash with whatever the unliving have planted," Gemidir said. "If you see new destinations appearing in the teleportation screen, it means it's working. For the time being."

"For the time being?" Zac repeated skeptically.

"Our array will probably only last a minute or two against the jammers of the Undead Empire, so you can't dally or hesitate," Kenzie said. "Immediately pick an option, and we'll all jump onto the array.

We can't waste a single second. Just make sure you don't pick a town in the wrong direction."

Zac looked around, his eyes turning to Joanna and her squad of six Valkyries who silently stood behind her. Zac recognized all of them, as they were all among the oldest members who had followed him all the way from Greenworth. They had followed him to both close incursions and conquer the underworld. The constant battle had utterly reforged them into stalwart warriors.

Their gear had been swapped out since the last time he saw them, though. All of them wore massive shields made from chitinous shells on their backs, each one large enough to cover their whole bodies. Their goal in the upcoming fight wasn't to boost Zac's prowess, but rather use their newly acquired War Arrays to protect the rear against unanticipated attacks.

He couldn't always protect Emily and his sister, but this group of six would hopefully be able to stall long enough for him to come to their aid. Zac took a deep breath before he turned to the ancient Sky Gnome, who stood by to the side.

"Do it," Zac said as he opened his teleportation screen.

It only showed the handful of teleportation arrays that were studded across the island, but nothing beyond that. He heard some tinkering sounds as the gnome drew some lines to connect the final power outlets, and a hum suddenly echoed out from the array as Zac felt his vision doubling for a second.

However, Zac forcibly ignored the odd effect and chose a town he recognized. It was one of the newly created settlements close to the shore of Pangea, as he figured a shorter jump would have a higher success rate.

Zac jumped into the array, dragging a swearing Ogras by his lapel just in case the demon chose to change his mind at the last second. The array whisked them away, and his surroundings were replaced by darkness.

However, something felt wrong. It was as though he were being squeezed through a too-thin pipe. The discomfort quickly turned to pain, but there was nothing he could do about it. He wasn't in control of himself during these types of teleportations, and he could only endure the pain and pray that the others were fine.

DEFIANCE OF THE FALL FIVE | 555

But the darkness of subspace suddenly cracked, and Zac found himself far up in the sky, heedlessly tumbling from the wind as droplets of blood rained down all around him. Screams echoed out from every direction, and he saw multiple bloodied people flailing about. He was obviously wounded as well, judging by the blood around him, but they were flesh wounds at worst, considering his sturdy frame.

However, his sister and Emily weren't so lucky, and they were utterly drenched in blood as they fell toward the ground. The scene made his heart burn with anxiety, and four chains shot out as [Love's Bond] transformed to its backpack form. The emerald leaf appeared beneath him the next moment, and five seconds later, the whole group was collected and safe.

Ogras and Kenzie had appeared on top of the leaf by their own means, whereas Joanna had managed to throw out ropes to half the Valkyries. Zac only needed to snatch up a screeching Emily and the rest of the Valkyries. Thankfully, everyone was fine, apart from getting bloodied. No one had died, and no one sported a crippling wound.

Only then did Zac take stock of their whereabouts, and he frowned when he realized they were above the open sea. No matter what direction he looked in, there was nothing, just sky and water. There was a pretty nasty storm cloud in one direction, but there was not a hint of shoreline.

"Is everyone okay?" Joanna said with a hoarse voice from the side.

"I'm fine," Kenzie said as she ate a healing pill. "I think they booby-trapped subspace by filling it with spatial tears or something. If we had continued the whole way, we would probably have emerged as chunks of meat. Thankfully, we installed a fail-safe in the array that would take us out of subspace if it got deadly."

"You did?" Zac said with surprise.

"Do you think I would gamble with all our lives?" Kenzie retorted with exasperation.

"Where the hell are we, though?" Ogras muttered from the side as shadows rushed through his alabaster hair and face to remove any blood.

"We can't be anywhere close to the Dead Zone," Joanna said as she looked around. "The array in the sky is massive, yet we can't see it at all. I think we might be some distance away from the continent."

"Well, we'll just have to fly," Kenzie said as she pointed in a certain direction. "We should hit land as long as we move in that direction."

Zac guessed that Jeeves had calculated it for her based on the suns in the sky or something, and he sent a mental command to the leaf. However, Zac soon enough handed over the task of steering the vessel to Joanna, as he wanted to take the opportunity to start leveling up in earnest.

The leaf was terrifyingly quick, but New Earth was also shockingly large, so now was as good a time as any to start eating his stock of node-breaking pills. There was the issue of pill toxicity, but right now wasn't a time to worry about that.

Besides, his new Hidden Node might even have some ability to deal with toxicity. He didn't feel any better after getting bled by the spatial tears, but he also shouldn't carry a lot of toxicity just yet. He doubted it would let him eat pills indiscriminately even if it worked, but it would still be a great help since he didn't have access to things like cleansing arrays at the moment.

Now that Zac knew what kind of energies he was dealing with, he felt confident enough to swallow two node-breaking pills at once. He wanted to see whether they attacked different nodes, or if there was some sort of system to which nodes were opened.

"Lunatic," a disgusted grunt came from the side as the demon looked on with shock. "The Heavens won't abide with you forever, you know?"

Zac only flipped the demon off in response before he focused on the two balls of fire that had erupted in his belly.

He was happy to see that they both stopped by one of the nodes in his left leg after having skittered about for a bit, as that proved that he would be able to improve his leveling speed as long as his body could take the extra strain. But Zac started sweating from pain the moment the two streams of power entered the nodes.

There wasn't a simple doubling of pain when taking two pills, but rather an exponential increase by ten times. It felt like his leg was getting continuously stabbed, but he gritted his teeth and endured it until the pain finally stopped after half an hour. Was this what it would feel like to brute-force nodes in the future?

This time, the node didn't even break open even after ingesting two pills, so Zac simply slammed two more of them. Another bout of agony lasting for half an hour passed, and the second node had finally been opened. He took a shuddering breath before he kept going. It felt like torture, but he wanted to gain as many levels as possible before he reached the Dead Zone, especially now that he had brought his people with him.

Zac didn't know how much time had passed as he crammed one pill after another down his gullet as though he were possessed. Sweat streamed down his body, and soon enough, the sweat had turned red as he actually started bleeding from his pores. His sister tried to stop his manic assault on his nodes multiple times, but Zac shrugged away the attempts, as he felt it was working.

But finally, he couldn't take the pain any longer, but he had already broken open his fifth node and gained its equivalent level by that point. The suns had started to set by that point already, meaning that Zac had been occupied for at least four or five hours.

"Just what did you eat growing up?" Ogras muttered from the side when he saw that Zac had finally stopped abusing himself. "This was not what I meant that it was fine to start taking node-breaking pills. Taking pills like that should be a straight ticket to the morgue, or at least the infirmary."

Zac could only respond with a weak smile, and he guessed that this wasn't the time to explain that he was actually a bit disappointed with the results of the experiment. When he had been forcibly instilled with the Miasma from tens of thousands of Zombies, he'd managed to eat ten purification pills in one go. Just three was supposed to be a death sentence, but he'd survived just fine.

He had thought that he would at least be able to take four or five node-breaking pills in one go to speed up the process, especially after gaining the odd Hidden Node. But he honestly didn't dare to even try three of them at the moment.

The experiment also indicated that the **[Void Heart]** did not have much of an effect when ingesting pills. He couldn't sense his heart doing anything at all, really, compared to the noticeable effect when absorbing a Miasma Crystal. Did it perhaps only work on natural sources of energy rather than refined ones? The man in the vision had eaten the void and a sun, after all, not a mountain of pills.

Another stark realization was that he couldn't simply eat node-breaking pills continuously. He felt that he was quickly building up a resistance as they traveled, and by the time he had cracked open the fifth node, he wasn't very confident there was any point in continuing his mad consumption. He knew that one couldn't simply keep eating pills for a few days and reach the peak of the E-grade, but he still felt it was too early to feel this kind of response.

"Isn't there anything I can do?" Zac asked. "I still have a lot of pills."

"The resistance will decrease with time, but the process is pretty tedious. And you won't get the full effect again no matter how long you wait." Ogras leered. "But gaining levels through killing and culti-vation also helps reset your body, so to speak. I guess you've reached your cap for now unless you find some Natural Treasure with similar effects."

Zac sighed, but he guessed he should be thankful there was a limit to how much you could gain from just cramming a bunch of pills down your gullet. If there were no restrictions, then the incursion leaders would all have been level 150 rather than 80 to 90 by now. Gaining five full levels in one day was still extremely good, and it had boosted his attributes by a shocking degree.

However, he still wasn't out of things to use just because he couldn't eat any more node-breaking pills. Zac swapped over to his Draugr form and took out one of his D-grade Miasma Crystals. He didn't have too many of them, but Zac figured it would be enough to fill up the five empty nodes on his undead side.

Terrifying waves of death-attuned energies slammed into his body as he started absorbing a D-grade crystal for the first time. It felt like he was deep inside the liquid Miasma that surrounded Be'Zi for a second, almost drowning from the waves crashing through him. But he soon managed to steady himself, and it felt like he had ascended to the heavens because of how good it felt.

He could barely restrain himself from moaning out loud, which would have become an eternal point of embarrassment in front of this group. He would rather stab himself to snap out of it than be forced to listen to Emily's and Ogras' taunts over the following centuries.

Zac noticed that the death-attuned energy from the Miasma Crystal didn't have any idea where to move, in contrast to the pills, which almost seemed to have homing capabilities. Still, it wasn't too hard for Zac to push the excess Miasma into the sluggish whirlpool in his right arm. It felt like the whirlpool was like a bottomless hole as more and more energies burrowed into the spot, gradually filling it with vigor.

The stagnant whirlpool slowly started to pick up speed, but it took Zac well over an hour before he felt a shudder through his body as the node stopped consuming Miasma. The time it took wasn't too bad, but it was still more than expected.

He had leveled pretty damn quickly with E-grade crystals in the F-grade, and he was already in the 40s by the time he got his hands on some. If he got some E-grade crystals at level 1, then he'd blast through levels like they were nothing.

It only got worse from there, though, as the second node took almost 50% longer to fill up until another wave of power spread through his body. He simply kept going, though, as land was still nowhere near in sight.

The third node took over three hours to fill, and the fourth node took five. It had cost him nine D-grade crystals to complete, which was pretty bad news. It had almost emptied his stock, and this was just for filling already opened nodes. The node breaking was the most energy-demanding part, and it seemed like using Nexus Crystals to level up would already be impractical for him by the time he reached level 80 with both his classes.

Zac still had one more node to fill with energy, but he stopped, as they finally could see land far in the distance.

DEATH DEFIANCE

At first, there was just a thin green line, but they were able to make out the landscape soon enough. Zac breathed out in relief when he saw that it was a pretty normal coast with some leafy growth and grasslands.

It wasn't the sandblasted desert of the scorched continent, as the only greenery there was the strip of palms along the coast. Zac still couldn't see any massive array in the sky, though, which meant they were still quite far from the Dead Zone.

"We'll have to keep going until we find a settlement," Zac said as he put away his Miasma Crystals. "We will need to make another jump."

"Finally," Emily muttered. "It's so uncomfortable to sit next to you while you absorb that stuff. Feels like I am both cold and feverish at the same time."

"Sorry about that." Zac smiled as he turned back to his human form. "I needed to get some levels for my second class as well."

Zac opened his screen again and marveled at the progress over the past day. Rushing levels in the E-grade was just putting himself further and further apart from the rest of the humans of Earth.

Name: Zachary Atwood
Level: 80
Class: [E-Epic] Edge of Arcadia

Race: [E] Human
Alignment: [Earth] Port Atwood – Lord

Titles: […] Tower of Eternity – 8th Floor, Heaven's Triumvirate, Fated, Peak Power, Monarch-Select
Limited Titles: Frontrunner, Tower of Eternity Sector All-Star – 14th
Dao: Fragment of the Axe – Middle, Fragment of the Coffin – Middle, Fragment of the Bodhi – Early
Core: [E] Duplicity

Strength: 1988 [Increase: 91%. Efficiency: 199%]
Dexterity: 766 [Increase: 65%. Efficiency: 170%]
Endurance: 2004 [Increase: 99%. Efficiency: 199%]
Vitality: 1278 [Increase: 89%. Efficiency: 189%]
Intelligence: 492 [Increase: 65%. Efficiency: 170%]
Wisdom: 814 [Increase: 70%. Efficiency: 170%]
Luck: 321 [Increase: 91%. Efficiency: 179%]

Free Points: 90
Nexus Coins: [F] 6,896,098,998

Zac's Strength had already passed his Endurance by this point, though **[Forester's Constitution]** was barely keeping it ahead in his human form. It was no surprise, as his class choices heavily leaned toward Strength.

It was crazy to think that his Strength wasn't even 1,000 just two days ago, and it was a clear justification why so many he met believed that choosing low-rarity classes was the way to go.

It made sense. He felt he had pushed the F-grade to a point that was almost unprecedented in his whole sector thanks to his combination of having two classes and snatching up almost all the progenitor titles of Earth. He had then risked his life multiple times inside the Tower of Eternity to push himself even further.

Yet he had gained just as many attributes by simply gaining a couple of levels in the E-grade.

He also knew it would be an extremely taxing challenge to form a

Cultivator's Core that was high quality enough to be able to support someone like him, whereas a genius who chose an Uncommon E-grade class would barely meet a bottleneck at all.

Zac's eyes turned to the 90 Free Points next, but there wasn't really a question of what he needed to do for now. He threw it all into his Dexterity, pushing it to 914. The flat points from the class had skewed his ratio, but the allocation had righted the ship once more.

However, he wasn't sure whether he could keep putting all his free points into Dexterity as he had done during most of the F-grade. His fighting style didn't only rely on his massive strength, but also his nigh invulnerability. The latter would take a hit during the E-grade, as he only got 8 points in Endurance per level from his Fetters of Desolation class.

Meanwhile, he would get more than three times that in Strength if you counted the Strength coming from both his classes. Perhaps putting part of his free attributes into Endurance to help it stay up was his best shot at keeping himself sturdy enough. That, combined with the boosts from his Daos, would probably be enough to stay an unkillable juggernaut.

Zac put the matter aside for now, as he wouldn't gain any more easy levels in the short run. However, he was still a bit leery about the attribute cap, and he ate one of his basic Race-Evolving Pills to push his attribute cap forward a bit. It was obviously not enough to completely evolve his Race to D-grade, but he could still improve his attribute cap from 2,500 by at least a few hundred this way.

That was all that Zac needed for the moment, as it was enough to avoid any issues in case he had some Dao Epiphany during the battle with the undead. An exuberant energy entered his stomach, and an intense warmth spread throughout his whole body. Streams of power entered every single pore, filling them with power.

His cells were like a bottomless abyss, and they greedily swallowed everything he could give them. Unfortunately, the pill only contained so much energy, and the warmth quickly abated as his body absorbed the last of the energies. He hadn't made any breakthrough, but his body felt extremely good, like he had just had a full-body massage.

Zac took a deep breath to enjoy the fresh air, but an abominable smell hit his nostrils and immediately dragged him out of his reverie, only to be met with ten appalled stares. He quickly looked down at his body, only to find his skin covered in an oily brown substance.

"You stink," the demon said with a disgusted snarl. "Why are you improving your Race in this cramped space?"

Kenzie didn't even speak up before she blasted him with cascading waves of water with the help of one of her skills, utterly drenching him and almost throwing him off the leaf. The torrent of water continued for a few seconds, but all the gunk was blasted clean when it abated.

"Uh, thanks," Zac said as he spat out a mouthful of water. "I'd forgotten that would happen."

It almost felt like he had made a social faux pas akin to releasing a fart in a cramped elevator, and he turned his gaze toward the horizon to hide his embarrassment, instead focusing on finding a town. Thankfully, he had the perfect item for an occasion just like this, and he took out the [Automatic Map] from his Spatial Ring.

The area it showed was a bit limited, but it was still twice what they could see with their naked eyes, and there were even markings of Nexus Nodes on it. It didn't take them long to find a settlement with the help of the map. It was a walled-off enclave with about two hundred houses hidden in the shadow of a mountain, with no roads leading to and from the place. Zac didn't bother announcing their presence; they landed in the middle of the square.

Unfortunately, it looked like the place was one of the weakest settlements, and it hadn't even bought a teleportation array so far.

They were a small community completely cut off from the world, and seeing the flying treasure and the weird retinue was a huge shock to them. However, Zac had no time for an orientation with these people, and they simply found the leader, a nondescript middle-aged man who had reached level 32.

There was a small exploit he had found while traveling before. Zac essentially explained who he was and exposed his level, and the mayor was more than willing to join his banner as a subordinate. Judging by how gaunt everyone looked, they had a hard time even getting enough Nexus Coins for food, and joining the strongest man in the world was no doubt a godsent opportunity.

A small hovel like this would never have unlocked the ability to buy a teleportation array normally, but now that they were part of Port Atwood, the mayor suddenly had a large increase in available purchases, including a slew of arrays. There were limits to how many places Zac could "boost" like this, but he was still well within his limits, as he only had a dozen towns or so under his command.

Zac then donated enough money for him to buy the array, and he breathed out in relief when he saw that almost all of his connections were still there when checking out the array menu. The advance forts belonging to the Marshal Clan weren't available, though, meaning that anything inside or even too close to the Dead Zone was blocked out by jammers or the death-attuned energies.

They were gone from the remote village a few seconds later, having teleported over to one of the strongholds closest to the Dead Zone. It was a base controlled by the Underworld Council, and Zac felt it was their best bet at getting updated intelligence from the front lines.

"Halt!" a man mounting a massive machine gun shouted upon their appearance, but he quickly realized who they were and stood down.

"I need to speak with the Council," Zac said, and he was soon led out of the building housing the teleportation array.

However, Zac stopped in his tracks the moment he exited the building, and he gawked at how the whole world was tinted in aquamarine. The blue sky of Earth had been completely supplanted by the chilly light-blue tint of death-attuned energies. If it weren't for the normal Cosmic Energy in the area, he would have thought the world was already realigned.

However, there was an unmistakable hint of death in the ambient energies even though this camp wasn't inside the Dead Zone, proving that the alignment was already in progress.

The turquoise hue was unexpected, but the most shocking scene was the gargantuan lines crisscrossing the sky, forming fractals whose size beggared comprehension. Just how much energy had been siphoned out of their planet to form this array? Zac started to worry that Earth would end up crippled even if they managed to deal with the undead somehow.

He hated to say it, but was this world even worth staying on if that happened?

Death Defiance (Unique, Limited): The war between life and death is as old as time. Stop the realignment of your world. Reward: World Core Upgrade. Individual rewards based on contribution. (0/1).

"Did you guys just get a quest?" Zac asked with confusion as he looked at the screen that had suddenly appeared in front of him. "To deal with the undead?"

"Yep!" Emily said with excitement shining in her eyes, and the Valkyries nodded their heads as well.

Zac frowned in confusion as he looked away from the ominous skies. Why was the System giving out a quest like this? It hadn't done that when he fought any of the other incursions. Did the System perhaps feel that people weren't struggling enough against the Undead Empire, and wanted to push for a final cataclysmic battle?

They soon walked into a command tent, where six of the Underworld Councilors were already waiting.

"Thank god you're here. We were starting to get a bit worried," Gregor said, and it almost looked like he wanted to run over and touch Zac to make sure he was actually real. "We were even contemplating paying the fee to enter the Ark World. But seeing you shoot up in levels the past hours felt like a stay of execution."

Zac nodded at the human councilor with a smile before he frowned in confusion at the unfamiliar word.

"The what? Ark World?" Zac asked with confusion, almost forgetting about the quest he just got.

"The New World Government approached us two days ago, shortly after we lost connection with Port Atwood. They said that they have discovered a spatial tunnel leading to a safe Mystic Realm. They call it the Ark World. They are currently shaking down the elites of the Earth to allow them to join the exodus," Gregor explained.

"So they're abandoning Earth?" Zac asked with a frown.

"Well, honestly, I can understand them. There's not much we can do. We can barely hold the lines against these undying bastards.

Reaching the heart of the Dead Zone and taking out the leaders? Impossible. At least for us…" Gregor said pointedly.

"That's why I'm here," Zac said. "If the array in the sky activates, then I have failed. At that point, you might as well leave for the Ark World if you can. Humans won't survive long on a death-attuned planet."

"Is there anything we can do to help?" Romal, the official speaker of the council, said. "I would be honored to join you in battle. I would rather fight for our shared planet than hide in some cramped Mystic Realm. Our people have already done that once, and I know what future such a decision will lead to."

"And it's not like the unliving are stupid," another councilor added. "They will find us sooner or later hiding in that Hidden Realm. I bet they have ten ways of forcing a passage open for every way we have to keep it closed."

"I will just take a very small group that will help with the arrays. I will deal with the Lich King myself. But you can still help me in other ways. Do you know if any of the undead generals are out on the battle-field?" Zac asked.

"We believe one still resides within the closest horde." Gregor nodded. "It has stayed extremely cohesive compared to the other two hordes."

"Can you make sure the horde and their army are occupied for the next two days?" Zac asked. "Things will go smoother if the Lich King isn't aided by any generals or his hordes."

"We'll do what we can," Romal promised. "When are you setting out?"

"The moment we're done here. The sooner the array in the sky is turned off, the better," Zac said. "By the way, have you guys received a quest to stop the undead incursion as well?"

"We received it yesterday." Gregor nodded. "Everyone who is above level 30 and beneath this cursed sky has it. I guess the rest are considered irrelevant in this fight."

ATTUNEMENT

"Are there any merit exchanges that have cropped up?" Zac asked, as the quest reminded him of the beast waves back on his island. "And have you figured out what the World Core upgrade entails?"

"Merit exchanges? Not that we know of," Gregor slowly said with some confusion. "We don't know anything about the core either. Perhaps it will upgrade our planet to C-grade? The System did mention it was D-grade when we got integrated, after all."

"You wish," Ogras snorted from the side, drawing everyone's glances. "This world is as wretched as D-grade worlds come. The energy and insights feels abundant now, but wait until the Origin Dao is gone and you've reached Peak E-grade. There is no way that a single quest will bump you all the way to a C-grade Planet. Our whole demon horde with tens of thousands of forces only has one of them."

"So what do you think?" Zac asked.

"It might push the world a bit further, to something like middle D-grade. It might increase the size of the world as well, as it is quite small. A larger planet would allow larger forces and higher overall strength, along with the formation of more resources that can be used to birth powerhouses. Or it might even give the world an attunement, which would probably be the most valuable reward."

"An attunement?" Zac repeated thoughtfully.

"It might not be useful for us, but for the following generations," Ogras added. "A fire-attuned world would generate a lot of fireaspected treasures and herbs, attuned crystals, and even the fire affinities of cultivators would slowly increase. Specialization begets power."

Zac nodded in agreement. Such a scenario would probably be the best for Earth, though it was useless for him unless the attunement was life. The planet becoming death-aspected for his Draugr side was obviously not going to happen, as that was the very thing the quest goal was designed to stop.

The councilors also tried to discreetly inquire why he had been missing the past days and how he'd managed to gain so many levels in short order. Zac explained it by slightly mixing truths and lies. He said he'd left for the Tower of Eternity in order to evolve his Daos and gain achievements to the point that he could evolve. That was the only way he would gain enough power to assault the Dead Zone.

Lying about going to the Tower of Eternity was a waste of effort. It was just a matter of time before his activities were made known across Earth. It shouldn't be too hard for people to figure out he was the one who caused such a ruckus the moment they went to the Tower themselves.

As for the levels, he didn't bother hiding it and told them about the node-breaking pills. He had a massive surplus of them now that he couldn't use any more for the time being. Most would probably be put into his Merit Exchange, so they stayed within his force, but he could also consider selling some of them to outsiders.

In fact, Zac was already thinking of holding an auction of his own sooner or later, provided their whole planet didn't fall to the Undead Empire. He had a lot of items right now that were pretty common in the Multiverse, but still unheard of on Earth. It was a perfect opportunity to make some money before people managed to find their own business connections.

No one on Earth was nearly as wealthy as he was, but the accumulated wealth of tens of thousands of elites should be pretty impressive by now. It was a bit unethical to overcharge his fellow countrymen, but it could be considered a fee for closing pretty much all the incursions for them.

Zac didn't want to stay in the base any longer than that, and he left after he had transferred all the latest intelligence reports to a tablet.

The bad news was that the Dead Zone was enormous by this point, having grown more than twice in size since he visited the last time.

The Realignment Array had not only increased the density of the death attunement, but the forces of Pangea left multiple kilometers every day. Death spread forth like an intractable wave, and you could even see the process with your naked eyes. Every single one of the border towns was long gone, having turned into unlivable ghost towns by now.

Teleporting closer wouldn't work either due to the jamming. That meant that there was no time to waste, as the distance they needed to traverse was simply massive. He guessed that it would take over half a day to reach the core of the Dead Zone even with the flying treasure.

They still had some time according to Kenzie's estimate, but he didn't want to be late once more. The desolate landscape flashed past them as they soared through the air, this time hidden from sight with the help of a mobile illusion array that made them perfectly blend in with the surroundings.

He had gotten the idea from the seer during the climb. He had mentioned that his descendants had placed a treasure on a flying treasure and hid in the sky, making them impossible to find. The Dead Zone was no doubt crawling with those ghost scouts, but this would give them a small chance at arriving to the core unnoticed.

At the beginning of their flight, they could see not only the undead horde far in the distance but also trucks and armies moving about on the ground. However, after one hour had passed, there was no activity from the living. They saw a smaller horde move toward the larger one at the edge of the Dead Zone, but that was about it.

The hours passed, but no one could relax. Everyone was afraid a storm of ghosts would blast through the clouds and attack them at any moment. But it really looked like their approach went by unnoticed. The Dead Zone was perhaps too big to monitor by now, allowing them to pass by unnoticed.

Zac was about to return to his meditation, but something in the distance caught his attention.

"Wait, stop for a second," Zac said as he pointed at a specific spot. "Set down the vessel over there."

He had kept **[Cosmic Gaze]** running to keep watch for any hidden threats. But rather than ghosts, it had allowed him to see something unexpected, a beacon of life in a sea of dour death. Joanna wordlessly changed course, and they landed where he indicated, and Zac's eyes widened with recognition as he looked around. He had been here before.

He had once sat beneath the tree in front of him.

"What is it?" Ogras asked with confusion as Zac walked over to the mutated tree. "We don't really have time for a botanical study."

"I just want to confirm something," Zac said as he closed his eyes with one hand against the magnificent tree.

It was really the same one. He had found this mysterious tree once more, hidden in a sea of death. It felt like there was some sort of fate behind the second encounter.

"Hopefully, you can help me in the future," Zac muttered as he ran his fingers across the bark. "I'll come back again after I've dealt with the undead."

"Heavens help us," the demon muttered from the side. "He's lost it."

"Shush," Kenzie said as she kicked Ogras' shin before turning to Zac. "What is it?"

"Life and Death," Zac said as he stepped back onto the leaf. "It's pretty amazing. If I could bring it with me without killing it, I would. I feel I can use it as a base to study my Daos."

Seeing the small beacon of life in the sea of death not only resonated with his Daos, but it also made him remember his Skill Quest. Splitting Life and Death was such an obscure concept, but perhaps this natural oddity might guide him down the right path.

"Take note of this place," Zac said to the Valkyries and his sister. "We need to return after we've dealt with the incursion."

The group kept flying through the Dead Zone, but the dense death attunement was, unfortunately, having an impact on his vessel, drastically slowing its speed. It was still a lot quicker compared to the old disk he had, but it felt like a crawl after the shocking speed it had exhibited when infused with the Dao of the Bodhi.

Zac didn't dare waste his mental energy on speeding up the vessel, though, in case something happened. He knew he was the muscle of the expedition, with the others acting as backup. The delay gave him enough time to finish filling his fifth node on his Draugr side though, allowing him to balance out his two classes at level 80.

He put the 10 points into Dexterity once more before he turned back into his human form. He still didn't want to expose his Draugr side to the undead invaders unless necessary, especially after learning about Catheya and her master. What if that Peak C-grade monster became interested and tracked him down?

He was already traveling in search of something to break through, and wouldn't Zac's body make an interesting study? Even Yrial said so. Zac sighed for the umpteenth time over the fact that there was no one to turn to for help regarding these issues. No old ancestor who could make their problems go away with a wave of his hand. Everything was up to him to solve, but he was out of treasures that could help him become stronger.

He instead turned his attention to the next thing, his skills.

With him having reached Peak mastery of multiple skills along with having evolved, then upgrading his skills was the next logical step. He had already learned some of the paths from Galau and his visit to the undead kingdom, and he had shored up his knowledge from the following encounters.

There were a few ways to upgrade his skills, demanding various degrees of interaction from himself. The simplest method was to adjust the skill fractal so that it would be useable in the E-grade as well. That wasn't to say that his old skills suddenly had turned useless, but there was a limit of how much energy they could contain.

His Miasmic bulwark would only be able to block so much damage, and the wooden hand he conjured with [Nature's Punishment] would only be able to unleash so much destruction. But this could be changed.

The skill fractals were right now like crude drawings placed in the masterpiece that were the intricate E-grade pathways. You could adjust these drawings to blend better, to take advantage of the higher amount of energies that could flow through them. The process of doing this was the same as when he'd manually drawn the pathways for his two classes back in the F-grade.

However, there was no blueprint provided this time. This meant that you were required to not only understand the skill to a great degree, but also how the skill fractals worked. You could actually ruin the skill altogether, forcing you to redraw the fractal from scratch.

Even worse, skill fractals were in a sense perfect as they were provided by the System. So every time you ruined them and remade them from memory, you were bound to add some small imperfections because of your lacking understanding. Too many failures, and the power of the skill might become just a shadow of their original power.

Even then, this method was generally considered the easiest way of progress, but that wasn't really the case for Zac. Most people had grown up in a world of cultivation, spending their entire childhood studying fractals and pathways and the Dao in preparation for when they could finally start cultivating. He could still somewhat intuitively understand what parts of the fractals did, but his understanding was still far worse compared to any average cultivator in this regard.

The second method was to upgrade through epiphany, and Zac guessed that this was his best shot at rapid progress. The odds of having such an Epiphany mid-battle like a Dao Epiphany were pretty slim, but there were treasures that could put you in a unique state of mind.

Galau had also mentioned Skill Arrays, which was something that most forces and academies used. You could even say they were an integral part of a proper Heritage. They were like assisted guidance systems that helped you upgrade certain skills. They resulted in slightly worse compatibility compared to doing it yourself, but they would drastically reduce the risk of messing up, ruining the skills altogether.

There were even generalist arrays that worked on most skills, but they put much greater demand on your personal understanding of runes, patterns, the Dao, and fractals. In either case, it was moot, since Zac had no way to get his hands on these kinds of arrays at the moment.

Finally, there were the Skill Upgrade Quests that the System would reward, but the first one wasn't until level 90 as far as he knew. It was usually a branched quest that would either allow him to upgrade a skill or transform it, and that this was the best chance to fuse two of his skills into one.

Certainly, one could fuse skills without the assistance of the

System, but you needed an extremely strong understanding to do something like that. It was probably something better left alone until you had reached a much higher understanding.

Perhaps Yrial could assist him a bit the next time he entered the Inheritance, but that was still a decade away.

Zac didn't really have a lot of options right now, but he kept looking inward at his skill fractals and their connection to the pathways. He figured that if he got a better grasp of the fractals and how they were lacking compared to the pathways, then he might be more likely to be able to gain an epiphany mid-battle.

Sort of like the heat of the battle was how he'd managed to form the bronze flashes inside the Tower.

However, no matter how hard he tried over the following hours, he simply couldn't make heads or tails about it. He would no doubt be able to redraw all the fractals in his sleep by now, but that didn't really help him in his predicament.

"I think we're just two hours away by foot now," Kenzie suddenly said, waking Zac up from his reverie. "What do you want to do?"

"Let's go by foot from here," Zac said after some hesitation. "We'll see if we can reach the core unnoticed."

GO TIME

Zac wasn't confident that their mobile illusion array would do them any good against the defenses of the Undead Empire. He figured that they would be able to hide more efficiently as a small group of humanoids in a forest that was no doubt teeming with Zombies, rather than on top of a lustrous giant leaf ripping through the otherwise dour sky.

There was no way that the Lich King hadn't erected any defensive arrays now that the realignment was so close, but there was a very big difference between a passively running array and an array actively controlled by an Array Master. Perhaps they would be able to crack open the entrance if they caught the Lich King by surprise.

Besides, they would have to be on the ground anyway if they wanted to deploy any of the Array Breakers they had brought.

The group landed inside the forest, and everyone already wore some sort of equipment that hid their life-attuned aura. Ogras and Zac increased the effect even further by adding a layer of shadows and dousing them in his Dao Field for the Fragment of the Coffin.

The coffin wasn't strictly death-attuned just yet, but it was death-adjacent, and it helped them blend into the surroundings a lot better than if they just walked in as is. They soon got a chance at testing the efficacy of their disguise as they spotted a mob of Zombies lumbering about. But they could breathe out in relief when their small group walked by completely unnoticed.

The Zombies treated them as though they were air, and the group kept running further toward the core of the Dead Zone. Of course, that small encounter wasn't enough for them to relax. Those Zombies were still unawakened, which meant they were as dumb as they came. Real Revenants might not be able to sense that their group was alive, but they would no doubt understand that something was amiss with a group of strangers running toward their stronghold.

Luckily, it seemed that the undead hadn't bothered planting any spectral scouts in the forest. Perhaps they figured that the increasingly dense number of Zombies would be enough as an early warning, or perhaps they didn't even care if anyone came all this way, confident in their defensive capabilities.

But the group of eleven still avoided any undead they spotted as they inched closer to their target. It forced them to take some detours, but it still only took them three hours until they reached their target, the true inner sanctum of the Dead Zone. Or rather the barrier that blocked them off from it.

Massive pitch-black runes hovered in the air, each of them humming with strength. They formed a long wall that stretched kilometers in each direction, and Zac could vaguely spot massive Unholy Beacons some distance behind them, no doubt powering them with a steady flow of power.

There was no physical wall acting as a foundation, but that didn't mean the barrier would be any easier to deal with. This was something that made use of the Dead Zone itself, and it would no doubt require a massive blast to crack open. However, reaching the target wasn't the only trouble they faced.

There was also the even thicker wall of Zombies that stood between them and the array. The density of the undead lumbering about in the forest had gradually increased as the density of Miasma did, and they currently had Zombies within thirty meters in pretty much every direction by now. However, they almost formed a solid wall of putrid flesh along the defensive array in front of them.

The swarm of Zombies was well over twenty meters thick, and it seemed to stretch endlessly in each direction along the barrier. Millions and millions of former citizens of Earth turned into nothing more than an unliving fortification. At least that was what Zac figured they were, as this band of Zombies definitely hadn't come about naturally.

"How the hell are we supposed to sneak in like this?" Ogras spat. "There is no way that the people inside won't be alerted if we start killing this rabble."

"Can't we just walk past them?" Emily asked. "Isn't that what our talismans are for?"

"No way," the demon said as he threw a humored glance at the teenager. "They're stupid, but not *that* stupid. Besides, I bet there is some fail-safe for that."

"Some sort of diversion?" Zac muttered.

He briefly considered using the thing he had gotten from Void's Disciple, but he eventually decided against it. This was still just an outer shield, and the real forces of the Lich King were nowhere in sight. Using that thing right now was a waste, and it was better left to use as a surprise when Zac was right in front of his target.

Besides, Void had said that he was meant to activate the black crystal inside a "castle," and there was nothing of the sort in sight just yet. That point alone made Zac a bit worried. It meant that his whole idea to sneak attack the leaders had already failed. Even if they rushed inside after blasting through the wall, the Lich King would probably be ready to meet their assault.

Still, they had managed to get pretty close without being noticed, which was worth something. It would be too late to recall larger forces to defend by this point, and there was no way undead general stationed in the horde would be able to come back in time.

"Can't be anything big," Ogras slowly said. "We want these rotting bastards out of the way without causing a scene. We need to hit the shield before the owners inside notice us. If they take active control, it will be twice as hard to break inside."

"What about Miasma Crystals?" Emily ventured. "We throw a few of them to the left and one to the right. I heard that Zombies search out things that benefit their strength instinctively. Shouldn't that split them up?"

The idea of throwing out Miasma Crystals as breadcrumbs sounded extraordinarily stupid, but it quickly became apparent that no one had a better idea. Joanna proposed they dig a tunnel, but Zac remembered how the slightest tremor in the earth had been immediately exposed by geomancers when fighting the second beast wave.

Ogras also suggested for Zac to somehow telepathically control them in his Draugr form, but he simply had no way to do that.

Though, to be fair, turning into a Draugr might push the Zombies away, as there was a massive inherent difference in caste between the noble Races and some newly turned Zombies without sapience. But he wanted to keep that as an ace in the hole, so they had no better option than going with Emily's plan.

Dozens of F-grade Miasma Crystals soared through the air and landed in the densely packed groups of Zombies as Zac started to throw them to their left and right. It took a few seconds for the undead to register what was going on, but they slowly started to congregate toward the energy-rich crystals on the ground.

It created a five-meter-wide corridor almost completely devoid of Zombies in front of them, and the group wordlessly rushed forward to set up an illusion array right next to the barrier. A few Zombies seemed to feel that something was amiss, but they soon joined the others in the struggle for Miasma Crystals after they couldn't see anything odd in their surroundings.

This close to the barrier, they could finally spot an almost completely transparent black film blocking them like a wall, proving the shield covered every inch of the core zone. Kenzie set up a set of mobile arrays that blocked out their presence, meaning the Zombies wouldn't find them even if they lost interest in the Miasma Crystals.

However, there was clearly no love lost between the Zombies, and the attraction of the crystals was beyond their expectation as undead fought tooth and nail for them. It was just a matter of time before the ruckus was exposed or the Zombies started getting ripped apart, so they were still against the clock.

The group had gone over the plan multiple times on the leaf and as they ran through the forest, and now was the time to put it into action. Zac and Ogras were both imbued with a fiery axe, whereas Kenzie got the one crackling with lightning that improved Intelligence and Wisdom. This was the benefit Emily had gotten from upgrading the proficiency of the skill. She could now boost three people in total, but she was only able to get one boost per type.

The six Valkyries each took out a large engraved spike and stuck it into the ground, forming a perfect circle within their bubble. They then placed their massive bulwarks outside them to prevent any interference while further isolating their small circle. Kenzie withdrew a densely inscribed skull that emitted scorching heat, along with a bunch of Flame Crystals they had dug up from Zac's new mine in the underworld.

Six chains were attached to the skull in various positions, and the six Valkyries each took one and attached it to their respective spike, effectively fettering the head to the ground. Kenzie made sure that the inscriptions held and that the array flags were properly planted, and Zac couldn't help but look at the odd scene with bemusement.

This was one of the Array Breakers he had found in the mentalist's Spatial Ring, and Kenzie had chosen this one for two reasons. First of all, it was fire-attuned, which seemed pretty effective against the undead based both on Zac's experiences and looking at the Church of the Everlasting Dao. Secondly, it was one of the breakers that were simple to use, with the downside that it carried low strength on its own.

Its strength was rather based on the power of the people infusing it. The users would feed it with their energy and Dao, and the array would convert it into an attack especially suited for burning a hole in an array. It would allow Zac to not only take advantage of his recent boost in energy circulation but also release a blast of power without wasting any of his long-cooldown attacks on the wall.

"Give me a few seconds," Kenzie said as she pushed one spike after another down into the ground, forming yet another array surrounding the treasure in the middle. "Get ready to infuse the main array with your Cosmic Energy and Daos. The more chaotic, the better."

Ten spikes turned to dozens that embedded themselves in the ground as Kenzie threw them in rapid succession, forming an increasingly large array that soon enough spread even outside the confines of their illusion array. Small spikes shot out between the Zombies with pinpoint precision and lodged themselves in the ground.

"These spikes will destabilize the energy flow in the area, making it harder for the shield to feed off the ambient energy. They might even disconnect this section of the barrier from the Unholy Beacons. They will burn out quickly, though, so you need to activate the Array Breaker the moment it's ready," she said.

Zac and the others nodded, and Cosmic Energy was already coursing through Zac's body as he readied himself.

"Go!" Kenzie said the moment she had finalized connecting the inscribed skull with the six spikes that the Valkyries controlled.

Zac, Ogras, Kenzie, and Joanna placed their hands on the skull, which was as large as an elephant's, and the whole area started to twist and turn as a massive congregation of power started building inside the hollow head. Its eyes started to flicker with chaotic colors as the Daos of the four clashed with increasing ferocity. It even started to vibrate, causing the chains to rattle, but it still seemed like it could swallow more.

Emily was instead dancing around inside the array, waving her tomahawks, and Zac realized that his mind felt extremely refreshed. Whatever she was doing was actually dispersing the negative effect of standing inside Miasma. It was a lot like [Hatchetman's Spirit] in that regard, as it felt like the inhospitable atmosphere had suddenly turned into something uniquely suited to them.

It helped Zac move his energy with a lot more vigor as an unceasing torrent of energy coursed through his arm and into the inscribed head. He infused the head with his Fragment of the Axe as well, as he felt that Dao Fragment would increase the destructive might the most. In a perfect world, he would have wanted to use all three Fragments, but he simply wasn't able to do that.

The hollow skull was quickly approaching the limits of what it could contain, while the six remaining Valkyries focused on keeping the supportive array flags stable. The ground shuddered and heaved by this point, and the Zombies finally realized something was amiss.

There was no way for the illusion array to block out the terrifying amounts of energy they were churning inside, as it was affecting the whole area by this point, and the Zombies roared as they charged at the source of the disturbance.

"Shield!" Joanna shouted, and six streams of silver Cosmic Energy flowed from the Valkyries and fused to form a sturdy wall surrounding them, using the chitinous shields as a base.

The Zombies desperately tried to cut through, but the War Array the Valkyries had gotten from the quest showed its worth, as it didn't even shudder from the onslaught. Of course, these Zombies were far from being the elites of the Undead Empire, but there were over a hundred attackers in just a second.

The stalwart shield allowed Zac and the others to wholeheartedly focus on the skull, and it finally rose into the air, stretching all the chains taut.

"Get ready to run!" Kenzie said as she swiped straight at the chains, breaking them in three swift motions.

A piercing screech seemingly from the abyss emerged from the mouth of the skull, and a blinding flame illuminated the sky as it exploded into motion. Zac's heart lurched when he saw that the flaming skull actually flew straight into the sky, and he started to worry that the weird treasure would simply fly away. However, his worries were alleviated when Kenzie threw out a flaming spike straight at the closest of the black runes that was twenty meters away from them.

It looked like the skull had found its prey, as it immediately did a 180 and shot toward the barrier with extreme momentum. It instantly broke the sound barrier as it flew toward the wall, causing waves of multifarious flames to incinerate everything close to its path, including dozens of Zombies.

A terrifying blast spread out the next moment as the flaming skull actually bit into the black fractal, and Zac's eyes lit up when a small crack in the rune appeared in an instant. The crack quickly grew as the flames increased in intensity seemingly without limit, and Zac took a steadying breath as [Verun's Bite] appeared in his right hand.

It was go time.

83

PILLARS AND BEAMS

The whole array of black runes lit up in an instant, but the runes around Zac's group were still dim thanks to Kenzie's efforts. However, explosions erupted in every direction as the array flags burnt out in quick succession. Thankfully, the barrier couldn't hold it any longer, and it suddenly shattered as the maw of the fiery skull closed with a snap.

A massive crack provided an ingress for the group, and they heedlessly braved the flames as they rushed inside, protected by the still-running War Array of the six Valkyries. A victorious roar sent a fiery discharge in each direction before the skull crumbled to white ash. Zac summoned **[Nature's Barrier]** and blocked out the fallout, but the Zombies on the other side of the array weren't so lucky.

Hundreds of them were incinerated in one fell swoop, and the shield had already mended itself before any new unliving could take their place. It looked like these pitiful creatures really weren't considered part of the Undead Empire just yet, as they were utterly incapable of following Zac and the others through the intangible barrier.

Zac knew that an advanced force like the Undead Empire would be able to erect arrays that could discern friend and foe, especially when there was such a striking difference between the living and the dead. But it looked like the Lich King had elected to keep even his own outside the core area. Perhaps too many Zombies would be a drain on the limited Miasma in the atmosphere or something.

Of course, it wasn't like there weren't any Zombies on the other side of the enclosure.

Large mobs of the undead were already rushing toward them from the distance, while Zac spotted clumps of Corpse Golems guarding the Unholy Beacons. These ones were the real deal as well, the crafty and ruthless elite Zombies that probably were on the precipice of evolving into sapient Revenants.

Zac flashed away and gripped one of the Zombies, who shrieked as he tried to dig his rotting teeth into Zac's arm. Its assault was obviously futile with Zac's 2,000 plus Endurance, though. Zac shook the undead man for a bit to make him release his grip before he flung him toward the defensive array.

The nearby Zombies roared in anger as they tried to mob Zac in retaliation, but they were dismembered by a few lazy swings of his axe. The projectile Zombie flew straight through the array, confirming Zac's guess. It worked like his own [Town Defense Array], only keeping people out in one direction. It was valuable information in case they were forced to flee later on.

"Let's go," Zac said. "They definitely know we're here by now."

The squad started running toward the shining incursion pillar that was barely discernible in the distance through the thick Miasmic haze. However, they barely had time to move a few hundred meters before the sky changed, and one aquamarine fractal after another started appearing.

These runes were clearly not the Realignment Array, but rather something meant to deal with intruders.

"Uynala, you were right," Ogras groaned. "It's not worth it."

"What?" Kenzie asked with a frown from the side.

Zac ignored the two as he activated [Cosmic Gaze] and turned it toward the sky. The arrays were obviously made from Miasma, but Zac frowned when he saw that they contained something that could best be described as condensed death, and this weird energy was quickly accumulating more power. It was like the array was taking the death-attuned Cosmic Energy and taking away the energy itself, leaving just the concept behind.

He didn't know what use that stuff was, but it felt extremely dangerous. He needed to stop them from activating.

"Destroy the Unholy Beacons," Zac said as a massive fractal edge grew out from [Verun's Bite].

He activated [Loamwalker] the next second, and within moments, he found himself in front of the closest beacon. It was more than three times the size of the mobile pillars he had seen so far during the two invasions of his island, and the hair on his arms stood on end from the extremely condensed Miasma surrounding it.

A fractal blade grew from his axe, and a wide arc swept through the guarding golems, causing them to fall apart into stale clumps of meat. A small amount of energy entered his body, but Zac frowned when he realized that it didn't target any specific node in his body like he would have assumed. It instead started to spread out across his limbs until it finally started to dissipate.

Did he need to direct the energy himself?

Zac quickly took hold of the energy and condensed it into a ball, and it was thankfully an easy process to figure out the next step. He quickly pushed the ball of energy through his pathways until he felt some pliability from a node in his left leg. But he barely had time to push the small amount of energy inside the node before almost a hundred translucent green balls poured out of the massive brazier at the top of the beacon.

They caused an extremely uncomfortable weight to descend on him, and it felt like a mix of mental and physical pressure. However, Zac's Wisdom had shot all the way up to 800 over the past days, a number that even most early E-grade mentalists would be hard-pressed to match. Combine that with a soul that had been forced to endure the continuous pressure from the Splinter of Oblivion for months, and he was starting to truly shore up his old weakness.

He didn't even need to infuse [Mental Fortress] with the Fragment of the Bodhi to effortlessly shrug off the mental pressure, and a few quick swings caused the tower to crumble. However, his mind warned him of danger the moment the beacon started to collapse, and he hurriedly flashed away.

It was just in time as well, as a chain of explosions turned the whole area around the beacon into a frozen hellscape. At least half of the odd spheres had been filled with ice-attuned energies, it seemed, and while their individual destructiveness wasn't too threatening, they still were a cause for concern when there were almost a hundred of them balled together.

Zac glanced at the sky and was relieved to see that a handful of the newly appeared fractals had dissipated, but most were still going strong as they condensed their energies. One of them suddenly activated, and a wave of darkness shot down at Ogras and Kenzie, who were whittling down another one of the beacons.

Ogras had already taken out the Corpse Golems and was working on the tower, whereas Kenzie waved her staff to conjure dozens of fireballs in an instant that shot out at an incoming wave of Zombies. The flames seemed to have a life of their own as they hopped from target to target and caused an extremely impressive amount of destruction for how little energy she seemed to have consumed.

However, there was no time to admire his sister's growth, as the wave from the sky was almost upon them.

"Watch out!" Zac shouted at the demon, who was immediately swallowed whole by a shroud of shadows.

Another ball of shadows started to rise around Kenzie, but she had already flickered away in a gust of wind, narrowly avoiding the darkness. The demon wasn't as lucky, as he was actually forced out of the shadows a few meters away from his earlier position as the wave swallowed him whole. The area turned back to normal the next moment, but Zac knew something was wrong when he saw how pale the demon was.

He flashed over and was alarmed to sense an overwhelming death-attuned aura coming from the demon. It was like he was being forcibly converted into a Revenant in front of his eyes, and the process looked extremely painful. Zac quickly grabbed the demon's shoulder and flooded him with the Fragment of the Bodhi as he gobbled up the large amounts of death-attuned energies for himself.

He felt a bit queasy from the incompatible energy, but his [Void Heart] would deal with it soon enough.

"Urh," the demon groaned as he spat a ball of black phlegm. "Zombifying beams. Just great. Thanks, by the way."

"No problem." Zac smiled. "Thank you for protecting Kenzie."

"What protecting, just making a fool of myself," Ogras grunted as he shakily got back to his feet.

The next moment, he disappeared and reappeared next to the Unholy Beacon once more. A storm of strikes slammed into the base as a forest of shadow spears rose to meet the falling balls, piercing all of them with expert accuracy. The beacon toppled the next moment, but the demon was obviously out for blood, or at least unwilling to let the arrays in the sky keep shooting at them.

The demon didn't even stop to loot the potentially valuable pillar as he shot toward the next one, repeating the process. However, the arrays in the sky were all starting to power up by now, and they clearly didn't only rely on the closest Unholy Beacons for power. Staying around and taking out the pillars was a waste of time, and the group instead started rushing toward the core.

Wave after wave of elite Zombies appeared to impede their path, but Zac's group was like a grindstone that turned anything that came too close into shreds. Zac was occasionally shooting out a fractal blade or flashed away to take out another beacon, but he mainly relied on the others to break open a path so that he could reserve his strength.

It was rather Kenzie and Joanna who did the heavy lifting. The Chief Valkyrie seemed to have gained a repeatable area strike upon reaching level 50, and she was using it freely at the moment. It was a pretty odd one as well. She kept conjuring a silver ball in the air in front of her, but the moment it appeared, she attacked it with a powerful stab with her spear.

The ball cracked like a broken mirror, and sharp shards reminiscent of all kinds of crude weapons shot into the Zombie horde with even greater momentum than her strike had. Some of the shards were shaped like spear tips, and they punched gruesome holes into the undead. Others were bladed weapons like swords or axes, and these shards cleanly cut limbs or heads off any Zombie they passed.

Zac shot a surprised glance at Joanna, feeling that she was walking down an interesting path. It made him think of the War Stele and the Dao of War, one of the possible upgrade paths of the various weapon-based Daos. If Joanna managed to walk down that road, she would have a chance to become as powerful as the great general in the vision.

Kenzie's side was an ever-changing scene as well, where the undying got incinerated one second and flash-frozen the next. She had also summoned a mysterious wheel that hovered above her head, and every time it turned 90 degrees, a devastating blast from one of the four elements was launched.

It reminded Zac of a drone as it kept pace with Kenzie, but he could quickly confirm that it was a construct made from attuned energies with the help of **[Cosmic Gaze]**. Zac didn't understand what kind of skill it was, but it felt a bit like the massive demonic angel that Iz Tayn had summoned. Was the wheel some sort of companion, but perhaps more akin to a golem than an elemental?

However, while the recent improvements of the two were impressive, their low levels was an undeniable weakness. Each strike could only kill so many of the unthinking rabble, but there was an unending stream of them that kept trying to tire them out before they reached the core. At least that was what Zac thought the undead were trying to do.

They were beset by an endless number of elite Zombies as they ran, but they had not encountered a single Revenant or another elite unit of the Undead Empire since taking down the Unholy Beacons. Worse yet, the group was constantly bombarded by waves of death from above, and they often had to interrupt their strike to desperately scramble out of the way.

Kenzie was already panting from the exertion, but she insisted that she could keep going. Zac didn't say anything, as he knew they were trying to help as much as they could while allowing him to save his strength. Because these waves of unliving were just the appetizer, whereas the main course was finally coming into vision just ahead.

A massive black fortress, reaching toward the sky with a backdrop consisting of an aquamarine pillar that pierced the Miasmic haze.

This was the first structure Zac's group had encountered inside the Dead Zone, aside from the endless ruins of the countries it had gobbled up. But Zac guessed that this monstrous structure would have no problem housing every single elite that had been brought over from the undead kingdom of the Zecia Sector, along with tens of thousands of the best Zombies who had been "recruited" here on Earth.

It might even be more apt to call it a city than a castle if it weren't for the fact that it really seemed to be one cohesive structure. Its pitch-black wall rose almost twenty meters into the air, wrought from some stone that Zac didn't recognize. It was covered in both turquoise fractals and intricate carvings reminiscent of European Gothic architecture.

Dozens of towers protruded from within the walls as well, each of them well over a hundred meters tall. They all seemed to house terrifyingly powerful Unholy Beacons at the top, probably responsible for providing energy for the whole building. They almost looked like fountains as dense clouds of Miasma billowed down along their lengths as though they were liquid.

They could vaguely spot the roof of many more sections, but the towering wall made it hard to make out any real impression of the layout inside. However, finding their way inside was the least of their concerns at the moment, as they first needed to break through the army waiting at the wall walk.

Thousands of Revenants, Golems, and Corpselords stood at the front, their killing intent palpable as they looked down at their small squad from above.

"Super Brother-Man, or should I say Zachary Atwood?" A decrepit voice full of power flowed down from up high, which helped Zac spot an all-too-familiar hooded being. "You came after all, not that you had much choice. But you'll find the Undead Empire a completely different target than the invaders you've fought until now."

Fury surged in Zac's chest as he looked at the man on the wall.

It was him. The Lich King.

84

WALLBREAKERS

It was the man who had almost killed Alea. The man who had left him no recourse but to either let her die or turn her into a Spirit Tool, not to mention causing the creeping death of their whole planet.

His appearance was all too familiar, as it was the very same one as the four ghosts he had fought back in Port Atwood. Zac had already known that the hooded beings he killed were clones or projections, as destroying the four identical copies provided no Cosmic Energy. He had also suspected him to either be the Lich King or one of his generals, but it looked like he had his answer now.

He was accompanied by a powerful-looking female to his left, and a wretched ghost to his right. If one of the generals was occupied in the Zombie horde, then these two might just be the last two generals of the undead incursion. The Abbot had killed two of the six when they tried to take down Mount Everlasting Peace, and Zac had dealt with Mhal himself, leaving just three. A host of ghosts hovered behind them in the air as well, perhaps there to provide the three with War Arrays.

Anger burned inside his chest, and his mind worked a mile a minute in figuring out a way to get up on that wall walk to rip that man into pieces. However, he was surprised to sense the demon next to him sporting a similar killing intent.

"It's that bitch," Ogras muttered from the side, his eyes trained on the ghastly woman standing to the side of the Lich King.

She looked almost like a pale human with long, black, flowing hair, but her hands were replaced by grisly claws with unnaturally long fingers.

"You know her too?" Kenzie asked with surprise. "She's the one who almost killed me and Ilvere. I thought we had killed her by detonating the mecha."

"All the more reason for me to skewer her," the demon muttered. "That crazy banshee almost caught me inside an array when we fought last time. This time, we'll see who will be the Scuttlecreeper and who'll be the Gwyllgi."

A roar from behind interrupted their discussion, and Zac turned around to see that the Zombies pretty much had caught up with them. There were thankfully no Zombies between themselves and the wall, though. Perhaps the Lich King was afraid of friendly fire.

The undead saw Zombies as something between children and potential recruits, after all. They both were and weren't part of the Undead Empire just yet, and while they wouldn't really mourn their true death, they also weren't keen on killing them with their own hands.

The six Valkyries set up their War Array once more, and they started a methodical slaughter of anyone who came too close, under the direction of Joanna, allowing Zac and the others to focus on the castle.

"Do you people have any better ideas than charging right at them?" Zac asked.

"They are obviously prepared for a siege," the demon said with a frown. "I can't sense anything, but I bet this place is covered in both defensive and offensive arrays."

"He's right," Kenzie said from the side. "The wall itself is full of array flags. Those huge towers contain offensive arrays as well."

"We can't dally too long," Joanna said from the side as she looked behind them. "We will be overrun in a few minutes without assistance."

"I can't keep boosting you either for very long," Emily muttered. "It drains way more energy now than it did before. Perhaps because you're E-grade and boost me 100 points?"

Zac's brows rose in confusion as he looked over. Her skill was supposed to boost his attributes by 10% after having been upgraded to

High mastery. However, a glance at his Status screen confirmed that it truly only gave him 100 Strength.

Perhaps there were limits to how much the skill could provide, and 100 points was no doubt a huge amount for most people in the F-grade. It made sense that she couldn't use it on a B-grade monster and gain tens of thousands of points too, which would allow her to skip multiple grades and kill D-grade Hegemons without much effort.

But now was not the time to experiment with the limits of Emily's supportive capabilities.

"Let me see how the arrays look," Zac said as he shot forward, a surge of warmth entering his back as Emily reapplied her buff.

A pillar of light rose toward the sky as a shockingly large fractal edge appeared. It glistened with sharpness as it stretched almost a hundred meters into the air, far exceeding the height of the wall. [Chop] might not be able to evolve, but just being able to cram five times more energy into the skill fractal before he lost control made a huge difference.

The ground cracked for dozens of meters in each direction as Zac launched himself into the sky, and the air screamed as he swung the towering fractal edge straight down toward the Lich King, seemingly intent on cutting the whole fortress in two. The area heaved as a black shield materialized just before the blade would hit them, forcing Zac's edge to a stop.

The clouds of Miasma churned as blade and shield met, and winds buffeted the Zombies who were approaching. Zac grunted in annoyance, though, as he was incapable of cutting the shield open even after having infused the skill with the Fragment of the Axe. He lost control a second later, and the blade dematerialized while the barrier remained.

However, while the shield held against Zac's strike, it didn't do so effortlessly. It didn't crack, but it did shudder and fluctuate a bit, and Zac noticed that a few of the core members of the incursion took a step back or reached for their weapons upon witnessing the strike. The shield wasn't invincible after all.

It looked like the Lich King hadn't completely ruined his finances when erecting the defensive arrays around his fortress. Perhaps he had spent too much of his invasion budget on the massive fractal in the sky and thousands of Unholy Beacons. This was the only reason Zac had a chance at taking them down at all, as there were obviously way more powerful arrays than this readily available in the undead kingdoms.

But those were too expensive to bring, and a kingdom would rather cut their losses than overinvest in an incursion.

"Not quite enough, Monarch-Select," the Lich King snorted as a green fractal appeared in front of him.

He reached out a withered hand and tapped it, and a massive copy appeared above one of the Array Towers the next second. Danger screamed in Zac's mind as the fractal started humming with power, and a torrent of what looked like radioactive toxins shot toward him while he was still in midair.

Another fractal blade shot into the array with tremendous speed, this time forming a stab aimed right at the Lich King's head. The Lich welcomed the strike without a care, and the shield unfortunately held against the assault once more. However, piercing the shield with a normal [Chop] had never been Zac's intent.

He shot away from the rebound like a bullet, narrowly dodging an acid beam that would have swallowed him whole if he hadn't reacted in time. It was the downside of [Loamwalker]; the skill didn't do him much good while in midair.

However, Zac could always move around with the help of [Chop] as long as he had some fixtures to generate momentum with. He could probably even generate some push by simply swinging in the air quickly enough. He landed some distance from the wall and flashed away, appearing next to his squad the next moment.

They were currently embroiled in a moving battle where they kept running back and forth while keeping a safe distance from the fortress' wall while dodging the constant blasts from the fractals in the sky.

"It's strong," Ogras muttered as he threw out a barrage of shadows at a clump of Zombies. "But not impenetrable. What about that thing you used in Base Town?"

"It's too soon," Zac said with a shake of his head after sending a mental thread into his Spatial Ring. "It is still drained from the last strike. I'll have to use [Nature's Punishment]."

"Wait," Kenzie said. "I still have a few ideas. We should use some treasures so you can save your strength."

"What do you need us to do?" Zac asked, agreeing immediately.

"Can you hold their attacks off for a few seconds while stationary if we get closer?" Kenzie asked.

"Those Array Towers are pretty scary, but it shouldn't be a problem." Zac nodded. "Worst case, I'll have to use a defensive treasure."

He was out of powerful offensive treasures from the mentalist's collection, but he still had a few defensive ones. He figured he might as well use them sooner rather than later. Being Early E-grade treasures, they would become useless soon enough with his rapid growth in attributes in either case.

"Good," Kenzie said as she took out a golden eye that was a bit reminiscent of the skill that the mentalist had used to fracture his soul during the climb. "This thing should both weaken the shield and give its controller a backlash."

"What if it fails?" Joanna asked with some worry.

"The drones are not completely restored, but they'll be able to launch one strike," Kenzie slowly said before she turned to Ogras and Zac. "If that fails as well, you'll have to do the rest yourself."

"What are you doing playing with those cursed things anyway, girl? Don't you know you'll draw the ire of the Heavens by getting involved with that stuff?" the demon muttered.

"It's not like we have a lot of options right now," Kenzie said as she put away her staff. "Oh, and this attack will cost some of the Soul Crystals."

"That's fine." Zac nodded, feeling it was worth the exchange if it gave a shot at wounding the soul of the Lich King. "Ogras and I will guard Kenzie; the rest stay behind."

The group didn't tally any longer as they rushed toward the wall as one. A storm of attacks quickly descended from the undead elites at the wall walk, but between **[Nature's Barrier]** and Ogras' ability to slightly move the trio by holding their shoulders, they reached their targeted distance without wasting too much energy.

Of course, the attacks were not the full force of the Undead Empire, as neither the Lich King nor the generals had made a move. That changed, though, as the Lich King swung his hand, causing a full five of the Array Towers to light up and form a series of different runes in the sky. Each of them contained even more power than the toxic attack from earlier, far exceeding Zac's expectations.

Zac's eyes widened as he turned to his sister, who was fast at work with the golden eye.

"How long?"

"Ten seconds," Kenzie said as a sheen of perspiration covered her forehead, mostly from the pressure of the situation, Zac guessed.

The two generals, at least Zac assumed that the unmoving ghost to the Lich King's side was a general as well despite his weak energy signature, were thankfully still unmoving. Zac still gave up any thought of defending that long with the help of [Nature's Barrier], as the arrays alone would prove too much to handle.

His defensive skill in his human class was designed to withstand many smaller hits, not to take on extremely powerful blasts like this. His Draugr side would probably be able to deal with it, but it was still too early to expose that side. He instead activated one of the rings on his finger. A golden gate appeared in front of them, each door branded with a fractal that emitted extremely dense power.

"What?!" the Lich King exclaimed, seemingly taken by surprise for the first time since they arrived.

Zac wasn't surprised, as the quality of his defensive treasures wasn't something that should exist on a newly integrated world, perhaps not in the Zecia Sector at all. But it was too late to cancel the attacks as they shot toward the defensive treasure. The whole area was suffused in a storm of chaotic energies the next moment, but the divine gate held fast, protecting the trio behind it.

However, the threat wasn't over, as Zac sensed something that he had been ready for the whole time. He stomped on the ground with his full force, causing a massive explosion that spread out in each direction. Rampant waves of his Dao spread through the cracks, as Zac had flooded his leg with the Fragment of the Bodhi as well, and Zac felt a small amount of Cosmic Energy entering his body.

Kenzie hadn't been prepared for the massive shockwave, and she helplessly fell over, barely managing to hold on to the Array Breaker.

"Sorry, there are ghosts in the ground," Zac explained, and Ogras instantly disappeared.

He reappeared among Emily and the Valkyries the next moment, just in time to rip two spectral assassins to pieces with a barrage of swings. A vast sea of shadows spread out from their position the next moment, no doubt making it impossible for any more backstabs to take place. Zac had already seen this tactic being used before, and he wasn't about to fall for that trick, especially not after having learned how to deal with the ghost warriors during his climb.

Kenzie shot another glare at Zac before she crammed a bunch of Soul Crystals into the eye as she realigned the pedestal that came with it. It was covered in dense inscriptions as well, and Zac felt his mind blurring a bit just from looking at them. His sister wasted no time as she adroitly activated the Array Breaker, and a gargantuan sapphire eye appeared in the sky.

The blue eye didn't launch an attack, but it rather shot straight toward the Lich King until it hit the barrier. However, no explosion wreaked havoc on the barrier. It rather looked like the eye had jumped into a pond of water, as the whole barrier started to ripple like a pond as the Array Breaker entered the defensive layer itself.

It somehow seemed to have managed to brand itself on the barrier, like an enormous sticker on the shield that gazed down on the soldiers on the wall. Multiple warriors keeled over from its stare, and even the Lich King hunkered over from its assault.

But the shield still held true.

85

DEATH'S EMBRACE

The Lich King was clearly hit by a psychic attack, but he still seemed very much in control of the shield. And while the barrier had dimmed by a certain degree, it wasn't to the point that a swing or two would break it.

"I guess we have no choice," Kenzie muttered as drones started appearing above her in rapid succession, each of them independently dodging any errant attack that came too close.

This was the first time Zac had seen his sister control more than one or two of them, and his eyes widened when he saw that she had summoned almost a hundred of them and had them coordinate with perfect precision as they charged up a beam. Something like this would no doubt demand great control even if she was assisted by Jeeves.

If he had a tenth of this skill when controlling his Dao Fragments, then he would be nigh unstoppable.

The brand of the eye remained on the barrier no matter what the Lich King tried, but he obviously wasn't dismayed to see the appearance of the drones. Zac's brows rose when he saw the arrays on the wall light up as an uncountable number of the same balls floated out to create a second barrier.

They were similar to those that had poured out of the beacons earlier, but Zac felt some disgust when he noticed there seemed to be screaming faces inside the balls. They only appeared for a second before they were replaced by churning mists, making Zac wonder if his eyes were playing a trick on him.

"These are the souls of your people." The white-clad general laughed to the Lich King's side. "Are you ready to sacrifice them to break our shield? They can still enter the Wheel of Samsara, but not if you destroy them like this."

Zac froze as his eyes widened. Those things were really the souls of former earthlings? Were the Unholy Beacons of the Undead Empire actually powered by souls? Kenzie paled at the words, but Zac put a hand on her shoulder.

"Keep going. I'll deal with these things. Destroying the balls is the best thing we can do for them. Imagine being trapped by these lunatics forever," Zac said as Cosmic Energy surged to the fractal close to his heart. "Besides, there's no way that E-grade people are strong enough to affect the afterlife."

Zac at least hoped that was the case.

There was no time to lose. He felt that these things would impede and weaken the strike of the drones, ruining their best option to break inside the fortress. He needed to do something about it, but a couple of [Chop]s wouldn't be enough. It was a bit of a shame to bring out his big guns early, but it was time to activate [Deforestation].

Zac figured that at least only one of his swings would be wasted on these floating spheres, and his arm grew taut as a huge surge of Cosmic Energy entered the skill fractal. This time he didn't feel any pain or pressure at all, and he swung his axe as he imbued the [Axe of Felling] with his Fragment of the Bodhi.

It wasn't as powerful as his Fragment of the Axe, but that was against normal targets. He wanted to purify these souls and release them to the afterlife if there was such a thing. The Fragment of the Bodhi was no doubt his best chance for accomplishing that.

A green ripple of destruction shot forward, and a deafening wail made Zac stumble for a second. It was the innumerable souls being cut apart, causing a massive backlash to rush back at Zac. If this had been before, then his soul might have actually cracked like during the climb, but now he only felt a splitting headache as he started running forward.

The way was paved, and Kenzie seized the opportunity to follow through on her end. Heat blared down on Zac as dozens of beams of pure energy passed above him before they tore into the weakened shield, right on top of the blue eye. Cracks spread across the whole barrier as multiple fractals on the wall broke.

The wound quickly started to close, though, but a massive torrent of shadows followed the blast, and they wriggled inside the cracks in an instant. A few of the shadows stayed inside the cracks, reminiscent of the scars on Zac's own soul, whereas others continued through the cracks and shot toward the Lich King.

Ogras was obviously not trying to kill him, but rather to divert his attention by forcing him to deal with an attack while controlling the array. The desiccated Lich was unfortunately a powerful E-grade warrior, and a swing of his staff was all that was needed to disperse the dozens of shadowy spears.

However, the small delay was all Zac needed, as his second swing of **[Deforestation]** was already in full force, and the **[Infernal Axe]** unleashed a rampant wave of flames at the weakened barrier. This time, he did utilize the Fragment of the Axe, and the splintered shield was quickly cut to ribbons before the wave continued forward into the physical wall.

The flames climbed up the pitch-black fortification, utterly destroying the remaining fractals and ornamental details before it reached the crest of the wall. A large number of the elite soldiers of the Undead Empire were instantly incinerated, but the Lich King quickly prepared a response. An enormous avatar appeared in the sky, a chained-down corpse that spewed an unending stream of green bile from his mouth.

The putrid liquid fell onto the flames of Zac's attack, and a rapid shockwave of noxious gasses shot down in Zac's direction as the green bile was vaporized by the wave of flames. Zac also sensed that his skill was quenched in one move, though it was slightly expended already from breaking the barrier and destroying half the wall.

The cloud rapidly closed in on him, and Zac's hairs stood on end as he realized just how potent the toxin was. There was no way that his sister or even Ogras would survive taking a single breath of that stuff.

"Back away!" Zac shouted and was relieved to see Kenzie flashing away to rejoin the others, but he didn't follow his own advice.

The Fragment of the Coffin churned through his body, and he thanked the gods for his recent boost to his Vitality as he rushed through the broken barrier before the Lich King had time to repair it. Even then, he felt extremely weakened for a few seconds, but his heart suddenly thumped with increased vigor.

It was the [Void Heart] that had activated once more, and Zac's heart beat with enough force to cause some ripples in the noxious fumes around him. Of course, it was nothing like the massive effect of the man in the vision, but the poisonous vapors right next to him slowly seeped into his pores and were absorbed into his heart. Zac couldn't worry whether this was a good or a bad thing right now, though, as he was in the middle of a battle.

His vision was completely obscured by the extremely dense poison, but he could still spot death-attuned hotspots when activating [Cosmic Gaze]. However, he noticed something odd when he looked around. The general stood like a beacon of power on top of the wall walk, but the Lich King standing next to her barely contained a third of her power.

Had he somehow swapped his real self with a clone the moment Zac lost vision of his target due to the toxic fumes? And where was the original? Zac had planned on taking them all out in one move by unleashing the third swing now that the barrier had been breached, but it looked like that idea was out the window.

It felt a bit of a waste, but he couldn't keep the [Axe of Desolation] on the back burner for too long. If he didn't use the swing within a minute or activated another skill, then the skill would reset and enter its cooldown period. The last thing he was lacking at the moment was Cosmic Energy reserves, so not using the attack with this many targets in front of him would be a huge waste.

He quickly ran up the wall, using the cracks from his previous strikes as a foothold to reach the crest with a few jumps. The ghost was gone, but the female general launched a swipe with enough power to make Zac's danger sense prickle. A shield appeared on his left arm as his amulet transformed into its defensive form.

The massive swipe was blocked without issue, but it had left a few small marks on the surface of [Love's Bond]. Still, seeing his new Spirit Tool get damaged like that filled Zac with a towering fury, and he rushed straight toward the banshee, utterly destroying the clone of the Lich King with a sideswipe, almost as an afterthought.

Zac was in far better control of his emotions now that the Splinter was properly locked up, so he didn't completely give in to his anger. However, that didn't mean he couldn't utilize it, and he channeled his churning killing intent into **[True Strike]**, launching it toward the undead general's back.

With Zac's amount of accumulated killing intent, the skill could barely be considered a feint any longer, but almost a compulsion. It probably felt like a D-grade Hegemon was bearing down on her from behind, and the general couldn't ignore it, just as expected. She quickly turned around to meet the attack as a shimmering shield appeared to block out Zac, but nothing met her furious swipe toward the rear.

The general immediately understood she had been duped, but she didn't have time to retreat before she was slammed in the face with a shield-bash powered by 2,000 Strength and rage. A crunching sound echoed out as she was thrown back like a ragdoll, black ichor spewing in every direction.

Zac couldn't activate **[Loamwalker]** at the moment, but the wall collapsed beneath his feet as he pushed forward to catch up to her flying form, and **[Verun's Bite]** keened as a Bodhi-infused swing ripped through the air. The general unfortunately had enough mental presence to desperately block the swing with her claws.

However, she couldn't match Zac's power output at all and was flung toward the inner section of the fortress with a wail of pain, four of her fingers cleanly cut off. Her bad luck didn't end there, though. The coffin shield quickly returned to its necklace form while Zac growled as he swung **[Verun's Bite]** in a wide arc toward the general. A massive half-moon of death spread out as the final swing of **[Deforestation]** activated.

Zac figured that if he couldn't locate the Lich King, then he might as well just destroy everything.

There was no need to even use **[Hatchetman's Rage]** to activate the third swing this time, his evolved physique more than enough to handle the massive strain. A coruscating wave of destruction ripped into the inner structures of the fortress, causing a chain reaction of buildings collapsing. The ground shuddered as almost a third of the fortress was leveled with one attack.

A series of interlocking shields in front of the Miasma Towers eventually managed to exhaust the energy of the strike, but the ground still shook for a few seconds as a few structurally unsound parts of the fortress collapsed. A shocking surge of Cosmic Energy entered his body, as the [Axe of Desolation] no doubt killed hundreds of the undead who were staying inside the buildings he destroyed, and he directed it toward the node he'd located earlier.

He dispatched the few Revenants foolish enough to actually attack him before he turned his sight inward for a second. He had started feeling some discomfort in his node when he kept infusing it with energy, and it even resisted his attempts at pushing more of his accumulated energies inside.

He wanted to see if it was ready to burst open, but was quickly disappointed. The node looked pretty much the same as before, apart from there being a decent amount of energies swirling about beneath the surface. Even more Cosmic Energy was needed, it seemed, and he tried instilling some of his leftover kill energy again.

This time, it worked, but he really had to cram it inside. It felt like the node was completely full, and he was currently increasing the pressure inside by forcibly instilling more Cosmic Energy. The pain was gradually increasing, but Zac sighed in relief when the pain abated a few seconds after the last of his surplus energy had been pushed inside.

Just how much energy would be needed was something he would have to worry about later, as bursting nodes mid-battle seemed like a spectacularly stupid idea. He instead activated [Cosmic Gaze] again as he looked around for his next target. The incursion was still very much active, which meant that the Lich King still hadn't left Earth even after Zac had made his way inside.

That meant he was currently hiding somewhere in the area, most likely protecting the core of the Realignment Array. The ghost was nowhere to be seen as well, and Zac didn't remember killing it. However, that was of lesser concern, as it didn't seem to be a combat-oriented cultivator. Perhaps he was the strategist of the invasion or something.

However, Zac frowned in annoyance when he noticed that the other general was still alive as well. She had probably managed to flicker away just in time to avoid getting engulfed in the wave of desolation, and was now standing on top of one of the Array Towers.

Her face was completely disfigured, and black ichor stained her dress, and her aura was clearly a bit unstable. She touched an array atop the tower before she floated down again. Zac saw her running further into the fortress before slinking inside a massive palatial section that was built on top of the roof of a more common-looking barrack.

He was just about to go after her, but he sensed a presence to his right.

"You go find the boss," Ogras said as his eyes were trained on the fleeing form of the undead general. "I'll deal with that one. I want to see what she has prepared inside her own lair."

"What about the others?" Zac hesitantly asked. "There might be more of the ghosts."

"They can keep the trash at bay for hours if need be." The demon shrugged. "And your sister has erected some anti-ghost array. If my clan had someone half as talented in formations as that girl back home, we wouldn't just be a bottom-feeding clan at the edge of our planet."

Zac nodded in agreement, but his eyes widened in alarm when he saw the surviving towers all light as one. It looked like the undead planned on unleashing everything in one massive blast before Zac dismantled the rest of the forest.

"Run!" Ogras screamed as he was swallowed by shadows, but Zac shrugged off the demon's attempts at bringing him along.

Instead, he instructed [Love's Bond] to retake its defensive form before activating the circular fractal on its lid. This was the first time Zac actually activated one of the two skills, this one called [Death's Embrace].

The whole coffin shook as the chains that held the lid shut twisted and moved until a small opening appeared. A dense black cloud spread out and rose into the air until it formed a massive torso, making it look like he had summoned a genie. But Zac's heart was still thrown into chaos, as it was no ordinary elemental that had appeared.

It was Alea.

SCOURGE

Zac froze as he looked up at the sky with shock in his eyes, but he quickly regained his wits. However, he couldn't dispel the lingering sense of sourness in his heart as he looked at the familiar figure, as he knew it wasn't Alea come back to life.

The avatar looked a lot like the poison mistress, but there were also undeniable differences. Its eyes didn't have the signature red irises, but they were rather pitch-black and without emotion. The same went for her usually expressive features, as it was the same delicate face but without any of the emotions.

The previously beautiful horns that shimmered in red like a sunset or crystallized fire were replaced by far longer curved horns, these ones tainted by green and purple. She no longer looked like the Torrid Demonkin that all the members of Clan Azh'Rezak belonged to, but was rather an avatar of corruption.

Perhaps this was what she would look like if she had managed to perfect and awaken her poison constitution before she fell, though Zac felt her appearance had more to do with the materials that went into the creation of [Love's Bond].

The skill didn't create a whole body either, which was yet another reminder it wasn't actually Alea. Beneath her upper torso, there was only black smoke that reached down into the coffin. Yet this semi-corporeal avatar was still more than ten meters in height, and it completely blocked Zac from the Array Towers' barrage of attacks that were bearing down on him.

The demonic avatar's arms were formed as well, and they reached up toward the incoming attacks as though she wanted to embrace them. A small sphere appeared in between her outstretched hands, a small seed that started to rapidly spin around its own axis. It was as though this unassuming ball was a black hole, and the air around it started to twist and distort.

The torrential downpour of poison, ice, and Miasma was seemingly unending, but it was all dragged into the small seed. It almost looked like the attacks tried to ignore the suction, but they were distorted and bent beyond their normal shape as they were dragged inside kicking and screaming.

Zac first thought the attacks were weaker than expected, but then a trail of ice broke free from the suction of [Death's Embrace] and slammed into the wall twenty meters from him. The wall immediately froze right over, creating a huge ice block that sealed over thirty unlucky Revenants inside. Even Zac felt some pain in his feet as the ice spread across the wall walk, and he had to circulate some energy to not get frozen as well.

But there were only a few such examples, as most of the attacks were sucked into the rapidly rotating ball. It grew larger and larger until it had turned into a chaotic sun that illuminated the whole fortress in green and aquamarine light. Only then did the offensive arrays run out of steam, and the arrays slowly stopped radiating power.

The ball stayed where it was between the arms of the avatar, though, and Alea's avatar slowly cradled it in her arms as she put her cheek against its surface in an embrace. Zac couldn't help but feel some trepidation as he looked at the ball. If that thing destabilized and exploded, then it would probably be game over even for him. He wouldn't get away without some serious wounds at the least.

But the ball appeared completely inert, and Zac's eyes widened as Alea's maw opened wider and wider until it swallowed the thing whole. It looked absolutely horrific, as the glowing sphere was even larger than Alea's head, but it was still gobbled down whole. The whole avatar lit up with terrifying power, but it didn't unleash a strike or something with the excess energy.

Instead, it started to dissipate into clouds that receded toward the coffin.

Zac couldn't help himself, and he tried to send his mind to the avatar in hopes of getting a response, but Alea didn't so much as look at him. There was no connection like the one he felt with Verun either, and Zac shook his head before he gave up. The lid snapped shut the moment the avatar had returned to the coffin, and Zac didn't even get a chance to look inside.

A few violent shakes rocked the Spirit Tool, but it still seemed fine overall. In fact, it felt like it had just eaten a treasure, and it gained a slight green luster as it turned back to its necklace form again.

This was the first skill of [Love's Bond], a terrifyingly powerful summon that could not only defend against most kinds of attacks, but it could even take the energy for itself. The full-powered blast of the undead fortress would probably have been able to seriously harm him in his human form, but now it was turned into food for his new Spirit Tool instead.

However, while the skill was extremely powerful, it wasn't without its limits. It would take days for the skill to be usable again, perhaps over a week if it took longer to refine the ball of poison. But it was still just what Zac needed. The defensive charges on his robes were essentially useless for someone like him by this point, and this was an excellent replacement.

His life wasn't in danger very often, but when it was, he needed an extremely powerful, and preferably reusable, skill that could turn calamity into opportunity.

Having stolen a full-powered blast of the Array Towers meant he had avoided crisis for now, but he still didn't want to wait around for the towers to recharge for another salvo. He rushed into the fortress toward the closest tower, but he was immediately beset by attacks from hidden mechanisms from every direction as the remaining soldiers on the wall followed him into the fortress, joining the hidden defenders in assaulting him.

Arrows, ice spears, and blobs of poison shot toward him from hidden vantages, and Zac could barely see the dour sky any longer from the chaotic waves of power. It looked like the Lich King had already expected his outer shields to be broken, so he had set up a second layer of defense. These attacks by themselves weren't a threat to someone with 2,000 Endurance, but they still required him to either dodge or block with [Nature's Barrier].

It would slowly drain him of his energy, which had already taken somewhat of a hit from activating [Death's Embrace] and [Deforestation]. However, his recent increase in attributes came with a massive boost to his Cosmic Energy reserves, while his skills were still all F-grade. It meant his endurance was through the roof, and he would be able to keep going for a lot longer even in a frantic situation like this.

A fractal forest rose from the ground, turning the dour fortress into one filled with greenery. It was immediately beset by a storm of Miasma, causing a battle between life and death inside the fortress. However, even if he couldn't utilize the skill to its utmost potential, he still gained most of its benefits.

It felt like he had gained a thousand eyes, and fractal blades started to shoot out in seemingly random directions as his right arm was turning into a blur. One wall after another crumbled, exposing squads of soldiers hidden within.

More Cosmic Energy entered his body, and he kept forcing it into the node in his leg as he reached the first Array Tower. He finally reached a point where he didn't dare to infuse any more, as he clearly felt the node was on the verge of cracking open. He could only reluctantly let the remaining energy dissipate, as this fight was too important.

He couldn't risk crippling himself from an experiment while the Lich King was still standing, but he could always open the node at a later date.

Zac grunted as [Verun's Bite] screamed through the air as he focused his frustration on the tower in front of him instead, but a fractal appeared on the surface of the stones the moment the edge was about to bite into bricks. A concussive mental wave exploded out from the inscription, but Zac was barely fazed as he swung again.

This time, the defensive array was expended, and a fifty-meter fractal edge cut the massive tower clean off after Zac bombarded the skill fractal for [Chop] with Cosmic Energy. Zac really felt that the skill description was right; there was greatness in simplicity. Now that he could control far more energy thanks to his improved pathways, [Chop] had grown all the more lethal.

A terrifying punch followed, and a cloud of dust billowed out as the lofty structure crumbled.

Zac wouldn't stop there, and he destroyed one tower after another in quick succession, taking out over fifty squads of elite soldiers along the way. A shudder in the distance told Zac that Ogras had begun his assault on the general as well, and he couldn't help but worry about the safety of his sister.

However, not only did she carry two of his defensive treasures, but she also had Jeeves to detect any surprises coming her way. He would be able to return and help the squad in case they were starting to get overrun, but he felt that he would be able to deal with this place before it came to that.

A crash resounded next to him as his unique fractal blade blasted through a wall, utterly ripping it apart. Zac had instructed the special fractal blade to cause maximum structural damage, and it was like a hurricane that accompanied him on his rampage through the fortress. It kept expending Cosmic Energy, but Zac had more than enough to spare.

The last Array Tower finally crumbled as Zac unleashed a barrage of furious strikes at its base, and it toppled over and crushed another section of the wall. With the Lich King staying out of the way, he had become completely unstoppable, and the towers didn't even get the chance to launch a second round of attacks before they were all smoldering ruins.

The gargantuan Array Towers also doubled as Unholy Beacons, and their destruction would hopefully put a stop to the various arrays in the area, including the ones in the sky that kept shooting down waves of death toward the ground. It was pretty clear to Zac that the Lich King was an adept Array Master, perhaps even having that as his main class.

So taking out the towers was in a way directly cutting limbs off the incursion leader, as he wouldn't be able to utilize their power any longer.

However, even though a battle between Ogras and the banshee raged in full in the distance, whereas Zac was running around inside the fortress like an enraged bull, the Lich King still hadn't shown his face. Zac could tell the Lich was cooking up something, and his eyes turned toward a seemingly inconspicuous structure to the side of the fortress.

Or rather toward the ground beneath it.

He had kept watch for any suspect energy fluctuations during his rampage, but the Lich King had truly hidden himself well. There were no hotspots of death-attuned energies anywhere that could give Zac a clue to either the location of the incursion leader or the core of the Realignment Array. Zac had first thought the Lich would go to some throne room to prepare his last defense, but the cathedral-like castle in the back of the fortress was completely devoid of both movement and energy.

However, Zac had made some discoveries.

The towers actually seemed to form a pattern around the building he was looking at, almost forming a star shape if you would draw a line between their placements on a map. Zac felt it possible that the Lich King had used those towers as a conduit to the Realignment Array, and he might therefore stay inside that building, where the power would be concentrated.

It was either that or the Lich had fled through a hidden tunnel toward the incursion beacon that was placed some distance behind the fortress.

Zac dismissed his fractal edge as he ran over to the building and simply punched a hole through the wall before he walked in. A normal door might be booby-trapped, so it was better to create his own entrance. However, the structure was just as unexciting on the inside as outside. It seemed to have been some sort of administrative building, with dozens of desks placed with some distance between them.

It was empty now, but the place was stacked with various missives and reports, somewhat skewing Zac's impression of how the invasion had worked. It looked a lot more structured from this side, compared to the seemingly mindless hordes that had spread across the continent like locusts with just the smallest of inputs from a few leaders.

But this showed a lot more refinement.

However, that wasn't why Zac came here, and he walked back and forth through the building until he found what he was looking for.

There really seemed to be something beneath this building, though he couldn't find an entrance. There were occasional waves of death-attuned energies rising from beneath him, indicating something was going on. They were pretty minute, though, and he probably wouldn't have noticed them without [Cosmic Gaze].

The ground shook, and pieces of gravel flew in every direction as Zac started to cut a path down, and he quickly destroyed the floor as he dug a twenty-meter-deep hole. The cuts started to sound hollow at that point, and Zac made his way forward with greater care. Finally, the edge cut straight through the ground, displaying a dimly lit hall beneath.

There was no way his digging had gone by unnoticed, so a sneak attack was out the window. He still took out a corpse from his Spatial Ring and threw it inside, waiting for any potential trap to spring. A thud echoed out a second later, and Zac guessed the hidden chamber had a fifty-meter ceiling.

There was no response, so Zac simply activated [Nature's Barrier] while infusing the always-running [Mental Fortress] with a Dao Fragment as he jumped down. His eyes glared in every direction as he fell, but there was no attack coming at him. Instead, he found himself in an enormous room full of inscribed pillars. The only light came from purple crystals embedded in the room, giving it an oppressive feeling.

Was this the core of the Realignment Array? Zac decisively moved to start destroying the pillars, but he froze when he suddenly heard a voice on the other side of the room.

"It seems I made a miscalculation." A sigh echoed out across the vast chamber. "To think that your power had increased to this degree in just a few short days. It shouldn't be possible, yet here we are. You stole my precious poison corpse and somehow turned it into a treasure shield, and now you are ruining my mission. You truly are a scourge."

"And you killed countless people and almost converted our world," Zac said as he looked around. "How about this? Undo what you've done with the realignment, and I'll let you leave this world alive, or your version of it at least. I let bygones be bygones, and your kingdom will give up any claim to this planet. I don't think that your kingdom wants an enemy like me anyway."

Zac's biggest worry right now was the Realignment Array. Kenzie was coming along with her knowledge of arrays, but there were no guarantees she'd be able to deal with such a massive formation. That left Zac's far cruder method, finding the Array Core and bashing it. But none of them had any idea what that would result in.

What if doing so would cause the array to go out of control, completely crippling the planet?

The best outcome would be the Lich giving up and backing away, based on the potential of Zac's future growth. Besides, revenge was a dish best served cold. Zac definitely would deal with the Lich King because of what he'd done sooner or later, but it didn't have to be today. He could always visit the undead kingdom as his Draugr persona in the future and track this guy down. Saving Earth was more important.

But a laugh echoed across the halls as a robed figure emerged from the darkness, and a glance with [Cosmic Gaze] confirmed that this was the real Lich King. The hooded undead teemed with power, far more than he ever had on top of the wall.

"What makes you think it is reversible? Death is the shadow of life, a natural absolute of the universe. Our arrays only speed the process up." He laughed. "You're long past the point of return."

"Bullshit," Zac growled without hesitation. "The thing hasn't even started up."

"Perhaps. Perhaps not." The Lich snickered as the fractals on the hundreds of pillars lit up in an instant. "But does it matter when you are about to join us?"

The energy density of the chamber grew by a terrifying degree in an instant, and Zac's danger sense prickled as he looked around with a frown. He shot out a series of fractal edges toward the closest pillars, but the blades actually crumbled in midair as it looked like a million motes of darkness fed on them until they couldn't maintain their form.

Zac activated **[Loamwalker]** to flash to a pillar instead, but it felt like he was trying to move through solid matter. Was nature blocked out in this place? He activated **[Hatchetman's Spirit]** next to rid himself of the effect, but it didn't work either. It was like he had lit up a weak candle of life in a raging storm of death, and his skill was ripped apart in an instant.

"I've reinforced this array for a year, and it contains the will of the Undead Empire. It is powered by an enormous fortune of crystals and is perfected by the ancient sages. How could your little domain possibly resist it?" The Lich laughed. "You are indeed powerful and bursting with potential, but you are too confident in your strength. You are not fighting me, but an empire, and the only result is death."

The intensity kept increasing, and Zac soon found himself on his knees. His skin burned like someone had thrown acid on him, but it was the black motes that tried to burrow into his skin. He tried to block them out with the Fragment of the Coffin and the Fragment of the Bodhi, but neither could help him for more than a second.

This array was just terrifying. It had created an absolute zone of death, and he as a living being was completely restrained. However, he still had one more card to pull, and a pitch-black crystal appeared in his hand as he readied himself. He quickly infused it with Cosmic Energy to activate it before he slammed it into the ground.

The whole area shuddered as the darkness turned into a vast nebula, and Zac felt the immense pressure of the array disappear. He pushed all the Cosmic Energy he could muster into [Chop] as [Verun's Bite] lit up with sanguine luster. He wanted to take out the pillars and the Lich King alike in one massive swing.

However, Zac had barely time to begin his swing before he found himself on the ground again, the vision of the cosmos so brief that it might just as well have been a figment of his imagination. The crystal lay cracked on the ground, completely devoid of power.

"Void's Disciple," Adriel snorted. "A supreme talent, to even have managed to catch a glimpse of the Dao of Space at such an early stage. He would be welcomed with open arms in most forces of the Zecia Sector. It's his bad luck to have been attached to such a wretched master."

Zac sighed as he looked at the cracked crystal in front of him with mixed emotions. It was a big setback that this thing didn't work at all, as it would force him to expose his Draugr form. But it was also a bit of a relief. He had built up Void's Disciple into some sort of mysterious powerhouse after their last encounter, but this was a good reminder that the Zhix warlord was just someone with an incomplete Heritage and a bit of a head start.

He had wanted to deal with this without exposing his undead form, but he was just restrained too much by this array of death. He sent the command to his Duplicity Core while he circulated some energy to shoot out a feeble fractal blade toward the Lich King. Of course, it didn't even make it halfway before it crumbled as well.

"You knew?" Zac croaked, trying to stall for a bit.

"He is talented, but just a native barbarian in the end. Just like you. How could I not notice him scanning the arrays in my domain?" Adriel said. "But there is time for us to discuss all this after you have awakened anew."

Zac was just about to complete his transformation, but his mind suddenly screamed of danger. He used everything in his power to slightly adjust his torso as a pitch-black spike descended out of nowhere, aiming straight for his heart. He just managed to adjust his chest enough to avoid getting his heart pierced, but the weapon still punctured his lung.

Bad turned to worse as a massive storm of Miasma tore through his body, and Zac knew he would have died then and there if it weren't for his unique constitution. Zac arduously looked around only to see a gaunt spectral assassin shrouded in a robe of pure darkness. He had never seen this assassin before, but he radiated a dense aura of killing intent.

Who was this? His aura was even stronger than that of the banshee general he'd fought earlier. And his mind had only managed to warn him at the very last second, barely allowing him to avoid getting his heart ruined. Was that ghost from before not actually the last general, but there had actually been one more lying in wait all this time?

If that was the case, then he was a true assassin. Zac had never seen a hint of his aura or his impressive killing intent, something that would only be born from a lot of carnage. He didn't do anything while Zac tore down half the fort and killed most of the soldiers, but waited to strike until he was confident in succeeding.

"Don't soil the body," the Lich said from the side, though he clearly seemed to be in a good mood. "I lost the poison-constitution lass, but we can still submit this body. It might be even better for my purposes. The dreams of the Heartlands are not yet dead."

Zac's chaotic mind wandered, but he snapped back into focus as the transformation into his Draugr form finished. The waves of Miasma that crashed through his body due to the spike were no longer harmful, but rather invigorating. The spike still hurt, but getting gored by a small spike wasn't a wound that really bothered Zac any longer.

Zac had been in this exact situation before, and there was no need to change a winning concept. A bladelike fist full of the Fragment of the Bodhi punched into the chest of the spectral assassin as Zac leaped to his feet.

"Wh–" the ghost said, but he didn't have time to react before his throat was caught in a viselike grip.

The extremely powerful array that had once threatened to crush his body and soul was no longer an impediment at all. In fact, Zac had never felt this comfortable in his undead form before. This place felt like a paradise for cultivation, and he already started thinking of whether he could bring these pillars back home to create a proper cultivation ground.

This was why Zac had been confident in jumping down into the hole at all. Most of the attacks that the Lich King had brought forth had either been based on death or poison. And in this form, he was confident in dealing with either.

There was no crunch as Zac ripped the ghost general's head clean off with another infusion from the Fragment of the Bodhi, but a surge of energy entered his body as he followed it up by crushing the head.

"What!" the Lich screamed as he fell back. "Draugr? It's you? It has been you all along?! This is impossible! Life and Death can never be one!"

"You keep saying that," Zac said with an abyssal voice as a child-sized coffin appeared on his back. "You should know by now that nothing is impossible in the Multiverse."

Four chains shot out the next moment, each of them aiming for the Lich with a palpable eagerness. Zac followed suit as black armor covered his body, and Zac stomped down on the ground to appear right next to the Lich.

The Lich King was clearly frazzled by the turn of events, and Zac couldn't blame him. This array he had set up would be the bane of almost any living warrior dumb enough to get caught inside, and even if Zac could withstand it, he should have been severely weakened. But how could the Lich have expected to run into one of the few living people in the Multiverse that the array was utterly useless against?

The fractal cage sprang up while Zac simultaneously pushed the taunting function of [Vanguard of Undeath] to its peak. He had already shown his hidden ace, and he couldn't let this man escape no matter what. The Lich King screamed as he unleashed a barrage of poison from his body, and Zac noticed that the real body of the Lich had once again been replaced by a copy.

However, the real body appeared just ten meters away, and the chains of [Love's Bond] were already twisted around his body before he had time to realize that he hadn't escaped as he had planned.

The massive avatar once more appeared in the sky as a waterfall of toxins started to fall, but the chains effortlessly moved the Lich out of the way. Bursts of poison emerged from his own mouth next, but if there was one thing the chains were unafraid of, it was toxins. They twisted even harder until sickening crunches echoed out through the subterranean hall as one bone after another snapped from the pressure.

Zac suddenly felt a tremendous surge of energy entering his body as the Lich finally couldn't take it any longer. Zac had been worried that there would be even more tricks to the Lich King, but he and his personal assassin had placed too much trust in the arrays in this chamber. It allowed him to take them out in quick succession, and Zac could already confirm that the invasion had failed, as the familiar prompt appeared in front of him, telling him that the area had come under his control.

There shouldn't be many surviving invaders after Zac had torn the whole place apart, but they would probably be fleeing toward the incursion by now. Zac didn't care about that, as he hadn't exposed his Draugr form to anyone on the surface, and unless there was another ghost that could hide from his scans, there were no witnesses down here either.

They would only be able to retell the situation of a terrifying progenitor, and they would sooner or later connect that with "Zac Piker" of the Tower of Eternity, which would explain how this was all possible. Hopefully, that meant that any issue with the Undead Empire would end then and there, as Catheya had indicated that she would make sure no problem would crop up even if he booted the local undead from Earth.

But honestly, Zac couldn't bother going over every eventuality. He closed his eyes as he felt a sense of calm spreading through his body. He had done it. He had defeated the Undead Empire, which would allow Earth to keep going for a while longer.

At least until the next threat came along.

88

BROKEN

Zac took another look around before he released **[Profane Seal]** as he gazed down at the corpse of the Lich King. This wretched half-man half-corpse had caused so much trouble for Earth, but he hadn't even been able to resist one attack of his new Spirit Tool. He shook his head with a sense of exhaustion before he bent down to look for treasure.

He pried a low-quality Spatial Ring from the man's hand and found a top-quality Cosmos Sack hidden within his robes before he threw the body into his Spatial Ring. He walked over to the ghost next, which had turned into a pile of shimmering sand upon dying.

It felt a bit weird digging around in a pile of ghost ashes, but Zac found a Spatial Pouch and a set of throwing darts inside. He popped a healing pill next as he explored the chamber, and he could quickly confirm there were only two points of interest apart from the numerous inscribed pillars. The first was a pedestal holding a large black rock, and the second was a proper entrance in the direction of the palace.

It didn't require a genius in formations to figure out the pedestal, or rather, the rock, was the core of the array, but Zac left it alone so that Kenzie could look at it instead. As for the entrance, it was sealed shut, and Zac had more pressing things to do than to look for treasure in the palace. A massive amount of energy coursed through his body after his two kills.

The Lich might have been the highest-leveled individual on Earth apart from the Dominators, and the amount of energy he had gained from the kill was staggering. This energy alone was more than all the kills aboveground, and it would probably take him weeks to grind the equivalent with any targets he could find on Earth.

He really needed to make sure everything was okay on the surface, though, and he ran back to the hole in the ceiling, speeding against the clock, as the accumulated energy had already started to dissipate from his body. But he froze just as he was about to jump up before he looked down at his chest.

The wound to his lung had mostly healed by now thanks to the pill, and he activated his Duplicity Core again. With **[Profane Seal]** expended, his undead form was severely weakened, not to mention there might still be curious eyes upstairs. He felt a stabbing pain in his chest when the transformation completed, but it wasn't too bad.

Zac jumped up through the entrance he came from, and soon enough found himself back in the open air. It wasn't too different from how he left it, but he saw a clear change as he jumped up on one of the tallest buildings that were still standing after the battle. Streams of the surviving undead were rushing toward the incursion pillar, and the fortress was fast losing its population.

This was just how it usually went. The invaders all got a warning the leader was dead, and the countdown before the Nexus Hub closed had begun. A glance over in his sister's direction showed they had moved away even further from the fortress, and the unthinking Zombies seemed to have lost interest in them by now.

Perhaps they were unsure what to do after having lost connection to the Lich King.

"Good job," a bloodied Ogras said as he emerged from the shadows. "That girl suddenly lost her composure. I'm guessing she got the prompt of her leader's untimely demise."

"I dealt with the other general as well. There should be no more threats, but are you okay to guard the others for a bit?" Zac asked. "I think I found the array, but let these people clear out a bit before I bring Kenzie over. I want to use the energy to break open a node before it's too late."

"These guys don't seem to have any fight left in them." The demon nodded as he looked around. "Go ahead. I'll look after things."

Zac nodded and entered the building he stood on, finding a secluded spot. There was no point in him going after the fleeing Revenants and Corpselords, as that would only result in a net loss of accumulated energy with the speed he was losing energy from killing the Lich King.

He only hesitated for a second before he sat down on his prayer mat. The fighting above had only left him with some grazes, and the stab wasn't too bad either. Most of the danger had come from the torrent of Miasma, which had been completely neutralized and absorbed the moment he turned into a Draugr. Apart from having spent most of his big skills, he was essentially in good condition.

He couldn't discard this opportunity to become stronger, and he directly started pushing the remaining energy toward the node in his left leg. The Undead Empire was dealt with, but he still needed every advantage he could get in the upcoming fight against the Dominators. He needed to break open a few more nodes, and he turned his vision inward.

The node in his leg was just like before, partially opened and chock-full of energy while still impeding energy circulation. Seeing that nothing had changed from swapping classes back and forth, he started to forcibly infuse it, and the pain quickly grew to uncomfortable levels.

The minutes passed, and Zac started to brace himself for what was coming, but even he hadn't expected the extreme agony when the node finally exploded. His white robes were drenched in blood as a chunk of his leg exploded to the point that bone was exposed. But that pain was still nothing compared to the agony he felt on a spiritual level.

The nodes were something between corporeal and intangible, fixed on what Ogras called a Spirit Body. It was essentially an energy copy that perfectly matched your physical form, and it was the housing of the pathways. And now this Spirit Body was wounded from the explosion, causing the pathways in his legs to become messed up.

He finally understood the difference between opening a node the normal way and forcing it open. The normal way was akin to unclogging a drain by pouring down some solvent before snaking it to dislodge whatever caused the bad flow. Forcing a node open was rather like throwing a stick of dynamite down the drain and blowing up the clog, along with half your house.

This self-inflicted carnage not only hurt a lot, but Zac also realized it had weakened him drastically. His energy circulation was all out of control, even in the parts of his body that weren't harmed. He urgently took out another pill, this one intended to heal souls.

It helped with the pain somewhat, but there was no time for him to properly heal, as an immense pressure suddenly descended upon him. Zac barely had time to get on his feet before a blinding golden light bled through the cracks in the wall, and then he was falling as the building collapsed.

A blistering heat was pushing down from above as well, almost immediately making the stones burn upon the slightest touch. A new set of shallow wounds covered his body as he was buried in an avalanche of stones, but he started to dig himself out. But there were just golden flames and smoke all around him, robbing him of his visibility. He didn't even know if he was digging in the right direction.

Worry gripped his heart as Zac pushed the heated stones out of the way. What the hell was going on?

The strength required to unleash an attack with that kind of impact was not something anyone in his group could deal with, and it didn't look like something that the undead would use. There was only one group who could conjure something like this.

The cultists.

He quickly circulated energy as he tried to forcibly push himself out of the mountain of rubble. But a blaring pain erupted in his left leg after putting too much pressure on it, almost making him black out from the agony. The events had made him forget about the wound from blasting open the node, but at least he had managed to break free from the building.

Only to be met with an utter inferno.

Golden flames had embroiled the fortress in every direction, and scorched corpses of elite undead warriors littered the wall. Zac had already killed most of them through his earlier rampage, and there couldn't be many still around after this salvo. The cultists must have bombarded the fortress with massive siege weapons to cause this kind of destruction in an instant.

Panic really started to set in, but opening the Ladder screen allowed Zac to breathe out in relief. He could spot both his sister and Emily on the Dao Ladder, and Joanna on the Level Ladder. Whatever was going on right now hadn't affected them just yet.

That didn't mean he could relax, but he simply couldn't find any target. There were just flames and corpses everywhere, and a sky on fire. He hobbled toward one of the broken towers, each step feeling like he was getting stabbed. A few jumps later, he found himself on the broken peak, looking across the landscape.

Nothing.

There was no zealot army amassing outside the gates, just a gray haze in every direction except for the incursion pillar. The bombardment was thankfully confined to the fortress, and he believed that Ogras was experienced enough to avoid getting scorched. Zac felt a fluctuation from his Spatial Ring, and he took out a communication crystal with surprise.

These things hadn't worked since they had reached the core of the Dead Zone, but now he heard his sister on the other side of the line.

"What's going on?" Zac asked. "Is everyone okay?"

"It's the cultists! A huge flying vessel suddenly appeared in the sky, and we fled into the woods to not implicate you," Kenzie said from the other side. "Ogras shrouded us, so we're fine."

"Stay hidden," Zac said. "I can deal with this alone."

"Be careful. I don't think they just came for the undead. They are probably here to deal with you as well," she said.

"It seems that way." Zac sighed as a storm of flames was falling straight toward him.

Cosmic Energy surged in his body, but a blazing pain made itself remembered as the recently opened node flared up. He could only grit his teeth as he forced the Cosmic Energy to move. However, he barely managed to form a thirty-meter fractal edge with [Chop] this time, compared to the hundred-meter blade he'd easily conjured earlier.

It wasn't enough. The blade cut into the wall of flames like a knife, but it was swallowed whole without breaking apart the attack. Zac didn't hesitate to activate a defensive treasure, and a sphere enclosed him and the top of the tower in an instant. The flames slammed down like a furious waterfall the next second, and Zac felt the scorching heat even within his protective bubble.

The base of the tower was quickly incinerated, and the tip was just held in the air with the help of the barrier. But the flames finally subsided, which allowed the skies to clear out. Only then did he finally spot the source of the attacks. A large vessel in gold and red hovered a few hundred meters above the fortress, something that looked like a mix of a flying treasure and a floating island.

Zac couldn't see how it looked from the top, but it seemed to be kept in the air with a massive ball of flames. Zac sighed with a shake of his head as he took out his own flying treasure. The cultists really liked their fire. He quickly rose into the sky as the tower fell to the ground behind him, no longer supported by the shield.

Nausea and double-vision plagued him from the pain of opening a node, so he needed to end this fast. He forced the unruly Cosmic Energy into his arm as he prepared his last skill of mass destruction. He had used up **[Deforestation]** in his earlier fight, but there was still one more card he could bring out: **[Nature's Punishment]**.

His whole body was covered in sweat from the pain of forcibly utilizing his maimed pathways, but he couldn't stop at this juncture. Space cracked, and the familiar hand flew out, though Zac was a bit disappointed that the hand hadn't changed at all from him evolving.

It still radiated terrifying might due to the Fragment of the Bodhi, though, and it shot straight through a burst of flames without even getting its leaves singed.

The hand placed itself straight above the floating warship, and Zac didn't delay a second before the familiar branch started to descend. There was no way to tell what these unhinged lunatics had planned, and he needed to strike before it was too late.

The branch quickly grew in size as it shot down at the ship, but a burning whip covered in white-hot flames shot up to meet its descent. Zac spotted a lizardman standing at the fore of the vessel, his eyes lit up like two blazing beacons as five swirls of pure-white globes of fire circulated behind him.

Zac had fought one of the other generals just the other day, but the power this man emitted far eclipsed him. In fact, this man felt even more threatening than the Lich King himself, though much of the danger from the undead leader had come from his command of formations.

Had the leader of the Church of the Everlasting Dao come in person?

89

FATE'S OBDURACY

If this really was the incursion leader of the Church of Everlasting Dao, then a massive chance had presented itself, as Zac still didn't know where the cultist incursion was located. They had somehow managed to hide their base of operations all this time while sending out roving death squads that killed everything in their path.

The best idea his people had to find these guys were to investigate the zones of Pangea that had no reports of human activity. They figured the lack of surviving towns could mean that everyone had already been killed by the Church, and the incursion pillar was close. But killing the leader here would save them all that trouble, as the incursion would still end if he died.

However, the head priest of the church was clearly no chump. One of the flaming balls hovering behind his back entered the whip as it elongated to reach well over a hundred meters. The very air burned while the whip ripped through the sky as the weapon's flames increased in intensity many times over. Zac instantly felt a blistering pain in his arm as the damage to the branch was transferred over.

It was like the whip was a boa constrictor that tried to squeeze the life out of the branch as it looped around it multiple times over, preventing it from freely growing in size. The white-hot flames had quickly latched on to the branch as well, and an inferno raged on across its surface. Burnt bark fell like rain from the sky as new layers grew out at the cost of even more of Zac's Cosmic Energy.

Zac felt like a fool when he saw the scene. The pain from opening his node had made him activate the skill as usual instead of thinking things through. He had always used the wooden punishment since gaining the Fragment of the Bodhi, as the two resonated the best, but he would clearly have been better off using the mountain or water punishment this time around. Still, there was no point in crying over spilled milk.

The fight had turned into a battle between destruction and creation in a sense, and Zac intended to emerge the victor of that struggle.

He kept infusing **[Nature's Punishment]** with his Dao and Cosmic Energy while he tried to force the branch to descend. The priest, on the other hand, was forced to infuse one globe of flames after another into his Spirit Tool to power the fires raging across the swelling branch.

Zac still hadn't met anyone who was able to outlast him in a clash of endurance, but he actually felt the skill starting to destabilize much quicker than usual. He had no choice, and the energy around him veritably exploded as he activated **[Hatchetman's Rage]**. The branch suddenly radiated powerful waves as well, and the flames were quickly subdued.

Zac saw his chance as he made a final push, and the whip simply snapped as the branch exploded in size. Newly born branches spread in every direction before they all turned toward the warship, like hundreds of falling spears. The wooden punishment had finally gained its momentum, and it crashed into the warship with enough force to push both the Miasmic clouds and the flames aside.

A golden shield appeared to block the strike, but it quickly broke as the main branch punched a massive hole. Flame and metal rained down toward the ground as both the ship and the sun that powered it broke apart, and screams echoed across the golden sky as dozens of cultists plummeted toward the ground. Zac managed to kill most of them with a rapid flurry of fractal edges, but his focus was still on the leaders.

The head priest was still alive, as the surge of Cosmic Energy he felt was nowhere big enough to correspond to killing someone that powerful. Finally, his target emerged through the smoke on top of a far smaller flying vessel with four powerful warriors to his side. Zac prepared himself for a final clash, wanting to end the battle before the timer for his buff ran out.

But his eyes widened in shock when he realized that there would be no cataclysmic battle in the sky. The so-called zealots left a burning trail in the air as they fled for their lives.

Zac couldn't believe his eyes when he saw the Church leader escape with enough gusto to almost punch a hole in the sound barrier. Was this the same faction as the one where pretty much everyone was ready to blow themselves up just for a shot at dragging you with them to hell? Where was the fanaticism?

The leaf ripped through the air as Zac instructed his flying vessel to pursue, as he didn't want to let the cultists get away. A chance like this wouldn't come again. The smaller vessel shot away with shocking speed, but Zac's own leaf wasn't any worse than whatever some local cultists could bring to the table.

It whizzed after the group of five, taking advantage of the fact that the cultists were actually burning away the death-attuned haze in front of them, forming some sort of wind tunnel. But Zac soon realized that he actually was unable to catch up to the group, as they seemed to have an endless supply of fire-attuned Nexus Crystals that they fed into the vessel, allowing it to burn through the Dead Zone.

Zac started peppering them with fractal blades from behind, but he sighed when he saw the man with the whip crush them one by one without overtaxing himself. The Spirit Tool in the head priest's hand was no doubt top tier, and he was clearly some ways into the E-grade as well.

Zac kept trying to take them down while **[Hatchetman's Rage]** was still active, but he was out of cards. The sense of power was soon replaced with weakness, and he wasn't sure what he should do. He didn't want to leave these guys alive. But he also couldn't leave Kenzie and the others alone in the middle of the Dead Zone while he harried the Church of Everlasting Dao for god knows how long. Besides, there was still the Realignment Array to deal with.

A few more minutes passed as he adapted to the state of weakness while they flew further and further. But finally, he had an idea, and the amulet around his neck slithered to his back to gain its backpack form. The inscribed circle on the lid was dimmed out after having used

[Death's Embrace], but there was another set of inscriptions that were still in working order. Zac infused a large chunk of his remaining Cosmic Energy, and the two lines of fractals running along its length lit up.

The scripture started to slither back and forth across the coffin lid for a second before they suddenly rose into the air, forming two actual chains wrought from darkness that shot toward his targets. However, the head priest unleashed a massive arc of flames that crashed into the two chains, causing them to shatter in an instant.

However, a skill from [Love's Bond] obviously wouldn't be defeated so easily. The two shattered chains suddenly regrew into four before they resumed their pursuit. The cultists desperately swatted them down over and over, but it was useless. They just split and grew back when they broke apart, just like the heads of a hydra.

Zac had already gotten a hint of what the skill would do, but his eyes still widened in shock when he saw the sea of darkness rushing after the vessel with wild abandon. Finally, the cultists couldn't hold the tide back any longer, and they were swallowed up by a ball of chains that frantically writhed as it tried to crush everything within its cage.

The ball was quickly dragged back toward Zac, who could hear crunching sounds and screams from within. However, a massive blast of flames suddenly erupted from within, forcing the chains away long enough for a flash of light to escape the stranglehold.

A frown marred Zac's face as he looked at the river of flames that rushed toward the horizon, the stream having a speed that superseded his flying leaf by many times over. He knew it wasn't an errant burst of flames, but rather some sort of escape skill or treasure, something in the same vein as the top-tier escape skill that was in Thea's possession.

Zac sighed, as he knew that there was no way he'd be able to capture whoever had fled, and he turned his attention back to the ball of chains that hovered in front of him. The chains of darkness had pretty much turned into a solid by this point, and things had turned completely silent by this point as blood dripped down from the bottom.

This was the second skill of [Love's Bond], called [Fate's Obduracy]. This skill could be used, like now, to wear down a single target with an unceasing wave of chains. Another strategy could be him sending the set of chains out to cause widespread destruction, where any attempt to stop the advance would worsen the situation. In either case, it was a nigh-unstoppable skill of destruction.

Just like [Death's Embrace], it had a pretty long cooldown. He wouldn't be able to use the skill for a full two weeks, and he would need to feed the coffin with some energy-rich treasures to recharge itself.

There was also a limit of just how many times the chains could reproduce. The cultists hadn't actually been that far from shaking off the attack. If the head priest hadn't burnt all five of those globes of flames to deal with [Nature's Punishment], he might have been able to exhaust the skill completely.

Zac instructed the mess of chains to unravel, and it displayed an utterly crumpled ship along with three barely distinguishable corpses. That meant that the burst of flames had contained two people, one of them being the man with the whip. Zac sighed as he instructed his leaf to fly back toward the undead fortress after looting the corpses.

He was still extremely disappointed with himself failing to kill that man. If the leader had just died with the rest of the cultists, Zac would have been done by now, having dealt with the two most troubling incursions in one fell swoop. But he guessed he couldn't always luck out, even with a Luck of over 300.

The emerald leaf whizzed through the air as Zac returned toward the undead fortress. However, he started to worry again as he flew, as he saw terrifying numbers of Zombies streaming toward the core of the Dead Zone as well. He had already noticed that the outer shield had been deactivated, perhaps as a result of him breaking the Array Towers in the base, and now the enormous number of Zombies who were previously stuck outside were on the move.

Zac didn't hesitate to infuse the leaf with the Fragment of the Bodhi to speed up his return, but he quickly changed course when he saw a group of familiar faces some ways from the ruined fortress. It was everyone except Ogras, and they had planted themselves on top of a small hill. The Valkyries had once again erected a shield wall, which was no surprise considering they were utterly surrounded by a sea of Zombies.

However, it barely seemed necessary. The shield occasionally received a swipe from a close by Zombie, but there was no concerted effort to push past the barrier. They all kept moving forward, streaming toward the fortress as though they were under a spell.

"You're back!" Kenzie said with a relieved smile. "What happened?"

"I've dealt with the cultists, but a few got away. What's going on?" Zac asked with bemusement as he landed next to them. "And where is Ogras?"

"He went off to check things out," Kenzie said. "As for these guys? We think they are heading toward the incursion; it started just a minute or two after you flew away. It's like something luring them toward the teleporter."

"We think the undead kingdom is doing something to attract the Zombies to bring them over to the other side," Joanna added.

"Why aren't you fighting them?" Zac asked curiously. "It should be a good opportunity to level up."

"It feels weird," Kenzie said. "It was one thing when they were attacking us, but now they are just ignoring us. They are former earthlings, after all. We were thinking it would be better to simply let them go if it means they'll get to at least live on in some way. And we figured there's no need to antagonize a faction like the Undead Empire even further."

"Besides, we've even gained a lot," Emily said with a wide grin.

"Oh?" Zac said with confusion, but he suddenly remembered the teenager should have gotten a part of his Cosmic Energy due to her buff. "How much did you gain?"

"Six," she said, her widening grin almost splitting her face in two. "I gained more than six levels thanks to you! I told you we should go out hunting together. I'd pass Thea Marshall in a week or two."

"If you always ride the coattails of others, you'll turn into a useless vase," a voice echoed out across the hill as Ogras appeared from the shadows. "You need to rely on yourself."

"What about you playing all cool and saying you'd deal with that lady general? Kenzie detonated a bomb right in her face just a few days ago. Zac almost knocked the soul out of her body and then cut off her hand. It's not like you're any different," Emily retorted with a teasing glance.

"You were a lot cuter after Zac picked you up from the streets. Feels like I've lost a daughter." Ogras sighed with an exaggeratedly forlorn expression.

Or perhaps it was just his wretched appearance that gave that impression, as he looked like he had been oven-roasted for a few hours. His body sported multiple new scorch marks that weren't there when they'd met earlier, and even his white hair had been singed clean off.

"What's with your look?" Zac asked with a snort, as the demon really cut a sorry sight. "I thought you left the fortress before the cultists arrived."

"Those netherblasted lunatics really didn't hold back. Who knows how much wealth was destroyed? I tried to salvage what I could before it was too late," the demon explained.

"Hey, you two are matching now," Emily said with glee as she pointedly looked at Ogras' bald head.

"Shit, don't lump me together with that eunuch," Ogras spat as his white hair quickly grew back until it reached his shoulders again. "That's better."

"Did you find anything?" Zac asked with a frown.

"Not much." The demon shrugged. "A storeroom full of half-burnt herbs. I don't recognize the thing, but there were massive quantities. I am guessing it's something used on Zombies from how much of it they had. So what happened with the cultists? Did you get the leader?"

"I don't think so." Zac sighed as he retold his encounter with the zealots.

"A whip? That's a pretty rare weapon for a man," the demon muttered. "I never heard of him from any reports either. It should be the leader of the incursion, who only ventured out to deal with you. Shame. Such life-saving measures usually come with a price, though."

"Let's hope so. I'll go check things out at the incursion," Zac finally said as he took out the flying treasure again.

However, the moment he was about to instill the leaf with some energy to activate it, he felt the whole world shudder and turn slanted.

An agonizing pain ripped through his body, and he felt his vision close in on him.

TRIV

Zac woke up with a start, his head a chaotic mess, but he instinctively shot to his feet with his weapon at the ready. He barely had time to stop himself from bisecting a shocked Valkyrie before he remembered where he was.

"Sorry about that. How long was I out?" Zac asked with a hoarse voice.

"Around forty minutes," Kenzie said with worry. "What's wrong? Are you poisoned?"

"It's nothing," Zac said as he rubbed his temples. "I broke open a node by force earlier because of all the energy I gained. I think I overextended myself a bit."

"I completely forgot after seeing you zip around as usual. I'm surprised you could fight like that at all," Ogras said, his eyes wide. "I guess that even the Heavens has finally had enough of your luck and sent some cultists in your direction. Karma always comes knocking sooner or later."

Zac turned his sight inward, and he was a bit better than before. His pathways were still a mess, but his flesh was on the mend already. He guessed that he had fallen unconscious because he had used his pathways when he should have been resting. It was a valuable experience, though, learning what kind of effect exploding a node had on his body and combat readiness.

But the node wasn't the only problem that ailed his body at the moment. He thought a second before he walked a few steps away, and shocked exclamations echoed across the hill as he stabbed himself in his arm. A large spurt of blood stained the ground, but the wound quickly scabbed over.

"Don't worry, just expelling some toxins," Zac said as he took out his flying treasure. "I feel a lot better already. Get ready. I'll check out the situation around the pillar for threats before we deal with the Realignment Array."

Zac really did feel a lot better after having exsanguinated himself. [Void Heart] had absorbed both a bunch of Miasma and poisons during the fight, and having been bled a few times helped him get some of the impurities out. He still would have preferred to rest up some more, but there was still the aftermath of the invasion to deal with. He gingerly tried activating the flying treasure again, and this time, it went smoothly.

He soon closed in on the turquoise pillar, and he actually saw a familiar figure fretting back and forth some distance away from it, the ghost who had hovered right next to the Lich King earlier. It looked unsure whether to enter or not. However, the moment it spotted Zac, its visage turned even ghastlier and became marred with horror, and it desperately shot toward the Nexus Hub.

The ghost wasn't all that quick, though, especially not compared to a top-tier flying treasure like Zac's. Just a second after the ghost spotted him, he had been caught, held firmly in Zac's grasp. A few Revenants were overseeing the Zombies as well, but they desperately jumped into the teleportation array, abandoning their colleague to its fate.

"Who are you?" Zac asked as he shook the ghost for a bit.

"Sir, I am just an attendant to Lord Ad– ah, I mean the Wretched Lich Adriel. A thousand blessings upon you for freeing me!" he hurriedly said. "Please spare this useless one. I am not a threat to you or your planet. I am just a custodian, a noncombat class ordered to come to this planet against his wishes."

"Shameless enough," Zac snorted. "What's going on here?"

"We're bringing back the children," the ghost explained, not hesitating to spill the beans. "They will have a better future coming with us than staying here, and it will rid your planet of these walking Holy Beacons."

Zac frowned as he looked at the Zombies, who mindlessly shuffled forward until they disappeared into the incursion pillar. Perhaps the ghost was right. The death attunement should dissipate sooner or later, and what would become of these people?

Some might turn sapient and find themselves stuck on a planet with a hostile environment full of enemies. But most would simply be cut down by cultivators gathering Nexus Coins and Cosmic Energy. At the Undead Empire, they would at least have a chance to be born anew.

"Fine, I'll let them go. Now, tell me how to turn off the Realignment Array," Zac said.

This was the most pressing issue now. The quest to stop the realignment still hadn't completed. He had actually noticed that the massive lines in the sky had started to fade while he hunted the cultists, but it seemingly wasn't enough. The most likely suspect was obviously the array below the surface, but he still believed that having this attendant turn it off was the safest bet.

But his hopes were quickly dashed as the ghost frantically shook his head.

"I can't!" the ghost cried. "I would love to explain to the young master, but I can't."

"The first directive?" Zac asked with a frown.

"Yes, yes! You are very well-read. The first directive precludes me from helping you no matter my personal wish to assist!" The ghost nodded.

Zac frowned as his eyes bored into the squirming specter. Catheya had never really explained exactly how binding the commandments were, but they didn't seem like complete compulsions to Zac. There should be some wriggle room, and Zac felt he might as well do some name-dropping to see if the Draugr girl could help him one last time.

"I recently became friends with Catheya Sharva'Zi from the Empire Heartlands when I visited the Tower of Eternity. It appears she is visiting your kingdom while her master is in secluded cultivation," Zac said as he took out the Teleportation Token she'd given him before he flashed his Tower Title. "She gave me this token; you might recognize it."

"This! Ninth floor! And you know that exalted mistress?" the ghost veritably screamed as its incorporeal eyes darted back and forth between the title and the token.

Catheya actually hadn't given him a token representing her force, but he was willing to bet that some random ghost wouldn't know the difference. For all it knew, it might very well be a Teleportation Token leading straight to the Empire Heartlands rather than Twilight Harbor.

"I can put in a good word for you the next time I meet her, or I can do the opposite." Zac shrugged. "I will turn off the Realignment Array sooner or later, even if I have to rip this whole fortress apart. I don't mind turning you into a pile of ghost dust first, though."

The ghost sputtered for a few seconds until it calmed down.

"Did you know that the attunement of a planet is based on its World Core? It is a magical crystal residing in the deepest core of a world. Some believe that a World Core is essentially alive, and the planet's attunement is a result of its cultivation, where it absorbs the energy of the cosmos. What do you think would happen if such a core was flooded with Death while it was sealed off from the cosmos?" the ghost said before it dimmed as though it were wounded.

Zac's eyes widened as he looked at the wretched appearance of the ghost. Was it actually wounded from divulging some information like that? However, it still hadn't answered his question, at least not straight out. Most of what it said was just general information and theories, and nothing that he wouldn't be able to piece together himself.

However, Zac obviously understood the implied meaning behind the ghost's words.

"The array in the sky was just blocking out the cosmos," Zac muttered before he looked down at the ground.

It seemed as though the people of Earth had gotten things a bit backward, if Zac had understood the ghost's explanation correctly. The enormous array in the sky wasn't actually the Realignment Array. It was at best half of it responsible for isolating the planet from the universe, preventing it from absorbing normal energy. The real realignment was taking place underground.

Both parts were important to stop, but the most important might be whatever was going on in that underground chamber. It looked like he would have to bring his sister after all. Catching other undead wouldn't do him any good either, as they no doubt would be implicated by the same compulsions.

"You'll be coming with me for a bit," Zac said to the ghost as [Love's Bond] transformed into a coffin on his back.

The next moment, four chains wrapped around the screeching ghost, each of them imbued with the Fragment of the Bodhi. One twist would rip the hostage apart if he tried anything, but it looked unlikely, judging by how weak it felt. Zac still kept his eyes on the ghost as they flew back to his group to pick up his sister.

Ogras might be helpful as well, but he seemed pretty wrung out. Zac left him on the hill instead so that he could protect the group while he recuperated. After all, there was still one undead general on the loose who could appear at any moment.

"What's this?" Kenzie asked as she curiously looked at the captured ghost.

"Young master, you should not mix with the forces of the Boundless Path," the ghost said, pointedly ignoring Kenzie. "Living or dead, we still follow Heaven's Path. Consorting with heretics will only lead to a lifetime of suffering."

"She's not a Technocrat. She's my sister," Zac snorted. "I just closed a Technocrat incursion and picked up some tools that are helpful until we've grown stronger. And you talk pretty big after almost having killed our planet."

"A thousand apologies, mistress!" the ghost exclaimed, his attitude taking a dramatic turn. "This humble one is called Triv. I worked as a caretaker of the previous Lord of this manor."

Zac suddenly realized that the ghost would be a pretty good source of knowledge. It obviously wouldn't be as knowledgeable as someone like Catheya, but he was still the right-hand man to the Lich King. He should have listened in on all sorts of conversations and had free access to a lot of intelligence.

Perhaps keeping him on Earth wouldn't be such a bad idea, provided he could be controlled.

"I thought he might be useful in turning off the Realignment

Array," Zac added. "It is obviously still going since the quest hasn't completed."

"But the massive arrays in the sky seem to be weakening," Kenzie skeptically said. "They should clear up in another hour or two."

Zac quickly recounted his experiences below ground as they reached the entrance to the hidden subterranean chamber. The group jumped down as one, but Kenzie immediately fell over, completely pale and shuddering. Only then did Zac remember the extremely dense death attunement in the air.

It wasn't too bad for him now that the Lich King wasn't there to amplify the effect, but someone like Kenzie was clearly worse off. He quickly handed her an E-grade Divine Crystal as he spread out his Dao Field for the Fragment of the Bodhi. It helped alleviate her symptoms, but it also made the ghost scream in pain until Zac moved the chains out of the field.

"Thank you," Kenzie said with a hoarse voice. "That was pretty scary."

"No problem," Zac said with a smile as he looked around. "What do you think?"

"These things are part of one array. I think the condensed death energy in here is just an aftereffect. Kind of like radiation in a power plant or something," she muttered as she looked around, her eyes flashing red for a few seconds before they dimmed again.

"How do we turn this thing off?" Zac asked.

Kenzie walked over to the closest pillar, and she went over every line for a few minutes. They also tried to go over the mysterious core, but they couldn't even get close before the aura of death became too overpowering.

"I think we can deactivate the pillars if we make our way from the outside," she hesitantly said. "We'll leave the core for last."

Zac nodded as they moved to the edge of the chamber, where Kenzie started breaking a few inscription lines that connected the pillar with the dense runes on the floor. Zac helped out by ripping crystal after crystal out of the sockets, rapidly expanding his stockpile of Miasma Crystals. They spent the next hour going back and forth, where Zac essentially acted as a mobile counterforce to the death attunement in the air.

However, even he was starting to grow tired, as it was a constant drain on his mental energy to keep his Dao Field active in this environment. Zac initially wanted to start smashing pillars, but Kenzie was afraid that would cause a massive final discharge of death energies that might hurt the World Core.

But Kenzie got more and more skilled at turning off the pillars, and soon enough, they had all dimmed down, leaving just the pedestal. It emitted a terrifying amount of death-attuned energy even though the pillars were all turned off. The energy clearly came from the rock. It was pitch-black and polished smooth, making it almost look like an egg.

The egg emitted mysterious fluctuations as well, and Zac frowned when he realized that it rendered his Dao Field utterly useless. Kenzie couldn't get close to it at all, and they had to retreat after a short while.

"What is that thing?" Zac asked with a frown as he turned to the ghost, who was still chained up. "And don't tell me you don't know."

"I'm not exactly sure what it is," the ghost said. "They are called Seeds of Undeath. Our kingdom receives them from the empire along with this array."

"Like a realignment kit?" Zac asked.

"Precisely." The ghost nodded. "Even small kingdoms such as ours can obviously convert a planet on our own, but our means require high-graded items that are impossible to bring through an incursion. But the empire provides these things as a sol–"

It didn't get any further, though, before massive convulsions racked its intangible form. Zac sighed in annoyance, as it looked like they couldn't get anything more out of the ghost without it exploding for breaking the commandments.

"So now tell me. Why shouldn't I kill you now that we know everything?" Zac asked as his eyes bored into the translucent orbs of the ghost.

LUMP OF COAL

"Kill me?!" Triv shrieked with dismay. "No! Let me stay on this planet. I can be useful to you!"

"You'd stay on a life-attuned planet rather than return to your kingdom?" Zac snorted.

"I'm fine while my master is dead. There is no way I will survive returning to face Lord Rexus. My soul will be tortured until it finally crumbles from age," Triv hurriedly said, the words veritably spilling out of his mouth. "That's why I resisted the call earlier."

"I thought you couldn't resist the compulsions of the empire?" Zac said.

"That's different. The one calling was Lord Rexus, Lord Adriel's master, and the investor of this invasion. I'm technically part of his force, though he didn't awaken me. Adriel did. His call is hard to resist, but it's nothing compared to the rules imprinted onto our very souls."

"What level are you?" Zac slowly asked. "And what can you bring to the table?"

"I'm a level 73 Custodian, and I have even gained two Dao Seeds after staying here," the ghost said with some pride piercing through his fear as he shared his Status screen. "I am practically guaranteed to advance to an E-grade Butler in the future. I will be better assistance to your daily life than any custodian burdened with a corporeal form could hope to be, provided you help me purchase Miasma Crystals for my survival."

Zac shook his head in bemusement when he saw that the ghost really was telling the truth. Its class was **[F – Uncommon] – Spectral Custodian**. There were really all types of classes in the world. He also noted with some interest that the ghost only was aligned to the Undead Empire. Normally, it wouldn't look like that.

You were aligned to your local force, not the empire it was a part of, just like Zac was aligned to Port Atwood rather than Earth itself. Triv should have been aligned to his master's force, but he must've had mentally cut ties with it, leaving only an alignment with the Undead Empire.

"A ghost butler," Kenzie mumbled, her mouth rising with intrigue. "Might be pretty convenient with your situation."

"Sign a contract to serve me properly, and you can stay on Earth," Zac said after a brief hesitation.

He knew how it would look taking in an undead after what they had done to Earth, but Port Atwood had long since passed the point of no return in picking up stray aliens. If it had been one of the generals or the Lich King, he wouldn't be so willing to leave them alive, but a noncombat attendant couldn't be considered as culpable. Noncombat classes almost never had a say in the decisions of a force, after all.

"Nothing would please me more," Triv said with a sigh, though Zac felt he didn't really mean it, "but our commands preclude me from entering contracts with the living."

"Oh? Is that so?" Zac said as his eyes slowly turned pitch-black. "That won't be a problem."

The cooldown for his change had passed while he was unconscious, allowing him to turn into his Draugr form once more. The ghost looked on, frozen with incomprehension, its mouth ajar.

"Now," Zac said with his abyssal voice. "The contract!"

"It was you the whole time… The mystery undead! This is impossible!" the ghost screamed.

"The Lich King said the same thing just before he died." Zac shrugged.

"Such a pure bloodline… No wonder the noble Lady made your

acquaintance!" The ghost spoke, and his whole form shuddered as his excitement quickly mounted. "I'll sign, I'll sign!"

The next moment, the ghost had entered a lifetime Contract of Servitude with Zac, and Zac finally released him from the chains that bound him. The ghost had obviously just wanted to serve as means of survival before, but now it looked beyond excited.

"Why are you so happy all of a sudden?" Zac asked with confusion.

"I'm a custodian, a caretaker of the elite. When our master is strong, we benefit as well. Our bloodlines become stronger if our master's bloodlines are stronger."

"So you're like a parasite?" Kenzie asked from the side. "Will you slow down my brother's cultivation?"

"No, no, not at all," Triv hurriedly said when Zac's brows furrowed together. "This comes to no detriment to our master! You can see us as a mix of a supportive and noncombat class."

"Can you buff me in combat?" Zac asked curiously.

"Alas, no," Triv said with a shake of his head, but he quickly followed up when Zac's eyes dimmed with disinterest. "My skill set is more linked to your home. I can help improve its environment to better suit your needs. Lord Adriel's Dao Chamber was largely set up by me, for example. It will take some time until I can sync with you to that level, though."

"What else?"

"I am there to deal with all the small things that flitter on my Lord's periphery. Cleaning, lighting incense, keeping track of servants, maintenance of private arrays, poison and threat detection. As I evolve, I will also gain some small healing capabilities and the ability to deal with unwanted spying or Karmic manipulation. We allow our masters to focus on what's important: becoming stronger," Triv hurriedly said.

Zac had to admit it sounded pretty convenient having a butler, though that might just be Triv upselling his usefulness. But he first needed to deal with the Realignment Array before he went into detail about what Triv could do and what limitations he had from his compulsions. However, Zac suddenly felt a weird presence appear in his mind, and his eyes once more turned to the ghost.

The chains of [Love's Bond] trapped the ghost the moment he felt the foreign presence in his mind, and the ghost wailed as he was about to be ripped to shreds.

"What did you just do?" Zac growled as Kenzie looked on with confusion and worry.

"My apologies, Lord! It's my skill called [Deathbound Attendant]. This is just our connection that you can use to send me commands," he screamed.

Zac took a steadying breath. He had overreacted a bit due to his history with getting his soul cracked. But there really was nothing wrong with the mark after a second glance, not that the ghost could harm him with a Contract of Servitude active. He dropped the subject and once more focused on the Seed of Undeath.

"We'll talk more about what benefits you can bring later," Zac said as he turned to his sister. "What do you think? Just yoink that thing?"

"The podium seems to be some sort of absorption array." Kenzie nodded. "I think it will be fine to just take it. But perhaps put the thing in a separate Cosmos Sack?"

"Okay, stand back just in case," Zac said as he walked over.

The closer he got to the egg, the fiercer the death buffeted him. It felt like he was inside an extremely refined Dao Field of death attunement, but it wasn't painful at all in his Draugr form. The Seed of Undeath wasn't fastened to the podium itself, but rather placed down into a groove.

Zac simply reached over to put it into his Spatial Ring, but a surge entered his arm the moment his hand touched the smooth surface. A storm of death spread through his body, and his recently opened node was instantly filled with Miasma to the point that he gained a level in his undead form as well.

He had already reached level 81 in his human form earlier. He had lost most of the energy from killing the Lich King due to the cultists' interruption, but he had gained enough to at least fill up the opened node by killing most of the zealots shortly after. Now his classes were once more in balance.

His eyes lit up as he felt just how magical the thing was, and he already had an idea what to do with the egg.

There was already a life-attuned cultivation cave back on his island that used the lotus as a core. What if he created an adjoining cultivation cave steeped in death, using this egg as a core? With the help of Kenzie and his new butler, it would quickly be turned into cultivation heaven that would give him a leg up on his cultivation, no matter if it was his [Nine Reincarnations Manual] or pondering on the Dao.

The egg calmed down after the initial burst, and Zac safely stowed the thing away. A prompt appeared the next moment, confirming that the quest [Death Defiance] had been completed. Zac sighed in relief, as that meant that Earth was finally safe from being turned into the latest branch of the Undead Empire.

As to whether the planet would rid itself entirely of the Miasma, it was too soon to tell.

The quest being marked as completed was just the beginning of the good things coming his way. An inscribed box had appeared next to him just as expected. It was the same with Kenzie, who eagerly reached for her own reward and opened the box.

A small tool was placed inside the chest. It looked a bit like a pen, but there were a couple of attachments that reminded Zac of the bits to a screwdriver. Finally, there was a small crystalline bottle containing some dark-purple liquid.

"What's that?" Zac muttered with some interest, as he hadn't seen anything like it before.

"It's an inscription kit." The ghost sighed. "The small parts are for inscribing on different surfaces, such as array flags, stone, or skin."

Zac's eyes lit up when he heard the explanation. It looked like his sister had gotten a reward tailored for her needs, or perhaps based on the fact that she had mainly contributed by erecting arrays. In either case, it probably meant that a customized reward was waiting for him as well rather than some random thing that might be useful or just something to throw into the Merit Exchange.

But before he opened his own box, he noticed that it looked like the ghost was on the verge of tears.

"What's with you?" Zac asked with some bemusement.

"I just failed a quest," Triv groaned. "As the custodian of the incursion leader, I would no doubt have received an extremely valuable reward."

Zac realized that the ghost probably had an opposing quest for [Death Defiance]. After all, Catheya had mentioned that the System was very much in favor of the Undead Empire causing struggle all over the Multiverse and that it brought some special benefits. He only snorted in response and instead focused on his own box.

A grin was spreading across his face as he opened his box, and Kenzie walked over with interest as well. He was the one who took out the Lich King and two of the generals, after all. His reward should be the best one around.

But he couldn't believe his eyes when he saw what was neatly placed inside.

"A lump of coal? Have you really been that naughty?" Kenzie laughed, and Zac once again found himself questioning his relationship with the System.

However, he somewhat got his hopes up as he noticed Triv staring at the box with greed in his eyes.

"This! High-grade Bloodline Marrow!"

Zac was about to ask what the ghost knew, but a shudder suddenly rose from the ground, like a small earthquake.

Was it the World Core?

"Anything?" Ogras muttered as Leech flittered back and forth among the ruins like a snake extending from his arm. "You'd better find something to evolve, or I'll figure out some way to eat you. Blocking my evolution, you really have a death wish."

A few coruscating waves rippled along the tentacle, and it started to look through the rubble for Race-boosting opportunities with more fervor. Ogras snorted as he kept looking as well.

He really couldn't catch a break.

Ogras didn't ask for much. Some good wine, a few pretty girls to accompany him, and a decent class evolution. Hadn't he earned that much by now after being dragged through one near-death experience after another by that walking calamity? But no, this bastard attached to his soul wasn't ready to evolve, which meant that Ogras wasn't ready to evolve either, apparently.

Now he was stuck looking for something to help this netherblasted Planeswalker take the next step. He had already found a few valuables among the ruins, and there were also quite a few natural treasures in the Cosmos Sack of the general he'd killed, but nothing that would help Leech evolve.

It didn't help either that the blasted shadow couldn't tell him what it needed.

"And you'd better gain the ability to communicate soon enough," the demon added. "I'm tired of guessing what ails you every day."

A sudden shudder spread through the whole fortress, and Ogras stopped his search for a bit. It looked like Zac and the lass had finally managed to turn off the array. A box appeared to his side as well, and he snatched it up without hesitation before he flashed out of the ruin. Ogras looked around with anticipation, but he frowned when he couldn't sense anything in the air.

There was no influx of Cosmic Energy, and neither was there any new attunement that he could sense. Then again, anyone would be hard-pressed to make any real assumptions after the undead and the cultists had tainted the air of the area. Not that he really had any idea what a World Core upgrade actually entailed.

He had sounded pretty confident in front of the humans, but he was honestly just spitballing. They needed to be reminded of his value as that human cockroach knocked off one threat after another, after all. So that the demons, or more importantly himself, weren't left by the wayside the moment the last incursion was closed.

He turned his attention to the small box in his hand, and he opened it with some anticipation. Getting a last-minute boost before evolving couldn't hurt.

"What the hell is that?" the demon muttered with a frown, but the tentacle on his arm vibrated with glee.

BLOODLINES

The time was finally up, and the turquoise pillar winked out of existence, leaving yet another inert Nexus Hub behind. If things worked as usual, it would soon disappear without a trace like the others, leaving just the one on his island behind. The last Zombies in the area had passed through the portal over an hour ago, leaving the surroundings of the fortress bare.

It was nice to get a confirmation that the undead incursion truly was over, but Zac still had a hard time celebrating.

Zac sighed as he looked around the rubble. The Lich King was dealt with, and the array was turned off, but he didn't really feel like a victor as he looked out across the desolate landscape. No matter what the "World Core Upgrade" entailed, it hadn't cleaned up the dour atmosphere at the core of the Dead Zone at all.

In fact, they hadn't noticed any change at all after that weird tremor. Ogras said that the upgrade would take a while, though, so there was no point in completely giving up on this area.

But Zac had to admit that this place felt dead in a completely new sense of the word. Was there really a return from this? Getting blasted by the furious flames of the cultists at the eleventh hour had turned things from bad to worse, and it had turned the whole area into a desolate region. Whatever those flames contained had somehow canceled out much of the Miasma in the area, causing it to become almost completely void of any Cosmic Energy at all.

It felt like just breathing was a chore right now, like there was no oxygen in the air. The Lich King had probably been spouting the things about Earth's death to mess with his mind, but there was perhaps a nugget of truth hidden inside the taunt. His new butler was no use either, as it had quickly become apparent that Triv wouldn't turn into a wellspring of information, as Zac had hoped.

Any question that was related to restricted knowledge of the Undead Empire caused a battle between the Contract of Servitude and whatever compulsion the ghost was born with, and it started to shake in pain as the two orders clashed. Zac was forced to cancel his questions to save him a few times until he finally gave up learning anything of use.

They did, however, manage to confirm that Triv could be used as a confirmation of source if Zac already had the answer. For example, Zac could say that there was one general alive, and the ghost could confirm it. But probing where he was and what skills he or she possessed was impossible.

There were also no limitations on general knowledge or nonclassified intelligence of the Undead Empire, meaning that he could still be useful in the end. He might not be able to talk about his own kingdom, but he was more than happy to spill any rumors he could think of about the living forces of the Zecia Sector.

The ghost had left him alone to recuperate earlier, instead joining Kenzie in her attempts to take control of the large number of arrays that were still active in the area while Zac kept watch and recuperated. But now that the incursion was closed and there was no sign of the cultists returning, there was finally time to go over his gains.

The Cosmos Sack of the assassin unfortunately didn't contain a lot. There were a set of similar spikes like the one he used during the fight, along with two daggers shrouded in darkness. They seemed to be decent Spirit Tools, but Zac couldn't think of anyone they were suited for at the moment. Perhaps Ogras, but that demon had already gotten more than enough benefits for free, and he would have to purchase the daggers with Merit Points if he wanted them.

There was also a cultivation manual and a few information crystals. One of them contained surprisingly detailed intelligence of the forces of Earth, including up-to-date dockets on the top elites. His own report was actually decently accurate as well, though it was based on the period when he was closing incursions left and right. Which was a shame for the assassin, as Zac was many times stronger compared to back then.

However, there was one piece of information that was a bit shocking. There was actually a mention of the Tal-Eladar and their recent actions. They had been seen together with the Brindevalt Clan, which apparently was the name of one of the three remaining incursions that neighbored the Dead Zone. There was even a small notation that the Brindevalt Clan had some sort of business dealings with other factions of the Tal-Eladar.

Was this their plan? Give up on Earth and somehow leave through the Nexus Hub of another force? Zac didn't even know whether that was possible or not, but he couldn't see any other reason for Verana to contact some random force. He had always wondered why the Tal-Eladar hadn't stepped up and fought with Port Atwood when they had their backs against the wall, but it looked like he had found the answer.

They had always had an exit strategy in case things turned south.

The intelligence was days old, though, and Zac still didn't know what had come from the discussions, but it still left a bad taste in his mouth. However, his annoyance was quickly alleviated as he turned toward the next Spatial Tool. The Assassin had traveled lightly, it seemed, but the Spatial Tools of the Lich King were a different story.

The Cosmos Sack contained a large number of Unholy Beacons, though Zac realized they weren't activated. It further confirmed Zac's guess that the souls of earthlings were used in their creation, while these things were just spares brought from home.

There were also several siege tools left completely unused, along with a vast array of cultivation resources. The Cosmos Sack was clearly a superior variant of the sack he'd looted from Rydel, the de facto leader of the demon incursion. That meant the Spatial Ring was Adriel's private stash, and Zac could quickly confirm that the quality of the things stored inside was a lot higher than the things in the Cosmos Sack.

One look was enough to confirm that Adriel truly was a formation master. There were at least a thousand array flags in the Spatial Ring, though most of them seemed to be empty flags waiting to be inscribed.

There was also a large number of herbs and powders, and Zac quickly realized they were poisonous after taking out a few of them. There was also a large cauldron that reminded Zac of the one he had seen the Imp Herald use in the heart of the cave systems of his island. There were a large number of crystals as well, but most interesting was a milky-white crystal as large as a washbasin.

He took it out with interest, and his eyes lit up after instilling some Cosmic Energy into it. It was suddenly showing an enormous horde that looked ready to completely crumble. An army comprised of all four Races of Earth was nibbling at its heels, but the real problem came from within.

The Zombies had gone crazy, attacking anything around them, which usually meant they were attacking other Zombies. It was like the horde had lost all cohesion, and it was suddenly everyone for himself. Zac figured that the death of the Lich King had removed or lessened whatever restraint kept them from killing each other, and it had turned into pandemonium.

Zac tried to change the scope of the long-distance spying array, but his vision was stuck in place until he finally was forced to give up. But Zac believed that Kenzie or someone on the island would be able to figure the thing out. Having this thing mounted in his courtyard would be pretty convenient, as it would allow him to check in on all his islands without alerting anyone.

He had always been a bit leery about Big Brother until now, but surely it was a different thing if he was the one watching?

The crystal and everything else of interest was thrown into his own Spatial Ring, where he spotted the lump of coal once more. Or rather, the Bloodline Marrow. Triv had no idea what kind of beast it came from, but he did know what they were used for. Not surprisingly, it affected bloodlines, but not as Zac had expected.

It was actually akin to poison to warriors with a bloodline. If whatever genes were preserved inside the marrow entered the body of someone with a bloodline, there would be a clash. The resident bloodline would become agitated and force out the intruding bloodline. It didn't sound very useful on paper, but it actually had a very specific purpose.

It would force a slumbering bloodline awake, and the struggle would condense and strengthen it. It was just like normal cultivation, where fighting for your life ended with you stronger, provided you survived, of course. There was also a small chance of gaining whatever bloodline hid inside the marrow in case you didn't have one originally, but that was generally seen as a waste.

It was also something that could help upgrade what Triv called Beastcrafted Spirit Tools, which essentially meant Spirit Tools that used animal parts. Zac still didn't trust the ghost even with a Contract of Servitude active, but he seemed to be telling the truth based on the fact that [Verun's Bite] really wanted the thing, while [Love's Bond] was completely indifferent.

It was a relief, as that meant there wouldn't be any conflicts of interest in case he decided to feed it to Verun. Zac figured that he could finally provide his axe with a feast when they returned to Port Atwood, providing all the things he had saved up until now. However, he was still leaning toward only giving his axe the Dragon Core, while keeping the marrow to himself.

The recent opening of his Hidden Node and talking with his mother had made him think more and more about his Heritage. Not really in terms of wanting to reunite with Leandra, but rather to make the most of the odd constitution he had been given. [Void Heart] clearly felt like a special node based on a bloodline, and he was sure that there would be exponential benefits the more Hidden Nodes he opened.

Especially if he managed to wake up a bloodline to match them.

But Zac felt that simply boiling a piece of marrow and drinking it as a soup was too crude, and he wanted to do some more research to improve his odds of waking up his constitution. He kept going through the Cosmos Sack a while longer, but he soon got tired of the dour view, and he started to make his way down from the peak of the broken tower.

The wound in his leg had mostly healed over the past six hours, but his pathways were still a bit of a mess. He believed he'd be back at full power in a week's time tops, though, provided he wasn't forced to go all out in another battle. The biggest issue was redrawing the broken pathways, which was both painful and took a lot of time and effort now that they were so intricate.

Zac was pretty disappointed with the long recuperation times, but he soon enough remembered Galvarion's experience. The aquatic cultivator had spent over a century in the E-grade, most of it on a sickbed. Being slightly weakened for a week per node was nothing compared to that. Of course, that was provided that the damage didn't get worse with each successive node.

Triv was hovering just by the base of the broken-down tower, apparently having left Kenzie's side some time ago.

"You're really stuck here with us now," Zac said as his eyes turned to the spot where the miasmic pillar had once stood. "Come with me."

"It is my pleasure to stay with the young Lord. How can I be of assistance?" the ghost asked as they walked around the rubble.

"Take me to my sister," Zac said, and they found her resting in an emptied warehouse with Joanna keeping guard.

Zac figured this was as good a place as any, and he bought the teleportation array. However, he frowned when he couldn't see any towns on the teleportation screen.

Was this place still jammed?

Kenzie immediately realized something was wrong as well, but she simply threw out a large number of Nexus Crystals.

"It's working, but it will cost a huge number of crystals to teleport out," Kenzie muttered. "The teleporter can't use the energy of the atmosphere here because there is none. I don't know if it's because of what the cultists did or if it's an effect of the Dead Zone itself."

"Well, we have more than enough crystals." Zac shrugged. "Most of the Zombies in the area have left, and we have broken the Unholy Beacons. Perhaps the array will work by itself as soon as the area clears up a bit. But what about the jamming?"

Port Atwood had appeared on his Teleportation menu after Kenzie had thrown out the Nexus Crystals, but that didn't really alleviate Zac's fears after their last experience. He couldn't stop himself from throwing a glare at the ghost, who floated by the corner, and Triv could only weakly smile in return.

"Either the jammers broke from us pushing through it, or more likely our people have found the arrays and disabled them," Kenzie said.

"We should send something over with a note to make sure it's safe," Joanna suggested from the side, sharing Zac's sentiments. "In case there are still some traps."

Zac nodded in agreement. No need to play with your life when there was no hurry to go home.

"I guess," Kenzie said as she got to her feet. "Have you found anything interesting?"

"A few things," Zac said. "I've been busy recuperating for most of the time. I guess Ogras has gotten his hands on anything of value by now. Do you need my help taking apart those pillars belowground?"

"No, it's fine now that they've been inactive for a while. Joanna helped me pry them out of the ground. By the way, I found out something interesting from your ghost butler earlier."

"Oh?" Zac said as he looked over at the ghost, who seemingly tried to make himself look agreeable.

"Did you know? It seems that a surprisingly large number of all earthlings have pretty good bloodlines, some that are completely unknown in the Zecia Sector?" she said.

"Is that unusual?" Zac asked.

"There are sometimes some interesting bloodlines that pop up when visiting a newly integrated planet, but not like we've seen on this see– ehm, on Earth," Triv said from the side. "It is no doubt from the escaped test subjects."

"The what?" Zac asked, but he soon realized what the ghost was referring to.

The Mystic Realm.

"The undead believe that the Mystic Realm was used for researching bloodlines. Some of the test subjects escaped thousands of years ago, and they became our ancestors. Isn't that crazy?" Kenzie said with excitement.

Zac's thoughts went back to the lump of coal in his Spatial Ring once more, and the mysterious Hidden Node in his heart. A mysterious base researching bloodlines?

Wasn't that just perfect?

Defiance of the Fall continues in BOOK SIX!

THANK YOU FOR READING DEFIANCE OF THE FALL, BOOK FIVE.

We hope you enjoyed it as much as we enjoyed bringing it to you. We just wanted to take a moment to encourage you to review the book. Follow this link: Defiance of the Fall 5 to be directed to the book's Amazon product page to leave your review.

Every review helps further the author's reach and, ultimately, helps them continue writing fantastic books for us all to enjoy.

DEFIANCE OF THE FALL
BOOK ONE
BOOK TWO
BOOK THREE
BOOK FOUR
BOOK FIVE
BOOK SIX
BOOK SEVEN
BOOK EIGHT
BOOK NINE
BOOK TEN
BOOK ELEVEN
BOOK TWELVE

Where to find Aethon Books:

Facebook | Instagram | Twitter | Website

You can also join our non-spam mailing list by visiting www. subscribepage.com/AethonReadersGroup and never miss out on future releases. You'll also receive three full books completely Free as our thanks to you.

For all our LitRPG books, visit our website.

96565028R00381